Echoes
of the
Past

Maya Mitra Das

INK START MEDIA
265 Eastchester Dr Ste 133 #102
High Point NC 27262

Echoes
of the
Past

For my aunt
The late Mrs. Bina Pani Ghosh

"What is history? An echo of the past in the future,
a reflex from future to past."

—Victor Hugo

"The past is always with us nothing that
was time can ever depart."

—Rabindranath Tagore

Prologue

This is the tale of two distinguished gentlemen, both products of their time, both artists in their own right as they used their hands to hold their respective tools: one to mold, sculpt and breathe life into his art, while the other to heal and repair brains and therefore save lives.

While both men lived in different eras, separated physically by time, they are connected by their own individual talents: Niccolò, the sculptor's legacy lives on centuries later in his medical successor, Rudy, who, by his own design, breathes new life into his patients. Niccolò, the quintessential renaissance man remains immortal not only through his famous sculptures that stand all over Italy and beyond but also through the timeless lessons found in his biography that Dr. Rudy Sen had read through the early years of his medical practice. Though on the surface it may appear these two distinguished gentlemen may have nothing in common, their tales of adventures in two cities—Florence and Newcastle—have eternally bonded them throughout the test of time. And as Rudy had discovered while reading Niccolò's biography, that while their experiences seemed to differ on the surface, their lessons on life, love, sacrifice and endurance continually bond the two men, as history repeats itself even centuries later through the echoes of the past.

* * *

Rudy had the most serendipitous fortune of being given a gift from an Italian friend he met on board a ship bound for England. Little did he know then how much of the sculptor Niccolò's life paralleled that of his own. And to Rudy, it was just a testament that no matter where one had lived and in what era, you could be connected on a higher, a more spiritual plane, by simply sending a message out to God and the universe that which you most desire to be your life's true calling. And then the universe will respond in

i

kind. That was what Rudy had experienced firsthand on board a steamer bound for England, and among the books he carried with him was the biography of Niccolò given to him by his friend.

And now as he stands on a floor of a hospital building under construction in Kolkata, India looking at the view of the city below, he remembers the time he set off on his journey to England and how his own life had paralleled that of Niccolò Bardi whose biography he now tightly holds in his hand.

Rudy recalls, as though it were only yesterday when he sat on a deck chair aboard the ship, the time he turned to the first chapter of the biography only to find himself immediately immersed back to the time of Niccolò.

The Journey of Niccolò: The Making of an Artist

The octagonal baptistery stood majestic against the blue sky in the Piazza del Duomo and Piazza San Giovanni across the Florence Cathedral and the Campanile of Giotto. At the end of summer, the sun spread its alchemy to the top of the lanterns and to all that it shone below: the cathedral, duomo and campanile of Giotto that formed a perfect trifecta in the piazza.

The year 1401 marked an event of far-reaching importance in the history of Italian art: a competition by Arte di Calimala, the cloth importer's guild, to design doors at the Florence Baptistery. These doors were to be a form of celebration as Florence had recently been saved from the Black Death.

Having decided to erect bronze doors for their Baptistery, the Florentines invited all artists to submit competitive designs. Each participant was given four tables of brass and was required to make a relief of sacrifice of Isaac. Each artist was given a year to prepare the doors and the artist who was judged the best was to be given the commission.

The artists of the city of Florence and from outside of Florence gathered their tools and started on the relief, chiseling out and shaping the figures at their utmost ability. Hours, days and nights passed without any rest or sleep.

This was to be their lifetime honor if they were selected by the judges appointed by the guild. The participants were in their own secluded places and no one was allowed to communicate until the project was complete. The piece of artistry had to be the best to win the competition.

1

The city of Florence and its people were more than excited to finalize the decision. Swinging in dilemma, Florentines were gathered in different corners of the city discussing and speculating their ideas and guesses as to who would win among each other and their conversations rose in chorus to fill the air of the city of Firenze.

After a preliminary trial, seven artists were selected. They were directed to make a bronze relief that was the size and shape of the door panels. The trial plaques were to be sent to the judges. A jury of thirty-four experts, among whom were goldsmiths and painters as well as sculptors, assembled to deliver the final verdict. All the artists were doing their work in private; no one was allowed to communicate their progress until they finished their work and sent it to the board of judges.

The judges eliminated most of the artists for faulty drawing, badly proportioned figures, lack of elegance and delicacy, or when figures were convoluted and unharmonious.

In 1402 it was evident that Lorenzo and Filippo were the most able competitors. Both of them were very close in the competition. The judges were hesitant before making a decision and decided to award the commission to both of them. But Filippo withdrew in favor of his younger rival and declared that he was going to Rome to study architecture, so the commission was entrusted to Lorenzo.

The decision was a wise one. Lorenzo's model was technically and aesthetically practical. Bardi, who was an influential member of the wool comber's guild and very actively involved in organizing the competition, passed away just before the competition was announced.

Niccolò, Bardi's fourteen-year-old son, had taken on the responsibility of representing his father. The boy's father, who had been in his mid-fifties, passed away suddenly just two weeks before the competition in his sleep. No one knew the cause.

The fourteen-year-old boy was being educated by a wealthy family of Martelli through his renowned father's influence and received artistic bearing from the goldsmith. He also learned metallurgy and fabrication.

Niccolò, being a boy, did not dare to be close to the competition, instead, he was a silent observer. He was mentally and physically familiar with every stage in the contest.

He had observed the last seven artists work very closely. Though he was still grieving, having recently lost his father, he knew he had to work to support his family that consisted of his mother and sister who was abandoned by her husband. But he did not yet know where he would obtain employment.

The other guild members were aware of young Niccolò's state but were at a loss as to what they could do. Lorenzo closely observed the keen interest of this young person in the project. He asked other guild members about Niccolò's background. All of them confirmed that his father had sent him to the Martellis, a very wealthy family where he lived and had the opportunity of learning metallurgy and working as a goldsmith.

Lorenzo was impressed with the skills and background of young Niccolò and thought the boy would prove to be very handy to work on this project.

So Lorenzo called Niccolò one morning as the sun was just peeping through the patches of gray clouds, its rays slanting over the Baptistery imbuing it with a divine glow.

Niccolò was pleased that a maestro personally sought him out. It was beyond his imagination. At their meeting, a happy Niccolò cast sparkling eyes at Lorenzo as he asked, "Maestro, why did you ask for me?"

"I patiently observed your skills and attention for detail with each step of the competition so now I want to ask you, Niccolò, are you willing to work hard?"

His question surprised Niccolò who did not know what to answer. His legs shook and his heart started beating faster.

"Maestro, are you really asking me to work in your shop? If so, then I will be more than happy to oblige for it is my dream come true."

Lorenzo nodded. "I want you to start work as my assistant at my workshop. When can you start?"

"Maestro, I am honored. I can start anytime you wish. I am ready to work."

"How about tomorrow?"

"Thank you, Maestro. Thank you very much."

Niccolò could not contain his excitement and was eager to tell his family the good news. His eyes sparkled with joy as he bid goodbye to Lorenzo, thanking him profusely as he told his mentor he was looking forward to tomorrow.

With a spring to his step, Niccolò started running faster towards home. Some of the passersby who recognized him called out for him to slow down but he ignored them, urging himself to run faster, faster.

The swaying trees and houses he passed became a blur, moving backwards faster as laps of the boat oars became fainter and fainter. Finally, he slowed down a little and saw he was rapidly approaching his cottage.

Panting heavily, he entered the cottage just as his mother and sister came running to him. Then he burst out, joyfully and loudly declaring, "Maestro Lorenzo has asked me to work with him on the project of a special bronze door!"

Shrieks of joy erupted as the women gathered Niccolò in a warm hug. His sister, Tia brought a glass of orange blossom water as Niccolò's mother, Orissa started wiping the sweat off her son's forehead with a cold, damp piece of cloth. The end of summer cool breeze blew through the jasmine patches and the scent of flowers filled the air. The apple and peach trees murmured their joyful song as a bunch of sparrows started chirping from their backyard.

* * *

Amid the bustle of the city life in India as he stood in front of a hospital building—once was his dream that has now become a reality—after accomplishing so many triumphs and hurdles, Rudy remembers how he came to this point in his life as he continues referring back to the biography of Niccolò.

Rudy Boards a Ship to England

With the cool sea breeze softly caressing his cheeks as he lounged on the deck chair of the ship, Rudy closed the biography of Niccolò momentarily as he closed his eyes, remembering his own humble beginnings.

Rudrendu landed in England with minimum resources. The resource was he himself—a young medical graduate from Calcutta, India with a strong determination and enthusiasm that he would have his dream fulfilled with hard work and patience.

After finishing medical school, he was restless as he thought there was no hope for him to do a post-graduate degree in Calcutta.

In fact, he attended medical school with a scholarship given to the refugees by the government of India encouraging them to get on with their lives after India was divided into two countries: India and Pakistan. His home town was Chittagong which was in East Pakistan.

Rudy aimed to become a surgeon and with the knowledge that it was possible to do an FRCS (Fellow of Royal College of Surgeons) while working in the National Health Service, he decided to go to England.

He managed to get some money after he finished medical school and out of desperation, boarded a ship, with a discount-managed cheap fare.

He boarded the Italian ship "SS Roma" at the city of Bombay, which was fitting given Rudy's affinity for Italian art and in particular the works of Niccolò. With only one suitcase, as he started walking on the causeway, his whole body seemed to sway with the ripples of the ocean. He turned his head towards the shoreline, saw the tall trees were swaying with the breeze, and his heart squeezed with sadness. To him, it seemed like a goodbye to all familiar and dear things and diving into the depths of the unknown.

A stewardess came and showed him his cabin down in the lower level with no window but a curtain was there to make believe that there was a window.

He put down his luggage and stepped out to the upper-level balcony, where all others were standing and bidding goodbye to friends, family and dear ones. He stood there, six feet tall, with dark brown skin, a pointed nose, a triangular face, and dark, black sparkling eyes. His straight black hair parted on the side.

He was uncomfortable with his anxiety and Bombay's sultry weather, so he pulled his red and brown tie out from his blue-colored, full-sleeved shirt and put it inside the pocket of his dark navy trousers.

As he tightly held the railing of the balcony, Rudy fixed his eyes far off into the horizon which was painted orange by the sunset. The reflected orange of the horizon and the blue of the ocean met and danced happily with the sea breeze.

Then suddenly, there was a big jolt as the horn of the ship blew, for now was the time to break the ship loose from the harbor and start the journey. The sound of the horn reminded him of Chittagong where the ships used to come and dock.

He had to pinch himself to experience the reality of making a voyage to a faraway, unknown place by ship.

The ship started moving slowly at first and cheering voices were heard in chorus as hundreds of white handkerchiefs waved from the people bidding farewell below.

Slowly and steadily, the ship gained its speed, the arch of the gateway of India surely got smaller and smaller and then disappeared in the horizon.

Rudrendu stood there for a while taking in the vast ocean all around, feeling as though the ship seemed like a paper boat floating on the vast blue ocean.

He took a deep breath, his heart pounding faster with anxiety and fear of the unknown as he slowly started moving towards his cabin.

After a day or two, he came across some friendly people from India and also some Italian people returning to Italy. The ship would end its voyage in Genoa where Rudy would have to find other means of transportation.

In his mission to reach London, Rudy found some friendly Italians eager to help him plan his journey by train which runs several times; from Genoa to Victoria Station in London it would normally take about twelve hours and fifteen minutes. He was advised that it would be better to take the early morning train in order to reach London by the early afternoon.

Rudy felt relieved and grateful having these friendly people around him. The burden of facing this lonely voyage to the unknown was suddenly light and he was confident the rest of the trip would be smooth. *I am glad I decided to choose this ship for my voyage.*

The passengers from India were from Bombay and also from Calcutta. A very happy Rudy was delighted with the serendipitous nature of discovering that a few passengers from Calcutta suggested they plan to celebrate Rabindranath Tagore's birthday on the ship as it just happened to be the 8th of May, Tagore's birthday which coincided with the ship's approach at the Suez Canal.

Rudy remembered reading about the Suez Canal which happened to be a sea-level water canal running north and south across Suez in Egypt to connect the Mediterranean and Red seas. He thought it was interesting that the canal separated the African continent from Asia and provided the shortest maritime route between Europe and lands around the Indian and western Pacific oceans.

"Suez Canal," Rudy murmured, "so much history, so much happened along this stretch of water and who knows many more would be happening in the near future."

So far, he remembered that when he was graduating from high school, Britain threatened to use force against Egypt over the Suez Canal. And then at medical school, almost at the end of his first year, headline news flashed in *Amrita Bazar Patrika*, a newspaper in Calcutta:

"Britain Gives Up Suez Canal: End of 72 years of British Occupation."

Rudy recalled people and students around in medical hostels talking about the exciting news with no one knowing whether the outcome would be good or bad only that it was the end of 72 years of British occupation and that alone seemed important to everyone.

This excitement went on for a short time when headlines dominated the local newspaper that British Prime Minister Anthony Eden informed President Nasser that he cannot have the Suez Canal. Rudy recalled the news bothered the people and students around as they struggled with their own survival.

Then on the 14th of September, 1956, while rushing from one class to another, Rudy saw the headlines in the newspapers in the common room that Egypt was in full control of the Suez Canal.

Suddenly he came back to the present and headed to the deck to see the body of water that is the Suez Canal. He took a deep breath and sighed and addressed the canal:

"Suez! I hope you remain calm with no more trouble from around the world."

Now Rudy whispered to himself, "Today is the 8th of May, an important date to arrive at the Suez Canal and coincidentally, it is Tagore's birthday. Happy Birthday, Gurudeva," said Rudy calling the great poet by the affectionate moniker used by the people of India, especially those from Bengal.

To celebrate Tagore's birthday, Indian people eagerly participated in events such as reciting poems, singing songs and talking about Tagore's life and work. In addition to the Indian passengers, some of the other non-Indian passengers also joined the celebration which elevated the moods of the passengers.

9

At the celebratory gathering, Rudy recited a poem that Tagore translated himself— song offerings, from *Gitanjali*:

Rudy Said -*"I am carrying the verse as it gives me strength*
This is my prayer to thee, my Lord
Strike, strike at the root of penury in
My heart,
Give me the strength lightly to bear
My joys and sorrows.
Give me the strength to make my love fruitful in service.
Give me the strength never to disown
The poor or bend my knees before
Insolent might
Give me the strength to raise my
Mind high above daily trifles.
And give me the strength to thy will with love."

The people gathered at the deck of the ship cheered Rudy on as most of them were familiar with the poem and were very happy to learn that the poet himself translated it.

Rudy happened to meet some Italians on board including one of them who happened to be a post-graduate student of art. Flavio immediately became close friends with Rudy, enthusiastically introducing Rudy to the lives and work of Renaissance artists and sculptors including the famous Niccolò.

Rudy was very much inspired by the Renaissance artists especially Niccolò whose life and artistic journey had been difficult and frustrating yet he, like many other artists like him, had continued to move on to reach their goals. Niccolò's triumphs, as well as his sacrifices and struggles, had imprinted on Rudy's mind long after his discussion with Flavio who presented Rudy with this most treasured biography of Niccolò.

Finally, they reached Genoa, bidding goodbye to newfound friend. Rudy and Flavio exchanged addresses and phone numbers maintaining their connection with the prospect of future visits in Uffizi or the Academia in Florence.

It was early evening when he reached the train station by bus from where he would board a train early in the morning. While buying the ticket, he came to know that there were five stops between Genoa and Victoria station London and the travel time would be twelve hours and fifteen minutes. The train would reach Victoria Station in London between 4 to 5 in the afternoon.

He was standing in front of a bench on some platform, looking around as to where to go and spend the rest of the hours, when a person with a deep blue jacket with gold buttons and a red tie asked him, "Pardon me, but which train are you boarding?"

The man inspected the ticket Rudy presented. "Ah, it is a long wait for you," the man said.

He then asked Rudy to follow him as the man took him up and down the escalator and over bridges until they came to a platform where Rudy would board the London-bound train. Then he took him to a waiting room which was very nice and equipped with cushioned sofas and chairs where Rudy could rest. After that, he showed him some cafés.

Just a level up from the waiting room, Rudy was very happy as by chance, he happened to meet a friend in the Victoria Station who happened to be from the same town where he grew up. This new friend, Mihir, invited him to stay with him for few days which made Rudy very happy to receive this unexpected invitation. He contemplated how lucky he was to get a place to stay for a few days, having just newly arrived in England.

He accompanied his new friend to his residence at Finsbury Park in London and got a small room to stay for few days. Before long, he started looking for a job but the problem was he had no work experience, not even as an intern or resident level.

But Rudrendu kept looking for a job to train himself as a surgeon. He was not sure which area of surgery and would randomly apply to any position he could get his hands on.

His spirits would be up when he would get a phone call or a letter for an interview for a job, but disappointment would soon knock at the door in the form of not getting the job. In between one of those events, in the process of interviewing, he happened to be sitting in a café with a bowl of soup and hot tea taking a break, when he allowed his imagination to fly back to where he was born and grew up as a child.

Chittagong was the farthest east of India that lies between the India and Burma plate. Before the independence of India in 1947, it belonged to India then became part of East Pakistan. It straddles between the coastal foothills of Chittagong.

The river Karnaphuli, which runs along the southern bank of the city including the central district, enters the ocean, a vast body of water, named Bay of Bengal, which meets the Indian Ocean further down south.

Rudy remembered how the morning sunrays would glitter the beaches like gold and in the evening, it would turn orange red. At the backdrop, the blue of the ocean would meet the azure sky in a seamless curve.

The white gulls would cruise across with a distant cry. Their voices would blend with the ships' mysterious horns, the signal of their arrival to the port.

Rudrendu used to feel that the calls were giving him a signal to travel far, far away and yet, at the time, he did not know where. The country was so beautiful to him, the river, green jungles and waterfalls and so many flowering plants.

Chittagong had so many invaders, the relics still exist to the present day, all of them were attracted to the port. He remembered reading that Chittagong was mentioned in Ptolemy's note.

The language of Chittagong was Bengali but it became a completely different dialect, comprising of fifty percent Arabic, some Persian, and Portuguese. It was interesting Rudy would try to speak in Calcutta in his dialect and nobody would understand.

Suddenly a sweet memory appeared and he saw he was talking to Manashi, his girlfriend in medical school, about Chittagong. It was raining heavily in Calcutta, there was thunder and lightning and they were in the corridor of the medical school where the wind was blowing hard and the landscape was misty. He leaned closer to Manashi and said, "You know a Chinese traveler named Xuanzang described Chittagong as a sleeping beauty arising from mist and water."

He remembered the expression on Manashi's face. She seemed to be lost with the beauty of the description, the breeze blowing through her black wavy hair. As a few locks softly covered part of her forehead, loose ends of her green saree that draped her left shoulder started flowing. Her face lit up with each stroke of lightning, her bright dark eyes appeared moist and soft and when she looked up, her vision was fixed on the young man in front of her.

"Oh Rudy, I wish I could go see and feel the misty beauty."

Momentarily returning to the present, Rudrendu took a deep breath and sighed. He finished his cup of tea. Outside the sky was gray and still drizzling. He checked his purse and determined he could afford to splurge on a strong cup of coffee that he could take without any cream or sugar.

Soon, he returned back to his past memories. He was the second among five children in his family. They lived in a modest home, away from the city. His family lived with a limited income, with his mother as a full-time housewife and his father who had a medical practice in homeopathy. Both hard working parents equipped themselves with a lot of determination and idealism to which they raised their children.

Rudy's mother grew vegetables at the garden to provide for the family and used to spin her own thread to make clothing, a practice inspired by Gandhi. Rudy's father taught the children to be hardworking and honest.

They instilled in their children the importance of hard work with determination, and Rudy remembered his parents telling him and his siblings those values would make a difference in their lives. And while striving to work hard, they should also be compassionate with others and help people who are most in need.

Rudy recalled a time when he could not buy books so he would borrow books and would spend evenings writing down the pages of assignments.

He would work at the fruit stand selling fruits to earn money to help the family, while showing compassion and giving back to his parents, his family and to others, sharing his earnings in whatever way he could.

Sometimes he would sell the fruits grown in their backyard and on other occasions, he would buy them in retail from other orchards. Interestingly enough, he had no money, so he would strike some sort of deal with the farmers that he would sell the fruit and give the money back to them.

The owner of the orchard would be very compassionate to see the youngster's efforts. He would price down the fruit and let him have the most gain.

Outside, a church bell started to chime and Rudy snapped back to the present mindful that he had to take a bus to his destination and again, to another interview.

When he reached the interview site, he found there were a number of candidates. They were called one by one, but none of them were selected. One of the candidates who came from Scotland told them that the selection committee had already made up their minds on someone who worked here for a few months as a locum, a temporary position.

One of the doctors who was already working in the hospital, took Rudrendu for a courtesy orientation and showed him the cafeteria. The doctor, having sensed great potential in Rudrendu, had taken pity on him upon hearing about the long journey it took for him to finally land in England all the way from India, and was fascinated to hear more about Rudy's dream to be trained as a surgeon.

While they were walking through the corridors and courtyard of the hospital, he told Rudrendu that there was an opening in a hospital in Manchester, a junior position, he could try applying there and get his training. Rudy jotted down copious notes and advice from this doctor which he intended to follow. Rudy had never looked back on his younger past before, but now, the remembrance of those days frequently appeared. It seemed the struggle and survival of those days had inspired him to move forward in this unknown land as a foreigner. He would get lost in his past memories while he took public transportation. Even on board a train he would hear the distant sound of another train, a train from his past as he witnessed the landscape of the English countryside moving backwards. It would bring back memories of the place where he was born and raised.

Hardship and survival were the first values he learned in his childhood. He recalled when his family often had only one meal a day, and struggles and hunger prompted his parents' encouragement they would move forward and persevere but, to Rudy, the religious teaching from his father sounded very empty and he saw no solution for his personal needs and, seemingly at the time, no end to their suffering and sacrifice.

As the family went through hardship to provide the children with only one meal a day, Rudy's father immersed himself in religious books, as well as Hindu philosophy, to forget the distress as a failed provider for his children.

However, one story from the Mahabharata appealed to Rudy where Karna, one of the warriors said, "It was the will of god where I was born, but it was up to me what I make of my destiny."

An auspicious day appeared in front of him when he was thirteen, he got a chance to become a house teacher to look after two toddlers in a neighboring village in exchange for food and lodging and an opportunity to go to school. But he had to live in a roadside outhouse close to a burning ghat or place where the dead bodies from near and far around the villages were burned. Families would administer their last rites of their relatives. He used to get the smell from burning bodies when the breeze blew strong and at times sad laments were heard from the relatives of the dead. He remembered he would plug his ears with cotton balls, his fingers and feet would get cold with fear and anxiety.

Rudy's vivid memories gave him chills and he had to remind himself that was the past and now he was in England traveling by train going for an interview for a job.

That night, exhausted from the job hunt and ensconced in bed at a room where he stayed temporarily, Rudy turned his attention back to Niccolò's biography as a source of comfort and inspiration.

Niccolò's Early Apprenticeship with Maestro Lorenzo

Sometimes Niccolò could not believe it was real—that he was actually chosen by Maestro Lorenzo to work on the bronze doors. To him, being awarded an opportunity to work for this maestro on such an esteemed project was like a gift from heaven so that he could support his mother and sister who lived with him.

He would get up very early every morning feeling nervous while at the same time reminding himself that he would put his mind and body together and concentrate so he could follow the maestro's instructions as he keenly observed him.

On the first day of work, he started a running pace from home to reach the Baptistery as the morning glow of the sun flooded the city of Florence. A gentle breeze nudged the tall trees along the way to move gently as the shrill of seagulls interrupted the chirping of birds. He sped by very few people along the way as the shops had yet to open, except the bakery whose owner and a friend of Niccolò's family came out quickly to hand him a freshly baked loaf.

"All the best my dear Niccolò and congratulations," the baker, Luigi said. "I baked a resin bread for you to enjoy during your break." He patted the boy on the head. "You will be fine, my boy. I know your father will watch you and bless you from heaven."

Niccolò was almost in tears. He stopped for a few minutes to take some deep breaths before continuing his sprint, running even faster. After a few minutes, he saw the sight of the majestic Baptistery shining like gold with the soft morning sun against the sky. Right then, it appeared an invisible force was drawing him closer and closer to the Baptistery. The last few feet seemed effortless as he felt as if he were floating in the air. After he entered the Baptistery, he felt very calm and safe.

At a distance in the hallway, Maestro Lorenzo welcomed him with open arms. "Niccolò, you are right on time. I will show you where I keep my tools. We will ask some helpers to get us a comfortable bench and we shall start our work."

Since the first day with Maestro Lorenzo, Niccolò would be the first person to arrive in the Baptistery and he was the one who would arrange the tools for his master. Niccolò was very happy to help his maestro carve the door at the Baptistery and was very excited to learn the technique in much detail. His hands and fingers moved so easily in a way that surprised him, as if some unseen energy was helping him to perfect the craft.

Every day so many people came and visited the Baptistery specifically to watch the doors being made. People from the cathedral, important people from all over the city and quite often people from the Medici Palace. Cosimo de' Medici visited a few times with his brother, accompanied by children of the de' Medici family.

These young children, around seven or eight years old, came and gathered around Niccolò to watch what he was doing. They were especially drawn to him as, given his young age, he seemed to be approachable and was the youngest person working at the Baptistery.

One girl, who was about nine or ten-years-old, was fascinated by the whole process and would ask Niccolò so many questions such as: "Where did you learn your carving? How many years of training did you have? Who was your teacher?"

Niccolò simply answered, "Maestro Lorenzo is teaching me and I follow his directions as I learn while I work."

The girl was then formally introduced as Beatrice, the niece of Cosimo de' Medici.

Niccolò continued being the center of their conversations as he was the youngest worker there. Yet despite his young age, he worked like an expert, an observation by others that made Niccolò very self-conscious and shy.

Another reason was that most people were attracted to Niccolò as he was a very handsome young man with olive skin, tall, slim, with a triangular face, pointed nose, big, sparkling eyes, and brownish-black hair. And he was always humble with a pleasant smile. Above all, he gave an impression of a hardworking, sincere, honest young man who seemed to know what he was doing.

Maestro Lorenzo seemed to be very pleased to have Niccolò, as he was trained in the field of metallurgy so the young man would be a huge help in the process of gilding the doors.

Every day Niccolò would arrive at 8:30 in the morning and work up to 5:30 in the evening, some days beyond that without taking a break.

Maestro Lorenzo would often insist that his young apprentice take a much-needed break. Lorenzo would approach Niccolò to say, "My dear Niccolò, you must go out and breathe some fresh air. It will not only do you good but will make your carving finer."

Niccolò would arrive home in the evening tired but happy and satisfied that he was working and earning whatever he could to support his mother and sister, Tia, who both tried their best to meet his needs and made him comfortable. Mother Orissa would cook Niccolò's favorite dishes like homemade gnocchi, freshly baked bread with raisin or almond. Very often she would cook almond rice for dessert which was Niccolò's favorite. Then his sister would make sure his bed was properly made and that enough water was left for his bath.

Water had to be fetched from their well and kept in an open tank like a reservoir made of stone or a cement-like material and in Niccolò's house, it was made of stone.

19

Niccolò really appreciated his mother and his sister's efforts toward making him comfortable, often thanking them. "Please do not work too hard to spoil me," he often told them.

* * *

After a while, Niccolò grew accustomed to his daily routine. He would get up early in the morning and, as his living quarters was way in the outskirts of Florence, he felt compelled to walk as fast as he could to reach the Baptistery. For now, he'd earned a good reputation as a rising sculptor.

In addition to being meticulous at work, Niccolò maintained a routine at home where he would check everything from making sure the cooking utensils were clean to ensuring there was enough wood for their brick stove. His mother liked everything to be very clean so he would check the kitchen, their paved patio and would sweep the courtyard of their modest home.

The sudden demise of Niccolò's father had put a burden on Niccolò whose father had been a member of the wool comber's guild and at that time, his family lived reasonably well. So Niccolò was trying hard to meet the needs of his family.

Niccolò would start from his home almost in breakneck speed that even a friend from the neighborhood had to catch his attention. "Niccolò, what is the hurry?"

"Sorry, I have to be at my workplace before maestro reaches there."

"How much are they paying you for your hard work?"

"I do not know. He just offered two gold coins to start with. I needed it very badly. Maestro is kind."

"You should be little firmer. You should ask for more and if you do not ask, you will miss out on an opportunity to earn an honest day's wage."

Niccolò paused for a second. "We'll see. I love my work. I think maestro knows that I am working hard and I trust him. I think he is very considerate and understands my situation."

"You do not understand. You have to be more assertive, otherwise people will take advantage of you."

"Dear Alfredo, I have to go. I want to reach my workplace before maestro does. He chose me for this work and I am very much in need of the job."

As Niccolò started running to reach his workplace he kept talking to himself. "I have been selected for this job and I think Maestro is very considerate. I trust him and he trusts me to do the work." He breathed heavily and uttered to his friend even though he was no longer beside him. "No, Alfredo, no. I cannot listen to you although you are one of my best friends since childhood. Why is Alfredo doing this? He should encourage me, instead he is confusing me by wanting me to stand up against Maestro. What could be the motive?" He could not think straight so he ran faster until he reached the studio. He saw his maestro and smiled at him.

Niccolò would start working on the door as Maestro Lorenzo stood by his side to show him the angle to place the chisel, to get the desired depth, and also advise him to take less material out at the beginning so that he could control his carving without mess.

*   *   *

More than two years had passed since Niccolò worked with Maestro Lorenzo on the bronze door of the Baptistery. On one spring day, a gentle breeze blew through the connecting bridge of Ponte Vecchio where Niccolò saw Beatrice, the young girl from the Medici family, standing where the wall curved. He guessed that the girl, who may be about thirteen or fourteen years-old, had grown taller and prettier, clad in her blue flowing dress, her brown-black hair cascading down her neck and shoulders. She had a triangular face, a pointed nose which suited her face, bright olive-colored skin and dark brown, moist eyes which were fixed on Niccolò.

Beatrice had been thinking of meeting Niccolò away from his workplace to tell him that she was very interested in observing Niccolò's methods of sculpting and she had already made up her mind to refer to him as "Maestro" which she deemed to be fitting given his position as apprentice to a master at the Baptistery.

Niccolò's heart started beating faster, he stood spellbound as he remembered the time she came to the Baptistery to watch him sculpt with Maestro Lorenzo.

She started moving towards him and said "Maestro, I admire your sculpting."

Niccolò blushed. "Thank you, my honorable lady, for your kind words."

Beatrice glanced at his work then gazed up at Niccolò. "You are very devoted to your work and I observed that you do not pay any attention to your surroundings except your work."

"My dear young lady, I come from a very ordinary family. I have to look after my widowed mother and my sister who was abandoned by her husband," he said emphatically. "I do not have the luxury to pay attention to anything except my work."

"Oh Maestro, I was only trying to praise you. It saddens me that my words were misunderstood. I am really sorry."

"My honorable lady, I must go now. Maestro Lorenzo awaits me."

It so happened that Beatrice would meet Niccolò at the corner of the bridge often and try to start a conversation with him. One more year of work went by for Niccolò at the Baptistery, and by now, he had grown accustomed to his daily routine. Suddenly he felt an urge to learn more techniques and study further to refine his sculpting skills.

Niccolò also harbored some anxiety regarding his sister and his mother. He tried his best to provide for his family by working hard. Maestro Lorenzo remained very pleased with him and he could work as long as he wished.

Yet there was that strong desire to study sculpture in Rome which started brewing inside him. He became restless and anxious to request the maestro for a leave of absence.

He heard Maestro Filippo was already in Rome and he felt so strongly that it was the right time to go to Rome and study with him. At night he would wake up and feel restless when a cloud of thoughts would start gathering inside him. In the morning while he strode faster to work, he would see Beatrice standing at the corner of the bridge and would try to talk to him. Some days he would stop for a few seconds, other times he would ignore her and hurriedly walk by. Niccolò wished he did not have to ignore Beatrice; he liked her and wanted to talk though his heart simmered, his mind warned him not to get involved with a young lady from the Medici family. The tension and anxiety exhausted him.

Yet on other occasions, Beatrice would stand at the corner of the bridge at Ponte Vecchio and would insist on addressing him. "Maestro, I know you are in a hurry…"

Niccolò would stop for a few minutes, smile and say, "Thank you, my dear lady," simply to appease Beatrice and assuage his guilt for the times he ignored her.

One fine morning at work, Niccolò was determined to ask the maestro about his leave of absence from the Baptistery. He tossed and turned the previous night with an uneasiness to continue his work at the Baptistery when his mind was constantly telling him to go to Rome and join Maestro Filippo.

Niccolò was worried and nervous, his feet were trembling and his hands were sweating as he faced Maestro Lorenzo. "I humbly request a leave of absence from work, Maestro, if that is possible."

To Niccolò's relief, Maestro Lorenzo was very supportive. "Niccolò, you have worked so hard. Some time away from this work will do you good. This project will be going on for a while. You will always have some work to do when you come back."

Niccolò was so happy he was almost in tears. "Maestro, I cannot thank you enough. I need a break very badly. I learned a lot from you. Thank you very much from the bottom of my heart for including me in this project."

"Dear Niccolò, I am always pleased to have you work with me."

Niccolò went home and told his mother, Orissa and sister, Tia that Maestro Lorenzo granted his leave of absence from the Baptistery to join Maestro Filippo at Rome to study and learn the finer details of the sculptures.

Niccolò was worried about mother Orissa and sister Tia. Both were happy that he was taking a break and assured him not worry about them. At present, they had enough money saved for some time and neighbors and friends were always there to help if they needed anything around the house like repairs or getting provisions from faraway shops.

Niccolò felt better and slept that night peacefully. He woke up, got ready and started his sprint to the Baptistery.

The morning soft rays of the sun touched the city of Florence as a cool breeze blew through Niccolò's black hair. He took a deep breath and felt fresh and energetic.

"If I see Beatrice, I will stop and talk to her as today is not the same as other days. I have some news to tell her," he murmured to himself. He felt that his heart was racing as he breathed heavily.

A shrieking seagull flew over his head and he realized he was very close to the bridge as he heard the laps of cruising boats along the river. Then he saw a silhouette of a young lady and, sure enough, it was Beatrice in her olive-green dress standing at the corner where the wall of the bridge curved.

She was holding something in her hand. A gentle breeze blew through her cascading brownish black hair as she gracefully moved towards Niccolò. Her big moist eyes were fixed on Niccolò as she seemed determined to start a conversation today.

24

Waves of sensations that started from her feet kept on rising upwards. She began breathing heavily seemingly unsure of what exactly to say. Then she composed herself as she drew closer to him. "Maestro, I made some snacks for you. Please enjoy them during your break from work."

"Thank you, my honorable lady. I have some news to tell you."

"Maestro, what is it?"

"I am taking a leave of absence from the Baptistery to study in Rome and learn the sculptures. I am excited that I will be joining Maestro Filippo there."

"What exciting news!"

"My dear lady, it appears you are interested in watching my sculpting. I will still be working there next week so please come any day you wish."

"Maestro, I'd be most happy if you would call me Beatrice."

"I will try..."

"Maestro, please let me know what particular aspect of sculpture you wish to study more."

"Well, that is a very good question but I will study the master sculptors' approach to how they make the sculptures so remarkable and unique and then I want to make my figures come alive."

Beatrice blinked her eyes in wonder. "That is wonderful but how would you do that?"

"I do not yet know but without it, the sculptures do not mean anything."

"Maestro, do you mean to say you want them to have emotion like joy and sadness?"

"Yes, and adding to your list: triumphant, contemplative, peaceful, happy—a combination of all these."

"That is wonderful and a very new idea, but how could a piece of stone do all of that?"

"My dear, do you have a pet?"

"Yes, I have a cat."

"How do you know if he or she is hungry, happy and wants your attention?"

"Oh, she will purr and call me with a meow and wail when she is in trouble."

"You know a sculptor gets the same sort of vibration from the stone when he is sculpting," Niccolò said, matter-of-factly. "It is a different vibration as it comes from the bond between the sculptor and his sculpting material. It is difficult to explain and hard to understand."

Beatrice nodded empathetically. "Maestro, I learned something very unique today and I wish you all the best. May I ask you how long will your leave of absence be?"

"I am not sure but around one year or so, maybe less."

The young lady grew quiet for a few seconds. Then tried her best to smile. "I will see you when you return then. I wish you a safe journey and return to Florence."

Niccolò smiled. "Thank you." And before he could process any further what had just transpired, he walked a faster pace then disappeared at the bend of the road.

Beatrice just stood there for some time before bending over the railing of the bridge where saw her reflection in the water which was slowly but surely rippling away to the other side of the shore.

And just as Niccolò was embarking on a new adventure in his life, centuries into the future, another young man was traversing new territory in his own line of work.

Rudy Arrives in England

In London, Rudy realized he had no registration, no post-graduate qualification nor any contacts but still, he had to find a job to survive. He also found that the job market around London was bleak with hundreds and thousands of Indian doctors arriving each month.

He was on his way to Manchester, as on his last interview, a physician at that particular hospital mentioned a possibility of a job in Manchester.

An urban county located in north western England, Manchester was a historic county of Lancashire which also included an area of the river Mersey of Cheshire. For Rudy, it was yet another new place in England where he would be interviewed. While the search and excitement about the prospect of getting a job led him to becoming accustomed to familiarizing himself with the different places of England, his main focus remained on obtaining a job to survive.

He boarded the London underground tube to reach Euston station which was in central London where he could board a train to Manchester. Rudy observed how the compartment of the fast-moving underground tube was of full of people; some were reading their newspaper holding it directly in front of their faces, some were dozing off, while others just looking out the windows blankly. There was nothing to see except the fuzzy dark and grey sheets, the fast-moving linear lines formed optical illusions giving the perception of moving faster backwards. The movement caused passengers to sway gently as they sat on red and black striped cushioned seats. Since the compartment was full, there was no place for Rudy to sit. So he grabbed one of the hand grips hanging from the ceiling of the compartment and concentrated deeply on his present situation.

A memory from the past flashed in his mind again this time focusing its lens on the time he was awarded a scholarship when he finished high school.

Newspaper headlines flashed about the wonder boy highlighting him and his hometown: "A village boy receives free college education and another house tutorship sponsored by a kind businessman from an affluent family who provided food and lodging," one news article touted. Being a recipient of this blessing certainly endowed Rudy a chance to explore uncharted territory beyond his life growing up in the village. Yet another thing he had in common with Niccolò who in his youth had been sponsored by a wealthy Italian family.

Bolstered with confidence by that happy memory, Rudy suddenly felt refreshed as recalling the past event provided a surge of energy and courage. He got down at the Euston underground station and strode in a fast pace to reach Euston railway station.

Thanks to the help of some passersby, he reached the railway station with no problem. All he had to do was walk up then down the escalators and stairs and walk a few feet to reach the station, a huge building that impressed him.

After buying his ticket, he found out that from Euston, there were trains heading to Manchester every two to three hours and the travel distance and time to travel was around two hours and thirty minutes. He could breathe easily now knowing he didn't need to rush to get to a train.

Though Rudy carried a portfolio with all his credentials and a small bag for his personal belongings, he did not know where he would spend the night.

To shake off the uncertainty, he started to walk with an easy pace aboard the Manchester-bound train waiting at a platform as more people scurried around at a hectic pace. He noticed how the station was well-illuminated, clean and signs that hung from the ceiling showed clear, easy to read and follow directions.

English gentlemen dressed in their dark trousers, plain blue or striped blue shirts with a tie or a bow draped by their long raincoats strode in a faster pace presumably to catch their respective trains. Some ambled carrying canes with a gold and metal hand grip. The canes swung with the rhythm of swinging arms and in one case, a cane lifted up in the air while the owner was trying to read directions to a destination. Women mostly clad in their miniskirts, long raincoats and high heel shoes that were tapping away on the shiny station floor on the way to their compartment.

The flag man gave the signal. "All aboard!"

Rudy got in a compartment and took a seat at the window. He made himself comfortable as the train whistled and started off. He thought two and a half hours would be a long trip and thought of ways to pass the time like go to the dining car. He checked his pocket to see if he could afford a cup of tea and some food. He was really hungry.

He pulled out a book of quotes from Swami Vivekananda which his parents gave him a while ago when he went to college. He was anxious and nervous at the same time. To calm himself, he sat at his window seat and started reading the quotes from Swami Vivekananda.

After a few minutes, through his peripheral vision, Rudy saw a person take a seat by his side.

Rudy turned his face towards him and both of them looked at each other. Something in the man's eyes encouraged Rudy to start a conversation. "Hello, I am heading to Manchester Piccadilly. And you?"

"I am heading to Manchester too, I live there."

"Oh, it will be my first visit. I am a new arrival in this country."

"I see that. I saw the book you are reading with a picture of a monk. I can tell you it is hard to adjust at first in a new environment and the weather could be harsh. After a while, you will get used to it. Anyway, what is the book about?"

"It is a collection of Swami Vivekananda's quotes."

"Who was or is he?"

"He was a Hindu monk and a most celebrated, spiritual leader of India. He was a thinker, great orator and a passionate patriot. He carried on the free-thinking philosophy of his guru Ramakrishna and forwarded it to a new paradigm. He was responsible for the revival of Hindu spiritualism and established it as a revered religion."

"When did he live?"

"He was born Narendra Nath Dutta in Calcutta and lived from 1863 to 1902. He was a spokesman of Vedanta and he presented Hinduism at the First World Parliament of Religion in Chicago in 1893. He was an instant success and subsequently was invited to speak all over America and Europe."

"Oh, that is quite an achievement to be invited and accepted in other foreign societies."

"When I am confused and nervous, I read his quotes to search for a direction."

"Is this like a Bible?"

"No, it's just a book of quotes. I can read one of the quotes if you would like."

The man nodded. "Go ahead."

"Okay, here goes:

Take up one idea. Make that one idea your life, think of it, dream of it, live on that idea. Let the brain, muscles, nerves, every part of your being, be full of that idea and just leave every other idea alone. This is the way to success."

"Oh, that is tough to maintain quite a lot of strength of the body and mind. Tell me, what would you like to become in this new country?"

Rudy didn't hesitate. "I had long wanted to be trained as a surgeon in this country and, armed with that hope and determination, I now venture forth."

To himself, Rudy reflected on what he had read about Niccolò's own journey to be trained by a master when he ventured as a young boy to Rome so long, long ago.

"Well then, I wish you all the luck and best wishes. I feel we do not have to exchange our names but when you succeed, hopefully, you will remember me and our conversation. And at any rate, perhaps, I might see you on a news flash someday in the future."

"I am honored by your words, sir." Rudy gave the man a slight nod and both of them smiled heartily and shook hands.

He started towards the dining car as there was yet one hour more to spend. Through the glass window, Rudy saw the green countryside was moving backwards as small cottages, fenced lawns, patches of flowerbeds, curved pebble or paved paths leading to the front door. Then framed by the train's window like a movie reel, miles of green pasture, flocks of sheep grazing on the green field, and a watch dog with his master to chase them to huddle in one particular place to graze played out before Rudy like a scene from a movie.

The train whistled as the telegraph poles passed one by one backwards as the train moved forward. Inside the dining car, rows of tables and chairs were set to accommodate four people at one table arrangement on both sides of the compartment.

Rudy admired the table covered with white tablecloth and decorated with small flower vases with yellow and white primroses, napkins and silverware arranged neatly. Male waiters adorned with white overalls and wide, red cloth belts were busy taking orders from the passengers.

Rudy took a seat at the window and ordered fish and chips, a small tomato bisque and a pot of hot tea. He was thinking that this was all he was going to eat for a while, so he thought, *Let me enjoy this meal as I don't know where and when I would get another chance to eat.*

The tomato bisque arrived first and while he was spooning the hot soup into his mouth, he realized that he was in a much more dire situation when he decided to leave the only life he had ever known in a part of the country which became East Pakistan after India's independence. He took a daring step to go to India without knowing anyone there to fulfill his dream to be a medical doctor.

He recalled the time he visited one medical college to another during the heat of the April sun in Calcutta with no hope in sight. One day after a days-long travel, hungry, thirsty and tired, Rudy sat on a bench in a place called College Square in front of an artificial small lake landscaped with trees and patches of grass to beautify the area.

Something out of ordinary happened. A man walked up and sat on the same bench. He started to engage Rudy in conversation wanting to know why Rudy was looking so sad. It seemed the man was worried that Rudy was contemplating suicide by drowning and as a good Samaritan, he was trying to talk him out of it.

Eventually Rudy, after taking a deep breath, opened up about his problem. After thoughtfully regarding Rudy, the man muttered, "I wish I could help you."

Then he remembered a famous doctor from his village who was the principal of a medical college. That man practically dragged Rudy onto the street where he showed him the house of the principal of the medical college. He advised Rudy to arrive there at 8 in the morning and wrote an appointment note on a piece of paper.

Then, as suddenly as he appeared, the mysterious man disappeared. In all the excitement and initial confusion, Rudy forgot to ask for the man's name as he was in a dream-like state and everything was moving at a faster pace.

The next morning, Rudy arrived at the house and gave the piece of paper to the doorman. After ten minutes, the doorman ushered Rudy in with a plate of snacks to munch on. Very shortly after that, the principal came—he was an orthopedic surgeon—so he asked Rudy to name the bones of the legs.

He was very pleased when Rudy could name all the bones and agreed to help him. The doctor advised Rudy to apply to a private college as an outsider from Chittagong East Pakistan. He could not apply to Government College and this surgeon was a principal of a Government College. With the surgeon's help, Rudy got admitted into a private medical school named National Medical College.

Sudden awareness he was still on the train's dining car, Rudy snapped back from his past and immediately absorbed the present, focusing on finishing his tomato bisque and starting his fish and chips.

The train's whistling pierced the air as the various conversations of passengers in the dining car reached its highest with the swaying reflective images of passengers' heads and faces on the glass windows.

Rudy felt this perpetual state of vacillating between his past and present as he remembered his anxiety seeking accommodation in Calcutta and sustenance, all essentials that required money of which he accumulated very little by teaching private students which he saved for medical school. So he decided to work as a paramedic in exchange for decent lodging in a nice neighborhood. Again, an unseen grace brought news that he got the refugee stipend from the government of India. He breathed easily and moved to the medical college hostel.

Rudy realized that both his mind and body were being transported; his physical form destined to discover new territory for the job hunt and his mind lapsing back to his past.

The train's chug chug sound was interrupted by a sonorous whistle and Rudy once again returned to the present and sipped his hot tea from a white tea cup with a strawberry design and whispered to himself, *The unseen force moved me here.*

He wondered if Niccolò, the artist he admired so much, had experienced the same life transitions as he had. Rudy was about to find out as he turned to Niccolò's next adventure.

Niccolò's First Visit to Rome

Far into the future as a young man contemplates his own past in India, he's reminded of Niccolò's own journey into the unknown. If only the young Niccolò had back then foresaw what an influence he'd become to the success of a certain future neurosurgeon, he would have been proud.

City of Rome 1405

A Florentine wandered like a stranger with a well-known sculptor who was a friend and adviser. He knew Niccolò's father and the Martelli family where Niccolò studied and trained in many different artistic crafts.

Niccolò worked for the maestro continuously without a break for three years at the Baptistery spending most of his time there that it had become as familiar and as pleasant as his own home. And while the sight of the octagonal Baptistery since the early Christian period that stood against the majestic blue sky across the Florence Cathedral and campanile pleased Niccolò every single day, he needed a break from his routine and took a leave of absence from his maestro there.

Niccolò's family was also very pleased that he was visiting Rome with a senior sculptor and adviser who would take care of him. It was the beginning of summer, the weather warm yet pleasant in Rome, the flowering oleanders of different colors like ruby red, pearly white and pink had just started to bloom, its scent filling the air of the bustling city with a gentle breeze.

Niccolò's eager eyes observed each and every marble sculpture, the parts of the body, hands, legs and feet, especially the face. Wanting to get a closer look, he beheld the sculptures from all sides, front and back, top to bottom where he could reach and touch them whenever he would get a chance.

Then he would sit down with a frown and sigh, resting his chin on his right knuckles and would try to gather his thoughts as he fixed his eyes to the infinite.

Niccolò soon got lost in the thought of ancient Rome. "From what I learned from my past studies," he murmured to himself, "from the beginning of history, the Romans had to prove themselves to the outside world. The Appian Way constructed so many years ago still exists and directly leads into the cities. It was constructed to link with military roads in the east and west of the empire and join Spain, Macedonia and Asia. The Roman forum, with its elegant columns and spaces copied in every major city in the empire as a place in which debate, ideas and the creation of the rule of law, provided the focus for the city."

All of a sudden, like an epiphany, Niccolò saw in his mind far into the future a young man whom he didn't know but with whom he felt a kinship toward. He wondered if this was a premonition of some sort, if he were connected with this person in some way. Then he shook his head and continued his observation of Rome.

* * *

The noise of horse-driven carts on the paved path woke Niccolò to his present. The bustling city life rolled on along with the clip-clapping sound of horses on the paved stony path.

Then the sound of water flowing from a fountain added to the background harmony. The pigeons were seen bobbing their heads across the patchy green grass, some were peeping carefully behind the fountain.

Niccolò sighed and exclaimed, "Rome, this same city has stood the same way as it continues to today and has seen so many events and so many changes. If only the pieces of stone could speak and tell me stories of the events that rolled one by one in front of them."

He continued to talk to himself. "I feel something but I cannot quite figure out what it is yet. I know something is missing. If I could get a clue from the sketches of the figures and their background, I would."

Niccolò's companion and adviser, Filippo, suddenly approached him, his voice sounding excited and happy. He rested his right palm on Niccolò's left shoulder. "Niccolò, did you study the sculpted head and the standing figures?" Filippo inquired.

"Yes, I did, but Maestro," he spoke in a mellow voice as he replied, "there is something I want to do with my hands so they—the sculptures—should come alive and I cannot figure out how and I want to get a clue to solve the problem. It is very painful that I cannot see the path to solve the problem."

"Niccolò, please sit down and I will tell you and show you the sketches I did and I will show what I came up with all those." He pointed his index finger and slowly moved over the sketches. "Here I see the outline of the path, but you know," he again put his hand on Niccolò's left shoulder and said excitedly, "I have to light it up with my knowledge of engineering and experiment it with the space and perspective of the creation."

Niccolò went back again and looked at the figures and touched their hands, faces, eyes and their stance. Then, eyes wide with excitement he said, "Maestro, I know what I want. I would like them to stand elegantly without support. The eyes of the figures will light up with a smile or a shadow of sadness will cover their face and they will cry. Can I try?"

"Sure, you can."

"Is there anybody to help me light up my vision?"

Filippo spoke very softly and looked with his luminous eyes at Niccolò. "Listen, my young apprentice, you have to think and go deep inside to light up your path. You are a rising, young sculptor. You can definitely discover what you want while working with your hands. There will be disappointments along the way but do not give it up. You know, I had my disappointment and I let go of the project and gave a chance to a younger person. I am not stopping now. It gave me more vision and energy and I will passionately proceed. My dear, Niccolò, I will give you a clue when you are ready but your work needs your own vision and passion to go forward."

The noisy, bustling city kept on rolling as horse-driven carts' monotonous sound harmonized with conversations of passersby. The orange rays of the sun veiled the treetops as the tired people of Rome headed home at the end of the day. The gentle breeze blew through the trees and the fountains murmured.

"Niccolò, let us go and rest and we will start tomorrow again from where we left off today."

A flock of pigeons flew over their heads.

Niccolò Returns to Florence

Niccolò and his companion took a sailboat on their way back to Florence. It was the summer of 1406 when Filippo wanted to visit Siena on their way back home to Florence. Maestro Filippo always wanted to study the architectures of the churches and abbeys in Siena. He thought it was a good chance for a visit.

Niccolò hesitated thinking about the expenses, but Filippo put his right palm on Niccolò's shoulder and said softly, "Niccolò, I like you and your passion for this art. It is very important to me to visit Rome and Siena that is why I sold a part of my property to pay for this trip. I will take care of it. My dear, Niccolò, you looked after my needs so much I cannot thank you enough."

Niccolò was delighted. "You make me so happy and I learned a lot and am still learning from you. You are my friend, adviser, and teacher. Maestro, you gave me so much strength and encouragement. I will always remember that whenever I am in doubt."

The two very happy sculptors boarded the sailboat that started its journey on the Mediterranean Sea which looked majestic with different shades of blue, an image that mesmerized both of them. There was light and dark blue and then divine, heavenly and sunken blues that left both Filippo and Niccolò awestricken. "It is impossible to catch all the hues," they agreed.

Their journey took a break in Siena where it was evident the cultural influence of Florence and Siena proved overwhelming on Italian history and there was always a power struggle between Siena and Florence. Filippo was very keen in visiting and studying the medieval architecture of Siena.

The elegant appearance of the skyline beyond the russet Tuscan hill with medieval towers and rust rooftops crammed with churches and abbeys overwhelmed Filippo with joy and excitement. "Niccolò, it is great we are in the city of Siena."

Niccolò beamed. "Yes, Maestro, we are."

Filippo and Niccolò wandered around the city of Siena, visiting the churches and abbeys as much as they could, studying the architectural designs and artistic decorations.

On the last evening, Filippo sat down with Niccolò as the sun was about to disappear beyond the Tuscan hills. The last rays of sun painted the hills and valleys with orange gold and one could see some riders racing their horses as one by one they disappeared in the dust cloud created from the racing horse hoofs on the winding path.

Filippo came close to Niccolò and took a dried twig from a tree and started explaining to Niccolò how to make a landscape or any other creation to be three-dimensional and started drawing lines and points on the dusty unpaved path. He put a horizontal line then put a vanishing or imaginary point some distance above and in the middle of the horizontal line. Then he drew parallel lines below the horizontal line leaving enough space and made the parallel line converge to the vanishing point.

"Niccolò, do you see, my dear, I gave you a clue."

Niccolò was very excited to get the idea. "Maestro, I see the created depth made by these lines and the point."

Soon, it was time for them to return to Florence. They looked at the city at dusk for the last time and boarded their sailboat that started off again to sea, leaving the bank and their memories behind.

As the sun set, its glow reflected on the sea then broke into pieces and danced with the waves far, far away, where the sea met the horizon.

* * *

Filippo and Niccolò reached Florence and bid goodbye for now promising to meet in the near future. Filippo was on his way to his family while Niccolò was on his way home to meet his mother and sister.

Happy to be returning home after a year, Niccolò could not wait to see his mother and sister, hoping everything was well. Thinking about the workplace and his maestro excited him and he was eager to share with fellow sculptors and trainees about his experience in Rome.

When his horse-driven cart turned towards his home, he saw the bridge Ponte Vecchio and his mind flooded with memories of Beatrice for this was the place where Beatrice would wait for him to talk. He looked at the bridge but asked the cart driver to move fast. He wanted to reach home before dark to surprise his mother. He sent a message from Rome through another friend to his mother and mentioned an approximate time and date for his arrival.

While away from his home city, Niccolò thought about his home, a small cozy cottage tucked away beyond the busy city of Florence. The family cottage had three bedrooms and a small courtyard accented with patches of flowering beds in front and a landscaped backyard with some fruit trees, a small kitchen garden and small patches of scented flowers which circled the well like a lace for drinking water.

He thanked his late father often for working hard and being considerate enough to build this property for them. He was excited thinking about a home-cooked meal lovingly made by his mother. He thought about his mother's homemade gnocchi, one with a special sauce in which she would add turmeric, fresh garlic from their small kitchen garden, ginger, and a pinch of salt and pepper and fresh herbs.

There would definitely be salad with cucumber, lettuce and celery fresh from their garden. The thought of his mother's preparation of almond milk and rice dessert or fresh pear from the garden cooked in red wine and sugar made Niccolò's mouth water.

Niccolò reached home and his mother and sister came running and hugged him. Tears rolled on his mother's cheeks with joy. His mother promptly prepared Niccolò's favorite gnocchi and almond milk rice and all the while, the three of them talked and talked; there were so many things to talk about. Mother Orissa asked about the meals Niccolò and Filippo ate in Rome.

"I learned to make so many things myself that I will try at home, if you will allow me to," he said excitedly.

He described some special bread dishes and a melon tart recipe which made his mother happy. Then he whispered to his mother and sister that he and his maestro found a treasure while leisurely walking the outskirts of Rome.

There was an open space full of shrubs and the paved path continued further to another city. It was the hour when the evening was settling in that they heard in the distance foxes calling that sounded like a series of quick, high-pitched barks followed by a screeching bark. The barks emitted as *ow, wow, wow, wow*, and when they decided to return to their place, Niccolò stumbled on a mound as his foot caught in a hole and both the maestro and Niccolò started digging the ground energetically until, with their combined strength, they freed Niccolò's foot. And that's when they found a small iron box. Niccolò was not so badly injured so they managed to carry the box back to their place and with their sculpting tools, they opened the box and found gold Florins coins.

After a considerable amount of thinking, they decided to keep it a secret and divide the coins between them as it would be a problem for them to tell anyone. Mother Orissa and sister Tia were happy to now be in possession of a little more money.

Niccolò told his mother and his sister that Maestro Filippo was very kind and taught him so many things. Sister Tia commented that they were pleased that Niccolò had thrived in Maestro Filippo's company. Then they hugged each other and felt proud for Niccolò that he had a very successful visit to Rome.

At this point his mother said, "We should all go to bed."

Mother Orissa and sister Tia bid good night, *"Buona Notte*, Niccolo."

"I will sleep late and go to my studio late in the morning," Niccolò told his mother who bid him a restful night.

Late in the morning the next day, Niccolò started his way to the studio. On his way there, he felt very happy and started walking faster and faster; the path and the area were so familiar to his heart it seemed he was lifted up in the air and floating. As he approached closer, he saw the Baptistery that stood majestic against the deep blue sky in front of the cathedral.

On his way, there were some peddlers pushing their carts who stopped and greeted him. When he entered the studio, everyone was busy working on their projects but then looked up when they noticed his presence, stopped what they were doing and cheered the returning young sculptor.

"Niccolò!" They all gathered around him as he greeted them with a smile and hugged them one by one.

They were all excited to hear about his stay in Rome and expressed that they all missed him very much.

After pleasantries were exchanged, Niccolò wanted to see his maestro and ran further inside the studio. His maestro approached him with outstretched arms and hugged him tightly.

The maestro's eyes sparkled. "I have good news for you."

Niccolò's eyes were luminous and his face lit up. "Maestro?"

"The church has given a project to work on two prophets," Maestro announced. "The church will explain to you about the work and sixteen gold florins are being offered depending on how you do the work. Then they will decide final compensation."

"Maestro, that is indeed good news, thank you very much!"

He wanted to share the news with his mother as soon as he could but suddenly, at this moment, he thought about Beatrice and also wished he could talk to her.

One of the younger members of the studio approached him and said quietly, "Maestro, a young lady from the Medici family came inquiring about your approximate time of return from Rome. And I told her it may be soon so she might come again."

Niccolò looked through the open door where the bridge at Ponte Vecchio curved.

Before he left the studio that day, he asked his maestro when could he begin the new project.

"Any time you wish," was the maestro's reply.

"Maestro," Niccolò said softly, "tomorrow then, at my usual time."

"Wonderful, I know you will excel."

Niccolò left the studio that early afternoon. He saw a boat full of people cheering the people at the bank of river Arno. The afternoon sun bathed the city of Florence. It was warm yet a cool breeze blew through the trees as a flock of seagulls were busy diving in the river in the quest for food.

He paced faster and faster to reach his home and once there, his mother and sister came out anxiously to greet him. They thought something went very wrong at work or he was not feeling good.

When Niccolò told them the good news, they were so elated that Mother Orissa went straight inside and knelt down at the altar to thank the Lord.

"Oh, we are going to make a special dinner to celebrate," his sister said. "I am making a list of ingredients to buy. Niccolò, my dear brother, please see whether you could find these things at the market. It is getting late."

Niccolò took the list from Tia and went to get the ingredients.

The following day, Niccolò arrived at the studio at his usual time. He was very happy now that he had his own project to work on.

The studio was full of marble slabs that came from a place called Carrara. Some were opaque white, others had yellowish streaks, some slabs had a silver-gray hue.

He scanned around the room and saw a slab lying in a corner looking at him. He quickly picked it up and started feeling it. Then he murmured to himself, "How does it feel?"

It seemed that the stone started to transform in front of his eyes. He remembered a past conversation with Beatrice when he told her that he wanted to make the figures come alive.

"When you see them, they would seem as if they are trying to tell a tale of their own life."

"How would you do that?" Beatrice had asked then.

"They convey their senses to me," Niccolò had replied.

"How could a stone do that?" she asked.

Niccolò remembered asking her, "Do you have a pet?"

"Yes, I do have a cat and she purrs and looks at me with her beautiful green eyes when she is happy."

"The slabs do the same. They convey their feeling with their silence. You have to view things from their perspective to understand that."

The slanted sun rays through the window fell on his marble slab and became more lucid to him. His spirit elevated and he was happy yet calm. "I am happy to choose the marble slab that I wanted."

Niccolò was happy that he got the list of things from his sister the day he told his mother and sister he got a project by the Domopera or the cathedral authorities. Total payment would be sixteen florins with the first payment of ten florins to be paid on November 1406 while the rest would be decided after he finished his work.

He told his sister and mother that he was going to invite their neighbor, Giorgio, who helped his mother a lot when he was away from home in Rome and also one of his *garzoni,* a younger assistant. He mentioned that he planned to prepare a type of dish.

It was a special dinner to celebrate Niccolò's new project and his return from Rome. Mother Orissa made gnocchi with a special sauce and herbs, Niccolò's favorite almond milk and rice while sister Tia made fresh salad with cucumber, tomato, and lettuce with herbs and olive oil. The herbs and vegetables were fresh from their garden. Niccolò surprised everyone by preparing Panutocon Provatura Fresca, a sweet and sour spicy fried bread with mozzarella.

They had a marvelous dinner with beer and ale as the conversation centered around Niccolò's success with his work-in-progress. They all agreed he was hard working and sincere and passionate about his work. Above all, he was a very good person always ready to help anyone in need.

They all wished him great success in the future and congratulated him from the bottom of their hearts.

Niccolò's Invitation to the Medici Palace

The studio was full of marble chips around different corners, the young energetic student sculptors trying hard with their different chisels, hammers and rasps to sculpt with keen attention. Their strong hands and long sturdy fingers kept working without rest, the long blood vessels bulged blue while the palms and fingers wrapped around hammer and chisel.

White marble chips dusted their bodies and their hair like snowflakes. Some grimaced with stooped heads to concentrate on their figures, some whistled, while others took deep breaths observing the ray of sunlight from a window with floating, fine shiny marble chips.

Niccolò took a deep breath and stood up to take a break. Everyone turned their faces towards this tall handsome body covered with marble chips. His long white outfitted stride started moving toward the door. He made a gesture that he was going out somewhere for some time.

No one asked but they were surprised that maestro's attention was not on sculpting.

The young student's whistling in the studio brought back some memories of a conversation regarding a concert. His face had an anxious look with brows contracting close together and lines appearing on his forehead

The Medici Palace would be the site of the concert that Beatrice invited him to attend. Beatrice had visited about three weeks ago in the afternoon when the sun was going down beyond the horizon, as she stood at the curve of the bridge at Ponte Vecchio. Beatrice knew that Niccolò would usually return home this way and around this time.

She was looking at the path, expecting any moment she would be seeing the handsome figure. She paced fast around a small circle around a gaslight post, her olive-green flowing dress almost sweeping the pavement and she was repeatedly trying to fix her dark brown hair and the locks on her forehead in place as it moved with the summer breeze.

Beatrice saw at last Niccolò's figure on the path and she almost bumped into him in her rush to greet him. Breathing heavily, she exclaimed, "I am so glad to find you here."

Niccolò stopped his fast pace and with wide eyes said, "What is the matter? Is everything all right with you?"

"Yes, Maestro. I have an invitation for you from my uncles Cosimo and Lorenzo."

"You do!" Niccolò couldn't contain his excitement.

She again took a deep breath. "Maestro, there will be a music concert organized by my Uncle Cosimo who's inviting musicians and singers from Florence and outside Firenze. Some musicians are coming from Germany. Both my uncles Cosimo and Lorenzo asked me to invite you as they know that I am interested in sculpting and painting and they also came to know I have visited your studio to see the process. They both liked your work and what you did for the cathedral.

Beatrice kept on luring him with compliments and attractions to get him more interested in attending the concert.

"There will be the trombonist from Germany and musicians from Padua and Venice and singers performing operatic excerpts from classical Greek operatic tragedies. Ladies from the Medici family might also take part."

Niccolò was listening very carefully and quietly, the color of his face changed from olive to blushing red and as he looked at a distance, his eyes were fixed to the infinite.

He took a deep breath and after some pause, he replied. "Beatrice, I appreciate the invitation very much. And I shall try my best to attend."

Niccolò Attends Music Concert at Medici Palace

Niccolò started walking faster and faster to his home. It was late afternoon and the sun was about to retire for the day. The orange sunrays flooded the tiled rooftops of the Florentine houses especially the plaza where the cathedral stood elegantly watching the city of Firenze.

Niccolò took a deep breath and murmured, "Madame Andre came to meet me in the studio which is very exciting that I must tell my mother about it. I wonder what she cooked for dinner? Well, whatever it is, it will be delicious." He picked up a faster pace and reached home in no time.

As usual, Mother Orissa and sister Tia were happy to see him and thrilled to hear about Madame Andre who they talked about as they sat around the dining table.

Soon a typical before-sunset dinner was served with soup made from carrots and eggs accompanied by freshly-baked bread, roasted salmon with spices like turmeric, ginger and garlic topped with fresh cilantro from their garden.

Niccolò started talking about his project when his mother announced that somebody from the church came and was looking for Niccolò.

The sculptor paused, his eating utensil in mid-air. "Did he say why?"

His mother shook her head. "No. He just said he wanted to talk to you."

Niccolò became anxious. "I completed the two prophets. They seemed to be satisfied."

"Yes, I am sure they are but they did not tell me exactly what they want to discuss only to find out if you are busy with any other work. I told them that I do not know and that they should talk to you. They asked me to tell you that at your convenience you can visit the Domopera, the cathedral authorities."

Sister Tia and Mother Orissa then jointly assured him, "Let us enjoy and have some wine today. Our prayers have been heard. Niccolò will get more commissions."

* * *

Niccolò got up early the next day to start his workday early. He was thinking about Madame Andre's commission as he walked towards the studio in his usual pace amid the seagulls' ear-piercing cries and the usual laps of the boats along the river Arno.

He missed Beatrice at this moment and wished he could see her soon. Suddenly he felt that "It is wishful thinking, a mere luxury to get involved with a beautiful, young lady from the prominent Medici family."

He started walking faster to reach his studio and whispered to himself, "I have work to do. I must focus for I cannot afford to have these thoughts slow me down."

On the way he saw the baker friend of his father waving to him.

He stopped to say "Hello." The bakery owner, Luigi, called, "Niccolò, here are some bread loaves baked with green olives. Please accept and enjoy these with your mother and sister and for you, here is a bottle of water flavored with orange blossoms to enjoy while you work. I am very pleased you are working hard. God bless you."

Niccolò was very pleased and happy. "Please let me know if I could help you with anything."

"Do not worry, my son. I will let you know if I need anything."

Niccolò's mood elevated as he sped faster to reach his studio. Once there, he selected a piece of marble then started feeling it. Then he viewed it from all directions possible, set it down and started drawing an outline of the figure carefully. When he was satisfied with it, he took his hammer and chisels of different kinds like a point chisel, tooth chisel and started subtractive sculpting and smoothing the surface with a rasp, a flat steel tool with a coarse surface most sculptors used, with sweeping strokes to remove excess small chips.

He was very pleased to have the flavored water Luigi gave him. Since he had been continuously working soon as he arrived at the studio at 6 that morning, he checked the clock and saw it was ten past 11 in the morning.

A fellow sculptor, Baccio, who was older than Niccolò, and Niccolò's student, Paolo arrived and insisted that Niccolò take a break for lunch. Baccio told Niccolò, "Let us try this place, an Osteria where the artists like us and the literati usually gather for *comestio*."

Niccolò was reluctant at first but on Baccio's insistence, he agreed.

"I'm sure you will like it," Baccio said. "This place serves simple but delicious food like home-cooked soup, millet porridge, mashed vegetables and egg. And, Niccolò! The place has locally-brewed beer that we must certainly taste." The young men started walking towards the piazza.

The breeze through pink and red oleander groves was refreshing, the scent of the flowers through the air made the paved path a pleasurable journey. Along the way, they came across people who gathered in some spots, urging themselves to take a break as others passed by leisurely.

Paolo, Niccolò and Baccio passed the oleander groves and the bakery then took the bricked-layered narrow path close to the river Arno until they reached the eatery.

The climbing vine with green triangular leaves and orange flowers covered the front of the building. The entrance was an archway layered with red bricks. All three sculptors were happy and relieved to find the place. Inside walls of Osteria was made with red bricks. At the middle there was an open fire oven, the semicircular wall above the oven was made with red bricks. The place was furnished with wooden benches and a wooden stool, all polished. There were clay vases with pink, white and yellow lupins which beautified the polished wooden table.

As expected, artists and literati were gathered as Baccio, Niccolò and Paolo took their seats and ordered soup, mashed vegetables and eggs. The three of them started a conversation with their hearts' content sipping the local beer.

Baccio started talking about Niccolò's commissions. "Niccolò, I heard the Domopera are talking about giving a commission to you."

"Dear brother, Baccio, I respect you as my elder brother, it is good news indeed but how do you come to know this?"

"Oh, Niccolò that is very nice that you respect me as your elder brother. From today, we shall bond with each other with our love and affection. To answer your question of how I came to know, I was called to see the Domopera in the cathedral in time to witness they were having a discussion about the commissions. Nanni de Banco, our sculptor friend gets St. Luke, I get St. Matthew and you, Niccolò, get St. John. I was in the corridor behind the big door so they did not see me. After I heard this, I went back again to the entrance, and returned as quickly as I could to reach there, breathing heavily to let them believe I had just arrived and was walking faster to reach in time."

"Oh, my brother Baccio, I thank you from the bottom of my heart," Niccolò said.

Paolo, the student, was quietly listening to their conversation. "Maestros, please take me with you if I could be of any help. It will help me to learn from you and I need to survive on my own so I need to earn some compensation."

Baccio and Niccolò both assured Paolo. "Do not worry. Work hard and learn everything carefully. We will definitely help you."

"Baccio, please advise me," Niccolò pleaded. "I am very anxious and nervous about going to the Medici Palace to attend a concert. Beatrice, the young lady from the Medici family somehow became acquainted with me and it seems that she wants to be friendly with me and she off and on appears at the curve of the bridge near Ponte Vecchio to talk to me about my work she shows a keen interest in.

"I used to be very brief with her but for the past few months, I stop and talk to her about my projects and my goals. She encourages me and that feels good but I do not know what else to do besides talk to her. I remind myself often that she is from the Medici family and she came to me two to three weeks ago and invited me on behalf of her uncles Cosimo and Lorenzo. She is very interested to see my studio while I am sculpting."

"My dear Niccolò, I want to know how you feel about this pretty lady."

"I feel extremely nervous and confused. A pretty young woman from the Medici family becoming closer to a person of my class is like Heaven falling on me; it is an absurd situation and I think I will be in trouble. I also I want to be a sculptor—that is my passion, that is what I want to be good at."

"Dear Niccolò, just keep on being a nice gentleman to this pretty lady but as you continue to be friendly, try to remain at a safe distance if you know what I mean." He winked his left eye with a smile. "You should definitely attend the concert. Who knows, it is likely that Cosimo heard about your work and he also contributes to the cathedral not openly but he is always ready to contribute whenever it is needed."

Baccio gave a friendly hug to Niccolò and Paolo joined them. Then Niccolò, Baccio and Paolo followed their path back to the studio.

Niccolò was happy to know that he was getting another commission. It was a special day when all three of them bonded together.

As the boat full of people cruised along the river, laps of oars harmonized with the cry of seagulls diving in water while people passed by.

On the day of the concert, Niccolò paced back and forth in his room. The thought that he in fact was going to the Medici Palace and would meet Cosimo and Lorenzo face to face made his heartbeat quicken.

He remembered Baccio's advice to attend the concert though he advised not to get too close to Beatrice. So after several bouts of hesitation, he decided to go.

He tried to look his best as he put on his brown three-forth, cut-out brief which reached just below the knee with a gold-colored button at the side, a beige, full-sleeved top with ruffles and a gold-colored button in front. His black hair was parted to the side which accentuated his clean-shaved face with his prominent nose. Overall, Niccolò thought he looked all right in the mirror. His leather shoes looked like sandals which were tied above the ankle with lacy strips of leather.

He started walking from his house and forced himself to arrive on time at the Medici Palace. It was a long walk as Niccolò lived on the outskirts of town and the Medici Palace was in the central part of town way past the Baptistery and cathedral piazza about five to six miles.

The concert would start at 5 in the evening but guests were supposed to arrive early. As Niccolò continued walking faster, he passed the houses of local people on a paved path and entered the sidewalk of the river bank adorned with oleander groves and some tall cypress trees where people were walking back home at the end of the day.

The year was 1407 and cypress trees moved back and forth with the summer breeze. Finally, Niccolò saw the piazza where stood the Baptistery and the cathedral.

He took a deep breath and murmured, "I am almost there."

As he came closer to the Medici Palace, it seemed to him from the outside that it looked like a huge, two-story building made with a big block of grayish black stone with a wide Cornish curled inside and a number of kneeling windows with iron bars were seen on the outside wall.

An enormous gate opened in front of him as he entered the courtyard which was paved with light gray and light pink-colored marble slabs. Huge clay flowering pots with orange and lemon trees were placed alternately all around the courtyard giving an impression of a citrus grove.

Right in the middle there was a cemented oval tank filled with water where large pink lotuses floated with their green dinner plate-sized leaves. At the far end of the courtyard stood a white marble sculpture of Orpheus with his flute. Apollo and Mercury were situated on the either side of the middle of the courtyard. Niccolò paused for some time to view them from various angles and whispered to himself, "classical Greek sculptures."

Passing the courtyard, Niccolò saw the covered corridor that stood painted in yellow with wide over hanging edges and at the middle of these hanging edges there was a Medici family court of arms on a relief.

Passing this corridor was the garden that Niccolò walked through on a gravel path. Someone came to guide Niccolò to the direction of the concert. He explained that the garden was in different levels as an extension to the house so there was always a chance to get lost.

As Niccolò and the guide passed through arches of climbing roses and wisteria, he was already feeling a sense of being a misfit in the House of Medici.

Finally, they entered the concert hall where Niccolò felt like an outsider amid the grandeur and beauty of the place. Silk tapestries hung on the walls of the big hall, some showing hunting scenes, others with beautiful maidens swinging on a decorated flowery swing. Some of the tapestries featured beautiful and playful, young maidens leisurely spending their time and others with ladies playing their lyre.

The upper part of the wall near the ceiling was bordered with flowering creepers with gold, blue and green. The painted ceiling resembled a blue sky where patches of white clouds floated with angels coming from different directions.

Beautiful chandeliers made with fine glass lighted the hall, each and every one unique with most of them looking like flowers with petals and in the middle of each flower there was a candle. Each chandelier was made with bunches of glass flowers, some had a pinkish hue others were opaque white with a perfect shape of flowers of different kinds, like roses and lilies.

In the middle of each flower was a place for a candle and all were lit when the concert started. In the middle of the hall there was a huge chandelier shaped like a lotus with open pink petals lit with candles reflecting pinkish hues that created a soft and sweet haze over the concert hall.

Niccolò appeared dazzled and lost himself when he suddenly realized that the hall was full of the Medici family and also wealthy members of the nobility who came from different parts of Firenze and beyond. They were all seated in their designated seats. Niccolò sat in one of first few rows. He was feeling out of place and shy when he spotted Beatrice.

Her hair up in a bun, her figure was adorned with a long pink flowing dress. She wore a wristlet made with pink roses and there were red and pink roses around her bun. Her ruby pendant with diamonds sparkled like a rainbow when she turned to look around.

Soon, the singers and lute players started performing. The audience became quiet as the sound of music filled the air. Niccolò enjoyed and savored every moment. He fixed his eyes on the divine expression on wBeatrice's face when the music started to fill the hall. He wanted to keep this moment forever inside him, fresh and new as the morning sun. He promised he would not get this impression lost for any earthly desire.

* * *

At intermission, the audience continued moving from their seats wanting to mingle with their acquaintances. This span of time—getting acquainted in conversation with others—proved challenging for Niccolò as he was not familiar with any other person except Beatrice. He stood up to take a walk across the hall and as he started to move, he saw Beatrice accompanying an elegant lady slowly gracing towards him. She was tall, her velvety maroon dress slowly floated on the pink and black mosaic floor. Her gold necklace was a piece of art: the teardrop diamonds hanging from a leafy creeper made with gold cuddled her long neck. Having been a goldsmith, Niccolò was amazed to see fine work on the jewelry. Her fair complexion possessed a tinge of olive tan that complimented her triangular face accentuated with big, bright hazel eyes and a sharp nose. Black hair was neatly arranged in a bun and adorned with diamond studded hairpins which sparkled when she turned her head to talk with others. Besides the beauty and the attire, there was something magnetic that exuded in her presence.

Beatrice approached Niccolò with an introduction. "Maestro, this is my Aunt Contessina, my Uncle Cosimo's wife."

Niccolò bowed. "Honorable Lady, I am very happy to meet you."

Lady Contssina seemed eager to start conversing with Niccolò. "I heard so much about your work from the cathedral people." She glanced at her niece. "And our Beatrice talks about you so much. Beatrice is like our daughter. She is Cosimo's cousin's daughter and very much interested in studying art and Greek literature so Cosimo asked her to come and stay in Florence with us. So she is our daughter now and she is my favorite. By the way, my husband is also very interested in art and literature."

Beatrice beamed and brightened with her aunt's comment, her glowing expression made her look prettier.

Contessina turned towards Niccolò. "Maestro, I will be very pleased if you would do some sculptures for our garden and also for our courtyard."

"As you wish, my dear lady, I will always try my best to reach your expectations and desires."

It was about time to get back to their individual seats for the rest of the concert. Before returning to their seats, Contessina told Niccolò, "Please wait at your seat after the concert is over. Someone will come and accompany you to Cosimo and Lorenzo as they want to talk to you about some future project for our new home in Florence."

Niccolò bowed and Contessina and Beatrice gracefully started back to their seats when Beatrice suddenly turned and approached Niccolò to say, "Maestro, I'm so very happy you came tonight."

Niccolò smiled in reply. The concert continued with a variety of artists playing their instruments. The trombonists from Germany played solos and also ensembles with others. Three of the lute players played individually exquisite performances.

Five beautiful ladies played the lyre. They were all clad in light blue and green flowing dresses with hair up in a bun, a flower wreath wrapped around the forehead at the hairline and tied at the back.

The sound of five lyres filled the air with divine music which elevated the audience to another level of human consciousness. Then the concert finished with loud cheering and a thunderbolt of applause.

Niccolò waited at the same spot and soon someone with a beige puffed full-sleeved top and sea green brocade waistcoat and tight hose approached him. The presence of the man who took off his brown cap and bowed nearly startled Niccolò who, because he thought him to be a member of the nobility, stood up. The person of average built with a broad face and black eyes and pointed nose said in a heavy voice, "Maestro, I am here to accompany you to master Cosimo's office."

Niccolò followed the man as they both traveled through the garden. By now dusk had settled in, the twilight just spread its veil, as several fountains kept murmuring, as the hanging lantern of different colors nearby reflected light around the bushes. A summer blast of cool breeze brought a wet smell of the surrounding green bushes which were trimmed flat and round alternately to harmonize with the potted plants down below. Some were only leafy green, others were blossoming plants like daisy and jasmine. The air was filled with a sweet smell as flying and chirping birds going back to their nests at the end of the day dotted the sky.

Finally, the moment of Niccolò's meeting in the chamber where Cosimo was waiting had arrived.

The meeting space was called a tapestry chamber where Cosimo would meet people and where he would spend days going over matters to be discussed. The walls were white, with frescos bordering the ceiling and the wall featuring designs of vine with flowers and fruits. The ceiling painted with a blue sky background with floating white clouds and angels hovering over them, showing in all its glory in different corners the mesmerizing winged white horses carrying different riders cruising across the sky.

The chamber's floor was paved with amber-colored tiles. A big, round glass top table with golden rim and gold-colored legs was placed in the middle of the room. Red silk cushioned chairs with gold-colored arms and legs surrounded it. Large windows were draped with white, lacy see-through curtains. Colorful tapestry decorated all four walls with hunting scenes and landscape scenes with hills and valleys with frolicking deer.

Cosimo sat on one of the cushioned chairs facing the entrance. He was in his high collar, full-sleeved, crimson, velvet long outfit, a houppelande with a matching cap on his head. Wavy brown black hair showed at his temples and also peeped at the back of his head below his red cap. The dark navy inner garment's neatly pleated folds were fashionably seen through the unbuttoned opening of his long outfit.

His triangular olive face with pointed nose and bright sparkling eyes seemed to absorb all the detail around him.

Niccolò entered the room with hesitation just as Cosimo welcomed him warmly and uttered, "*Buonasera*, Maestro, have a seat."

Rudy Arrives in Manchester

Rudy arrived in the big city of Manchester. At the train station he met a physician of Indian origin working in Manchester who happened to be there to bid goodbye to his friend who was going back to London.

He was very pleased to meet another Indian unexpectedly and one that was also a young physician. After a brief conversation, the physician discovered that Rudy was desperately seeking for a job. The man Rudy met was an experienced doctor working for a while who was aware of a few jobs available for junior doctors around that area.

The physician invited Rudy to his house to spend the night and have a leisurely conversation with him. Rudy was pleased to get the invitation as he did not know the area and it would be convenient to spend the night with his newfound friend.

Moreover, he might know someone around the area who can help him get a job.

The doctor drove a blue Audi with black leather seats. Rudy was riding with him in the front seat. They passed through the sprawling Manchester metropolitan area where buses and cars sped by and on two sides of a pavement, people strode faster to reach their homes.

On a late summer evening half past six, the sun was still shining bright around this part of England where the sun would usually set late in the evening around 9:30 to 10 p.m.

Soon as they left the city, Rudy could see the open fields and small cottages. Rudy's new friend drove off the highway, circling around the town center and followed a wooded area to an open space where Rudy saw peaceful picturesque cottages.

The car continued on a winding country road and coasted along a paved path of a stone thatched cottage that boasted a brick chimney. The pale-yellow cottage home that stood on a narrow pathway looked like two floors with the second level resembling an attic from the outside. The glass windows were framed in wood but painted white. The blossoming wisteria climbed up the roof and displayed its color. There were several birch trees on both sides of the house. The green bushes on either side of the paved path led to the main entrance. Flower beds of different colored daisies lined up along the bushes. Beyond that were several rose bushes. The garden seemed overgrown and hemmed by a white-washed garden wall where there were more garden beds on either side.

Rudy heard about cottages and gardens in England and that English people liked their cottages to resemble those in a village.

Once Rudy entered the cottage, he was greeted by the lady of the house who was also from India. They sat down and chatted for a little while and then they sat down around a small table for a simple light supper: potato and leek soup, slices of bread and butter, some cheese and slices of red apples with cinnamon sugar.

A white tablecloth covered the small rectangular table at the kitchen adorned with yellow and pink roses in a vase. When Rudy sat down, he saw the rose bushes at their backyard.

The new friend seemed to be older than Rudy so Rudy started calling him "*Dada*," which means "elder brother," a title that was the Indian way of paying respect to the man who was trying to help Rudy.

The physician *Dada* told Rudy that in the proper city of Manchester he would not get a job as he was new and the hospital board would probably preselect the local young doctors from the university. So the best thing to do would be to go to a relatively small group hospital where there would be more possibilities of getting a job.

Rudy agreed and this *Dada* of Rudy knew few people in the selection board at the relatively small group hospital. Rudy and his newfound *Dada* would visit the hospital the next morning as he somehow managed to arrange an interview for Rudy to apply for a position as a junior house officer.

Rudy felt relieved that if he was granted this position, a free place to live and food would be provided daily by the hospital. The hospital cleaning staff would come and take care of everything like bedsheet changes, clean towels and laundry service were all provided.

Rudy was very pleased and excited but at the same time nervous and shy of the completely new environment to adjust in and nervous about the work. Furthermore, Rudy had never taken a clinical training for the routine procedures in patient care.

Rudy returned with his *Dada* at the physician's house to spend the night so he could start his new job at the hospital the next day.

He thanked his newfound friend with warm words and gestures like holding his hands warmly. Rudy thanked the lady of the house for giving him delicious food and letting him stay in their beautiful cottage.

That night he could not sleep. He was anxious as to how he was going to cope with the new job as he never had preliminary clinical training. Rudy recalled reading Niccolò's biography where the sculptor had been nervous about his new job in Rome but then he eventually persevered. Taking inspiration from Niccolò's own sense of adventure to embrace a new opportunity, Rudy then realized there was no other way but to be strong and face his new situation.

And speaking of a new situation, Rudy contemplated again how his own experience venturing out into the unknown in his line of profession might have paralleled with what he read about Niccolò's situation at the time when the sculptor had his first commission with none other than the great Cosimo de' Medici.

Niccolò and Cosimo

Niccolò took his seat on one of the chairs made with finely polished walnut with carved legs and arms. The back rest of the chair was designed with the face of a gargoyle protruding from curved creepers. Cosimo reached out his right hand to greet Niccolò whose fingers shook as he was nervous as he always was when encountering a new person and, in this case, Cosimo, one of the important and richest men of Florence. Deep down inside, Niccolò felt proud that Cosimo invited him as he was only an artist, not on par with a man of Cosimo's stature.

His hands were moist. "Pardon my hands," Niccolò said.

"Do not worry, Maestro, working hands tend to do that."

On the glass top table sat silver goblets and a silver wine pitcher with the engraved name, "Medici," along with a stack of white, heavy, medium-sized, thick glass plates with a painted border of blue-colored vines and yellow pears. Several of them were filled with small fruit tarts and others with sugared chips and triangular pastries filled with cream and some filled with chunks of cheese.

Cosimo asked the attendant standing nearby to pour some wine for both of them then he filled an empty plate with a variety of pastries using a silver tong and offered it to Niccolò who hesitantly said, "*Onorevoli* Signore, I will just take one, thank you very much."

Cosimo asked Niccolò about his family and the sculptor related that he lived with his widowed mother and his sister whose husband abandoned her.

Cosimo's eyes sparkled as he warmly said, "Niccolò, it is wonderful that you are looking after your family. I really want to help you, Maestro. Let me know what your needs are."

"Signore, I really appreciate your concern and offer. I am a sculptor who works passionately with my two hands. I pray to work on artistic creations which truly come alive and meet your expectations and in return as appreciation for whatever you offer, I will respect that. One more thing: I want my creative freedom. You can give me your idea and I will work hard with all my sincerity to create it. But when I start the work, something happens at that moment. My hands with the tools take me to the world of creation and I immerse deep down in that world where no one can enter."

"Dear Niccolò, I am so glad that you told me all this. I am impressed. I welcome you as my creative friend." Cosimo sipped some wine. "Niccolò, my wife, Contessina likes you very much and we are planning to build a new palace that will be our home in the near future. She would like you to sculpt some figures for our garden and also for the courtyard. I have a list of things which I want to you sculpt. Anyway, we will both meet on several occasions to discuss. This is just an introduction."

The attendant in the meantime lit all the candles inside the big dome-shaped chandelier in the middle of the room. The big teardrop crystals which were hanging from the chandelier started refracting light like a prism.

The breeze through the large windows on both sides brought the sweet smell of jasmine from the garden which filled the air as shadows of flickering candles and the murmuring of the fountains together made the chamber magical and dreamy.

They both looked at each other as Cosimo said, "It turned out to be a pleasant evening. I am glad that we had a heart-to heart talk. Lorenzo, my brother, also wanted to meet you." As soon as he uttered the sentence, Lorenzo, who lived on other side of the palace, appeared at the door.

An average-built man, Lorenzo had a round face, pointed nose, tanned olive skin and a thick, black moustache. His wavy black hair was parted in the middle and his large, sparkling hazel eyes definitely attracted attention of the people around him.

He wore a brown, three-forth, cutout brief, a yellow silk shirt with ruffles in the middle and also around his full sleeves he was wearing a blue brocade vest and a navy-blue cap with a feather on it.

"*Ciao*," Lorenzo said to Niccolò with his baritone voice and bowed his head slightly to show respect to his elder brother, Cosimo, who warmly welcomed his brother stretching his arms to him and inviting him to join their discussion of the list of sculptures.

Cosimo poured wine in a goblet which he offered to Lorenzo who asked his brother whether he had shown Niccolò the plan for the new palace and garden.

"Not yet, my brother. I think maestro Brunelleschi's plan is grand and beautiful, but I do not want to show that grandeur to the Florentine people so I am thinking of choosing Michelozzo's plan which is a little smaller scale and not so grand in fact from the outside. It will show like a two-story brick building. What you think, Lorenzo?"

"Yes, I think that it will be very practical to go along the flow especially. We do not want to show our grandeur or greatness, building a grand palace. We want to show our work which will help the Florentines for generations to come."

"Oh Lorenzo, my brother, you spoke of my heart's intent."

Lorenzo looked at Niccolò and said, "Maestro, I hope you heard that my sister-in-law, Contessina, and our niece, Beatrice, like your work very much. Both of them want you to sculpt for our new home and garden."

"*Onorevoli* Signore, I will try my best to meet your expectations."

Niccolò looked outside, not knowing what else he could say. His eyes went beyond the large windows where the shadowy trees were moving with a gentle breeze.

Cosimo asked, "Maestro, are you working on some commissions right now?"

"Yes, I am working on Madame Andre's two prophets which will be finished, very soon I hope."

"Any other commission?" Lorenzo asked.

"I am going to meet the Domopera soon as they want to talk to me about probably working on some project."

Lorenzo was very eager to talk to Niccolò. "Maestro, I have a question for you."

"Please, Signore."

"I wonder if you can start on a separate project with the permission of my brother, for us, like some sculpture for our new courtyard and garden and then when the plan gets through and the real construction work begins then ultimately done, there would not be any problem of placing the finished sculptures in places where they will belong. What do you think, my brother?"

"Excellent idea, my brother," Cosimo said, "If it suits maestro's work schedule."

"I will be glad to work on the subject you want me to sculpt and in that way I can plan ahead and do my work."

Evening settled and soon crickets were chirping as Niccolò was ready to go back home. Cosimo and Lorenzo assured Niccolò that their carriage would take him home.

Niccolò felt overwhelmed and shy. "Thank you, but I can walk home."

"Of course, you can but we would not let you do that," Lorenzo said.

Niccolò smiled and bid goodbye to both of them.

The carriage was run by two large, brown horses, dressed up with a golden bordered blue silk material covering their back as a garment, the leather reins had fancy gold stars. The carriage driver dressed in tight black pants and a fluffy black and white striped shirt with a black cape hanging on his back.

Niccolò sat on the black cushioned seat of the carriage. The roof was open and a summer breeze gently blew through his hair. A very pleasant yet unfamiliar feeling overcame him.

The carriage driver drew the reins and called out to the horses, "Come on, boys let's go!"

The horses trotted for a short time and then started galloping on the paved road.

With a clip clap and later, a galloping sound, the silhouette of the palace with its open flame torches soon disappeared in the darkness as they passed by the slumbering city and the shadowy trees. The dark sky with blinking stars watched them pass until Niccolò reached home and said good night to the carriage driver who bid him a *"Buona Notte."*

Rudy in Bury

Bury was a town in greater Manchester about eight miles northwest of Manchester on the river Irwell. After going through past disappointments, the house officer job in Bury was more than a welcome reprieve.

Now he had to deal with his limited knowledge of practical medicine and overcome his fear of being ridiculed by other doctors. At his orientation, Rudy familiarized himself about Bury, a town that emerged in the Industrial Revolution as a mill town famous for its open-air market, art museum and the local dish, Black Pudding of which there were special stalls highlighting the local dish.

Traditionally made with pigs' blood, Black Pudding consisted of oat cereal or other types of cereal, sometimes spices. After preparation, it would look like a sausage patty. It also contained some fat considered a super food presented fried or baked.

Rudy started his work in the early morning when the nurses were already at work and the doctors had yet to arrive. He realized that the nurses knew as much as the house officers who were also known as junior doctors.

So Rudy started being friendly and nice to them and his catch phrase would be, "How do you do this in your country?"

They were very happy to be given so much importance. Every day as the time passed, he would learn how to do an EKG and how to draw blood from patients when the technician was not available in the odd hours of night and wee hours of the morning.

The nurses also protected Rudy from the senior doctors if he lagged behind on the work and some routine work ordered by a senior doctor that had yet to be done. Thus, the learning process continued.

Rudy, all prepared to take on the day, would listen to the patients' histories and examined them; he excelled in bedside etiquette with the patients and their relatives and would show kindness and humility to their inquiries, distresses and demands.

The nurses, called "ward sisters" in England, helped Rudy a lot and were very friendly. All the sisters wore uniforms which were usually long-sleeved or half-sleeved, deep sky-blue dresses that fell below the knees. The long-sleeved uniform would be broad starched, a white cuff at the end of the long sleeve with a gold-colored button to keep it in place. Half sleeves would add a tailored, lightly frilled white cloth band to go where the sleeve ends.

Over their heads in the front, a white cloth kind of cap or crown would be placed just behind their hairline, fully stretching across the front of the head from side to side.

When these sisters made their rounds to take care of their patients, they would look very graceful and professional working in their uniforms. The ward was fully controlled by the sisters. Doctors of all levels had to respect, listen and go along with the rules which were established by them.

On one particular occasion, Rudy was asked by his senior doctor to do a lumber puncture to draw spinal fluid from the spinal canal. This was one of the diagnostic tools for the investigation of certain patients. Rudy was nervous as he lacked prior practice of this in the past and did not want to poke the patient the wrong way. Thank goodness, the sisters were saviors as they usually prepared the patient while doctors had to scrub and put on a scrubbing outfit to do the procedure.

The sisters proved to be present and reliable as they did the scrubbing, cleaning and applying of aseptic dressing on the area where the procedure would be done. One sister handed the lumber puncture needle to Rudy and pointed to him exactly where and how the needle would go in and how to place it in between the two lower lumber vertebrae.

Rudy, with his gloved hand, followed exactly what the sister showed him, going in the spinal space and taking out the stylus from the base of the needle. The clear fluid started dripping; the clear spinal fluid was collected in several white test tubes for a laboratory test. Rudy's heart started beating faster with the joy of success, his face, though covered with a mask, stretched a little with a hidden smile. It made his day and the sisters around congratulated him.

From this point, the sisters would call him Rudy most of the time and not Dr. Sen or his full name, Dr. Rudrendu Sen, except in very special circumstances.

Soon, Rudy's time in Bury went by faster and, armed with a lot of learning experience, he was confident enough to seek some other job.

Yet, a part of him was reluctant to leave as he somewhat became attached to his current working place and the people but now the time had arrived to move on.

It was evening after work when he went back to his living quarters which was inside the hospital camp. He wished he could confide in someone. He looked out the window to see that it was nearly sundown as the rays passed through the tall pines that reflected over an open space, coloring it orange. Birds like tiny black dots flew up at the distant sky. Rudy wondered and whispered as the flock flew to their home peacefully. He took a deep breath and looked at the distant horizon with a fixed gaze when suddenly, a flash of Manashi appeared to him as he murmured hope that she was doing well.

Rudy pondered to himself, "Why would she not be doing well? She's a young woman full of energy and determination who can do whatever she wants. Her compassion, thoughtfulness, imagination, and grace will serve her well in the years ahead. Though my survival has always been challenging, I anticipate more of it as it will only make me stronger." He paused to reflect on his past with Manashi.

"Yes, I think I couldn't have faced the situation bidding her goodbye. It would have been too tough and yes, I didn't have the courage to let her know of my true feelings—that I loved her and wanted to be with her. Why did I not express this? I ask myself repeatedly. Was it shyness? Was it my pride? We did do fun things and enjoyed studying together. We were young.

"But yes, I always enjoyed being with her but I was anxious and fearful. She came from a respected, well-established family and I was a refugee, a person without a radar or compass in the vast empty space." He remembered reading in the biography of Niccolò that the sculptor didn't think he was good enough for Beatrice in the same way Rudy thought he didn't deserve Manashi, who was stations above him.

He paced inside his room a number of times, taking deep breaths and then sat down on the couch and put his right hand on the right side of his head just over his temple. Rudy sat like that for a few minutes, breathing heavily then got up and went to the mirror and said to himself, "I will keep the image of my love in my heart forever but now, I must move on."

And for him, moving on meant he would do as he read Niccolò had done when he received his first big commission, one big step towards a new beginning in Niccolò's as well as Rudy's own life.

Niccolò Gets St. John Commission

Niccolò was lost in his thoughts as one by one the events passed like a dream. He lost his father as early as fourteen then, with the maestro he worked on the bronze door then on to his visit to Rome with maestro Filippo.

Back in Florence he acquired the two prophets commission from the cathedral and then Madame Andre's commission and a visit to the concert in the palace and a pleasant evening with Cosimo and Lorenzo.

It was hardly a year ago that he heard from Baccio the rumor of getting a commission from the church people known as the Domopera.

Today, a bright summer day in June 1408, he was going to see the Domopera for hopefully another commission from the cathedral. Could it be that someone divine was guiding his path, or was it some sort of energy beyond this world that was showing the light to him?

He was confused, but he felt deep inside him that it was beyond his control that the events were manifesting themselves.

Suddenly he felt a deep affection and appreciation for Beatrice. The connection with Cosimo and Lorenzo at the palace was only made possible through Beatrice.

He could not fathom how a pretty young Medici girl became so interested in sculpture and also interested in him. Niccolò murmured to himself that Beatrice would serve as an inspiration, a bundle of energy, and not an earthly desire.

He started walking towards the cathedral to meet the Domopera. Walking along the paved path by the white oleander bushes, he thought about the white marble ready to be picked up and would take a shape of whatever you want it to be, then suddenly it would wake up with all its senses morphing into whatever you or anyone wished it to become.

He felt confused and cheerful at the same time. He was almost at the gate of the cathedral and took a deep breath as he strode faster through the corridor and arrived at the chamber where the cathedral people were waiting.

They all smiled at Niccolò and asked him to sit down on a bench close to a rectangular table where the Domopera sat. Niccolò bowed with respect and sat down.

Then one of them said, "We are very pleased to commission St. John the Evangelist to you. When can you start on this project and how long do you think it will take you to finish it?"

"Respected bishop," said Niccolò, "I can start tomorrow, even today, if you give me your permission to start. What is the estimated time that you would like St. John to be finished?"

"Say about five to six years."

"I will try hard to keep your expectation. My dear Bishop, I would like my creative freedom, allow me to explain. You can give me your ideas about the sculpture but when I sculpt, I am immersed in my own world and my mind goes deep in the ocean of creation and my hands follow it. At that period of time, I am cut off from the present world and the true form evolves from the stone, I have no external control."

"We understand and hope your creation of the St. John the Evangelist sculpture would come alive for future generations of Florentines. God bless you. You have our blessing to start the work."

Niccolò was very happy but he wanted to make the sculpture unique and to display his uniqueness, he wished to apply the idea of perspective. Before starting his work, he desired to talk to Beatrice as she never failed to encourage him to go ahead and display his unique ideas.

Furthermore, a friendship with Cosimo and Lorenzo in the palace was possible as Beatrice introduced and mediated the process.

Beatrice came in the afternoon at the usual place where the bridge curves. She prepared an almond rice dessert, Niccolò's favorite, and was patiently waiting at the spot for that was the time when Niccolò usually took a break.

Niccolò was very happy to see the silhouette of Beatrice from a distance. She was adorned in her light amber dress as the summer breeze blew through her wavy dark brown hair. She seemed anxious and not sure exactly of the time of Niccolò's arrival as she was aware that sometimes Niccolò did not take a break.

Suddenly, a seagull passed by with a shriek and Beatrice jumped to the other side of the road when she saw Niccolò's figure at a distance. She was very happy and greeted Niccolò with a smile. "Maestro, I am so glad you took a break."

"Yes Beatrice, I got a new commission of St. John the Evangelist. If I can finish it within the allotted time, it will be in the niche of the Duomo."

"Oh Maestro, that is so wonderful to hear."

"Beatrice, I have a new idea of making it towards naturalism. It will be placed far above the eye level of the people who will be visiting him, so to correct the distortion, I will lengthen the torso."

He brought a paper and a marker and started to sketch as he explained the process to Beatrice. Then he held the paper up lifting his arms above Beatrice's eye level and showed that if the torso was lengthened and the legs were shortened, it would look normal."

"Maestro, you are genius."

"Beatrice there is another thing. He is depicted as young, but I want to show the wisdom in his personality. So he will not look as young."

"Maestro, I understand you will make a unique creation."

"Beatrice, I want to thank you very much. Your uncles Cosimo and Lorenzo, both of them treated me very well. They are planning to give me a commission of some sculpture for the new palace. They even said that it will be soon. I do not have enough words to express how much I am grateful to you. I appreciate it very much."

"Oh, Maestro, please do not even mention it. You are highly qualified and the right person for the job and we are lucky that you will be a huge part of it. Maestro, I have some news. Uncle Cosimo plans to expand the library and it will also be available to the Florentine people and he has given me some responsibility in the literature section to work and arrange it. I am very pleased and I shall cherish this kind of responsibility to work on."

"How nice. It will be a big workload for you and I am amazed and proud that you offered up yourself to do this project."

Beatrice's face beamed with joy as her eyes sparkled. "Maestro, you have made me so happy." She handed him his favorite almond rice dessert.

After thanking Beatrice, he bid her goodbye as he had so much to do.

Niccolò hurried back to the studio and started to search for a piece of stone which would be the best one that he was going to sculpt with and found a colossal piece of white stone. With the help of other sculptors in the studio, he placed the particular piece at the end near a corner then stood back a few feet away trying to visualize the figure. Then he went close to the particular piece and started to touch it from different angles. Suddenly his face illuminated and he ran to get a paper and a marker and started sketching the figure. He murmured to himself that the figure would be more naturalistic.

Niccolò took time to sketch the figure and was very careful about all the aspects of the figure like his stance, the position of the hands, legs, his face and eyes.

He started sculpting St. John and every single day, other fellow sculptors could see him murmuring to himself. "I know that he was the pillar of the

Church but I want to portray him with deep feeling—the feeling which comes from the bottom of my heart so that I may do justice to St. John, a noble and introspective prophet."

He started concentrating on sculpting with his deep feeling of humanism. As time went by, there were times that Niccolò forgot what day it was so immersed was he in his project.

He would start his work early in the morning, and hours of the day would pass, sometimes without any break until the end of the day when the sun would go down.

The last rays of sun reflected through the studio window full of fine dust particles that would emit various colors of refracted light.

Niccolò would get up to stretch his arms and legs and whisper, "Oh, daylight is already receding!"

Other sculptors and visitors from church kept on coming to see Niccolò's progress. Beatrice visited with her Aunt Contessina, Cosimo's wife. The visit of Beatrice and Contessina was very inspiring to Niccolò. They were all amazed to see this colossal figure take shape and come to life.

The prophet was seated in traditional flowing robes that hid his body but showed off graceful sculpted arms and torso which was elongated more than his legs to correct the distortion as the sculpted figure would be placed above in a niche in the Duomo.

Niccolò sculpted St. John's arm placing it carefully atop a book of scriptures. He depicted his expression of wisdom as an aging prophet with some lines of wisdom on his forehead and his eyes fixed far to search for some deeper truth.

Niccolò Starts Work on St. John

October, 1410

Niccolò started work on St. John in the summer of June 1408, and now it was the middle of October,1410. The cathedral people wanted him to finish in six years. There was a chill in the morning as Niccolò paced faster from his home to the studio and he noticed some of the trees already painted their leaves in autumnal colors.

The gray and white clouds against the blue sky seemed to be grouped together and were racing each other to reach somewhere unknown. The morning sun was still sleepy as it peeped through a misty screen. Niccolò strode swiftly until he reached his studio.

Paolo quickly approached Niccolò. "Maestro, some guild people are waiting inside to meet you."

"Which guild people?"

"I do not know, Maestro, but they are waiting and said it is important and urgent that they see you today."

Niccolò went inside and saw three people waiting. They all got up and said, "Buongiorno, Maestro, we are from the Armor Guild. We heard news from the south that an army led by a tyrant from Naples moved north to attack Florence. Now Florence is in danger of being invaded. We are commissioning you to sculpt St. George as this saint was known as a military man and patron saint of the Armors Guild. He was the one who was with the crusaders."

Niccolò patiently listened to them then asked, "When would you like me to start this commission?"

"It is very urgent, Maestro, today or tomorrow at the latest. Another thing is that you have to work in the niche where he is going to stand in the Orsanmichele. We and the people of Firenze are depending on you."

Niccolò took a deep breath, his eyes looked far off in the distance as he sat down on his work bench and looked at the unfinished St. John as he kept on breathing heavily.

The guild people were anxious for his answer. "For the people of Firenze, Maestro, please accept it."

After a few minutes Niccolò stood up. "I will accept it after I inform the cathedral priests about it. They commissioned for me to work on St. John as well. So I anticipate their granting approval, that way I will divide my work time on the two saints."

"Maestro, the Domopera already know that and have asked us to reach you and talk to you."

"I will juggle my time between the two saints as St. George must be completed early. I will work on St. George for four days then the rest of the week on St. John. Another thing, Paolo, my assistant, will be helping me there in the church."

"We thank you very much and we welcome Paolo to work with you in the church."

Niccolò asked Paolo, "Please gather the tools we have to take with us and my drawing papers and work bench and whatever else you may need, Paolo. Please put them together and some transportation is needed to carry all of these to the church. I have duplicates of my tools that will help but other times, we will need help carrying back some tools to my studio."

A spokesman from the guild said, "We can arrange a horse-drawn cart to transport all the essentials back and forth from the church to your studio. We can also arrange a carriage from here in the afternoon to transport your tools. If you would please put them in one place and show the men who will be coming to pick them up which tools to bring that will be very helpful. It is no problem that we can arrange bringing back some of your tools to your studio."

"We will both be here when they come. What about the sculpting media?" Niccolò asked.

"Maestro, the guild can only afford to sculpt it in marble as bronze will be too expensive for us."

"That is all right. Slabs of marble will be delivered to the church?"

"Yes, Maestro, there are marble slabs already delivered in the church. You have to choose yourself which slab you want."

"That is all right then. We will wait here till your men with the cart come to pick up our tools."

The guild people seemed very pleased that everything was arranged and soon they bid goodbye to Niccolò and Paolo. Niccolò examined St. John and when Paolo handed over the rasp, chisel and hammer, Niccolò worked on his unfinished torso which was proportionally bigger than his legs. He was pleased to see that Paolo had started on the back side of the sculpture.

"Paolo, we have to be in the church of Orsanmichele around 8 o'clock in the morning."

"Yes, Maestro, no problem."

Niccolò was lost in his thoughts as he was planning to finish St. John much earlier.

Now this commission came to him as a blessing from some unseen force. Suddenly he felt that he was waking up from a daze to a clear, lighted path to follow his journey forward without looking back.

Niccolò finished his day and started walking towards home as thoughts passed by one by one. There was a chill in the air as branches of the birch trees swayed with a murmur passing the message of autumn to the beech and oak trees. The blue sky met the blue of the ocean at a distance as a tinge of the setting sun reflected in orange broke into pieces and carried away by ripples of ocean to shore.

He heard that people of the linen guild were eager to meet him. Were they also thinking about another commission for him? He decided not to think about it right now. Tomorrow he would start St. George and determine to finish it as soon as possible.

And on that note, Niccolò started walking faster to reach home.

*   *   *

St. John, as he desired, came alive in front of him. To him, the saint was alive, searching for a deeper truth. As the morning sun brushed the sculpted figure, Niccolò cried out loud, "He is alive!"

Then he circled around the sculpted figure and took note of the area of the figure that he had to smooth out with his tool.

As he worked, he started talking to himself, "Within two to three months, I can give St. John to the cathedral people. I will miss him but he will grace the cathedral with his divine presence."

Niccolò and Family Receive a Message from his long-lost Nephew

Niccolò on his way to his studio would always walk faster to warm up his body and mind to welcome his day of creativity and on his way, the landscape seemed to recede backwards. The landscapes were usually imprinted inside him pleasantly unless it was disrupted by an out of ordinary event like a cart full of vegetables toppled on the road side or a repair of the paved road, such unusual incidents as that. The cool breeze, the familiar path, greetings from known faces along the way inspired him to dedicate time to his often challenging yet satisfying artwork.

Along his way, thoughts about his mother Orissa and his sister Tia passed one after another like wandering clouds. His mother expressed anxiety about Tia's welfare and what would happen when Orissa no longer existed in this world. Niccolò gave his word of honor not to worry about that since he was going to take responsibility for her.

His sister was also very artistic in her own way as she embroidered with fine designs on dresses and on other daily utility clothes and shawls. She was a fine dressmaker too.

Tia learned her artistic technique from her aunt on her mother's side. Her aunt's husband had a shop in Venice and her aunt was one of the main artists who helped her husband provide materials to sell. Her aunt would come and stay with her mother almost every year to take a break for a month to stay with her sister Orissa and she would teach her niece Tia who would pick up the technique very quickly and easily. She was lucky and it helped her a lot after her husband left her to keep her busy and obtain whatever meager amount of income available to contribute to the family fund. Her mother Orissa and brother Niccolò really appreciated her efforts very much.

There was no one to promote her and she was reluctant and afraid to put herself out there to look for business. She usually depended on word of mouth through neighbors and known contacts.

Then Niccolò suddenly remembered that his sister Tia was completely cut off from her only child, Amadeo, which was another painful situation. Her husband took their son, and threatened her not to contact them at all. Amadeo, who had been between four to five years old at the time and had no awareness of the matter, followed his father to Siena.

Niccolò's father, Bardi, was in a wool comber's guild and reasonably established. He was more than ready to provide for his helpless daughter. Bardi welcomed Tia to come and live with the family. She took his offer and had since been staying with mother Orissa and her brother Niccolò.

Just a few days later, Angelo, Niccolò's friend, another sculptor in Siena, sent him a message that his nephew, Amadeo, who lived in Siena came and talked to Angelo and wished to send the message to Niccolò that his father passed away and he owned a few acres of land that he would like to turn into a local winery. Amadeo was now nineteen years old and single and wished to see his mother and the rest of the family, but was hesitant and nervous as he did not keep contact with his mother and her family.

Angelo was a sculptor and a close friend of Niccolò. He worked at the Baptistery in Florence at the same time Niccolò was working there.

Niccolò thought it would be a good idea to share this latest news with his mother and sister for discussion at the dinner table. Even though he barely remembered Amadeo, he felt some affection for this nephew he hardly knew.

* * *

The cool air made Niccolò's walk pleasant as summer would take leave soon. The rays of the sun had become milder and there was this thin veil of mist which covered the city this early morning.

A horse-drawn cart with fresh vegetables like fresh flat beans, celery, lettuce, tomato, capsicum, and carrots, displayed their flash of colors and rolled away, as a pair of doves came flying down on the cart and tried joyfully to nibble on them.

Niccolò passed the bend of the bridge at Ponte Vecchio and reached his studio. He could foresee a ray of hope in his sister's life but warned himself not to expect too much.

He put his totebag on a hook and started to work on the sculpture of St. John which was already done. Now it would take a very meticulous process to go through all the details to make it livelier. Next it would entail cleaning the rough surfaces and markings of the tools used and finally polish the whole sculpture which had to be meticulous but tedious. The whole process was slow and exhausting.

Paolo, the young assistant and sculptor-in-training was very eager to hand the tools to Niccolò. He handed him the rasp, a flat metal tool with a course surface Niccolò used to remove excess stone and small chips.

Then he also wanted a smaller version of that tool which looked like a pen to refine it as the hours and days passed by.

Niccolò concentrated on refining the sculpture as much as he could. His left palm and fingers were flexed for gripping as his right palm and fingers worked continuously scraping and chipping small excess pieces with his eyes almost fixed on that area, brows knitted with prominent vertical lines on his forehead between the eyebrows.

Paolo reminded Niccolò, "Maestro, it is ten minutes past five and the sun is going down so we should finish today."

Niccolò appeared ready to go home. He got up and started brushing his whole body with his two hands. As marble dust filled the air, the rays of the setting sun refracted on the dust particles. Niccolò came out quickly of the rainbow dust cloud and stepped out of the studio, took a deep breath and stretched his arms over his head. "Paolo, thank you very much. I will see you tomorrow morning."

"*Maestro ci vediamo domani*," Paolo said.

Niccolò briskly walked towards his home and along the way he came across the bakery as the smell of baking loaves filled the air. He realized he was hungry and thirsty.

The vendors at the end of the day were pushing their carts very slowly. Some carts were almost empty while some still had a few vegetables left. All the vendors called out, "*Ciao*, Maestro." Niccolò waved to them but was very exhausted to engage in conversation.

The sun went down the horizon as its setting rays colored the Arno River in gold. Some boats were still cruising the rhythmic laps of the oars and shrieks of seagulls harmonized the day's end.

Niccolò felt a blast of cool breeze and strode faster to reach home. He had an important agenda today for his family: tell them about Amadeo's news. His mother and sister welcomed him home.

"Dinner is ready, Niccolò, whenever you want," his mother said.

A tired, hungry Niccolò said slowly, "*Mamma, affamato.*"

His mother Orissa and sister Tia were more than happy to put the cooked dishes on the table. Today's menu was salad with punslane succulent which was supposed to have many healthy nutrients and minerals, cucumber, tomatoes, celery, dressing made with ginger, cilantro, dash of turmeric, olive oil, wine vinegar, and homemade sourdough bread. There was also salted herring and flat beans in tomato sauce with basil. Dessert was pears cooked in wine and brown sugar.

Niccolò was very happy to hear the menu and shortly after he changed from his studio clothes, they sat together for dinner. They were halfway through dinner when he said to his mother and sister, "I have some unexpected but exciting news for you."

"Is it another commission?" Tia asked.

"That might be later but what I want tell you now is really unexpected."

Tia and her mother looked at each other.

Niccolò took a deep breath. "Tia, your son, Amadeo, sent me a message through my friend who lives in Siena, that his father passed away. He got a few acres of land and decided to start his own winery business and wanted to visit us, but he's been feeling shy and nervous as he did not keep in touch with you, his own mother, and our family."

Tia was overwhelmed with this message. She was shaking nervously with emotion and her eyes welled with tears.

"I know it is hard to get this news suddenly," Niccolò said, "but in my opinion, with our mother's permission, we should send a message that we will be very happy to see him here at our home. There's no need to be shy or nervous."

Tia stood up and hugged her brother. Mother Orissa was overjoyed with the news and tears rolled down her cheeks.

Now, let us celebrate the occasion with some wine," Niccolò said.

The three of them sat around the table and started talking and sipping their wine. Mother Orissa slowly said, "We saw him last when he was a boy. He looked sad when his father asked him to get in the carriage. He must be a handsome fellow now."

Tia could not say much and just uttered, "So many years passed. He must be a grown man." Tears rolled down her cheeks.

"We will welcome him affectionately and allow him to tell us what he wants to say and we will listen to him then decide from there how to proceed with the relationship," Niccolò said. "I can take some time off before I finish St. John."

Mother Orissa and sister Tia was very happy that Niccolò got the commission.

"God heard our sincere prayers. Niccolò got the commission," his mother said.

"Yes, depending on the circumstances and attitude of Amadeo and his plan, how much he wants to keep connected with our family, we can proceed and I can spend time and help him, if he wants, to get him established in his life however way he wants."

Overwhelmed with emotion, Tia hugged Niccolò. "Dear brother, I cannot thank you enough for what you have done and are now doing for me. God bless you, my dear brother. I wish and pray that your name as a sculptor should go far and wide beyond our own country."

Niccolò gave his sister a warm hug.

Mother Orissa kissed her son on his forehead and muttered, "God bless you."

They sat down around the table for some time quietly before retiring for the night.

Niccolò and St. John

Niccolò was determined to concentrate on St. John and his promise to the cathedral people. All he had to do to put his mind and body in sync with St. John was to focus on making the saint come alive as much as he could.

"Paolo," he addressed his faithful young assistant and fellow sculptor, "starting tomorrow, I am going to start the work pretty early in the morning. You do not have to come so early. Just arrive at your usual time, start your project and I will ask for your help when I need it."

"Maestro, at what time will you plan to be in the studio?"

"As early as 6 tomorrow morning I will start my work."

"I will set your tools close to your work space in the evening before I go home. I will arrive here by 7:30 in the morning." Paolo surveyed the tools on a table.

"Do not worry. Arrive whenever you can."

"Maestro, please teach me how to polish the sculpture. I promise you, I will handle the areas that still need work when your hands and fingers get tired."

"That will be a big help, Paolo. Sure, I will teach my own technique using my special tool which I enjoy doing."

Soon, Niccolò's day was half over as he continued polishing the selected areas of the St. John sculpture. So far, he was using the rasp which was a flat spatula-like tool with teeth on the surface. One had to be careful with it as sometimes it would leave a scratch on the surface while you were working with it.

The small selected areas would be marked and would be worked on starting from the lower part of the sculpture moving upwards. That was the way Niccolò would do it. The face would be the last one feature to be worked on.

Paolo and Niccolò worked together closely on the wider part of the sculpture's body and often Niccolò would allow Paolo to try his hand on the sculpture. The grooves and bends and folds of the clothes and in between, the crevices of the body were all features that required Niccolò's care as it was difficult to work on those parts.

Paolo would sigh often and say, "Maestro, my fingers and hands are getting tired."

Niccolò would say firmly, "Take a break then. Do not spoil the work which is already done. You might leave scratch marks on the area."

Paolo would take a break but Niccolò would continue to work, his exposed body and face would be covered with white marble chips and dust till the sun soared to the west and his studio would be covered with dust shimmering with different colors of refracted sunlight.

"Paolo, I am going to leave soon as I would like to see my friend, Alberto. He is going to Siena to visit his cousin and I want to send a message to Angelo, my sculptor friend in Siena who will get in touch with my nephew, Amadeo."

"Maestro, you have a nephew!"

"Yes, I do, he is now nineteen years old and the son of my sister. His father took him when he was five-years-old and left my sister. But his father is no more and now the son wants to visit his mother and his grandmother and me after all these years."

Paolo clapped his hands. "Maestro, that is good!"

"Which is why I will take some time off to be with my family especially my nephew when he comes to visit us."

"That is fine with me. I will try to keep myself busy with the relief the cathedral commissioned." Paolo dusted off small white particles that accumulated on his clothes.

"Do you mean the elongated slabs that look like borders with grapevines and the creepers?"

Nervous about how to tell Niccolò that he went to see the bishop about getting some work, Paolo's voice became louder and he started scratching the back of his head.

"Yes, Maestro, I went to the cathedral and talked to one of the priests and mentioned that I am your assistant and humbly requested that I need some work. So they just told me to do the borders which are the elongated reliefs. The cathedral authority will put them as an added decoration in places between the niches and sculptures. Maestro, I need money to help my family, my father's trattoria business needs investments for hiring people. My father and mother are getting old. They cannot work that hard anymore. My brother helps and my sister will be getting married soon. That is also an added expense."

Niccolo nodded. "I understand. You do not have to explain that you need money. Anyway, hopefully there will be more commissions from recent and future projects and you can help me with that."

"Oh, it makes me so happy that you want me to help you with other commissions."

Niccolò patted his assistant's shoulder. "See you tomorrow, Paolo. Remember, I will start work early but you can come at your usual time."

* * *

Niccolò visited Alfredo on his way back home. Alfredo worked on the other side of the river Arno. As he crossed the bridge, there were boats filled with people waving to the people crossing the bridge and also to the people standing on the bank.

Niccolò wanted to pass the shops which were very close to the bridge as you walked across. In this area, his friend, Alberto, worked and owned a gold jewelry shop which he inherited from his father.

Niccolò strode faster to reach the store. Alberto, who was more than happy to see Niccolò, came forward with his outstretched right hand to pat him on the back.

"Niccolò, *Buonasera!* Oh, I am very happy to see you!"

"*Ciao* Alberto, I am happy to see you too."

"Niccolò, I heard you are working on the commission of St. John. I am very happy for you."

"Alberto, I came here to send a message through you to Angelo to tell my nephew, Amadeo, he is more than welcome to come to Florence to see us and his mother. I heard that you go often to Siena for work-related visits. I would really appreciate it if you do this favor for me. Amadeo knows Angelo. Alberto, you remember that Angelo was a close friend of mine and we worked together for some time."

"Absolutely, that is no problem." Alberto gave Niccolò a heavy pat on his right shoulder. "I do remember sometime in the past we used to get together and talk and I used to tease you that you should be firm to get more money for your hard work while you were working on the bronze door, remember?" Alberto started laughing and patting Niccolò on his back.

"Alberto, that is very amusing. I took it very seriously and I used to get upset."

"Niccolò, those were the days when we were at an age when we would make fun of each other. And now, look at you. I am so proud of you. You will go a long way in your career. We all hope and pray that you succeed, my dear friend. No problem. I will give this message to Angelo myself and see to it that it is delivered soon."

Just then, a man entered Alberto's shop to look at some pieces of jewelry. Alberto asked his assistant to take care of the customer. The place was illuminated with a covered lantern since the customer came. A bigger lantern with more light was brought in so the pieces could be more visible.

The alley where the shop was located was busy with passersby walking and looking at the different kinds of shops. There were shops where potteries were displayed. Artists' paintings were on display for the public alongside shops featuring such offerings as spices, rugs, silk scarves and shawls for sale.

A constant chorus of people talking and passing kept flowing as Alberto and Niccolò continued talking.

"Have a drink. I have orange blossom favored water or homemade beer."

"I will take orange blossom water. I have to go home soon as my mother and sister always wait for me for dinner."

After drinking the water, Niccolò hugged Alberto and was on his way, picking up his pace towards home just as the evening had set in.

Lights as tiny specks were shining on the other side of the river bank just as the chirping of birds serenaded the air from the treetops and a few seagulls still focused on the river to dive in the water for fish. Some gulls were shrieking to call their mates to the nest. The sun's last glow of orange had just been covered with the evening's mist as the call of the autumn breeze through the air accompanied Niccolò's stride home.

His mother and sister Tia who were, as usual, waiting for a while for Niccolò, were relieved to see him home.

After Niccolò changed and joined them at the dinner table, he announced that he had sent a message to Amadeo saying, "that he is very much welcome to this home whenever he would wish to come."

Mother Orissa and Sister Tia were very happy to hear this.

Niccolò told his mother that he planned to work very early every day starting the next morning. That way he could finish most of the project so he could take some time off to spend with family, especially with Amadeo.

Both mother and sister were overwhelmed with joy. Tia hugged her brother. "I am so fortunate to have a brother like you. As a sister, I pray your dream of being a successful, famous sculptor would come true."

His mother kissed Niccolò many times. "Dear God, please bless my dear son Niccolò with a long, healthy life. We give thanks for the blessing of his dream as an artist is coming true."

They all bid good night with a pleasant feeling of loving and caring for each other.

Niccolò and St. George at Orsanmichele

Upon awakening early in the morning from Niccolò's cottage the rays of sun felt soft by the time he strode briskly towards the church just as a misty haze wrapped the city of Firenze.

The city was just waking up as there were few people walking on the paved pathway. Few boats cruised along the river Arno. The morning sun colored the river in gold. The partly cloudy sky showed puffy white clouds racing somewhere unknown with a message.

Lost in his thoughts about the commissions, Niccolò was very happy that he was getting these commissions but was anxious about getting them done in time. He also wanted to put his energy and effort the way he wanted.

Niccolò also remembered that he promised Cosimo that he would sculpt figures for his new palace and garden.

He snapped back to the present with the shrieks of seagulls. One shrieking seagull chased another gull who was holding a dangling fish tightly with its beak which amused Niccolò who smiled as he murmured to himself, "Every corner of the earth the same events are happening. One gets it and the other is deprived. The protest of the deprived usually runs in vain."

His swift pace led him to the church of Orsanmichele. As soon as he entered, he saw Paolo standing at the corner with a beaming face and a big smile. "Maestro, I arranged all the tools one after another near the niche where you will work."

"Thank you, Paolo, you are very prompt and efficient."

Niccolò went inside where the niche was. The slabs of marble were scattered around. He went close to the marble slabs, looked around one by one at them and then touched them. Then with his two palms, he stroked them as one would do to a pet. After a while, he picked one which was hiding in the middle among all others. His eyes sparkled as he made eye contact with Paolo. "This is the one."

With wide eyes and a beaming face, Paolo said excitedly, "Maestro, so we start right now?"

That was the day when the sculpting of St. George began. Niccolò had a plan as to how he would depict St. George. His depiction seemed to reflect the idea of standing tall against an approaching enemy. It was a spirit that must have been shared by Florentines of the day on account of contemporary events and Niccolò liked to use it as the source for the disposition of this statue.

Niccolò divided his time to be with St. George as it was urgent. It seemed that almost every two weeks messengers would come and read messages which they received from various sources in the piazza where the Baptistery stood.

The message contained details as to the whereabouts of the enemies and how far they were from Firenze. This caused pressure for Niccolò who wanted to finish St. George as soon as possible as the people of Firenze believed that St. George was going to save them against this tyrant from Naples.

Niccolò concentrated with his body and soul as much as he could. He would hold his hammer and chisel to carve the sculpture then he would take his rasp and his own handmade sandpaper-like device to smooth out the carved parts.

Niccolò made the spirit of St. George stand strong against the enemy and this strength seemed to be reflected in the face of St. George. Niccolò sculpted the saint's neck turned slightly to the left, mouth barely opened, his eyes showing a glance which was lifted and to its left rather than directly in front. His expression was of one of intense concentration reflected in his wrinkled brow. This was a figure of courage and resolve and a figure who would not back down. Niccolò whispered to St. George while sculpting, "I am carving you with a confident posture, St. George. You stand tall with a shield in front of you as if you could rotate on the small base which is touching the ground. So that you are ready to confront enemies coming from different directions."

The guild made a special adornment for the metal sword projected forward and out of the niche created a very visible statement to all who were walking down the street in front of Orsanmichele.

The saint's legs clearly supported the saint's weight although the front of his left foot was not completely planted on the ground but partially hung off the front of the base. The purpose of the stance was stability and immobility. He was not to be interpreted as moving instead he was stable and immovable. To Niccolò, this was a very defensive posture.

Two years passed since Niccolò started St. George. One afternoon, Niccolò went on a break at Ponte Vecchio where the bridge bends to meet Beatrice. She was standing and waiting for Niccolò with her light blue flowing dress, her dark brown hair secured in a bun at the nape of her neck and a gold-colored scarf hugged around her shoulder and neck.

She was more than happy to see Niccolò as she ambled quickly towards him.

"Maestro, Uncle Cosimo will send someone to you with a message about a commission of sculptures for his new palace and garden. He knows that you are busy with St. George and St. John yet he wants you to be informed about a list of the sculptures he would like to commission to you so that you can start gradually working on them one-by-one without pressure. He has a lot of confidence in you and expressed that he would like you to get a fair amount of payment whatever that amounts to. I came to let you know ahead of time and want you to know how much he admires your work and confidence about your capability."

"Beatrice, I really appreciate you letting me know, thank you very much. You have done so much for me."

"Maestro, I did not do anything. I am glad and thankful that Uncle Cosimo has publicly acknowledged that he appreciates and honors your talent in this manner."

"Thank you for your good words and encouragement."

"Maestro, I brought you some almond rice. Please enjoy this with your assistant."

After bidding Beatrice farewell, Niccolò hurried toward Orsanmichele, his heartbeat rapid thinking about Beatrice.

"She is so thoughtful and conscientious. I hope she understands that I cannot do more than appreciate her. I hope that whoever ultimately gets her hand will understand her inner beauty and treats and respects her in a manner that she deserves."

He ended up breathless when he was almost at the door of Orsanmichele. Paolo came running to Niccolò just as he arrived.

"Maestro! Maestro, the people from the linen guild are waiting for you." Even though Paolo was out of breath, his eyes sparkled with excitement.

Niccolò calmly said, "Why are they looking for me?"

"I do not know. They were asking me about you and how busy you are."

Niccolò walked inside and one of the members from the linen guild came forward to greet Niccolò. "Maestro, we know you are busy but we humbly request that you please sculpt St. Mark for us. He is our saint and he will be placed in another niche in Orsanmichele. So you can sculpt St. Mark in his place. Since you have already started working here, please consider our request. Also, we would like St. Mark to be facing the front so he will be looking toward the people while his back will be against the curve, the hollow of the niche so there will not be too much work there at the back. Maestro, please consider this: we are not so rich like the other guilds but we thought you would be kind enough to consider our commission."

Niccolò gazed off into the distance as wrinkles appeared on his forehead. He sat down on his work bench near St. George and took few deep breaths.

"I was thinking of taking some time off. When do you wish for me to finish it?"

"Maestro, it is all up to you. We have limited funds so we wish to compensate you with whatever we can. So we are at your mercy and the rest is your decision."

"All right, I accept as long as you agree with my way of looking at St. Mark and my artistic ability to take creative license to sculpt him the way I envision St. Mark to be."

"Maestro, we are very pleased you have accepted our request and trust that you will begin the project at a time most suitable to you."

And with that the guild people left.

Paolo started to stammer in disbelief. "Maestro, how will you manage to juggle all these commissions?"

"Look, Paolo, I cannot refuse them for they help me by introducing me to the people and other guilds when my father passed away. At any rate, if good fortune is bestowed on us, let us welcome that. We will finish St. George within another year and a half. St. John will have to wait. St. Mark will be looking towards the people so we have to carve the front part and of course, it is a commission from the linen guild so we will sculpt the folds of his clothes around his body so they hang perfectly."

"Maestro, whatever you say."

"Paolo, let us enjoy the almond rice first and then we will finish the face and eyes of St. George. I have to see his stern look towards the enemy before I go home today."

Niccolò Juggles St. George and St. Mark

Niccolò and Paolo enjoyed the almond rice which Beatrice made for Niccolò as it was his favorite dish. They determined to keep working until Niccolò was satisfied to see St. George's stern expression towards the enemies. They both worked hard and late.

Finally, Niccolò stopped. "Paolo, please go home. I see his expression now. We will work on putting the finishing touches tomorrow and polish him later. We have to start St. Mark tomorrow."

"Maestro, what about St. John?"

"Paolo, I want to concentrate on St. John later. I want to finish St. Mark and St. George and after that, I want to take a break and ask my nephew to come spend some time with us. Then I will put my heart and soul in St. John. So Paolo, it is already evening so you should go home now and rest."

"Maestro, what about you?"

"Do not worry. I will leave soon."

They bid goodbye. Niccolò started walking faster than usual to his home. At this early autumn evening, the sky studded with stars seemed to dome over him as it met the horizon beyond the Arno River. All he could see were the stars against a black dome staring at him. It was as if they were blinking and trying to say something. Niccolò never before looked at the horizon like this; he took it for granted that it was there.

As he started moving even faster, the cool breeze blew through the shadowy trees. Firenze moved at a slow pace. By now the roads were almost empty as few passersby were making their weary path towards home.

Niccolò attempted to move swiftly, thinking of the dinner prepared by his mother that awaited him. He knew that his mother had also kept some warm water for his bath in a big iron vessel heated over an open fire and the very thought of this comfort encouraged him to pick up his pace even more until at last he reached his house.

As usual, his mother and sister happily welcomed him home.

"I need to wash myself and change and then I will talk to you at the dinner table." After he said this, Niccolò bathed and changed into his comfortable attire. Then the three of them sat around the table.

This evening, his mother, Orissa, made vegetable soup in beef broth with carrots, peas, pieces of turnip and dried tomato, some grated cheese with some basil on top. Freshly-baked garlic bread complemented the main course: fettucine with freshly-made tomato basil and mushroom sauce. Soon, they enjoyed a dessert of fresh sliced apples, cinnamon and small pieces of toasted bread spread with orange blossom honey on top to soak the bread pieces.

Niccolò thanked his mother for cooking the delicious meal and thanked his sister for arranging the dinner table and helping his mother.

He was excited to give them an update. "I have started sculpting St. George, St. Mark and St. John."

"Niccolò!" his mother said, "I am happy though I am worried. How will you manage to finish all three pieces? What kind of time frame do you have?"

"Mamma, please do not worry. I started sculpting St. George and I progressed the way I wanted when the linen guild came and asked me about the commission of St. Mark. They said St. Mark will be in a niche in Orsanmichele. The niche is already made and is waiting for him. The sculpture will be facing front and the back portion will not be seen. I think that it will be a little less work as I am not going to give a finer touch at the back and I do not have to polish the back portion also.

"I have to work in Orsanmichele for St. George so when I am there already, with all the best wishes and prayers, I can squeeze in work on St. Mark. Sister Tia and Mamma, I want to finish St. George and St. Mark and then take a break. So Amadeo can come and spend time with us then. What do you say?"

"Niccolò, that is fine with us," Mother Orissa said.

"Good night. Sleep well and rest," his sister said.

* * *

Niccolò got up the next morning just as the autumn sun, misty and hazy, was lazy to rise in the east. Niccolò covered his ears and his neck with a woolen comforter as he started striding towards his studio. There were few passersby who covered themselves with thick wraps or a sweater around the body.

Their warm breath that blew against the cool air was making a misty smoke around them. Seagulls were bravely diving in the river for fish. The chorus of their shrieks filled the air as a wake-up call for the sleepy city.

Niccolò now warmed up from exerting effort of his brisk walk towards the Orsanmichele. Once there, he was moved to see Paolo standing right at the door waiting for him.

When both of them entered the building, Paolo pointed out the niche where St. Mark would be placed. Niccolò looked around and found a person from the linen guild and asked him where the marble slabs for sculpting were located. The person happily took both Niccolò and Paolo to the place where marble slabs were kept. The sculptor and his assistant spotted huge pieces of marble slabs strewn on a wide, long rectangular shaped hallway. Niccolò hurried towards the slabs and kept on crisscrossing the marble slabs which were lying on the floor ready to be picked up. He approached a relatively long marble slab and stopped there, inspecting it from the side then from one end. He touched the marble with his hands as if he was getting a sensation of some kind from the marble. He performed this ritual with both eyes open and then with both eyes closed. Then he jumped for joy and asked the person to bring the slab with the help of other people close to the niche where the sculpting would take place.

After Niccolò selected the marble piece, he was in a state of peace. His eyes continued to sparkle and his face gleamed with joy. He asked Paolo to accompany him to the niche where St. Mark would stand.

Paolo quietly observed his maestro. He was restless trying to balance his body and walk steadily. He started stammering as he said, "Maestro, Maestro, why did you choose the long piece of marble?"

"I will show you the sketch on my sketching paper." He eyed his assistant curiously. "You ask why I am doing this?"

"Please Maestro, please!"

Niccolò took the sketch paper and started sketching St. Mark. "I want to sculpt a larger-than-life sized sculpture."

"Why would you want to do that?" Paolo inquired insistently.

"St. Mark will be placed in the niche so the front will be visible and the back will not be carved."

"Maestro, I understand that but why a larger-than-life size?"

"St. Mark is for the linen guild so I have to emphasize the garments on the figure so the clothes over his body fall over him as though it will fall over an actual human body so I need a larger and longer space to carve it."

"Oh Maestro, you are really a genius. I understand now."

"Every day we will take our lunch break at one o'clock. We will work from 8 in the morning to one in the afternoon straight on St. Mark and from 2 to 5 in the evening on St. George."

Paolo said he had no problem with that and agreed to go along with his maestro.

So every morning they would start their work on St. Mark and in the afternoon they would switch their focus on St. George who possessed a different expression and attitude so Niccolò was very meticulous with every step to bring out the expression and stance of St. George.

Niccolò wanted to finish St. Mark earlier so he can concentrate more on St. George who would be an embodiment of powerhouse to slay the attacker.

As Niccolò explained to Paolo, he wished to emphasize his sculpting of the garments on the figure of St. Mark to strive for a more realistic depiction. The cloth covering his body fell over him like it would fall on an actual body with clothing on it. This way of modeling a body with garments was quite different from the way it had been done from times during the earlier period when artists would depict a body hidden inside a mass of garments.

Niccolò showed how St. Mark's right leg carried the weight and was made a column for emphasis. His left leg and left knee were clearly detectable under his robe. His left hand was used to hold the gospel book and his right hand on his side as if he was receiving divine inspiration to write the Gospel. He stood atop a pillow which was typically a symbol of holiness.

The result of Niccolò's work was profound. He revived the use of *contrapposto*, a counterpose in a free-standing sculpture. Niccolò sculpted this large-scale free-standing sculpture by giving St. Mark a natural look through the use of counterpoise.

In addition to counterpoise, Niccolò made St. Mark's head, hands and torso elongated a bit so that they compensated for the angle viewed a bit above eye level. The work was placed along the street which was a bit above the eye level.

This was a breakthrough from the international gothic style that preceded it and ushered in a new era of increasingly natural figures carved and cast in life-size and larger.

Niccolò and Paolo glanced at each other and took a deep breath. "We can concentrate now on St. George."

"Yes Maestro, starting tomorrow morning."

They both examined St. Mark and put their hands slowly over the carved sculpture as Niccolò whispered, "Thank you, your holiness for standing tall and natural to give us your inspiration."

Niccolò and St. George Save Firenze

When Niccolò and Paolo started working on St. George they had dedicated so much time to this sculpture that, at the moment, it was now just a matter of polishing and giving the saint a finishing touch.

Niccolò whispered to St. George, "Please save Firenze." He took his rasp and started to smooth out the extra chips. Then he used his own way of polishing the sculpture with his handmade sandpaper-like device.

Niccolò just finished the final touch. He would again inspect him to see whether St. George's facial expression complemented the posture of his body to create a memorable statement not only about this man in particular but about the Florentine spirit in general.

He looked at him and murmured, "I concentrated sculpting you with my whole body and my whole soul. Please come alive and save Firenze."

People in Orsanmichele came to help St. George in his niche. It was spring 1415 in the middle of a morning in Firenze and the sun rays were soft and misty. Alongside the paved road, the tall birch trees with shiny green leaves were swaying gently with the cool breeze as oak trees murmured their songs which drifted away beyond the Arno River.

Birds chirped happily in unison as the roadside landscapes were colored with daffodils and varieties of tulips waving happily at the passersby.

Then suddenly, the galloping sounds of horses were heard from a distance causing the passersby to become anxious. They saw two mounted soldiers come in front of the Baptistery who stood on the plaza against the misty blue sky. They dismounted from their horses and called the passersby to hear what they were going to read from a scroll.

All the people came running as one of the soldiers started reading loudly: "An army from Naples, led by a tyrant moved north and was preparing to

103

attack Firenze. Along their way, the Neapolitan tyrant was struck by some disease and slain, so the army is receding and Firenze is saved!"

The people cried out loud with joy. "Firenze is saved! Firenze is saved!" The chorus grew louder and louder with an interrupted loud accent of a joyous cry: "Nic-co-lò! Nic-co-lò!"

The news reached Orsanmichele as everyone applauded with joy. Cheers roared inside to congratulate Niccolò and his assistant Paolo. Niccolò approached the sculpture of St. George and touched him as he whispered, "Thank you for coming alive to save Firenze."

It was a miracle the day when the sculpture of St. George was placed in the niche with an armor and a stern look and as a result, the attacker was slain suddenly by a disease. The city of Firenze came alive with banners and slogans cheering Niccolò's name.

Paolo and Niccolò longed to go home but when they stepped outside of the Orsanmichele, they were swept up amidst a river of the crowd flowing from different directions with banners and flags and shouting in joy, "Nic-co-lò! Nic-co-lò! Firenze is saved!"

Paolo turned to his maestro. "Goodbye and see you tomorrow, Maestro. Looking forward to talking about your vacation and St. John."

"As soon as I get paid for both sculptures, I will pay you for assisting me. You worked hard. Let me know if you need some money right now, I will try to pay you."

"Maestro, I know you are very kind and generous. I will let you know if I need compensation earlier before they pay your contract."

"Thank you, Paolo."

Niccolò navigated his way along the stream of the crowd, covering his head and half of his face with the piece of cloth he usually ties over his head while he sculpts to prevent marble chips from getting in his hair.

It was twilight of the evening as darkness lay herself just below the horizon where a few stars were twinkling. The cool breeze of spring blew gently while the chorus of the joyous crowd became stronger and stronger as with it, the lapping sounds of river Arno were muffled and became fainter. The mighty Arno River rippled with reflected light from the shore as a few people joyfully cruised along the human wave.

The startled shrieking seagulls flew over the crowd as birds settled in their nests and the branches of birch and oak trees remained quiet, ready to rest and welcome the spring evening. Niccolò managed to pace faster and faster while the spring breeze echoed the joyous chant of the people of Firenze: "Nic-co-lo! Nic-co-lo!"

The renowned sculptor finally reached home happy to announce that he finished St. George and Firenze was saved. Mother Orissa and sister Tia were overjoyed.

Niccolò took a deep breath. "I can take my vacation now."

Niccolò and Family Reunites with Amadeo

Niccolò strode as fast as he could to reach home just as the summer evening was settling in. The evening glow of the sun bathed the whitewashed cottages as birch trees and beech trees swayed with the gentle breeze and the fragrance of white and red oleanders filled the air.

He paced so fast that pearly sweat drops appeared on his forehead. As soon as he entered the door, his mother and sister came running to introduce Amadeo who was standing next to them.

Amadeo was a handsome young man with olive skin and black hair parted on the side. An oblong face, sparkling brown eyes, and an aquiline nose rounded out his facial features. His strong stature yet trim figure stood about five-feet nine inches tall, a little shorter than Niccolò who was five-feet and eleven inches tall. A brown knee length brief, a loose yellow shirt and a brown vest completed the young man's attire.

After initial introductions, Amadeo embraced Niccolò. "Uncle, I am very pleased to meet you."

Even though Amadeo was a child the last time Niccolo saw his nephew, it was like they were meeting for the first time.

"With God's grace, we are all together again," said Mother Orissa who then turned to her son. "Niccolò please change your clothes. We will start dinner soon."

Tia decorated the dinner table which she covered with one of her best white tablecloths embroidered with pink roses and green creeper all around. Then she put a crochet white tablecloth and through the crochet one could see the embroidery. In the center of the table there sat a vase with pink, yellow and white daisies.

Large, long candles were placed on either side of the vase. A number of tall candles were placed on different corners of the dining room. White heavy dinner plates with silverware and white napkins were placed for all four of them.

Mother Orissa made gnocchi, salad from the garden that included celery, lettuce, carrots, tomatoes, chives, fresh cilantro dressing with vinegar and olive oil. Homemade bread with green olives, smoked salmon and almond rice rounded out their meal.

Niccolò changed quickly into his up to knee, navy blue brief with gold buttons at the end, a white, round-neck silk shirt and navy-blue vest with gold buttons.

Mother Orissa's long salt and pepper hair was secured in a bun on the top of her head. Her face was round with graceful wrinkles on her forehead and her eyes were deep brown with long eyelashes. She was adorned with an olive-green dress at knee length with lacy frills at the end and a V-shaped neck with frills around her three-quarter sleeves.

Sister Tia was about five-feet and four inches tall, a slim figure with light olive skin, a triangular face, black brown eyes, a pointed nose and wavy brown hair which cascaded down her shoulders. She wore a forest green, long silk dress up to her ankles, puffed short sleeves with a round, deep neck and a lacy frill. A wide, green, long silk belt wrapped around her waist and tied in front at the left side in a bow.

All four of them sat at the table. Mother Orissa was very happy to announce that, "It is a special day and with God's grace, our dear Amadeo is with us."

Niccolò turned to his nephew. "How long will you be staying with us? Let me know if I can help you in any way."

"Thank you, Uncle. I would like to stay here for seven days, if I may. I want you all to know that I am not with my father's family anymore. I mean, with my stepmother and her children. I left them about four years ago when I was fifteen. I managed to work in a farm and also in a winery.

"The person for whom I was working was nice and kind and gave me shelter and advised me to build my own future. At his advice, I borrowed some money from him without interest and bought a piece of land where I now grow grapes and started a winery on my own.

"I inherited my share of money after my father passed away so I plan to build a cottage in the near future. I am single at present and I still rent a place close by which belongs to my friend.

"I left my father and my stepfamily as I was not treated well, in other words, I was abused and could not continue my studies after school. Even school was very difficult. I am pretty surprised that I was able to get a bit of an inheritance."

With a sad expression on her face, Tia patted her son on the arm reassuringly.

"I am very sorry that you had gone through these difficulties," Niccolò said. "I wish we knew about your situation then but dear Amadeo, what happened to you is now in the past, we cannot change, so let us work hard sincerely in the present to make the future pleasant and comfortable. You are young, you can surely make your wishes come true and as your uncle, I will do my best to help you if you wish for me to."

Amadeo was overwhelmed with joy and hugged Niccolò. "Dear Uncle, I really appreciate it."

Mother Orissa and sister Tia hugged Amadeo. They were all in joyful tears.

Four of them enjoyed the delicious dinner especially Amadeo who thanked his grandma Orissa and expressed that this experience was a rare and joyous reunion after a long time.

"However way you would like to spend your time in Florence, you have the liberty to do that," Niccolò said to his nephew. "I have free time to spend with you if you wish. I have some suggestions for places to visit, if you are interested."

Niccolò and Amadeo sat out in the paved patio to chat after dinner. On a cool summer evening, a gentle breeze blew on this starry night as the sky studded with stars seemed to cover the earth with a thin veil. The sweet smell of jasmine filled the air casting a dizzy spell on the evening.

Orissa and Tia brought out some wine to celebrate the evening and they all sat on wooden chairs around a round wooden table as they planned for the days ahead.

Amadeo wanted to spend his days with his mother, grandmother, and uncle exploring the Baptistery and a short cruise along the river Arno.

Niccolò said that he would like to explore Siena with Amadeo where he knew people there who can help Amadeo built a cottage. He ran this idea by his nephew whose faced beamed at the suggestion.

"I would love that," Amadeo replied, "though I do want to burden you. I am sorry I did not contact you all when my father was alive as I was afraid and not sure if I was welcome."

They all assured Amadeo to let the past go and all that mattered was that they were now all together. They sat for a while contemplating a bright future ahead.

"Let us go to bed now as it is past midnight. We will continue making plans again tomorrow," Mother Orissa said.

"I am not going to work tomorrow so I can sleep late," Niccolò said.

"I will sleep in Grandpa's library as that big, padded sofa looks so comfortable," Amadeo said smiling. "I already tried it."

Tia hugged her son then ran her fingers through his hair and kissed him on his forehead. "Good night, dear son, I am so glad to have you here."

Grandma Orissa hugged and kissed Amadeo good night.

The last blessing came from his Uncle Niccolò and then Amadeo happily went to bed in his grandpa's library.

Amadeo Visits Niccolò's Studio

Amadeo happily accompanied his Uncle Niccolò to his studio to see where his uncle creates great sculptures. Paolo was working on a relief project with a design of a creeper with flower and fruit. What he saw impressed and excited Amadeo very much as his eyebrows rose in wonder and awe, his eyes sparkled with a beam of amazement as he tried to balance from one leg to the other.

Paolo greeted Amadeo with a smile and shook his hand heavily when Niccolò introduced them.

"Maestro, let us take Amadeo to the Osteria for lunch," Paolo said.

"Would you like to eat at the Osteria where they serve simple food like soup, salads, some light fish dishes and vegetables either roasted or cooked with spices like basil and chives, orange blossom water and homemade beer? They also serve freshly baked bread with olives, gelatos, fruit tart and fresh fruits."

Amadeo smiled broadly, with sparkling eyes replied joyfully, "Yes, Uncle, I would love to."

Before they left the studio, Niccolò invited another sculptor, Salvatore, to join them.

White clouds floated against the blue sky bright with sunshine. Almost the end of summer signaled a cool breeze that blew through the oleander bushes and filled the air with a sweet smell. Tall birch and beech trees happily murmured along the paved path. The sound of boat oars and shrieks of seagulls along the river Arno became fainter as they proceeded past the Baptistery and cathedral where people were passing by, some of them smiling at Niccolò. Then all four of them reached the piazza where daily vendors with vegetables sold their produce. They soon made a sharp right turn and passed a narrow alley before arriving right in front of the brick red structure of the Osteria.

The creeping honeysuckles with their orange and yellow blossoms covered most of the front wall of the Osteria. The four young men, Niccolò, Paolo, Salvatore and Amadeo, sat around a rectangular table made of polished walnut wood. They took their seats on four, round three-legged stools. There were fresh yellow and white daisies in a small vase on the table.

An oven ensconced in a brick wall was right in front of them. Steam and the aroma from the huge iron container cooking vegetables in some broth filled the air.

There were people sitting on their right and also at the far-left corner talking as they spooned their soup and enjoyed their beer. The Osteria was filled with the sound of people's voices and frequent laughter.

They all ordered soup, eggs and roasted vegetables like potato and carrots and freshly-baked green olive bread, orange blossom flavored water and fresh fruits like cantaloupe.

Salvatore started talking to Amadeo while putting his right palm on the young man's left shoulder firmly. *"Mio Caro*, Amadeo, what is your plan for your future and how long will you be in Florence?"

"Zio Salvatore," Amadeo said addressing him as "Uncle," "I will stay for another five days in Florence. My plan for the future is to start a winery on a smaller scale. I already bought a small vineyard in Castellina which is twenty-two miles from Florence and nine miles northwest of Siena which is part of the Chianti hills."

"Niccolò, your nephew has a good head on his shoulders." Salvatore's face flushed with excitement as he patted Amadeo firmly on his left shoulder. Then he stretched his hands in front and started clapping.

The food was served on the table. "Let us enjoy this food and then Amadeo can tell us more about the place and the rest of his plans."

"Buon appetito," Paolo said.

Soup was especially prepared as ordered with beef broth simmered with vegetables such as celery, tomato, corn kernel, bits of potato, barley, grains, and a few basil leaves. Fresh eggs were added on the top to be cooked then and there in the hot soup.

While spooning it into his mouth, Amadeo expressed loudly, *"Delizioso! Delizioso!"*

The freshly-baked bread with olive was Salvatore's favorite. "Niccolò, I am glad that you asked me to come with you. Thank you."

After few minutes while eating Salvatore asked Amadeo, "Tell me about Castellina."

"Zio Salvatore, what I heard and learned from people there is that it has a long history dating back to the Bronze Age. Etruscan men came from Etruria, a place between the Tiber and Arno rivers at the west and south of Appenines Mountain. They came to Tuscany around 7TH century BC and evidence of civilization still exists there in Castellina. They had a very rich civilization and many features of their civilization were adopted by the Romans. The pebbled road made by the Etruscans reached as far as the Adriatic Sea as a gateway for trading with the East. There is still evidence of that road around Castellina. The town sits on a dramatic rise of ground between the valleys of the Pesa, Atria and Elsa rivers. The roads wind through the hills and valleys. It is a picturesque town and the sunset is spectacular beyond the hills with its orange glow when the sun is slowly sinking. When the valleys and towns flood with orange at that time, it seems that time stops and we all get trapped in that timeless glow of orange.

"I am especially interested in growing olives and grapes as many of the people there do, such as the farmer who grows olives there has a big farm and inspired me to start the winery. I borrowed money from him to buy a few acres. He is very kind and helpful because I worked for him and that is why I decided to settle there."

"*Caro* Amadeo, that is quite a story and I congratulate you that you decided to go ahead with your plans. God bless you. Niccolò, my friend you have a very bright nephew," said Salvatore.

"Thank you," Niccolò told Salvatore. "I am taking some time off to go with Amadeo to see the place in Castellina."

"Niccolò, I am glad that you are accompanying him to visit the place," Salvatore said. "You might know someone in Siena."

"Yes, my friend, Angelo, the sculptor lives there."

After finishing lunch, they all bid each other goodbye. Salvatore gave a big hug to Amadeo while Paolo shook Amadeo's hand and said, "*Arrivederci.*"

Niccolò and Amadeo ambled from the Osteria towards Piazza Del Duomo and Piazza San Giovanni where the majestic Baptistery stood against the blue sky.

Amadeo was really taken by its beauty. He could not remember whether he had seen it before. He wanted to see the Gilberti's door that Niccolò worked on when he was only fourteen. So Amadeo went to the door and was amazed to see the intricate work laid with gold.

He said to himself that, "Niccolò, my very own uncle did the work when he was just fourteen years old. Isn't this amazing?" His eyes sparkled with joy as he turned to Niccolò. "Zio, you are really amazing."

Niccolò patted his back and smiled.

Amadeo's days went by very quickly in Florence. Niccolò and Amadeo agreed to travel twenty-two miles by carriage which would take a whole day. It was likely possible they might transfer to another carriage in the middle of their journey if needed.

Saying goodbye to his mother and grandmother was difficult for Amadeo as the last few days they lavished him with so much affection, care and comfort and delicious dishes his grandmother cooked. But he promised them, "I will be back soon."

The carriage's arrival in front of Niccolò's home signaled their departure. Tia hugged her son and said, "I am glad you made an effort to come and see us, my dear boy. Take care and be safe. May God bless you."

Tears rolled down her cheeks just as grandmother Orissa was already weeping and hugging her grandson, planting several kisses on his cheek. "May God bless and protect you."

"Arrivederci! Arrivederci!"

Amadeo was overcome with emotion. His eyes were sad and moist. "I will be back soon, I promise."

Niccolò put his arm on Amadeo's back. "Let us go. The carriage is waiting for us."

It was almost the end of summer at 9 in the morning. The sun was bright yet there was a cool breeze which blew through Amadeo's hair. The smell of jasmine from the backyard of the cottage made Amadeo sullen as he remembered the past few evenings he would sit at the backyard of the cottage and relax, looking at the sky while talking with grandmother Orissa.

The carriage driver signaled the horses who started to move. Niccolò and Amadeo looked at the cottage where Orissa and Tia were standing outside the door waving as slowly and surely the two figures moved backwards and became smaller and smaller until they disappeared.

The carriage soon picked up speed and as the horses galloped, the city of Florence moved backwards while the carriage moved forward towards Siena.

Niccolò and Amadeo Travel to Castellina

Carriage horses started galloping along the paved road of Florence towards Castellina. On this late summer, nearly autumn day in 1415 after they left the cottage of Niccolò, the morning sunlight was softer, sun rays bathed the orange-tiled houses and tiled-roof buildings. The city started its day with people walking faster on its paved road to their workplace, peddlers carrying their carts with fresh vegetables to the market square and some netting their cart carrying fresh fish. The seagulls eagerly followed those carts, shrieking and flying around in frustration unable to get the fish. The Arno River was busy with passengers on boats with their rhythmic laps of oars swaying monotonous and lulling. The tall swaying birch and beech oak trees passed by as the smell of oleanders became lighter and lighter until they came to an open green field.

They passed bushy shrubs and then the path winded round the open green rolling hills, the farmland of wheat and olive trees on the slope and valleys passed by as they moved from one village to the other. The red-tiled top houses sat cozily on the slopes of the hill. As the carriage horses galloped, one could see the silvery green olive orchard surrounded by tall, swaying cypress trees miles after miles. The magical soft veil of the morning sun lifted slowly as they approached the afternoon. Now the rays of sun flushed the valleys in bright yellow as the grayish-blue distant hills met the blue horizon where a few white lazy clouds were wandering.

Niccolò and Amadeo sat dozing on the padded, black leather seats of the carriage. They had to get up early that morning to get ready for their departure from their home in Florence. The journey was their time to catch up on their sleep.

Soon, they had awakened to see where along the journey they were now situated.

"Zio Niccolò," Amadeo said, "see, we can stop at one of these villages for lunch and there will be food and drink for the horses too."

"That is an excellent idea. Do you know what is the name of this town?"

"Uncle, Greve and Panzani are still fifteen miles away, but there are these small villages in between where we can stop. They have places where you can eat and rest and sample their homemade wine. We can stop at Greve and look around and have some drink and snack before we reach Castellina."

"Amadeo, I know you told me you share a room with your friend. So when we reach Castellina, I shall seek my own accommodations. Do you know of any places where visitors can stay?"

"Oh, do not worry," Amadeo replied. "Marcello, who has acres of farmland, has a beautiful red-tiled roof cottage that is spacious and it snugs on a slope of a hill. From there, you can see the area around and also his farmland where he grows wheat and olives on one side and has a fruit orchard on the other side of the hill. He has a wife and their son is my age. I share a space with their son who is my friend and we are very close. Stefano's hobby is painting, so Marcello extended Stefano's side of the cottage for his art work. I am lucky Stefano has shared part of his studio space for my living quarters. Stefano and I work on Marcello's farmland and help with whatever is needed. I am paid by Marcello but for Stefano it is different, it is his farmland too, so whatever is needed, he does it. During harvest time, Marcello employs extra people from town to help. Marcello and Angela already asked me to invite you to come and stay with them before I left for Firenze. I was not sure that you would have time to come. But it worked out so well and I am so happy that you came. Marcello, Angela and Stefano will be very happy to see you."

"I am so happy, that I could come, and I'm grateful that Marcello and his family are extremely kind and nice and so helpful to you. I do not have enough words to thank them," Niccolò gushed.

"Uncle, they are like my parents. Yes, I am lucky and I feel I am the person I am today as a result of their kindness and love. So it was through Stefano who was my schoolmate that I got this opportunity. I hope we remain close as we are now for the rest of our lives."

"Amadeo, you know that I was working on a St. John commission then after two years, the Guild of Armorers and Sword Makers of Florence commissioned St. George which was very urgent as Florence was on the verge of a threat by a tyrant in Naples around 1410. They were already getting ready when I got the commission of St. George by the guild. I took a break from St. John and worked long hours day and night to finish St. George. I had to take my tools and my assistant to the building of Orsanmichele church to work on the sculpture in a niche there exactly where the church people wanted to place St. George. They believed the popular tale involving St. George defeating the dragon came from a collection of stories called the Golden Legend. So they wanted St. George there to defend themselves against the tyrant. I placed my utmost concentration on St. George and whispered to him every day while I was sculpting, urging him to come alive and save Firenze and its people. The news kept on coming from different sources that the army was ready and coming from the north.

"I put my mind and body to complete St. George with my assistant Paolo working hard to help me. Early summer this year of 1415, I had just finished and the guild decorated the marble statue of St. George with a metal sword and armor when news came that the tyrant of Naples suddenly died of some disease and the marching army receded. Firenze was saved. So I wanted to take few weeks off before I start again with St. John."

"Uncle, you are a great motivator. What an achievement! I wish to have your stamina and concentration. Uncle, from where did the name Orsanmichele originate?"

"The name means St. Michael's Kitchen Garden but now you know it is a church. You are doing fine, Amadeo, I am really proud of how you came this far with so little help. I want to help you have your own place then your mother and your grandmother can visit you. What do you say?"

"That is very nice and kind of you, Uncle."

The carriage took a side pathway winding around a hill. They came to a small village with a small square surrounded by three small green hills. There were about ten cottages which were visible.

They stopped in a small open space where four cottages were overlooking part of the open space that was paved and there was a place for the horses to rest. Moreover, there was a bale of hay and water for the horses.

The cottage where the carriage stopped had a small gate and a narrow-paved path that led to a door. Either side of the paved path lay patches of flower beds, jasmine alternating with white and yellow daises. Oak and birch trees stood tall and green on either side of the cottage.

As soon as all of them, including the carriage driver Francisco, arrived near the door, a middle-aged man and a woman greeted them, *"Benvenuto nella mia casa."*

The man was in his brown brief, white full-sleeved shirt and brown vest with a square, tanned face, black eyes, and a prominent nose. His head was covered with a white cap and he wore leather, sandal-like shoes which were buckled by the leather straps around the ankles.

He was very excited and happy to see them. His outstretched hands made a sweeping motion, making a sign to come in and sit down on the dining table which was near a window at the far end of the room.

The lady wore a printed, floral cotton dress which was below her knees, her brown hair tied up in a bun. Her round, light olive-skinned face highlighted a pointed nose and soft brown eyes. Wearing a red apron tied at her back, she approached them with a smiling face and announced, "We have pepper sausage, spinach, parmesan soup, corn biscotti, minestrone soup, pane ciabatta, and tomato basil soup. We also have fruit such as grape and cantaloupe."

They ordered pepper sausage soup with corn biscotti, cantaloupe and extra bread with olive oil. Uncle and nephew along with the carriage driver enjoyed their lunch while talking and looking through a window at the green landscape surrounded by hills and valleys before they started off again towards Castellina.

The horses were energized after food, drink and rest. They galloped away toward the winding path surrounded by hills. The afternoon sun washed the hills and valleys as the magical light with a little haze transformed into a dreamy landscape.

The carriage reached Greve, a small town which was once occupied by Etruscans and then by Romans, their old relics still remained. There was a church from the 11th century.

"Please go around so my uncle can see the town," Amadeo requested the driver who took the carriage around the town that impressed Niccolò.

By late afternoon, Francisco, the carriage driver, alerted Niccolò and Amadeo, "We have to get going and reach Castellina before dark." Then Francisco gave the horses a signal to gallop faster passing the dreamy landscape along the way.

Finally, they reached Castellina where Amadeo lived with the Casini family that consisted of Marcello, Angela and their son, Stefano, his best friend.

The carriage carried them up a winding road to a hill where they stopped in front of a cottage. Niccolò was amazed and could not imagine the size of the area where Amadeo and his adopted family lived. The sprawling area boasted of three hills and their valleys and farmland expanded into the distance that even by evening the vast landscape stretched as far as the eyes could see to meet the horizon.

Outside the cottage on the wall from projected iron hooks, covered lanterns were hanging. Out at a distance from the door, the flames of fire were seen burning from a big torch in a small iron tower with a covered iron railing.

Amadeo stepped out and paid the carriage driver and asked whether he wanted to spent the night.

"Thank you for the offer but my cousin lives not far from here," the driver said. "I would like to spend a couple of days with him."

Niccolò told Amadeo, "Nephew, I was supposed to pay for the carriage ride."

"Thank you, Uncle, but you promised to pay a much bigger amount for me to have a place of my own."

Just then, Stefano ran out the front door to greet Amadeo and Niccolò. Marcello greeted the visitors with outstretched arms to shake hands with Niccolò.

"*Benvenuto,*" said Marcello. He was of average height, with tanned skin, a round face, sharp nose, brown eyes, and black hair parted in the middle. He wore a beige brief, white cotton shirt and a brown vest.

Angela approached them with a smile. She wore a long olive dress with puffed small sleeves and a round neck. Her gold pendant with rubies reflected lights from the burning candles and a covered lantern light. Her light olive complexion highlighted a triangular face, big sparkling hazel eyes that complimented her light brown braided hair that went up and around the middle of her head and pinned at the nape of her neck.

After an initial welcome they all sat for a drink in the paved courtyard where they enjoyed a light supper. Marcello poured wine in silver goblets to celebrate and enjoy this special occasion of Niccolò's visit to Castellina. Soon, darkness fell and the vault of the sky studded with stars met the horizon at the distant void down below the valleys and mountains wrapped in a shadowy veil as a few wandering clouds drifted across the sky.

Just then a sickle moon peeped beyond the shadowy hill as a night bird shrilled and crickets started chirping to signal a good night's slumber.

Niccolò in Castellina

After spending the night in Marcello's cottage at Castellina, Niccolò got up early in the morning with the chorus of chirping birds on the branches of an oak tree.

The tree was just outside the room at a distance where the hill sloped down. He came close to the window and saw the range of green hills that seemed to be holding hands with each other. One slope would go down and the other slope of the hill would start rising. This cottage of the Casini family was hugged by green hills all around.

Niccolò quickly changed to his short brown brief and beige, long-sleeved shirt and brown vest from his long, white flowing overhaul. He was ready for the day.

The soft rays of the sun reached parts of a hill. There were areas yet to be kissed by the sun. Between the green hills, light and shadows played their joyful game when the sun slowly ascended the horizon. The distant green of the hills met the greens down below where trees swayed in the gentle breeze.

Niccolò was totally immersed with nature's play as he thought nature was trying to teach him how to deal with areas of light and shade viewed from different angles while he was sculpting.

Then he heard Amadeo's voice in the background and turned towards the voice where he found his nephew standing at the door.

"Good Morning, Uncle. Marcello wants to show you his farmland and also show you which part of the land will belong to me. I will pay him back by working at his farm and later when I start earning from my own farm."

"Amadeo, that is a wonderful plan."

"Angela left some fruits for your breakfast and there is freshly-squeezed grape juice if you like."

"Grape juice sound delicious."

Marcello, Niccolò, and Amadeo started to walk downhill around the valley until they came to a vantage point from where they could view the area. Marcello's land stretched far including three hills and the valley. He possessed huge olive orchards as far as you could see. Vineyards and fruit orchards were on the slopes of the hills.

The two hills hugged a smaller size hill and valley which was designated for Amadeo. Niccolò was very pleased to know what Amadeo planned to accomplish.

Niccolò thanked Marcello by holding Marcello's right hand with his two palms together. His eyes moistened with tears. "I cannot thank you enough."

Marcello hugged Niccolò and shook his hand very firmly. "The pleasure is mine. Amadeo is like a son to me."

Niccolò thoughtfully regarded Marcello. "May I ask you something for my nephew?"

"Anything you like."

"I want to help Amadeo have a place of his own. Now that you have helped him with the land and his future business, will you be kind enough to guide him with acquiring a home of his own? I know you know so many people around here."

"Of course. I am so glad you are willing to help." Marcello turned to Amadeo who had been standing by them. "Your process of settling in will be sooner, my boy."

Amadeo's face beamed as his eyes sparkled with joy. He was restless, balancing his body from one leg to another. Then he hugged Marcello and Niccolò.

Niccolò asked Marcello about hiring a carriage to Siena where his friend, Angelo lived. Marcello who had his own carriage said, "My carriage will take you wherever you want to go. The driver knows Siena very well. My friend, you are my honored guest. I am lucky to have you here. People in Firenze and Siena know what an exceptional sculptor you are. You took all the commissions and finished them in time and Firenze is saved from the tyrant soon after you finished St. George. I heard the Siena church wants to contact you for another commission."

Niccolò was overwhelmed by Marcello's hospitality. His face flushed and he was speechless for a few minutes. Then he stretched his right hand and shook Marcello's hand firmly.

Accompanied by Amadeo, Niccolò met Angelo in Siena. Angelo came running from the cathedral to welcome his longtime friend.

"Oh Niccolò, I will never forget the days When we worked in the Baptistery. I learned so much from you."

Niccolò smiled, hugged and thanked his friend, grateful for the messages sent to Niccolò and Amadeo. The three of them spent almost all day together talking about old times and going around the cathedral.

While Niccolò walked around the cathedral and abbey with Angelo, memories came alive of the time he came near a wooden bench under an oak tree. Here he remembered the time Filippo took a twig and taught him the linear perspective by drawing and illustrating it on the dirt. He wanted to sit down for few minutes to bask in that moment so all three spent some time here to relax. Then it was time to have lunch. Angelo took Niccolò and Amadeo to an inn for visitors where they serve meals. The semicircular-shaped inn only had a ground floor with brick walls and a red-tiled roof.

The courtyard spread all around the front and back. Tall cypress trees lined the flower beds with white and yellow daisies which wrapped around the paved courtyard like a garland. On the paved courtyard there were big clay pots with citrus plants, some had yellow, others had green citruses which proudly swayed with the breeze. Some plants still had citrus flowers, their light lemony fragrance filling the air. Niccolò and Amadeo eagerly stopped at the courtyard and took few deep breaths and enjoyed the pleasant moments.

Then they went inside to dine and ordered big bowls of soup with plenty of different vegetables and basil topped with cheese. Red tablecloths and yellow daises in a vase decorated the tables.

The kitchen was at the far end but they could see the open brick oven where fresh breads were baking. The waiter brought the food and homemade beer as a complimentary drink to honor Niccolò. Siena seemed to recognize Niccolò as an honored guest and for that, Niccolò was pleased but very surprised.

"Niccolò, people from Siena went to Firenze and saw you work," Angelo said, "now Siena church is thinking of contacting you after discovering that you are coming here."

The prospect of working on a commission for the Siena church made Niccolò happy. His faced flushed and his eyes sparkled with joy.

"Thank you, Angelo, and my gratitude to the people of Siena. Let me know Angelo, when you would like to visit Firenze."

"Sure Niccolò, I will definitely let you know. Now that I know Amadeo, it will be easy for me."

"Angelo, do you also know Marcello?"

"Yes, I do."

"Marcello told me that you are invited any time you want to visit them in Castellina."

They bid goodbye to each other for the time being. Then Amadeo and Niccolò returned to Castellina.

The next morning the carriage which brought Niccolò and Amadeo to Castellina arrived at the gate of the cottage. Soon it was time to say goodbye to Marcello, Angela, Stefano and his dear nephew, Amadeo.

Niccolò tried hard to speak a few words but his face was flushed and his voice cracked and he repeated sentences many times. "Marcello, Angela and Stefano, I cannot thank you enough for your hospitality." Amadeo came running and said, "I love you," and hugged him. "I will miss you but I know I can go any time to see you, my mother and my grandmother."

Marcello, Angela and Stefano bid him, *"Arrivederci!"*

Niccolò boarded the carriage. The horses started trotting as Niccolò waved to all of them until the horses started galloping down the hill and the figures in front of the cottage suddenly got smaller and disappeared in the green of the olive orchards.

Niccolò's Return from Castellina

When Niccolò returned from Castellina, his mother Orissa and sister Tia were very happy to hear about the place where Amadeo lived. They were more than happy to know about the Casini family of Marcello, Angela and their son, Stefano. Mother Orissa said that Amadeo was very lucky to have a family who treated him like their adopted son.

Niccolò described the land Amadeo acquired by taking a loan from Marcello promising to pay him back by working at his farm and the rest of whatever would remain he would eventually pay him by earning money from his own business. He wanted a place of his own there. Niccolò informed them that Amadeo was sharing a place with Stefano, Marcello's son, who was his close friend.

His mother and sister were very happy and tears of joy rolled down their cheeks that this nineteen-year-old son of Tia had accomplished much for himself.

Niccolò then started talking about his work now that he was back from vacation. He would go back and finish St. John. There was just the final touch and polishing left.

His mother and sister were happy to know that St. John would be finished soon and will be placed in the cathedral.

When Niccolò left his home to set out for work, the sun was up but there was a misty haze. Some of the trees already started to paint their leaves orange and brown. The morning breeze felt cool and fresh. Niccolò almost reached the plaza where shops were just opening and street vendors were pulling their carts as people strode briskly to reach their destination. He passed the bridge on the river Arno at Ponte Vecchio walking rapidly when suddenly a strong feeling kindled inside him to work and finish St. John's sculpture as soon as possible.

Niccolò murmured to himself, "This is almost the end of 1415 and I started the project at the end of summer 1408. I remember the church people requested me to finish St. John in about five to six years. I could not finish it in the time stipulated as I had to sculpt St. George and St. Mark. But right now, there's no excuse. I must finish St. John."

When Niccolò reached the studio, Paolo welcomed him with a huge smile and he saw all the sculpting tools were arranged carefully on a small bench near the sculpture of St. John.

"Thank you, Paolo, for arranging the tools. Let us start working on St. John," Niccolò said.

"Maestro, I am so glad to see you back."

"Paolo, allow me to share with you my thought process of creating of St John's sculpture. I would like to shift the artistic view of gothic mannerism to naturalism, yet I kept some of the gothic mannerism as to sculpt the hands graceful and stronger, a well-built body and the figure as a whole but the torso is big and strong, do you notice that Paolo?"

"Yes. Maestro, I do. But why a bigger torso?"

"Good question. I want a three-dimensional effect: the torso is made bigger and his leg shorter. He will be put on a niche and the people will be looking from below the niche above their eye level so it will make sense and the whole sculpture will be seen in that perspective to be together and proportionate."

"Maestro, Maestro, that is brilliant!"

"Let us polish now. Start from the legs and go upwards including the flowing robes which covers the body."

They worked together continuously for three to four hours from 9 in the morning to one in the afternoon. It seemed that St. John was almost done except the finishing touches.

"Let us take a break for fifteen to twenty minutes and will try to finish the work today and tomorrow," Niccolò said. "We will just inspect the sculpture and see if we have any unfinished areas to take care of."

Niccolò and Paolo stepped out of the studio and started to walk towards the river Arno. The breeze was cool and moist. They saw Baccio, Niccolò's sculptor friend who was also taking a short break. His studio was further down the city center than Niccolò's. They were very happy to meet each other. Baccio gave Niccolò a small loaf of pumpkin bread to enjoy for his break.

"Thank you, my friend," said Niccolò about the snack. "This will help us to work another four to five hours."

They turned back to walk towards their studios as the lapping of the boats along the river Arno could be heard in the background interrupted by shrieks of seagulls.

When they both reached the studio, Niccolò said, "Let us enjoy the pumpkin bread with cool orange blossom water from the pitcher."

Once they finished their snack, they continued working on St. John. Niccolò concentrated on the prophet's face especially the prophet's expression which was depicted as deep and penetrating as if he was looking up towards heaven for a deeper meaning.

"Maestro," Paolo inquired, "please tell me why you want to portray St. John as older. He was a young prophet, wasn't he?"

"Good question Paolo. I want to portray St. John as a noble introspective, a prophet with a lot of wisdom. His graceful hand sits atop the book of scripture as he was a writer of the Book of Revelation and a writer of the fourth gospel."

"Maestro, you are a genius."

Both Niccolò and Paolo worked hard until the sun went down in the west and the last rays of sun struggled through the fine marble dust in the studio. The reflected sun rays on the dust particles created a rainbow at the feet of the prophet's sculpture. The sight was far from any earthly scene. Niccolò and Paolo could only stop in awe at the sight as they uttered, "Amazing."

"Maestro, the light is fading."

"Yes, I am almost done. I think we did what we intended to do today. Tomorrow we will look at the sculpture and see whether some areas need some final touches."

The western sky was still orange red as the chirping of birds at their nests filled the air when Niccolò and Paolo stepped out of their studio and headed home.

St. John Goes to the Cathedral

Niccolò looked at St. John, his creation and started talking to him. "I sculpted you, how I visualized and feel you in my heart. I did not show you as very young. I want to show your maturity and wisdom that is my heart-filled respect, love and affection for you.

"Please pardon me. The cathedral people will soon come to take you away. They will put you in a special niche. I will miss you but I will always be with you. You are my first big commission to which I gave all my concentration, sincerity, and all the love I have."

He looked at him for some time and took a deep breath just as Paolo arrived.

"Maestro, the cathedral people are coming to take St. John today." When the cathedral people arrived—all ten of them—they brought a crate carefully padded with jute bags and soft cloths which they secured like a bandage carefully all over the sculpture then covered him with jute bags padded with cotton.

Then eight, strong men holding the covered St. John slowly pushed him to a strong, thick padded wooden plank that had holes on either end to pass the thick ropes.

Slowly and steadily, the cathedral people pulled the padded plank with ropes attached at both ends towards the crate. The iron crate had bars with an opening as a door on one side through which the sculpture could go in. There was also space for the men to stand inside the platform to hold the sculpture tightly.

Eight of the strong men holding the statue all around inch-by-inch slowly pushed the padded statue to stand on the padded platform of the crate. Then workers tied the statue all around with ropes which ends were tied to the iron bar of the crate.

To be more careful, the workers held the sculpture tightly and the whole crate slowly dragged by rope to an inclined padded plank then onto a horse-drawn cart.

The driver of the cart gave a signal to the horses to trot slowly while the strong men held the covered St. John tightly. Before his signal to the horses, the driver of the cart said, "Maestro, the cathedral is about three and half miles from your studio so it will take four to five hours to reach the cathedral. Do not worry. We are going to take good care of St. John."

"I know that St. John is in good hands," Niccolò said.

People stood on both sides of the road to greet and pay their respects to St. John.

Niccolò strode at his usual fast pace just as the sun was going down in the west painting the sky in orange. Though there was a gentle breeze, he felt an emptiness inside him. St. John occupied his heart for a long time yet there was a feeling of comfort and ease that he finished the work he had set out to do.

Niccolò saw local people of all ages, from working class to the rich and poor, from all social and work backgrounds standing on either side of the road to cheer and bless the covered St. John on his journey to the cathedral.

Paolo joined Niccolò and together they stood side by side as they witnessed the covered St. John moving slowly in a procession towards the cathedral.

They stood there for a while until the horse-drawn cart became smaller and smaller. Niccolò fixed his eyes towards the distance until the sound of horse hooves mellowed and the seagulls' shrieks filled the air. He took a deep breath and heavily put his feet forward to move. He bid goodbye to Paolo. It was almost evening as Niccolò walked briskly towards home, still feeling empty inside yet in the depth of emptiness there was tranquility and a call for a new creation. When he reached home, his mother came running to reward him with a comforting hug.

"I am so glad that you finished St. John and he is on his way to the cathedral," his mother told him. "You did your very best and now the people can enjoy the fruits of your hard work."

Niccolò replied to his mother's reassuring words with a grateful embrace.

Rudy as House Officer
on his way to Newcastle

This was certainly a time of new beginnings yet again, thought Rudy as he took a break from reading the biography of Niccolò's life. Rudy bid goodbye to the entire hospital staff in Bury being especially thankful to his newfound friend and *Dada* whom he first met at the Manchester train station.

An epiphany came to him—he was a lot better off now that he had gained more confidence in the friendly work environment in Bury, moreover, he had been appointed as a house officer in the emergency department. This was not a dream job but the realization hit him that the job market was bleak and thousands of international medical graduates were arriving each year. So for the time being, he considered it a blessing.

Rudy decided to go by bus so he arrived at the coach station in Bury and took his seat. To him, this mode of transportation seemed to be a luxury coach with plenty of leg room, comfortable reclining seats, air-conditioning and more affordable than airfare. He did not have enough money yet to buy a car.

The travel time was shorter but then he would have to transfer to another train. The coach ride would be more time consuming but it would take him directly to the city center without transferring to another vehicle.

The coach started from the city center around midmorning. Rudy was very tired as he did not sleep for the last two nights due to work related tasks: he had to finish clinical assignments and hand them over to the person who would be taking over.

Paperwork included the history and summary of patients who had been discharged during his time as well as their discharge summary. He was thankful that he completed those tasks and now in the coach, he looked forward to taking a long nap.

The coach cruised along the motorway, pushing the landscape of the hills and valleys backwards. The coach route was longer—almost three hundred miles—as it stopped at a few cities and towns.

The bus would stop at their designated area for forty to forty-five minutes to fill up the needed fuel and give passengers a break to stretch their legs and move around. The stop also allowed passengers to have tea and coffee and dine in the café.

Rudy would get down the bus with the other passengers to walk around but realized he was still tired so he ended up back in his seat without going to the café.

By the second designated stop, Rudy regained his energy to go to the café for a snack and tea when he saw a group of four young women in their mid-twenties huddled together. Rudy had immediately noticed that one of them who wore a blue-colored saree most likely hailed from India.

Since Rudy had been preoccupied and anxious most of the time with uncertainty about concerns such as wondering what a new workplace would be like with new people and new surroundings, any pleasant distraction that would take his mind elsewhere, such as the sight of the young lady in a saree would set his mind at ease.

He turned his attention to the landscape that could be seen from the window of the bus and noticed the rounded hills, grassy shrubs and trees swaying with the blast of wind.

The sky was covered with patchy gray and white clouds that seem to be racing towards their unknown destination. Down below, the landscapes went from rocky to alternating with a patchy green meadow and a dancing brook would make its busy journey along the landscape.

Rudy met a few tourists in his coach who came all the way from the US, from California and Nevada who were teachers and hikers going to see Hadrian's Wall. Some of them planned to hike the entire length of the wall. A tour guide accompanied this group who intended to get off in Newcastle.

Rudy heard the guide introducing this group with the history of Hadrian's Wall. Ken, one person from the tour group asked, "How far does Hadrian's Wall stretch and approximately how long?"

"It is approximately seventy-four miles long; to hike it all the way would take six to seven days," the tour guide replied. "It stretches across the breadth of North England Wallsend and the bank of River Tyne, Newcastle on the eastern side of the North Sea to Bowness on Solway and the Irish sea in the west. When we hike there, I will detail some historical details to you. For now, as an introduction, it was a wall which was built by the emperor Hadrian to keep the barbarians of the north out from the Roman empire."

"Is Newcastle its original name?" Marty, another tourist asked. "Did the city exist for a long time since Roman occupation?"

"Yes, it did. The Roman name was Pon Aeilus. The name Newcastle has been used since the Norman conquest of England. Due to its prime location of the river Tyne, the town developed greatly during the Middle Ages and it was to play a major role in the Industrial Revolution. The town is famous for brown ale, nightlife and Giordie, the native dialect.

Rudy was very pleased to know the background and history of the area. He finished his tea and returned to the coach where the driver announced there would be one more stop before the bus reached Newcastle.

Rudy kept on thinking about what and where his new home will be and how his new workplace would be like. The area of work itself was not very interesting to him; he would take care of patients for a short time just to deal with the acute phase and then the patients would go to his or her doctor for treatment and care with their respective area of ailments.

For example, a person with head injuries would go to a neurosurgeon, someone who had a heart attack would go to a cardiologist, someone with broken bones would go to orthopedics, he thought to himself. *So as an emergency doctor, I would just sit there and deal with initial care which is not very much, just to ensure a patient remains stable and gets relief from his pain. No, this is not my area. But anyway, what other alternative do I have? There seems to be nothing at present.*

As he pondered about the uncertain future and the opportunities that lay ahead of him, Rudy thought about how Niccolò had handled any new commission or project that came his way. Rudy's studies of Niccolò taught him that with sheer will and determination, anything was possible. With that comforting thought, he surrendered to a much-needed nap. After dozing off for some time, he heard the driver announcing that within half an hour the bus will take another stop.

A person from the backseat tapped the seat where Rudy sat. "Hello, I am done with the newspaper, you can have it if you wish." He handed the newspaper to Rudy who turned his head.

"Thank you." As Rudy got up to greet him, he found a local British man dressed in a tweed jacket, blue shirt and striped necktie who could be in his late twenties. He had a triangular, freckled face, a pointed nose, greenish-blue eyes and rustic gold hair parted on the side. The man greeted him with a smile.

"I am heading to Newcastle for the first time," Rudy said, cheerfully.

"Whereabouts?"

"I got a job at Newcastle General Hospital in the accident and emergency department."

"Good, I am heading there too," the man said.

"Oh, that would be nice as you might show me where to go."

"Sure, no problem. I can give you a ride, if you'd like. I left my car in a lot which is not very far from the coach station."

Rudy appreciated the offer by this kind stranger. *Is this what they refer to as an English gentleman? I lucked out,* he thought to himself.

The driver announced the bus would stop within fifteen minutes and would take a break about forty-five minutes. When the bus came to a stop, Rudy headed towards the café only to find himself facing the four young ladies he saw from the bus stop earlier. Three of them appeared to be local to the area and the fourth one dressed in a saree captivated his attention.

He decided to not let shyness get the better of him. A surge of courage coursed through Rudy. "Hello, I am Rudy, a newcomer to this country and also new to this area. How about you, young ladies?"

Smiling, they introduced themselves one by one: Julie, Carolyn, Sharon and Sharmistha.

"We plan to stay in Newcastle for two days then we are heading to Durham," Carolyn said. "We are students from Durham University."

"Oh, that is wonderful," Rudy said. "Are you residents of the area?"

"No, me and Carolyn are from Bristol, Sharon's from Dublin and Sharmistha— Sharmi, for short— is originally from Calcutta, India," Julie replied.

"All the way here from India! How interesting," Rudy gushed.

Sharmi narrowed her eyes. "Why is it so interesting? People from India like me attend Oxford and Cambridge. I chose to attend university at Durham."

"That is true, you are right. I am sorry that I mentioned it."

"No problem. People ask me where I'm from all the time especially when I am dressed in my saree. Anyway, I'm guessing you're from India yourself?"

"Yes, I am," Rudy replied, eager to gain more information about the young Indian lady without being too obvious. "If you don't mind, may I ask what subjects you are all studying?"

"Oh, we are all graduate students majoring in English Lit, different periods, of course," Sharon replied.

All too soon, the young ladies bid Rudy goodbye and went inside the café to have snacks and beverages. Rudy grabbed a table near the window and started sipping his tea. Thoughts of the young lady, Sharmi, filled his mind just as the gentleman who sat behind him on the bus, the one who gave him the newspaper showed up.

"May I?" the man motioned to the seat at the table.

Rudy was pleased he could join him. "Yes, of course."

"I apologize for not properly introducing myself earlier. I'm Robert. And you are?"

"Rudy."

The man nodded. "Nice to make your acquaintance, Rudy. I could tell when I saw you on the bus that you are the one the hospital has appointed. I'm working there as a registrar that is an equivalent to a fellow, you see. A person becomes a fellow after finishing their internship and residency. It is really a coincidence that I met you on this particular bus."

Pretty soon, it was time to board the bus again after the break to head towards Newcastle.

As Rudy returned to his seat, he started thinking about the amazing luck bestowed on him during this journey. How each event happened one by one: a kind gentleman would give him a ride to an unknown place he worried about and what a pleasant surprise to meet those pretty young Durham University students, especially the young lady Sharmi—all the way from India, brave woman! The bus was in full speed cruising and winding along a hilly path while green landscapes moved backwards on both sides of the blue sky as they continued to play hide and seek with hips of white and grey clouds.

Finally, the coach reached downtown Newcastle which seemed like a big city to Rudy.

Robert, his newfound friend, approached him. "Rudy, I am ready whenever you are to give you a ride."

"Thank you very much. I am ready."

As they got down the bus, Rudy saw the four young ladies standing on the pavement. They greeted him with a smile as Rudy smiled back.

"All the best to you," he said, "and if I should ever come to Durham, I would love to see you, though where should I look for you?"

"Oh, that is simple. Just search for the Department of English Literature," Carolyn replied. "Someone will point you in the right direction."

"In the Department of Philosophy and in the Department of Religion, there are visiting professors from India, most likely from Calcutta."

"Our dear Sharmi is from Calcutta but she was from somewhere else before Calcutta that is not in India now," Sharmi added.

"That is very interesting," Rudy mused.

"And why do you find this interesting?" Sharmi inquired.

But before Rudy could answer, the coach driver called Rudy.

"Sir, you paid too much bus fare. You may claim your extra money at the window just around the corner beyond where two beige buses are waiting for passengers."

Rudy hurriedly bid goodbye to the ladies. "I am a physician about to start work at Newcastle General Hospital." He waved to the ladies and took one last glance at Sharmi.

It dawned on him that Sharmi was petite yet very pretty with light, wheat-colored skin, wide black eyes, a triangular face, a pointed nose which fit her small-size face. Her long black hair was secured in a bun which loosely sat on the nape of her neck. The blue saree with a green border wrapped her petite stature and draped loosely on her left shoulder.

They looked at each other for few seconds when Sharmi blushed and fixed her eyes on a distant object. Then the group of four young ladies said goodbye as their ride had arrived.

While they were walking away from Rudy, Julie called back to Rudy, "Keep in touch. You will meet a few more from your part of the world in Durham. Our university is very renowned and a diverse people from all over the world come to study there."

Rudy walked towards Robert who was waiting for him at about fifty yards under a birch tree. Rudy felt that he just woke up from a dream as he followed Robert to his car, a green Austin England. When Robert started the car, he turned to Rudy.

"Are you all right?"

Rudy had a feeling that this was indeed the start of such a wonderful life that lay ahead for him both personally and professionally. He smiled. "Yes, Robert, I am fine, thank you."

That night before Rudy settled in bed, he reached for his biography of Niccolò and continued reading.

Niccolò Acquires Marzocco

Niccolò's trip to Castellina was pleasant and satisfying all at once. He was pleased with Amadeo who took a big and brave step to establish himself while at the same time, maintaining contact with his mother, grandmother and uncle when he got a chance. He could feel and envision Amadeo as a dutiful, rising young man with a depth of feeling in his heart.

Niccolò felt very happy to see the expression of joy, relief and contentment in his sister and that his mother was assured that everything would be fine with her daughter's future.

Yet there was still some emptiness which bothered Niccolò as he thought about Beatrice. He did not have the strength yet to tell her the truth directly—that it was impossible for him to have a certain relationship with her. The kind of romantic relationship he felt she longed for.

"This is 1418 and I am thirty-two years old," Niccolò mused to himself, "and Beatrice will be around twenty-two or twenty-three so this is the right time for her to get married and settle down with somebody in her social class. I do not know how to put this fact in a gentle way."

He felt shaky as some strange feelings kept on creeping from his lower extremities, ascending throughout his body and his heart started beating faster as he breathed heavily.

On this late summer afternoon, Niccolò longed for a break from his studio for a leisurely walk to empty his mind of the thoughts which were passing by like clouds. He stepped out of his studio and felt a cool blast of breeze and heard the rhythmic lapping of the boats' oars cruising along the river Arno.

He moved towards the wall of the bridge and saw one seagull chasing another seagull which looked a little smaller than the chasing seagull when suddenly, the smaller one took a dive in the Arno River. The other seagull angrily flew in a circle and shrieked loudly when a bunch of seagulls joined and started shrieking.

Just then Niccolò heard somebody calling, "Maestro, maestro, we need to talk to you soon."

Niccolò snapped back to the present; he wanted to create some distance from his studio at least for a little while but now he had to turn back towards his studio to welcome these two men who were eagerly waiting for him.

"Maestro, His Holiness Papa Martin V wishes to commission you for Marzocco, the heraldic lion, the Insignia of the Republic of Florence," said one of the men about the Pope's request. "It will stand at the top of a column at the foot of the stairs which leads to the Papal apartment at Santa Maria."

"Maestro, we urge you to please accept His Holiness's request," said the other man holding a scroll.

"Well, let us go inside my studio to discuss this further."

The three of them entered the studio where Paolo hurried over to them.

"Maestro, I am glad you are back," Paolo said breathlessly. "There were some people looking for you."

Niccolò raised his eyebrows. "Oh, and who are those people? These here are two honorable persons sent by His Holiness Pope Martin the V—"

"No," Paolo said quickly, "they were different visitors who were here to see you, Maestro. They will be back tomorrow."

The representatives of the Pope followed Niccolò. "Maestro, on behalf of His Holiness, we would like to express how fortunate we are to approach you first before others could garner your immediate attention. We respectfully urge you, Maestro, to please accept His Holiness's honorable request."

Niccolò listened with intense focus, mentally organizing his thoughts as the men outlined and described the project further. He took a deep breath.

"All right, I agree to sculpt Marzocco but I must have my artistic freedom and also since this is the summer of 1418, to complete the work, I estimate it will be around the summer of 1420."

The expression of relief on the men's faces was palpable. "Thank you, Maestro, His Holiness appreciates your service and would graciously accept your conditions."

"Oh, and another thing, I will choose my sculpting material—a fine gray sandstone of Tuscany called Pietra Serena."

After the men glanced each other, they nodded.

"There will be no problem. We will deliver the slabs after you choose them."

Then they said goodbye after thanking Niccolò.

Niccolò smiled at Paolo. "It felt empty after we sent St. John to the cathedral so it's best if we start working soon."

"Maestro, people keep on looking at the sculptures you sculpted earlier," Paolo said. "They gaze at them and say, 'Amazing, they seem to come alive and looking at us.'"

"Thank you, Paolo for your good words. For now, let us go home."

Sundown was upon them as they trekked towards their homes. Beyond the other side of the river, the orange horizon painted the sun rays as orange ripples of river moved towards the shore. The birds flew to their nests quietly as seagulls rested on the wall of the bridge. Then there was a moment of silence as if time stopped and held the beauty in a frame.

Rudy's New Position in Newcastle

As he sipped his coffee that morning, Rudy closed his Niccolò book and set it aside, thinking about how Niccolò must have really felt about Beatrice. To have affection for someone you wanted but couldn't have…ah, Rudy thought pensively, as he knew exactly how that felt. But now he had to focus on his new position in a new place.

Being in Newcastle excited Rudy though the job was in the ER. Young doctors usually like to be in a specific department to be trained and develop a relatively long-term relationship with patients that includes a follow up. But he had no choice as the options were limited then and Rudy was grateful for the stability his new job provided at least for a year. He soon established a rapport with the nursing staff, charming them with his polite and humble attitude of learning new things about patient care. He would say things like, "Please show me how you do this in this particular hospital," a show of humility that endeared him to the hospital staff.

As a result, people around him seemed more than willing to help him get acclimated with routine procedures. Life was tolerable and pleasant highlighted by meeting and getting to know some friendly people from India.

One pleasant evening, Rudy was invited by a fellow physician and his wife from India who was recruited recently to the same hospital. They were both from Kolkata and had been residents of Newcastle for six months.

Rudy arrived at their home in due time. On this winter early evening, the wind blew hard through the whistling trees, amid the silent flakes of snow.

Since Rudy lived nearby, he was so determined to walk fast through the strong wind and snow to reach his destination.

He entered his new friend's home, wiping his feet on the mat outside as he brushed snowflakes from his overcoat with his hand. As soon as he entered, an unexpected surprise greeted him in the form of the young lady, Sharmistha, whom he met on the bus on his way to Newcastle and immediately their eyes met and locked.

Rudy was warmly welcomed by his friend and fellow physician, Samir, who was dressed in a polo white sweater and dark blue pants. His wife, Amita, was adorned in a red silk saree with a black border and black embroidered shawl wrapped around her body.

Amita led Rudy into their cozy living room. The sight of the blue and yellow rising flame drew Rudy closer to the fireplace where he put his two palms out to warm them. The hospital management provided the couple's small two-level cottage.

Downstairs featured the kitchen, dining and living rooms with the bedrooms located upstairs. The living room was decorated with a sofa padded with olive green silk upholstery framed with walnut colored-wood complete with armrest. There were four, olive-green padded chairs and a walnut wooden rectangular coffee table and two small side tables. A framed watercolor landscape with daffodils hung on the wall just above the fireplace.

Two tall standing lamps with white shades provided just the right illumination for a cozy evening with friends filled with a lively evening chat. A light yellow, shaggy carpet covered the floor. All this time Rudy had focused his attention on the details of the living room so it wouldn't be obvious that he was too taken with the young lady present.

Sharmistha sat on a padded chair in a corner across the fireplace. Dressed in a forest green saree with a wrap-around red shawl embroidered with yellow borders over her upper body, she was the vision of loveliness.

Rudy couldn't contain his surprise. "It was beyond my imagination that I would ever meet you here."

Sharmistha just smiled. "It is rather a pleasant coincidence. Amita is my friend since I was at school."

How interesting, Rudy thought, but didn't dare to say aloud.

All four of them started their evening chat in Bengali, which brought comfort as they smoothly conversed in their mother tongue.

There were a lot of things to talk about: their daily routine in a new country, new workplace, manners and food.

When food came into the conversation, Amita excitedly mentioned, "I prepared a simple Bengali meal with rice, dal, and cabbage with shrimp. Sharmi helped me by adding two more items: a dish of Hilsa fish made with mustard paste and yogurt and pineapple chutney."

"Oh, that sounds so delicious. I cannot wait to taste it," Rudy said.

Sharmistha, who Rudy learned was called Sharmi, for short, blushed in embarrassment. "Amita, you are making a big deal about my cooking. I do not know whether it tastes as good as it sounds."

Samir and Rudy both confirmed that they were sure the dishes will be delicious. "We are far away from our homeland and you both tried hard to bring a taste of home by cooking our favorite dishes for us. That is enough to boost our appetite," Rudy said.

The foursome headed to the dining area where a smorgasbord of food was displayed on the table. A stack of dinner plates was placed at the further end of a rectangular dinner table covered with a white tablecloth but over it, a transparent plastic sheet was placed to protect the spillage as silverware and napkins accompanied the plates.

The four of them sat around the table to eat as Rudy inquired whether there was Hilsa fish in the UK's waters.

"No, never," Samir replied, "these are imported from east Pakistan. This particular catch comes from the Padma River in east Pakistan. Here in the UK, we have herring but it's not even near the taste of Hilsa. If you get Shad that could be the closest fish but Hilsa has a richer taste. Both Shad and Hilsa are the bonniest fish."

Sharmi and Amita joined in on the discussion about the Hilsa fish.

"How long are you going to work at the emergency room?" Samir asked Rudy.

"It is going to be over soon. I can't believe a year has already passed."

"Are you looking for another position in the same hospital?"

"Yes, I actually got an offer at this hospital in the orthopedics department."

"Oh, that is nice, but be careful of sister Frazer. She's tough to deal with."

"How do you know?"

"I just heard from others."

Ever the gentleman, Rudy wanted to involve the ladies in the conversation, politely asking Amita and Sharmi about their daily routine.

"I am finishing my training as a speech therapist and then I'll start looking for jobs," Amita said turning to her friend. "Sharmi is studying the influence of religion on literature during the 14th and 15th century England. She is a graduate student at Durham University." Amita beamed proudly at her friend.

"That is so wonderful that you've both carved out your particular path where your passions lie," Rudy said. "I am a wandering star as I do not know where exactly my orbit will be."

"Oh, do not worry. You will find out soon," Samir said. "You should keep in touch. We meet here every now and then and Sharmi comes and joins us so please be our guest if you are not too busy. Do you know anyone else from India?"

"Besides the three of you, none at all." Then Rudy suddenly thought of an idea. "I can cook some Indian dishes, the only thing is, I live in a bachelor's quarters so it is very cramped."

His new friends agreed that won't be a problem.

Rudy cast a thoughtful gaze at Sharmi. "I met Sharmistha on the same bus as I was riding to Newcastle for the first time. And now, I'm pleasantly surprised to see her here. I'm happy to see you again."

"Thank you," Sharmi said with a small smile. "Yes, I remember you said 'all the way from India to Durham.'"

Rudy emitted a chuckle. "Yes, I recall thinking how very brave you are and passionate to travel across continents to follow your dream. I thought that was quite admirable but somehow, I could not express it properly with the right words."

A thoughtful silence passed between them as the crackling fire soothed their thoughts.

"By the way," Rudy asked, "may I ask you what part of Kolkata are you from?"

"Well, I am originally from Chittagong. We are displaced from there at present. My family resides in the south part of Kolkata."

"How serendipitous that I am also from Chittagong and also displaced. My family is at present in North Bengal but I studied in a medical institution which is also the south part of Kolkata."

"What an amazing coincidence," Samir gushed.

"Well, as much as I thoroughly enjoyed this evening, I must say goodnight to you all and hope to see you soon."

Amita and Samir both affirmed that, of course, it would be a good idea to meet regularly. "It was fun," they said. "Sharmi visits us every two weeks and stays with us on the weekends so we can definitely plan for all four of us to get together."

Outside, the wind died down as the overcast night darkened. Through a cloud, the moon tried hard to gaze at the earth, as a struggling moonbeam brushed the path in silver. As he made his way back home, thoughts about the evening, his new friends and a certain young lady came into view and Rudy found himself wondering what had his favorite artist, Niccolò had done in such a situation. Had he acted on his feelings regarding Beatrice as his special young lady and how did it feel like? The more Rudy read about Niccolò, the more he admired his tenacity and determination, qualities he strived to incorporate in his life. But as for matters of the heart, one can only guess where Niccolò really stood, conflicted as he seemed to be. As Rudy strode on, following the silvery path towards his apartment, it was as though he floated in a dreamlike state.

Once settled in his apartment, before bedtime, he reached for the biography of Niccolò and continued reading.

Rudy Settles into New Job, New Friends

Rudy was happy that soon after finishing his emergency room tenure he got a position in the orthopedics department. He was still not sure whether he wanted to be an orthopedic surgeon for the rest of his life. Anyway, he thought there was no alternative. The job market was very bleak so he should accept this as a blessing. Rudy thought about the book he had been reading, a biography of his favorite sculptor, Niccolò, and all the commissions he received as a result of the artist's talents. Rudy realized that both he and Niccolò worked with their hands—hands could do so much for others, for the whole world. Like create sculptures and, in Rudy's case, perform life-saving surgery. He resolved to be more patient using the lessons of perseverance from Niccolò as his guide.

In the meantime, he was determined to learn and give it a try as a junior house officer or resident. The orientation with the senior house officer went fine. The orthopedic unit was almost full; patients were afflicted with different kinds of fractures of the hands and lower extremities who needed surgical reduction and casts. Some patients with bone tumors had to have their lower extremities amputated.

The unit was a long rectangular hall with patients' beds on either side. The patients had their side table and individual curtains pushed at the head end. Each patient's individual telephone was at their bedside and a TV monitor hooked up high in between the beds.

Nursing stations were on either side of the long hall, presenting a very tidy and clean unit with sisters walking back and forth in their navy-blue knee length dresses with white cuffed, three-forth sleeves and a white starched cap which was placed at the middle of their crown.

Rudy's introduction to the patients in the ward with consultants and his immediate senior house officer and the nursing staff went pretty smooth. Yet something was bothering Rudy. He remembered his friend, Samir warned him about a sister named Frazer whom he had not yet been introduced but his anxiety increased which bothered him. He continued to absorb with utmost concentration what new instructions his co-workers were trying to teach him. He thought it was good to learn from everybody regarding a new patient care situation.

It was almost at the end of the day when Rudy just finished the history taking and examination of his patients and was about to settle down to write individual patients' history and examination when the sister in charge of the ward appeared with a stern look and somewhat upset expression on her face. She headed straight to Rudy, peering at him through her glasses as she attempted to read Rudy's name on his badge. Her brows furrowed as she appeared to struggle with his name as it was a long and unfamiliar name: Rudrendu Sengupta. Since she had no idea how to pronounce Rudy's name, nor did she know how to address him, this made her even more upset. Her eyes flashed, jaws clinched, brows arched and fine lines appeared on her forehead.

Rudy was flustered to see her so upset and sensing her struggle, he said, "You can just call me Rudy for short. My last name is Sengupta but you can shorten it to Sen."

She seemed satisfied by what he said. "So, Dr. Sen, have you worked in the orthopedics department before?"

"No, this is the first time."

"Oh I see!"

She sized him up with her fiery eyes from head to toe.

"With the help of an experienced sister like yourself and your staff, I can learn quickly," Rudy humbly said.

"We have a very strict routine and protocol here." She cast Rudy another stern look then abruptly left to the next unit.

Rudy was confused and didn't understand why she was very upset with him. In his flustered state, he wasn't able to catch her name and was afraid to ask. Soon, he finished his work for the day and it was time for dinner at the doctors' dining room before heading to his quarters.

The next morning, he was in the hospital ward with his patients when the sister or nurse in charge whom he met the previous evening, arrived carrying a patient chart. She was upset complaining about an order of prescription where the exact time was not written when it was ordered.

Rudy wanted to see the chart but before he could check it the nurse in charge was in an angry mood and told him that omission had caused serious confusion among the nursing staff. Then she went on and on. When Rudy calmly looked over the chart, he found that indeed he did write down the time, not where he wrote the date, but at the end of the order where he signed his name.

He calmly showed it to the sister-in-charge which made her more upset. She frowned and said in stern voice, "That is not acceptable here."

Then she stormed out of the unit leaving noisy clicks of her shoes on the floor.

Again, the encounter with the sister in charge left him confused, anxious and frustrated. He decided to confide in the senior house officer to ask for advice. He told Rudy that sister Frazer, the sister in charge of the whole nursing staff, a position she had held for a number of years, demanded that everyone must adhere to a certain protocol and that should anyone dare to counter her expectations, "it will make matters worse."

Rudy continued to exert concentration and effort to work in the unit, meticulously going over every detail in order to meet the sister-in-charge's expectations.

It so happened the sister-in-charge took some time off during the Christmas holidays giving Rudy a chance to relax a bit and breathe comfortably in her absence.

One of his forms of escape was at Samir and his wife Amita's place along with the special attraction of Sharmi who visited their place every two weeks.

He started to know Sharmi a little better and promised her he would visit Durham in the near future.

Meanwhile, the tension between the sister-in-charge and Rudy escalated when sister Frazer came back from her vacation. She complained that Rudy did not attend a call-in time and arrived late to attend to a patient.

Rudy came late to her call because he was attending to another patient in distress just before sister Frazer gave him a call. Her complaints went on and on: like the time Rudy misplaced a patient chart and illegible writing on patients' orders.

Rudy asked help from the consultant and matron—the head of the nursing staff—but nothing helped. Eventually Rudy discovered that he had unknowingly dislodged the doctor who had wished to continue in his position as he had been in a romantic relationship with none other than the ward sister—sister Frazer.

Knowing the reason sister Frazer had been hard on Rudy was disconcerting. Dealing with the disgruntled sister-in-charge exhausted him. He was really tired and wanted to give up his position. So he wrote a resignation letter which he handed over to the secretary who pleaded to him to not be too hasty as he had to move out of the hospital living quarters if he resigned. Instead, he asked if Rudy would be interested in doing a locum, a temporary job in neurosurgery as they were unable to find a junior doctor.

He was initially scared to jump on the decision but with his present position and the anxiety and tension of losing his accommodations if he left his job, forced him to say, "Yes."

Later on, Rudy contemplated on yet another career move as outside the winter storm kept howling as flakes of snow formed a blizzard in broad daylight. As he watched the snow through the window, Rudy took a deep breath of relief.

He flashed back to the past and remembered the days when he was desperate and some unknown energy brought him the news of hope.

Suddenly the secretary's voice pierced his thoughts. "I just called the neuroscience center to let them know that you are interested in the position there."

That was enough to bring Rudy back to the present. He looked at the secretary, with eyes full of hope. "Thank you," he said.

Feeling incredibly lucky, Rudy couldn't help but think that reading about Niccolò's good fortune of acquiring great opportunities was starting to rub off on Rudy who was eager to continue reading more about Niccolò's new adventures.

The Making of Marzocco, the Heraldic Lion

On a sunny day about mid-morning in the summer of 1418, people representing the office of Pope Martin V delivered the slabs of Pietra Serena, gray sandstone, to Niccolò's studio. Paolo and Niccolò were there to receive it with anticipation.

Paolo reminded Niccolò that other people had also planned to meet him possibly regarding another commission. "Maestro, shall we wait or start working?"

"No, we wait. These people are from the palace of Cosimo."

"What should I do then? Stay here or go?"

"No, stay here."

"Before the palace people arrive, I will explain to you about the heraldic lion and how I want to sculpt it." Niccolò's face showed seriousness and contemplation. "Paolo, the heraldic lion is also known as Marzocco, the animal symbol representing the free republic of Florence. Legend goes that the Florentine Republic chose the symbol of a lion over other animals because lions are able to tear apart the eagle which is the symbol of imperial power. So I want to make the lion very strong and powerful, yet I will add some expressions as if it is alive."

"Maestro, will you sketch it before we start?"

"I believe I will." Niccolò's attention was diverted. "Paolo, I see that people from the palace are coming towards our studio."

Indeed, two people from the Medici Palace dressed in blue knee-length briefs, beige cotton shirts, and brown vests approached and one of them opened a scroll.

"Maestro, the honorable Cosimo de' Medici sends you the details of his commission," said one of the messengers.

"Thank you," Niccolò said, gesturing Paolo to bring wooden stools so the guests could sit down. "Paolo, please bring the jug of orange blossom water and two glasses for the guests."

While Paolo offered water to the visitors, Niccolò read the commission. There were a number of sculptures Cosimo wanted him to sculpt. The top priority was a sculpture of a young lady pouring water from a conical vessel which would be a fountain. This particular one had to be sculpted first after a real model—his niece, Beatrice as she was planning to get married in the early part of the year 1420.

Niccolò's heart sank, his face flushed as beads of sweat like pearls appeared on his forehead. He knew this day would come yet secretly, he wished it would never come to pass: the inevitable day Beatrice would belong to another man. To hide his expression, Niccolò said, "I have to look at the list carefully so I must sit down to take some notes. Paolo will attend to you."

"No problem, Maestro. Take your time. We can wait."

Niccolò sat down, took some deep breaths and thought to himself, *I cannot refuse Cosimo, but God help me, it will be a very tough challenge for me to sculpt with Beatrice sitting as the model.*

He sat there for a while pretending he was going over the list. At last he took a few more deep breaths and tried to calm himself before rejoining the guests and handed over the signed list.

After the two representatives from the palace left, Paolo eyed his maestro with concern. "How you are going to handle both commissions? I cannot go to help you when Lady Beatrice is modeling."

"That is true. I will start Marzocco in the morning and will leave some parts of Marzocco which you can do on your own. I will go in the early afternoon to sculpt in the palace." Niccolo wiped the sweat from his brow. "In the meantime, let us pick the slab from where the lion will come alive with our touch."

"Maestro, where did the name Marzocco come from?"

"I am not sure but I believe the name came from the word *Marte,* the Roman God statue noted by Dante and carried away by the flooding of the river Arno in 1333. It previously served as an emblem of Florence. However, it may have come from St. Mark the evangelist whose emblem is a lion. So Paolo, this is my plan."

"Yes Maestro, I am very much interested to know how we are going to sculpt Marzocco."

"Marzocco will look real, the eyes of the lion will look wise and delighted," Niccolò said, his eyes sparkling as it always did when he was excited about a new project. "The top torso of the lion will be prolonged to spotlight a luxurious mane and its posture as human. Marzocco's head will be pleasing since it has the attribute of a living being. The lion will be on a quiet stance, no longer competitive, his front paw will be curdling the red Iris court of arms of Florence. It will be definitely a warning sign for the enemy of Florence. The lion is portraying the town. Paolo, every day before I go to the palace to sculpt, I will sketch the outline on the slab and you can sculpt that part alone in the afternoon."

"Will you be going to the palace to start sculpting tomorrow?"

"I have to go and see them tomorrow afternoon. That is what I mentioned to the people who came from the palace to visit us. We have the rest of the day together so let us start."

"All right, Maestro."

The huge slab that was already on their work bench was standing erect. Niccolò took the medium-size ladder, placed the drawing paper, hung it from the top of the erect slab, measured the area with tape and started sketching the face with a black drawing pencil. After finishing the face, he roughly sketched the mane and the prolonged torso.

The lion would be in a sitting position and the paw will be holding the court of arms of Florence with red lilies.

He finished sketching within two hours. Paolo watched carefully while holding a big sheet of drawing material with utmost concentration. When his eyes were almost fixed on the area where Niccolò was sketching, his jaws clenched and he kept his body still, holding his breath for a long time so as not to disturb his maestro with any sort of movement.

"Maestro, this was the toughest time I have had so far in my sculpting career," Paolo said after Niccolò finished sketching.

Niccolò smiled. "I really appreciate your efforts, your dedication, your patience and hard work. I am glad that you held the drawing sheet tightly otherwise I could not have finished it within a relatively short time."

Niccolò stood up to stretch after a long work session. "Paolo let us drink the rest of the orange blossom water first and I will explain which part you are going to sculpt when I am not with you in the studio."

"All right, Maestro."

As they enjoyed the orange blossom water, Niccolò explained to Paolo that he would work on the prolonged torso part on his own in the studio. Then, in the morning Paolo would help Niccolò with the face and mane or whatever else needed sculpting.

Paolo beamed with joy. "I am so happy that you are trusting me to sculpt some parts of Marzocco by myself."

Though it was early afternoon, both of them decided to go home early and would start working early the next morning.

* * *

When Paolo arrived the following morning, he thought about arranging all the tools for Niccolò and they would start working. But upon his arrival at the studio, he saw his maestro was already sketching Marzocco.

Niccolò greeted Paolo. "I sketched the part of the torso you will sculpt in the afternoon when I am not here. Now we will start working on the face and head of Marzocco."

"Thank you, Maestro. I will get all the tools ready for you."

Niccolò started with the lion's face, sketching roughly on the stone, the area of the head and mane. Then he started working on the area with his hammer and his tooth and point chisel.

Niccolò kept on subtracting pieces of stone from the slab and created the area of the whole face with the special area of the nose and mouth roughly. He kept the place for the eyes as it was and more details would follow. He kept the area of the mane thinking Paolo could do that part.

The paw of one hand would touch the marble slab where the lion would sit. He sketched the hand and the paw on the area of the slab from where it would be carved.

"Paolo, this is another part you are going to carve when I go to sculpt in the palace. You choose which one you want to start first. I think this is enough for me today. I will start again tomorrow in the morning where I left off today."

"Maestro, you made amazing progress so far. I will work on the part you sketched for me."

"Thank you, Paolo. I will see you in the morning."

* * *

Niccolò strode purposefully towards the Medici Palace as the afternoon sun was strong. He wore his long, white, flowing cotton outfit and had on a black cotton turban-like cover on his head. He carried a medium-sized, beige cotton bag hanging on his right shoulder with sketching paper and pencil. He also toted a closed clay bottle of water.

As he walked faster, he felt the warm sultry weather as sweat collected on his forehead. He took a sip of water and as he passed the river Arno, he noticed the peddlers moved under the trees with an open umbrella. The bakery put a curtain of straw half the length of the door and windows and the shopkeeper's assistant put water to keep it moist and cool.

Not too many people were seen walking around and the few who were tried to walk under the shadow of the trees whenever possible.

When Niccolò finally reached the palace, someone at the entrance welcomed him. Niccolò soon recognized him as one of the men who came to his studio. The man wore the same outfit of blue knee-length brief, beige cotton shirt, and brown vest.

"Maestro, I will accompany you to Lady Contessina's chamber."

Niccolò nodded and followed him. He realized that the outfit the person was wearing must be some kind of uniform of certain employees of the palace.

They passed the paved courtyard which had several big clay pots with citrus plants. The smell of citrus blossom was refreshing as they passed the sculpture of Mercury then both of them came out in the garden.

They followed the paved path of wisteria and climbing rose pergolas. The flowers of wisteria were gone but vines arched over the trellis. Patches of iris of different colors were on both sides of the path. There were patches of pink, yellow, and white roses, their sweet smell filling the air; the patches of flowers formed a rectangular shape; in between the patches there was a paved path and big clay pots with different varieties of citrus plants which broke the monotony. Beyond that, there were varieties of trees, some Niccolò could recognize like birch, maple, oak, and slender pointy cypresses.

But he was amazed to see one big tree with red leaves that looked out of the ordinary but beautiful. Niccolò inquired about the identity of the tree.

"Maestro, that is Red Oak," his guide said.

Niccolò gazed at the tree with awe. "It is beautiful."

"Maestro, we are almost there," the palace staffer said, "we just have to climb up a few steps which will lead to a small courtyard with a garden and beyond that is her ladyship's section of the palace.

Niccolò and the staffer passed through another potted citrus grove where a big oval clay water tank sat as pink lilies floated with their round green leaves. Once they passed that, they entered a lighted chamber with large windows and chandeliers hanging from the ceiling.

On the wall there was one tapestry depicting a scene where ladies engaged in different activities, some of them playing their lyres while some were on the swings. In the tapestry landscape, there were flowers on the trees and small daisies on the grass.

The room was furnished with pink, floral, silk padded chairs with gold arms and legs and an oval table with a gold-framed, glass top and golden legs, a chandelier hanging in the middle was designed with pink iris petal made in frosted glass.

Niccolò clutched his bag which hung on his right shoulder. He was restless, shifting from one leg to the other, breathing faster, as thirst overcame him so he took a gulp of water from his clay bottle.

Lady Contessina appeared through a swing door on the other side of the room. Adorned in a long, olive-green dress, her ladyship's pretty olive tan skin was visible through the three-quarters of see-through, lacy sleeves. An oval-shaped emerald pendant lined with diamonds rested below her neck. A golden star hairpin secured her hair in a bun. Her presence was magnetic; her large hazel eyes sparkled when she started talking.

"Please make yourself comfortable," Lady Contessina welcomed Niccolò. "Beatrice will be joining us momentarily. I shall stay for a short while but there will be a maiden who will attend to you and help you if you need anything."

"My honorable lady, I want to know exactly how you would like me to sculpt Beatrice."

"Maestro, it is up to her. We would like her beautiful figure to be sculpted in white marble. Beatrice would like the sculpture to be clothed."

"My lady, I want to let you know my schedule," Niccolò said. "I will come in the afternoon for the first few sittings as I have to sketch her and then I will sculpt on the marble. After the initial sculpting is done, I will do the finer detail when she need not pose. At the end when it is almost done, I might need her to pose for two or three more times to give it a final touch."

"Maestro, we trust you to do whatever needs to be done. Beatrice is the one whom you must consult with regarding the schedule," Contessina said. "She is the person who you will spend more time with and the schedule should fit her daily routine."

Niccolò nodded, affirming that Lady Contessina was right. He needed to run his schedule by Beatrice. But before he could regain his composure and prepare for the young lady's arrival, Beatrice glided through the swing door. Upon seeing her, Niccolò inwardly gasped.

Beatrice was breathtaking, a vision of beauty. She was just as beautiful as he remembered her, even more so now. Her brown-black, wavy hair cascaded down her back. Her hair naturally parted right around the middle, a wavy tendril loosely resting on each side of her triangular face.

Her big, hazel eyes below the perfectly arched eyebrows and thick eyelashes looked at Niccolò. Once those eyes met Niccolò's, she shyly turned away to look at the floral carpet which almost covered the chamber.

Niccolò's eyes scanned his muse's attire. Beatrice wore an amber-colored silk flowing sleeveless dress that reached to her ankles. The dress featured a V-shaped neck and round back. Fastened on the front side at the end of the V, was an amber-colored silk rose tailored with the same material of the dress that gently moved as she stepped forward. At the waist the tailored dress narrowed in a honey-combed design. A red ruby pendant lined with diamonds cradled her neck.

She wore red slippers with lacy red leather straps tied around her ankles. Two teardrop rubies dangled from her ears which sparkled with her movement.

"*Buongiorno,* Maestro," Beatrice said softly.

"*Buongiorno* Beatrice," Niccolò said bowing slightly. "I trust you have been well." Wanting to get right down to business and not really wanting to know about her engagement, he quickly asked, "What would you wish for your sculpted figure to be—standing or sitting sideways with your face turned in front?"

"Maestro, sitting sideways facing the front, please."

"So you have to sit on a comfortable, cushioned bench or stool and I will start sketching."

"I will ask Pietro to get a comfortable, cushioned stool," Lady Contessina said. "I bid you farewell for now. I shall be back in the late afternoon. In the meantime, Miranda will attend to your needs. Maestro, is there anything else you need for your work?"

"My honorable lady, I will need the conical vessel which Beatrice's sculpture will be holding as if she is pouring water that will be the fountain as that is exactly what is mentioned in the commission I received from the palace."

"No problem," Lady Contessina said. "I will ask Pietro to acquire one and he will soon bring it to you."

"Thank you, my lady."

Lady Contessina hugged Beatrice before she left the chamber.

Pietro arrived promptly with a rectangular maroon velvet cushioned stool made of rosewood which Niccolò asked him to place close to one of the windows.

Then Niccolò softly asked Beatrice to sit on the padded stool and turn sideways, not fully so her legs will be angled sideways while her body and face would turn towards the front.

In the meantime, Pietro returned with a medium-sized clay vessel with a round opening, the body of the vessel gradually tapering at the bottom. Niccolò then asked for a wooden board on a stand which he would use to tape his sketching paper on. He started sketching immediately, beginning with her legs and he could see through her fine silk dress the beautiful shape of her legs. He inwardly acknowledged that she was not sculpted by human but by divinity. For a few moments, he lost his concentration and as his hands trembled, he started breathing faster. He pulled himself together, reminding himself that he was commissioned by Cosimo and indeed, this was a job for him. He was at work. For a while, they were without attendants just when Beatrice started talking in a very soft voice as her face flushed a deep pink.

"Maestro, you must know—I do not want to get married. I would like to study and help people around the palace and…and I want to spend time watching you sculpt."

Niccolò paused briefly and sighed. "Beatrice, you know that is not practical. The reality is that you must blossom in your own way and experience this world. Going through your life, you will be presented with opportunities to help people around you as well as yourself. My body and soul are bonded with sculpting. I do not see beyond this; my two hands and fingers only feel the hard sculpting vehicle that I make come alive. I try sometimes to break the invisible boundary and bondage and it seems that some invisible force drags me gently to where I belong. Beatrice, you are my inspiration, my muse, and I will carry with me those special feelings as long as I breathe and sculpt. Beyond that I am useless to you."

Beatrice was overwhelmed with emotion. Her whole body shook, her face was flushed as her eyes welled with tears. She was at the point of sobbing.

Then she looked around the chamber to see whether anyone was spying on them before turning back to Niccolò.

"Maestro, you have made me happy and very sad at the same time. My boundless joy is that you have said I am your inspiration. But there's the sadness that I will never get close to you the way I would like you to for I really want to be so very close to you."

Suddenly, she came out of her pose to open a window allowing fresh air and a gentle breeze to enter. The sweet smell of roses filled the air. Miranda brought a jug of water and two silver glasses and a tray full of fruit and snacks for Beatrice and Niccolò.

Niccolò asked Beatrice if she wanted to take a break for water or move around. She replied that she would like to take a break after half an hour. So Niccolò finished sketching her legs then started the front of her body.

Finally, they both took a break just as Miranda poured some water in two glasses and served some fruit and snacks on plates for the sculptor and his muse. They practically ate in silence exchanging a few casual words between them.

After their break Niccolò asked Miranda to assist Beatrice in the next pose guided by Niccolò's instructions: to hold the vessel with two palms below the lip of the vessel tilting it slightly at an angle downwards.

The instructions were meticulously carried out yet it was still not quite as right as Niccolò wanted. So then he tried to impart guidance one more time as he moved forward to Beatrice and lowering his voice, he whispered, "I am going to place the vessel where I would like it to be." Then he placed his palms on Beatrice's hands and moved them forward where he wanted. He could feel Beatrice's whole body slightly tremble, as her face flushed and glossy eyes softened. Niccolò breathed heavily and returned quickly to his sketching and fixed his eyes on Beatrice.

Miranda remained a silent observer as she poured more water in two glasses then offered one to Niccolò who accepted it gratefully as he needed that glass of water desperately.

Miranda then approached Beatrice and offered her water holding the glass close to her lips. Beatrice reached out with her slightly parted lips to sip the water.

The rest of their time flew quickly. Niccolò realized that he had to stop for today as he saw the sun went down in the west coloring the sky orange.

"That is all for today," he told Beatrice, with a slight bow. "Thank you for sitting for me. It was quite a good productive session. I will see you tomorrow at the same time."

She blushed as soft tendrils fell over her face. "Thank you, Maestro."

* * *

The next morning Niccolò returned to the studio to find that Paolo was already there. His assistant eagerly showed Niccolò the part he sculpted.

"Maestro, I finished carving the paw of Marzocco where it will be on the slab."

"Let me see." Niccolò peered closely inspecting Paolo's work. "It is pretty good but you must take out some stone chips around the paw area to be more defined. Overall, you did good sculpting work."

"Thank you, Maestro." Paolo eyed Niccolò curiously. "And how did your work at the palace go?"

Niccolò sighed. "Well, yesterday was the first day. It took a while to start but I was able to sketch Beatrice, except for her face. I plan to roughly finish the sketching today but will spend two more days to detail it further." He took a deep breath and paused. "Then the sculpting will start on marble."

"Maestro, that is wonderful you have already planned it out."

Niccolò nodded a bit absentmindedly as thoughts of Beatrice filled his mind. "Let us start with Marzocco's face today. That is very important to me and then we will work on his mane."

Work, thought Niccolo as he sighed, would provide a much-needed distraction from the other major beautiful distraction that awaited him at the Medici Palace.

Rudy Takes Some Time Off

Rudy was happy to be selected as a house officer, or resident in the neurosurgical unit at the regional Neuroscience Center. It was like an unknown and uncharted sea to him. He wanted to start with a clear mind to give his utmost concentration to the field of neurosurgery.

So he planned to take off for a few days to be away from the hospital environment and decided to visit a few places around the area. One of them on his list that he promised to visit was Durham where Sharmi was a student.

Rudy told his friends about his plan and Samir and Amita were happy and encouraged him to take some time off for a few days from hospital work. They knew that he went through a tough time in the orthopedics unit with the charge nurse who was always picking on him and gave him a hard time to the point that he was on the verge of submitting his resignation. A position in the regional neuroscience center was a pleasant change for Rudy transitioning from one department to another which gave him the opportunity to try something absolutely new. He was excited and happy at the same time.

So to celebrate his time off, Rudy explored the area to visit historic places. One of them was Hadrian's Wall which he came to know from tourists and their guide traveling with him on the same bus he was riding on his way to Newcastle for the first time.

Rudy called Sharmi from a phone booth before he boarded a train from Newcastle which took only twenty-five minutes to Durham. Sharmi was happy and excited; she couldn't believe Rudy would come from Newcastle to visit her.

She assured Rudy not to worry about his accommodation; she would arrange a bed and breakfast place close to where she lived with her friend, Sharon whom Rudy had seen on the bus on his way to Newcastle. Rudy was pleased to know that Sharmi would arrange a place for him and that it was close to Sharmi.

The short train ride was pleasant as the train moved fast curving like a snake through the verdant hills and valleys of Northumberland.

Durham, located North East of England, was a most picturesque city. Upon arrival, Rudy was received at the train station by Sharmi and Sharon. The three of them were excited to see each other, especially Sharmi whose eyes sparkled with joy and her voice cracked. She was wearing a green saree with a red velvety border, a red long-sleeved open breast cardigan and a beige overcoat.

Sharon wore long boots, plaid navy skirt, beige cable-knit thick, high neck sweater, a woolen red cap, and a khaki raincoat. She came forward to shake hands with Rudy, welcoming him to Durham.

Then they took a taxi and headed to their destination. Sharon and Sharmi suggested that Rudy take a guided tour of the campus.

"It is worth visiting. What do you say Sharmi?"Sharon asked. "I think Rudy would find our campus interesting. We can take you on a tour of our English department."

"Okay, ladies whatever you say, I am up for anything," Rudy said.

"Sharmi, you should take a few days off and accompany him," Sharon said.

"I will think about it," Sharmi replied. "Let's go and check in at the bed and breakfast place."

"And how would you like us to address you? Doctor with your last name?" Sharon asked.

"Oh no! Please call me Rudy."

The two young ladies exchanged glances. "Okay," Sharon said. "Let's go!"

The three of them arrived at a cottage with a thatched roof and a garden in front. It was the middle of January and the garden looked bare except for the trimmed evergreen hedges. The tall bare trees swayed with the breeze. At one end, a heap of fallen leaves tried to fly with the breeze instead. They were huddling together with a rustling noise.

The owner was a middle-aged lady, blonde and blue eyed with her hair up in a bun with golden barrettes on each side of her crown. She donned a bright floral skirt below her knees, a high-neck, cable-knit long-sleeved, white sweater, black wooly high socks and brown boots tied with lace.

She introduced herself with a pleasant smile. "I am Mrs. Ainslee Johnson, your host. I will do my best to take good care of you. Now, I will show you your room." Mrs. Johnson took Rudy to his room which was in a split-level above their garage, very neatly decorated with a comfortable rosewood bed, a thick comforter, two big pillows, a bedside table with a lamp, a desk with another small lamp, and two padded beige chairs. The room had one small chandelier on the ceiling which looked like a few pink tulips, and a bathroom with a shower.

The room's two windows featured white sheer, thick lined curtains with red roses on a beige background. Rudy was more than happy with his room as it looked very comfortable and cozy.

Mrs. Johnson said breakfast will be served from 8 to 10 in the morning in the dining room downstairs. "Anything you need let me know."

Rudy thanked her and took the keys for the room and the front door. Mrs. Johnson mentioned that if Rudy returned late, after midnight, he had to inform her ahead of time.

Rudy shook her hand, thanked Mrs. Johnson and went down to rejoin Sharon and Sharmi. Soon they boarded a bus which was just two stops from Rudy's bed and breakfast place. The living quarters of the post-grad students were an extension of Durham University just on the other side of the road which was one of the entrances to the campus.

They reached their destination—a two-story apartment building with trees and greens hedges in the front, a security checkpoint at the entrance. Sharmi and Sharon led Rudy upstairs to their living quarters which turned out to be pretty cozy with two bedrooms, a living space and a kitchen, a dining area and bathroom.

As soon as they entered, Rudy was surprised to see Carolyn and Julie sitting on the pink padded couch. "Hello, surprise!" they gleefully said in unison.

Indeed, Rudy was happy to see the whole group. "What a nice surprise to see you all again."

The living room had one big sofa, two small sofas, two padded stools, a rectangular coffee table, standing lamp, a wooden floor and a wine-colored shaggy rug.

A framed watercolor print of Durham University with its landscape hung on a white washed wall. There were two windows with thick amber-colored curtains. The dining table with four chairs, placed against the wall in front of the kitchen, was covered with an amber-colored tablecloth and a small vase stood in the middle with an evergreen pine twig.

"To celebrate Rudy's visit, we will have some champagne but Sharmi will have baby champagne," Julie said.

"For dinner, I made saffron rice, dal with meat balls and aubergine curry with yogurt and mustard paste and some cucumber salad," Sharmi said.

Carolyn was excited. "Oh, I love it. We made some bread pudding so it will be a gala dinner."

"Sharmi, we can open the bottled Ahmed's Mango Chutney that we bought from the Indian store the other day," Sharon said.

Since Rudy hadn't brought anything for dinner, he said, "Can I help you with anything?"

Julie raised her hand. "That would be great if you could help me bring the dinner plates and silverware from the kitchen while I arrange those on the table. You can open the bottle of champagne and pour it into glasses. If you're an expert, you won't spill a drop on the floor. Don't forget to serve the baby champagne to Sharmi."

They all sat around the table and feasted on their food and drink to the last morsel.

Julie and Carolyn already booked the guided tour the next day for Rudy and Sharmi. The weather forecasted that a snowstorm was expected in couple of days.

The girls were excited for Rudy to see their Durham University campus.

"I have a car so I can take you around," Julie said. "When the weather gets worse, Rudy can visit the library and other indoor areas."

"The next two days I'd like to spend long hours in the library," Sharon said, "so Sharmi and Rudy can spend time here whenever they need to."

Rudy was overwhelmed with everyone's generosity and hospitality.

The clock tower chimed ten, and Rudy excused himself saying he wanted to go back to the bed and breakfast place to retire for the night.

He bid goodnight to Sharon and Sharmi who reminded him to meet her at her apartment at 9:30 in the morning as she knows where the tour starts. She gave him directions on how to reach her apartment. Then Julie and Carolyn gave Rudy a ride to the B and B.

The car ride was short. It was dark and misty and the wind was blowing through the shadowy tall trees with a whistling sound that echoed through the surrounding campus and came back again. The cycle repeated through the dark dome of the sky as a few stars tried hard to gaze at the mysterious earth below and just when the breeze died down, the silence prevailed.

Deeply ensconced as he settled in for the night at the bed and breakfast, Rudy thought about how this could be the beginning of something wonderful with Sharmi and wondered, as he picked up Niccolò's biography again, how Niccolò was able to navigate his own feelings for Beatrice.

Niccolò Splits Time Between Marzocco and Beatrice

Niccolò's plan was to start the lion's face and mane. He already told Paolo that he would start the lion's face. Niccolò was very particular about the eyes of the lion.

"The eyes of the lion must be wise and delighted," he emphasized.

"I understand," Paolo said, "but please show me how to do it."

Niccolò took his marker and drew the eyes of Marzocco to be large and open. He took his pointed chisel and made grooves both in the upper and lower part of each eye on the stone where the eyelids were supposed to be; the grooves were not very deep but almost flashed with the upper and lower eyelids. Niccolò started chiseling out the stone to create an eye socket.

"Will the eye sockets be deep?"

"No, not at all. I told you that Marzocco is no longer competitive. He is in a quiet stance. Deep sockets will create a stern look. I will still be working with Marzocco's eyes. But please start on the elongated torso to spotlight on the luxurious mane. I will sketch it on paper and will leave that to you for the afternoon when I am not here. Please be ready to hold the paper while I sketch the luxurious mane."

"Yes, Maestro, I am very pleased that you are giving me some opportunity to work on the mane. You have always talked about how the sculpture should come alive. What exactly do you mean by that?"

"Paolo, you ask a very good and serious question. I hope I could explain to you clearly what I mean. If you do not understand, please let me know. I will try my best to explain this to you again. And also think it is not your fault but that I am the one who might have failed to explain it to you properly.

"To start with the last few centuries, the sculptor followed the scholastic style around Italy and around the other places like Greece. The sculptures are perfectly sculpted in proportion and measurement. They do not have any expressions, they just stand. I want the sculpted figures to show emotion: to be happy, sad, angry—all those things and more. They will be geared more towards humanism."

"What a unique idea. Is this what you have always wanted?'

"Yes, I have always wanted it this way. When I went to Rome with Brunelleschi, I always told him this is what I want and he encouraged me. He taught me many things. But he told me one day, 'My dear Niccolò, you have to find out your own way of doing things and that it will come sooner than later your unique imagination and technique of sculpting will be mingled together, when your passion will carve the path to meet the vast ocean of artistry."

"Maestro, today is very special day for me as I came to know you in depth which is beyond my reach but it is deep as the ocean. "Thank you."

Niccolò continued to concentrate on the sketching of the lion's luxurious mane, while Paolo held on to the paper patiently.

Then after a while Paolo reminded him, "Maestro, it is past noon."

"Yes, thank you for reminding me."

Niccolò handed over the sketch to Paolo.

"Please sculpt exactly what I sketched," Niccolò said. "Do not try the finer edges just sculpt the mane as sketched. We will do the finer touches together. I will work on his eyes and face to give the expression that I envision. See you tomorrow."

Niccolò sat down for a few minutes and took his bag and the clay water jug with a lid. He grabbed a white piece of cloth, covered his head and tied the two ends of the piece of cloth on the right side of his forehead making sure that the ends hang behind his right ear and touched the upper part of his neck.

After he bid Paolo goodbye, Niccolò stepped out of the studio and started his brisk stride.

* * *

A summer afternoon walk to the Medici Palace in Florence was not enjoyable this time of day due to the occasional humidity. But Niccolò murmured to himself, "It is not too bad as there is a gentle breeze. Today, I must be in the proper frame of mind to sketch Beatrice's upper portion of the body. I must instruct her on how she should position herself so that the contours of the breasts with nipples is to be sketched as natural as it could be through the sheer of her dress."

He took a deep breath and whispered to himself, "It is such a difficult task. Is some superior energy testing me? Please help me God or whoever is watching me so that I can put myself together and finish the project."

He strode faster and faster while taking sips of water from his container.

The sound of oars of the cruising boats along the river became fainter and fainter as few familiar faces of passersby waved at him.

At last, he reached the palace where the guards again escorted him inside through the maze to Contessina's section of the palace where Niccolò would work.

When he entered the room, he found Contessina and Beatrice waiting for him.

"Maestro, please come in," said her ladyship. "I have some chilled orange blossom water. You must be thirsty."

Niccolò bowed to both ladies. "Thank you very much, my honorable lady. I really appreciate your kindness."

"Maestro, Angela will be attending to you today but she will be coming in about a half an hour to forty minutes as Miranda is not well today."

"Thank you, my lady," Niccolò replied as he started to arrange the materials for his sketching.

Lady Contessina bid farewell to Niccolò then gave Beatrice a kiss on her forehead.

Today Beatrice styled her wavy, dark brown hair in a bun which softly rested on the nape of her neck. A wavy tendril hung loose on the left side of her face, her olive-skinned neck adorned with a piece of jewelry—a neck collar which was strung with four rows of pearls which was again strung to a big, oval-shaped pink opal in the middle surrounded by a row of small diamonds. Two oval pink opal eardrops swayed as she glided forward.

She wore a long, sheer light fuchsia sleeveless dress whose upper part was just made to fit the contour of her breasts, narrowed at the waist and then flared to touch her ankles.

A pale pink sheer scarf studded with silver sequins was draped over her right hand.

She took her seat on a padded bench facing her body toward the front, positioning herself a few feet away Niccolò who was ready to start his sketching.

Beatrice wrapped her body with the sheer scarf. Niccolò looked at Beatrice and asked her to sit upright with her back straight and her legs tucked together slightly on the left side.

Niccolò started sketching but now he asked her to shift her upper body to face towards him. Beatrice's heart started beating fast feeling her legs weakening.

Niccolò then asked her to remove the sheer scarf from her upper body. She followed his instructions as though she were in a hypnotic state. This time she felt some kind of sensation passing through her body starting from her legs then surging upwards. This feeling caused a jolting yet numbing pleasure leaving her feeling beyond control as her whole body including her face became flushed. Her eyes were sparkling and gleaming.

Niccolò continued sketching her upper body, concentrating on the contour of her breasts and the cleavage in between. He looked at Beatrice's contour and mentally noted to himself, "She is a virgin and untouched. The nipples are looking upwards with their enchanted look and the contour is round and perfect, seemingly soft, yet firm. This is the divine beauty of Beatrice and I am the first one who has a chance to view it."

Niccolò's leg started trembling as sweat appeared on his forehead. Thankfully, the attendant Angela arrived with a tray of snacks and a jug of water.

"Maestro, I need a break," Beatrice said softly.

Niccolò looked at Beatrice meaningfully with eyes that glowed with inner light. "Of course."

Niccolò took a glass of water from the tray and walked to a nearby window. The afternoon sunlight had spread over the citrus grove as a gentle summer breeze blew through the water in an artificial tank where the pink lilies floated. Big, round, green leaves of lilies moved slowly with the breeze where two birds perched.

Niccolò was lost in his thoughts. Suddenly he came back to the present when he heard a soft voice calling him, "Maestro."

He turned towards the center of the room and saw Beatrice and Lady Contessina.

"Maestro, I came to see whether you need anything. I hope Angela has been attending to you well."

"Thank you, my honorable lady. I am fine and have everything I need. I am happy and honored by your presence. I will need another day to finish sketching then I will start sculpting. I would like to request a space here in the palace, a corner or a small room, where I can sculpt. This request is for convenience purposes as there will be much traveling to lug the sculpted figure to the palace. Also, there are many people and other sculptors in my studio so it is very distracting. I prefer this sculpture not be exposed to visitors while it is a work in progress.

"Now my honorable lady, it is your decision whether my request is possible or not. One other matter is that my assistant usually helps me when I sculpt yet for this sculpting project, I shall accomplish all by myself."

Lady Contessina seemed quite content. "Absolutely, we will arrange a room close to the garden by the steps where you enter this part of the palace which shall be accessible and convenient to you. Just let us know whatever else you may need there and we will arrange it all for you."

Beatrice peered at Niccolò with her big moist eyes. "Thank you."

Niccolò bowed to Lady Contessina. "Thank you, my lady. You have been so gracious to me."

When the last rays of sun peeped through the big windows, a reddish orange glow emitted outside as the chirping of the birds filled the air.

Niccolò bid farewell to Lady Contessina and Beatrice who gazed at Niccolò with a beaming expression and a look of yearning.

"*Ci vediamo,*" she said softly.

Rudy Visits Sharmi in Durham

When Rudy arrived the next morning at Sharmi and Sharon's apartment, he found both girls in the middle of having breakfast.

"Can we offer you breakfast?" Sharon asked after pleasantries were exchanged.

"No, thanks. I just had breakfast." Rudy eyed their food curiously.

"A cup of tea or coffee, then?"

"If it is not much trouble, I'll have a cup of coffee," he said.

"It's instant coffee."

"No problem."

Sharmi appeared happy that Rudy arrived on time. "Rudy, we have to walk to the entrance of the campus and wait for our guide."

"Have fun both of you," Sharon said. "Sharmi, I will be late tonight. I'm going to spend time in the library today."

"What about dinner?" Sharmi asked Sharon.

"Don't bother," Sharon replied. "I'll eat in the cafeteria when I am hungry. I have to finish part of my research assignment."

"So long, see you."

Rudy and Sharmi started walking towards the entrance of the university. They both wore long, black, wool-lined raincoats and thick gloves. A thick, red scarf covered Sharmi's head.

The morning was very cold and crisp with the sun up in the horizon as the misty rays of sun peeped through the tall trees. The stony paved path towards the entrance of the university was wet and shiny with freshly melted frost.

Rudy and Sharmi moved closer together to avoid a narrow stream of water from the melting frost. Patches of grass were yellow and frosty. They walked towards the entrance of the castle, belonging to the university, that featured an arch with all its mystery seeming to draw them with invisible force. The castle stood proudly, sturdy and stony against the cloudy gray sky. The tour guide stood there already waiting for them.

A young graduate of Durham University who majored in ancient history, the tour guide had reddish-brown hair, freckles, a triangular face, pointed nose, hazel eyes, of average height and weight. He wore a tweed jacket, a blue long-sleeved shirt, red tie and navy-blue trousers.

He greeted Rudy and Sharmi with a smile. "Hello, I'm Paul, your tour guide. From your reservation, I trust you are Rudy and Sharmi?"

They nodded.

"Welcome!" Paul said. "Right now, you are standing in front of Durham Castle. Shall we proceed with the history of this place?"

"Yes, please," Rudy said.

"May I ask you where are you from?" Paul addressed Rudy.

"I'm originally from India and at present, I live in Newcastle. I'm going to start my training at the Neuroscience Institute in Newcastle."

"That is excellent. I am sure you know about Rudy Kipling and his writings on India?"

"Yes, I do and I've read some of his books."

Paul turned to Sharmi.

"I came from India too," she said. "I'm a graduate student here at Durham University in the Department of English Lit."

"So, you are one of us. That's wonderful," Paul said. "Sharmi, I'm sure you know that Durham Castle has been occupied since 1837 by the university college of Durham after its previous role as the residence of the Bishop of Durham. This castle stands on a hill above the river. We are on the Durham peninsula opposite the Durham Cathedral. The construction of the castle, which follows the Motte and Bailey design favored by Normans, began in 1072 under the order of William, the conqueror six years after the Norman conquest and soon after the Normans came to the north."

"What is Motte and Bailey design?" Sharmi asked.

"Good question," Paul remarked. "A Motte is a mound, a higher place where the building of the castle is on and Bailey is the inner and outer fenced or walled area. Can anyone guess what's the material of the building?"

"Stone!" Sharmi replied.

"There was some debate whether the original building was wood or stone but archeological evidence suggests that even in the 11Th century, much of the building was in stone. Substantial elements of the castle survive today incorporated into later buildings. There was a major blaze in the 12TH century and portions were rebuilt. As well as being a military hold, the castle was the bishop's ceremonial palace." He paused. "How's that for historical information, so far? I will give a brief account from here onwards so that you can connect Durham Castle's utility to Durham University and its students."

Paul added that in the Middle Ages with less and less emphasis of defense the focus became more on convenience for living and display of status and wealth.

"What kind of convenience for living and display was going on?" Rudy asked.

"Oh, I should have impressed upon you that these bishops who took over the castle were called "prince bishop," they were like powerful rulers. Northeast of England stayed too far from Westminster; the Bishops of Durham enjoyed extraordinary powers such as the ability to hold their own parliament."

Paul paused to look up at the castle. "I want to give you an idea of how the castle changed when a new bishop took over the castle. A great hall was built then rebuilt and then the hall was converted to an apartment in the 15Th century."

He then told Rudy and Sharmi that in the 16th century, major additions were made to the north side of the courtyard including a new chapel and its attendants, stair turrets and a two-story gallery that leads from the great hall.

Paul further stated that in 1680 following the restoration of the monarchy, huge amount of work was undertaken by Bishop John Cosin and his most spectacular addition being the great staircase in the northwest corner.

The last prince bishop was William Van Mildert who was credited for the foundation of university in 1832. In 1837, when Durham University took over the castle, building alterations were made to increase the quality of student living.

"I'll give you a break to wander around at your own pace and see if you have any questions, I will do my best to answer them," Paul said. "Will an hour and a half be enough time for you to explore? I can meet you at the Palace Green."

He pointed to an area as Rudy and Sharmi followed Paul's directions. "You see the space spread out close to the castle? We'll be visiting the adjacent building and the cathedral next. I'll be standing over there so you can't miss me. Oh, and there's a cafeteria right at the corner where you can also find the men's and ladies lavatories. I guess you'll have to drop a penny."

While touring around Durham, Rudy kept thinking that while he was enjoying Sharmi's company, his mind continued replaying the scenes he had been reading in the biography about Niccolò being in such emotional turmoil during the process of working on Beatrice's sculpture and Rudy's heart went out to Niccolò and the heartsickness he must have felt wanting a young woman he couldn't have.

Work on Marzocco and Beatrice Sculptures Continue

Niccolò was escorted out by the palace guards and while he was walking along the paved path, the rays of the setting sun felt softer. There was a mild haze in the air and then he suddenly realized fall was knocking at the door.

He silently reminded himself within a few months he had to finish Beatrice's sculpture. As he neared the gate of the palace, Niccolò bid farewell to the guards.

They bowed. "See you tomorrow, Maestro."

Niccolò nodded, and started his stride towards home. There was a gentle breeze that nudged tall pointed cypresses to sway gently as birds chirped at the end of the day. He looked toward the horizon at a few scattered clouds drifting slowly.

The sleepy sun set to retire for the day, spilling its orange glow over Firenze. Niccolò again, found himself in deep contemplation. "I want to finish within the end of this year. I do not want to linger on in the palace beyond that. Beatrice should not see me beyond that. Her thoughts should be focused on her future world and with whom she will eventually settle with." Niccolò's pace increased with intensity until he reached home.

* * *

The next morning Niccolò picked up his pace to reach the studio and along the way, the cool and misty air blended with the morning glow of the sun reflected on the tiled roof of the buildings. The tall pointed pine trees swayed through a misty veil as the shops along the way were just opening their doors as the smell of freshly baked bread filled the air. The owner of the bakery waved at Niccolò who returned the baker's greeting with a smile as he continued his brisk trek to the studio. He had much to explain to Paolo before he returned to the palace to work on Beatrice's sculpture.

Once Niccolò reached the studio, Paolo, who was already there, greeted him with a smile. "Good morning, Maestro. I kept the tools ready for you. I did part of the mane. You can inspect the work I have done."

"Before I start, I want to talk to you about how we will proceed with Marzocco's sculpting. The initial sculpting should be finished by the beginning of spring next year and then we will proceed with the finer touches and polishing. That will take us both to fall. We shall send a message to the Pope through his messenger to have him come and look at it. If they are satisfied, then we will spend a few more days to see whether everything we planned is done and whether Marzocco is ready and alive to protect Firenze." He raked his fingers through his tousled hair. "And I plan to spend more time at present on Beatrice's sculpture so that I can finish it by the end of this year."

"Maestro, how do you plan to do that?"

Niccolò sighed. "Paolo, that is a challenge but I will be working late in the evening with that sculpture."

"Late in the evening?" Paolo's eyes widened.

"Yes. I have requested for a special room or an area where they will accommodate me so that I can concentrate on the rest of my work there. It will be more convenient and more efficient that way so I will be able to finish the project on time. That is why I must work there late."

"Maestro, it will be too much to work those long hours."

"I know, though it will only be for a few months and I will be done. I do not want to prolong the period till next year when the palace will be busy arranging Beatrice's wedding."

Paolo nodded. "Ah, now I understand."

"Let me see how far you are with the luxurious mane." Niccolò took time to inspect his assistant's meticulous work. "Paolo, it is very good. You have progressed a lot. You can fill up the prolonged torso of the lion up to a point where I will mark you to end it. That will take quite a number of days as the finer details we will do together."

"I am so glad that I have this opportunity and I am learning a lot."

"Now, I am going to work on Marzocco's eyes. Please continue to work on the luxurious mane."

Niccolò started working on Marzocco's eyes, carefully chiseling out the sandstone to flash the eyeballs just below the designated eyelids. He started working with his jaw clenched, brows knitted together. As the work progressed, he started to relax his jaw and after hours of work, took a deep breath, exhaled and said with a smile, "I am done with Marzocco's eyes and I will give the finishing touches later."

"Maestro, it seems Marzocco is smiling and looking directly at me."

"You see it will look more alive and illuminated with expression when it is finished." Niccolò wiped the sweat off his forehead and took a deep breath. "I will rest for a few minutes and drink water. Before I leave, you can continue with the mane of the lion. I will see you tomorrow."

"Thank you, Maestro, and please take care of yourself. Sorry I cannot help you with the project at the palace."

"Do not worry Paolo, I will be fine."

Niccolò walked more rapidly towards the palace more than his previous visit as he was determined to finish the sketching of Beatrice's figure. "What is left?" he mused to himself. "Her face! Her very pretty face. I want her eyes to be soft and looking slightly downward. Oh sure, I must ask my muse what she prefers," he assured himself, taking a deep breath.

186

Once he reached the palace gate, guards escorted him inside the palace. When Niccolò entered the grand building, Lady Contessina welcomed him. "*Buongiorno,* Maestro. Before you start your work, I will take you to a designated area where you can sculpt. The room is ready for you. Let me know if there's a special table or other furniture you need for your sculpting. The room is well illuminated with large windows and also has a chandelier and special areas to place extra lamps for more illumination."

"Thank you, my honorable lady, I really appreciate your accommodation and your kindness."

They both started walking through a swing door which led to a few steps down. Niccolò was anxious about the spot where he was to sculpt. As he followed Lady Contessina, clouds of thoughts passed one by one. It seemed to him one could never predict what may await one on the other side. Momentarily, they arrived at a glass covered corridor. Through the glass, one could see the creeper with orange flowers almost covering the outside of the glass. Niccolò sensed as if he was passing through a mysterious veil yet one that was pleasant just as Lady Contessina said, "We are almost there."

Niccolò snapped back to the present and saw a moderate-sized rectangular room with large windows and doors. Through the windows he could see a fountain and his favorite oak tree with red leaves. Niccolò took a few deep and easy breaths and felt refreshed.

He spotted a comfortable, padded chair and a small table. There was a reclined padded sofa closed to it placed at the far end of the room near the window. In the middle of the room, there was a moderate-sized sturdy, rectangular wooden working table that Niccolò was very pleased to see already there. The only thing he needed was a working stool to sit on while sculpting.

He bowed to Lady Contessina. "My honorable lady, everything looks fine. But I need a working stool and some sort of chest or box where I can keep my tools so that I do not have to carry them every day."

"Maestro, there is no problem arranging that. And should you need anything else, someone will always be around. Do you see the door on the other side? There is a bell attached to it. Just pull the chord and it will ring."

"I cannot thank you enough. You are too kind."

"Do not mention it, for it is my pleasure. Let me know when you are ready to select the marble slab. They are inside a storage room on the far side of the garden."

"My dear lady, I will try to finish my sketching today. Hopefully tomorrow, I will select my marble slab first and then I will start working on it when the slab will be brought to this room."

"This will be done entirely according to your instruction."

"Thank you, my lady. So today, I shall return to my sketching if Beatrice is ready."

"Yes Maestro, she is waiting for you in the same room and today, Miranda is there to look after both of you. I will walk along with you to the room."

Lady Contessina and Niccolò arrived at the room where Beatrice was waiting then her ladyship bid them both farewell for now.

Beatrice sat on a padded stool near the window. Today she wore her long, deep olive-colored dress. For the model of sculpting, one can change the color of their dress and accessories but not the posture and pose; those had to remain the same.

Beatrice looked fresh and stunning. Her hair was in a bun which rested in the middle and top of her head, secured with star-shaped gold pins on either side. It pleased Niccolò to see her hair up in a bun as it highlighted the contour of her face fully making it convenient to sketch. He bowed his head slightly in greeting.

As he assessed her with beaming eyes, Beatrice softly spoke. "*Buongiorno*, Maestro."

Niccolò then arranged his sketching stand and paper and promptly started sketching. Beatrice resumed her pose, sitting with her upper body straight and her feet together, pushing them a little towards the left, face forward, head with a slight tilt to the right.

She would be holding the vessel with both hands to create the illusion of looking at it and pouring water. It was a difficult pose to sit for at least forty to forty-five minutes at a stretch before taking a break and starting again with whatever needed to be done to get it completed. That day would be the final day of sketching.

After that the sculpting would start; for Beatrice, she would see Niccolò a few more days, not so often. Her heart was heavy thinking that she was not going to see Niccolò as much, only a few sessions of sculpting and then, no more. So close and yet so far. Soon and then not at all.

"Beatrice, would you like to cast your eyes downwards at the vessel or would you like to face forward?"

"Maestro, it is up to you. Whichever you prefer."

"I think it would be appropriate to look slightly down."

"I shall do as you wish. Whatever you feel is best." She looked down then peering at him through her thick eyelashes. "I trust you."

Niccolò felt his face flush and promptly asked Miranda to bring the conical clay vessel to give to Beatrice. Miranda followed Niccolò's instruction and handed it to Beatrice who held and looked at it with her face tilting slightly to the right.

There was some difficulty on Beatrice's part in following the instruction so Niccolò had to pause his sketching to help fix her pose, putting careful touches on Beatrice's forehead with his left fingertips and the lower part of her chin with his right fingers to position her exactly where he wanted.

The touch of Niccolò's fingers and palms aroused a wave of sensations. Through Beatrice's body the pressing fingertips were gentle, the palms firm, yet loving and caring. The energy traveled all around her body and she started to feel warm and shaky. She felt heartbeats around her throat.

At that moment, she closed her eyes for few minutes to savor the moments, breathing deeply. Then reality set in, and the ethereal moments were soon over.

Back to the task at hand, Niccolò started sketching her face and neck, at times stopping to look at her face. To him, every single feature was perfect, making depicting her pretty and divine face easy to render in a sketch. The two lovely, expressive eyes beneath two perfect brow lines, the rosy cheeks and pointed nose were made to fit her face and the lips to him were like two rose petals close together that were about to open and blossom.

He was so overwhelmed with the beauty of Beatrice as this was the first time he focused on her so closely. Waves of sensation ran wild from his feet, climbing upward to his body, pounding his heart heavily, making him breathless. His face was flushed and drops of sweat appeared on his forehead.

He stopped, needing a break to drink some water.

Beatrice's feet were numb and weak. She was relieved to have a break. She seemed to be in a state of hypnosis and moved slowly from her seat as Miranda held a glass of water and whispered, "Please take a sip."

It was already late afternoon and the rays of sun were soft and diffused as a cool breeze through the windows refreshed the room.

"I will take another fifteen to twenty minutes to finish my sketching. Tomorrow, I shall select the marble slab and arrange the room and my tools properly so Beatrice, you need not be present. I will let you know which days I will need you." As he said this, he detected disappointment etched on her face.

Beatrice tried to regain her composure with a wan smile.

"Thank you for your patience. It was a real pleasure to have you as a model," he said. "I will do my best to carve your very essence in marble."

"Maestro, I am fortunate to have you sculpt me," she said breathlessly. "It will stay for an infinite amount of years, even when I am gone, your touch and your name will stand out and remain for centuries to come."

Beatrice was overwhelmed with emotion as her voice cracked and her big eyes pooled with tears.

Niccolò came closer and grabbed her hands warmly as he softly uttered, "Thank you, Beatrice, for your good words."

He wrapped up the sketching and other paraphernalia and bid goodbye affectionately to Beatrice and formally to Miranda and left quickly along with the guards while Beatrice watched as his tall figure slowly disappeared in the evening mist.

Rudy and Sharmi Tour Durham Cathedral

Paul stood at the open space between the cathedral and castle watching as a couple walked back to the designated meeting place.

Rudy and Sharmi seemed to enjoyed their break as they were holding hands, talking and smiling while looking at each other with a meaningful sparkle in their eyes. Once they came close to Paul, they said, "Hello."

"Welcome back, shall we continue our tour?"

"Looking forward to it," said Rudy.

"It will be an interesting journey through history. I can give you an outline and direct you to different aspects of the cathedral but I encourage you to explore further the other aspects that interest you."

They started to amble slowly as Paul continued his narration.

"Durham Cathedral is the great experience of Europe to the eyes and minds of those who appreciate and understand architecture. To some, it appeared as a dream, of a river valley cut in a landscape with wooded sides as the river bends and around the bend on a hillside lies the old town. First the castle and then the cathedral dominates the skyline with its solemn and majestic grandeur. Famous poets wrote about the beauty of the cathedral."

Rudy and Sharmi were mesmerized as they looked at the skyline from where they stood, with Rudy's one hand gently holding Sharmi's lower back. As they started moving forward to the entrance of the castle, Sharmi looked like a small doll compared to Rudy who stood almost six feet tall.

Paul looked at them and smiled. "We are almost at the cathedral entrance." Then Paul paused allowing Rudy and Sharmi to catch up with him. "I will first give a brief history of how it all started as you probably know that one of the most significant moments of English history was the Norman conquest of 1016. William the Conqueror became the first Norman king of England and set about building a new English monarchy. Not only did this have impact on English culture, but also had a major impact on architecture. The Norman architect swept through England with the first great example being the Durham Cathedral. The work on the Durham Cathedral commenced in 1093 not long after King William died. Can you guess why they built the church here?"

"Is there a story behind the reason?" Rudy asked.

"Good question," Paul said. "The story dates back to St. Cuthbert, the 7th century Bishop of Lindisfarne. Fearing the Vikings might raid the monks of Lindisfarne, they fled with St. Cuthbert's remains in the 9th century until the coffin became too heavy to move. Taking as sign that saint had decided that this was a good place to be interred, they built a shrine."

Paul went to narrate that considering that they were fleeing the Vikings, the monks decided to build a new home here in the peninsula naturally guarded by steep river banks. Over the next few decades, the church was built and was a popular pilgrimage site. King William appointed William of Calais as first Bishop Prince who had multiple duties and he had to protect the land and spread the faith. Part of this mandate was building a grandeur cathedral and accommodate a growing number of pilgrims. The remains of Venerable Bede, the most influential scholar of medieval England, came to rest in Durham Castle. Paul paused, turning to smile at Rudy and Sharmi. "Are you still with me so far? I know it's a lot of information to take in."

"Is there another name for the cathedral?" Sharmi asked.

"Good question. This is the Cathedral of the Blessed Mary, the Virgin and the home of St. Cuthbert. This is also a seat of the Bishop of Durham, the fourth-ranked bishop in the church hierarchy."

Paul looked thoughtfully for a few seconds before continuing. "I will give a brief background of the architecture of Durham Cathedral but you have to see for yourself to appreciate the concept as a whole entity."

Paul further explained that Durham Cathedral was to be entirely of stone, though no one really mastered stone architecture since the fall of the Roman Empire. So, it was an ambitious undertaking. Luckily, there was a sandstone quarry nearby. The style of the time was Romanesque where buildings were entirely made of stone. They only support that much weight by being thick and heavy. So I ask you, what would have happened if they followed the Romanesque style?"

"It would collapse," Rudy said.

"That's true," Paul said. "On the other hand, they would become very small and cramped with no windows so it would be cramped and uncomfortable. Now, let us go inside and you can see it for yourself."

They entered the cathedral amazed to see its spacious interior. Rudy and Sharmi exclaimed, "Wow."

"You see, the engineers had to come up with a theory and technique so they decided the columns be built into an opposite wall that would extend to the ceiling, arching up and meeting at a point in the middle. By creating a corridor of these arches, the ceiling would be taller and wider allowing more interior spaces." Paul beckoned them with a flickering of his fingers. "Come look up and see for yourself. What you see?"

"I see a ribbed vault," said Sharmi, peering above.

"Good observation. The builders realized that this system worked better than expected. In a traditional Romanesque church, the walls carried most of the weights. However, the structural ribbed vaulting dispersed the weight into the columns making most of the wall between the columns redundant."

Pleasantly surprised by this discovery, the builders realized that they could actually take out part of the walls and insert windows instead allowing for more natural lights, Paul added.

"I will now give you some time to wander around the rest of the cathedral. If you want to see the shrines and the treasures, you must have permission, otherwise you can go and see the Galilee Chapel of the Cathedral where people stand and pray, the altar and stained-glass windows. I will be at the entrance for another half an hour if you have any questions. Just enjoy yourself it was wonderful to be with you. I hope you liked the tour."

Sharmi and Rudy thanked Paul.

"We enjoyed every bit of it," Rudy said.

"Hope to see you in future," Sharmi said.

After Paul's departure, Sharmi and Rudy enthusiastically explored around the cathedral. Rudy couldn't help but think what it must have been like for Niccolò to pass by the cathedral at Florence often—how fortunate was Niccolò to be surrounded by such marvelous art and architecture every day. And now here was Rudy, enjoying the beauty of this amazing architecture that, like Niccolò's sculptures, have stood the test of time.

Feeling the spontaneity of this auspicious day, Rudy boldly asked Sharmi if she would like to spend some more time together and he would buy some food on the way to his place.

She did not say anything and kept quiet. But on Rudy's second request she accepted.

Rudy and Sharmi spent most of the evening at his place. The evening was windy and cool, one could hear the windy whistle through the tall trees. The sky was gray yet the moon behind the clouds spread a veil of light which lit up the sky.

The happy couple, Rudy and Sharmi, enjoyed each other's company until the clock struck ten.

"It was a very pleasant and memorable day for me. I wish we could spend more time like this in the near future," Rudy said, looking into her eyes.

Sharmi blushed as she moved closer to Rudy. "It's been a pretty remarkable and pleasant experience. It seemed to me a life changing experience. For the first time in my life, I wish I can freeze this moment in time and space to let it flow eternally."

They both hugged each other tightly.

"I have to get back to my place," Sharmi said, "Sharon will worry about me."

They both stepped outside to look for a cab, just as the wind blew strongly, the moon peeped through the clouds, as the misty moonlight flooded the earth below.

Rudy opened the door of the taxicab for Sharmi and slid inside next to her to accompany her back to her apartment. As they rode through the town, Rudy's heart swelled with warmth despite the cold outside.

And judging by what Rudy had been recently reading about Niccolò's life, he realized that the great sculptor did at least experience romance in his life in some form and hoped that Niccolò had found some solace in knowing that.

Niccolò Demonstrates His Slab Selection to Beatrice

Paolo was relieved to see Niccolò, who usually arrived at the studio before 8:30 in the morning, enter past 9 o'clock that morning.

"Maestro, I am very glad to see you."

"Thank you, Paolo."

His assistant eyed him curiously. "How was your work yesterday at the palace?"

Niccolò attempted to appear nonchalant, as if his recent encounter with Beatrice had no effect on him. "Oh, I finished sketching. Today I will only arrange my tools and ask the people at the palace to arrange the room as well. I will select the marble slab today and the palace people have to bring that slab in the room and put it on the table where I will work."

"Maestro, that is wonderful you progressed so much."

"Today, I will work on Marzocco's face and you can keep working on his mane. Anyway, I can go little late to the palace as I will not be sculpting. The next two days I will put my sketching paper on the slab and mark another copy on marble."

"You told me that you will make Marzocco alive. Do you mean to say expressive like a live human?"

"Yes Paolo, I am so happy that you understand the idea. I am bringing back a long-forgotten, classical idea that was buried in time. This will be a new artistic taste and beauty in keeping with time blossoming and moving closer to humanism. I have Filippo to thank for his advice and guidance while I was with him in Rome."

"I am so glad to work under your guidance as I learn from you." Paolo's eyes brightened. "For now, I shall go back to work on Marzocco's mane."

"And I will try to work on Marzocco's eyes which should look wise and proud."

Both of them engaged themselves in their work. Hours passed while nothing except the chiseling sound of the stone filled the air of the studio. At times, the distant chorus of the lapping oars of the boats along the river Arno could be heard. The day was sunny yet there was a veil of haze around. A blast of cool breeze and the piercing cry of seagulls suddenly drifted through the windows just as Paolo looked at the wall clock.

"It is past one o'clock in the afternoon," Paolo noted.

Niccolò turned to his assistant. "I finished Marzocco's eyes. Take a look at it and tell me what you see."

Paolo peered in for a close inspection. "He is so confident and alive and looking at me and trying to say something."

"Yes, he is proudly wise, as you say, confident. He is alive, Paolo, he is alive!"

Then as Niccolò prepared to leave for the palace, Paolo handed over a rectangular box to him. "Maestro, these are the tools for your sculpting and pens for marking on the marble slab."

"Thank you, Paolo. I would like to keep these tools there so that I do not have to carry them every day. I appreciate the box. Now it will be more convenient to carry it especially with the handle. Paolo, I cannot thank you enough. I will see you tomorrow."

"Do not mention it, Maestro. It is my pleasure."

* * *

Niccolò ambled towards the palace along his usual way and as he approached the bridge where the wall curved near Ponte Vecchio, memories of the time he used to meet Beatrice flashed before him. This was where she would wait patiently for him eager to talk. He saw at that very spot on the wall some seagulls were standing with one of their legs up, resting peacefully with closed eyes.

Niccolò murmured to himself, "These gulls are in peace. They do not have to dive deep into past memories to hurt themselves." He sighed with a deep breath and continued his quick stride.

When Niccolò reached the palace, once again the guards who were waiting escorted him to a different direction as they walked around the garden along a path through a citrus grove, passing by a fountain that resembled small cascading falls draining in a semicircular pool with floating pink water lilies.

Past that, he came close to his favorite oak tree with red leaves realizing that he was approaching his work room. He entered the room and was pleasantly surprised to see Lady Contessina and Beatrice waiting for him, each of them extending Niccolò a warm welcome to which he bowed to them both in return. Niccolò and Beatrice exchanged warm glances.

"Maestro, we would like to accompany you when you choose your slab of marble."

"Yes, of course, my lady. You shall see how I take time to select each piece which is a process I will explain, if that is all right with you. My steps to choosing the right piece are the following: first, I have to like, actually love that piece. Next, I start to closely inspect the piece then I touch and feel the piece of slab, putting my palms lovingly to the entire length almost like a living being. Then I wait until it starts speaking to me which only I can hear and then I pick up that special slab."

Lady Contessina's eyes widened in amazement as she covered her mouth with her right palm and took a step back, while Beatrice suddenly became still, her eyes moist, face flushed as she started breathing rapidly as if she was out of breath. Suddenly she remembered, in the recent past, Niccolò had asked her:

"Do you have pet?

To which she answered, "Yes, a cat."

"Do you understand when she is happy and what she needs?"

"Yes, by her expressions and gestures."

"Well, I feel the same way about the slabs."

Beatrice allowed the memory of that conversation to sink into her consciousness until it was time to return to the present.

Niccolò followed Lady Contessina and Beatrice to where the slabs were housed, beyond the fountain along a paved brick road that led to a solid, big iron doorway to a large, high ceiling room with very few windows that were placed high up on the wall.

The room was packed with different types of stone slabs and marble was one of them. Niccolò had to look around for the marble slab he liked.

He went around so many times where the marble slabs were lying waiting to be picked up.

Finally, he decided on a slab which stood against the far end of the right wall. This one was quite unique with a touch of amber and some grayish fine veins running along the entire slab.

Niccolò went close and hugged the rectangular piece as though it were a living being. He started to feel the piece with the palms of his hand then moved his palms, touching the entire length of the slab lovingly which he repeatedly did for a certain length of time. Then he waited there very close to the piece quietly, touching his right side of his face and right ear on the marble. Suddenly he came back to the present and announced, "Would someone please carry the piece and put it on my table where I will sculpt?"

All this time, Beatrice and Lady Contessina were silently observing Niccolò so far. At this point, Lady Contessina softly answered, "No problem, Maestro. I will request to have your marble slab transported and placed on your working table." She took a deep breath. "We are amazed and really fortunate to have observed your process of selection."

"Thank you, my honorable lady. The stones speak to me." He breathed with relief. "I want to keep my tool box in the room where I will sculpt and with your permission, I would like to leave early today and start again in the afternoon tomorrow. I shall let you know in few days when I will need Beatrice to model again for me."

"Please do. I think Beatrice will gladly accept your invitation to pose as a model again," she turned to Beatrice, "Won't you, my dear?"

Beatrice looked at Niccolò and said, "Gladly." Then she shyly turned away, casting her eyes downward.

It was already the twilight of evening when Niccolò bid goodbye to Lady Contessina and Beatrice. Again, the palace guards escorted him towards the exit of the palace. After bidding goodbye to the guards, he began walking at a brisk pace toward his home, trying hard not to think about Beatrice and instead looking forward to the dinner his mother cooked.

The cool breeze refreshed Niccolò. Though it was not quite dark, the sky was grayish dark with a few stars dotting the sky. To Niccolò, it seemed to be a very peaceful moment as he gazed up at the sky just as the stars twinkled down at him. Then he continued his eager, rapid stride home.

Rudy's Last Few days in Durham

When Rudy got up the next morning, he could feel that it was misty and windy as the room filled with diffused daylight. He had a good night's sleep yet was lazy to get up from bed. He was reminiscing about yesterday's tour with Sharmi while surrounded by the spectacular architecture of Durham Castle and Cathedral. Flashes of their time spent together after the tour when he invited Sharmi back to his place in the late afternoon and evening where they bonded over dinner danced merrily in his head. Then he remembered his heavy heart when he took a cab to drop Sharmi back at her place and once there, before she got out of the cab, she turned to give him a hug that, though warm and sweet, still kept her distance even as her eyes sparkled with what Rudy hoped was love and affection.

He decided he would like to spend more time with Sharmi, either a revisit, or perhaps she could visit him at Newcastle.

"Now that I have a position as a senior house officer, the hospital will provide me with a place to live, so she can stay with me but will she or won't she?" Rudy murmured to himself in the same way he imagined Niccolò doing the same when pondering the present and future. "It's very likely she will not stay with me and prefer to stay with her friends. I have to stop thinking too far ahead. I must be patient, take my time and let things progress at their own pace and see where the future takes us."

Suddenly the bedside telephone rang, jolting him from his thoughts. Rudy eagerly answered it hoping it was a call from Sharmi. His wish was granted—it was her.

After "Good Mornings" and other pleasantries were exchanged, conversation quickly turned to planning the activities for the day. Sharmi expressed that she and Sharon would like to give Rudy a tour of the university library and English Department then have lunch somewhere in the campus. Later, they'd make evening plans.

"Your plan sounds good, Sharmi thank you," Rudy said. "I'll be there at your place between 9:30 to 10 this morning. I'll get ready soon, have breakfast then head on over there."

He looked at his watch; it was twenty minutes past eight in the morning. Rudy eagerly started to get ready and within half an hour, went to the dining room for breakfast. The dining room was very cozy with a fireplace, tables all covered with white cloth and the silverware set in the right order with white napkins shaped as ladies' hand fans were placed on white plates with golden borders.

A young lady waiter with a medium-length floral dress and a frilly white apron approached Rudy with a smile and handed him the menu. She was a fair woman with golden hair secured neatly with a hair net. Her big blue eyes complemented her pointed nose and triangular face which turned reddish when she smiled.

Rudy was hungry for bacon, poached eggs, baked beans, fried half tomatoes, crispy wheat bread and a pot of tea. As he enjoyed his breakfast, he had a view of the foggy and windy day from his seat by the window.

After breakfast he started to walk fast to reach Sharmi's apartment as a blast of freezing wind compelled him to take a cab. Rudy arrived at Sharmi and Sharon's place on time. The young ladies were very happy to see him and immediately offered him coffee made specially to warm him up.

Soon after Rudy finished his coffee, Sharon, Sharmi and Rudy headed towards the library of Durham University all warmly dressed in their winter clothes. Though still fall, it was already cold but in general, snow didn't start until sometime later but for Rudy, the Durham weather seemed unpredictable and might even feel like snow was on its way if the windy conditions were to be any indicator, a harbinger of winter to come.

While ambling along the campus towards the library, they could feel themselves walking against the strong, cold, gusty wind that was whistling through the tall oak, birch and pointed cypress trees. It was hard to walk against the gusty wind, their noses and faces seemed to be frozen and numb as they reached the library with a sigh of relief.

At the entrance another postgrad student friend of Sharmi's and Sharon's was waiting for them to arrive. He was as tall as Rudy, fair, with red hair, blue eyes, a freckled face, pointed nose, wearing a light blue shirt, navy blue trousers, a crimson tie and a tweed jacket. The young man strode towards them with a smile as Sharon introduced him to Rudy.

"This is Brian our very close friend and a postgraduate student of ancient history who will take you on a tour of Cosin's Library the oldest one."

After exchanging pleasantries, Brian said to Rudy, "I will give you a short history to let you know the names of the other libraries that belong to Durham University."

Sharmi and Sharon both had some commitment in their department for about an hour so they bid "bye for now" to Rudy, agreeing they would all meet at the Palace Green where Rudy and Brian will conclude the tour.

"So where are you based here?" Brian asked Rudy as the two began walking.

"Right now, I live in Newcastle and was interested in visiting Durham which I've been enjoying. I'm finding this area has a very rich ancient history."

"So glad to hear that you are enjoying Durham and our weather is not hindering your enthusiasm." Brian pointed ahead to Rudy. "We are on our way to Cosin's Library at Palace Green."

As the young men headed towards the large area of grass at the center of Durham, Brian started narrating the brief history of the library. "Durham University Library was founded in January 1833 at Palace

Green. One hundred eighty volumes of printed material were donated by the then bishop, William Van Mildert. At present, it houses 1.6 million printed items."

Brian added that several sections were big enough to be individual libraries with different names including this large library: the Bryson Main Library, Leazes Rd Library, Palace Green Library, International Study Center Library and Durham Business school library.

"So we are going to visit the library in Palace Green?" Rudy said.

"Yes, you are right," Brian replied. "You can't possibly see everything all at once. If you are interested, you have to take your time to leisurely browse to maximize your experience." Brian paused to gauge Rudy's attention. "Shall I proceed with the history?"

"Please," Rudy said.

"After the donation by Bishop William Van Mildert, a suitable location to house the library materials had to be constructed on to the Cosin's Library, a Diocesan library founded in 1669 by bishop John Cosin located in Palace Green. While the original Cosin's Library is still located with its collection of medieval manuscripts and early printed books, it eventually came under the trusteeship of the University in 1937. Rudy, you are standing in front of very old bookshelves and stacks of books and printed materials. Take your time to browse around and ask if you have any questions."

As Rudy explored, he was fascinated to see the stacks of old books on the old bookshelves and amazed to see the portrait panels located above the bookshelves.

He rejoined Brian and asked him about the portrait panels. Brian explained that Cosin's Library "is a grade one listed building and is located in a UNESCO World Heritage Site now." The original portrait panels above the bookshelves were painted by Jan Baptist van Eersel from 1668 to 1689.

Nearly three hundred years later, a former university librarian David Ramage completed Cosin's original plan for a library by painting further the portrait panels, he added.

"Did I answer your question?" Brian asked.

"Oh yes, thank you," replied Rudy who was amazed with all the historical background and thanked Brian for showing him around.

They were just discussing where should they wait for the ladies to meet them when Sharon and Sharmi appeared at the far end of the library and strode towards them. The young ladies were pleased to find themselves just in time for them to have lunch.

They all agreed to go to a nearby restaurant where fish and chips was the specialty. A drizzle and wind met them as they started to walk, that they almost ran to reach the place. They were relieved to find the restaurant warm and cozy with the fireplace lighted with a wooden log. Most of the dining tables were occupied by students and staff of the university, their collected conversations echoing through the air.

Beige tablecloths covered the tables set with medium-sized thick, white plates with silverware on either side and beige napkins folded in a triangle were placed on the plate. Sharmi, Sharon, Rudy and Brian fortunately got a table close to the fireplace. They were pleased to sit down and eager to order.

"Are the students enrolled here from different parts of Britain or are there students from other countries too? I know there are students from India," Rudy said, looking at Sharmi.

They all laughed. "Yes, we are aware you know of one very well."

"They come from different parts of Europe like Poland, Austria, France, Italy, Germany, and Switzerland as well as from Africa," Brian said. "Very few come from Durham but there are a few here who usually enroll in the south, mainly in London and the greater London area and some in Manchester."

A young man, a student of the university, was their waiter. He was fair, average height, with a freckled face, big hazel eyes, a round face, aquiline nose and brown wavy hair. He was almost covered with a red apron but one could see his black trousers and beige cable-knit, round neck sweater.

"I am Mark," he said cheerfully, "are you ready to order or need more time?"

"We are ready," Sharon said. "I'll have the beer-marinated fish and chips and a cup of tomato bisque." She glanced at her group. "I think we'll have tea so a big pot of tea, please."

"A bowl of leek and potato soup and a grilled cheese sandwich," Sharmi said.

Rudy and Brian both ordered fish and chips and French onion soup.

After Mark took their orders he said, "It will take about half an hour but I'll bring the pot of tea right now."

Sharon asked Rudy, "How was your library tour?"

"Oh, it was wonderful and I came to know so much about the history of the library thanks to Brian," Rudy said.

"If you are interested, we can take you to our English department but a forecast for another storm may deter that plan," Sharmi said.

"We've already made plans for the evening," Sharon said. "We will have a get together and Julie and Carolyn are arranging it in their place and Brian will be there too."

The invitation touched Rudy. "I cannot thank you enough for all you are doing to make me feel welcome."

"You're welcome."

"So, what is your plan?" Sharon inquired.

"I should leave tomorrow afternoon so that I can start my new job the day after tomorrow in the morning at 9," Rudy replied.

"Tomorrow's forecast is not that bad," Sharmi said, "but it might rain."

"I have a car so I can take you to the train station or will you be traveling by bus?" Brian said.

"Thank you," Rudy said, "I'm going by train."

Mark arrived with the orders just in time for the hungry group to devour their hot lunches. As they ate, they saw through the window a view of snowflakes falling, silently hitting the ground.

Sharmi suggested that perhaps they forgo visiting the English department for another time and instead take a cab to their apartments.

"What about Brian?" Rudy asked, as apparently, Brian had left his car at home.

"Don't worry," said Sharon. "Brian lives on the other side of our apartment building."

They continued enjoying their lunch as they chatted about the evening's activity.

"I wonder, while we are all out enjoying, who's working hard to arrange the party tonight?" Rudy inquired.

"That's very nice of you to ask but Carolyn and Julie are arranging the party at their place and we've already cooked the food. We each made one dish each ahead of time so it will be fine," Sharon said.

"Thank you all for making my stay in Durham memorable," Rudy said.

After finishing a few cups of hot tea, Sharon and Sharmi suggested grabbing a cab to their apartment. So after the four of them got up, they headed to the front desk of the restaurant where Sharon used the telephone to call a cab.

The weather was gray with flakes of snow silently filling up the ground. Though the wind was not blowing hard—not a biting cold at present, it was still very cold.

Once they reached the apartment building, Brian said bye for now and that he would join them a little later at Carolyn and Julie's place.

Sharon said wanted to freshen up. "I'll take the food to Carolyn and Julie's and will call you both after sometime when you're ready to join us."

Sharon left a half an hour later with the food, leaving Sharmi and Rudy to spend some alone time together.

Aiming to avoid any awkward silence, Rudy started the conversation. "Sharmi, how many years or months do you have left for your postgrad study?"

"I still have more than a year. What about you?"

"Mine is just beginning," Rudy replied, "let's see it's now 1964 so two years as a senior house officer, then a registrar for two years and then a senior registrar which is almost at the level of consultant but I will have a position and living space and earnings. In the meantime, I have to finish my Fellow of Royal College of Surgeon examinations which is in two parts. The first part of the exam is pretty tough but I can finish it within a year from now, then at the end of my second year of training, I can appear at the final one, provided I pass the first one." He eyed her curiously. "So Sharmi, what is your plan after you finish your graduate study?"

When she slowly shook her head, Sharmi's shiny dark hair cascaded down her shoulders. "I have no plan yet. I will pick and choose from among the options presented to me at a certain time."

"That is nice." Then, clearing his throat, Rudy asked, "Do you plan to visit to Newcastle?"

Sharmi blinked her thick eyelashes. "Well, I could. Would you like me to?"

Rudy nodded. "The invitation is always open for you to visit Newcastle especially now that I have my own place. You're always welcome there."

Sharmi remained silent for a few seconds. "At present, I will stay with Amita but I can surely visit you."

"That will be very nice." Rudy extended his hand to shake hers.

Their palms remained locked for few minutes until a shrill sound at the far end alerted them the telephone on a side table was ringing. Sharmi hurried over to answer it. "Yes, Sharon, we will be heading out in a few minutes. See you soon."

Rudy had a nice time at the small gathering hosted by Sharmi's friends that evening as it gave him more time to spend with Sharmi. By the time he went back to the bed and breakfast, his last night there, he was ready to go to bed but before drifting off to sleep, he stayed up to read the next chapter of Niccolo's biography that always helped him relax before a good night's sleep.

Between Marzocco and Beatrice

This morning when Niccolò arrived a little early at the studio, Paolo was not there yet so Niccolò walked over to the sculpture-in-progress. He noticed Paolo was almost done with the mane of the lion, just a few inches yet to sculpt up to where he marked on the torso.

Niccolò was very pleased to see that he himself wanted to finish the face of the lion, then go over the legs, paws and other parts of the body very carefully and mark them then teach Paolo how to sculpt the unfinished parts.

"I want to finish the face today then apply a finer touch on it later," he murmured to himself.

So Niccolò started working on Marzocco's face.

"His expression should be confident, yet relaxed." As soon as he thought aloud to himself, he heard Paolo's voice.

"Maestro, you are already working!"

Niccolò glanced at his assistant. "Do not worry. I came early today and want to finish Marzocco's face. You did very well nearly finishing work on the lion's mane."

"Maestro, whatever is left I will finish it today."

Niccolò nodded. "We have to carefully sculpt the legs, paws, and part of the body; he will be seated. He will also be cradling the coat of arms of Florence so I will sketch that for you. On the stone, you can do that part when I am not in the studio."

"Thank you, Maestro."

Niccolò started the lion's face with determination to give him an expression of confidence yet relaxed as protector of Florence with his point chisel and rasp. He worked hard with his new idea of sculpting that imagined lines converging at a point on the horizon

He wanted to bring his idea of a new appreciation of artistic taste and beauty with time blossoming and moving closer to humanism in his sculpting. It seemed time passed very quickly when Paolo announced, "Maestro, it is twenty minutes past noon."

A reminder for him that it was already time for him to go to the palace.

Niccolò took off towards Cosimo's palace. Today, he took a much slower pace as his mind was occupied with Marzocco. He kept on thinking about how to make Marzocco's face confident yet relaxed. Some familiar faces passed by along the road addressed him, "Maestro!" yet he did not reply. Then after a few minutes, he realized it was one of his students so he stopped even when he had already traveled a distance and then turned back, called out his student's name, waved his hand and smiled.

He was deeply immersed in his thoughts of Marzocco and found himself at the gate of the palace where the palace guards greeted, "*Buona Giornata,* Maestro."

He followed the palace guards to his designated sculpting room. Today, he planned to copy the figure of Beatrice on the marble slab which he sketched on his art paper during last few days.

The slab was already on the table, standing quietly, waiting for Niccolò. He began to glue the sketched paper carefully, missing Paolo's assistance as he was always eager to help him hold the art paper as long as he needed.

Then Niccolò took a deep breath and started thinking of how to copy and mark the marble from the sketch in a wise way.

From the lower limb, he started to snip off, bit by bit, with scissors and marking it with marker from the art paper. He had to balance holding the sketched sheet and mark it with his other hand.

The chandeliers illuminated even in the daytime to brighten the room. Through the window, the pleasant breeze and murmur of a nearby fountain filled the air. At times, the chirping of birds could be heard and then fade away, sounds that relaxed Niccolò as he kept on working.

Soon, it was in the twilight of the evening when he saw in his peripheral vision two figures. He stopped and looked surprised to see Lady Contessina and Beatrice followed by attendant Miranda who held a jug of water and some snacks on a plate.

Lady Contessina was in her flowing orange, flowery silk dress with a V-cut neck. Her hair was in a bun at the back of her head with a golden hairdress and a see-through veil draped over that which hung up to her neck, pinned with some gold barrette on either side. She wore a necklace with a row of medium-sized diamonds and teardrop diamond earrings reflected different colors of lights while she moved.

Beatrice wore a deep square neck, sky blue flowing dress with sequins, a pearl necklace cradled her neck, her ears adorned by teardrop pearl earrings. She looked so fresh and pretty it seemed to Niccolò that she came out of the sky with stardust on her dress and landed on earth. He felt a warmth which was radiating throughout his body, his heart racing and drumming in his chest.

"Maestro!" Lady Contessina addressed him in her smooth voice. "We would be very pleased if you would take a few minutes break to have some orange blossom water and some peach tart, and," she glanced at her niece, "if you would like, we can ask someone to hold the sketched paper for you."

Beatrice must have suggested to her aunt that he needed assistance, Niccolò thought. "Thank you, my lady, I would be very happy to drink some water and it will be quite a help for me if someone holds the sketched paper."

"Very well, then." Lady Contessina turned to the attendant. "Miranda, please summon a palace staff member while Beatrice and I will attend to Maestro."

Niccolò's face flushed as drops of pearly sweat appeared on his forehead.

Beatrice, with a beaming expression and a look of longing, fixed her eyes on Niccolò. Though her feet trembled and her heartbeat raced, she took a few deep breaths and with a loving smile, started speaking softly, "Maestro, you are working so hard. Is there anything else you need?"

It took sheer willpower for Niccolò to resist replying that all he needed was her. Instead, he replied, "No thank you, I want to finish the marking on the slab today."

"Maestro, our carriage will take you home so you do not have to walk," her ladyship said.

"My lady, you are very kind. But I prefer to walk."

"No, Maestro. You will make us very happy if you take the carriage. We insist on it."

Niccolò knew better than to counter her ladyship's offer. "Thank you, my honorable lady."

Lady Contessina then informed him that Miranda brought a male attendant strong enough to hold the sketched paper for a few hours.

Beatrice and Niccolò exchanged their loving looks of longing to each other as they knew the time to part hovered upon them once again.

Lady Contessina thanked Niccolò and bid him "*Buona Notte.*" Then she, Beatrice and Miranda left when Niccolò started marking the slab again while a palace attendant held the sketched art paper.

Niccolò concentrated to finish the rest; he was up to the bust. He picked it up from there and moved carefully to the arms holding the pot and carefully sketched the neck and the face. He thought he would mark the area of the eyes and the contour of the face and detail it later. At that point he would need Beatrice to pose again. After an hour passed, he said to the attendant, "I am done for now. Thank you for holding the sketched paper. It really helped me to finish it."

"Buona Notte, Maestro," the attendant said. The carriage is waiting outside. I shall accompany you to the carriage."

By the time Niccolò reached his ride home, the carriage driver recognized Niccolò from the time he gave Niccolò a ride one evening to visit Cosimo.

"Maestro, please sit down and relax," the driver said. "There are few pillows for your comfort and so you can rest your back. I will take you home in no time."

Niccolò remembered seeing the two large open fire torches, one on either side of the big iron gate of the palace which were going backwards as the tall shadowy trees swayed with a gentle breeze. When the carriage started to move, the galloping sounds of the horses became fainter and fainter then suddenly he heard the carriage driver calling him, "Maestro, you are home."

Niccolò woke up from his nap dazed and in disbelief. "I am home?"

"Yes Maestro. We have arrived at your home."

He thanked the carriage driver and went inside where his mother and sister anxiously awaited him at the dinner table.

"Niccolò, we are so happy and relieved that you're finally home," his mother said.

The next morning Niccolò arrived at the studio around 9:30 to find Paolo already there.

"Good morning, Maestro. I finished the mane of the lion."

"That is wonderful. Today both of us have to work together with the paw of Marzocco which will cradle the insignia of Florence. Paolo, this is important. What I will create for the insignia, if you recall what I told you, Florentia is built by former legionnaires as consecrated to the god, Mars. When Florence started to flourish, they adopted a new symbol, the 'lily' which was used by the Florentine army in the first crusade but they did not forget their origins. A lion was kept in a cage close to the

Baptistery. So I will make the shield with a lily and Marzocco will be cradling that shield."

"Maestro, you are a genius. This will be a unique insignia."

Both of them started working on detailing the paw and the insignia. Niccolò explained to Paolo that the front paw would be holding the shield with the insignia of a lily, a clear warning that the lion, the god Mars was protecting the city.

Paolo already sculpted the limb out from the slab as Niccolò marked the slab before. The paw began taking shape when Niccolò started taking out the chips of stone with his fine chisel and smoothed the part with his rasp.

Then Niccolò already marked the area on the shield with his marker thinking that Paolo could work on it while Niccolò worked at the palace.

Soon, Paolo again alerted him that it was already fifteen minutes past noon. Niccolò reminded Paolo that Marzocco was not centered entirely on the earthy realm of religion—it explored the man's abode inside the natural world. Paolo thanked Niccolò for the reminder.

Once again Niccolò headed towards the palace murmuring to himself, "The breeze is cooler, the trees are changing colors, this year will be ending soon. Now I must focus my body and mind towards sculpting Beatrice. I want to finish soon and stop going to the palace for a while. The rest of Cosimo's projects can wait next year until I finish Marzocco." The pace of his stride increased as the rays of the sun on red-tiled roofs looked milder. There was a haze through which the sun rays struggled to reach.

At the palace, the guards promptly guided him to his work room where Niccolò sat down on his work bench and tried to plan how he was going to proceed.

He decided to start with the lower extremities up to the waist then proceed with the upper body, arms and her face would be the last part. After finishing each section, Niccolò would need Beatrice to come and pose for a day so that he could make it as perfect and as natural as possible.

Now that Niccolò had come up with a plan, he decided to inform Lady Contessina and Beatrice ahead of time as to when he would need Beatrice to pose for him.

Niccolò worked on the lower extremities, chiseling the chips of marble from the slab. Through the window, the mild afternoon sun rays reflected on his work bench. The room started filling up with marble dust as the reflected rays of the sun on the fine dust made a hollow of the rainbow on the unfinished sculpture.

Niccolò paused for a moment, lost in thought, as he pondered that Beatrice was a fleeting moment of beauty and illusion in his life. Yet he longed to hold on to that moment, feel the depth of it and be inspired to immerse himself in his creation.

Then he continued his work, chiseling and rasping until the sunlight faded and the chorus of chirping birds filled the air as Niccolò told himself, "Time to stop today and go home."

* * *

The next morning when Niccolò arrived at the studio at his usual time, Paolo was arranging the sculpting tools on the work bench. He was very excited to see Niccolò.

"Maestro, I worked on the insignia after you left. You can look at it and let me know whether it is all right or not."

It impressed Niccolò that Paolo had worked on the insignia. "Paolo, it looks fine but we have to carve out the lily more and of course, later, the finer touch on the shield's border and polishing."

"Maestro, how did sculpting at the palace go?"

"I finished the lower part. Today, I will work on the upper portion of the body. Then I will ask Beatrice to pose again to see whether every part is sculpted as natural and as perfect as possible. Then I shall focus on the face when Beatrice poses for me again. Then it is on to polishing for maybe a few days or more. I do not know how long it will take. Perhaps a week more or less. Then, finally, the finishing touches."

"That is great you are making progress."

"Shall we go back to focus on Marzocco's face again today?"

"Yes, Maestro."

"So today, we will again work on the facial expression. I envision Marzocco's eyes to be wise and proud. I have already sculpted the eyes in position; they are large but flashed with the eyelids. The eyeball curvatures will be slightly bulging but not too much, also a slight rotation on one side so that he will not stare at people. This whole combination will make Marzocco appear not in the mood for competition. Let us carefully finish the eyes today and then I will mark the jaw which should be also relaxed."

Niccolò and Paolo both worked together for a while to create the expression of Marzocco as Niccolò envisioned. Niccolò stopped for few minutes and looked at Paolo who understood that look.

"Yes, Maestro?"

"I want to make Marzocco's lips slightly open as if he is trying to address the people."

"What an excellent idea. It makes it more humanistic, as you have said."

"I am so glad you understand what my creative heart desires, Paolo."

"Thank you, Maestro."

They worked together in silence for a while until again it was time for Niccolò to leave the studio and start heading towards the palace.

At first, Niccolò wanted to hurry yet today something made him slow down, a force that hindered his usual pace. Thoughts of Beatrice passed like clouds across his mind—there was some sort of sadness slowly seeping into his body and mind. He wanted to brush it off once and for all yet he could not. So he started assuring himself, "For the past few years, Beatrice had always been there, waiting patiently for me at the bridge where it bends, always with a smile, eager to talk about my project as she encouraged me. She never talked about herself; she was always very humble, graceful, even though I sometimes tried to ignore her or cut her short to show her how very busy I was. But still, that did not deter her to continue greeting me in her own special and graceful way. I will surely miss her and perhaps, after this day, I might never even have a chance to see or talk to her privately after I finish sculpting her."

He felt a sensation of loss which felt like a painful squeeze on his heart.

So he paced more slowly to prolong the inevitable parting from Beatrice. He felt like he was sinking inside his own body, unaware of himself, unaware of how he arrived at the palace gate when suddenly a voice snapped him back to the present as one of the guards spoke to him. "Maestro, are you all right?"

He tried very hard to smile. "I am all right, just too many things on my mind."

The guards then accompanied him to his work room. Today he planned to sculpt the upper portion of Beatrice's body. He smoothed out her narrow waist and proceeded to her trunk where he carefully sculpted the tailored design of her dress and moved upwards to sculpt her beautiful virgin breasts. With his knowledge of perception of depth, he created an illusion, as if the shape of her virgin breasts were visible through the thin layer of her dress. He concentrated very hard for hours since he arrived, taking deep breaths as he worked and looked outside. It was twilight in the evening and he could hear the chorus of the birds returning to their nest.

Suddenly, he realized he had not taken a break and neither did he send a message to Lady Contessina as to when he needed Beatrice to come and pose for the sittings. He thought for a while then decided he would need three more days to sculpt and finish everything including her face. After that, Niccolò would ask Beatrice to come and pose for him for at least two days so that he could see her in front of him for the purpose of improving, enhancing and sculpting the minutest details—the areas he would check to see if there was something missing then would start to polish—on the already sculpted figure.

Suddenly he had an idea. "I can ask Paolo for help." Then he changed his mind, whispering to himself, "No, that would not be a good idea. I shall do this all by myself, that way I will bring her beauty the way I want to see her. She will be close to me and be mine only." Niccolò breathed heavily, feeling warm and shaky.

He took a few deep breaths to compose himself and then wrote a note to Lady Contessina informing her when he would like Beatrice to sit for him. He handed the note to the palace guard. "I am done for the day. See you tomorrow."

"Maestro, the carriage driver is waiting to take you home," the guard said.

"I can walk. It is not that late."

"Maestro, it is our honorable Lady Contessina's order and desire that the carriage will take you home every evening until you finished your sculpting."

"That is very kind of Lady Contessina. I am extremely thankful to her."

Once he got in the carriage, the horses trotted then started galloping, the hooves sound echoed through the air while the misty sheet of darkness receded backwards. Niccolò fell asleep unaware of the time until he woke up just as the carriage stopped with a jolt. When he realized he reached home, with a sigh of relief he said to the carriage driver, "I was very tired. I appreciate that you brought me home."

"You are welcome. *Buona Notte*, Maestro."

* * *

Niccolò arrived at his studio the next morning as usual. Paolo was already there with the sculpting tools already lined up in order. Niccolò invited Paolo to sit down.

"Let us discuss our plans first before we start working on Marzocco."

"Of course, Maestro."

"The next two to three days my schedule at the studio will be the same. I will be coming in the morning and leaving around noon. After that, for the next three to four days, I shall be working all day at the palace. I will mark with my marker Marzocco's torso and hind legs as a sitting position which you will carefully carve while I am not here. I will start marking it from today and will finish that within the next two to three days as I also continue to work with you on Marzocco on the days I am here. Does this plan feel comfortable to you?"

"Yes, it is no problem."

They worked together for a while as Niccolò marked the torso and part of the hind leg in a sitting posture. Then Niccolò had to finish and head to the palace.

On his way to the palace, he started planning during his swift walk to get there. "Today, I will finish the sculpting and tomorrow, I will go over the sculpted figure to see and feel it with my own hands to make sure that I sculpted her the way I wanted. Then Beatrice could pose for the next two days and then I will be done with the sculpting part and then polish the figure myself no matter how many days it takes."

Suddenly Niccolò felt an emptiness again. "Then that will be it with Beatrice." He started breathing heavily as an uneasiness crept deep inside his chest as if a heavy hammer pounded inside. He was startled when he heard a voice.

"Maestro, welcome!"

Niccolò then went to his work room and gazed at the sculpted figure of Beatrice. He drew closer to the figure and touched her; to him, she felt alive, so alive that he was shaking and had to sit down to rest and compose himself.

"I have to finish this task," he murmured to himself. This is my creation and I need to touch the areas so tenderly so that her beauty will glow and radiate to the people who will be looking at her—my beautiful creation. At least this sculpture, this version of Beatrice, will be absolutely mine and I will be bonded with her for life."

He sat down on his work bench for a while before taking a deep breath. Then with his trusty tools—the rasp, fine chisel and hammer—he promptly finished her neck before the face which needed to be defined more as well as the eyes. Then he would sculpt a lock of hair just loosely laying on the right side of her temple up to her eye level.

Her face looked forward, yet there was a slight tilt to the right as she looked at the vessel while pouring water from it. Niccolò devoted long hours to sculpt her eyes; he wanted an expression of innocence and softness that would radiate through her eyes. By late afternoon, the rays of sun reflecting through the window was mild. He proceeded to her forehead to sculpt a lock of hair loosely lying on her right temple as he preferred the rest of her hair to be in a bun.

Now that he finished the sculpting part, he sat down to gaze at her. He did not know how long he was looking at her until a guard approached him.

"Maestro, the coach is waiting to take you home when you are ready."

He slowly got up from his work bench and sighed. "I am ready."

Paolo was already in the studio by the time Niccolò arrived at 9 the next morning.

"Good Morning, Maestro. How did your day go at the palace yesterday?"

"I finished sculpting and today I plan to spend my time inspecting the sculpture very closely to find out if I missed any detail. And if that is the case, then I will make a note of it. Tomorrow Beatrice is scheduled to pose for me while I check all the details in the necessary areas. I requested she pose for two days. The first day to focus on the legs and lower portion of her body up to the waist and then, the next day I shall concentrate on the upper body and face. After that, I will begin polishing which could take two to three days."

Paolo was focusing on Marzocco. "Maestro, that is wonderful you have already marked Marzocco so I can continue to sculpt those parts and then when you come back, we can work together to finish the sculpting."

"Yes Paolo, that is right, we will finish the sculpting then we can go through the necessary details and then polish which will take time. So Paolo, I will work with you on Marzocco's torso as long as I am here and then I will leave for the palace and come back after four to five days. If you need to urgently reach me, you can relay that message to my mother or my sister at home."

"Do not worry Maestro, hopefully everything will run smoothly here."

Niccolò and Paolo began sculpting the torso and then Paolo took the lead with his hammer and chisel and started to shape it by taking out the stone chips from the slab while Niccolò helped him smooth out the rough areas.

"I am very confident that you will do a great job of sculpting the areas I marked when I am not here."

"Thank you, Maestro."

Niccolò bid goodbye to Paolo. As he started making his way to the palace he kept on thinking about the way he envisioned how the polished sculpture of Beatrice would look and then he tried to visualized how peaceful and pleasing it would be to place her somewhere in the garden where the sound of the water would flow from the vessel as it cascaded through different levels against the steep wall or look like cascading falls and then flow like a stream to carve its path along where ducks would be swimming with their babies.

He realized he was already approaching the palace so he woke up from his daydream, striding purposefully to reach the palace gate. Once Niccolò reached his work room, he gazed at Beatrice's sculpture, sat on his work bench slowly and began touching and feeling her legs, starting from the ankles before moving upwards toward the knees.

There he felt the sculpted folds of her dress and the design he sculpted on her dress. Slowly and steadily, he moved his hands to the upper part of her legs which started shaping the beginning of her buttocks covered with the sculpted folds of her dress. Then when he stopped at her waist, which he held firmly with both palms, his face became flushed and his eyes gazed afar. He longed to say something but it seemed he was at a loss for words. He released his palms from her sculpted waist and sat down on his work bench. He felt warm and thirsty so he rang the bell for an attendant. This was the first time that Niccolò had to ring the bell for an attendant who promptly appeared.

"Maestro, how can I be of service?"

"I would like some water while I take a break, please."

In no time, the attendant brought a jug of orange blossom water and pieces of melon and fruit tarts."Maestro, I shall put these on that table and bring that red cushioned chair for you to relax." He served the pieces of melon in a bright blue bowl and the fruit tarts on a thick medium-sized white plate bordered with green creeper and yellow flowers. Then he poured the orange blossom water in a tall, shiny silver glass.

Niccolò reached the table and sat on the red, velvety cushioned chair. After he sipped the water from the silver glass, he said, "Thank you. I was very thirsty."

After quenching his thirst, Niccolo sat breathing heavily, willing his mind to continue focusing on Beatrice's sculpture as work even though his heart was veering in another direction.

Rudy at the Newcastle Neurosurgery Center

Rudy got up early to have his breakfast at the doctor's mess hall so he could have an early start at the neurosurgery department.

At the doctor's dining room, as he was looking for a table to sit down, an average height, red-haired, freckled, square faced, blue-eyed, pointed nose young man in his late twenties or early thirties approached Rudy. Dressed in a blue, long-sleeved shirt, a red tie, navy trousers and below-the-knee white doctor's coat bearing a name tag of "Dr. Harry Jones, Neurosurgery," he shook hands with Rudy.

"Hello, I think you are the Dr. Sen who was appointed recently as senior house officer."

Rudy was pleased to meet this man who came across as a welcoming person who worked in the neurosurgery department. After Rudy's harrowing experience at his previous job, he aimed to start out on a positive note. "Yes, you are right. I am pleased to be here."

Dr. Harry Jones asked Rudy to join him at a table close to the fireplace. "Please sit down and have breakfast leisurely as there is plenty of time."

Tables were covered with white starched tablecloths set with white plates and shiny silverware. Napkins folded as hand fans complemented one side of each plate. Ladies dressed in forest green dresses served as waiters distinguished by their knee-length frocks with white aprons, their hair neatly secured with a hair net and bobby pins. To Rudy, they all seemed to be local residents around Newcastle judging by the way they spoke with the same accent.

Rudy thanked Dr. Jones for the invitation to join him.

"Dr. Sen, you will be working with our group. I will take you around and introduce you to the nursing staff and others in our unit. You will meet Professor Harkinson, head of neurosurgery who will also welcome you. I work as a registrar

225

so most of the time I'll be in the O.R. assisting Professor Harkinson with surgery. You will be taking the history of the patients and order all the diagnostics tests on them and will be doing all the lumber punctures to get spinal fluid from the patients and order the laboratory tests for them. When you are done, then you can come and join us in the operating room to watch and stand by. I will help you so you can ask me any questions or whenever you need help."

"Thank you. I really appreciate it."

"We address every doctor by their last name like Dr. Jones, Dr. Sen, etc."

"I will follow the same custom you mentioned, but I don't mind if you call me Rudy, short for my real name."

"Thank you," Dr. Jones said. "For when we meet outside our clinical duties."

Rudy thought to himself, *I'm glad he's my immediate supervisor. He seems to be nice.*

Rudy finished his breakfast and put on his doctor's white coat and name tag which he got from Margie at the doctor's quarters who sent it the day before he arrived from Durham. Dr. Harry Jones, the registrar, was very pleased to see that Rudy was very organized. "Very good, you are all prepared to start."

Rudy followed Dr. Jones to the neurosurgery department where his supervisor introduced Rudy to the nursing staff, comprised of sisters who all welcomed Rudy who was pleased with their chorus of "Good morning, Dr. Sen, welcome to neurosurgery."

Dr. Jones showed Rudy his own cubicle where he could sit down and do his paperwork. Then Dr. Jones showed him his own office as well as Professor Harkinson's.

Then they proceeded to the wards where patients lay in the same arrangement of beds similar to other hospitals—side by side with space in between and an arrangement of curtains which could be drawn whenever needed for privacy. Each patient had their own bedside table. Several TV monitors were placed higher up on the wall for the convenience of patients who would like to watch programs.

Sisters—nurses—dressed in white collar and white cuffed half-sleeved, deep blue uniforms with a white cap were busy moving back and forth tending to patients.

On this particular Monday, there was no list of surgeries for Professor Harkinson who usually made his clinical rounds at the ward where he would go over with each and every patient's clinical and detailed diagnostic status and ask his junior doctors how they would take care of these patients in terms of further diagnostic tests and future treatment.

Professor Harkinson arrived at his office at 9 in the morning ready for rounds with his patients a half an hour later usually joined by doctors like Dr. Jones. Rudy felt welcomed by Professor Harkinson who said, "Very pleased you have joined our group, Dr. Sen."

Dr. Jones provided Professor Harkinson with a brief history and diagnostics test results done so far of the patients one by one. Then Dr. Harkinson went to each and every patient to say hello, chat briefly, then do a quick clinical exam, jotting down his findings before moving on to the next patient.

By 11 a.m., the clinical round concluded then the three doctors went to a conference room joined by other doctors, nurses, social workers and physical therapists to discuss matters relating to tests and treatment for each patient. Everyone in the group gave their expert opinions on further tests and treatments to be carried out in the immediate future. By noon it was time for lunch break then time to tend to the outpatient clinic from 2 to 4 p.m., a regular routine for Dr. Harkinson on Mondays.

Rudy's first day at his new position was shaping out to be a long day. At the clinic, Rudy had to get the detailed history of two patients for which he performed clinical examinations for. Then he had to present these cases to Professor Harkinson. Initially, Rudy was very anxious about this process but he sailed smoothly through it.

Further proof of Rudy's success was Professor Harkinson saying he was impressed that Rudy had performed pretty well on his first day. This praise made Rudy feel proud of what he accomplished.

As senior house officer, it was Rudy's duty to clerk daily notes on the patients, order laboratory tests and do the procedure of putting a special needle between the fourth and fifth lumber vertebral space—the lumber puncture—from outside and get spinal fluid for laboratory tests then report to the registrar who was Dr. Jones. After finishing these Rudy would go to the operating room to watch the surgery.

Rudy at times felt that what he was allowed to do was not real neurosurgery but would remind himself to be more patient that these were the steps he had to climb to reach where he wanted to go.

Professor Harkinson continued to observe Rudy's keen interest and enthusiasm and would call him at times to watch the surgery up close and explain to him about the pathology of the brain while at surgery.

Then a day came when registrar Dr. Jones was absent and Professor Harkinson needed an assistant to hold the retractor—a stainless steel surgical instrument used to make the surgically opened space wider by pushing the incised skin and tissue further apart—while removing a brain tumor. When Professor Harkinson called Rudy, with a great sense of achievement and joy, Rudy rushed to the operating room and the nurse-in-charge helped Rudy with careful hand scrubbing, gowning and gloves.

With considerable trepidation, Rudy stood quietly by the side of the surgeon. When Professor Harkinson asked Rudy to hold the retractor, he followed the surgeon's orders and to Rudy, those few minutes felt like hours. Still, those few minutes were forever memorable as it was the first time Rudy saw a living brain which was so unlike the ones preserved in formalin that students studying the brain encounter in anatomy dissection halls. To Rudy, the living brain resembled a sponge compared to a preserved brain which was soft and firm. There were fissures and sulci, gaps between the brain matter and blood vessels running along.

Rudy also marveled at how close the speech center area was. If the surgeon made even a slight error, the patient would never speak. So that surgeon would have to deal with the costly mistake on a human's most precious organ that would result in causing the patient's confusion, paralysis, inability to talk and even death.

A millimeter here or a millimeter there made so much difference to the quality of the outcome so Rudy concentrated more with full strength to hold the retractor when the surgeon removed the tumor quickly. Afterwards, Professor Harkinson congratulated Rudy on a job well done.

"You passed with flying colors," Professor Harkinson said. "I will be sure to call you again soon for assistance."

Rudy was ecstatic with inner joy and satisfaction as though he were floating above his present surroundings.

The sister-in-charge of the operating room told Rudy, "Dr. Sen, Professor Harkinson is very pleased with you and asked me to add your name to the list to call you whenever needed. You know, Dr. Sen, you are very fortunate as a senior house officer rarely gets a chance like this."

Rudy felt honored. "Thank you very much for your kind words. I really appreciate it."

Feeling celebratory, he thought to himself, *Now is a good time to reward myself with a nice meal and relaxation.* Then as he ate lunch, Rudy couldn't think of a better person to share his recent triumph with than dear, sweet Sharmi.

This success reminded Rudy of the times he read about similar triumphs and accomplishments in Niccolò's career as he learned new techniques and imagined the sculptor feeling as triumphant and elated as Rudy was feeling at moments like this.

Niccolò Marvels at the Sculpture of Beatrice

After drinking cool orange blossom water and taking a break, Niccolò took control of himself and started looking at the sculpted Beatrice from the waist upwards. He found some rough areas around her neck and wanted to make her cleavage a little deeper. So he started to chisel out some of the stone in small chips from the area between her breasts to deepen the cleavage. He stopped when he felt satisfied with what he wanted to do. Niccolò proceeded towards her sculpted neck, smoothing out the rough areas with his rasp.

Then he looked at her face, thinking he would just feel her face with his fingertips and palms, close his eyes, holding the image for a few seconds inside him.

He opened his eyes and felt he had given all he could give: the expressions and the radiance through his sculpting. Now it was time to wait, to see Beatrice again in person as she posed to find if there was anything missing that he needed to complete.

He looked at the sculpture one more time and whispered to himself, "Time to go home. It is early, the sun is still up. I can be home early to sit outside on the bench under the pear tree in my backyard which has already started changing colors. Then I will be refreshed with a blast of cool breeze as I hardly ever have time to enjoy the little things like that around me."

He got up and told the attendant that he was done for the day.

Once he arrived home, Mother Orissa and sister Tia came quickly to greet him.

"Niccolò, it is so nice for you to come home early," his mother said.

"Dear brother, I have some news from Amadeo," Tia said. "Come, let us sit down in the backyard patio and talk. There is still light."

He, along with his mother and sister, sat on benches basking in the still reddish glow of the sun on the western horizon, a chill in the air a reminder of the arriving winter.

Niccolò was very excited. "I cannot wait to hear about Amadeo. Is he all right? What is his new project? Any news about that?"

Tia clasped her hands together eagerly. "He has a new project! He already started harvesting grapes to make wine on a small scale. He already made some structure where the wine will be processed. He wishes to come and stay with us a few days during Christmas."

"That is wonderful." Niccolò beamed. "I can take a few days off to spend some time at home."

"What about *your* project? When will it be done?" Tia inquired.

At the mention of "project," Niccolò's mind immediately went to Beatrice. Internally, he shook those thoughts away. "No, Marzocco will not be done completely. Only polishing will be left to do but the sculpture for Cosimo's palace will be finished within a few days." *There*, Niccolò thought to himself, *I actually said it.* He sighed at the inevitable finality of his time at the palace, his time with Beatrice.

"Oh, that is amazing, my dear brother."

Mother Orissa nudged closer to her son. "Niccolò listen, Amadeo is already planning to build a house so that Tia will have her own space: a two-bedroom living space and another small space for her sewing and embroidery, a separate kitchen, front and back patio. Her space will be in the same building where Amadeo will live in his portion of the house."

"That is amazing to see how deeply he loves his mother," Niccolò gushed, "and he is very compassionate and understanding. I am very impressed. I will try my best to see that his dream comes true regarding his building this house and building his winery."

Tia was almost in tears. "Dear brother, I really appreciate your kind gesture to help Amadeo."

The twilight of the evening set in as a cool breeze felt even cooler. A chorus of chirping birds became fainter and, on the horizon, a few stars twinkled down at the Earth.

Mother Orissa rose from her seat. "I will serve dinner in fifteen minutes."

Tia and Niccolò got up offering to help their mother.

Soon, they all sat around the dinner table with flickering candles enjoying mother Orissa's homemade tomato bisque with basil, cucumber salad with homemade mint dressing, lightly fried salmon with pickled and sliced black olives sprinkled with chopped cilantro and freshly-baked bread and Niccolò's favorite almond rice for dessert.

Besides dinner, they enjoyed conversing about Niccolò's Marzocco project which Niccolò explained was almost done but that he would spend more time detailing and polishing the sculpture with his assistant, Paolo.

He also shared that in the next three to four days, he would be working at the palace where he will spend entire days to finish the work. Cosimo and his wife would also like him to work on future projects for their new palace garden but that will be after the Marzocco project is complete.

Soon a tired Niccolò was ready to go to bed. He kissed his mother goodnight and thanked his sister for helping their mother with dinner.

"*Buona Notte*, Niccolò," Mother Orissa and sister Tia said together.

* * *

When Niccolò got up early the next morning, he heard birds chirping from his backyard while he was still in bed in a state of wonderment. He never realized the sound of chirping felt so pleasant until that day. Though the sun was not up, a haze could be seen through a half-open window where one could view the misty landscape outside that appeared as though the entire landscape and beyond was covered with a veil that looked gray and mysterious.

Niccolò took a deep breath, murmuring to himself, "It really feels empty that after two or three days, Beatrice will barely exist beyond that misty veil, like a shadow to me, and memories of her would haunt me every now and then."

He almost dragged himself to get ready for his trek to the palace. As usual, Niccolò started off in a fast pace along the avenue of trees as the cool breeze helped him remain in the present. The sun was up in the horizon and the eastern sky still imbued an orange-red color.

The ripples of the Arno River happily moved towards the shore while the boats carrying people cruised along the river. The peace of the morning was frequently interrupted by the piercing cry of seagulls.

When Niccolò reached the gate of the palace, a guard promptly accompanied him to his work room.

The soft morning sun flooded the room as the sculpture of Beatrice bathed by soft rays appeared radiant. Niccolò gazed at the sculpture, getting lost with its beauty. He touched the figure and murmured softly, "I am going to hold this image inside me to inspire my body and soul with creativity and I will feel the soft and tender touch of you when I am tired."

Suddenly a palace attendant arrived, piercing his thoughts, to announce that Beatrice and Lady Contessina would be arriving shortly.

Niccolò thanked the attendant and started to line up his tools in preparation of working immediately. He was halfway through polishing the forehead of the sculpture when Beatrice and Lady Contessina arrived.

Beatrice gasped immediately upon seeing her very image and likeness. She wore her olive green, flowing dress with a four-stringed pearl neck collar adorned with an oval emerald in the middle lined with one layer of diamonds reflecting various colors of light. Her emerald earrings layered with diamonds swayed gracefully when she stepped forward to greet Niccolò after she composed herself.

"Good morning, Maestro, I am ready. Let me know where and how I should stand or take my seat," she said in her mellifluous voice.

Acknowledging her with a polite nod, Niccolò pondered the options thoughtfully, his observance of her initial reaction to the sculpture forever imprinted in his memory. "That is a good question, Beatrice. For now, I want you to sit close to the window and I will start from your feet and proceed from there."

Contessina addressed Niccolò with a cheerful and excited voice. "Maestro! The sculpture looks so beautiful and alive. You really are a genius."

"My dear honorable lady, I am glad that I could fulfill your expectations. Your praise is appreciated and makes me happy."

"I will take my leave," Lady Contessina told Niccolò. "Miranda will be attending to your needs shortly. At the end of your day, I will be very much pleased to talk to you if you have time."

"Certainly, my lady, whenever you wish to talk, I shall make the time."

Once Lady Contessina left, Niccolò concentrated his work on Beatrice's feet though since there was not much to be added, he started polishing, fully aware of his muse's presence.

Beatrice cleared her throat. "Maestro, I will really miss seeing you work and... I already feel very sad and empty." Her voice trembled.

Niccolò kept working unable to meet her gaze. In truth, he shared her sentiments yet could not express them aloud. "Beatrice, you will be very much involved with your new surroundings and meeting people. You are about to embark on a new life so there is no need to be sad. Yours will be a smooth life of leisure, affluence and frivolity. You are young and have your whole life ahead of you, whereas I will eventually become an old sculptor doing the same tasks every day, chiseling out the chips of stone with my hands. You will soon get bored with such a life like mine which is not very exciting, with very little amusement, only hard work. I cannot afford the luxury of living a life of leisure."

"But Maestro, you are not only so creative, you are truly passionate about your work and that in and of itself brings you much joy and fulfillment that is something beyond this material world of affluence and amusement. You are living your soul's calling and that is what I also wish for myself."

"Beatrice, you are so sweet, young and innocent, and immersed in your fantasy world," he told her a bit firmly, "so try to maintain that world and you and I will both be at peace. I will not be gone forever. I shall always be there whenever you need a friend or confidante for I intend to keep you inside my world. For when I am tired or would like some encouragement, I know I can call upon our wonderful memories which I shall always cherish. And knowing that you will go on and be happy will bring me immense joy." Niccolò took a deep breath. "I shall miss you too, Beatrice, but this is the best course we could take, for it is what the universe has intended to give us and I accept it."

Beatrice was in tears. "Maestro, will you continue to accept any creative project from my family?"

"I am an artist," Niccolò said. "I will see whether I am capable of doing a certain project or not. And if I deem that it is feasible, then yes, I shall comply."

This seemed to brighten Beatrice's mood. "Maestro, I would like to see you as often as I can then." She came closer and grabbed Niccolò's hand tightly. Niccolò gently took her beautiful hand with long fingers, touching them gently, then placing her hand on his broad chest and beating heart for few minutes before kissing her hand very softly.

Niccolò's face was all flushed, his eyes soft and moist, his body swaying with emotion. Beatrice started shaking; she was breathing heavily and felt as though her heart would leap out of her body.

Niccolò slowly grabbed her with his hands and gently steered her to the seat at the window. She looked prettier as the blood rushed to her face, her whole body.

Miranda had been on the other side of the room and as she approached them, she pretended to arrive late then asked Beatrice if she would like anything to drink.

Miranda poured cool orange blossom water for both Niccolò and Beatrice whose face was still flushed as she stole glances at Niccolò.

Meanwhile, Niccolò tried hard to compose himself by staying calm and taking control of the situation. He started working on the sculpture and as he found there was not much to add, he just scraped and smoothed the rough surface on both hands of the sculpture and the vessel which the sculpture was holding.

Time passed and soon, the soft rays of the sun reflected over the sculpture just as Lady Contessina arrived. She was in awe by the radiant look of the sculpture bathed by soft rays of the setting sun that she covered her mouth with one hand and closed her eyes.

"Maestro, it is a masterpiece," she said, "it is so beautiful I have no words to express how truly magnificent this is." Lady Contessina turned to her niece. "Do you agree, Beatrice, that it is exactly your image and likeness?"

Beatrice turned her solemn face to her aunt and nodded with a wan smile.

Niccolò glanced at Beatrice then slightly bowed his head to her aunt. "I am honored, my lady.

"Maestro, it is priceless. What shall we offer you? I am asking very humbly."

"My dear lady, you are correct, it is priceless therefore no price tag is necessary."

"Maestro, what are you saying? I do not understand."

"My honorable lady, I wish to present this sculpture as a wedding gift to Beatrice as a token of my gratitude for her enthusiasm for my work. And because I wish her a long and blissful life." He did not care to mention "wedded life" as the thought of Beatrice belonging to another man was too unbearable.

Aunt and niece emitted an "ahh," in understanding and Beatrice rushed over to Niccolò, clasped her hands, bowed as tears sprung to her eyes. "Maestro, oh Maestro, how can I ever thank you? I don't have the right words to express my appreciation."

Niccolò wished she could reward him with a warm embrace but he resisted the urge to show affection in light of Lady Contessina's presence. "You do not have to say, do or give me anything, Beatrice. Only that your present and future happiness is my reward for I cannot thank you enough for your presence and admiration of my sculpting work all these years."

Beatrice shook with emotion as tears rolled down her cheeks. "Maestro, you are a very kind-hearted person and I pray that your glory shall spread far and wide all over the world."

Lady Contessina approached Niccolò to shake his hand. "Maestro, what Beatrice has said is all very true and I completely share her sentiments. I cannot thank you enough. You are a very special person with a huge heart and on behalf of the Medici family, I am bestowing you a very special, eternal place in this family. You are always welcome here."

"Thank you, my honorable lady. You are too kind." He cleared his throat and continued with the task at hand. "I just want to let you know that tomorrow I will come and start polishing. Then just before the end of day, I will send a message to Beatrice to come and pose for the rest of the day to see if I find anything I missed to be detailed or not. Then I will proceed to apply my finishing touch."

He paused to catch his breath. "Then one more day, I will take my time to look at the sculpture and I will touch the sculpture with my hands as a final inspection. I do this with every sculpture. Then when I am all done, it is all yours."

Lady Contessina nodded. "Maestro, my husband, Cosimo, would like to have a word with you when you have time. Are you very much occupied at present?"

"I shall make time," he replied. "At present, I have a commission from the Pope that I am still working on which I hope to complete within a few months."

"Thank you, Maestro."

"I believe I am ready to leave work right now," he said.

Miranda offered him fruit tart and a glass of cool orange blossom water.

"Maestro, before you go, you must taste the fruit tarts that I made myself," Lady Contessina said. "They are peach tarts which are, in fact, a favorite of Beatrice's." She turned to her niece. "Beatrice, have you had some of the tarts already?"

"Certainly, my dear lady," Niccolò said, taking a couple of tarts from the plate. "Thank you for the treat."

They all exchanged goodbyes—with the ladies profusely thanking Niccolò again then all too soon it was time for the palace guard to escort Niccolò to the carriage.

Niccolò was awash with sadness, yet relieved that he provided the utmost care and attention to this precious sculpture that he was happy to present as a wedding gift to Beatrice.

He recalled Beatrice's expression when he took her beautiful hand and placed it on his chest. She was sad, yet fulfilled, surprised and excited that Niccolò acknowledged her love and he not only made a gesture to acknowledge her love but also tried to show her how much her feelings were reciprocated in the best way he knew how that did not give her any hope or expectation that what she ultimately desired will come into fruition.

When the carriage arrived at home, Niccolò went straight to the dinner table and said listlessly that he felt very tired and would only have the leak and potato soup with pieces of home-baked bread after which he would go to bed early.

Niccolò arose early the next day to start his journey towards the palace. The morning breeze felt refreshing as the city of Florence was just waking up from a slumber. There was an orange glow on the eastern horizon as the sun was not entirely up yet and the sky was partly cloudy. Shops along the plaza were just beginning to open as vendors pushed their carts full of vegetables to reach their destination. Along the way, Niccolò stopped for few minutes at Ponte Vecchio where the bridge curves, where Beatrice used to wait for Niccolò. He missed seeing her here and almost wished she would continue her ritual of waiting for him. But they each have their own separate lives now.

Two seagulls stood with closed eyes as they sensed Niccolò and they cried out with a shrill shriek. One of them approached Niccolò as if to bite which snapped Niccolò out of his fantasy world and back to the present where he strode faster to reach the palace.

At the gate the guards accompanied him to his work room. "Maestro, someone will be soon here to attend to you."

As Niccolò began working, he murmured, "Today, I would like to finish polishing most of the sculpture before Beatrice arrives as I do not know how to cheerfully bid goodbye. I must remind myself to do what is best for her." He thought of a list of things he planned to do but his heart was thumping sadly.

All day he worked polishing the sculpture until he saw the rays of the setting sun bathing the sculpture and that moment, he stopped to send a message to Beatrice to come and pose for one last time.

The sculpture looked radiant bathed by sunlight. When Beatrice arrived wearing a flowing orange dress, he asked her to take a seat very close to the sculpture. It was an exquisite sight to behold that moment forever. To Niccolò, it seemed time had stopped.

He remained silent, immersed in the beauty of Beatrice and her sculpture, side by side.

The muse herself was silent as her large eyes welled with tears. She tried to speak but no words would come out. And when she did begin to speak, she burst out sobbing. Niccolò was just about to draw closer to console her when Lady Contessina arrived.

Upon entering, when she saw the sculpture and Beatrice side by side, she cried out, "Maestro, what an amazing job you have done. I am utterly speechless!"

An attendant came to announce that Cosimo was on his way there.

All of them stood up to greet Cosimo who, dressed in his long, red velvety outfit, came very close to the sculpture. He looked at Beatrice and then to the sculpture and exclaimed, "What a beautiful sight, my dear friend, Niccolò! Such a wonderful job you have done and all your hard work presented as a gift is something beyond my imagination. You are indeed generous. You have the kind of riches beyond any wealthy man could ever have in the world. What can we do for you in return for your generosity?"

"My honorable lord and friend, I am an artist and I want to flourish with my artistic endeavors. That is my life's motto and that is the ultimate joy for me."

"My dear friend you are an idealistic, noble-hearted man and truly an artist. My family and I shall support you in all your artistic endeavors as much as we can."

"Thank you, my honorable friend for supporting my cause."

Lady Contessina, Cosimo and all the attendants bid farewell to Niccolò as Beatrice lingered behind.

As evening drew its curtain, Beatrice came closer to Niccolò. "Thank you, Maestro, I hope it will not be long before we see you again soon." Her voice cracked and she looked at Niccolò and burst into tears. Niccolò tried hard to control himself, his body trembled with emotion, his face was flushed. He searched for the right words to say to Beatrice and finally uttered softly, "I shall pray for your happiness always."

Beatrice's eyes filled with tears as she looked at Niccolò for what may be the last time. Then she took a deep breath and turned to leave the room.

A few minutes later, Niccolò walked wearily towards the door where a palace guard accompanied him to the carriage. Once he boarded the carriage, a brooding Niccolò sat looking out the window, a lump forming in his throat as he tried to stifle a sob.

It was dark but the horizon was illuminated by the moist moon peeping through the clouds as the horses galloped and the dark landscape moved backwards.

To occupy his mind, he murmured to himself, "I will bring Paolo to the palace tomorrow and show him the sculpture and spend some more time inspecting it and touching it. I do not want to be alone anymore with the sculpture. I have to move forward in time. It should remain in its own timeframe, the time when I created her and let her live there ever after."

Two years in the Newcastle Neurosurgery Center

After two years as a senior house officer—a senior resident—Rudy felt very accomplished and was in a celebratory mood just thinking about it.

He had thought that all this time he'd hopefully made a good impression on Professor Harkinson who might give Rudy chances to assist him in future surgeries and that would help him thoroughly learn brain surgery techniques.

Newcastle would open another social aspect of his life: having a close friendship with Dr. Samir Basu and his wife, Amita. And to top it off: Sharmi would visit her friend Amita, a wonderful added benefit that gave Rudy more opportunities to see Sharmi.

Rudy concentrated fully, with his body and soul, to learn as much as he could in the neurosurgery department and all his efforts had paid off as Professor Harkinson was very impressed to see Rudy's keen interest and amazed to see his tireless, hard work always performed with a pleasant smile.

Despite Rudy's days seeming to fly rapidly, he made time to call Sharmi at least twice a week and managed a few times to go to dinner at Samir and Amita's place where he heard Sharmi would be arriving on the 22nd of December and return to Durham on the 7th of January.

During Christmas, the workload of the hospital would be light as there were less patients on the operating list two weeks during vacation unless there was an emergency.

Rudy suddenly noticed there were Christmas decorations almost everywhere in the patients' ward, the clinic, doctors' offices and nursing stations. The mood inside the hospital was very cheerful yet the weather was harsh, stormy with snow and rain.

Rudy got his schedule of night on-calls. He was on call on Christmas Day but off on Boxing Day and three days thereafter. He was off on New Year's Eve and New Year's Day, but on call on the second and third of January respectively. His work schedule was tolerable, even managing to convince himself, *I am glad I came to know the grueling unpredictability of it so I can plan around it.*

He thought he would let Amita and Samir know about his schedule as they had already planned to arrange a few activities around the Christmas holidays. He looked at the calendar and thought to himself, *I have already been working for three months and this is the first week of December.*

Rudy's daily routine was structured and busy. He would get up around 7 to 7:30 in the morning, get dressed and have breakfast at the doctors' dining room before starting work at the hospital patients' ward. He would go and talk to each and every patient very compassionately and friendly and while doing that, he would assess a patient's speech and level of awareness in their surroundings. Once a patient became more familiar with Rudy, he would ask, "Sir, good morning, anything bothering you physically today?"

When the response would be, "I have difficulty walking and a problem with balance," Rudy would help a patient walk and discover him scraping his feet while walking, the whole body flexed with having difficulty in speaking. For this one particular patient, Rudy gave a physical examination and found that the patient had a rigidity of muscles that led Rudy to estimate it was Parkinson's disease and he ordered an initial diagnostic test then proceeded to other patients.

If there was pain, a patient would be questioned to elaborate what it felt like: throbbing, pinching, pins and needles, where the pain exactly was and whether it radiated anywhere else in the body.

Rudy keenly observed how patients walked or could not walk, how they talked and then would test for patients' muscular strength and sensation by lightly touching with a pointed pin any abnormal movements like tremors and tendon reflexes with a simple knee hammer to tap lightly on the knees, ankles and upper extremities to find whether the reflexes were absent, normal or exaggerated.

Rudy was very thorough in his examination of the rest of the body as he would feel the abdomen for any mass or enlarged liver or spleen, listen to a patient's heart and lungs.

Routine blood tests would be ordered and then the cases would be presented to Rudy's immediate supervisor and then to the consultant. After presenting the cases to the consultant, more necessary diagnostic tests relevant to individual cases would be ordered.

Professor Harkinson was very much interested in Parkinson's disease. He had an ongoing research project of the effect of giving electrical therapy deep inside the brain. Rudy found out about it and studied fairly well about Parkinson's disease so that he would not miss any signs of the patient while taking their history and examination.

Rudy experienced a wide spectrum of presentations with Parkinson's disease. Some came with a classical presentation of symptoms like tremors at rest, slow movement of the body, rigidity of muscles, difficulty in walking and speaking due to rigidity of the facial muscles, flexed posture of the whole body and balance issues.

There were few who came without any of the above classic symptoms but were very vague about their surroundings and disturbed emotionally. For example, a patient would complain someone was trying to kill him or spying on him. Rudy was very thorough with his examination and with his keen, observant eye, he could detect some signs of Parkinson's disease in these atypical presentations and in one of them, he found a patient's hand was not moving with his leg as normally the hands also swing with the legs while walking. Another aspect he found was that he was scraping his foot.

Rudy presented his cases to Professor Harkinson and when the professor asked what was his diagnosis, Rudy replied that his impression was Parkinson's disease, a deduction that impressed and pleased the professor.

After going through other diagnostic tests, the patients were diagnosed and treated for Parkinson's disease. As a result of his diligent efforts, Rudy established himself as a very capable senior house officer, or senior resident.

That opened up a number of future opportunities like a good recommendation for the next job and opportunities to help Professor Harkinson in surgery.

Rudy wanted to share his excitement with Sharmi but he controlled himself thinking it might seem very immature and childish to talk about himself and his accomplishments.

By the end of the day, he realized it was a Friday and he was off for the weekend. When a sister on duty called him and said, "Dr. Sen, a telephone call for you," a surprised Rudy immediately thought, *Why? I am not on call this weekend.*

He picked up the phone and found it was his friend, Samir calling.

"Rudy, we will be pleased if you could come and join us for dinner," Samir said. "It will be fun. You'll get to meet someone too."

Samir's secretive tone intrigued Rudy. "Do I already know this person?"

"You'll soon find out."

Rudy was excited that he would soon be with his friends and he went to his apartment, took a quick shower and dressed in his winter attire and took a small bag with extra clothes in case it snowed in and he had to spent the night. He took a taxi just as the wind was howling, threatening to turn into a blizzard.

When he reached his friends' place, he was surprised to see Sharmi there. Immediately, the foursome settled into a happy huddle.

"I told Rudy to stay tonight," Amita said. "There is a forecast of snow and gusty winds. There's a spare bed in the study upstairs so it's no problem."

Rudy gratefully accepted the accommodations and they sat as close to the fireplace as they could. The temperature of the house was comfortable yet it felt cozy to be close to the fireplace to watch the blue and yellow rising flames with the crackling sounds of the burning logs.

Soon they were warmed up with their mulled wine except Sharmi who had hot apple cider. Dinner consisted of chicken curry, cabbage with shrimp, Dal cooked with green peas and rice. The sight and smells of the delicious dinner made them move towards the dining space but they all wanted to sit in the cozy living room and enjoy their dinner. Amita announced that something important came up they needed to discuss.

Rudy asked anxiously, "What is it?"

Amita looked at Sharmi and said, "May I?"

"Go ahead," Sharmi said.

"Sharmi's parents want her back in Kolkata during Christmas vacation," Amita said then took a deep breath. "They are planning to get her married to someone, a young and handsome lawyer who recently passed a competitive civil service exam to start a judiciary job. His mother is in failing health and the groom's party wants the wedding soon. The groom's parents and Sharmi's parents are longtime friends, and they know each other very well. The groom's parents always liked Sharmi."

Rudy's whole body felt rigid as he sat there listening to Amita tell of Sharmi's predicament. It was like an out-of-body experience.

"Oh gee," Samir said. "Sharmi, what do you think about this?"

Sharmi shrugged her shoulders and sighed. "If I go, I lose everything I've worked so hard to achieve—my studies, my opportunities. And my professor with whom I've been working with, would be so disappointed as I'm supposed to finish my thesis by spring and there are lots of unfinished work which has to be completed in the month of January and February. I have already committed to university to do a research project after I finish my graduate study. I will have a position as a Post Doc and it would be a dream come true."

She sighed again, her shoulders deflated. "To me, it is unfathomable to get married during Christmas vacation and then leave after years of hard work. My parents always encouraged me to pursue a higher education. I wonder why this proposal of marriage reversed their ideals and thoughts."

"Sharmi, did you let them know that it is not possible."

"I did but they do not understand. In fact, about three years ago, they wanted to arrange an elaborate engagement ceremony with this particular person and to set up a final wedding date just when I was frantically looking for somewhere to enroll for graduate study outside India and fortunately I got into Durham."

Samir scratched his head. "Sharmi, I wonder…if you like this particular person or was it that you had chosen not to get married or that it wasn't the right time for you?"

Sharmi quickly glanced at Rudy. "I was never attracted to this man. I could be wrong, but I always had a sense that he was arrogant and a show-off."

Upon hearing that Sharmi had no feelings for this man, Rudy heaved a sigh of relief yet the looming threat that Sharmi could return to India to marry this person to please her parents shook him to his core.

"What would happen if you say no to your parents," Samir said in a firm yet gentle tone resembling that of a big brother. "Sharmi, I have to be very firm and strong with my parents. My relationship with them will be strained and I might lose some financial help but that's the risk one takes when asserting oneself for the sake of one's own happiness."

Although he was listening quietly all this time even while anxious thoughts were swirling in his mind, Rudy finally couldn't stay silent any longer. "Sharmi, I wonder what is most important to you right now."

Right then, Sharmi and Rudy shared a look loaded with emotion.

Sharmi took a deep breath. "Well, the most important thing now is finishing my graduate studies and my work on this research project which is so close to my heart. It could open a new path to boost my career."

Rudy felt a tinge of disappointment that Sharmi hadn't mentioned that *he* was among her list of what was important to her but then he realized Sharmi's tongue was tied as they had yet to privately acknowledge their feelings to each other. "You should follow what you strongly believe and follow your heart. Parents want their children's security and also there's the generation gap: our generation will encounter the same thing when the time comes. Parents always come back, but for the time being, we friends are here to support you and we can stand by and help you as much as possible. I speak for all of us here." Rudy turned to Amita and Samir. "I hope it is all right."

Amita and Samir both nodded said together, "Thank you, Rudy."

"We are in total agreement with you," Amita said.

They all insisted Sharmi take some time to think about her situation and suggested that Sharmi should call her parents this weekend to explain to them about her commitment to finish her thesis and that it was not possible to take vacation.

Nor was it feasible to marry this man, Rudy thought silently as thoughts continued to swirl rapidly in his head.

"In the meantime, let's all try to come up with possible questions and counterarguments that may arise from her parents' side along with some effective responses from Sharmi," Amita said.

Sharmi sighed again. "Well, they will ask me 'When can you come?' and I will answer that 'I can't come home for at least six to eight months.' So I will invite them to come in the summer for my graduation ceremony."

Rudy, Amita and Samir agreed that was a satisfying response.

Sharmi clasped her hands tightly. "But I do not know what their actual response will be and the proposal of marriage will be lurking somewhere which they will for sure bring up in the conversation."

"That will be inevitable, Sharmi," Samir said. "So you will have to deal with it directly whether you want to get married to this particular person or not."

"And my answer is 'no,'" Sharmi said firmly.

"Also, you must be prepared in case there will be questions like whether there is someone else you may be thinking about."

Sharmi and Rudy exchanged shy, quick glances. Then Rudy cleared his throat.

Sharmi nodded and sat up straight, a determined look on her face. "I will call my parents and see how the conversation goes and if I feel that I can't respond to certain delicate questions they may ask me, then I can say I need time to think and call you later."

"Let us all think about it and start fresh tomorrow," Samir said. "Amita, when do you think we will have our breakfast?"

"We should be ready for breakfast around 9:30. After breakfast, Sharmi can call her parents in India where the time there will be 1:30 in the afternoon," Amita said.

Outside, the snow blizzard continued signaling time for everyone to curl themselves in their own beds. The high sound of the storm was somewhat mysterious at first with its high-pitch whistling before lulling all to sleep.

Yet, sleep was slow to come for Rudy who, after reading Niccolò's immense sadness at not being able to have a relationship with Beatrice, felt the weight of the first stumbling block in his own courtship with Sharmi. If only things could go smoothly in both one's career and love life, thought Rudy as he drifted off to sleep.

Beatrice's Last Visit, a Final Farewell

Niccolò woke up in the morning with a heavy heart with thoughts of Beatrice swirling in his mind, passing like clouds. Yet he felt relieved that the work was done and offering the sculpture as a gift to Beatrice consoled his heart.

As he began his swift stride towards his studio, he did not realize that winter had already arrived. He walked faster to warm up his body. The passersby were dressed in their winter outfits like woolen cloaks, some wore long rectangular warm woolen wraps around shawls, also covering their heads with it. The trees were almost bare except the pines. The cold blast of strong wind rustled through the dry leaves on the paved path and at intervals, it sighed harshly through the bare trees.

He passed the plaza when a family friend from the bakery started calling him, "Niccolò, Niccolò!" He turned back and went to the bakery where Luigi gave him two freshly-baked loaves, one with raisins and the other with green olives. Niccolò was grateful and happy. "Thank you, Uncle Luigi, you are so thoughtful and nice to me."

"You are welcome, my dear. You are like my son. I am very proud that you are the gifted son of Firenze."

"Thank you for your good words."

"God bless you."

Niccolò strode faster to reach the studio. Paolo greeted him with a big smile.

"Maestro, Good morning. I have already arranged the tools, if you want to start sculpting on Marzocco."

"I am happy to be back in my studio. Let us talk and plan our day."

"Yes, of course, Maestro."

"First, let me tell you Luigi gave me two loaves of freshly-baked bread. We will have the one with raisins as a snack, while the other one I will take home to my mother and sister. Then both of us will go to the palace to see the sculpture of Beatrice which we will carefully inspect. As you know, I always try to feel the sculpture. We will also work on Marzocco today for some time. Then starting tomorrow, we will devote our time fully to Marzocco.

"There is another thing. My nephew wanted to spend Christmas Eve and Christmas day with us. He is planning to take his mother and grandmother to Castellina where he lives for about two weeks. I am not sure, but I may go there along with them for two to three days and will be back to Florence. Then I might start doing whatever there is left to do on Marzocco and then start polishing. If you wish, you can take more days off for your Christmas vacation and start after New Year's Day."

"Maestro, that sounds pretty good. For Christmas, I will spend time with my family and after that, I will help my parents around the house, and relax a little and we will start our work on Marzocco again when you come back. I will see if I might come back to work even before New Year's."

"What do you think? Shall we to go to the palace after lunch or now?"

"I prefer going after lunch, we can work on Marzocco now, then have our lunch and then go to the palace and from there we go home."

"Yes, Paolo that sounds good, and perhaps from the palace, they can offer us a carriage ride home"

"That would be wonderful."

"So let us work on Marzocco."

They approached the sculpture of the mighty lion.

"Paolo, let us go over the areas we have already finished again to see if anything could be added. You work on the torso and I will go over the face and eyes."

Paolo and Niccolò started working on the places they had already worked on before. The torso had to be smoothed out so Paolo took the rasp and fine-pointed chisel and started from the lower part of the torso moving upwards, taking small parts at a time. Then the rasp to smooth out the surface and the pointed chisel to take out the uneven bumps.

Niccolò started with the eyes. He smoothed the eyeballs with his handmade sandpaper-like device and with a fine chisel, chiseled out the grooves of the eyeball to make the exact depth to flash out with the eyelids. The jaws were made more relaxed with no tension and the lips were slightly open as if he wanted to talk to people.

It was already noon when Paolo and Niccolò took a short break and enjoyed the raisin bread from the bakery before they dashed towards the palace.

"Maestro, the sun feels good, and we can walk faster. I will try to keep up with you but my legs are shorter than yours."

Paolo, a young man of twenty-six, was five feet nine inches tall, smaller than Niccolò. His face was triangular with a pointed nose and black sparkling eyes, tanned skin and black hair which was parted in the middle. Dimples on his cheeks appeared when he talked, bursting with energy when he smiled.

Niccolò liked him very much as he was very sincere and very attentive when learning the trade.

He was usually dressed in his brown cut out brief at the knees with a yellow cotton round neck shirt and dark brown vest with red buttons. Paolo dressed in his long-sleeved warm brown coat to protect himself from the winter cold.

Niccolò was always in his long white overhaul and a black hooded warm cape to cover himself from the harsh elements.

They passed the Baptistery, followed the paved path and arrived at the front of the palace gate. Palace guards approached them. "Maestro, it is nice to see you again."

"This is Paolo, my assistant. We would like to look at the sculpture for one last time to see if there is anything missing before it needs a final touch."

"As you wish, Maestro," said one of the guards. "I will accompany you inside the palace and someone will attend to you. Then I will inform the carriage driver when you are done so he should be ready to take you both home."

Paolo was amazed to get all the attention. While walking through the garden Paolo was awed by the huge landscape and buildings of the palace with sculptures in the courtyard.

They came to the room where Beatrice's sculpture was. It was a winter afternoon as the soft sun rays bathed the sculpture. Paolo was amazed to see the beauty and likeness of Beatrice made in marble form.

"Maestro, you created a heavenly beauty. You are so creative and talented and I am lucky to be learning from you."

Niccolò nodded his appreciation. "Paolo, let us start working. Try to inspect from the lower extremity and carry on towards the upper body. Let me know if there is anything needing a final touch and I will feel it with my hands starting from the head then going towards the lower extremity."

Miranda, the attendant, arrived. "Maestro, I will bring some water for both of you and Lady Contessina and Beatrice wish to greet you both before you go home."

Niccolo thought he had bid his final farewell to Beatrice and although it was more than a pleasure to see her, it pained him to endure yet another long goodbye. He nodded to the attendant. "Thank you, we will be honored."

Paolo started doing what Niccolò told him to do. He looked at the entire sculpture carefully and found a small area around the elbow of the sculpture that was rough and smoothed it out.

Niccolò found a small bump under the chin on the left side, chiseled it out and polished it. The late afternoon sun slowly descended as the orange glow was still on the western sky. Down below on earth, the chirping of birds filled the air.

They were almost done when Miranda brought fruit tarts on a silver tray and a jug of orange blossom water.

She was pouring water in two glasses when Lady Contessina and Beatrice arrived. Both Niccolò and Paolo bowed at the presence of these distinguished ladies.

Lady Contessina was dressed in a gold-embroidered, maroon, round-neck dress with three-quartered sleeves. Teardrop pearl earrings and a four-strings pearl necklace adorned her ears and neck with her hair done up in a bun at the back of her neck where gold star hairpins shone through the black hair net.

Beatrice wore her olive flowing dress, her black brown hair cascading at the back of her neck as her emerald pendant studded with diamonds rested around her neck. Teardrop diamond earrings reflected rainbow colors when she moved forward.

"Maestro, I am so happy to see you again!" Beatrice gushed.

"Thank you, Beatrice," Niccolò said, his heart beating faster. "And I am also happy to see you again."

Paolo looked up from polishing, his eyes darting from Beatrice to Niccolò.

"Maestro, the palace will send you a special invitation to attend Beatrice's wedding which will commence the first week of January in 1420. However, I am personally inviting you and…hello there, I assume this young man is your assistant. I would like to extend an invitation to you as well," Lady Contessina said eyeing Paolo.

"My honorable lady, you are correct. Paolo is my assistant. Thank you for the invitation. We are honored. If I am in town then I will attend otherwise I might be visiting Padua on a special invitation."

"Oh that is wonderful Maestro. It could likely be to talk to you about a future commission. It is unfortunate if you will not attend. We will miss you."

"Maestro, I shall hope to see you when you return to work on future projects for the new palace as I will be working on my uncle's library project," Beatrice said.

He nodded politely, though inside he was excited at the prospect of future sightings of Beatrice. "Thank you, Beatrice. Again, I wish you all the best for your future and may you be granted a very happy and prosperous life."

She paused as if lost in thought before saying, "Thank you, Maestro."

It was already evening, time to say goodbye. Niccolò once more thanked Beatrice for her encouragement and introducing him to the Medici family.

"It has been my honor to recommend you for you are so talented and gifted, you do not need any introduction. Thank you for your kind words which I shall treasure for as long as I live."

Quite suddenly, Beatrice started sniffling. As she drew closer to Niccolò and bowed, lifting her face to gaze up at Niccolò for the last time, her whole body trembled and she burst into tears.

Niccolò shook her hand, wishing he could do more to comfort her further yet he maintained his composure in the presence of Lady Contessina and Paolo. "I wish you all the happiness in the world." His voice cracked and his eyes became soft and moist. He gazed at Beatrice softly one more time before turning to face Lady Contissina whose expression appeared confused and curious yet warm at the same time.

Niccolò thanked Lady Contessina for her hospitality and for accommodating his work space to ensure he had everything he needed including a palace carriage to take him home.

"It has been my pleasure," she said. "We look forward to the next time when you return whenever that may be."

Once again palace guards accompanied Paolo and Niccolò to the carriage waiting to take them home as a sullen Beatrice and Lady Contessina stood there watching the figures of the two men disappear beyond the evening dark.

Rudy's Admission at Samir and Amita's House

The morning was clear with hazy sunshine, rooftops were covered with snow and as far as one could see, the roads were clear but heaps of snow were piled up on both sides of the roads. At a distance in an open space, children were playing with snowballs trying to make a snowman.

Inside Samir and Amita's house, everyone was up and ready around the breakfast table near the kitchen. Everyone's plate except Sharmi's was nearly full with baked beans, sausages, poached eggs and toast and they were all holding a steaming cup of tea. Sharmi was anxious as well as nervous as she held onto her cup of tea very tightly and her hand was trembling.

She sat quietly on a chair stooping towards the table and looking at a distance.

"Sharmi, if you're ready, you can make your telephone call now just to get it over with," Samir said. "Remember, we are close by and here to support you and help you communicate with you parents. Just repeat what they are saying so we are in on the conversation and so that we can guide you as to what you can say if you need our help."

Finally Sharmi made the phone call and the first few minutes appeared to be jovial moments as her parents did not expect a call from Sharmi and were happy to hear her voice.

Then when Sharmi told her parents that it was almost impossible to take a break from university now as all her hard work and studies would be wasted and that she had to finish her thesis and her graduate studies, a frown etched across her face.

Her father and mother insisted that the wedding could be postponed after her graduation. But the engagement had to be arranged without delay in England as one of the parents from the groom's side would attend.

Sharmi was visibly upset, her face flushed and she shook uncontrollably. "I do not understand. What is the matter? Why is it so urgent that I get engaged?"

Her parents remarked that Sharmi was behaving so strangely.

"Is something brewing there?" Her father demanded. "They have stretched so far to accept you as their future daughter-in-law. May I remind you, they are from a very respectable family and their son is established in his profession. You should feel lucky enough."

When Sharmi repeated her father's words for Amita, Samir, and Rudy's benefit, their expressions changed to anger. Amita was whispering and shaking with disgust as she felt that Sharmi was being degraded. Samir was not happy either shaking his head.

Rudy was quiet, but thinking that most of the educated middle-class parents wanted to protect their children very badly even if they were grown up especially the daughters.

Sharmi kept quiet for few minutes, then finally said, "I cannot agree with all these sudden arrangements." She took a deep breath. "I am sorry, but I refuse to marry this person under such pressure and even without pressure, I must refuse. I cannot continue the conversation any further."

"Then we cannot support you and your behavior," her father replied. "We gave them our word a long time ago and you have let us down. You will put us to shame. Think about what this is doing to our family. You must marry this man."

"You are pressuring me into marrying someone I do not love nor will I ever love."

There was a long pause, Sharmi kept on saying, "Hello, hello," until a few minutes later, her father replied sternly, "So go ahead and do what you want. We cannot support you any longer."

Then Sharmi's father slammed the phone down and the line disconnected. Sharmi could no longer hold her emotions in and burst into tears, her whole body shaking when Amita hugged her tightly and made her sit down on a comfortable sofa.

Samir and Rudy drew closer to Sharmi and Amita.

"Sharmi, we understand what you are going through," Samir said, "but I believe all these things are happening for a reason and that something good will come out of this in the near future."

"Sharmi, please, you must eat something for your strength," Rudy said. "Let us all sit down and finish our breakfast and drink our tea and try to come up with a solution that will benefit Sharmi in the long run."

Rudy went to the kitchen and filled up a breakfast plate of fresh toast with orange marmalade and poached eggs for Sharmi then filled up the teapot with more hot water and put extra tea bags to make the tea stronger.

At first, Sharmi refused to eat breakfast, then after everyone insisted that an empty stomach did not help to solve problems only caused more issues to her health, she finally relented. They all resumed their breakfasts with cups of hot tea.

"Sharmi, as Rudy said yesterday, we are all friends here and will see that you finish your graduate studies and that we all believe that your parents will eventually come around. So please, try to relax."

"You must concentrate on your wellbeing and focus on your graduate studies as you mentioned these are what's most important to you," Rudy said, "Try not to worry about other things you cannot control. Everything will fall in place at the right time."

Amita took a deep breath as she patted Sharmi gently on the arm. "All right then. Let's lighten up our mood and talk about our plans for Christmas vacation."

A while ago Sharmi had already planned with Amita that she would stay there from the 22nd of December to the 7th of January then return to Durham to concentrate on her thesis.

Slowly but surely, Sharmi returned to her usual self and then started to talk excitedly about her work and studies at Durham. Sharmi said the next six months would be more or less busy with January, February and March occupied with work and writing her thesis and the rest would be dedicated to preparing for the final examination.

"Please refresh my memory about the title of your thesis," Rudy said.

"It is 'The Effect of Religion on the 14th through 15th century English Literature.'"

"Wow," her friends said.

"Rudy and Sharmi," Samir began, "I would very much like to ask you both about something personal. As you know, we are close friends here, really like a family so it will be better to discuss the sort of issues that come up that will further tighten our bond as we get to know each other better."

Samir looked directly at Rudy. "What are your specific plans?"

Rudy blinked momentarily curious about the sudden inquiry. "You mean about my profession, well, that is simple. I will finish my stint as senior house officer then look for a registrar job when I will take part one of the Fellow of Royal College of Surgeons examination and then after part two, look for a senior registrar job which is difficult to get as after this one becomes a consultant."

"That can't be your only plans for the future," Samir teased Rudy. "I mean, what do you plan to do in life other than your career?"

Rudy took a deep breath. "Well, I am really open to whatever may come."

"I have to interrupt," Amita said, "otherwise I can't focus my mind on other topics, mainly our Christmas holidays. Samir, what's your holiday schedule?"

"I think I'm off on Christmas Eve and off on Boxing Day and thereafter up to January 2nd."

"And you, Rudy?"

"I am working on Christmas day and then again on the 2nd and 3rd of January."

"Interesting both of you are working on Christmas day," Amita said, "so we will arrange a party on Christmas Eve with some of our other friends from India."

"Sounds good," Samir said.

Amita turned to Sharmi. "What do you say?"

"It's all right with me," she said. "We can just spend Christmas day cleaning up and then relax here at home."

"That sounds very nice and we will chat to our hearts content," Amita said.

"Oh no, we will miss the two of you talking behind our back," Samir said with a chuckle.

"Don't worry, we will keep you informed. I am thinking of a plan," Amita said, her eyes sparkling. "Wouldn't it be nice if we could take a short trip somewhere for three to four days and then be back on the 30th of December in time to welcome 1965?"

"That would be nice. Where are you thinking we could take this short trip?" Samir asked.

"Either we can go to London to see the Christmas decorations which is really spectacular or to Paris which is a very short flight and spend three to four days there. I enjoyed looking through some promotional packages—"

"I'm not sure whether I can afford it," Sharmi said abruptly.

"Sure you can," Amita said quickly. "It's not that expensive and with your student status, you get a huge discount. And don't worry. We will do a package of four so we get an even greater discount. How about you, Rudy? How does this sound?"

"It sounds wonderful," Rudy said. "I am all for it."

"What kind of deal are you looking for in Paris?" Samir asked Amita.

"This is what I am thinking," Amita said, excitedly, "we leave on the 26th of December to Paris in the afternoon. There are several flights but I think the one at 3:45 p.m. will be best. We will get there around 5 p.m. Then when we reach the hotel, we'll have dinner and there is an evening bus tour to see Paris decorated with lights." She took out a sheet of paper. "See, it's written here that on the 27Th of December, we can take the city tour bus from 10 a.m. to noon. For our free time, we'll go to the Louvre. The rest of the day, we could do some sightseeing and leisurely explore or spend more time in the Louvre. And evenings are free for us to have dinner or explore the city."

Amita consulted her travel brochure information sheet again.

"On the 28th of December morning and afternoon, we can explore some more on our own. Then that evening we can get tickets for a show, a can-can at the Moulin Rouge. When we arrive, there will be a free bottle of champagne with dinner and Happy Hour. There will be time for dancing before the show starts at 10 and goes on for three hours with an intermission in between for half an hour. So we return to our hotel in the wee hours of morning, sleep for a bit then on the 29th of December, the day is free to go wherever our hearts desire. And then on December 30, we take a flight at 11a.m. back and reach home by early afternoon. And that's about it."

"Wow, you really did take some time to plan this whole itinerary out for us," Samir said. "Are we all in favor of this plan?"

"I like it very much," Rudy said. "It will certainly break the monotony of the usual Christmas parties around this time."

"You have to arrange another hotel room and I know Paris is expensive, so I think I will pass," Sharmi said.

Amita shook her head. "No way. Actually, you are the pivotal person that absolutely needs to have this escape before your thesis and graduation. You need this getaway as a good distraction to clear your mind and to help you relax and have fun."

Samir scratched his head. "Okay, not to change the topic but I have been wanting to ask you both this for a while now. Rudy and Sharmi, you both have become very dear to Amita and me so as I am about to ask you a very personal question, you understand the level of trust we can both assure you. So, here it is: how do you both feel about each other? I hope this is more than just a passing fancy and certainly I, as your friend hope that what you both have could extend to more than just a casual friendship. But, as your friends, Amita and I would both like to know if you are going to continue the relationship seriously?"

Rudy knew this was coming but wasn't really prepared to address this matter so soon especially given the fact that he and Sharmi had not yet made an official commitment. *They all must know how I feel for Sharmi and figured it out since my visit to Durham to see her and since then, they have arranged to invite me whenever Sharmi visited them. Also, they must have observed from our body language that Sharmi and I feel so happy and excited to see each other. Whatever I say now in front of my dear friends and in front of Sharmi will be my sincerest wishes and thoughts.*

Rudy took a deep breath. "I would like to continue to see Sharmi on a regular basis and I am pretty sincere about it. Do you know what I mean?" He paused as Amita and Samir nodded. Then Rudy faced Sharmi whose face had suddenly flushed. "I adore her and the fact that we come from the same city which is now in East Pakistan, is like kismet. How serendipitous that destiny brought us together here in England. I tried my best to open my heart as much as I can but I admit that I have been feeling shy to fully express my emotions until now."

Amita clasped her hands eagerly. "Sharmi, my dear friend. What would you like to say?"

Placed in a spot suddenly though she was expecting it, her face color grew ruddy.

"Well, I am not very outgoing like other girls," she said, her voice trembling. "I have been raised to be humble and modest, to not to show emotion in front of others."

"But do you feel the same as Rudy? That he wants to continue the relationship with sincerity and affection? He did not mention the word 'love' as he was shy in front of us. And Samir and I do apologize for making you both uncomfortable if that is the case. But as your friends, if we know what both your intentions are, then we will know how best to support you."

Sharmi took a deep breath and bravely faced Rudy. "Yes, I feel about the same. With Rudy, I feel safe and protected."

Amita and Samir cheered. "Then what are we waiting for?" Samir said.

Amita held up her hand. "Well, first it's best to wait for Sharmi's thesis and graduation and then let them decide how soon they wish to proceed with their future."

"At any rate, this calls for a celebration," Samir said.

Rudy drew closer to Sharmi. "Dear Sharmi, may I kiss your hand?" he asked softly, with sparkling, moist eyes.

Sharmi blushed and looked at Rudy who knelt down in front of her and kissed her hand very softly. At this tender gesture, Samir and Amita cheered as Rudy's eyes sparkled with joy and Sharmi blushed, feeling shy. And though her eyes were fixed at a distance, she looked happy. Though she did not know what to say or tried to say something and then paused, her heart pounded with excitement. She sat down and somehow started speaking slowly with a tremulous voice, "Everything seems to be moving fast. But I feel as though a burden has been lifted and that's a good thing."

"We are going to celebrate today so we should order take-out food," Amita said. "What do you think Sharmi?"

"You decide, Amita. I cannot think straight right now," Sharmi said, in a bit of a daze.

"I'm going to take care of the food. All of you just sit back and relax," Samir said.

"And I'll help you," Rudy said.

They looked at the clock. "It's 1:30 in the afternoon," Amita said. "I have some vegetable stew and dinner rolls we can warm up which will go well with the vegetable stew. I'll plug in the stew pot and it will be heated soon.

"Whenever you feel like having the stew, feel free to serve yourself," Sharmi said. "I should make myself useful and make a pot of tea."

"Don't worry Sharmi," Amita said, "just relax. This is your day."

"For the take-out dinner, I suggest, we call in the order around 6 tonight," Samir said. "That way, it will be ready for pick up by 7 then we can have dinner at 8. So there's no hurry. Today is Saturday. It will be a relaxing day for all of us."

Amita loudly cleared her throat. "So, if I can have everyone's attention. Let's again come back to our Paris trip."

She explained that the package includes transportation from the airport and back again on their last day; hotel accommodations with continental breakfast every morning during their stay; a bus tour of the city in the evening on Dec. 26th; advanced tickets for the Louvre and Eiffel Tower; a bus tour morning till afternoon on Dec. 27; and transportation to the Moulin Rouge. Tickets for the can-can will be extra.

"I am going to buy the can-can tickets for all of us," Rudy said. "This will be my Christmas gift for you all."

"Wow, are you sure? It is a little expensive," Amita said.

"I am sure," Rudy replied. "The National Health Service takes care of food and accommodation and all utilities, so I will spend my paycheck for the tickets and other essentials for the Paris trip. This is an investment, I assure you as this is a very special time of my life." He glanced at Sharmi.

Amita and Samir expressed that they would take care of dinner on the 26th and 27th of December. And Rudy said that dinner on the 28th and 29th would be on him.

"So what should I contribute?" Sharmi said. "You are all so generous taking care of everything and the least I could do is take care of our lunches."

"Sharmi, you can make lunch bags for us," Amita said. "We will buy groceries from a nearby store: bread, meat, cucumber, mayo, butter, nuts, and we will be happy to have whatever you offer."

"Okay," Sharmi said. "But now, I want to know about the hotel room arrangements."

"We'll be getting a place where they have an extra place for kids but it is fortunately a separate room attached to it. So don't worry. You can have that room with no extra charge. All you have to take care of is your airfare."

"You are stretching yourselves too far to include me," Sharmi said.

"This trip is planned around you," Amita said, "so we will be lucky to be in Paris because of you."

"So let's make this Paris trip a real special one," Samir said.

"A very special one for me as it will be the first time I'll be taking a trip of this kind," Rudy said.

Sharmi looked anxious. "I don't know what kind of explanation I would give my parents."

"About what exactly?" Amita asked.

"About the trip and my decision."

"Sharmi, you are entitled to have a break and some fun," Amita said, "and you are an adult woman able to make your own decisions in life. You are not regretting your decision, are you?"

"No, not at all. I feel a heavy burden on my shoulder has been lifted. I'm so relieved."

"Anyway, you don't have to tell them anything or everything right now since you won't be talking to them by phone anytime soon." Amita shrugged her shoulders. "I told you what I think, the rest is up to you."

"I know. I just worry about how I will eventually face my parents."

"Oh, you will figure it out when time the comes," Amita said. "Anyway, they told you to be on your own, so you are free to make your own decisions. Now just relax and enjoy the present."

"It is very painful to be in a position like this to be detached from your parents," Sharmi said.

"Sharmi, right now your goal is to finish your thesis and graduate study and when it is done, you will give this news to your parents. And within time, you will find their opinions and attitudes will change eventually. Do not worry so much."

"And remember, you are not alone. You have all of us," Rudy added looking directly at Sharmi. "You have me."

That seemed to appease Sharmi who flashed him a bright smile.

Soon, they all sat around the fireplace until afternoon when they took a TV break with their bowls of vegetable stew and cups of tea.

Amita liked a TV program titled "Lost in Space," a kind of children's show about a family lost in space who were in their spaceship traveling and stopping in different planets whenever possible with the ultimate goal to reach Earth safely. Amita liked the characters including a boy named

William who was about eight years old, a robot, and Dr. Smith, a middle-aged doctor, who was funny and a troublemaker always getting messed up with some problem. The boy's parents also traveled in the spaceship, in fact, the boy's father was the commander of the ship. Amita's favorite was the part when the robot warned Dr. Smith that there was danger ahead and William would say, "Dr. Smith, Robot is giving us a warning."

Dr. Smith would say, "Never fear, Smith is here" but then would slip and fall in a ditch or become entangled by an alien plant and cry out for help. Then the robot and William would go to help free him when the robot would give a robotic laugh while flashing his light inside his face and the laugh would sound like, "*Hee hee three hee, hee hee three hee Dr. Smith*," and he would say "Shut up, you bubble head dummy." Then they would all return to their spaceship. End of episode.

It was something that also turned out to be entertaining for Sharmi who, with Amita, sat around the fireplace talking about the Paris trip and what to pack. The consensus was mainly warm clothes, a raincoat or trenchcoat with a hood and umbrellas.

Much later that evening, Rudy and Samir arrived with their take-out dinner.

They laid out the food on the kitchen table: Mutton Biryani, spiced rice with pieces of cooked meat, Mutton Kebabs on a stick, cauliflower roasted with spices, and Mango chutney.

They ate their delicious meal sitting around the fireplace as outside the wind started howling and through the window, they could see the misty landscape dotted with amber colored lights.

Sharmi had to get back to Durham the next day in the afternoon by train and from Durham station one of her friends would pick her up to take her to the apartment where she lived.

They were all ready to go to bed after the meal.

"For the Christmas Eve party, I decided we will order food from the Kebab Place so we can just clean up and then we can start getting ready for our Paris trip," Amita said. "Samir and Rudy are both on call on the 25th and on the afternoon of the 26th we are leaving for Paris."

"I will bring beverages to the party," Rudy said. "Anything else I could contribute?"

"That should be enough," Amita said.

"I will help with whatever you need on the day of the party and before that," Sharmi said.

"I know you will," Amita said.

"Good night, all," Samir said, "see you in the morning at breakfast."

"Good night."

They each retreated to their respective rooms to curl up in their beds while the stormy wind whistled through the trees and rain pattered on the windows to lull them to sleep.

After reading more of Niccolò's biography, Rudy lay awake in bed thinking about his recent declaration of feelings and intentions for Sharmi feeling so incredibly fortunate that Sharmi's feelings were mutual. He wished the outcome between Niccolò and Beatrice would have been different, thought Rudy as he finally succumbed to much-needed sleep.

𝔐arzocco 𝔖tands 𝔖upreme

When Niccolò arrived at the studio, it was almost nine in the morning and he wondered why Paolo was not there yet. He was about to hang his bag on the hook when suddenly he heard a scraping sound and found Paolo was working on the end of Marzocco's torso trying to simultaneously chisel out and smooth the area. He saw Paolo's forehead and two sparkling black eyes which made him smile.

"Paolo, you are a very sincere and hardworking sculptor. You will rise in this trade. You know you looked very amusing hiding behind Marzocco's torso."

"Maestro, I appreciate your kind words. I wanted to hide as sometimes there are other student sculptors and people keep on visiting. I want to see and hear what their comments are."

"Oh, that is interesting and funny too that you hide so you can find out exactly what their reactions are," Niccolò said with a smile. "Paolo, I am going to start again with Marzocco's face. I will try my best to make his expression as human as possible. He is wise and proud, a powerful protector of Firenze. The enemies will be fearful yet the people of Firenze relaxed as he is giving a powerful message to the people of Firenze to never fear though his powerful figure gives a warning to anyone wanting to harm Firenze. His lips are a little open as if he is speaking to people and there is a hidden smile on his face, a sign that he is relaxed and very confident."

"Maestro, that is a very powerful message that I can see already."

Niccolò concentrated on the expression of Marzocco and kept on working with his fine tooth and point chisel and then he smoothed the working surface with his small handmade rasp. Paolo was also working hard on Marzocco and suddenly he felt that his hands were tired; the work was not progressing as fast as he wanted. He looked at the clock and saw it was fifteen minutes past one in the afternoon. Paolo stopped working and put all his tools down.

"Maestro, let us have a lunch break," Paolo said. "My mother prepared some salmon tart with dried fruit and spices and golden leek. I got some orange and lemon rind flavored water."

"That sounds so delicious, thank you and your mother very much. It is very nice of her to prepare food for us."

"As you know, my parents have a trattoria business. My mother helps prepare food twice a week. The rest of the week there is a chef. My two younger brothers help with the business and my father does the overall management."

"Yes, I remembered you mentioning about the trattoria. Where is it again?"

"It is on the other side of the river Arno in a crowded and busy area at the end of the bridge and close to a market which is convenient for us to buy things for the trattoria."

"Where do you and your family live?

"We live at the far end of Firenze. We are lucky to live with our grandparents. The house has two stories with enough rooms to accommodate us and there is a small cottage attached to the house where grandma and grandpa lives.

"My grandfather had an olive farm where he used to make olive oil. When he was quite successful, he built the house with the intention of giving it to his only son, my father, and built the cottage as well so that they could live close to their only son when he retires."

"Paolo, you are very lucky to have grandparents who are so thoughtful and affectionate."

His assistant nodded. "Shall we have our lunch now?"

The salmon tart with dried fruit and spices was delicious served with grilled golden leek on the side.

Niccolò kept expressing his compliments. "This is the first time I ever tasted this dish served this way and the golden leek goes very well with it. Please convey my many thanks and regards to your mother, Paolo."

"I will. She will be very pleased to hear that and you are very welcome. I am glad that you like it."

"Paolo, let's plan how long we should continue to work. My nephew will be arriving on the 20th of December and leaving on the 26th or the 27th to Castellina with his grandmother and mother. What is the date today?"

"It is the 10th of December."

"What do you say we work next week up to the 16th or the 17th of December and return in January, shall we say the 7th or the 8th of January. My goodness, can you believe it will already be the year 1421?" Niccolò wore an incredulous expression on his face.

"I know, time is just speeding by. All right, that sounds good. I might come to the studio and work on Marzocco or whichever area you would like me to concentrate on."

"That sounds good, Paolo. I will work on Marzocco's face and try to finish it today and give the finishing touch later. Tomorrow we will work on Marzocco's mane."

"That is a good plan."

"There is another matter, Paolo." Niccolo gazed out the window, his face solemn. "I do not wish to attend Beatrice's wedding which will take place around the 4th or 5th of January."

Paolo eyed his maestro cautiously. "You said you have to go to Padua."

"Yes I can do that when it is convenient for me. For that, I will take six days off. Two days to reach there and two days to return and spend two days in Padua with the people who want to commission me. With the carriage, it will take me within twenty-four hours to reach there but I do not want to travel at night."

"I never travelled far in a carriage. Please tell me how it works," Paolo said.

"Usually, it takes four horses to drive a carriage. There are padded seats inside for passengers, a covered roof, doors and small glass windows on both sides. The carriage driver sits at the front platform and might have an assistant with him. The horses run five miles per hour and can run at a stretch for twelve to fifteen miles and then a change of horses is required. In some places, they start again with changed horses. Padua is about 118 to 120 miles so it needs eight to ten stops. They start in the morning and reach their destination in the evening where you can spend the night and start again the next morning and reach Padua at dusk."

"Seems like a lot of time, energy and patience is needed and one must be prepared in the event matters do not occur as planned."

"Yes, indeed one must prepare himself for any delays and unfavorable road conditions you might come across that is travel."

"Thank you, for your advice, Maestro."

Paolo and Niccolò worked the rest of the day on Marzocco and they promised to come early next morning to work on Marzocco's mane.

Niccolò And Habakkuk—1422 to 1425

On the 22nd of December 1421 at 9 in the morning, Niccolò strode faster as usual to reach the studio. His mother Orissa and sister Tia already left for Castellina to spend Christmas and New Year with Amadeo. Niccolò promised to join them on the evening of the 24th and planned to stay through the 2nd of January.

Niccolò donned his hooded cape over his long overhaul. He wanted to reach his studio before it started to rain. The sky was gray and the clouds were racing faster to the unknown on their way, it seemed, towards threatening Firenze with lightning and thunder. The roads looked empty and few shops were open.

The pointed cypress trees on the road side were moving side to side, at times touching each other with their pointed ends. The screaming of the birds filled the air in the background when the blast of wind grew stronger.

The lapping sound of a few boats were heard and the splashing sound of the river Arno at the shore became stronger and stronger with intense wintery winds.

Niccolò reached the studio happy to see Paolo was already there.

Paolo came running to greet Niccolò. "Maestro, I was just working on the fountain commissioned by Cosimo de' Medici. Just smoothing out the petals of the lily."

"Thank you, Paolo. I have to talk to you about a new commission by the Florence Cathedral for its bell tower."

"Maestro, that is wonderful."

"Yes, this will be a large sculpture of an Old Testament prophet, Habakkuk. He must have lived in Jerusalem in the era of 612 BC when

274

Babylonian invaders repeatedly desponded the land of the Jews. He was the one who dare to complain to God: 'How long oh Lord, have I cried to you unanswered? I cried violence but does not save.' He detailed the savagery of raiders like swooping to devour the pray. Paolo, the book tells in brief but in an agonizing detail of what he suffered for his divine vision. So I want to sculpt this prophet with all my creative sensitivity so that it speaks to the people who will come close to him."

"Maestro, I know you will give all your creative energy to sculpt him. I am very eager to help you in the project if you want me to and I will devote my energy and concentrate on what you want me to do. This will be a unique opportunity and I feel very lucky that I am your apprentice watching you create great works of art."

"And I might add that your help has been so immensely valuable as I continue to sculpt," Niccolò said. "One other thing you should know is that the marble is metamorphic."

"Maestro, what does that mean?"

"This is the material when rocks are transformed by pressure or heat. Mostly the rock is made by calcite. Over centuries it had been nurtured by architects and sculptors who favor this marble for many reasons. One of them is that it is translucent. The translucency resembles that of human skin which helps give sculptures a lifelike appearance and adds to the realism of these sculptures."

"Maestro, that is amazing how nature makes this unique material and how when the architects and sculptors first discovered the material that is another mystery to be solved."

"Yes, Paolo, there is more to it. Newly quarried, the marble is easy to work with due to its softness. As the material ages, it hardens, it is durable, it cannot be destroyed by elements of water and wind. But it is susceptible to tear in the environment with acidic rain. Marble also absorbs skin oils as the artist works with it which may lead to staining.

The technique I am going to use to sculpt is known as a relief. This technique involves the use of light and shallow carving on the surface of the marble to bring about life."

"Thank you for explaining to me this process in detail that way I know how I can help you in the proper way."

"We will work today and finish up early before I leave for Castellina," Niccolò said. "I will ask the church to deliver marble at my studio. I will go tomorrow on the 23rd of December and ask them to deliver on 4th of January 1422. Do you want to accompany me?"

"Thank you, Maestro, I will be very happy to go with you."

"So we can meet here tomorrow at 9:30 in the morning and then we will start towards the cathedral. Later, we can have lunch at the Osteria."

The morning was cold and breezy on the 23rd of December, 1421 as the hazy rays of sun struggled through the misty air. Paolo, who was dressed in his brown brief with beige stockings, woolen brown vest and a brown woolen cape with hood, was eagerly waiting at the entrance of the studio when he saw a tall silhouette through the mist wrapped up in a long overhaul and black cape which soon turned out to be the figure of his maestro who was moving faster towards the studio.

Paolo greeted him with a smile. "Maestro, I am ready to go."

Niccolò joined Paolo and started sprinting towards the cathedral. During their brisk walk, Niccolò encountered familiar faces. A vendor who covered himself in a black wooly rectangular piece pushing the cart with fresh vegetables was looking for space to place his cart.

"*Buongiorno*, Maestro," the vendor said.

"Hello, your vegetables look so fresh. I wish I could buy some from you but I am leaving for Castellina tomorrow."

"*Grazie*, Maestro, some other time then."

Then they passed the bakery where Luigi, the owner, came out with two loaves of freshly-baked bread. "Niccolò, where are you heading?"

"Towards the cathedral. Uncle Luigi, this is Paolo, my assistant."

The baker nodded at Paolo. "My dear Niccolò, they are treating you well with some commissions, I hope?"

"Yes, they commissioned me to sculpt a prophet for the bell tower."

"I am happy," the baker said. "Please enjoy these loaves—one is with black olives and the other one with raisins. Merry Christmas, my son."

"Thank you, Uncle Luigi. See you soon."

They continued their rapid stride to reach the cathedral where fog and mist covered its tall spires. The misty air was cool and damp. Both of them entered the long corridor and on their right, they saw a priest waving at them to follow him. They followed the priest and entered a medium-sized room with large, uneven glass windows in an iron frame and a high ceiling and saw a walnut finished wooden round table around which three Domoperas in grayish long cloaks and black capes with their long, huge necklaces with crosses around their necks were waiting eagerly for Niccolò.

When Niccolò entered with Paolo, everyone welcomed them with a smile. They asked both of them to sit down just as Niccolò introduced Paolo to which they acknowledged his assistant with a smile.

One of the Domopera started addressing their guests. "Niccolò, we are pleased to have you and your assistant join us. We have decided to commission you to sculpt the prophet Habakkuk."

"I am honored and I humbly accept and will do my best to keep your trust," Niccolò said.

"As far as the duration of the project, how long do you think it will take?"

"I humbly ask when would you like the sculpture to be finished?"

The Domopera looked at each other. "Let us say in about two years?"

Niccolò and Paolo exchanged glances. "Then yes, it can be done." Niccolò took a deep breath. "Here are my conditions which, with all due respect, I request your attention. When I start the project, I wish to maintain my artistic freedom. I have no control over my hands or where the creative process will take me. You may let me know the size or some specifications, however, that is all I can consider."

The tall Domapera with a round face and a friendly smile who sat in the middle said, "We shall give you all the creative freedom that you wish."

"That is very kind of you. And one more matter, if I may: I would like the metamorphic marble to be delivered at my studio after I come back from Castellina around the 4th or 5th of January."

"It shall be done as you wish but you have to come back and choose your marble slab."

"I will return on the 4th of January, about ten to eleven days from today."

All three Domopera nodded. "We are all very happy that you will sculpt the prophet Habakkuk."

"It is my honor. Thank you for bestowing on me this opportunity."

After bowing their farewell to the Domopera, Paolo and Niccolò left the cathedral.

They briskly walked as the sun struggled to shine though the mist. A cold blast of wind whistled through the bare trees in harmony with the seagulls' cries.

Paolo pointed out an alley. "Maestro, we can take this alley, a quicker way to reach the Osteria."

Niccolò and Paolo entered through the oval, brick-layered entrance of the Osteria where they took a seat on a table close to the open fire oven with logs over which a huge iron vessel hung by big chains on hooks from the top of a brick laid wall as the smell of the cooking soup wafted through the air.

"Maestro, it smells like minestrone."

"All right, we will have a big bowl of minestrone and what else? We have two loaves of bread."

"No, Maestro, you take those to Castellina."

"Okay, I will ask them to serve us some bread then."

An olive-skinned young man with a square face, prominent nose, hazel eyes, brown hair, wearing red breeches and beige stockings with a long-sleeved, beige shirt and a brown vest, arrived at their table.

"I am Carlo, what would you like to order?"

"We would each like to have a big bowl of minestrone soup. Do you serve bread?"

"Yes, with the bowl of soup, we serve roasted garlic bread."

"Oh, that is very nice."

"Anything else?"

"Some orange blossom water."

"We can serve that too and today the specialty is mulled wine."

"That will be perfect for a breezy day,"

"I will be back in a few minutes," Carlo said.

Niccolò turned to Paolo. "I am leaving tomorrow and will be back on the evening of the 3rd of January. We must go again to the cathedral the next morning to choose the marble slab on the 4th of January and hopefully the slab will be delivered that day or the day after. Then we will start soon after the slab arrives at our studio."

"Whatever you plan I will do my best to help you."

"The sculpting of this prophet will be very special, Paolo. I want the sculpture to be alive with his all senses so that when people see him, they will see his suffering and the agony in his expression"

"I have faith you will do a fine job conveying this, Maestro."

Carlo brought the bowls of soup, garlic bread, two glasses of mulled wine and a jug of orange blossom water. Niccolò and Paolo enjoyed their soup and bread and the mulled wine was a perfect beverage choice to combat the cold weather. Outside the wind blew strongly as the sky grew gray and clouds were racing to threaten rain.

"We should get going," Niccolò said. "I feel that it will rain soon."

Paolo thanked Niccolò for the lunch and bid goodbye. "Maestro, pleasant journey and safe return. I will see you on the 4th of January in our studio at 9:30 in the morning."

* * *

December 24th 1421 around 9:30 a.m.—Niccolò was getting ready to go with his bag and also took his sketching papers and charcoal marker along with his marking pencils. He was nearly possessed with the idea of the Prophet so he took some art materials for the times he could express his thoughts when the feelings would get intense, he would sketch it even during his vacation.

He heard the trotting of horses and saw a horse drawn coach approaching his home. He came out with his belongings and waved to the coachman that he was ready. He embarked, greeting the coachman, *"Buongiorno!"*

Piero was an average-built adult with an elongated face, sharp nose and brown eyes dressed in black hose and brown breeches, a white, long-sleeved shirt, red vest and wooly coat with a long whip in his right hand who returned his greetings to Niccolò.

"Signore, it will take us almost seven hours to reach Castellina," Piero said. "We will make two stops where there will be a changing of horses."

"Piero, let me know when you would like to take a break and since you are more familiar with this route, you decide where we will stop and have lunch."

"*Grazie, Signore.* I will stop after three hours in a village before Greve and have lunch and change the horses. Before that, around two hours, I will stop for fifteen minutes at a place where I can feed the horses and let them drink some water. I know an olive grove where there is a facility to do that and where you can also stretch your legs before we stop for lunch."

"*Grazie,* Piero."

As the coach started clip-clapping on the paved path of Firenze, Niccolò closed his eyes and started to think about his commission of the prophet Habakkuk.

"The Prophet's body, his eyes and his facial expression of agony—he is humble yet he is brave enough to question God: why must there be this injustice and extra load of suffering on the people? Why is he not doing anything?"

The horses started galloping and in a short time they were in an open space where the gray sky carved to meet the green valleys with undulating hills all around.

Niccolò peered outside through the sliding window of the covered coach and saw different shades of green as far as the eyes could see, accentuated with wild, yellow mustard flowers and white daisies of different sizes. The snow sprinkled on top of the undulating hills as the sun played hide and seek through the clouds. The reflected rays lighted part of the hills while the shadows mysteriously hid part of nature's treasure. The coach made its way up and down the hills until the olive grove where the horses would be fed and where they would have a chance to drink water.

Niccolò was happy to stretch his legs while walking along a paved path. The owner of the grove, Francesco greeted Niccolò from the other end of the path.

"*Buongiorno,* Maestro."

Niccolò was surprised by the greeting of the middle-aged man with a robust built, muscular hand, terracotta face, tanned skin, big black eyes, bushy eyebrows, and lines on his forehead. He was wearing a blue, spotted brief-like outfit with a beige, long-sleeved shirt folded at his elbow. His head was wrapped like a turban by a piece of brown cloth.

He was delighted to see Niccolò in person and informed him that he was in the cheering crowd in Firenze when St. John was on his way to Cathedral. He was so pleased by his encounter with the great sculptor that he offered some of his cured olives to take for his nephew and asked him to stop by again on his return home to Firenze.

They left the place after fifteen minutes once the horses were fully energized. After they had their food and drink, the horses galloped through the red dusty road and climbed up the green hills. On both sides, there were olive groves. The trees of the fruit orchards were all misty and barren and it seemed they were casting their haunted look while the coach passed by.

"Signore, we are going to reach Greve in ten to fifteen minutes," Piero said.

"That is wonderful."

They reached Greve surrounded by medium-sized Chianti hills and the valleys of the rivers Greve and Pesa. An area of 169 Square, it was Langobardic, Tuscany who descended from a small tribe Winnili from southern Scandinavia in the early medieval era.

"Signore, the clock tower says it is 12:30 p.m. from the city center there is the castle of Verrazzano up on a hill built by Lombard which you can visit now or after lunch. When we leave Greve to Castellina I can drive close by and you can visit it. There is a monastery in the heart of the city and in the Piazza Chilesa, Santa Croce built in the 11th century and rebuilt in 1325, there is a trattoria in the piazza for lunch whenever you wish to go. While you are at lunch, I will take my carriage pretty close from there and change my horses. Signore, Greve is well known for its olive oil and red wine."

"*Grazie*, Piero. I will take a break for my lunch now and while we are on our way to Castellina, we can stop for few minutes at the Verrazzano castle. What about you? When are you going to have lunch?"

"Signore, do not worry I will have something to eat after changing the horses. What would you like to eat?"

"I want to go to an authentic Lombard place," Niccolò said.

"Oh, I know a place that is very quaint and homely. It is at Albion's house, the name is 'Tuscan Lombard' and he prepares authentic Lombard food himself."

"Piero, that sounds very nice, is it close by?"

"Yes, I will take you right now if you wish."

The buildings around the town imbued a medieval quality as all were made of stone with iron-framed windows and iron gates at the entrance. The path to the entrance was paved with gray colored stone. There were olive trees on the sides of each building with the shrubs jutting out here and there.

Winter took its toll on the landscape of flowering beds. Just beyond the center of town, through a paved brick path, a small two-floored house seemed to be made of stone with an iron gate and a paved path leading to a wide wooden door with a semicircular top. Doors had many iron bolts in their entire surface. At the middle of one door, an iron bell about five by three inches hung from a hook attached to the door.

When Piero rang the bell, a tall man with a bearded, square-shaped face, brown hair, a prominent nose, hazel eyes, and a strong muscular body opened the door.

"*Buongiorno*! I am Albion."

He looked charming with his brown breeches, yellow shirt folded at the elbows, and brown vest with gold-colored shiny buttons. "Welcome to my home."

Niccolò immediately took a liking to this man. "I would like to have lunch at your place."

"Certainly, I am at your service."

Piero nudged Niccolò's arm. "Signore, enjoy your lunch. I will be back between 1:45 to 2 in the afternoon and then we will continue our journey which will be around three hours, more or less. See you then."

Albion took Niccolò inside his home which was decorated with long, green garlands of pine leaves accentuated with a bunch of red berries at intervals. Garlands hung by hooks on a wall, around the windows and in two fireplaces logs of oak were burning. There was one in the dining room and one in the living room where stood a pyramid-shaped shelf and on the top, a silver metallic star.

There were candied fruit and nuts on the upper shelves and at the lower level, a Baby Jesus was placed surrounded by scenes of the nativity created with figurines.

Niccolò followed Albion to the dining room at another level. The room had two iron-framed windows overlooking the yard with some olive trees and a few pines. Beyond that, a green valley as far as the eyes could see lay surrounded by hills.

The room was again decorated with green garlands from pine leaves and branches. The room was cozy and comfortable from the heat of the fireplace. The green garlands were placed on the stone wall secured with iron hooks above the fireplace. Four tables were covered with red tablecloth and each had four chairs with red cushions. Each table had a small vase with some greens from pine and a bunch of red berries.

Niccolò sat by the window and saw a Christmas tree kept outside in the yard with hanging apples. He took a deep breath, remembering his childhood when he used to help his father put the tree outside and helped hang the apples and flowers made with papers of different colors, thinking now his sister and mother might introduce this tradition to Amadeo.

Albion approached Niccolò. "Signore, what would you prefer for lunch? I have Risotto Alla Certosina cooked with fresh crayfish and frog legs or Ossubuco Alla Melanese, veal shanks braised with vegetables, white wine and broth, garnished with shredded lemon skin, garlic and parsley or Pizzoccheri Lombard buckwheat pasta, which are strips of pasta cooked with leafy vegetables, potatoes and cheese."

"I will have the Pizzoccheri."

"And for dessert," Albion continued, "we have Panforte, a medieval-inspired dense aromatic spiced fruit, nuts and honey, the spices are cinnamon, nutmeg and cardamon; torrone, which can be soft or hard, made with egg white, sugar, nuts, almonds, walnuts and hazelnuts.

"I will have the soft torrone, a glass of red wine and some orange blossom water."

"Of course. I will serve your red wine and cheese gorgonzola and also a jug of orange blossom water with your food which will be about twenty minutes from now."

As soon as Albion left, Niccolò got lost in his thoughts. The blue and yellow flames of the fireplace mesmerized him as it kept on flickering, a sense of motion that calmed him. Niccolò mentally moved back in time to the 7th century Judah, the time of the prophet. Babylonians emerged as a world power. They rebelled against Assyria; Judah got a brief relief. The Babylonians crushed the Assyrians and quietly proceeded to defeat the Egyptians. Then the Babylonians overtook Judah. The curses were serious internationally, but even greater concern was national corruption. Josiah was a good king and when he died, his son rose to the throne. In three months, Egypt invaded Judah and removed the king.

Niccolò came back to the present when he heard loud cracklings from the fireplace and Albion approached with Pizzoccheri.

"*Buon appetito.*" Albion smiled.

"*Grazie*, Albion."

"Signore, I will be around. Please call me if you need anything. Enjoy."

Niccolò concentrated on his Pizzoccheri which he thought was delicious especially paired with a glass of wine. He gazed at the fireplace, fascinated with the motion of the flickering flame. This time he was thinking about the Prophet's sculpture.

"What if I add the motion-like appearance in some part of the Prophet's body?" He said to himself while focusing on the fireplace. "It could be done playing with creative shading with the lighter part reflected on the sculpture. Oh, yes then some parts will be thin and some rough. Well, that is it."

Niccolò finished his main dish when Albion brought his dessert and poured some orange blossom water in a glass. He then tasted the soft toronne. "The toronne is delicious. Everything I ate tasted delicious, thank you, Albion."

"Signore, you must come back again. By the way your coach driver has just arrived and is waiting for when you are ready."

Niccolò thanked Albion. "I will visit again when I travel to Castellina."

Albion escorted Niccolò to the coach and as soon as he stepped inside, he handed Piero a bag of food from Albion's restaurant. The driver thanked him profusely.

Then the coach started click-clapping on the paved road, and past the city center, the coach started to slow down. "Signore, up on the hill is the Verrazzano castle. We can stop and you can climb up and visit it."

"Thank you but I do not want to climb up. Thank you for stopping, I can see the castle from here and that is enough. I am eager to reach Castellina."

"That is fine. I will make it there even less than three hours. Signore, what is your plan for your return."

"Piero, I want to leave Castellina on the 3rd of January soon after noon so that I reach Florence in the early evening."

"Signore, I can drive you to Firenze, if you want."

"That would be nice, Piero. Are you staying in Castellina?"

"No, I will be staying in a place not far from Castellina with my parents for Christmas and New Year's this year. It is a place just before Siena."

"That is wonderful."

The horses started galloping along the paved path on the hills and down the valleys which were mostly of olive groves. On some slopes of green hills, winter battered vineyards holding their bare vines tightly waiting for spring and summer to turn green and bear their fruit. The top of most hills was covered with patchy snow. The horses galloped along the curved path of the hills where red-tiled villas were seen. Misty rays of sun brushed the meadows. It was a peaceful afternoon. Niccolò was lost again in his thoughts of creating a schedule of his time in Castellina until some time had passed and he abruptly came back to the present when he heard Piero's voice.

"We are very close to Castellina."

The horses started galloping in full speed as the green valleys passed backwards while the coach started ascending the hills.

Niccolò could recognize the olive groves on the slopes of the hills and beyond the valleys, the three hills looked like they were holding each other's hands standing there overlooking a green valley.

The first hill was the Casini family's house where Niccolò stayed last time. The evening was just settling in as a veil of mist spread over the dreamy hills and valleys.

As the coach curved along a path, a view of a rustic brick-layered L-shaped house was visible almost facing the Casini family's villa. The house looked like a two-story building with an extension on its side and a separate paved path to the extension. Yards in the front and back were fenced with iron rods and a moderate-sized gate. In front of the gate there was a tall iron cage where a torch with open fire was burning.

The coach stopped in front of the iron gate when Niccolò saw his nephew Amadeo open the front door, a covered lantern in his hand. He stepped out of the house to greet him.

Christmas Day and Preparations for Paris trip

Newcastle, 25th of December, 1964

Through the misty glass window, one could see the gray skies, the bare trees covered with snow, the flashing amber glow at the traffic light was warning drivers of the hazards ahead. At times the west wind blew its whistle through the trees and the snow collected on the branches was thrown on the ground by a blast of wind.

Amita and Sharmi sat in Amita's living room in front of the fireplace around 10 in the morning holding cups of hot tea in their hands.

"Let's clean up the mess from yesterday's party," Sharmi said. "I am glad it was all disposable so I am going to empty those in a big trash bag and put it outside in the big trash receptacle."

"Sharmi, please check whether it's still snowing."

"It doesn't matter," Sharmi said. "The can is just outside and I will put on my trenchcoat and boots."

"I will empty the leftovers and clean the containers," Amita said. "I think we don't have to prepare any food for our dinner tonight and tomorrow's light lunch. The leftovers will be enough for our two meals. Let us also pack our suitcases and check our handbags and travel documents. What do you say, Sharmi?"

"I agree with you," Sharmi said. "I have four sarees, two petticoats, one petticoat will be enough but I'll bring another in case I spill something and it gets wet, also matching blouses and enough undergarments. Sarees do not take much space, thanks to the smooth silk of the sarees one can fold into very small rectangles or squares and you can stack them inside the suitcase very easily in a small space. The matching blouse of a particular saree goes in between the folds of a saree for that particular match. Two cotton petticoats, one black and white, will not take much space so it is very easy to pack. Among the selection of sarees two are very colorful heavy silk sarees, one maroon color with fine gold work and another black with red borders and gold flowers inside the body. I don't know whether to take those. Maybe I'll leave those at your house before we fly to Paris."

"No, no you will need them," Amita said. "I'm taking a black dress to wear the day we go to the show. I'm also taking a heavy silk saree with gold works. For my western outfits, I'm taking two to three woolen pants, silk shirts and sweaters. Sharmi, I hope you also packed sweaters."

"Oh yes, two thick sweaters and a couple of lamb's wool ones."

"Sharmi, let me know if you need anything for the trip."

"Don't worry, I already packed my suitcase," Sharmi said. "I just have to organize my handbag and keep my clothes for tomorrow's travel handy. I'm always wearing a saree anyway so I already selected the one I will wear with a warm sweater and gloves. I bought a new, long coat that has a waterproof hood you can take out when you don't need it."

"That's wonderful," Amita said. "What is the color of the coat?"

"Oh, it is bright maroon."

"That's nice. I like maroon-colored coats."

"We are lucky the airport is very close so we can just hire a taxi and go," Sharmi said.

"Oh yes, but in Paris we're going to land at Orly International Airport. I don't know how far it is but it doesn't matter. The tour company will give us a ride."

"You know Newcastle-upon-Tyne also has an international airport."

"Yes, I forgot about it. Sharmi, we will eat lunch from our leftovers and keep some for our dinner. Let's make some plain rice—I just got tired of

Biryani. I don't think Rudy is coming today. He will arrive in the morning so we will have brunch as we have to leave home between 12:30 and 12: 45 in the afternoon. Our Air France flight is at 3:45."

"That's fine with me."

While Amita went to organize a few things around kitchen, Sharmi was left alone for some time looking outside through the window. *It is a gray day with rain and wind. I use to like these gray days for sitting quietly to read and contemplate on certain aspects of life that used to be a pleasure but now it is so different as I am disconnected with my parents and family,* she thought to herself.

Her mood changed to blue and mentally she took a flight to a faraway land, where her parents lived. Then she became sad and started thinking and whispering to herself: "It really hurts now that I cannot communicate with my parents."

It was a very big step for her to accept the Paris trip and Rudy's commitment to her—both these events were huge steps as well as joyous events that sadly caused her so much anxiety as thoughts of how she would face her parents in the future loomed darkly in her mind. She felt as though she was sinking in a dark abyss. Her feet and fingers were cold and moist as she started breathing heavily just when Samir arrived from work at the hospital.

"Hello! I am done for the day and if they need anything, they will call me from the hospital and just take my advice by telephone, unless there is an emergency." Samir paused as he realized his wife wasn't around.

"Amita!" Samir called out. "Where are you?"

Amita emerged from her trip preparations.

"I'm going to call Rudy to see what he is doing and if he can join us. If not, then we will see him in the morning. What do you think?"

"That is fine with me, go ahead," Amita said.

"Sharmi," Samir said. "How about a cup of tea?"

Maya Mitra Das

"Sure. I'll make us some." Samir's presence snapped Sharmi back to the present and she got up to make tea for them.

Meanwhile Samir called Rudy who appeared happy to receive the call.

From his end, Rudy told Samir, "There is not much going on here. Most of the patients have been discharged but I have to take a clinical round in the evening to see and greet all the patients. I can come and spend the day with you and then return and sleep at my place and then in the morning I will be at your place as soon as I get ready."

"That sounds good," Samir said.

* * *

Rudy concentrated on the patients' charts checking whether he finished writing daily notes on patients' physical examinations and changes and also the prescription of medication for the patients.

In that moment, a patient's relative arrived and asked Rudy if he could take his father, Mr. Irwin home for few hours to enjoy Christmas day with his family. Rudy relented and asked the nurse-in-charge to make arrangements for the visit.

Rudy saw how Mr. Irwin's face lit up with joy and his son was very delighted and grateful to get permission from Rudy to make arrangements on such short notice.

Suddenly, Rudy's imagination flew to north Bengal India where his family lived. These last few days, Rudy had been thinking about his family in India, and how that will impact the fact that he opened his heart to commit to Sharmi. He felt relieved for welcoming Sharmi into his world, yet without his family's knowledge.

Since Rudy's mother no longer dwelled in this world, his father lived with his sister in the northern part of West Bengal. His sister, married with children fairly settled, took care of their father. Rudy's brother was busy with his own family. All were busy in their own worlds and because of this fact, Rudy didn't

292

think it was that urgent to inform his family about his commitment to Sharmi. Yet, there was something inside telling him to communicate with his family. As Rudy often read about Niccolò's self-ruminating, he murmured to himself, "I will make it more official and announce my intentions in due time."

Just then, a misty shadow of his former love, Manashi, appeared in his memory. Immediately, Rudy thought of the heart wrenching part in Niccolò's biography which he read about Niccolò's secret and forbidden love for his muse, Beatrice, and realized how he shared this in common with his favorite artist. Rudy took a deep breath and exhaled. *She is beyond my reach but I will treasure my memories of her, my beautiful muse. I will frame her in the tide of my time, yet there is something which bothers deep inside me that I never opened my mind about my feelings. I believed that she is beyond my reach and left the country almost in secret so that she will never know just how much she meant to me.*

All these thoughts swirled in Rudy's mind while he was at work. He became restless, an uneasiness crept from his feet and spread all over his body. Because reading Niccolò's biography had given him so much strength, wisdom and inspiration, he made a mental note to pack the book in his luggage to read during quiet, restful moments at the hotel in Paris. He took a few deep breaths and started pacing inside the patients' ward where most of the beds were empty. Rudy took the clinical charts of the few who were there and read the detailed notes on each patient. Then he composed himself by the time a nurse on duty arrived.

"There's a call for you from Dr. Basu again."

Rudy came back to the present as he took the telephone call.

"Rudy," Samir said, "come and have lunch with us. Sharmi is making tea. Oh, one more thing, as you told me you are going to make an effort to make this trip a memorable one, how are you preparing for this memorable trip? For all of us it will surely be memorable but what I mean to say is that do you have anything special, anything specific planned for you and Sharmi? If you know what I mean."

Rudy sensed his friend's gentle encouragement. "Yes, Samir, I do have some idea as to how I would proceed but do you have any suggestions as to when I might do this?"

"Well, the afternoon of Dec. 27 will be perfect, after our morning tour. You and Sharmi can go your own way and we will go on ours," Samir said conspiratorially. "I suggest we go back to the hotel and change, then have dinner on a ship cruising the Seine. I will try to call today, if you want to make arrangements. I think the cruise starts at 7 that evening and will feature a two and a half hour-tour with dinner, music and dancing. We have to board the ship around 6:30. What you say to that?"

"That sounds wonderful, Samir. I cannot thank you enough for being so thoughtful in making this trip so special for us."

"This is special for all of us but especially for you and Sharmi. Now hurry up and finish what you are doing at work and join us soon, it is Christmas."

"I'll be there soon."

Rudy placed the phone down and ruminated to himself. *It feels like I am on a pendulum, swinging in the past, present and future. Very hard to control the passage of time which is unpredictable.*

He took a deep breath and whispered to himself, "I must move forward."

Rudy finished his work at the hospital and soon joined Samir, Amita and Sharmi. The pleasant afternoon brought a delicious lunch of leftover kabab, naan, and green salad. Cups of hot tea rounded out the meal. They were all in the holiday spirit and excited about the Paris trip, talking about the places they will visit as this will be their first visit to Paris.

Rudy sensed some change in Sharmi as she spoke softly and blushed, her expression brighter yet shy. On the other hand, Rudy felt bold being close to Sharmi, asking whether she would like some bread and a cup of tea as if he had known her for a while. He would take pieces of kebab from his plate to share with Sharmi and serve her a cup of tea and say, "This is in appreciation for all your hard work."

"What about me?" Amita teased. "I work hard here at home to keep you all fed."

"I mean for all Sharmi's academic accomplishments," Rudy said. "And of course, Amita, I am grateful for your cooking and will make a cup of tea for you too."

They all laughed as they enjoyed their delicious lunch. Then Rudy had to leave for his evening rounds so he bid his friends bye for now, assuring them he would meet them back here by mid-morning the next day.

That evening Samir, Amita and Sharmi double-checked everything for their trip before retiring to their rooms for the night.

By mid-morning the next day, the sun shone in the sky as the sun rays bathed the earth, snow-covered rooftops were glittering like gold through the window. One could see the snow and frost with refracted sun rays giving off several colors. The snow also covered the ground while frosty icicles hung from trees and windows.

At Amita and Samir's house, everyone was up and busy running around, putting their luggage in one place. Amita and Sharmi were in the kitchen, making sandwiches with kebab meat on naan bread with lettuce, slices of tomato and spicy cilantro. The electric kettle plugged in for tea was ready as they waited for Rudy to start lunch.

They were all happy to see Rudy arrive at 11:30 and immediately Amita and Sharmi served the delicious stuffed naan on plates for them. The boiling water was poured in the teapot and teacups were already displayed on the table.

Samir had already called a taxicab which would arrive at 12:30 that afternoon for the four excited friends anticipating their trip as they finished their delicious lunch.

Once the taxi arrived on time, they all rushed to the door with their luggage and hurried to board the taxi.

At the airport everything proceeded smoothly for the two couples. Once on board the plane, the couples secured window seats in different rows and happily settled in unable to contain their excitement. They couldn't believe they were actually on their way to Paris!

When the plane took off, Amita and Samir happily and tightly held hands and cheerfully started talking to each other.

"Amita, thank you for arranging this trip," Samir said. "I'm so happy that I want to keep this moment forever."

Amita drew closer to Samir. "Me too."

An elated Rudy moved closer to Sharmi. "I can't believe that I am going to Paris with you. It is beyond my dream."

Sharmi appeared bright and calm yet her eyes were fixed at the window looking far out in the distance.

"What are you thinking?" Rudy said.

"I'm still anxious and nervous," Sharmi said, "everything seems to be moving so fast around me and it feels like I'm about to take a difficult, decisive final test at the university."

"Everyone encounters these feelings—some experience them more or less than others," Rudy said. "Just try to stay positive, hopeful and in the present. Think about all the exploring we will do in a new place full of ancient history, art and literature. For you, Paris is a gold mine and you are going to learn so much."

With his caring words, Sharmi's mood improved, her outlook brightened as she warmed up closer to Rudy who put his arm around her shoulder that made her eyes soften and moisten. She tightly held Rudy's hand and smiled as the plane reached its desirable altitude. During the short flight, while Sharmi took a nap, Rudy dove back into Niccolò's biography as down below, heaps of busy clouds continued floating to reach somewhere very far and unknown.

Niccolò Explores Amadeo's Home

Niccolò saw his nephew Amadeo with a covered lantern scurrying towards the iron gate. Just behind Amadeo, he saw his sister at the door and his mother Orissa standing with another covered lantern waving her hand.

Niccolò paid Piero the travel expenses and confirmed with the driver the time when Niccolò would be picked up for his return to Florence on the 3rd of January.

"Grazie Signore, Buona Notte."

The coach turned slowly as the horses started galloping down the hill, the sound echoing from hill to hill and fading as the coach disappeared behind the mist.

The four family members were thrilled to be reunited again as they exchanged embraces and excitedly caught up on the happenings since they last saw each other.

Amadeo's new home featured the entrance to the living room which was after a covered patio. The wooden walnut-colored rectangular doors with shiny, golden knobs were on the right as one entered. Next on the wall was an iron-framed, large glass window with wooden shutters and lacy curtains blowing with the breeze. The flickering candles from the chandelier inside hung from the ceiling, casting some shadows on the white wall of the room.

As Niccolò entered he saw the white washed ceiling partly reinforced by wooden beams. In the middle of the room in a recess layered with bricks, the fireplace with wooden logs burned to keep the place warm. A medium-sized mahogany sofa for two with armrests on both sides, padded with raw red silk, was placed horizontally as you entered the room. In addition, two small sofas of the same kind were placed on either side of a gold-framed oval glass center table. There were two more wooden chairs with red cushions. An oil-painted landscape of Castellina hung over the medium-sized sofa on the wall. The floor was covered with grayish tiles and a red area rug with a floral design was placed around the area of the sofa and table.

Mother Orissa hugged Niccolò, as Tia and Amadeo followed. Niccolò's mother asked everyone to sit down to have some wine and almond milk cheese. Soon after, she announced that dinner will be served in about an hour.

Niccolò requested Amadeo to give him a tour of his house.

"Zio, would you like the tour now or after we have our drink?"

"It will be nice to have the tour first and then we can settle down for the rest of the evening," Niccolò said.

The living room and the kitchen were on the first floor. The living room lead to a room where closets had a wooden door with a semicircular top which led to an elongated anti-room with a large window. In the center there was a rectangular wooden dining table covered with a red tablecloth and a lacy cloth was spread over the red one in the center. A candelabra was placed on a green garland of pine leaves. Four white dinner plates with silverware were arranged and four fan-shaped red napkins were placed on the dining plates.

A chandelier with glass crystals shone with gold-colored candle holders over the top of the table hanging from the roof. Six mahogany finish wooden chairs with red cushions were set around the table.

On the white washed wall of the dining area, two oval recesses on each side of the wall held a covered lamp with large, thick burning candles.

Then a narrow corridor led to a moderate-sized kitchen that had a brick-layered wall in front with an open fire oven in a deep recess layered with bricks.The wall above and on both sides of the oven were brick-layered. Kitchen utensils hung neatly from hooks on the right wall.

The oven was still kindling. There were shelves on the white walls on both sides just after the entrance of the kitchen. Some were for kitchen utensils, shelves for spices, and others for cooked foods of the day. All had thin metallic mesh doors framed with wood. The kitchen floor was a gray and black, marble chip, speckled floor. Past the oven there was a wooden door which led to a small paved patio which overlooked the backyard.

Evening was settling in and there was still light. Niccolò saw a Christmas tree through the misty veil decorated with colorful paper flowers and apples hanging from the branches and a silver star shining on top as Amadeo held his covered lantern close to the tree.

"Zio, let us take a quick tour of the bedrooms upstairs and I will show you your room," Amadeo said.

Niccolò followed Amadeo as they climbed up the stairs next to the kitchen. The stairs were also speckled with pink and gray marble chips. They reached the upper floor and landed on a pink and black mosaic corridor which led to the bedrooms.

Two bedrooms faced each other with another in the middle. The wall was white chalk paint and floors were made with alternate black and white marble tiles with a black marble border.

Each room had two doors, one entrance after the corridor and another opened to the common hanging balcony facing the backyard. The rooms were furnished with high wooden beds, thick mattresses covered with rust-colored velvet bedspreads and pillows with lacy covers and a small side table with a covered lamp.

Each room had recesses on the walls for the covered lantern. There was a covered closet with wooden doors in each of the three bedrooms. Each room had two large windows, one by the side of the doors which opened towards the corridor and another on a side wall of the rooms.

"Zio, you can choose whichever room you want," Amadeo said.

"Thank you, Amadeo. I will stay in the room on the right as you climb the stairs so that I can see the hills as soon as I get up in the morning."

"That is fine."

"Now let us go down and have our drink and tomorrow, I will show you my mother's side of the house or my mother can give you a tour. Let us enjoy the rest of the evening."

"That is a very good idea," Niccolò said.

Once they reached downstairs, they took their seats in the comfortable sofas.

Niccolò suddenly remembered that Luigi from the bakery gave him two loaves of bread on his way to Castellina and the owner of the olive grove gave him some cured olives. He opened one of his bags and gave mother Orissa the two loaves and gave Amadeo the jar of cured olives. Amadeo thanked Niccolò and gave the jar to his grandmother.

Sister Tia poured wine in glasses and handed one to each family member.

Mother Orissa served some cured olives and cheese in small plates and asked everyone to sit down and grab their plate.

"Niccolò, when will you start your new project?" his mother asked.

"Mother, I have already started it— not carving yet; that I will start when I get back after the 3rd of January. I have my sketching materials with me and I will start sketching prophet Habakkuk during my vacation here."

"All right, my dear son, whatever activity gives you pleasure and satisfaction. Carry on with God's blessing."

"Yes, I enjoy the peaceful surroundings of Castellina, being close with my family and spending Christmas at my dear nephew Amadeo's new house. It is a grand occasion."

"Thank you, Uncle, if I could be of any help, let me know."

"Amadeo, that is very nice. I was thinking of putting the sketch paper on the floor and work on it whenever I feel like it. As you mentioned, if you can help me hang it somewhere on a hard surface, it will be easier."

"I have a better idea. My friend, Stefano, is an artist. He has different sizes of hard boards. He can loan you one for a few days, whichever one will be the right size for you."

"Oh, that will be very helpful."

"Do not worry. I will ask him tomorrow morning."

"If you are ready, I will serve dinner within fifteen minutes. After dinner, I will get ready to go to Midnight Mass with Marcello and Angela who will pick me up. After mass, I shall rest in their house and come back here late tomorrow morning."

"That is fine with me," Niccolò said.

"Do not worry, Mamma. I will take care of things around the house and will make tomorrow's lunch," Tia said.

"I can help too," Niccolò said.

Mother Orissa clasped her hands in glee. "That is wonderful. Now let us sit down for dinner."

Niccolò's mother served soup made with asparagus tips, eggs, chopped onions, olive oil and some lemon rinds in a vegetable broth. Grilled sardines on toasted bread rounded out the first courses. Then everyone bowed their heads to say, "Grace."

Tia and Niccolò took their seats on one side and Amadeo and Mother Orissa took the two other chairs on the opposite side so all were facing each other.

They took their glasses of white wine and said, "*Saluti!*"

The soup was delicious complimented with sardines on toast as everyone complimented mother Orissa for a delicious meal.

Tia helped mother Orissa serve the main dish.

"Today's meal is all fish but I did not prepare a variety of seven dishes just two items with fish," said mother Orissa.

"*Nonna,* I am very happy that you made just two items otherwise it would be too fishy," said Amadeo.

Everyone laughed.

The main dish looked very colorful and delicious. It was spaghetti in tomato base with peas, carrots, large grilled chunks of bass sprinkled with chopped cilantro and lemon rind.

After Mother Orissa served everyone, she said, "There's plenty of food left. Help yourself to more."

Tia and Niccolò enjoyed the dish very much and went back for another serving.

"Remember how Papa loved this dish?" Niccolò said to Tia.

His sister nodded. "I used to hate carrots and put them on my napkin so that I could throw them out later."

"And I would take all the peas and also steal from your plate to make you upset," Niccolò added teasingly.

They were in a jovial mood, enjoying their childhood memories.

Lastly, Niccolò's favorite dessert almond rice was served for all to enjoy. As they concentrated on their desserts, they remained quiet, lost in their own thoughts.

The day was in the phase of a new moon and as it became dark outside with occasional shrills of night birds, a cry of animals echoed through the hills which pierced the silence into pieces for some time then faded far away. The silence grew deeper to be one with the dark. The log of oak from the fireplace in the living room crackled. They all came back to the present.

Mother Orissa broke the silence first. "I shall get ready for Midnight Mass. I am thinking of inviting Marcello and his family for lunch tomorrow as I have plenty of cold cuts, fruit, cured olive, bread, and cheese to nibble on the whole day. And Marcello and Angela have invited us all for dinner tomorrow to welcome back Niccolò to Castellina."

"Mamma, do not worry. I will arrange everything for display on the table," Tia said.

"And I will help Tia with whatever she needs," Niccolò assured his mother. "You go and enjoy your time with Marcello and Angela."

Mother Orissa hugged and kissed everyone a good night.

Sculpture Thoughts Consume Niccolò

On a cool windy afternoon at Amadeo's new home in Castellina, Niccolò reflected on this visit to this small town surrounded by hills and valleys with its vineyards and olive orchards cozily hidden a few miles from Siena. He felt pride for his nephew Amadeo for inviting his mother, Tia and grandmother, Orissa and himself to his nephew's new home thinking it was a good decision to take a break from work and join his family for Christmas. Niccolò thought about the time he was Amadeo's age, as he now observed his nephew, a twenty-three-year-old handsome, young man about five feet nine inches tall with olive skin, an oblong face, aquiline nose and sparkling brown eyes celebrating Christmas Eve and Christmas Day with the reunited family, considering the experience as "the best Christmas he ever had."

Niccolò closely looked around his nephew Amadeo's house and was pleased to see that he did a great job building this house with a separate unit for his mother whose portion of the building was not yet complete but looked quite spacious and comfortable.

He offered to help Amadeo by providing money if needed and though his nephew was very grateful by his uncle's gesture, he said, "Do not worry. I am fine. I will ask your help when I need it, thank you very much."

After Niccolò finished exploring around the house, he toured Amadeo's own business and workplace—the vineyard and his winery which he thought to be impressive and wanted to enjoy the rest of the afternoon relaxing and viewing the landscape through the window surrounded by hills and valleys. The hills sprinkled with snow seemed to be standing one after another holding their hands and listening quietly to the overture of the wintery wind.

Then there were times in between when the wind stopped blowing when it felt like time had stopped, when a peaceful calm captured the landscape. Niccolò drifted away completely with nature, lost and unaware of the present time and space as the beauty and peaceful moments took him to his creative world where he was busy collecting his realm of thoughts. He felt fortunate to have brought some sketching materials with him should sudden inspiration dawn upon him. As much as he grew restless to return to Firenze to start working again, he promised himself and his mother that he would not repeat what he did the last time he defied his mother's wishes to enjoy his vacation. The memory of that experience played back in his mind taking him back to the time he cut short his Christmas vacation in Castellina to go back to work at his studio.

* * *

"Niccolò, someone from Florence sent a message inquiring about a sculpture," his mother said. "My dear son, you must finish Marzocco, the lion for the Pope."

"My dear mother, do not worry. It is almost done. I sculpted some putti, as the adornment of the young, naked child holding the garland would complement the sculpture. I have another project in progress that is prophet Habakkuk who I call "Zuccone," the bald headed. Besides there are a few other sculptures I need to work on for Cosimo's new palace garden."

Niccolò held on to his mother's hand for assurance. "I want to keep on going as long as my creative energy flows through these hands." He briefly held up his hand. "I wanted to enjoy these next few days of relaxation but I think it is not possible."

"You do not have to work so hard," she said. "Take few days off."

"Mamma, I cannot. Some unseen energy, a force is pulling me towards Firenze. I am getting restless and so before I leave, I want to tell you about my new mode of relief in the marble Schiacciato, a flattened-out technique involving extremely shallow carving throughout which will create a striking effect of atmospheric space than before. The sculpture no longer modeled his shape in a usual way but seemed to be painted with the chisel." Niccolò's eyes sparkled with excitement and enthusiasm for his work.

"That is wonderful, my dear son, but I believe some people would like it the conventional way," his mother said. "Maybe you must ask them—"

"I do not usually do that," Niccolò quickly interjected, "I do not have control over my creative idea. It just flows and takes shape on its own."

There was silence for few moments and then mother Orissa softly said, "I pray for you, my son. May God be with you."

Niccolò left that early afternoon. Amadeo was sad that his uncle was leaving so soon. Naturally, his mother and sister were equally sad.

The horse-driven coach soon started galloping as the hills and valleys of Castellina drenched with misty sunlight, moving backwards until lost in the mist.

Niccolò was in peace that his nephew's construction of his house and the portions in progress would be finished soon. He was so pleased to see his sister's joy that her son constructed the house all by himself and a portion of the house belonged to her.

Niccolò soon dozed off and when he opened his eyes, he saw some flickering lights of the hanging lamps of a few stores. Big open fire torches of the palace gate reflected on the paved path. There were hardly any people walking on the road except for weary vendors pushing their empty carts towards home.

"Oh, I am already in Firenze." Niccolò looked at city clock tower that showed it was 7:30 in the evening.

Good thing Mother Orissa packed some bread, vegetable soup, and gnocchi enough for two days, he thought.

Niccolò instructed the coach driver where to turn to reach their cottage. After paying the driver and bidding him goodbye, he turned towards his home. The cottage looked empty yet he felt very happy that he was going to sleep in his own bed. His mother kept everything at home ready for his convenience such as the open brick oven Niccolò used to warm up his food in no time. While he was eating his meal, he put the big iron vessel on the brick oven to warm water for his bath.

Soon he refreshed himself with a warm bath and was very happy to snuggle in his bed for a good night's sleep.

When Niccolò got up in the morning, through the misty window glass he could see the hazy sun rays struggling through the bare pear tree. He pushed himself to get up as he still wanted to snuggle a little more in his bed.

He remembered the note his mother gave him from someone inquiring about a commission. He dressed in his work clothes: a long, white overhaul reaching up to his ankles with sleeves, his head covered with a piece of cloth like a turban, and a woolen cape to cover him. Then he set off on his usual rapid stride towards his studio. A blast of cool breeze whipped his face numbing his nose. On his way he saw some vendors organizing their produce. He passed by the bakery where the smell of fresh-baked bread filled the air. He passed Ponte Vecchio where the bridge curved reminding him of Beatrice and the ache in his heart swelled by the fact that she will be married in a mere few days. He took a deep breath. *Yes, it was right here where she used to wait for me.* He was sad for a few minutes then tried to think about the commission as he hurried to reach the studio.

Once he arrived there, Niccolò was surprised to see Paolo there.

Paolo rushed to greet him. "Maestro, I am so glad to see you back in the studio."

"Thank you, Paolo. But I did not expect to see you as I thought you were still on vacation. I am glad to see you too."

"I arrived here yesterday and found Rossi Ormani's note pasted on the door. I figured he might send someone to check whether our studio was open or not. So I decided to come and see exactly what he wants."

"That is very nice of you. He sent a note through someone who was visiting Siena that he would like the finished sculpture before December 31ˢᵗ so you are right. Today is the 29ᵗʰ of December and we expected someone representing Rossi Ormani to come and visit us today."

"Maestro, do you want me to bring the relief of the putti in front?"

"I will help you. It is heavy, Paolo. I think we shall leave them there. Signore Rossi's men can figure out how to carry them."

"Oh, and Maestro, the putti look so lively, happy and playful. You are a genius for creating them."

Niccolò acknowledged his assistant's praise with a nod. "Remember you helped me with the garland they are holding? You are going to be a good sculptor."

"I am very fortunate to learn techniques from you."

"Paolo, let us start polishing Marzocco today."

As soon as Niccolò finished his sentence, they heard a galloping sound that drew closer and closer towards their studio.

"Maestro! Maestro! Signore Rossi's men are coming."

"Do not worry, Paolo. Let them come. Just letting you know that Signore Rossi is a businessman who is a close friend of Cosimo de' Medici."

Paolo was right. The horse-driven coach arrived at Niccolò's studio and stopped. Two men got out of the coach dressed in outfits made of fur trimming, one with a high-neck beige color widened from the shoulder down with a black hose, the other with a green, V-shaped neck with a beige hose. Both men wore black boots and hooded black capes all the way down to their ankles.

The one with the beige outfit had brown eyes and an aquiline nose. The other had a round face, hazel eyes, and a nose that suited his triangular face.

They walked to the door with wide steps, their shoulders back and chin high, looking directly at Niccolò and Paolo. *"Buongiorno."*

"*Boungiorno,*" Niccolò said.

"We are here to pick up Signore Rossi's sculptures," one of them said. "They are two separate pieces standing and holding a garland."

"Signore, do you see that piece? That is the one."

"Maestro, I see the relief which is one piece. I see two putti holding the garland. We are instructed to take two putti standing individually on the ground. What should we do?"

"I do not know," Niccolò replied. "I told Signore Rossi when he presented the commission that he can tell me his idea but I insist on having my artistic freedom. He told me that he wants two putti holding a garland."

"Maestro, please understand we must obey whatever he told us. He instructed us to pay the rest when we take the sculptures."

"Paolo bring me my bag," Niccolò said. Paolo got his bag which hung on a hook.

Niccolò took a bunch of florins and said to the men, "Here, take this money I am giving him back to Signore Rossi. Then get out. Do not disturb me. I am busy."

"Maestro, please understand—"

"Understand what?" Niccolò shouted. "He is just thinking about his idea will be sold to others." He turned to Paolo. "Please get me the hammer I will destroy the sculpture—"

"Maestro, no! Please do not!" Paolo ran to the sculpture and stood before it. He hugged the sculpture tightly, protecting the relief with putti so that Niccolò could not destroy the sculpture by breaking it in pieces with a hammer.

"Signores, please leave!" Paolo cried out. "Maestro is upset. Please leave our studio at once, I am begging you!"

Both men ran to their coach. Suddenly, the winter storm rustled through the fallen dry leaves on the paved path. The gray sky lit up with lightning and thunder rolled. The seagulls flying over the river Arno started screaming then big drops of rain started clattering on the windows as galloping sounds of the coach got fainter and fainter.

There was peace and calm for few minutes inside the studio until Niccolò broke the silence.

"Paolo, come out from there and let us have some olive bread and orange blossom water," Niccolò said quietly.

Paolo cried out loud with such emotion and said, "Thank you, my dear Maestro, for saving them. The putti are still alive! They are alive!"

Outside the wind whistled through the bare trees, echoing the sound: *The putti are alive, alive, alive, alive, alive…*

* * *

Suddenly, Niccolò heard his mother's voice and came back to the present. Niccolò turned to see his mother standing behind him, her arm hooked to the elbow of Amadeo who was proudly showing his vineyards to his grandmother. Then it dawned on Niccolò that he was still in Castellina with his family and the memory of that experience from a year ago was only that—a memory. He now had the opportunity to take his mother's advice and stay in Castellina to enjoy Christmas vacation with his loved ones.

Niccolò Spends Christmas in Castellina

December 25ᵗʰ 1421, Castellina—On this particular morning, though cool and breezy, the sun was struggling to come out through the mist and fog. Niccolò peered through the misty window and saw the green hills in the background of the gray sky. To him, it looked mysterious. He ruminated: *Peaceful with a touch of sadness—what is the message?* Just then he reminded himself he had to get ready soon.

He thought he slept very well, hardly recalling whether he woke up during the night. The last thing he remembered was that he put out the fire of the small charcoal portable room heater by putting some water on it and crashed inside his cozy bed.

Feeling rested and refreshed, Niccolò started to get dressed. First, he wore his round neck, long-sleeved, pleated, long white outfit, almost touching his ankles, tapered at the waist then flared down like folds. He looked at his wooly sweaters, one brown the other navy. He grabbed his navy one and selected his navy cap, and looked at the mirror on the wall of a small chamber attached to his bedroom.

He looked at his reflection in the mirror noticing his hair parted on the right side of his midline. Then he put on his navy cap after combing his hair. Pleased with himself, he was ready to welcome the day.

Niccolò was about to step out of his room to climb down the stairs when he heard Tia's voice. "I am making hot and spicy mead, a drink with berries."

Amadeo's voice was heard. "Mama, I will be there soon."

Niccolò looked forward to the honey and water fermented with yeast concoction his sister was making but just then, he remembered he had a gift for Tia so he returned to his room and took out a small rectangular package which he wrapped in his own art paper. He put the gift inside the long-hidden pocket of his outfit. It was heavy yet he thought it would be all right for a short time though he was anxious that the weight of the package might tear open his secret pocket and fall on the floor.

Niccolò slowly walked down the stairs and went to the dining area to meet Tia.

"Mamma baked some cookies, do you want some?

The sound as well as the smell of his mother's cookies lifted Niccolò's senses. "Of course. What spices did you add to the mead?

Tia was stirring her concoction in a pot. "Sage, rosemary, basil and anise."

Amadeo came running down the stairs dressed in his beige breech and red long-sleeved high neck sweater and beige vest with shiny buttons and crimson-colored embroidery of creepers.

Tia wore her green long dress, her hair in a bun at the nape of her neck. She wore a long, gold chain around her neck and two gold earrings. She appeared very fresh and happy in her green attire, her beautiful eyes sparkling with joy soon as she saw Amadeo climbing down the stairs.

Amadeo grabbed some cookies and a glass of hot mead drink.

"Uncle, I will be soon visiting Stefano and will bring your board," Amadeo said.

"Thank you, nephew," said Niccolò who turned to Tia. "When are you going to give me a tour of your part of the house?"

"We can do it now before we start setting up for lunch. Marcello, Angela, and Stefano will have lunch here and then we all are going to go to Marcello and Angela's dinner in your honor for coming to Castellina for Christmas."

"I am overcome with their gesture. It is really very nice of them," Niccolò said. "I will help you arrange the food for lunch but before that, I would like a tour of your part of the house."

312

"All right. Finish your drink and cookies and I will give you a tour."

Niccolò took a sip of his hot drink. "Delicious."

He was very eager to see Tia's part of the house so after he finished his drink, Niccolò followed Tia to the opposite side of the kitchen where there was a short, narrow corridor just behind the living room which led to a wooden door that opened to an anteroom, a small space with few closets and a big mirror on the wall and shelves on its side. There were different sized combs and barrettes, and hairpins on a small wooden tray. Niccolò figured out this was Tia's dressing room where there was an oval opening through which Niccolò saw a bedroom with lacy covered pillows and a thick, gold-colored comforter and side table with a covered lantern. There were oval recesses on the white wall where thick candles stood on a candle holder, a big window on the opposite side of the foot of the bed with a heavy, beige silk curtain. There was a door which led to another bedroom of similar décor.

As they entered the second bedroom Tia said, "This one is for mother when she visits."

Niccolò's face brightened with joy. "Wonderful. I am amazed Amadeo thought of all of this and planned to construct it with his family in mind."

There was a room next to it smaller than the bedroom which had shelves and counter tops with a big window facing the backyard. Tia said, "This will be my sewing and embroidery room."

Niccolò was overwhelmed with joy. "See, Tia, your son loves and respects you so much that he did not forget that you love to spend time with your artwork. I do not know how to express in words how very happy I am for you, my dear sister."

Tia was almost in tears. "Dear brother, I do not know how either. Let me show you my kitchen, the dining space and prayer room."

"Oh, there is a prayer room?"

"Yes, it is a small space with a white marble altar and two marble steps below the altar. The floor is made of polished wood. There are two small oval recesses on both sides of the altars for candles. There is an oval chandelier which hangs from the ceiling and two wooden polished benches. Now that you have heard about it, I will show you after the tour of the kitchen and dining room."

They started walking towards the kitchen which was a smaller version of Amadeo's kitchen with a brick-layered open fire oven in a recess, few closets and hooks for hanging kitchen utensils. Beyond the far end of the kitchen there was a room with a dining table with four chairs that looked mahogany polished and new.

At the end of the dining room, they stepped forward through a door to a small room and saw the marble altar and two small marble steps. There was a window on the side which overlooked the front yard. On the altar there was a mahogany wooden cross.

Suddenly Niccolò remembered the gift he brought for Tia. He turned his back to his sister whose expression changed with knitted brows as she emitted short breaths.

Niccolò somehow managed to get the package out from his hidden pocket and handed it over to her. This time, Tia was breathless for a short time as her knitted brows went straight upwards and with wide open eyes, she stepped backwards.

"Tia, please open it."

Niccolò watched as she opened the rectangular package and saw her mouth drop open in surprise to see a marble relief sculpted with mother Mary and the child Jesus. The background of the relief was painted in blue, the sky with white patchy clouds. There was a golden halo around mother Mary and her sculpted clothing folds were bordered with gold. The eyes of the mother and child were sculpted from marble and the apples of the eyes were painted in black. Mother was looking down at her child and the child gazed up at his mother, touching his left cheek on his mother's right cheek, his right hand resting across Mother's upper part of the chest. The child's sculpted marble clothes were golden in color.

Tia's voice choked with tears and with her cracking voice, she exclaimed, "My dear brother, this is a priceless gift! It is so beautiful!" Tears rolled down her cheeks while brother and sister hugged as Niccolò's face brightened with joy.

"My dear sister, I am very glad you like it," he spoke in a very low voice.

Tia put the relief on the marble altar, made the sign of the cross, bowed, then turned to Niccolò with a smile. "This is the end of the tour my brother."

"I am so happy for you. At last you got what you deserve," Niccolò said.

"Thank you, my dear brother. Let us start to set up for lunch before Mamma comes home. She will be happy to see us both preparing lunch."

"Yes, I agree."

They walked quickly to Amadeo's side of the house where the dining table was already covered with a red tablecloth and on the top of it, covered by another fine white, lacy cloth that Niccolò recognized was created by Tia.

"I will first decorate the room by hanging the pine garlands on the wall," Niccolò said. "Do you want me to border the table with some garland? Then we have to remove the lacy cover from the table."

"That is a very good idea, brother."

Niccolò started hanging pine garlands with red berries on both walls and some smaller versions around the recesses of the wall where the tall candles stood. Then he put some around the candelabra with three candles which were standing in the middle of the table.

Tia was impressed with Niccolò's decorative arrangement. "It looks very magical and Christmas-like."

"Thank you," Niccolò said. "How about your plan of displaying the food?"

"As we enter the dining space, there will be another small table by the side of this table with dinner plates, napkins and silverware, next to this dining table. At that end, we will place our big pot of tortellini soup and place some soup bowls close to it. Then sweet potato salad and parmesan brussel sprout salad, fried turnip slides on roasted garlic bread, Rigatino bacon, Salami Tuscano, grilled Tuscan sausages, prosciutto, glazed ham steak then the desserts: almond rice, Panforte and a basket of fruit with apples, oranges, pears and then a plate of roasted chestnuts."

"All right, I need your help in showing me the serving trays and containers for all the items."

"Do not worry, I will help you," Tia said.

In no time, the table displayed all the featured foods except the tortellini soup.

"Everyone is going to help themselves to their own food and we will sit in the living room, is that what you intend to do?" Niccolò asked.

"Yes, that is the plan."

"So there will be seven of us in the living room. At present, six of us have seats so I can move two chairs from the dining room to the living room then it will be enough for everyone and one chair will be extra."

"Oh brother, I cannot thank you enough. Amadeo will get the wine glasses for the drinks and he has several types of wine which he will serve; he took charge of that. I will place some cured olives and cheese on a tray and a few small plates there on the center table."

Niccolò was about to move chairs from the dining room to the living room when Amadeo and his friend Stefano arrived. Amadeo intervened and said, "Zio, I can do that. Here is Stefano, my friend, who got the board for your artwork."

"*Boungiorno* Maestro," Stefano said, "please show me where I can place the board."

"Grazie, Stefano," Niccolò said, "please take it upstairs."

"No problem."

Stefano followed Niccolò upstairs to his room. Upon entering, Stefano suggested, "Maestro, the wall between the door and the window will be the ideal place as you will get light and there is another window just opposite that will add more brightness to the room."

The board was around nine and half feet tall and more than five feet wide in a stable stand with a back rest. The surface of the board was smooth. There were clip-like devices to secure the art paper on the board.

"Maestro, I can fix the art paper on the board if you want me to do that."

"That would be quite a huge help for me."

The art paper was fixed on the board and Niccolò was overwhelmed with joy, his face flushed and his voice cracked. "Stefano, I do not have words to thank you. You have helped me a lot."

"You are very welcome. Let me know if you need anything else."

Niccolò gave a Stefano a warm hug. "Thank you. Now, let us join the rest of the family downstairs."

Stefano's parents, Marcello and Angela, had already arrived along with mother Orissa who went to her room to freshen up.

Excited to see Niccolò again, Marcello shook the sculptor's hand. After they shook hands very warmly, they sat down on the sofa where Angela greeted Niccolò.

"Nice to meet you again on such a special day like Christmas," Angela said.

When mother Orissa arrived in the living room, everyone said in a chorus "Merry Christmas!"

Amadeo went near the fireplace to add another log of wood as the flames of the fireplace started rising high with blue and yellow flames in concert with cozy and happy moments of the Christmas gatherings.

Mother Orissa asked Amadeo to serve the drinks. Everyone remarked that it was very special to taste the red and white wine from his winery. Mother Orissa served everyone the cheese and cured olives. She was pleased with Tia and Niccolò's lunch spread.

The mood of the Christmas gathering was in full swing with a chorus of cheers as everyone held their wine goblets up to toast to health, happiness and good cheer.

After sipping the wine, Niccolò, Marcello and Angela complimented Amadeo on the wine's remarkable taste. Angela said she was very tempted to sip more and more until she reluctantly warned then stopped herself.

Mother Orissa and Tia was very pleased to hear comments about Amadeo's selection from his winery. They both commented how pleasantly surprised they were that Amadeo could make such delicious wine.

Then Marcello stood up to say he had a special announcement. "The Siena Cathedral people found out that Maestro Niccolò is visiting so they requested me to ask Maestro if he would be very kind enough to spend a few minutes of his time at my home to speak to the person from the cathedral."

Niccolò kept quiet for a few minutes without any answer. Everyone in the room starting feeling uncomfortable and anxious thinking about what Niccolò's answer would be. At last, Niccolò took a deep breath. "Yes, I can afford to spend a few minutes with the person from the cathedral."

Everyone was relieved with Niccolò's response. Then mother Orissa announced, "Time to start our lunch with tortellini soup and freshly-baked bread."

Niccolò got up and asked everyone to proceed towards the dining space and asked his mother to relax and that he was going to serve the soup to everyone. Niccolò carried out the task of serving the soup and at the end, he brought two soup bowls with bread, one for his mother and another one for his sister. They both were overcome with emotion, with moist eyes and flushed faces. "Thank you. It is so thoughtful of you."

The misty Christmas afternoon passed merrily with tasting different food, joyous conversation and sipping wines. Outside, the gentle breeze grew stronger and stronger as inside, the crackling sound of the fireplace interrupted the conversation, demanding more logs.

"We are taking leave," Stefano said.

"We will see you soon at our house," Angela said.

"I am also leaving. Thank you for the scrumptious feast," Marcello said. "I have the responsibility to light the chandeliers and the fireplace. See you soon at our house."

Through the window, it seemed the misty daylight was fading in the evening shadow, though the Christmas celebration would soon continue.

Rudy in Paris

December, 1964

Their Air France flight safely touched down at Orly International Airport where the group of friends passed through passport, luggage and customs lines smoothly. When they exited the airport, they saw two gentlemen waving the banner of "Gateway to France Travel" alerting them of the agency that arranged their trip.

The men approached Amita, Samir, Rudy and Sharmi politely asking to accompany them to a big, black luxury car where the men opened the car doors and loaded their luggage in the trunk.

"Mesdames et Messieurs, please be comfortable during your ride," said the driver. "It will take more than an hour to reach your hotel."

They all said "Thank you" and sat on black, padded, shiny leather seats. The luxury car started slowly and soon took its speed to its fullest.

They were excited to see the roads and landscapes that lead to the Paris city center where cars buzzed along in traffic. Soon they immersed themselves with the spectacular architecture of Paris as they passed avenues with trees and large mansions with curled, leafy cornices. Noticing the mansions carefully, one could see that just below the cornice, decorated cemented creeper or garlands punctuated with cemented tassel as a border ran all around the mansion.

"Your hotel is very nice and is very close to the opera house which is one of the main tourist attractions," said the travel agency attendant.

"We have a bus tour at 8 tonight," Samir said. "Before we board the bus, we would like to eat. Is there a place where we can get some takeout food?"

"Oh yes Monsieur, but we will reach at your hotel approximately 6:15 and by the time you check in and go to your room, it will be nearly 7, so there will not be enough time to go to a takeout place to have your dinner. In the lobby, at the east corner there is a coffee shop that serves ready-made food like soups, bisque, potage, bouillabaisse, different kind of breads: baguette, croissant and also a heavy stew with herbs, vegetables, meat, thickened with marrow bone, called Pot eu Feu. Then there are different kinds of crepes: éclair, macaroon, crème brûlée and a variety of pastries."

"That sounds very good and convenient for us."

When they reached their Hotel Nolinski, they were really pleased to see the impressive hotel. The four friends went to the coffee shop at the corner of the lobby and ordered bouillabaisse, baguettes and mineral water. They really enjoyed their soup, a mixture of seafood, herbs and spices that went well with fresh baguettes.

The hotel rooms were very spacious and luxurious. Sharmi got a smaller, cozy room close to Amita and Samir but completely separate, a small unit on its own. They stored their luggage in their room and within minutes, had to go down to the main entrance of the hotel to board the bus for the evening tour.

Samir, Sharmi and Rudy kept thanking Amita for coming up with the idea and the planning of the Paris trip. They didn't expect to stay in such a grand place. Just as they stepped outside of their hotel and stood by the main entrance, the friends looked up in time to witness the buildings and hotels nearby, including theirs, lit up.

"Wow, it all looks so magical," Sharmi said. "No wonder why Paris is called the City of Light."

They all agreed and started teasing Sharmi that she initially resisted coming to Paris, jokingly reminding her of her words, "No, I will pass, you all go."

They had a good laugh just as the big tour bus arrived. Once they boarded the bus, the foursome chose the seats they liked: Sharmi at the window and Rudy close by her side. Amita and Samir sat three rows back from Rudy and Sharmi.

The tour guide took the microphone and introduced himself as Claude and acknowledged the bus driver, Bernard. "Raise your hand if you are visiting Paris for first time," Claude said.

Out of the thirty people in the bus, four of them raised their hands.

"*Merci*," Claude said. "Bernard is going to first take us to *Musée du Louvre*, which sits along the bank of the Seine River. Can anyone guess why the Louvre was built?

Allen, a British tourist, raised a hand. "It was built as a royal palace," he said.

"You are partly right," Claude said. "It was built as a fortress in 1190, but reconstructed in the 16th century to serve as a royal palace. During its time as a royal residence, the Louvre grew tremendously. In 1682, Louis XIV moved the royal residence to Versailles. In 1793, the National Assembly opened the Louvre Museum with 537 paintings."

The bus continued moving as Claude took a break. The four friends marveled at the way the cityscape of Paris illuminated, with the evening's magic touch on buildings they passed by. Christmas decorations accentuated the windows of the shops and the streets lined bare trees decorated with different colors of blinking lights, festive images that moved backwards while the bus moved forward through a thin layer of fog.

Claude took his microphone. "Mesdames et Messieurs, the Louvre of today was created by Napoleon who wanted to be in charge of creating a collection of art in the Louvre which he renamed in 1802, the Napoleon Museum."

Sharmi quickly took out a small notebook from her purse and started writing the date and other notes.

Rudy smiled at her. "I told you that you will learn a lot." He gave her a loving nudge. Sharmi smiled back and touched Rudy's hand softly.

"Napoleon wanted to create a museum in France with a collection of art from all over the world," Claude continued. "He enlarged its collection from his military campaign, private donations, and commissions he made. Napoleon's collections included the spoils from Belgium, Italy, Prussia, Austria. When Napoleon abdicated, 5,000 works were returned to the country of their origin. The name of the museum was then reverted to its original name."

The bus drew closer to the Louvre and from a distance everyone saw the lights and the expansive open courtyard.

"Madame et Messieurs, I will give you ten to fifteen minutes to stroll around the courtyard," Claude announced. "Please return promptly."

Everyone got down from the bus with their cameras and flashlights as they scanned their surroundings in awe of the grandeur of the building which looked majestic and colossal. The tourists were very excited about taking photos at night with diffuse lights all around the building, with a lighted lamp post at the courtyard and a lighted fountain in full force murmuring its song—all together felt like a mesmerizing call for the tourists.

When Sharmi, Rudy, Amita and Samir got down from the bus, the couples decided to take two different directions and agreed to meet at the fountain before they returned to their bus.

"Sharmi," Rudy said, "let us go back in time. First, close your eyes and imagine hearing horses trotting on the courtyard with royal guards. There is a royal coach waiting for the king—that I'm not sure who—Louis the—"

Sharmi enthusiastically interjected. "Can the royal guards see us from their own time zone? I don't know but they cannot catch us," she remarked with a teasing tone.

They shared a hearty laugh. Rudy was pleased that Sharmi seemed to have fun using her imagination. They looked at each other then exchanged a hug.

Rudy looked at the watch. "Oh no, it is already time to go to the fountain."

They arrived at the fountain where droplets of water sprayed all over and a distant, wet smell filled the air blending with a cool, moist breeze. They looked through a wet watery screen and saw Amita and Samir waving their hands gesturing it was time to board the bus.

Just as they returned to their seats, Claude took the microphone. "One more thing I want to mention about the architecture of the Louvre: it is an example of French classics composed of paired Corinthian columns, arches with pavilions at the corners of façades. These architectural designs influenced many buildings including the U.S. Capitol in Washington D.C. and the Metropolitan Museum in New York. I hope everyone has their daytime tickets to get inside the museum."

Everyone responded, "Yes."

"Our next stop will be the Arc de Triomphe."

The bus started moving as Claude took his microphone again. "I am going to give you a short history of the Arc de Triomphe. It was designed by Jean Chalgrin in 1806 and is iconographic, pits heroically nude French youth against bearded Germans in a chain mail. The arch has a height of 50 meters (164 feet) and a width of 45 meters (148 feet) and a depth of 22 meters (72 feet). Its large vault, 29 meters (95.8 feet) high and 14.9 (48 feet) wide. It is located at the right bank of River Seine at the center of dodecagonal configuration (3D polyhedron with twelve vertices and twelve edges) of twelve radiating avenues. It was commissioned after the victory of emperor Napoleon "Austeritz" at the peak of his fortune. Laying the foundation took two years and in 1810 when Napoleon entered Paris from the west with his new bride Archduchess Marie-Louise of Austria, he had a wooden mockup of the completed arch constructed.

"The architect Jean Chalgrin died in 1811 and the work was taken over by Jean-Nicolas Huyot. It was completed until the reign of King Louise Phillipe between 1833 to 1836 by the architect Louis Robert Goust. That is in short, the history, but I will mention a few important events just to let you know. Arc de Triomphe honored those who fought and died for France in the French Revolution and Napoleonic wars. The names of all French victories and generals are inscribed in its inner and outer surfaces. Beneath the vault lies the tomb of unknown soldiers. Any questions?"

"Can we go up?" Sharmi asked.

"Yes," said Claude, "you pay a fee and walk up 208 steps to the top and have a lovely view of Paris."

Everyone laughed.

"What kind of material is the Arc de Triomphe made of?" Samir asked.

"It's made of limestone," Claude said. "A few more details: on December 1840, Napoleon's remains were brought back to France from St. Helena and passed under the Arc on the way to its final resting place at Invalides. Prior to burial in the Pantheon, Victor Marcello's body displayed under the Arc during the night of May 1885. On August 7, 1919, Charles Godfrey flew his plane successfully under the Arc.

"All right, Mesdames et Messieurs, I will give you 10 to 15 minutes to go around the Arc and take photos. It is all lighted so there is no fee for walking round the Arc. Our next stop will be the Eiffel Tower where the bus will also stop for 15 minutes. Other places like Champs-Élysées you can have a view from the bus which will slow down and stop, but you must enjoy viewing these other landmarks from your own seats."

All the riders got down. Sharmi needed help to get down the bus as the steps of the bus were too steep for her but Rudy lifted her and delicately brought her down.

The group of friends walked closely together and stopped to take group pictures and savor the architecture and the city lights. As the evening drew its curtain, they felt a little tired as the day started out with their journey from England to Paris and proceeded with lots of sightseeing and excitement that began from the time they left home.

The impressive Arc was illuminated as it majestically stood there with its grandeur, reminding everyone of its colorful and eventful history as though it were only yesterday. After the photo session, the four of them gazed at the Arc one more time before moving slowly back towards the bus.

"It reminds me of the Gateway of India," Rudy said. "I was on a ship during my voyage to England and the ship blew the whistle and, slowly but surely, the Gateway of India moved backwards leaving the shores of India behind. Those moments of time made me heartsick because I felt I was leaving everything related to my past and diving deep into the ocean of the unknown."

When the bus began moving, all the passengers started speaking excitedly in fragmented and muffled sentences about the Eiffel Tower that filled the air of the bus.

Rudy and Sharmi tightly held hands and looked at each other with disbelief that they would finally see the Eiffel Tower together.

The bus stopped at a distance when Claude held the microphone. "Madame et Messieurs, I know you're all excited so I'll try to be brief about the La Tour Eiffel. This most recognizable landmark was built to celebrate the centenary of the French Revolution during the 1889 exposition Universelle at Champs de Mars, and the 100-year anniversary of the Fall of Bastille. The authority staged an open competition to design a spectacular centerpiece to the World's Fair. Out of 107 proposals, a committee selected the design submitted by Gustave Eiffel along with engineer Stephan Sauvestre and engineer Maurice Koechlin and Emile Nouger. For four decades, it was the tallest building until the Chrysler building was built in 1930 in New York. Construction lasted for two years, two months and five days. It is made of iron, to be specific, puddle iron."

"What is puddle iron?" asked Eric, one of the tourists from Australia.

"Good question," Claude replied. "It's when an excess of carbon is removed from iron."

"Is it the same as wrought iron?" Rudy asked.

"Yes, it is, it makes the iron stronger, durable and malleable and becomes easy to work with," Claude said. "I have to tell you that, although the Eiffel Tower is a worldwide symbol of romance, its radical design inspired anything but love in the hearts of 300 prominent Parisian artists and intellectuals including Guy De Maupassant who signed a manifesto that ran in Le Temps on Valentine's Day 1887 which I'll read to you: 'We writers, painters, sculptors and architects, passionate lovers of beauty until now, hereby protest with all our might and indignation in the name of French art and history against the construction of the useless monstrous Eiffel Tower.'

"Guy de Maupassant later used to dine in the restaurant of the Eiffel Tower so for that period of time, as he dined, he would not see the monstrous structure towering the city. Since Gustave Eiffel footed 80 percent of the tower's construction cost, he was permitted to have the structure stand for 20 years to recoup his investment before it passed to the Parisian government which planned to dismantle it for scrap as it was only built for the World's Fair. Seeking a way to prove the structure's strategic utility, Eiffel erected an antenna atop the tower and financed experiments with wireless telegraphy which started in 1898. The French military realized the value of sending and receiving wireless messages which caused the city to renew Eiffel's concession when it expired in 1909. The French military used the tower to intercept enemy messages. The French arrested and convicted legendary spy Mata Hari. That is in short, the history. Now the tower has 109 stories and 1710 steps, is 984-feet tall, weighs 10,000 tons and is usually illuminated by 5 billion lights. Every hour after sundown, the tower sparkles five minutes on the hour." Claude paused to catch his breath. "I will stop now and please enjoy the view of this monumental structure for 15 minutes to walk around this worldwide symbol of romance.

The passengers got down and walked around, gazing up at the amazing structure. Amita and Samir chose an ideal vantage point to take pictures as Rudy and Sharmi walked together holding hands still not believing that they were standing in front of this most famous marvel of the world.

"We must come back here tomorrow afternoon and climb up to the top," Rudy said. "Don't worry, they have a lift."

"Oh, I'm glad," Sharmi said with a light laugh. "I don't want to climb stairs."

Rudy winked at her. "Don't worry. I'm strong enough to carry you."

Sharmi gasped in mock shock. "Oh no, in front of a crowd? No way!"

Rudy laughed. "Sharmi, now that I'm so close to the tower, I think it's more appealing when I see it from a distance. From afar, I can see the tower as a whole."

"Yes, I see your point," Sharmi said.

"Look at how it's sparkling this evening! What time is it?"

"It's nine o'clock."

Rudy came closer and pulled Sharmi in a warm embrace until it looked as though she was almost hidden under Rudy's long unbuttoned coat. She was very cozy yet felt her heart pounding hard, a warm sensation emanating all over her body.

They were both silent for these precious few moments as if to tighten the bond between them deep in silence. They gazed at each other with moist eyes before they started walking hand-in-hand back to the bus.

Claude welcomed back all the passengers and counted them. "Please be comfortable while we will drive you through one of the most recognizable avenues in the world—the Champs-Élysées, which is French for "Elysian Fields," the place for dead 'heros' in Greek mythology. Champs-Élysées draws a perfectly straight line from the Louvre through Tuileries Garden and Place de la Concorde and where the Obelisk of Luxor bisects the Arc de Triomphe until the reign of Louis XIV. Champs-Élysées was largely occupied by the fields and kitchen garden and was laid out in 1667 by André Le Nôtre as an extension of Tuileries Garden."

"Who is André Le Nôtre?" Amita asked.

"Good question," said Claude. "He was a French landscaper, architect and principal gardener of Louis XIV. He was born in Paris in 1613 to a family of gardeners and lived in Tuileries where his grandfather and father were gardeners. André Le Nôtre designed the Versailles Garden and other places in Paris and abroad. He designed several places in Italy and designed the Greenwich Park in London and plans for Windsor Castle. Coming back to this renowned avenue, the Champs-Élysées has been the site of military parades. At present, it is known for theater, cafés and luxury shops."

As the bus entered the beautiful avenue, passengers kept chatting with each other about the unique characteristic styles that stand out as French. They commented how shops and cafés all looked very unique.

Sharmi and Rudy suggested they all come back to Paris again to leisurely walk along this famous avenue. Rudy put his arm around Sharmi who seemed to like the gesture very much and rewarded him a sweet smile in return.

Theirs was the last tour and by the time the tour was done, by 10 that evening, the group of friends grew tired.

"Sharmi, tomorrow will be another day for exploring," Rudy said. "After breakfast, we'll be at the Louvre and then we could eat at a café there and the two of us will visit the Eiffel Tower by ourselves."

"Why just us two?" Sharmi asked. "What about Samir and Amita?"

"Oh, they have their own plans too." Rudy said casually, trying to conceal his excitement. "Then in the evening, we'll all dine together aboard a ship cruising the River Seine. Of course, we'll have to go and change into more presentable clothes so we'll be fresh for dinner. I'll have to wear a tie as that is the dress code for this particular restaurant."

"Oh, so I have to wear something fancy?"

"Yes," Rudy said, "but anyway, a saree always looks quite formal." He paused to look at her intently. "Before we get down to the hotel, here is a good night hug."

Sharmi felt shy, all flushed and red as she saw two ladies watching them. When the bus stopped in front of the Hotel Nolinski, Amita, Samir, Sharmi and Rudy thanked Bernard and Claude and wished all their fellow riders a good night and a pleasant time in Paris.

Then the bus slowly proceeded to get the rest of the tourists back to their hotels as shadows of waving hands reflected through the glass windows as the bus moved towards the main street.

Settling in his hotel room that night, Rudy picked up Niccolò's biography pleased to know that as he was reading the part where Niccolò celebrated the Christmas holidays with his family, Rudy too was celebrating Christmas week with friends. Two men centuries apart yet connected in spirit.

Niccolò's Last Few Days at Castellina

Niccolò looked through the window and saw the three hills which surrounded the areas where Amadeo and the Casini family lived. The sky was overcast with grayish cotton ball clouds and the hills were shrouded by a misty veil as sunlight diffused through the veil of mist, scattering the color on the hills in different shades of grayish blue.

He looked at the sketch of the Prophet and started talking to his creation: "I was so engrossed with you that I forgot to ask our neighbor about their lives and let them talk about themselves." Niccolò shook his head. "It is unpardonable. Today, no more of you and no more work for now. I want to talk to Marcello, Angela and Stefano who seemed to be a nice, young man who helped me a lot."

Today, instead of his work clothes, he dressed in a brown brief just below his knee, a yellow, long-sleeved cotton shirt with ruffles and a brown vest with gold buttons.

He combed his hair in front of the mirror that hung on a wall and tried to put a dark brown band on his forehead below the hairline. While he was lifting up his thick wavy hair at the back to tie a band at the back of his neck, he found a few gray hairs peeping. He stopped for a minute and took a deep breath. *It is a reminder that time passes by. Time waits for no one,* he thought.

As he got ready to go downstairs to talk with his mother and sister, Niccolò took another deep breath and whispered, "Mother is getting older too. I have to pay attention and spend more time listening to her." His heart squeezed with anxiety and started beating faster. He rushed going downstairs and found mother Orissa and sister Tia waiting for him. He greeted them good morning and gave them both a warm hug.

Mother and Tia urged him to enjoy the hot drink they made with roasted barley and honey.

"I made Cornetti with cream," his mother said.

Niccolò beamed at the mention of his favorite flaky bread rolls. "That sounds delicious."

After Tia brought the hot orzo and the cream filled-croissants, they all huddled around the fireplace.

"This is delectable." He took a sip of the hot drink. "I want to discuss with you both your future plans. You know I will continue to do what I do best till the end, but I want you both to be happy and comfortable, not work too hard especially for me."

"What do you mean?" his mother asked.

"Well, you work hard preparing food for me and doing things for my comfort," Niccolò said. "Tia helps you but now, she has her own place so she will start living in her own house in the near future. Mother, your workload will be more."

"Do not worry, brother. I have a plan," Tia said. "I will spend two months with Mamma in Florence and then she could come to Castellina to stay with me as long as she wants. Then when she wants to go back to Florence, I will again stay with her for a month or so and then, we can all celebrate Christmas in Castellina whenever you can take a break and take some time off. How does that sound?"

Niccolò was pleased his sister had the foresight to come up with a plan that ensured their mother was taken care of. "That sounds good."

"If mother needs help when I am not in Florence, we can arrange someone to help her," Tia said. "There are some ladies willing to help Mamma during daytime."

"I did not know that could be arranged," Niccolò said.

"It can be arranged. That is not an issue at all, dear brother. You carry on your artistic dream. We are proud of you. It is God's gift to you and to us as we feel lucky you have answered your calling in life. Do not worry about us."

Niccolò took a deep breath, moved by his sister's assurance. He felt small, never thinking his sister loved him so deeply enough to give much consideration about his life as an artist.

"Thank you, dear sister, I wish I can do more. You are so thoughtful and considerate."

"Thank you, my dear brother."

All this time, their mother watched with pride how kindly her children interacted on behalf of her own care. But on to other matters. "We are going to spend our New Year's Eve at the Casini's home. I think I will leave the party just after midnight and Angela had so kindly offered me to spend the night there so that Stefano does not have to make an extra trip to take me back to our house. Then their carriage driver will come the next morning for his duty and he can drop me off at our house."

"That is a very nice plan," Tia said.

"Mamma, I wanted to tell you for a while that I really appreciate what you have done for me and what you still continue to do—work hard for my comfort." Niccolò took a deep breath. "I came to this level of artistry where I am now as a result of your support and encouragement."

"My dear son, that's what mothers everywhere around the world do."

"All right, Mamma, I plan to spend two more days here before I go back to Firenze as I will be busy with the Prophet and then with The Feast of Herod," Niccolò said. "Sometimes I feel as though I have taken for granted all that you do for me as I get deeply involved with my work. But I want you to know that I am grateful for all that you have done."

"Dear son, do not worry. You just keep enjoying what you do and that's what makes me happy."

Niccolò gave a big hug to his mother as Tia came closer and the three of them bonded closely together.

Niccolò was all ready for the day. "Can I prepare lunch for all of us?"

"That would be nice," his mother said. "I am baking bread. It will be ready by lunch time and something to go with it."

"Mamma, I can prepare potato and leek soup," he offered. "I know you have fresh leek from the garden."

"Wonderful Niccolò!" his mother said. "Please make the soup in a bigger pot so we can take some for the Casinis."

"Do we have some cooked ham?" Niccolò asked his mother.

"There's some leftover ham over there."

"I will cut them into small pieces and put them in the soup."

"That is a wonderful idea, my dear son."

Just then, Amadeo came down. "What is going on?"

"We are all excited your uncle is preparing lunch for us," Tia said.

"Amazing," Amadeo said, "Zio, can I help you?"

"Of course, you can," Niccolò said, "but it is not a grand lunch."

"It does not matter whether or not you are cooking a grand feast for us," Amadeo said. "What is on the menu?"

"Oh, it is just potato and leek soup and grandma's freshly-baked bread."

"I love that."

The house was filled with the aroma of baking bread as Amadeo put another log in the fireplace and Tia brought the hot orzo drink and Grandma Orissa handed a cream-filled croissant to Amadeo who took a bite and then a sip of mead.

"Oh, the two together go very well," Amadeo said, gleefully.

Niccolò busied himself in the kitchen chopping the leeks after cleaning them thoroughly.

Amadeo entered the kitchen. "Uncle, can I help you?"

"Please peel the potatoes. That would be a great help."

Niccolò looked at the handwritten recipe by his mother. "Mamma said to make this soup in a large container." So he placed a large iron container on the brick-layered cave of the open fire oven. Then he poured some olive oil in the cooking container but was not sure whether it was enough so he added a little more then put all the chopped leeks to sauté with a few cloves of garlic and some thyme.

Amadeo peeled the potatoes. "What is next?"

"Chop them in pieces and we have to sauté them with leek."

Amadeo followed instructions and Niccolò took the chopped potatoes and put them in the container and started to sauté the potatoes with the leek.

After Niccolò saw the leeks were already wilted, now it was time to put salt and ground pepper, a few bay leaves and chicken broth already prepared by his mother before covering the container with an iron lid.

He took out some of the burning logs from the fireplace and put them in a water-filled container. The idea was to simmer it for a while so that the potato and leeks were thoroughly cooked. After that, the next step was to thoroughly blend them with a hand-held blender made with iron wire. The elongated blender with a bulbous lower end and tapering elongated upper end, which was like a stem, had to be operated by rolling between the palms to blend the vegetables completely when some cream was added to make it tastier and smoother. Niccolò and Amadeo took turns in the blending process.

At some point, Niccolò said to Amadeo, "I think it is done and looks smooth enough. I added some chives, and oh, my special ingredient—small pieces of mother's roasted ham."

"Uncle, it looks delicious," Amadeo said. "I will ask Nonna and Mamma to come look at it."

An excited Amadeo rushed inside the living room to call his mother and grandmother who came to the kitchen immediately. Orissa and Tia were delighted to see the artistry of potato leek soup created by Niccolò and his assistant, Amadeo.

Mother Orissa was all smiles and Tia joked that both of them could open a business like a trattoria. The four of them laughed.

Then mother Orissa said, "Let me bring a nice container to pour some of this soup for Marcello and his family. I have baked some bread with green olives that will go very well with the soup."

Everyone agreed and happy that mother Orissa was proud to share with others another one of Niccolò's skills—his culinary talents.

Niccolò's Work in the Louvre

Dec. 27, 1964—After a good night's sleep, Amita, Samir, Rudy and Sharmi congregated at the dining hall on the third floor of the hotel large enough to hold sixty people at a time. Individual tables of four were decorated with fresh yellow daisies, silverware, round white plates, side plates, fine, white gold-rimmed teacups with matching plates and fan-shaped red napkins on a white tablecloth. The dining area, enclosed all around with big glass windows, felt like an open space with lots of lights on the ceiling and on the surrounding wall. The food display featured unique, fresh fruits cut and artfully arranged, some resembling flowers, others in different shapes: round, cubes, heart-shaped, displayed in different groups with contrasting colors. The charcuterie spread featured varieties of cheese, bread, pastries like a variety of croissants: plain, chocolate, and almond. And the beverage counter offered different fruit juice flavors. The four friends marveled at this self-service breakfast smorgasbord.

In addition to the breakfast spread, the dining hall offered a menu featuring specialized meal combinations that included sausage, bacon, eggs, and ham ready to be cooked the way guests preferred. Tea and coffee were also served by the waiters.

The group of friends grabbed a table near the window and filled their plates with fruit, croissant, eggs cooked-to-order in different ways: poached, sunnyside up and sausages. Since they were accustomed to preparation of good tea being a ritual in England, they were uncertain about the tea in Paris and ordered coffee instead. After the sumptuous breakfast, they went down to the lobby to take a cab to the Louvre.

Both couples planned their museum visit ahead, making a list of things they would like to see so they wouldn't drown in the Louvre's vast ocean of art collection. They reminded themselves this was their first visit.

The foursome boarded a cab and arrived at the Louvre amazed to see the grand, palatial museum during daytime. To them it was majestic, the size of the open courtyard seemed more open. It was beyond the limit of their eyes to catch the boundary.

They also saw the long line for tickets, noting the skip-the-line service of reserving tickets in advance was certainly the better option.

On this day nearing the end of December 1964, the sky was gray, and luckily not raining, though the cold wind blew fiercely through the bare trees. At times, it was strong enough to blow some of the ladies' woolen caps. Someone's cap got caught on Amita's feet while she was tightly holding on to her own headcover.

By the time the foursome came to the end of line, they felt the tips of their noses become frozen and numb. As soon as they entered the Louvre, a comfortable, warmth enveloped them that continued as they climbed the stairs to see the Winged Victory of Samothrace. The four friends felt lucky to hear a tour guide's commentary about certain works of art especially since they were unable to secure a tour guide. So they took an opportunity to enjoy the tourists' interaction with their guide.

"Is this the oldest statue?" One of the tourists asked.

"Yes," said the guide, "it is one of the oldest and most influential statues. Greek statues are much older than Roman statues and also rare to find. Only a fraction of them survived to present day and the Winged Victory of Samothrace is perhaps the best of the bunch."

"Why and who were the people it was sculpted for?" Another tour group member asked.

"Good question," said Romero, the tour guide. "The statue was placed by the Rhodian people in commemoration of a specific naval victory."

Then the guide asked if anyone noticed anything about the posture and the dress of the statue. Amita, Samir, Rudy and Sharmi kept quiet as they didn't belong to this guided tour. Instead, they whispered amongst themselves that she looked majestic and like a bird perched on a pedestal of her choice.

A boy about seven or eight-years-old from Lancaster, England raised his hand. "Oh, the lady has wide wings and her body is pushed forward."

"That is excellent, very good observation," the guide said. "It is a highly theatrical presentation with monumentally wide wings and forward thrusting of the body. The technical mastery of the work as the way it imagined the elements around it give an impression of a wet dress, the ways the folds were placed close to the body and also there was evidence of wind ruffling Victory's dress. The figure creates a deliberate relationship to the imaginary space around the Goddess, the wind that carried her and which she is fighting off sharing to keep steady. At the same time, expanded space heightens the symbolic force of work, the wind and the sea are suggested as a metaphor of struggle and destiny and the divine grace of God. All these made it one of the single most influential sculptures of western history, a lady who is 2200 years old and counting."

Sharmi and Amita expressed their amazement at how she was sculpted 2200 years ago. "She is so beautiful."

As the group moved to the sculpture of Cupid and Psyche, the four friends followed them and Rudy couldn't help but feel inspired and connected to his favorite artist, Niccolò. He wondered if he and his friends would encounter one of Niccolò's statues in the Louvre. To Rudy, Niccolò was more than a sculptor whose works one would admire—the life of Niccolò in many ways paralleled his own and Rudy could extract wisdom and life lessons from reading the biography of Niccolò if one chooses to read between the lines as Rudy had.

The guide asked the group to look at the sculpture and enjoy the two beautifully sculpted figures and express what they are seeing.

"Well, one of them that is Cupid is completely naked and other one modestly draped," one of the tourists commented.

The boy from Lancaster raised his hand again and with big sparkling eyes said, "Oh, the lady is placing a butterfly on the palm of the person with two wings."

"Good point," the guide said. "Anyone knows what it signifies?"

Everyone stayed silent until Romero said, "The butterfly signifies the soul which she offers in innocence to Cupid."

Rudy and Samir whispered to each other that it was a beautiful metaphor.

"The wandering of the soul was a concept of Neoplatonic philosophy in which Canova adhered," Romero added.

One member of the tour group asked, "Who was Canova?"

"Antonio Canova, a sculpture from Possagno, was only 30-years old when the sculpture was commissioned by a Scottish Colonel Sir John Campbell whom he met in Naples in 1787 and who also commissioned the Psyche revived by Cupid's Kiss that is also here in the Louvre." The group moved to Venus De Milo as Rudy, Samir, Amita and Sharmi continued to follow the group.

"This statue certainly revives the classical tradition but would appear to be classicizing, recreating the date of 2nd century B.C.," Romero said. "The goddess's air of aloofness, the harmony of her face and her impassivity are stamped with the aesthetics of the 5th century B.C."

One of the tourists in the group who introduced himself as Lorenzo, an art student from Italy said, "To me, the positioning of the elongated body gives an impression of three-dimensional space."

Upon hearing this, Rudy's ears perked up as though he had just heard Niccolò's own remarks about the positioning of a statue come to life from one of the scenarios detailing Niccolò's own creative process behind creating his own sculptures.

"You are absolutely right," Romero said, "the sculpture reflects innovation that appeared during the Hellenistic period between the 3rd and 1st centuries.

The spiral composition, the positioning of a figure in a three-dimensional space and a small-breasted elongated body are characteristics of this period. The goddess is arrested in time holding her legs together as draperies slide over her hips. Her nudity contrasts with the effect of light and shade of the finely detailed drapery. Based on the inscription on the plinth, the statue is now thought to be the work of Alexandros."

Samir and Amita admired the spiral composition of the sculpture and asked Sharmi what her impression was. "I like her the way she is. She is really beautiful," she said.

"Who was Alexandros?" Timothy, a tourist asked.

"Alexandros of Antioch appears to have been a wandering artist who worked on commission," Romero explained. "According to the inscription at the ancient city of Thespiae near Mount Helicon in Greece, he was a winner in a contest for composing and singing. The exact date of his birth and death is unknown. He is best known today for the statue of Venus de Milo. This statue was discovered at the Greek Island of Melos. Alexandros is thought to have sculpted the statue of Alexander the Great which is also displayed in the Louvre."

The group moved to the next room where Michelangelo's sculpted figures stood. A few of these sculptures depicted the expression of human suffering.

Samir and Rudy expressed that they have their own lists of paintings to see.

"It's now past 11:30 and we have a little over an hour to spend here," Rudy added, "I would very much like to see one bronze sculpture and relief by my favorite artist, Niccolò that my Italian friend suggested when I met him on board the ship when I was coming to England. He is an artist from Florence. There are a few more works in the Louvre by Niccolò we can see tomorrow when we have free time in the morning and afternoon. Then we have half an hour for our lunch break and for our next activity we have at least two to three hours so that we can reach our hotel by 4:30 to change clothes then leave our hotel at 5:30 to be at the dock for our Seine River dinner cruise that starts at 6:30 p.m."

Everyone agreed to the plan.

They started their list with "The Raft of Medusa" by Theodore Gericault. Samir, who had some notes, read, "Due to poor navigation, the French frigate wrecked off the course of the coast of Mauritius." To which they all commented that the painting was very dramatic and emotional.

Then they moved to face Delacroix's "Liberty Leading the People" circa July 1830. There were a number of people gathered, some seated on a bench close by quietly and contemplatively viewing the painting as though it was a form of meditation.

Standing a few minutes in front of the painting, Sharmi commented, "It represents a dramatic patriotism."

Next on their list was the Coronation of Napoleon by Jacques Louis David, circa 1804, a 33-feet by 20-feet painting secured in a large frame.

"I read that Jacques Louis was the official painter of Napoleon," Rudy said as Sharmi nodded her approval.

Then the Pastoral Concert, circa 1509, which Samir looked up in the guide book and read, "An unknown attribute to Titian, this is a turbulent period of the league of Cambral's war in Venice. The art historian suggested the painting was painted in response to the idyllic refuge from scheme that created ravages of history." Samir paused to ask whether he should continue reading.

Sharmi and Amita expressed they wanted to know more about the background of the painting which Samir read as "a subgenre of the Italian Renaissance painting unique to Venice."

"Venetian paintings are characterized as having rich color schemes that create a 'warm glow' and emphasize naturalism. The painting is also considered the origin of the Pastoral genre of art because of its connection to pastoral poetry as seen in the painting of young men gathering in an Italian countryside's lush greenery to start 'Pastoral Concert or Fete Champetre', a genre described as a gathering of picturesque landscape in a creative pursuit."

The four friends commented that it was a very peaceful landscape with colorful greenery.

Amita, Samir, Rudy and Sharmi next moved on to the painting "The Death of the Virgin." Sharmi started reading from the notes she collected: "It is a brutal view of a religious theme. Mary lies reclined in a simple, red dress, lolling head, swollen spread feet. This is a raw and realistic view of the virgin's mortal remains. The sacred character is evidenced by a thin layer of the halo. The apostles gathered around her are little recognized, their faces almost engulfed in shadow or hidden by hands. St. John kneeling by her side and the elderly man on the left is St. Peter. The woman isolated in the foreground has often been identified as Mary Magdalene. The painter made nuances of light and shadow to model the volumes of objects and clothing above all accentuates through this process, the physical presence of the virgin struck by dazzling light."

The four friends marveled at the fact that Caravaggio was a great painter and naturalist who utilized a special painting technique where his object of focus was illuminated against a dark background.

Next, they moved themselves in front of Leonardo's "The Virgin and Child with St. Anne." It was Amita's turn to share information she collected with the group.

"It is an unfinished oil painting by Leonardo depicting St. Anne, her daughter, Mary and the infant child Jesus Christ is shown grappling with the sacrificial lamb symbolizing his passion as the Virgin tries to restrict him. It is likely that painting was commissioned by King Louis XII of France following the birth of his daughter, Claude. It measures 68 by 130 cm and painted by Leonardo in 1510. Here he has arranged the figures as a pyramid set in a landscape. The theme of the Virgin Mary, her mother, Anne and Jesus is common. It is unusual here in this painting for Mary to be portrayed in her mother's lap. The background landscape whose crags are seemingly replicated in Anne's veil, virtually melts in a sfumato haze. The baby lamb is both a symbol of innocence and of Jesus 'sacrifice for humanity'."

"What is sfumato," Sharmi asked.

"According to this information, it is a technique for softening the transition between the colors mimicking an area beyond the human eye," Amita replied.

The next one was last on their list: Leonardo's the "Mona Lisa." Rudy, who collected notes about this famous painting, asked his friends to take time to observe the painting as he studied it with intensity as swarms of people continually gathered around the iconic Mona Lisa. Visitors took turns to go close to the painting but there seemed to be no break in the endless streams of onlookers.

Rudy and his friends tried to spend as much time as they could to view the Mona Lisa as they gathered close to listen to the artistic information and background he read about the iconic painting.

"It is said that the Mona Lisa is not the most artistically accomplished painting in the Louvre nor the most beautiful," Rudy shared. "It is not emotive, even awe-inspiring. What it has, more than perhaps any other work in the world, is a rare technical mastery. He painted Mona Lisa with a technique of his own sfumato in which he layered coats of semitransparent paint washes, one on top of another, to create a sense of three dimension using light and dark. At that time, it was revolutionary."

"What about her smile?" Samir asked.

"Good question," Rudy said. "According to this information, Mona Lisa's smile has been the subject of countless debate and criticism. Is she happy, sad, perplexed? It is exactly the kind of delicious enigma historians love to argue and they will continue to do so for the future. As for its historical background, the Mona Lisa is understood to be a portrait of an Italian woman named Lisa Gherardini which was commissioned by her husband Francesco del Gioconde 1503-1509."

Rudy paused allowing his friends to absorb this information. "Before we go to lunch, I would very much like to see some work by Niccolò, a famous sculptor introduced to me by my friend whom I met on the ship the first time when I came to England. This Italian friend introduced me to Niccolò's life story and his work.

"Today we will see the bronze relief crucifix and mother and child, and on the 28th, we have the morning and afternoon free so we can visit the Louvre again, if you like, but I wish to visit Florence maybe two years from now so I can see most of his famous work and visit my Italian friend who also lives there. The Louvre doesn't always have his work displayed, except just a few, although sometimes they would feature his work as a special exhibit."

Rudy recalled reading about a relief of the mother Mary and the child Jesus that Niccolò had given to his sister, Tia. In the Louvre's display, Mother Mary and baby Jesus, sculpted on a relief, were looking towards the future and what was to become of Jesus, their expressions evoking awe and horror. Their expressions seemed so real that it appeared both mother and child were alive—at any rate that was what Rudy's friend told him and now as Rudy and his friends observed this work of art, they were amazed to witness that what Rudy's friend said was true. From his reading, Rudy was also delighted to actually see proof of what Niccolò meant by his sculptures coming alive.

Next was a crucifix in bronze relief, which was very unique as beside Jesus on the crucifix, there were four figures: two soldiers and St. John to one side. The other side featured mother Mary weeping. Though it was a bronze relief, Niccolò's technique of making his work "come alive" was really visible and impressed Rudy and his friends who admired Niccolò's talent from just a few of his works they got to view.

"Looking at just a few of his works has inspired me to see more and really want to know about his life and want to know the man he was," Rudy said, feeling even more connected to Niccolò despite being separated by time and space. Viewing Niccolò's work up close today was like the wisdom and inspiration of the past echoing now in Rudy's mind and he walked away from Niccolò's work feeling so uplifted.

Then the four of them exited the gallery eager to have lunch. Sharmi prepared lunch bags for them with each bag containing two sandwiches, one peanut butter, the other cucumber, a small bunch of grapes and some roasted almonds.

Sharmi handed each friend a lunch bag. "We need some tea or coffee." They all found a coffee stand and devoured their lunches in no time. After lunch Amita and Samir bid Sharmi and Rudy bye for now promising to meet them back at the hotel at 4:30.

At first, Sharmi was hesitant being separated from Amita and Samir and was a bit confused as to why they were going on their own, yet she kept quiet.

Rudy on the other hand looked very excited and cheerful. He drew closer to Sharmi. "We are going to the top of the Eiffel Tower."

"I hope there is lift."

Rudy laughed. "Yes, there is and from the top, you and I will see the entire city of Paris."

Sharmi and Rudy took a taxi and in a short time they reached the Eiffel Tower. Since Rudy made reservations, they skipped the line and took the lift.

"You can't go all the way up in one lift," Rudy said. "There are levels, like a two hundred, four hundred, and nine hundred feet-level lift. What do you say, my dear Sharmi? Shall we take the lift up to the third level then spend time at the top level then descend with the lift and spend as much time as we can at the other levels one after another?"

"Sounds fine to me," Sharmi said. "It will be quite an experience."

The lift that ascended to the top floor was just occupied with a few couples. They all exchanged friendly nods and smiles with each other. Then Rudy and Sharmi stepped out of the lift with the others as Rudy held onto Sharmi's left hand and they headed to the observation deck. In front of them, the gray December horizon lay at their feet with a few white clouds curved at a distance seemed to be holding the throbbing city of Paris very close to its heart and at the top deck of the Eiffel Tower with their eyes fixed to each other, two loving souls, Rudy and Sharmi held one another closely.

After a few minutes of silence, Rudy looked into the eyes of his beloved. "Sharmi, I love you very much. Will you do me a great honor and marry me?"

Sharmi's whole body started shaking with fine tremors, her face flushed, heart beating faster as if it would leap out of her body. Then, with soft voice she looked up at Rudy and said "Yes!"

Then Rudy pulled out a tiny, red velvet box from his pocket, opened it, took a ring out and slipped the diamond ring in gold setting on Sharmi's left ring finger. Tears started rolling down her cheeks. Rudy drew her towards him and kissed her. Lost in their fantasy land, they moved in small circles, holding each other tightly yet very gently until they gradually came back to the present when they heard applause and congratulations from a crowd of tourists.

Rudy looked at his watch and saw it was 2:30. "We have only an hour and a half left before we go back to our hotel," he told Sharmi. "Let us go to the second level and enjoy the view."

Still dazed and dreamy, lost in her own space, Sharmi said "Whatever you decide."

"We will spend some time taking lots of photos and ask people around us to take photos of us," Rudy said.

Sharmi came back to the present and smiled. "That will be fun."

Rudy and Sharmi went down to the second level where they saw another nice view of Paris but from this level, one can see the city's interesting landmarks more distinctly. They posed and took photos and looked for tourists who wouldn't mind taking a few shots of both of them when suddenly they heard some familiar voices from the other end of the observation deck and—surprise! surprise!—Sharmi and Rudy saw Amita and Samir coming towards them. Rudy lifted Sharmi's hand up to show their friends the engagement ring. Both Amita and Samir burst into joy. "Congratulations!"

The four of them came together to form a group hug then Samir gave Rudy a strong pat on his back and joined their hands together to cheer for joy which burst spontaneously from them. After a brief photo session that included photos of the newly-engaged couple atop the Eiffel Tower, they descended to enjoy cups of coffee before taking a cab back to their hotel. Four of them found their choice of coffee shop. Rudy looked very cheerful and expressed that, after years of struggle, he seemed to finally be living in his dreamland—a nice career, a beautiful fiancée and a trip to Paris with friends. Amita and Samir were pleased to hear that. Rudy smiled thinking to himself how much his own life paralleled that of Niccolò Bardi who had also overcome struggles to achieve success.

Once they reached their hotel, Rudy said he needed to freshen up and change as Sharmi, Amita and Samir expressed the same as they walked to their rooms.

"Today is a very special day for you, Sharmi, so I am going to help you with your make up and saree," Amita said. "I ordered some flowers which will be stringed and tied around your hair bun."

Sharmi appeared embarrassed. "Oh, I appreciate it, Amita, but you do not have to—"

"Hush," Amita said, "today you just have to accept what I wish to offer you. Sharmi, when an engagement finalizes, we Bengalis celebrate with friends and family so we are celebrating yours in the same spirit. The girl to be wed is usually dressed up almost like a bride. This is the honor you deserve."

Sharmi kept quiet for some time and then said, "I feel a bit overwhelmed. Yes, today is a very special day as I turned my life in a new direction but I still cannot communicate with my family and I've kept them all in the dark."

"Sharmi, you are going tell them eventually," Amita said. "You are not in India and your marriage is not arranged by them. Your engagement happened spontaneously on a serendipitous path while you are building your future in a faraway land. So while it appears very different than the usual customs, you can't ignore that and you are going to rejoice and you are still very fortunate to have been given this opportunity to meet a man who supports the fact that you wish to continue your doctorate and pursue meaningful opportunities for yourself. And that, my dear Sharmi, is worth celebrating. So cheer up! We are going to celebrate as much as we can. Just remember, we might not have another day like this again. Once it passes by, it is gone."

Amita and Sharmi walked briskly towards their rooms.

"So I will go to your room to get dressed," Amita said. "Let me first pick up my things from my room and maybe the flowers I ordered for you have already been delivered to our room so I will bring those too."

Sharmi eyed her friend curiously. "How come you ordered flowers? Did you know that something special was going to happen?"

Amita smiled. "We guessed it when Rudy gave some hints to Samir and me and when he requested some time away from our group. We figured out from our chats, that Rudy intended to make a more official commitment of his relationship with you and look how he has done better by slipping a diamond ring on your finger. How wonderful! Sharmi let's start getting ready. I suggest you wear your maroon saree with gold embellishments and I will also wear my saree with gold work. Then I'll put make up on you with a big red bindi. I'll fix your hair in a bun and secure white roses strung together around your hair bun. A pair of gold dangling, pearl earrings will go perfectly well.

"Oh, what about you?" Sharmi asked.

"I have a pair of gold earrings to match my saree," Amita said. "I'll also put a rose in my hair and secure it with bobby pins then put on some make up. Let me do your face first and then I'll do mine."

Once they both dressed up in their chosen outfits, they looked in the mirror to make sure they looked pretty in the way they wished.

Sharmi blossomed into her five-feet tall stature, and with her light skin, black hair, pointed nose, triangular face and dreamy eyes, she looked like a beautiful young princess lost in her fantasy world. Amita looked equally as beautiful, standing taller at five feet, four inches, imbuing the quintessential essence of a young woman with wavy brown black hair that cascaded down her shoulders which complimented her olive skin, dazzling eyes and pointed nose. Both impeccably dressed young ladies were ready to explore and enjoy an evening cruising along the River Seine.

Checking the clock, they saw it was fifteen minutes past five in the afternoon and they hurried down the lobby where their men waited. Samir and Rudy looked very smartly dressed in their black suits. Rudy sported a red necktie with a pearl tie pin and Samir wore a striped red and black tie with a gold tie pin. The four friends complimented each other and Rudy could barely take his eyes off his beautiful new fiancée who smiled shyly at him.

Their tour company, Bateaux Parisiens' big black sedan drove up in front of the hotel's entrance and the foursome boarded the cab which cruised through a lacy curtain of fog. To them, it seemed like even the street lights, which were misty and dreamy, kept cruising along with them to an enchanted wonderland.

As they rode through Paris, Rudy savored the best part of the day— when Sharmi agreed to be his wife. He only wished that Niccolò had, like himself, been rewarded the gift of having the lifelong companionship of the love of his life.

Christmas in Castellina

25th of December—The evening shadow was just starting to spread its veil slowly on the landscape. Mother Orissa dressed in her long-sleeved maroon, long silk dress with lacy ruffles in front, a long gold chain around her neck swayed when she sat down on a red cushioned chair.

"When would you like to go to Marcello's?" she asked her family.

They all answered within half an hour or so.

"Stefano will be bringing their carriage driving himself as the carriage driver is on Christmas vacation."

"You have to see the surprise gift from Niccolò," Tia told her mother who looked at her daughter with surprise.

"A gift!" Mother Orissa said. "I can hardly believe it. He is always lost in his own world of work."

"You have to see it, Mamma."

Mother Orissa, Tia and Niccolò all entered the prayer room in Tia's side of the house. Mother Orissa instantly saw the relief of the mother and child and immediately recognized it was Niccolò's creation before anyone said a word. She was so happy, tears rolled down her cheeks and she planted many kisses on Niccolò's forehead and prayed for blessings to Niccolò and their whole family. Then she placed her right palm on Niccolò's head.

"I am so proud and happy that you are so thoughtful," she told her son.

"Thank you, Mamma. I worked several nights to make this possible."

Just then they heard the clip-clapping sounds of horses. "It is time to go to the Casini family's house," Tia said.

The three of them went to the living room to put out the flames in the fireplace and kept their portable charcoal room heater ready for heating their bedrooms. Then they boarded the carriage where Stefano, who drove his family's carriage, informed them that Amadeo was already in their house.

"My parents eagerly look forward to your visit," Stefano told them.

They all enjoyed their short ride to the Casini family's home where the open torch fire outside the main door burned inside a covered grilled iron cage. Just before the main entrance, the Christmas tree decorated with hanging apples and different colored paper flowers stood tall with a silver star on top.

La casa della famiglia Casini was decorated with green pine wreaths accentuated with red berries on the walls inside and on the front doors. Inside, different kinds of candles burned at different corners of the living and dining room, part of which could be seen from the living space. Inside the living room, the fireplace was burning with yellow and blue flames and a fine fragrance wafted as soon as one entered the room.

Marcello and Angela came to greet them with open arms. Angela escorted Mother Orissa to sit on a red sofa which was close to the fireplace. The living room was large enough to comfortably provide sitting accommodations for eight to ten people. There were two big size sofas with red velvet covering, one against the wall and another facing in front of it close to the entrance. There were two small red cushioned sofas in addition to two cushioned chairs. A gold-framed rectangular glass top table was placed in the middle of the room.

A priest with his grayish-black, flowing long cassock and a scapular with a metallic cross sat on a small sofa. He greeted everyone with a smile. His round face with big eyes beamed as soon as Niccolò entered the room lit with different candles all around.

The pink crystal chandelier hanging from the ceiling with flickering red candles cast a different glow inside the room in concert with other light sources.

Marcello welcomed Niccolò with open arms. *"Buonasera, Benvenuto."*

"*Buonasera*, Marcello," Niccolò said.

"My dear Niccolò, Reverendo Don Bianchi from Siena would like to talk to you for few minutes."

"Of course, I am honored to make time for you, Don Bianchi."

Niccolò bowed and approached the priest. Amadeo stood by and placed a cushioned chair close to the priest for Niccolò.

The priest welcomed Niccolò with a smile gesturing him to take a seat. "My dear Niccolò, the Siena Cathedral wants you to sculpt the execution of St. John and The Feast of Herod on bronze."

Niccolò, whose eyes were fixed at a distance, his head slightly bent and his right palm resting on his forehead, remained silent for a few minutes. He thought about the load of work and time it took to create this and considered it will be his first commission for casting in bronze. The minutes of silence seemed to stretch for hours that everyone present in the room seemed very anxious including the priest.

Then Niccolò took a deep breath and said "Yes, I can accept this commission. I wish to sculpt it with all my artistic freedom and I want to carve it in my studio in Firenze and the materials have to be provided by the Cathedral of Siena."

The Reverendo Don Bianchi stood up and approached Niccolò. "Bless you, my dear Niccolò, whatever you need, we will provide it for you."

"Don Bianchi, I cannot start until the later part of the coming year and it might take two to three years to finish it," Niccolò said.

"That will not be a problem," the priest said, "take as much time as you need. I am very happy that you are going to sculpt these commissions."

"It is my honor to do so."

A strong blast of wind whistled through the dark evening. Just then clip-clapping of horses could be heard which grew louder and louder and stopped just outside Marcello's gate.

Stefano bowed to the priest. "Don Bianchi, your carriage has arrived."

The priest bid everyone goodbye and thanked Niccolò again for accepting the commission of The Feast of Herod.

Marcello poured wine in goblets while Angela started serving cheese and cured black olives to the guests. The smell of roasted meat and spices made everyone hungry that it was a matter of time when the host would ask them to take their seats at the dining table.

Marcello asked Niccolò about the commission of the prophet Habakkuk. Niccolò explained to him that Habakkuk's life in the Bible was bleak as little information about his private life existed. He must have lived in the era of 612 BC when Babylonian invaders repeatedly desponded the land of the Jews.

"What made Habakkuk stand out from other prophets was that he was not afraid to question God about the injustice He allowed on the people of Judah," Niccolò said.

Marcello was very pleased to know the notion inspired Niccolò to start creating the sculpture of the prophet.

Angela came and asked everyone to proceed to the dining area. Then she escorted mother Orissa to take her seat at the head of the table close to the entrance of the dining room and Marcello requested Niccolò to sit on the opposite end of the head of the table. Niccolò was quite reluctant to do that and asked Marcello to sit there instead. After a brief discussion, Marcello agreed to be at the head of the table.

Varieties of food were displayed on a separate table: Pasta al Forno—baked pasta with long simmered ragu made of fried tiny meatballs—salami, hard-boiled eggs, cheese and rich béchamel sauce. Main entrées included roast shank of lamb sliced in pieces, baked chicken, salad with radicchio, olive, cilantro, and onions.

There was a special small table with Christmas dessert: Panetone, Panforte and Struffoli—small fried dough with Lemoncelle, citrus grind coated with honey.

Each one took their turn serving themselves except mother Orissa whose food choices were served to her by Angela.

Everyone commented that the food was delicious and thanked Angela for the feast. Marcello and Angela suggested that all the guests take their dessert plates to enjoy in front of the fireplace with some more wine.

The lively chorus of conversation went on for hours especially on the subject of Niccolò's stay in Castellina. Niccolò expressed that during daytime he would occupy himself with the prophet's sketching. Stefano asked whether he could observe him.

"Yes," Niccolò said, "you are very welcome."

Marcello and Angela told the guests that in the late afternoon they were all welcome to spend time and have dinner with them.

"We will prepare some items also so that you do not have to cook too much," Tia spoke to Angela and Marcello on behalf of her mother.

"Do not worry. If it is too much I will ask for help," Angela said.

They were all quite pleased to make this arrangement. "We are all very honored to have Maestro Niccolò spend some time with us," Marcello said.

"It would be nice for a change, relaxing in the evening and not rushing to go to the studio early in the morning," Niccolò said.

Christmas evening went by quickly. Stefano was standing by to take the guests home. They all thanked their hosts for a scrumptious feast, bid each other "Good night and we will see you tomorrow."

* * *

Day after Christmas

The lazy sun tried to emerge from the gray sky the next morning. The day diffused sunlight-covered hills and valleys. Ready to sketch with his marker, Niccolò opened the curtains of the windows letting the light pass through the window and brighten the art paper fixed on the board.

Niccolò stood in front of the sketching paper, his eyebrows knitted as he took his marker and murmured, "Where to start?"

He decided to concentrate on his subject's head and then his face. The head was bald, like a *zucca*, tilting downwards showing humility. The eyes called out to the viewer as they appeared sad and void but at the same time, acknowledging the presence of the viewer.

Niccolò clenched his jaw and took a deep breath. He looked at his marker, stepped forward, and murmured, "Prophet, with all this anxiety and sadness which is not easy, taking his breath and holding it inside until he can no longer hold it any longer as his face is pale then suddenly his breath blows out with a jolt. In the process, his eyes are sad and anxious, appearing as though they are bulging out of sunken sockets, with lips partly open, trying to say something. He looks like he lost weight. His body is thin and shrunken. There are horizontal markings on his forehead." Niccolò kept on sketching along while talking to himself until several hours had passed.

"Now," he whispered, "your shrunken body is covered with layers of clothes.

Niccolò forgot he was in Castellina and cried out loud: "Tell me what it is you are trying to say, Prophet. Speak to me, I demand that you speak to me!"

That's when Amadeo came running to him, an alarmed look on his face. "Zio, are you all right? Are you all right?"

Echoes of their speech reached far away and when lightning flashed over the hilltop through the window, Niccolò saw the dark clouds racing across the sky and daylight suddenly got covered by the evening veil.

Niccolò looked at the sketching board and put his marker down. Amadeo drew closer, patted his uncle's arm and said, "Uncle, let us go downstairs and relax with a glass of wine. We will go to the Casini family's house for dinner remember?"

Later, at the Casini family's living room, Stefano was busy putting logs in the fireplace. Angela came forward and took the bag of cooked food from Amadeo.

"The delicious smell of the food is making me hungry," Angela said.

Mother Orissa smiled. "There is minestrone and gnocchi with roasted red peperone."

"Thank you, Mother Orissa."

Angela asked everyone to take their wine glasses to the dinner table. In addition to Mother Orissa's minestrone and gnocchi, there was baked chicken stuffed with tomato and parmesan, green beans and for dessert, cannoli filled with soft ricotta cheese.

The topic of the dinner conversation centered again on Niccolò. Marcello asked how his work was going to which Niccolò replied, "I started sketching and will finish the face and a part of the body tomorrow then layers of his toga will take two more days. The folds of the clothes will be seen better once I play with different shades of marker. That will be another day, perhaps around the 30th of December or the 31st and on the 1st of January in the new year of 1422, I will relax and spend time with everyone and welcome the new year. Then on January 2nd, I will look at the sketching and put some coating on it so it stays the way I sketched it."

"Maestro, I have different shades of marker you can borrow and I have a liquid coat that's very thin and transparent," Stefano offered. "If you like, I can provide that to you also."

"I am very fortunate to have you around," Niccolò said to Stefano.

"What about your new commission?" Marcello asked. "If you do not mind me asking, I wonder whether you will do two simultaneously: the bronze casting one for The Feast of Herod and the other for the execution of John the Baptist? It will double the hours of your hard work, no?"

"You are right," Niccolò replied. "And no, I will somehow combine them together. I have not planned just how yet."

The evening went by swiftly as everyone soon bid each other *"Buona notte"* and Stefano began to take the guests home by carriage through a dark and stormy evening. The clip-clapping of horses' hooves blended with the whistling of the wind that echoed from one hill to the other then faded far, far away, spiraling into the evening darkness.

Cruising Along the Seine

Paris, December, 1964

When Rudy, Sharmi, Samir and Amita reached the dock where their cruise would start, they got excited when they saw that it was pretty close to the illuminated Eiffel Tower which was a magnificent sight to behold, standing tall and watching the city. They lined up to board the cruise ship that was also decorated with tiny lights.

Once they got on board the ship, Rudy and his friends followed a lady attendant who seated them at their assigned table and, wow! They found their table was by the side of an enormous window with a spectacular close-up view of the Seine. A candle was placed on the center of the table with a small wreath of red roses as a candle holder. On top of the white tablecloth lay silverware shone at the side of white dinner plates with amber-colored napkins shaped like birds placed on the plates.

They took their seats with Sharmi and Amita each grabbing a window seat on each side.

A very pleasant young gentleman came and introduced himself as Leon. "Mesdames et Messieurs, I am your attendant this evening."

"Thank you, nice to meet you," they all greeted.

As the evening set in, the live band on board started playing their orchestra pieces. From the large window, one could see the reflected lights on the River Seine shimmering away to the shore. Two large, white swans floated towards the bank and some noisy ducks were busy gathering their ducklings.

The music from the live band started playing a song, "The Way You Look Tonight," by Frank Sinatra.

For Rudy and Sharmi, the song seemed very appropriate for the occasion as well as for Amita and Samir as they had just marked their 3rd anniversary in early December. Both couples drew closer to hug each other's partner when Leon, their table attendant arrived to go over the dinner menu before taking their orders.

To start, their choices were: a crust pate, onion confit, or salmon tartare and vegetable minestrone; or a choice of other soups included a creamy pea soup with peppermint and fresh goat cheese. Leon explained that salmon tartare was raw fish marinated in lemon juice and herbs, delicious but the fish was raw, he emphasized.

The four friends chose the crust pate onion confit and creamy pea soup with peppermint and fresh goat cheese.

For the main course, there was: fillet of veal, parsley and potato mousseline with veal gravy; or Fillet of sea bream, Carrot and basil; risotto of black rice, coriander, and confit tomatoes. Then cheese and desserts: Bourdalone pear tart in glass; tea and coffee and beverage choices included Vin Mouten Cadet, or Medoc Bordueax France, Evian water and soft drinks.

Rudy and Samir chose fillet of veal, Amita ordered fillet of bream, and Sharmi wanted to try risotto of black rice. For the wine, three of them chose Mouten Cadet while Sharmi chose lemonade.

As the cruise ship started moving, the live band started playing Frank Sinatra's "Fly me to moon, let me play among the stars," through the misty horizon as the moon peeped through a patch of clouds and few stars twinkled through the drifting clouds while illuminated buildings and rows of light posts slowly but surely moved backwards.

After Leon poured wine in the glasses and served Sharmi her lemonade, he brought a variety of cheese and placed that at the center of the table.

Leon told the group that any particular song requests they might have he would relay to the live band before serving dessert. Then the floor would be open for dancing and their requested songs would be played so they could dance to their chosen songs or any other song they would prefer.

"I'll be back with your crust pate, onion confit, and soup in few minutes," Leon said.

Amita and Samir were very excited thinking about some Elvis Presley songs, first choosing "Love Me Tender" and second, "Can't Help Falling in Love." Rudy chose "Love Me Teender," to commemorate his and Sharmi's engagement.

Leon came to serve the crust pate, onion confit and soup. Amita, Samir and Rudy handed their song request lists to their waiter who was very happy to pass them along to the band. "I'll let you know once the floor opens for dancing and when your requested songs will be played."

Three of the friends were excited but a very anxious Sharmi said, "I have never danced like this before so I will just watch you."

Rudy and Samir assuaged her fears assuring her that ladies rely on the gentlemen to lead in a dance. "You leave that to us."

Rudy and Samir were very pleased with the crust pate and onion confit, commenting that, "It tastes delicious and is one of a kind."

Amita and Sharmi commented the pea soup tastes good but "very different from what we have in England."

The cruise ship slowly slid under a magnificent bridge illuminated with old gaslight-shaped poles. The body of the bridge was engraved with a stony flower wreath which ran along the arches. The shadow of the bridge glided over the boat while the lighted Eiffel Tower stood at the background.

Just then, the live band started playing "Ave Maria" as the guests cheered, "Notre Dame! Norte Dame!"

Sharmi, who was very excited and happy to see the Notre Dame, kept on repeating, "I can't believe I'm passing in front of the actual Norte Dame cathedral."

"I didn't know you are very interested in the Notre Dame," Rudy said. "We should spend our free half day there."

Sharmi smiled. "I've already put that on my list."

The four of them were excited to see this beautiful lady, the Notre Dame, the finest example of gothic architecture sitting on an island in the Seine like a queen on her throne. The façade seen from the cruise ship looked so harmonious.

"I am so glad we are going to spend some time at the Notre Dame which we get to see in broad daylight tomorrow," Samir said.

Leon came and started clearing the table to prepare for their main course. The music of the live band filled the air as the cruise ship glided smoothly along the Seine. The moon came out of the cloud and seemed to follow the ship with her dreamy eyes.

Leon served fillet of veal to Samir and Rudy, fillet of bream to Amita and the risotto to Sharmi.

After bidding them a *"Bon Appetit,"* Leon informed them that he submitted their songs to the live band who would first perform Elvis's "Love Me Tender." The friends thanked Leon for bringing their food and alerting them about their songs.

"Let us enjoy our food, it looks delicious," Samir said.

Amita agreed. "My dinner looks pretty good too."

Sharmi was very happy with her risotto and asked if anyone would like a taste.

Rudy took a spoonful of risotto. "Thank you, it tastes good." He then asked Sharmi if she wanted to taste his veal fillet, she said, "I don't eat beef," a fact that Rudy carefully noted and added to his mental list of his new fiancée's preferences.

"Try my bream," Amita said. "It tastes like some fish we used to eat at Kolkata."

Sharmi took a small portion of the fillet and agreed it tasted delicious.

The ship cruised smoothly along, pushing river water on both sides of the ship as the buildings on both banks slowly moved backwards. Some of the people strolling along the promenade and the river bank waved at the cruiser cheerfully. The reflected lights of the city on the river broke into linear pieces, fading away to the shore on both sides.

As Rudy engaged in conversation, his eyes sparkled and his voice cracked, punctuating his sentences with his mannerism of saying, "You know what I mean," then stopping and saying, "You know what I mean." He took a deep breath. "Today is the happiest day of my life." He put down his knife and fork on his plate and reached towards the other side of the table for Sharmi's hand and gave it a kiss.

Sharmi was overwhelmed with emotion, momentarily speechless.

Leon, the waiter, came back to announce that in ten minutes the dance floor would be open for the performance of the first requested song, "Love Me Tender."

Rudy was excited. "I would like to dance to my requested song with my new fiancée." He looked at Sharmi.

"By all means this will be yours and Sharmi's special song and dance," Amita said.

Sharmi replied nervously, "But I don't know how to dance."

"My dear, you do not have to know how," Rudy said gently. "I will guide you how to move with me."

Amita and Samir were very happy to hear that and soon they were all excited and ready to head to the dance floor. Once the newly-engaged coupled reached the dance floor, the band leader announced, "Here's to

Rudy and Sharmi who just got engaged at the Eiffel Tower earlier today and in their honor, we will play 'Love Me Tender,' by none other than the great Elvis Presley."

There was applause from the other guests as Rudy put his arm around Sharmi and gently guided her to the middle of the dance floor. Sharmi glowed in her maroon silk saree, her triangular face and dreamy eyes gazed into Rudy's sparkling ones. Then she rested her head softly on Rudy's chest as they started slow dancing to the music. Sharmi felt this was where she now belonged, a place so peaceful and safe as if time just stopped and she reached the infinite. For Rudy, it was a different, more incandescent world as he felt like a winner holding his reward—his princess, as they both coasted along joyfully to their happy destination.

They both came back from their dreamland to the present when the band started playing Elvis's other song "Can't Help Falling in Love," a cue for Amita and Samir, two energetic dancers, to take to the dance floor. They continued having fun dancing as others joined them.

Time flowed happily until the songs ended. The ship sounded its horn to alert guests it was time for dessert and drinks. The band kept on playing as people settled into their seats at the table where they savored every sweet morsel of the unforgettable cruise that would soon come to the end of her journey. Then the ship blew her farewell horn at the dock where they boarded the cruise as the lighted Eiffel Tower welcomed them back to a peaceful evening as guests brought along with them pleasant memories of Paris cruising along the Seine bidding them "Au revoir, until we meet again."

Sketching of the Prophet

29th of December 1421—On a gray morning in Castellina, three days passed since Niccolò started sketching the Prophet's head, face and body. The head was bald facing front, tilted down, the manner showing him as a humble man. The eyes were sad, vacant and submissive, trying to acknowledge the viewer. His mouth, partly open, was trying hard to speak. Niccolò looked at him and said, "By some strange margin, all I am trying to do is capture the phantom of your life, your body as hollowed and ravaged by revelation wrapped up in massive drapery."

The slender man was covered with a long toga characterized by ruffles and layers of cloth. One hand gripped the strap which rested on his one shoulder. The other one clutched the robe's fabric. Niccolò murmured, "I am trying to show the sense of inner life of you, Zuccone! A sense one can feel from the hands, arms, one bare shoulder and sandaled feet where your figure ends, the whole of a gaunt, sinewy body which one can all but smell."

Niccolò paused, looked at it then he stepped away and tried again to visualize it.

"Oh! The neck should thrust forward and his gaze down resolutely mingling strength with doubt." He approached the window and gazed at the undulating hills.

Niccolò started to whisper, "The rhythmic folds of clothes which begins with a slow swirl and eddies under the Prophet's head is beyond sublime and terrible."

Niccolò suddenly heard some footsteps near his door and saw Stefano waiting outside the door, holding different shades of markers in his right hand.

Niccolò welcomed him with a smile. "Please come in."

Stefano entered the room and looked at the sketch, amazed to see the transformation of the sketched figure compared to how it first looked in the beginning.

"Maestro, you are a genius. I feel he is going to emerge from the sketch and speak to me."

"Thank you, Stefano, for that is exactly the mood I was going for. You know, the dream of a statue that can speak, breathe and move is a fantasy shared by many cultures around the world. I heard from a merchant friend of my late father, who used to travel by ship to the east, that there was a female sculpture somewhere in India. Early in the morning, when the rays of sun bathe this sculpture, a beautiful musical tune would emanate from the sculpture and would fill the air."

"Maestro, that is interesting and magical, I want to know what technique will be used to make Zuccone," Stefano said.

"The technique will be a light and shallow carving on the surface of marble to bring about the lifelike quality and then add the texture by contrasting rough and smooth. Instead of chiseling, it seems to be a painting."

"Maestro, that is an amazing and very original idea. I have the coating if you want, I can bring it. Oh, I remember we will be together in the evening for dinner at our home. I will bring it when I give you a ride back to your home. My father is waiting to hear about the technique of bronze casting of your new commission."

"Thank you, Stefano."

The evening set in early around 4 o'clock in the afternoon as wind blew strong through the hills and valleys and the gray clouds busily raced across the sky with frequent flashes of lightning.

Stefano and Niccolò went downstairs to the living room to meet Amadeo. Mother Orissa and Tia were surprised to see Stefano and welcomed him.

"You are already here," Niccolò's mother said.

"Oh, I was enjoying Maestro's company for a while and I saw his amazing sketch of the Prophet," Stefano said.

"Niccolò, have you already finished your sketching?" his mother asked.

"Yes Mamma, I am done. Stefano will provide a thin liquid for coating the sketch this evening so tomorrow it will be ready. Then I will relax for three days with all of you before I go back on the 3rd of January to Firenze."

"That is very nice Niccolò then we can spend time together talking and doing fun things and relaxing."

"I will help you with the cooking, Mamma."

"That is very nice, my dear son."

"If you are all ready, we will proceed to the carriage and I will drive you all to our home," Stefano said. "My parents are eagerly waiting for you."

The short carriage drive was uneventful except for the windy and dark conditions with frequent flashes of lightning. Once there, they found the living room cozy with the warmth of the fireplace. Marcello and Angela welcomed them to sit down and offered drinks.

Mother Orissa made tomato basil soup and risotto of rice with a variety of cheeses which she handed over to Angela. "Hope you will all like it," Orissa said.

"I'm sure we will all love it," Angela said.

Mother Orissa's eyes sparkled before she took her seat and then happily started to sip her wine.

Angela looked at the clock. "It is 5:30. I will serve dinner about half an hour from now if that is all right with you."

Everyone chimed a resounding, "Yes."

Angela announced that tonight's dinner will be Pappardelle with roasted tomato and meat, salad with lettuce, marinated beet and carrots. Also on the menu would be Mother Orissa's tomato basil soup and risotto.

Amadeo and Stefano said they cannot wait any longer. "Sounds delicious."

Marcello and Niccolò relaxed with their wine goblets in front of the fireplace.

"My dear friend, I am very curious about bronze casting, How do you do that?" Marcello asked Niccolò.

"It is very a laborious process. One has to be very careful and attentive. A sculptor makes a model with clay which is called core."

Niccolò was about to utter his next sentence when Angela announced, "Dinner is served. Please take your seats at the dining table."

"I will tell you the process of casting bronze later," Niccolò told Marcello.

Everyone started their dinner with mother Orissa's tomato basil soup and olive bread commenting, *"Delizioso!"* which made Orissa very happy.

Choruses of laughter and conversation went on with the crackling sound of wood in the fireplace and again, the topic focused mainly on Niccolò's stay in Castellina.

Angela, Stefano, and Marcello talked about how fortunate they were this year to spend Christmas with Niccolò and looked forward to welcoming the new year with Mother Orissa and her family.

Mother Orissa was very happy to hear that. "God bless you all and I love you very much."

"I cannot wait to hear from Maestro about the bronze casting," Stefano said.

Tia and Amadeo expressed they would love to hear about the casting technique while enjoying the cannoli dessert in front of the fireplace. Everyone laughed as they were all thinking the same thing. After finishing their delicious dinner, they all took their share of cannoli and settled in the living room in front of the fireplace as Stefano fed the fireplace with more logs.

With everyone gathered around, Niccolò started his story of casting.

"A sculptor molds the desired sculpture out of clay. This is called core. He covers the core with a thin layer of wax and makes details on the wax. Then he attaches the wax rod perpendicular to the wax surface covering the core. There will be channels from which the air and gasses will escape during the casting process. Bronze pins—chaplets—are inserted into wax and the core remain sticking out. Another layer of clay is placed over the entire wax covering. The whole structure is then baked as the wax melts."

"Very interesting but I wonder how the two clay shells will hold together the core and then the second layer of clay placed over the wax?" Marcello inquired.

"The chaplets are inserted to hold the two clay shells together. A mold has now been created. The whole structure is then baked up with earth and sand to hold steady and help the mold resist the pressure created when the molten metal is poured. The bronze is heated about 1350 to 1450 F.

"So what is bronze exactly?" Stefano asked.

"The molten bronze is an alloy of 90 percent copper and 10 percent tin. So this molten alloy is poured in the mold where the wax was. The clay core is most often scraped out to avoid interior corrosion. The bronze is rough and needs to be finished in a process called chasing. The limitation of direct method is that the sculpture is one of the original."

Marcello was happy to hear about the casting. "I am amazed to know about the procedure of casting. It takes so many careful steps to get it done."

"Maestro, you are amazing," Stefano said. "Did you perform this procedure before?"

"No Stefano, not exactly like this, but I have worked with Maestro Lorenzo on the door of the Baptistery and I learned a lot about casting from that experience."

The evening hours of the 29th of Dec 1421 passed at the Casini house as the shrill of a night bird welcomed a cold crisp night. The stars twinkled on Castellina as Stefano drove the carriage to take Niccolò, Amadeo, Tia and mother Orissa home.

Then Stefano drove back to his home, patted the horses goodnight just as the dark night pulled its curtain over the hills and valleys of Castellina.

* * *

30th of December 1421—Niccolò got up early and looked through the windows to see the sun trying hard to shine over the hills of Castellina. The sketched Prophet Habakkuk fixed on a board seemed to stare at him. Niccolò murmured, "Yes, Prophet, I know I have to apply a thin layer of liquid to coat you and then it will stay the way I sketched you and while traveling by coach to Firenze, you will remain fixed on the sketching paper. Then you will be at my studio where Paolo is eagerly waiting to welcome you and then every day both of us will slowly transfer you bit by bit to metamorphic marble which is so natural that you can see and talk to the people when they come and visit you at the cathedral. What do you say about this, Prophet? I know you do not want to talk. I take it that you agree?" Niccolò took his fine brush and concentrated on applying the thin layer of liquid to coat the sketch.

He passed most of his day applying the thin layer of liquid to fix the Prophet on the sketching paper. It was almost at the end of the day when he heard a knock at his door and saw Amadeo. "Please come in."

"Uncle, we are soon gathering at our living room for some drink and snacks. Stefano is already there and Angela and Marcello will be joining us soon. We will have dinner at our house. Marcello and Angela are in the process of arranging their house for a New Year's Eve party."

"Oh, that is wonderful. I am done with my work for now so I will put my sketching marker and pencils in my bag and will join you."

Amadeo smiled. "See you soon."

Downstairs Tia and Mother Orissa dressed in their long, silky dresses, Tia in her amber dress reaching down to her ankles with a black embroidered shawl and mother Orissa with her forest green, long-sleeved, below-the-knee pleated dress. Tia adorned herself with a necklace of green beads and gold earrings while Mother Orissa wore a gold-setting coral earing and an amber bead necklace.

Stefano and Amadeo wore their briefs and ruffled shirt with a brown vest.

Mother and Tia welcomed Niccolò who shook hands with Stefano.

"Maestro, now that you are done with your work, we are eager for you to join us."

"Yes, I am ready to enjoy the rest of my stay just enjoying all of your company."

Angela and Marcello brought platters of food, handing them to Tia. Angela wore her sky-colored long silk dress, her long neck adorned with a necklace of blue sapphire placed on a silvery case and two diamond earrings which sparkled as she moved forward to talk to mother Orissa.

The party started with drinking wine from Amadeo's vineyard and cured olives from Marcello's grove and a variety of cheeses.

"Dinner will be served at 6 o'clock, another half an hour from now," Orissa said. "The soup today is Ribollita which is a bread and winter cabbage soup. Angela made Fagiolle Al Uccelleto, white beans, puréed tomato and olive oil, and baked sourdough bread. I made gnocchi with spicy sausage from Siena. Dessert is almond rice."

"Sounds delicious," Marcello said.

"We will enjoy our dinner with Maestro as he talks about his studio and future commissions," Stefano said.

Everyone ate their dinner with bread and vegetable soup which was delicious, followed by Fagiolle and gnocchi. The slices of fresh sourdough bread proved to be a nice compliment to the meal.

Then they all gradually moved to the living room with their almond rice dessert, eagerly waiting for Niccolò to talk about his studio and other commissions.

"The studio is crowded with pieces of stones of different kinds left over from the sculptors. My current sculpted piece is approximately the size of half of your living room. The walls are painted with light yellow. There are two doors: one is in the front and faces the street and the other at the opposite wall opens up in the back to a small covered patio. There is a big window with iron-framed glass which faces the street. It is not far from Ponte Vecchio where the bridge curves in Florence. Inside the studio, there are hooks on the wall to hang our bags and sometimes tools. We have two working benches, two closets to keep our tools. There are two covered clay jugs for drinking water on a small wooden table and a few goblets for drinking water. There are a number of wooden stools to sit while sculpting and also for resting your body and two covered lamps. Extra-long candles are kept in the closet.

"Two buckets usually filled with water to wash hands are kept just outside the studio in the covered patio. Paolo, who is my assistant, takes care of the studio. We start usually 9 in the morning but sometimes earlier than that. In the summer, we work long hours till late afternoon. During winter, we stop working early afternoon as the sun goes down earlier and sometimes the sky is gray and cloudy so daylight is not enough, when lighted candles and covered lamps are not sufficient to do the precise work.

"While the studio is located in a quiet corner, you can still hear the screaming seagulls and clapping sounds of the oars of boats carrying passengers along river Arno. During breaks, we step outside to refresh ourselves with the gentle blast of cool breeze from the river Arno."

"It seems you like your workplace," Marcello said.

"Yes, I have no complaints. And working on my art is immensely satisfying."

"Maestro," Stefano began, "how do you handle so many commissions at the same time?"

Niccolò sighed. "Not at the same time. I usually work on one after another but sometimes I am compelled to work on two at the same time so I divide my time from morning till early afternoon for one project then the rest of the day I will sculpt the other one as much as I can."

The lines on Stefano's forehead creased. "That seems really hard."

"You know, Stefano, I am accustomed to this, that way my mind is occupied with my art and there is no time to think of anything else. My art keeps me busy and happy."

"Any further offers of new commissions?" Marcello asked.

"Yes, several in fact. Cosimo de' Medici's new palace will be built soon and he has ideas of several sculptures which will be placed inside the palace as well as his garden and he wants me to sculpt all of those. Then the Paduan people sent several messages to go there and meet the people who want me to sculpt their commissions. There is also a possibility of traveling to Rome with my friend and sculptor there."

"Wow, Maestro," Stefano said, his eyes widening. "You are so busy. I am glad that you are here for a few days and that we are honored to be in your company."

Suddenly, there was a flash of lightning as thunder roared. Marcello suggested he and his family set out for their home before it starts raining. While all took time to warmly bid goodnight to each other, Stefano heard the horses neigh, indicating it was time for them to go home too. Then the horses happily clip-clapped on the dirt road toward their home while thunder roared and lighting flashed often to pierce the darkness.

The Splendor of Notre Dame

December 28, 1964—Still enjoying and savoring their time in Paris, Rudy, Sharmi, Samir and Amita, dressed in their winter attire, grabbed a table at the Hotel Nolinski dining hall, by a large window where they had an ideal view of the street directly below where men and women with their winter clothes and umbrellas strode briskly to reach their destination while braving the gust of cold wind. The sky was gray and a veil of mist covered the city. Rudy and his friends kept reminiscing the unforgettable events of yesterday—the engagement of Sharmi and Rudy atop the Eiffel Tower followed by a celebration on a river boat cruise along the River Seine—that seemed to keep merrily swinging in their imagination. The attendant came to the table to take their orders with all of them ordering poached eggs and all three, except Sharmi, ordered sausages as well. Between tea or coffee, they all ordered coffee.

The dining hall was not yet full but there were a number of hotel guests, some from Japan, a few from the Middle East, others from United States, in fact, the Americans' conversations dominated the dining hall.

Amita, Sharmi, Rudy and Samir filled up their plates with fruit and pastries and enjoyed breakfast and conversation at their table. Samir started talking about the memorable events from that very special day that happened just yesterday and the cruise along the river was so perfect that it would remain in their memory for a long time.

For Rudy, it was his dream and fantasy come to life.

"Today will be a day of contrast," Amita said. "We are going to visit the Notre Dame Cathedral in the afternoon then attend a can-can show in the evening."

Sharmi asked whether they were going to take a guided tour to which Samir had replied, "Yes."

"How long will the guided tour be?" Amita asked.

"About two hours, we will start at 12:30 and will be done at 2:30 p.m. We can come back and have some snacks at the lobby and rest—enough time to get ready for the evening," Samir checked his watch. "The time is now 11:30. We should get a taxi to reach the Notre Dame."

By the time the four friends went down they luckily boarded a taxi that had been waiting in front of the hotel and soon they were off as the cab drove through the city covered with a misty veil. The hazy outline of the buildings and ghostly bare trees moved backwards and they reached within a short time the Parvis Norte Dame, the plaza of the famous Notre Dame Cathedral.

As the four of them stood in front of the west facade of the Notre Dame, they were amazed and speechless to feast their eyes on this iconic architectural marvel—a honey-toned stony façade, a remarkable gothic masterpiece of simplicity and harmony—during daytime.

"Now I agree with the famous architect Le Corbusier who called this a 'pure creation of spirit,'" Samir said.

As he finished speaking, they saw a young man about five-feet eleven inches tall with a pointed nose, hazel eyes, brown hair parted in the middle, who was waving a rectangular piece of paper with the names of Samir, Amita, Rudy and Sharmi in bold letters.

He wore a blue shirt, dark brown, long-sleeved cardigan, dark navy-blue trousers and a khaki trenchcoat which reached to his knees. The four friends approached the man and introduced themselves to the tour guide, Raphael who shook hands and greeted each one with, *"Enchante."*

"I will give you a short history and walk you through the Notre Dame as much as I can in a short time," Raphael said. "There are so many interesting things that's not quite possible to see in one visit."

Raphael took a deep breath. "Okay, the cathedral was built on a small island called the Ile de la Cite in the middle of this Seine River. Construction began in 1163 during the reign of King Louis VII and was completed in 1345. The cathedral is considered to be a jewel of Gothic architecture. I trust you all know that Notre Dame means "Our Lady" and is the seal of the Archbishop of Paris. After construction began, the flying buttresses were added—anyone have an idea why?"

"For support," Sharmi replied.

"Very good," Raphael said. "The flying buttresses were meant to support the structure, but also added to the cathedral's Gothic style. The cathedral was damaged and neglected in 1790 during the French Revolution. I'm sure you all know the novel, *The Hunchback of Norte Dame* by Victor Hugo. This book informed readers about the decrepit condition of the cathedral. The book also helped the spur of significant overhauls from 1844 to 1864 when architects Jean Baptiste, Antoine Lassus, and Emmanuel Viollet-Le Dac redid the spire and flying buttresses.

"I suggest you all take time to carefully observe the flying buttresses to get a good idea of what I am talking about. Let me know if you have any questions," Raphael said.

The four friends carefully observed the spire and buttresses from a closer angle that made all the difference as they felt the importance of having those to secure the cathedral in its place. They all expressed how very amazed they were to see the flying buttresses and could not believe how the architect figured out this whole marvelous design would work at that time.

"It is a medieval Catholic church and a finest example of gothic architecture with its pioneering rib vault and flying buttresses," Raphael said. "Now I will show and explain to you about the western façade which is 41-meters wide and includes powerful buttresses and three portals and took less than a century to build. Construction started in 1200. The façade is a harmonious ensemble based on a play between vertical and horizontal lines. Four powerful buttresses rise to the towers, an attempt to reach towards heaven and two horizontal strips seem to bring men down to earth. The height between the ground to the base is 43 meters. The façade is governed by a series of squares and circles treating symbolic significance. The square refers to limited created space, while the circle is boundless. That is a perfect figure without beginning and end, the image of God. Any questions?"

"No question but I am amazed how deeply they thought about every detail while constructing the cathedral," Samir said.

"I'm just giving you in brief an idea of the cathedral," Raphael said. "You have to explore everything in detail yourself and then you can take a guided tour again to go into even more details of the cathedral."

All four of them said they agree with their tour guide who continued his narration.

"Well, now look at the façade— which has three portals. The larger one is the portal of the Last Judgment. It is the middle one built from 1220 to 1230 and was the last one to be completed. The left north portal of the Virgin, the right south portal, the portal of St. Anne. The portal of the Virgin was completed between 1210 to 1220. The center of tympanum shows Mary's coronation in heaven, being crowned queen of heaven while she sits on the same throne as Jesus in the lintel below Mary in her death bed surrounded by Jesus and twelve apostles. Two angels are about to lift her up to heaven.

"The Portal of St Anne was built in 1200 and shows scenes from the childhood of Jesus, from the Annunciation of Mary to the adoration of the Magi." Raphael paused to allow the group to take it all in. "Now you may all go explore and see for yourself."

The group was very pleased to see those portals on their own and expressed their gratitude to Raphael for his detailed explanation.

"I recommend you all take time to visit the inside of the cathedral and suggest you pay close attention to the rose windows carefully; there are three rose windows, rose window being a generic name applied to a circular window for those found in gothic cathedrals and churches. It is a highly complex design which can be seen to bear a similarity to a multifaceted rose. In gothic cathedrals and churches, a rose is found above the west door. The common subject is the Last Judgment, when rose windows are used in the transept end, one of them will be dedicated to mother Mary. Use of blue and red are in abundance. The blue represents purity and the color of the Virgin Mary. The red represents the blood of Christ." Raphael paused to allow the group to contemplate these details.

"There are two more things I'd like to tell you in brief," he continued. "The first one is about the organ and the second one about the bells. The symphonic organ has been the voice of the Norte Dame since 1733. It has 8,000 pipes divided into 115 stops making it France's largest instrument. It has five keyboards as well."

"Wow, 8,000 pipes!" Amita chimed. "Just imagine the sound that comes out will be out of this living world!"

"Yes," Raphael said, "you'd have to listen to it to believe it. "There are ten bells—the Bourda which is tuned to an F sharp dated in the 15th century, recast in 1681 upon the request of Louis XIV who named it Emmanuel and weighs about 13271 kg. All others weigh less than Emmanuel and all are named after a saint."

After a pause to allow the group to assimilate the information, Raphael said, "Well, it has been a pleasure to meet you and I wish you all a pleasant stay in Paris. Please take your time to look around inside this amazing cathedral."

All four of them expressed their gratitude to their tour guide saying they all "had a wonderful time listening to all the details about the Notre Dame."

Amita, Samir, Rudy and Sharmi started walking inside the cathedral wanting to focus on the three rose windows. The first one they targeted was the west façade which they stood gazing at in front of the rose window for half an hour entranced by the mesmerizing colors. They all agreed the detailed depiction of the story was unique.

They all came to the conclusion that they have to come back again and devote more time to see all this splendor and enjoy it more.

Sharmi was very happy to gain this knowledge about the Norte Dame and considered how she might try to write about the cathedral and literature at that time period.

"That is wonderful," Amita said.

Samir and Rudy were anxious to get back to their hotel after spending almost half a day of the guided tour at the Notre Dame. They were very eager to have some tea and snacks and relax sitting around before getting ready to have fun at the Moulin Rouge.

The foursome took a cab from the Notre Dame back to the Hotel Nolinski, all excitedly talking about their eventful few days in Paris. The air inside the cab was filled with warmth from their conversation of their days in Paris with topics ranging from some sculptures they viewed at the Louvre, or some famous painting they all loved especially the ones they considered to be unforgettable and beautifully haunting.

Samir mentioned that "The Death of the Virgin" by Caravaggio still haunted him as the painting was a contrast of bright color of the virgin's clothes against a very dark background. The painter did not put any sign of divinity except a faint halo around the virgin's head.

"I read that Caravaggio fully exploited the nuances of chiaroscuro to enhance the three-dimensional nature of his figures and other objects," Rudy said. "He also used tenebrism to emphasize dark contrast to pick out weeping mourners and illuminated Mary's lifeless form with heavenly light."

"I read about that as well," Sharmi chimed in. "He showed Mary laid out like poor people and being mourned just like poor people were mourned."

"The Mona Lisa was beautiful but to my eyes there were so many other beautiful paintings," Rudy commented with a sigh.

"You know, Rudy, it's not the portrait itself, it's the technique," Amita said."What Leonardo invented was absolutely new at the time as he was using colors, layer after layer to make the background just blend in infinite. I like the Sfumato technique."

"We have to consider the background story which goes along with it too," Sharmi said.

Their back-and-forth conversation came to an end suddenly when they passed the opera house and the cab reached their hotel. The Hotel Nolinski was made of Carrara marble where the secrets of bringing in a space of contemporary and classical prestige met in an enchantment and flair.

The four friends entered the lobby stepping on the floor made with a blue hue of emerald green precious material. The custom-made pieces of furniture cushioned with amber-colored velvet and soft tweed waited for their tired bodies to rest on them. The background music and intimate setting scented with spice and musk was an invitation for their senses to roam and emotions to rise.

They sat in a corner where stood a table made of walnut finish and in its center a single red rose propped inside a slender tube-shaped vase.

An attendant named Adam came to hand a menu of different kinds of snacks and pastries. He asked the group, "Tea or coffee?" and they all chose coffee.

Adam took the ladies' order first. "Madame, what do you prefer?"

"What about the éclair de genie?" Amita asked.

"Oh, that is a wonderful choice," Adam said.

"And I would like the apple tart," Sharmi said.

"Good choice," the waiter said, "ours is one of the best in the area."

When it was Rudy's turn to order, he asked, "What do you suggest?"

"Oh monsieur, you see the name *Stohrer*? This is a puff pastry topped with bourbon vanilla cream and a caramelized glaze. This particular one was a favorite of Louis XV."

"All right," Rudy said. "I will have that."

Samir said, "What about this Pierre Herme?"

"Excellent choice," the waiter said, "it is a crunchy biscuit with hazelnuts and chocolate."

They settled down as their server, Adam set the table with off-white placemats and maroon napkins, gold-bordered white plates and silverware.

They checked the time which was just quarter to four in the afternoon and noted they had plenty of time. They discussed heading up to their rooms around 6 to change into their evening clothes and be ready by 7, well enough time to be at the Moulin Rouge by about 7:30, a half hour earlier.

"I'll go check at the front desk if there is any message," Samir said.

He was surprised that there was a message for Sharmi from her roommate, Sharon, who, like Sharmi, was a graduate student in the department of English at Durham University. Sharon had left a message for Sharmi to call her. When Sharmi got this message, she became very anxious, her hands and feet became cold and she started breathing heavily with interrupted sighs. She refused to eat her snack and preferred to go to her room. But her friends encouraged her to sit down and have her snack and tell them why she was so anxious. Rudy drew closer and patted her back gently for support.

"I have a feeling that there's a message from India," Sharmi said, her voice cracking. "Something must have happened."

"I think you are just overreacting," Amita said. "And until you know for sure, don't worry about it."

"Amita, you know how I feel when I'm anxious," Sharmi countered. "I can't just sit here. You all go and enjoy the evening. I must call and see what is happening."

Amita's expression softened. "All right, go ahead and call for your peace of mind. We are here to support you. It is just past four in the afternoon. Durham is a just one hour behind Paris."

Sharmi took Amita's advice and called her friend, Sharon, who immediately told Sharmi that the call was from her sister in India who wanted to relay the message that their mother is not doing well. Immediately Sharmi felt weak as she said goodbye to Sharon on the phone. Sharmi could not control herself as her whole body shook and she burst into tears just when Amita and Rudy came and hugged her. Her friends urgently suggested that Sharmi call her family in India to find out more about her mother.

After figuring out the time was now around 8:30 in the evening in Kolkata, Amita dialed the number and Sharmi started talking to her sister Urmi, who answered the phone.

"Ma will not eat anything unless you come home," her sister said, "we are just able to force her to take some liquids like milk, sometimes buttermilk and green coconut water. No solid food for the last four days."

Her friends told Sharmi, "You need to make arrangements which will take at least two to three days maybe more."

Sharmi told her sister Urmi and she in turn let their mother know. This time, Sharmi's mother took the phone and said in a very feeble voice, "I want to see you. Come home soon."

Sharmi started sobbing. "I will try to come as soon as possible, Ma, please try to eat."

"Let me know soon when you are coming," Sharmi's mother said, "if you do not, I will not even drink anything. Urmi is trying to force me to drink."

"I am going to go there as soon as I can arrange it. Please, please do not," she pleaded and started sobbing, "do not do this to us, don't do this to yourself."

Sharmi put the phone down. "I don't know what I'm going to do!" she wailed.

Rudy took Sharmi in his arms to comfort her.

"Try to book a flight from Paris to Kolkata tomorrow afternoon," Samir suggested. "Let us know the situation when you reach Kolkata and we can arrange your return flight."

"Sharmi, you must let your professor know that your mother is ill and you must visit her in India," Amita advised. "Tell the professor you will return to England as soon as possible."

After composing herself, Sharmi started dialing Professor Martin, the head of the department and her supervisor. Fortunately, she got a hold of him and explained her situation—that her dear mother was not well and wanted to see her.

Sharmi's voice was very sad and shaky and her professor was very nice and understood the situation.

"Do not worry my dear," he said, "if needed, I will give you an extension so that you can complete your thesis later. Keep me updated on your situation in detail and take care of yourself. I know it is hard on you. Just remember, the Universe sometimes brings problems for a reason but eventually situations resolve themselves within time."

Sharmi was overcome with emotion and burst into tears and with her tremulous voice said, "Thank you, thank you, Professor." And they exchanged a warm goodbye, each wishing the other well.

Meanwhile Rudy and Samir started searching and trying to get a flight for Sharmi to Kolkata. They came across a direct flight to Kolkata that leaves the next day at 1:30 in the afternoon and with Sharmi's consent, they booked the flight.

In the meantime, the attendant served coffee and snacks as the friends begged Sharmi to sit down and talk about how she was going to deal with the situation of her engagement with Rudy which she still kept secret from her family.

Sharmi took a deep breath as creases formed on her forehead. "That is a major problem and a difficult situation as my mother is on hunger strike because I refused to marry the person they selected. They had already made up their minds and thought this is the best although his parents and my parents are close friends and the person is well established, they took for granted that I will agree and will be happy with the arrangement." She looked at Rudy. "I never liked him and was just being courteous all along."

Her friends nodded in understanding.

"Just be gentle and try to express yourself to them the way you've done to us," Amita said. "Go visit your mother. Tell her gently that you must submit your thesis and show up for an examination to get your degree. But if you are prepared to do whatever is needed for your parents, then they should also respect what you want to do. Tell them you will not be happy otherwise."

Then the clock started striking at 5 as Sharmi became quiet, her eyes scanning the source of the sound. She thought there was something solemn in the repeated strokes of the clock: a remembrance of her childhood as there was a grandfather clock in their house that used to strike in the same way and oh! She could hear the playful footsteps of her youth, imagining a peaceful evening, the chirping of crickets, the scent of jasmine through a gentle summer breeze. Nothing could ever take the place of childhood in India, Sharmi thought as she sat there staring at the clock, eyes welling with tears.

Amita patted her friend's back. "Come on, Sharmi, your coffee is getting cold."

Sharmi started speaking very slowly. "Nothing is very clear to me. It's like a twilight existence in the midst of everything, I am on the crest of a wave. I do not know what to do."

Amita and Rudy took turns hugging Sharmi.

"Just think, tomorrow you are going to fly to India to go see your mother and your family," Samir said.

"Everything will be fine and you are going to come back and complete your thesis and get your graduate degree at Durham," Rudy assured his fiancée. "Life is giving you a sign to be bold and strong and the rest is up to you."

The four of them sat there for a while to finish their snacks and coffee.

Then the clock started striking at 6 o'clock. Her friends reminded Sharmi to call her family in India to let them know that she will be arriving at Kolkata at 11:30 a.m. on the 30th of December. When Sharmi talked to her sister, it made her mother happy.

Samir, Amita, and Rudy were relieved that Sharmi's mother felt better and that her daughter would be arriving soon to visit her. They all told Sharmi now there is no reason to back out of going to the Moulin Rouge that night.

"To me, it wouldn't feel proper," Sharmi said.

"What is proper, Sharmi?" Amita said. "To just sit alone in your room? To cancel the event tonight? That's not fair to us. That's not even fair to yourself."

Sharmi agreed in the end to spend the evening with her friends at the Moulin Rouge.

"You are lucky you don't have to pack much for your travel to India, just some personal essentials and a change of clothes," Samir said. "You might end up with just a carry-on bag and prepare that before you get ready for the evening."

"That's true," Sharmi said. "I guess I'll only spend about a half an hour to pack my things for the flight so I can get ready for the evening."

Finally, they all went to their rooms to change into evening clothes. The men wore neckties as was the dress code for the evening. Then they got a cab and were off to the Moulin Rouge.

Amita and Samir sat closely holding their hands while Rudy held Sharmi by her waist and pulled her towards him. Sharmi was overcome with emotion and started sobbing.

"No more tears," Rudy said, soothing her fears and tears, "we are all going to have fun for the next few hours."

The cab zoomed through the illuminated avenues of Paris until they arrived at the avenue near Moulin Rouge where all other nightclubs were dazzling with blinking lights, lighted images of dancing ladies spilling wine cups and the spinning windmill of the Moulin Rouge.

They were excited as they got out of the taxi and as soon as they entered, an attendant looked at their tickets and asked them to follow him to the grand hall with the big performance stage.

Rudy's group chose the section called Henri de Toulouse-Lautrec evening. Moulin Rouge opened in 1889 when Toulouse-Lautrec was commissioned to produce a series of posters, said Louis, the attendant while escorting them to their seats. "Henri Marie Raymond de Toulouse-Lautrec was a French painter, printmaker, caricaturist and illustrator. Mesdames et Messieurs, I can continue telling you about his life story in short, if you like, or I can stop here and let you enjoy yourselves."

The group of friends expressed that they would love to hear more about his life story and also wanted to know about the can-can.

"Henri de Toulouse-Lautrec was among the best known painters of the post-impressionist period along with Cezanne, Van Gogh, Paul Gauguin and Georges Seurat," Louis continued. "He lived between Nov. 24, 1864 to Sept. 9, 1901 and was a member of an aristocratic family."

"You mean to say that he lived among counts and countesses?" Amita said.

"Yes exactly that," Louis replied, "if Toulouse had lived longer, he would have inherited the title of count. But he had a congenital health problem and a disability. The condition attributed to family in-breeding. His legs ceased to grow. He had a short stature but developed an adult-sized torso with a big forehead, facial distortion with brittle bone and his dense bone easily fractured. He had the inability to exercise and sometimes difficulty in breathing. This condition was suggested as Pycnodysostosis."

"Did he get any medical help for his condition?" Samir asked.

"There was no treatment available for the condition itself at that time," Louis replied, "he only got treatment for complications like fracture of bone and difficulty in breathing. Toulouse always had difficulties with normal activities so he had to keep himself busy with his artworks. Toulouse's mother had high ambitions and tried to get him to renowned Bonat's studio to study under Leo Bonat. He was drawn to Montmartre the area famous for bohemian life and gatherings of artists, writers and philosophers.

"After training under Bonat, he moved to Fernand Cormon in 1882 and established a group of friends he kept the rest of his life. He met Emile Bernard and Vincent van Gogh. Cormon was more relaxed and allowed pupils to roam and look for subjects. Toulouse was fascinated by the lifestyles of the 'urban underclass' and incorporated those characters into his paintings."

"What was the connection between Toulouse and Moulin Rouge?" Rudy asked.

"Montmartre cafés were some kind of consolation to Toulouse, a way to forget his condition," Louis answered. "He met his muse La Goulue whose real name was Louise Weber. Moulin Rouge opened in 1889 and Toulouse was commissioned to produce a series of posters. Toulouse was a regular customer of Moulin Rouge shows every night relentlessly drawing everything around him. In 1891, he made the first advertising poster of Moulin Rouge which became one of the famous representations of the cabaret even today. He painted some of the famous personalities: Astride Bruant, Jane Avril, and Yvette Gulbert. His portrait of Jane Avril and his representation of Moulin Rouge were considered a masterpiece. Suffering from alcoholism owing to his unpleasant consumption of absinth and cognac and contracting syphilis at the same time, he was taken to a sanatorium before dying at the age of thirty-seven. And that's the brief life story about Toulouse. And you also requested me to give a brief account of can-can."

Rudy and his friends expressed wanting to know about the history of can-can.

"The can-can appeared in Paris in 1830. 'Can-can' in French slang at the turn of 19th century meant malicious gossip or scandal. At that, people loved to go to balls and the last dance of the night was with couples called a quadrille. The can-can originated out of this last dance with higher kicks and more energy. The dance challenged political convention and a call for change.

"Dancers, usually four in a group, hold up high the seams of their frilly dresses kicking their legs to reveal petticoats and underwear. The music is a march tune composed by Jacques Offenbach. Madame et Messieurs, that is in brief all about the can-can. Soon the music will start to invite the guests to the dance floor and after that, the dinner will start. So please enjoy," Louis said, "it was nice meeting you all."

Sharmi, Amita, Rudy and Samir thanked Louis for giving them a brief biography of Toulouse and a brief background of the Moulin Rouge and can-can. Soon after Louis left, the music started and guests were invited to the dance floor. Then the lights dimmed and live orchestra music came on.

After a few minutes, couples started to join others on the dance floor. It was mesmerizing to see couples with long dresses as they started waltzing, the different shades of light focusing randomly over the couples—it looked like a dreamland. Amita and Samir began to dance then Rudy guided Sharmi to the floor, holding on to her tightly as they moved slowly. Sharmi rested her head on Rudy's chest and moved slowly to Rudy's lead. It was misty and dreamy as the couples kept on moving with the music in their fantasy and enchanted lands of their own.

They all snapped back to the present when announcements of dinner started and Rudy's group approached their designated table which was covered with a red table cloth, gold-border white dinner plates, silverware, white napkins and candelabra with flickering white candles. The four friends promptly took their seats.

The waiter served them bulgar salad with black tiger prawns marinated and cooked with tandoori, pickle cucumber and pomelos. He then showed them the menu and asked if the group wished to order veal with grilled wild mushroom, or chicken fricassee with parmesan cheese or sea scallops with lentil and chives.

Rudy and Samir ordered veal. Amita asked for chicken fricassee with parmesan cheese, Sharmi ordered sea scallops, lentil and chives. Everyone commented that the salad was delicious especially as there was a touch of tandoori spice.

There was not much time left for the friends to talk to Sharmi as she would be flying to Kolkata by the next afternoon, so they all started to wish her "Bon voyage" to Kolkata.

"Remember to stay calm and prioritize your life first and see how they react," Amita said. "If your family truly loves you, then they would want you to be happy."

"There will be a lot of sensitive issues to make you feel guilty but remember to stay focused," Samir said. "You have to finish your thesis and also get your graduate degree."

"Please call us and keep us updated on what is going on with you," Rudy pleaded, squeezing Sharmi's hand gently. "Paris will not be the same without you and it will be difficult as we will be here in Paris one more day. We will miss you, but I feel that for your peace of mind you must settle things with your family. It will be good for us to start our future together if you make peace with your family. Remember, I am just a phone call away if ever you need me." Rudy smiled when Sharmi nodded and patted his hand.

The attendant brought the main course and a bottle of champagne and a special drink for Sharmi who loved the color of her drink as she asked what it was.

Adam, the waiter, said, "Madame, it is cranberry lemonade." He surveyed the whole group. "Take your time and enjoy and when you finish dinner, I will bring your dessert: white chocolate mousse, salted butter caramel apple compote and Jaconde Biscuit."

Everyone thanked him.

"I am especially worried about how they will react from the fact that I am engaged without informing my parents," Sharmi said.

"That is true, there is cause for concern initially," Samir said, "but I trust it will be all right when you let them know who Rudy is and what he is doing and what are Rudy's sincere intentions for the future."

"Take some photos of all of us together with you," Amita suggested. "Once your parents see that you are in good hands with me and Samir as your friends who will vouch for Rudy, then you will gain their trust. You have to be honest with them, Sharmi. Then they will eventually come around."

The waiter returned to check whether Rudy's group was almost done with their main course. The four friends all praised the chef for cooking such delicious main courses.

"This is the most delicious fricassee I've had in a long time," Amita said.

"And my scallop dish was scrumptious," Sharmi added. "It was the first time I had tasted this."

Adam was very happy, and in no time, he brought their dessert. "The show is going to start soon."

The dessert nearly melted in their mouths as the lights started blinking once the show started. The marching music was very exhilarating as groups of four ladies danced energetically with their frilly, colorful, long skirts, kicking their legs high almost over a man's hat who was doing some tricks with ropes at the side of the stage at the same time.

Rudy held Sharmi, putting his hand around her shoulders and occasionally squeezing the back of her upper arm.

On the stage, the first group moved to the side and kept on dancing with the music as another group of four women came with more energetic gestures, lifting their skirts high to show their undergarments.

Samir drew Amita closer to him and kissed her as Amita relaxed her head on Samir's shoulder.

Then the next group of four arrived dancing on the stage, doing splits and tumbles. There were jokers who performed with their funny faces in between the dancing yet the show kept on flowing seamlessly and they were almost at the tail end when the whole ensemble joined on stage and danced then the music paused and the light dimmed.

Then suddenly, there was a group of beautiful women who posed nude for a few minutes on stage like a framed painting amid the sound of "Ooo's and Ahh's" from the audience filling the air. Their figures looked so perfect, their radiant skin, the contour of breasts, their lean figures narrowed to their perfectly small waists and flat abdomens where the dimple of the belly button rested. With the allure of their eyes, their long shapely legs which complemented their sensual hips, they looked unreal, as though they seemed to appear from some unknown place and time.

The stage dimmed even further then suddenly, like magic, the lights came from different directions to brighten the stage with rainbow colors. At the end, all the performers, jokers, and dancers gathered on stage simultaneously to perform a spectacular finale with a gallant end.

The audience gave the performers a standing ovation for some time so the performers had to come back on stage twice as the audience would not stop cheering them on until they realized it was time to quit and leave the hall.

Rudy, Sharmi, Samir and Amita were all dazed as they got a cab and returned to their hotel. Rudy gave a good night kiss and a warm hug to Sharmi, and all four said that they would meet at breakfast at 10 in the morning and from there, they would accompany Sharmi to the airport.

At the hotel's breakfast hall the next morning, Rudy spotted a table by the window with a view outside of a gray morning. The streets seemed to be wet and he could see it was drizzling. He was anxious as he did not see the rest of his friends so he ordered poached eggs and sausages. After scanning around the hall, Rudy finally saw Samir, Amita and Sharmi coming from the other end of the dining room to meet him. After exchanging morning greetings, Rudy observed how much Sharmi looked tired and nervous as she informed everyone that she could not sleep last night.

Rudy attempted to reassure her as Samir and Amita joined him and together, they all tried their best to cheer up Sharmi so by the time breakfast was over, Sharmi felt a little better.

Rudy embraced Sharmi warmly reminding her she can call him collect from Kolkata as Sharmi nodded and tried her best to smile.

Then they all took a cab to the airport. Sharmi had no extra luggage so she went through checking in quickly and soon they all waved her up to the gate where she stopped, looked back at her friends and waved one last time before joining the other passengers on their way to boarding their respective flights.

Rudy took a deep breath and exhaled as Amita assured him, "She will be all right. When she reaches her home, her younger sister is very close to her and she will be a great help and support to Sharmi."

"Thank you," Rudy said, as he realized how empty he felt without Sharmi by his side.

"Let's all go back to our hotel and plan our day," Samir said, patting his friend on the back. Okay, Rudy?"

"Okay," Rudy replied, taking a deep breath as he longed for activities to distract him from worrying about and missing Sharmi. He was really glad and grateful he had the good sense to bring the biography of Niccolò book with him as reading about how the sculptor had overcome struggles had given Rudy the strength to go on.

He nodded to Samir and Amita. "I am open to whatever you suggest."

New Year's Eve in Castellina

December 31ˢᵗ 1421—In the afternoon at the Casini family's house, everyone was busy with the preparation of welcoming the year 1422.

They were all excited to have Niccolò join them to celebrate New Year's Eve. Angela was preparing food and Stefano placed candles around the house in different places. Marcello decorated the center of the dining table with a flower decoration where a few candles would be placed.

Long garlands of different colors of handmade paper flowers hung in various areas of the wall and over the fireplace. Logs were stacked in front of the fireplace. The party would last until early morning when the guests would get tired and ready to return home.

"Mamma, what time would you like me to go to Amadeo's house to bring them here?" Stefano asked his mother.

"Around 6," Angela replied. "I will serve dinner a little late, around 7."

"That is good. That way I have a few more hours to finish the decorations."

Stefano worked another couple of hours until he was satisfied with his New Year's Eve decorations. Marcello walked through the house and complimented his son on a job well done.

"Stefano, the house looks so festive."

"Thank you, Papa, you made my day. I will check whether Mamma finished her cooking and will help her set the food on the table."

"I will help too," Marcello said, "then it will be done sooner."

Marcello and Stefano entered the kitchen where Angela was cooking.

"We are here to help you if you need us," Marcello said. "May I ask, what is the menu today?"

It turns out that Angela conducted her own decorating scheme. On a wall hung a large piece of art paper given to her by Niccolò, where Angela decorated the border with flowers and wrote:

New Year's Eve Dinner Menu

*Mediterranean mixed seafood

*Chianina meat balls with braised sauce

*Calamarata pasta with shrimp

*Rissotto with roast chicken

*Dessert: Almond Biscotti and Pandoro

*Midnight snack: Zampone, Pork Sausage with Lentil

*Red and white wine

"That is an excellent menu," Marcello said.

"Mamma you already cooked everything," Stefano said.

"Oh, yes," replied Angela with a tired but bright smile.

"The Zampone," commented Marcello, whose favorite dish included this fennel pie with scalloped potatoes.

"Yes, that is a sign of good luck," Angela said, "but somehow I have to keep it warm by putting a large quantity of water in a big container with a lid and let the water continue to boil, wrap the Zampone with palm leaves and put that on top of the container lid two hours before midnight so it will stay warm."

"Mamma, you are a genius."

Angela ruffled Stefano's hair. "Thank you, my dear son."

"What is the time now?" Marcello said.

"It is quarter to 5," Stefano said.

"Let me change and get ready," Angela said.

"We should all change and get ready," Marcello said, "but before that, I want to put the containers, bowls and platters where food will be displayed."

"That is a very good idea," Angela commented. "Let me take those out and you can arrange them. I made some labels to place beside each food dish in the menu."

"That is great idea, Mamma."

"I will take the food to the table after our session of cheese and wine," Angela said. "Well now, we should get ready for the party. Stefano, get ready when you can and before you leave to pick up your friend's family, please hang those different colored lanterns on the hooks outside."

"Yes, Mamma."

Stefano got ready in a very short time, donning his maroon brief with gold buttons, beige, long-sleeved shirt with ruffles and a maroon vest with gold work.

Marcello changed into his long-sleeved dark green doublet, rust-colored hose and light brown tapered front suede shoes and rust color cap.

Angela took out her rust color, long-sleeved, square neck, floor-touching flared, velvet dress accentuated with gold piping and white lace around the neck and the cuff. She looked in the mirror to secure her black brown hair in a bun accentuated by a gold hairpin with a gold star on top. She wore three-tiered round pearl earrings and one string of round big pearls on her neck.

She looked at the mirror once more then went down to meet her husband and son who both commented, "Oh you look gorgeous." Marcello was pleased to see Angela's dress matched with Marcello's brief.

Soon, Stefano and the carriage reached the gate of Amadeo's house where his friend came out with a lantern to greet him. Amadeo was dressed in his gold-colored brief, white, long-sleeved shirt, a gold-colored shiny vest, and a black woolen cape.

Niccolò, who had been ready for a while, wearing his brown brief and brown vest, held open the carriage door for his mother Orissa, dressed in gold-colored puffed, full-sleeved, round neck, floor-touching dress, with a long, dangling gold chain around her neck and two gold earrings. A red embroidered shawl rested on her shoulders. Tia, who followed her mother inside the carriage, wore her long violet Venetian dress, which flared from the waist with a lacy square neck and puffed long sleeves with white lace around the upper part of the puffed sleeves and around the cuffs. She adorned herself with a three-stringed pearl necklace and her teardrop pearl earrings swayed as she stepped inside the carriage with Niccolò stepping in behind her.

Stefano was very excited to see them all comfortably seated inside. Amadeo took a seat next to Stefano that was meant for the carriage driver's assistant.

Everyone exchanged greetings with a hearty, *"Ciao."*

Though it was already dark outside, the sky was clear except for a few clouds drifting by and the air felt moist and cold with the fresh scent of the earth due to a recent rain shower. When the carriage reached the gate of Marcello's house, Marcello and Angela came to greet Niccolò's family.

Marcello gave Niccolò a hearty handshake as he stepped out of the carriage as Amadeo helped his grandmother and Tia step out of the carriage. Angela hugged mother Orissa and Tia while Stefano took the horses and the carriage back to the covered stable.

The living room at Marcello's house was cozy and inviting with the crackling of burning wood in the fireplace and a fresh lavender scent filling the air as guests and hosts mingled cheerfully holding up wine goblets.

Stefano urged the group to gather by the fireplace as he moved sofas and cushioned chairs closer to the hearth. As much as Niccolò longed to share his plans for the next year, he encouraged everyone to share their new year goals.

"I want to learn Latin," Marcello said. "I did when I was young but could not continue. I was busy trying to earn a living."

"That is great, Marcello," Niccolò said. "What about you, Angela?"

"I just want to learn embroidery and other handicrafts from Tia," Angela said.

Pleased with the compliment, Tia said, "I look forward to teaching you what I know about handicrafts."

"You would be surprised by what we want to learn," Stefano said. "Fauxbourdon produced by three voices."

"Then proceeding in parallel motion in intervals corresponding to the first inversion of the triad," Amadeo said.

"Here comes another twist: the upper and lower voices progressing an octave or sixth apart, while the middle one extemporaneously doubles the upper part at a 4th below."

"Wow," they all exclaimed.

"That is wonderful," Mother Orissa said. "Will the performances mainly be in the churches?"

"Yes," Stefano said.

"Who else wants to share their plans for the new year?"

"I will continue to do what I love—my handicrafts," Tia said. "I like to make a sizable tapestry—a family scene with a father, mother, a cozy cottage. While my brother is smoothing sculptures, I am busy doing my embroidery."

"What a wonderful idea, my dear sister," Niccolò said.

"What about you, my brother?"

"Just like you, dear sister, I will continue to do what I do best—my passion—sculpting. But I learned to play the lute. When I was young, my dear mother bought me a lute which I will start playing again and practicing regularly. In fact, I will play some tune after our dinner tonight."

Everyone thought a musical concert by the great Niccolò was a wonderful idea.

"I hope everyone knows about the lute," Niccolò said.

"Yes, a little bit. It is a string musical instrument, am I correct?" Marcello said

"That is right," Niccolò said. "A lute is a plucked string instrument with a neck and a deep round back enclosing a hollow cavity usually with a sound hole or opening in the body. It is pear-shaped with six pairs of strings tuned in 4th with a 3rd in the middle. It is 36 inches in length and 11-12 inches wide. The gut stringing sound is delicate and rich. Lute is a symbol of harmony."

Mother Orissa was listening very patiently to everyone. "I am very pleased that everyone shared their resolution. I want to add: please try to carry it out regularly throughout the year. Do not abandon your dream when life gets busy with other things. It will be my pleasure to watch you all carry out what you have decided to do."

Everyone expressed appreciation to Mother Orissa promising they will try their best.

Angela invited everyone to help themselves to the food displayed on the dining table. "You can take your seat anywhere you like either around the dining table or the living room by the fireplace.

They all decided to sit around the dining table. Stefano announced that after dinner, Uncle Niccolò will play his lute then he and Amadeo will sing alternately with an accompanying tabor.

"I would like to request my father to play his clarinet,"

Everyone cheered on Stefano's announcement.

Mother Orissa took her seat at the head of the table as Angela was ready to serve her. "Can I start your meal with the Mediterranean seafood?"

"Yes, please," said Niccolò's mother.

In fact, everyone started with the Mediterranean seafood. Only Stefano wanted to first try the fennel pie with scalloped potatoes.

The smorgasbord of food slowly but surely got consumed by the hosts and guests. Conversation about delicious dishes filled the air. The chorus of serving spoons' touching on platters and the comments of particular menu items moved spirally around the dining room.

After the sumptuous New Year's Eve dinner, everybody gathered around the living room with their goblets of red wine and a piece of Pandoro, the eight-facet fluffy cake-like bread.

Niccolò plucked the strings of his lute and started playing a tune he improvised. He explained to the group the scene of a calm voyage on a ship suddenly interrupted by a storm, the sound of big waves crashing on the deck of the ship, the fearful sound of the ship's crew and the captain's loud announcement, all spiraled like a twister. The captain ordered the ship to turn so the ship made a turn which made everything and everyone displaced from their posts. After a short, turbulent period, the sky cleared and the ship started cruising smoothly along the vast sea.

The improvisation of Niccolò was beautiful and everyone enjoyed the music. The sound resonated richly that all in the room cheered. Then Niccolò, Stefano and Amadeo started singing:

"When Siena sleeps, everything is silent

Moon lights up the tower, sense in the dark

Alone in peace, subdued Fonte Gaia

Niccolò accompanied with his lute and Marcello joined with his clarinet as everyone once in a while softly sung or hummed to, "Long live our Siena…"

The impromptu concert lifted everyone's mood somewhere far beyond their presence in the living room, with only the crackling of firewood and the flickering shadow of the chandelier reminding them of their presence in Castellina.

They kept on singing and drumming the snare drum very softly, tiptoeing the tune.

After this song, Niccolò started singing while plucking his lute.

"O Rossa bella (Oh lovely rose)

O Dolce anima (My sweet soul)

Non mi Lasser morte (let me not die)

In contesia in contesia (in courtly love)"

Everyone was surprised that Niccolò was singing this kind of song—a song like this reflected the heartbreak and pain of love and described the secret passion between aristocrats that was erotic, spiritual and uplifting.

After a while, the music lulled the group into a relaxed mode. Mother Orissa, who was initially wide awake, her expression of surprise glistening as she listened to the music, now grew tired and sleepy, her eyes distant and fixed, as if searching for some clue.

Marcello and Angela complimented Niccolò for the song he performed. They praised Niccolò for his baritone voice. They all praised Stefano and Amadeo for their performances as well and both young men were amazed to find out that their uncle Niccolò was a very good singer, saying "We will continue to perform together till midnight though it might not be as good as Uncle Niccolò."

The music filled the air of the Casini family's residence and at the hour of midnight, the strokes started chiming in the house, beyond the three hills, through the dark clouds. The dreamy moon started to play hide and seek with the light and shadow chasing each other around the hills and valleys. With the blast of wintry wind, the church bells at Siena started chiming as everyone cheered loudly "Happy New Year!" with their wine goblets. Mother Orissa sprinkled rose petals and Angela sprayed scented water with a silver sprayer over the revelers.

Angela waited until everyone settled down then served the Zampone, pork sausages with lentils to each person, a tradition for a prosperous and healthy year ahead.

All of them enjoyed the Zampone and talked to each other for a while until it was time to retire. Stefano happily agreed to drive Amadeo's family home.

Niccolò bid a warm goodbye as he would be leaving on the morning of January 3rd to Florence. "I enjoyed my stay in Castellina and was very pleased and overcome with the excellent friendship, love and entertainment from the Casini family. I am so pleased to see Amadeo in his new house and feel very happy to see that he will be living close to this wonderful family of Angela, Marcello and Stefano. I will be very busy when I return to Florence but, thanks to all of you, I will be very carefree and blissful."

Rudy and Friends' Last Day in Paris

While Amita, Samir and Rudy stood in a long line to go inside the Louvre in Paris, they remembered the last time they were there with Sharmi and wondered how she was doing. Thoughts of Sharmi kept dominating their mind, especially Rudy's, ever since they sent her off at the airport. After about fifteen minutes, the friends decided that because of the long line, they gave up going in.

"It's Dec. 29, only a few days after Christmas and it seem tourists from all over the globe are gathered here today," Amita said. "Since we've already been to the Louvre, perhaps we can find other things to do with what's left of our precious time here in Paris."

"We could walk along the Champs-Élysées and then sit at some streetside café to enjoy some coffee and tea and watch people passing by," Samir suggested.

Rudy and Amita both agreed this was a good idea.

"Anyway, I wanted to visit the shops at Champs-Élysées," Amita said.

Starting out in Paris as the fabulous foursome and now down to a threesome, they took a taxi to the Champs-Élysées and realized it was an avenue in Paris' 8th arrondissement that stretched 1.2-miles long and 230-feet wide running between the Place de la Concorde and the Arc De Triomphe. This area was full of theaters, cafés and luxury shops. Amita was very enthusiastic about visiting some of the luxury shops as Samir and Rudy followed her. After getting inside a few of them, she got disenchanted looking at the high prices. Then the weather suddenly became windy and cold and the gray sky began to drop a drizzle.

So they decided to go into one of the several cafés and order some food. All of them ordered Cassoulet, a stew with meat, vegetables and pieces of bread on top and Chocolate Au Paine croissant filled with chocolate paired with hot tea.

They loved sitting inside at a cozy corner of the café enjoying their food and watching people pass by with their umbrellas. This was their last day in Paris so they were not in any pressure or schedule but wanted to feel the throbbing pulse of the city in their hearts.

"We are going back home tomorrow," Samir said. "Rudy, why don't you stay with us till January 1st? You are not working till January 3rd anyway."

"Actually I am not working till the 4th," Rudy said, "the 3rd is Sunday."

Their conversation was suddenly interrupted when they found at the periphery of their vision four hands waving at them. There was a table nearly next to them where two couples sat with their coffee, bowls of soup and slices of bread stacked on their side plates.

There were two tall and sturdy white males with light-colored hair, one with blue eyes and the other light green. The one with blue eyes, a round face, prominent nose, thick, light brown eyebrows and a very hearty smile wore a blue, long-sleeved shirt and khaki pants. The other one who wore a striped blue, long-sleeved shirt and navy pants, had an elongated face and a prominent nose. The color of their faces had a reddish tinge, The one with blue eyes and khaki pants pointed a finger to himself and said, "Nikita."

Then he pointed a finger to his wife, Olga, a tall, slim lady with beautiful brown eyes, golden-colored hair secured in a bun, and a triangular face with a pointed nose. She wore a forest green dress that reached below the knee with a gold-colored belt around her waist.

They waved and said, "India! India!" then said, "Moscova," pointing to all of them seated at their table. "No English," the man said.

Samir said half-jokingly, "No Russian."

Then the other couple introduced themselves as Maxim and Natalya who looked like a dancer. She was tall and slim with her brown hair in a bun on the middle of her head. Natalya had hazel eyes, a triangular face, a pointed nose suitable for her face. She wore a turquoise three-quarter-sleeved dress up to her knee, a long silver chain around her neck and two silver dangling earrings. Her legs were long and shapely. She was about five-feet-seven-inches tall.

Maxim pointing to himself and said, "acoustic engineer" and pointing to his wife Natalya, he said, "ballet teacher."

Nikita said he and Olga were aerospace engineers.

"*Privet*," Rudy said "Hello," and pointed to himself and Samir and said, "doctors." Then pointing to Amita, "Rudy said, "*Logoped*," which meant "speech therapist."

"*Rad vas videt,*" Nikita told them, "nice to meet you."

Maxim said, "*Vozrashchoyusdomoy segodnya Moscow*," which Samir, Rudy and Amita figured out as the couples were going back home.

"Bon Voyage," Samir said.

The friends waved their hands and started their conversation where they left off.

"We were talking about when we start work again," Rudy reminded.

"Yes, I thought we start on the 3rd of January and now I realize that is Sunday so I am also off on Sunday."

"And I want to call Sharmi on the 31st to find out what is going on," Amita said.

"That is a very good idea," Samir said. Then turning to his friend, he said, "Rudy, I am very glad that you two are engaged, my friend. So what are your thoughts about settling down, I mean, getting married?"

"Good question," Rudy replied. "Well, Sharmi has to finish her Ph.D. as you know, and in the meantime, I will try to get through the first part of my FRCS. I've already submitted my application in November. The examination is usually in April. So, if Sharmi could finish her Ph.D., it will be nice, then we could think about planning our wedding for either June or July. Of course, I have to consult with Sharmi. I have already informed my father, my brother and my sister. They are very happy. I don't think they can come to the wedding but they said they want to see us together so I have requested for few days off to see if we could take a break and visit them in India."

"Where would you like to have your wedding ceremony?"

"Oh, I have suggested this to Sharmi and she and I want the wedding ceremony in Venice," Rudy said.

"Wow. That is fantastic," Samir said. "Do you mean in a gondola?"

"Well, that would be very nice and unique," Rudy said, "but I do not know whether the gondola association will allow an event like that."

"Then let's find out," Samir said.

"Rudy, do you and Sharmi want an Indian wedding?" Amita asked.

"Yes," Rudy said, "with the usual customs, the exchange of garland and all that."

Amita and Samir both said that was so wonderful.

"We will help you arrange to have a priest for Indian rituals," Samir suggested. "It will be easy to register the marriage in Newcastle and if you want, you can invite a small group of people and arrange an intimate party the hospital staff can attend. I think people who are very close and also Indian friends who are doctors will make an effort to attend the wedding in Venice."

"Yes, you are right," Rudy said. "I have to sit down and calculate the budget."

"You do not have to pay for the hotel accommodations for everyone except the priest and someone from Sharmi's side and your side who are attending the wedding. Depending on the number of people, we have to reserve two to three gondolas and a venue for the wedding reception dinner," Amita said.

"Yes, we have to inquire about the hotel accommodation and dinner and also the rules for the gondolas," Rudy said. "I have about five months to plan all this but I will do it within a very short time otherwise, I believe, booking will be difficult and once I finish this, I have to concentrate on my studies for the first part of my fellowship examination in April 1965."

Amita raised her hand. "Change of topic. I'd like to know about our New Year's Eve plans. How are we going to set up the New Year's Eve party?"

"How many people are invited?" Rudy said. He really didn't feel like celebrating without Sharmi but being among friends would provide a positive distraction.

"Including us—ten," Amita said.

"I suggest calling the Kebab Place to cater and include an attendant who will arrange and serve us and at the end clean everything so that we do not have to do anything except arrange midnight snacks and drinks for the guests. What do you think about that, Amita?"

"That's a great plan," Amita said, clapping her hands, "yes it's good if we could do less so we can just enjoy the first day of January by taking it easy." She paused to take one more sip of tea. "I suggest we go back to our hotel to organize our luggage then we can just relax at our hotel lounge and have our dinner at our hotel because our flight is at 10 tomorrow morning."

They went to their hotel and organized their belongings not wanting to waste any time on their last day in Paris. After packing their luggage, they went down and decided to stroll leisurely along the area around their hotel to mingle with the Parisians.

Though the sky was overcast, the City of Light was sparkling and pulsating through a veil of mist. The people promenading on the sidewalks dressed up in their raincoats and boots, some pacing faster, others in a slow pace talking, couples holding hands looking for a café to tuck into for warmth. The musicians at the street corners played their guitars and in one particular corner, there were people gathered listening to a guitarist, a young adult likely in his early twenties, with brown black hair, a pointed nose, with dark, large eyes who stood in front of a handwritten poster that read he fled from the Middle East to seek asylum in France to study music. People would stop and toss some money inside his guitar case on the sidewalk, some would stop and ask questions about his background. The cars and buses kept rolling along the busy streets, the cafés crowded with people and the smell of coffee and food would whet their appetites for good French food and beverages as they passed by the bistros.

Suddenly there was a strong blast of cold wind that caused people to become aware, to stop and think of where to go when the rain started pelting down. People strode faster, taking shelter under some tall buildings' projecting cornice. Some took shelter in front of the shop's projected roof while others escaped to cafés. Few people braved the rain and wind and kept moving to their destination. Amita, Samir and Rudy were among those who wanted to go back to their hotel.

The rain and wind became stronger and stronger and fortunately an empty cab passed by and Samir was quick enough to hail the cab to give them a ride. Once they reached their hotel, they promptly changed out of their wet clothes into warm dry ones to get ready for a nice dinner in the hotel restaurant.

After changing their clothes, the friends met at the hotel restaurant which was comfortable and convenient. Once seated at a table close to the fireplace, they perused the menu.

The main entrées featured steak, grilled chicken or salmon, with other side dishes that came along with the dinner menu: shredded carrots, radishes, or French onion soup. With the main dish, the options were pasta, rice, potatoes and green beans.

They all ordered French onion soup with Amita ordering grilled chicken with rice and string beans and Samir and Rudy ordering steak with pasta, potatoes and beans. Amita ordered a glass of white while Samir and Rudy ordered glasses of red wine.

Conversation turned to Rudy's and Sharmi's Venice wedding plans.

"I am going to take the primary FRCS in April," Rudy said. "I don't know when Sharmi's Ph.D. thesis will be completed."

"As far as I know, she has to finish it by March 1965," Amita said. "If she needs an extension, then it might be delayed but not beyond April. Then she has to appear before a board who will ask different questions regarding her thesis and if they are satisfied, then it will be done."

"So I'm guessing it will all be done by May 1965," Samir said.

"That's a nice outlook for the future," Rudy commented. "Sharmi knows a bit about what I envision for the wedding, but I have to further talk to Sharmi about wedding plans and ask her opinion too."

"Of course," Amita said.

"Then it looks like it would take place around June or July," Rudy said. "But right now, I can't really think about the exact date or other details quite yet."

"Let's call her and ask her about the plan and see what happens, if her family will cooperate," Samir said.

"We can try calling tomorrow once we reach home in the afternoon," Rudy said.

"You don't have to go to your place until January 3," Samir said. "Stay with us."

"Thank you, I will just check my mail, shower and bring a change of clothes then go to your home in the late afternoon. How about if I cook some simple Bengali dishes at your place, like rice, Dal, and some curry with fish and vegetables?"

"Wow," Anita said, "that sounds wonderful!"

Then the three friends went to their rooms to spend their last night in Paris.

* * *

Newcastle—31ˢᵗ December, 1964—At 9:30 in the morning, the sun was covered with gray clouds as the diffused sun rays touch the rooftops of the houses covered with frost and patchy snows.

The wind whistled through the bare trees and at times chunks of snow from bare branches blown by the wind ultimately took refuge on the ground.

Inside Samir and Amita's home, the fireplace burned with blue and yellow rising flames, at times the crackling sound of wood interrupted the morning peace.

Samir, Rudy and Amita, with their cups of hot tea, sat close to the fireplace to enjoy a fireside chat.

"I will put a bunch of balloons around the living room and hide the Happy New Year sign behind the Christmas decorations made with green pine needles on the wall and at the stroke of midnight I will remove the pine needle decoration and the sign will be revealed," Samir said. "We will use the flower petals of yellow and white daisies as confetti."

"Wow, that is a very neat idea," Amita cheered. "Rudy, last night you cooked a simple Bengali dinner. It was delicious."

"After a long time, it felt that I am back home in Kolkata so the fish curry with vegetables was really special," Rudy mused. "Any time you want that type of curry. I will cook for you both."

411

"It is 10 o'clock right," Samir said, "do you think we should call Sharmi now?"

"Yes, it's exactly the time I wanted to call her anyway," Amita said.

The three of them sat closely as Amita dialed Sharmi's number in India. Sharmi's younger sister, Urmi, answered the phone.

"Hello, how are you, Urmi? This is Amita, Sharmi's friend."

Urmi sounded very happy. "Oh, I am so glad to talk to you after a long time. How are you? Sharmi is right here…"

"Urmi, I want to talk to you first," Amita said. "I remember when you were a young girl. Now you must be a pretty young lady. You finished your master's degree, right?"

"Oh yes, I am teaching at present at a college nearby."

"That is wonderful, Urmi."

"Here comes Sharmi," Urmi said. "She's eager to talk to you."

"Hello, Amita," Sharmi said, her voice low, "hold on while I go to the other room to talk."

"No problem. Sharmi, how are you and how is your mother and what's going on over there?"

Amita heard Sharmi sigh. "I am doing okay but first I want to tell you, I decided to go back there on January 15. There is no direct flight to Newcastle so I have to change the plane at Paris and will arrive at Newcastle at 4:30 in the afternoon which will be a Saturday."

"That is wonderful," Amita said, "we will be there at the airport to pick you up. Tell me about how things are with your parents."

"Oh right. Ma is feeling much better. She knows about my decision to go back and finish my Ph.D. And I…" Amita heard heavy breathing on Sharmi's end. "I told my parents about my decision with Rudy and Ma accepts it with a

412

heavy heart, the reason is she has no knowledge of his background. But my father is not going to accept my decision and he wants nothing to do with me. So he's not in talking terms with me and he did not want to hear about my engagement with Rudy." Sharmi took a deep breath.

"So I decided to go my own way," Sharmi continued. "I have to talk to Rudy and ask him what his plan is. I cannot think straight but Urmi has been a big help and thankfully, my brother who lives in New Delhi is also happy with my decision."

"Sharmi, Rudy is here and he has big plans which you might already know a little bit about," Amita said. "Here, he wants to talk to you. Hold on…"

Amita handed the phone to Rudy. "Hello, I am really so happy to talk to you, Sharmi. I miss you sooo much! How are you?"

"Hello," Sharmi said, her voice cracking as she started sobbing unable to talk.

"Please don't cry," Rudy said. "It breaks my heart. I want you to know I have big plans for our wedding, for our marriage so you can tell everyone there we are going to get married."

"But when?" Sharmi's voice cracked with emotion.

"Soon after you finish your thesis say around June or July. You have to decide and pick a date and the place will be in Venice. I wanted to surprise you but I think you know how much Italy means to me and I want to share my passion of Italy with you."

Sharmi was shaking with emotion, at first, she was speechless. Then she finally found her voice. "Rudy, oh Rudy," she burst into tears, this time with joy and excitement. Urmi came running to Sharmi to hug her and took the phone from Sharmi.

"Congratulations, we are so happy."

Rudy was calm yet felt the joy to hear the word "congratulations" from someone in Sharmi's family. "Urmi, this is Rudy. Nice to talk to you. I will send airline tickets to Venice for you to attend the wedding and for anyone else who wants to fly there."

"That's so wonderful, Rudy!" Urmi cheered. "You make me and Sharmi happy. I will ask my brother too. Thank you. I *cannot* wait to meet you."

Urmi gave the phone back to Sharmi.

"Okay, I look forward to seeing you in two weeks," Rudy told Sharmi. "We will plan everything when you come and if you want to shop while you're still there, please go ahead and I will arrange to send you money for whatever you need. Amita wants to talk to you now. Please take care, I love you, Sharmi and I miss you. Oh, before I hand the phone back to Amita, I want to tell you my family—my sister and brother are all happy. They cannot go to the wedding but asked us to visit them in India when we can. Give my warmest regards and "*pronam*," said Rudy, using the Bengali custom to ask the blessing of bowing down and touching their feet, "to your father and dear mother."

"I miss you very much, Rudy," Sharmi said, breathlessly. "I love you deeply from the bottom of my heart." Sharmi's voice choked with emotion.

Amita took the phone. "Sharmi, ask Urmi to talk to me. I suggest you both go and buy the usual things for your wedding. Please choose a wedding Benares Saree."

Urmi took the phone and excitedly said, "I will definitely go and buy new sarees and whatever goes with it. Jewelry is already set and maybe Ma wants to add more—whatever we can do within two weeks while Sharmi is here. The rest I will take with me when I fly to Venice for the wedding. I am so happy and excited! I am going to call our brother."

"Urmi, please wish your parents a Happy New Year," Amita said. "Try to have a little celebration to welcome 1965 with your friends and cousins to help cheer up your mother."

"I am definitely going to start preparing and making arrangements right now," Urmi said. "It is such a happy occasion."

"Sharmi, Samir would like to say a word or two to you…"

"Congratulations again, Sharmi. You're like a little sister to me," Samir said. "See you soon."

"Thank you all for everything. See you soon," Sharmi said. "Happy New Year."

That night, his fears and uncertainty about how Sharmi's family would receive news of the wedding now put to rest, Rudy was able to curl up on the sofa to continue reading his favorite book.

ῼarzocco ῼeaues Niccolò's Studio

4th of January 1422, Firenze—On this first work morning of the new year, Niccolò dressed up in his usual outfit then covered himself with a long, black hooded woolen cape. When he stepped out of his cottage, his purposeful, brisk stride to reach his studio felt familiar, the air crisp, wrapped in a veil of mist. The bell tower started chiming signaling 8 o'clock in the morning. A vendor completely covered with a wooly rectangular wrap was pushing a cart full of tomatoes, carrots, beans, potatoes, different kinds of greens which surprised Niccolò as it was hard to get greens this time of year. The vendor waved his hand, it seemed he was trying to say something. Niccolò stopped walking and waved back at him. The vendor filled a basket with each kind of vegetable he had then showed the basket to Niccolò, making him understand that he was keeping the basket for him and welcoming him home.

Niccolò was overcome with emotion and nodded to the vendor indicating that he would gratefully take the basket home at the end of the day.

Then Niccolò's pace increased just as he heard the lapping boats along the river Arno, a familiar sound he had not heard for a while. He was close to Ponte Vecchio where the bridge curves as memories of Beatrice flashed in front of him. It seemed that he could even see her dressed in her olive-green flowing dress waiting there. He strode faster, the shrills of the seagulls further awakening him to this new day.

Then he stopped for a minute to take a few deep breaths. His heavy heart seemed to be squeezing in pain. He could feel the blood gushing from his heart to his head and all over his body felt warm and shaky.

"Beatrice is now happily married and moved on to a path where she belongs," Niccolò murmured, convincing himself of this new reality. "My path is my studio and…"

His mind and heart could not continue on this trajectory that was the past. So he quickened his pace to reach his studio where, upon his arrival, he found Paolo was already there to welcome him with a huge smile.

"Maestro, Happy New Year! I trust you had a wonderful vacation in Castellina." Paolo pointed towards an area in the studio. "I am polishing Marzocco—remember we have to get Marzocco ready as the church people want to get him soon."

"A very Happy New Year to you, Paolo. I hope you had a nice vacation as well." Niccolò cast his gaze towards his sculpture. "I am going to look at Marzocco and see what else needs some more work. Remember we are going to get a stone slab for the Prophet soon within a day or so."

Niccolò gathered his tools and wits together, acclimating himself back to his studio work. "Paolo, there is another commission from the Siena Cathedral. They want me to sculpt the execution of St. John and a scene of The Feast of Herod in bronze casting."

"Bronze casting! Have you done this before?"

"Yes, I helped Maestro Lorenzo so I have some experience. But this will be a huge new project and my very own first bronze casting."

"Where you will do this?"

"Right here in the studio. We will set the oven for melting the bronze at our partly covered patio and make some arrangement to let out the gasses from the melting metal. I will call my friend, Diego, to help me with that."

"Maestro, I am excited!"

"This is what I intend to do: from today, we will polish Marzocco and try to finish it two days from now and hope the stone slab for the Prophet arrives soon. I already finished the sketching which is in my cottage which I will bring tomorrow. I will try to transport it by horse carriage as it is now loosely mounted on a stand. I would like you to help me hold the sketch when I start sketching on the stone slab and when it is done, we will start sculpting.

"I will be very happy to do that. And I would like to help you with the scene of The Feast of Herod, but I have never seen a bronze casting before."

"Do not worry, I will teach you step-by-step as we go along with the project. For now, let us focus on Marzocco."

As Niccolò started looking at Marzocco, he could see that Paolo did a good job polishing Marzocco yet there were some places needing some finer touch, for example, the face around the crease of the nose, the eyes, the socket needing to be a little cleaner, around the lips. The sculpture's mouth was open as if he was talking to a passerby.

"Paolo, I see you did a good job polishing Marzocco. I think we will give him a finer touch today and at the end of the day, we will just go over the sculpture to see whether everything is done and then Marzocco will be ready to go."

"Maestro, that sounds very good."

As they started working on Marzocco, outside the sky was overcast, the wind was whistling through bare trees and the monotonous, lapping sound of the boats along the river Arno continued. Minutes and hours passed when Paolo took a deep breath and said, "Maestro, I need a break."

Niccolò checked the clock. "We should take a lunch break then."

"I brought some lunch for both of us and also some orange blossom water."

"Thank you, Paolo. That it is very nice of you."

"I am going to heat the stew," Paolo said. "I bought a small, portable charcoal oven for the studio we can use as a heater and also when we need to warm our food."

After acknowledging his appreciation to his assistant, Niccolò looked at the clock again which now showed it was 1:30 in the afternoon. Suddenly a distant clip-clapping sound of a carriage could be heard.

"Do you hear what I hear?" Niccolò asked as Paolo rushed closer.

"Maestro, the sound is getting closer and closer to our studio. It must be the church people bringing the stone slab for the Prophet."

Paolo was right. The carriage stopped in front of their building and six strongly built men carrying a stone slab slowly approached the studio.

Niccolò and Paolo welcomed them inside and asked them to place the slab on top of their work table, instructing them to place it upright against the wall for support. The men seemed pleased to follow the instructions as though they knew they were doing their part to create something magnificent and timeless.

Niccolò and Paolo offered some water to drink for the delivery men who were grateful to have a refreshment after carrying the heavy slab.

Niccolò wrote a note to the priest that "the Marzocco sculpture is ready to be picked up," and gave the note to one of the delivery men.

"Maestro, I will give it to *il prete* and, if I am not mistaken, I believe we will come back again to pick up the sculpture in a day or two."

Niccolò nodded. "I appreciate that."

When the people from the church left the studio, Paolo presented their lunch of stewed beef and vegetables, freshly baked sourdough bread and two goblets full of orange blossom water. As they ate their lunch, Paolo talked about how he and his family celebrated Christmas and the new year.

"How is your family doing?" Niccolò asked.

"Doing well. The family restaurant business was running smoothly during the Christmas and New Year season but right now, it is slow."

"Do not worry," Niccolò said. "The church people will pay for Marzocco soon so you will get your share of the money."

"Maestro, I am not worried. I know now that you are back, the work will continue to flow and so will the income."

Niccolò regarded his assistant with a thoughtful gaze. "Paolo, my sister now has her own house courtesy of her son, Amadeo, who built it for her. It is completely separate yet it is connected to his part of the house through a corridor. So she will start to live there. She told me she will spend a few months every year at our cottage with my mother who in turn, will also visit my sister in her new home. Yet there will be months when my mother will be alone with no help around the household. So I am kind of worried as she is getting older."

"Maestro, do not worry. I have a cousin whose children are grown and moved away. I am sure she will be happy to help your mother, if your mother wants to hire her."

"That is very nice, Paolo. I would feel better that help is around the corner if we need it, thank you." With his mind at ease, Niccolò stood up. "Paolo, let us start working on Marzocco. I think we will be done at the end of the day."

Feeling energized by their lunch, they continued working on Marzocco with a rasp and fine chisel, taking time to chisel out a small area and smooth it out with a rasp. With knitted brows and a clenched jaw, Paolo studiously worked with his fine chisel, his serious face flushed and eyes fixed on the area he was concentrating on.

Niccolò was relatively relaxed, chiseling and smoothing out automatically without any concern, mainly due, he thought, to his vow to maintain a calm demeanor after his visit to Castellina.

A few hours passed when they heard the church bell strike four times. "Paolo, we should stop working. The daylight is fading."

"Maestro, I have finished the area you had me work on. I would like you to look at it."

"Let me see." Niccolò inspected the work. "You did almost perfectly, the small area below his mane is a little rough. Just smooth it out it. It will take a few minutes. I will look at him again thoroughly and then you can check him again and that will be it."

"He looks very alive and happy as if he's trying to talk to us," Paolo said.

Paolo and Niccolò finished their work and bid goodbye just as the daylight faded away and evening set in around 5 o'clock. Niccolò remembered that the nice vendor was most likely waiting for him so he picked up the pace faster to catch up to him.

Close to Ponte Vecchio was where he saw the vendor coming towards him with his empty cart holding a basketful of vegetables. Overcome with emotion, Niccolò approached the vendor. "Good evening, Signore. I am very sorry I am late."

"No, problem, Maestro," the vendor said. "This basket is yours. Today I sold all the vegetables and eggs I had. It was a good day."

Niccolò took out some money from his bag and handed it to the man. "How much do you I owe you?"

The vendor shook his head. "Maestro, do you remember you gave me some money when I started my business? This is just a small gesture."

Niccolò frowned. "That won't be necessary. I cannot accept a handout from you."

"Please accept this as a gift, Maestro. Then whenever I need something so badly, I will ask for your help but for now, I am fine. As a token of my gratitude, once a week I will keep a basketful of fresh vegetables for you."

"Oh, that's so nice of you, Signore. And should you ever need anything from me, please do not hesitate to ask."

The vendor nodded, pleased with the deal. "*Buonasera, Maestro.*"

Niccolò strode faster to reach home as a wintery breeze blew through the tall bare birch trees, the avenues of tall pointed pine trees kissed each other with frequent blasts of wind. Niccolò realized that he would be the only one at his cottage. Memories of his mother flashed as he remembered his mother's advice to keep the brick-layered log oven ready in the morning before leaving home for work so that as soon as he reached home at the end of the day, he could prepare his dinner.

And so he decided to do just that, though he was very reluctant. Suddenly, a few horse buggies clipped-clapped along the paved road prompting memories to flash in Niccolò's mind of the time when he used to sculpt Beatrice at the palace. He recalled how Lady Contessina, Cosimo's wife, always arranged a carriage and driver to take him home. He remembered being so tired after a long day's work at the palace that he fell asleep during the ride home. Then a wintery breeze blew so strong, the freezing blast whipped at his face forcing him back to the present as he picked up the pace faster towards home.

After a somewhat restless slumber, Niccolò woke up to a cold morning. Through the window, he saw a layer of frost on the rooftops and on the ground. He got up to find the portable charcoal heater that felt comfortable during the night and vowed to make the brick layer oven ready for cooking dinner in the evening. He remembered to take the leftover vegetable stew, boiled eggs and bread for his and Paolo's lunch.

He took the sketched Prophet that stood at the corner of the bedroom and placed him close to the front door. Then he took a deep breath, murmuring, "I have to get ready and remember to put out the fire of the charcoal heater. The carriage will arrive at 9."

Sure enough, the carriage came when church bells started chiming at 9 that crisp, cold winter morning despite the sun being up in the clear sky.

Piero, the carriage driver, greeted Niccolò with a smile.

"Maestro, please get in. I will help you with your carry-on items."

Niccolò was relieved to get in the carriage that started to move slowly. Today he noticed the landscape passing by where the rooftops of the houses were covered with thin layers of snow. A few birds hopped on the frosted, patchy green ground as the bare birch trees shivered from the cold breeze and tall pine trees were shaking off snow from the their needles.

He murmured to himself, "I do not just pass by all the wonders of nature, I see them, lost in my own world. The sun looks glorious today. It is a new day where the soft morning rays of sun flooded everything as far as I can see so it looks so alive as if speaking to me. All my senses feel the touch of my surroundings in an extraordinary way. It is a blissful joy too much for a hard-working sculptor to accept. How do I control myself?"

Just then Piero called his attention. "Maestro, we will soon reach your studio."

Niccolò jolted back to the present, hearing the shrills of seagulls and the lapping of the oars of the boats along the river Arno. When they reached his studio, Piero helped him carry the sketched prophet on the stand. Then Niccolò took the rest of his things from the carriage as he saw Paolo coming out of the studio to help Niccolò carry his packages.

Niccolò thanked Piero and gave him the fare along with a generous tip for his help which made Piero very happy as he bid him, "*Ciao!*"

Paolo turned to Niccolò. "Maestro, the church people will be arriving this afternoon to take Marzocco."

"That is good so then the studio will have some space as the Prophet occupies a huge amount of space with all the tools around. Paolo, I prepared lunch for both of us."

"That is very nice of you."

"Let us now start to sketch the Prophet on the stone slab."

"Everything is ready, Maestro."

"Paolo, I want to start sketching from the head downwards. His head is bald like a pumpkin."

"Maestro, tell me how I should hold the sketch."

"Just climb up that stool and hold it closer to the upper end of the slab. It will be hard and difficult for you but I will try to finish it before noon. I need to sketch his round head, mark his hollowed eyes and mark the area of his partly open mouth. Then we have to ask for some help to put the slab horizontally on our work table."

"All right, Maestro. That is no problem. You can start whenever you are ready."

Niccolò took his marker. He could reach the upper part of the slab. With his knitted brow, eyes fixed on the slab, Niccolò held his marker firmly and started sketching the Prophet's head on the stone slab. Soon hours passed, and Niccolò took a deep breath.

"I need a break," he said just when the church bells started chiming at noon.

Paolo sighed. "Thank goodness. I need a break too."

"I finished sketching the bald head and eyes and marked his partly opened mouth. Do you think we can hire some people to move the slab horizontally after our lunch?"

"Yes, Maestro, that would be possible. Let me warm up the lunch you brought and I will ask around the plaza where the vendors are. We will surely get someone to help us."

Paolo warmed up the lunch Niccolò brought for them on the portable charcoal heater. "Maestro, it smells delicious. I did not know that you cook so well."

They enjoyed the vegetable stew, some bread and hard-boiled eggs that Paolo had sliced and put in the stew.

Niccolò brainstormed some ideas as they ate lunch. "I think I will keep the stone slab standing. We have to push the slab standing against a solid wall that way we do not have to ask them again to place it vertically. Once I finish carving the head, you will not have any problem helping with the lower part of the body and his layers of clothes wrapped around his body as a garment. What do you think?"

"It is absolutely fine." Paolo paused to chew his food. "I can help you for hours when you are working on the upper part of the Prophet's body and might need some break in between."

"So are you finished with your lunch? We need help to push the whole slab against a solid wall. You choose which people can assist us."

"All right, I will go now and asked some people for help."

While Paolo went to the piazza to hire some people, Niccolò started talking to himself. "The head of the Prophet will bend downwards, showing humility. The area of the neck on the bent side will be shorter, a smaller angle with that shoulder. The neckline on the other side will be longer and the angle will be much larger with the shoulder."

He went close to the sculpture and figured out where to mark the area precisely. Just then, he heard the clip-clapping of horses and realized the church people had arrived to pick up Marzocco.

Niccolò stood close to Marzocco's sculpture, looked at him, and whispered, "Marzocco, the insignia of the Republic of Florence, you are going to stand at the top of a column at the foot of the stairs leading to the Papal apartment of Santa Maria. You are an image of a powerful protector of Firenze. The enemies will be fearful. You are giving a strong message to the people of Firenze to relax because you will watch over them."

Eight people from the church asked Niccolò's permission to wrap Marzocco up with thick cotton material.

"Please wait a few more minutes," Niccolò urged, "Paolo, my assistant, will be here momentarily. He must see the sculpture before you wrap him up."

"As you wish, Maestro."

Niccolò explained that his assistant went to look for some people to help them push the marble slab against the wall.

As soon as Niccolò finished his sentence Paolo arrived. "Sorry, I could not find anyone willing to help us. Only the vendors were there and they could not leave as it is mid-day and they need to tend their businesses."

The church employees offered their help. "We can help you. Just tell us what to do," one of them said.

Paolo showed them where the slab was to be placed against the wall. Four of them took the task of pushing the stone slab against the wall while the others began wrapping Marzocco with pieces of cloth.

Paolo drew close to the sculpture of Marzocco. "Please enjoy the place where you belong and thank you for protecting Firenze," he whispered.

Niccolò and Paolo were pleased and grateful that church workers could push the stone slab of the Prophet against a solid wall. Niccolò took some money out of his bag and it offered them, though they were reluctant to take any money.

"If you do not take it, I will be very uncomfortable asking any help from you in the future," Niccolò said. "Please accept this."

With Niccolò's request, the men accepted the money and divided the amount among the eight of them. "Thank you for your generosity."

They wrapped Marzocco and pushed him slowly onto a rectangular wooden plank where at one end was the door of an iron cage. They then placed it on the back of the carriage which had a wooden platform without a roof. It was very tricky to push Marzocco to the higher slant of a rectangular plank at the door of the iron cage from the ground level. But with slow and correct maneuvering, the eight workers successfully managed to put Marzocco at the back of the carriage where four of them were situated with the other four in front holding the sculpture tightly. The half door device at the back of the carriage closed and locked.

Slowly but surely, the carriage started on its way as Niccolò and Paolo stood at the entrance of their studio watching as the carriage gradually disappeared in the mist of winter and the clip-clapping of horses muffled while a blast of wintery breeze whistled through the air in concert with the shrieks of seagulls at a distance.

Sculpting Zuccone Begins

25ᵗʰ of January, 1422—Inside Niccolò's studio on this afternoon in late January Paolo was lighting the big candles as daylight had already faded away.

One could see the studio full of pieces of different kinds of stone, a finished sculpture in a corner, a shadow of a stone slab against the wall and shadows of two sculptors moving on the wall with flickers of candles.

The church bell rang four times to remind everyone in the city what time it was in the afternoon.

"Maestro, it's time to go home. There is hardly any light and the candle lights are not enough."

"Yes, we must stop now," Niccolò said. "I am almost done with the sketching. I will check tomorrow if I have missed any area. If not, then we will start sculpting the Prophet tomorrow afternoon and also make arrangements to prepare for The Feast of Herod and St. John's execution." Niccolò paused to collect his thoughts. "So, Paolo, today is the 25ᵗʰ of January and the days pass by so quickly. It's hard to believe I came back from vacation on the 4ᵗʰ of January."

"Maestro, why do you want to start on two commissions at the same time? What is the hurry? You have two years to sculpt the Prophet."

"Listen, Paolo, we have to sculpt the Prophet and shape it, then there will be fine touches to make him come alive. His sad face, sunken eyes with layers of clothing, his lips will be open and he will start talking, telling his sad story of the injustice to his people, and he will cry out loud to the Almighty and ask, 'Why did you not save these people? Why did you tolerate the injustice to innocent people?' We want to capture the Prophet's questioning God in the people's time of need."

"I understand it takes time for the finer touch and polishing the sculpture, but—"

"Paolo," Niccolò interjected with urgency, "tomorrow morning on my way, I will talk to Antonio who lives pretty close to me. He is the one who will make a special partially covered furnace for us to melt the bronze. Oh, I remember my mother and sister will be back soon so that will be nice."

"Oh good, so you do not have to cook for yourself."

"That is true. Although I have been able to manage on my own," Niccolò said. "Now, I will tidy up everything this evening around my house so when they come back, they will be happy to see the house is not messy. I might be a little late tomorrow so you can arrive a little late also."

"Do not worry. I will prepare everything ready for you."

Then they bid each other goodbye and headed towards their homes.

* * *

When Niccolò got up the next morning, through the frosted window glass, he could see the rays of sun refracting the colors like a prism and a bathed marble sculpture of a mother and child placed on a round table just next to the window. Niccolò felt very energetic and happy as he went to the kitchen and checked the cooking utensils which were all clean and shiny. He scrubbed the floor of the kitchen and brought wooden logs for the brick-layered, open fire oven the previous evening.

He dusted the dressers of his mother's and sister's rooms this morning and went to check them once more to see if everything was fine. He had a feeling they were going to arrive that late afternoon.

Then he remembered he was supposed to meet his friend, Antonio, about building a half-covered brick-layered furnace for his bronze casting commission to melt the bronze.

Niccolò started from his home on this crisp, cold morning with a wintery breeze. The sky was clear and the red roofs of the houses were still covered with a layer of frost. The birch trees were moving their bare branches to host some birds to sit on them as pine needles were shaking their dews with a gentle breeze.

The paved path to his friend's cottage was all frosted and slippery green bushes on both sides of the path were covered with a layer of frost leading to a red door. As Niccolò walked along the paved path, he could see the yard on both sides of the bushes were frosted and covered with dry leaves, mainly maple, while the tall bare trees stood on both sides waving their branches slowly with a wintery breeze as if to welcome a guest.

Niccolò knocked at the door and within a few minutes, Antonio came and opened it. He was very happy to see Niccolò.

"*Buongiorno,* my friend. Welcome to my home!"

After pleasantries were exchanged, Niccolò wasted no time getting to the point of the visit. "Antonio, I need your help."

"Tell me what you need."

"I would like to request that you build a half-covered, brick-layered furnace to melt the bronze for my bronze casting."

"Where would you like me to build it?"

"Inside a covered patio in my studio."

"I have to go there and see whether it is possible, and Niccolò, you must know the city's regulation. They do not want you to do this every day. There are particular days in your area and also a particular zone of time."

"Oh! The city has its regulations." Niccolò expressed his frustration at this one obstacle. "Antonio, you can come with me if you have time."

"Okay, my friend, just give me fifteen minutes and I will be ready to follow you."

"Thank you, Antonio. I will wait."

Antonio was ready after fifteen minutes as promised and both of them started towards Niccolò's studio. The sun was up on the horizon as the rays of sun bathed the frosted roofs of the red-titled houses. The oblique sun rays pierced the screen of mist refracted and displayed in different shades of blue and orange over the patchy, frosted ground. As they strode faster, the shrills of seagulls and sounds of lapping oars of the boat along the river Arno could be heard.

"My friend, we are getting close to my studio."

"Do not worry. I am doing fine."

After a few minutes, they reached the studio. Paolo, who saw them coming, rushed out to greet them. *"Buongiorno."*

"Paolo, this is my friend, Antonio."

After pleasantries were exchanged, Niccolò said, "Paolo, we must show Antonio our covered patio."

When they all went out to the patio, Antonio's impression was that the patio was almost the size of the studio. He took some measurements and put it down on paper. Then Antonio came back again inside the studio muttering to himself while at the same time explaining to Niccolò and Paolo, "You see, as you enter, the door is at the entrance. There is a big window, next to it, the wall opposite the entrance is a solid wall where your work bench is, and on it, the marble slab is standing so that is good. On the left side there is a window and there are closets and a few stools and a small table. The right wall is almost solid except at the middle there is a door which opens to the covered patio. So my plan will be to build another room a little less than half the size of your studio."

Antonio scanned the area again and did a quick sketch. "I envision building a wall right next to the door which opens to the patio, leaving a comfortable space. In the middle of this wall, there will be a door which will open to the furnace room. The brick-layered furnace will be built just on the opposite wall of the entrance of the furnace room. On the left, there will be a window and for the hot gasses, I have to design a tubular structure which will open to a concrete cistern with some absorbent mixture and charcoal and water. Once or twice a year, designated people will come and empty it and add fresh absorbent and fill up the cistern with fresh water. Emptied material will be disposed by the designated people in a special and designated place."

"How long will it take to build?" Niccolò asked.

"Three months at least, might be a little early or maybe a little delayed."

"That is all right. I will concentrate on the commission of the Prophet and try to do as much as I can on him. Thank you, Antonio. Would you like me to give you some amount in advance?"

"No, I do not need it at present." Antonio's brows furrowed. "You did not even ask me how much I charge."

"No, I do not need to. I know you," Niccolò said. "Whatever amount you will charge, I will gladly pay it."

"You are the same as before," Antonio said. "There's no charge, my friend, you are a very special person and a very good friend."

"Antonio, thank you very much. I will however, donate any amount to a charity of your choosing," Niccolò said. "And as for the building, when can you start?"

"I will start a week from today. Will that be all right?"

"That will be fine. Antonio, are you sure you do not want me to pay you some in advance?"

"No, my friend, that is very nice of you to ask. I will finish it around April so how about you pay me then?"

Antonio shook hands with Niccolò and Paolo as they all agreed to meet again the following week when two assistants will be accompanying Antonio to help with the building project.

Niccolò looked at the clock. "Paolo, it is 11. Most of the morning is nearly done.Let us start sculpting Zuccone. I will see whether I sketched and marked all the areas."

"Maestro, I am ready and have arranged all the tools for sculpting.

Niccolò examined the standing metamorphic stone slab for several minutes. When he was done, he said, "Paolo, the sketching on Zuccone is done. Let us start."

"Would you like me to stand on a stool? I cannot reach the head from the floor."

Niccolo pointed. "Just stand next to the slab on the bench."

"I am standing the way you instructed me," Paolo said, appearing a bit frustrated. "Please tell me what I am supposed to do to help you."

"I am just chiseling out the bald head which is a little bent showing his humility. I am following the marked lines you just clear the chips with the brush." His maestro's tone sounded equally impatient.

Hours rolled by until the clock stroke one o'clock. Paolo gently reminded Niccolò, "I need a break. I cannot stand any longer."

"Paolo, I am so sorry. Just another few minutes, please. I am done with Zuccone's head and the finer touch will be applied later. The head was sculpted out of the slab."

After a few more minutes of work, Niccolò was satisfied. "Let us go out for lunch."

"My mother made minestrone soup and pasta with meatballs last night so there are some leftovers for our lunch. I will warm it up," Paolo said.

The charcoal heater, which worked for warming up the food and also as a room heater, was a small tube-like round iron container about one-and-one-half feet high with a diameter of eight to ten inches. It had a two-round, flat-iron platform like a disk one above placed six inches from the top which had vertical openings where the charcoal would burn and another solid iron plate placed six inches below from the upper plate to collect the ashes from the burning charcoal. There was a small lid which opened and closed next to the platform, a device to clean the ashes from the platform. To add to it, the charcoal heater stood on three small iron legs.

Paolo and Niccolò finally had their lunch at 1:30 in the afternoon.

"Paolo, I am sorry that I made you wait till this late hour to have our lunch so we will have our lunch break until 2:30. After lunch, I would like to work on both shoulders of the Prophet. I would love to work another two hours but we will see if the daylight will last. Otherwise, if it fades away too soon or the weather becomes stormy, then we have to stop early."

"Maestro, that is fine with me."

"So, this is my plan for next Monday: my friend, Antonio will start working so I want to sculpt out the Prophet's two hands. The right hand holds a scroll and clutches on to his toga not in all the details but whatever possible without the details of the toga which will be taken care of later as the left hand points downwards."

"Maestro, let me know how to help you so that the sculpting flows smoothly."

Paolo noticed that Niccolò became restless to resume his sculpting, so he said, "Maestro, let us go back to work and pick up where you left off."

"The neck and the shoulders, Paolo."

So they started sculpting the shoulders and neck area, paying attention to the side of the head which was a little bent. All of a sudden, out of nowhere, there was the sound of thunder with flashes of lightning.

"Maestro, please. We have to stop working. The weather is getting worse."

Niccolò stopped sculpting and rubbed his eyes. "Yes, I see. Let us close everything and get out of here quickly. I hope my mother and sister arrived safely."

Paolo and Niccolò exchanged a quick *"Buona Notte"* before they parted ways.

Niccolò strode as fast as he could until he came to the piazza and saw the vendor with his vegetable cart holding a basketful of vegetables for him.

"Maestro, I am glad that you came a little early. I was about to leave as the weather has turned out to be stormy."

"Thank you very much, Signore. But you should also head on home yourself. I hope my mother and sister arrived safely. They will be very happy to see this basket full of fresh vegetables."

"Maestro, I think they have arrived back in town. I saw a carriage earlier with two ladies."

"Oh, I should be heading home soon, then. Do take care, Signore. Thank you again."

Niccolò hurried his pace as the stormy weather continued with lightning and thunder, threatening to rain any second. The stormy wind whistled through the bare trees and pointed pines along both sides of the path madly causing the trees to kiss each other.

Niccolò moved faster and faster and even though he was expecting his mother and sister to come home, thoughts that they could not make it back today swirled like a storm in his mind.

"Oh no, I refuse to think like that," he murmured, shaking his head to rid his mind of negative thoughts.

He practically ran, sprinting closer and closer until he approached the family cottage. "Is this real? I see some light. Could it be that Mamma has lighted the candles and also the covered lamp outside?"

Finally, Niccolò opened the front door to see his mother and sister rush to greet him, all of them overcome with joy and relief. After they exchanged hugs, Niccolò presented his mother and sister with a basketful of fresh vegetables for which they were all grateful for the vendor's generosity.

Niccolò's heart warmed when his eyes spotted their dinner table with candles and a warm delicious dinner cooked by his mother and sister displayed on the table.

Outside the thunder rolled with flashes of lightning as the storm blew its whistle through the shivering trees. While inside the cottage, Niccolò, Mother Orissa and Tia stayed warm and cozy as they gathered for dinner to nourish themselves with Orissa's hot Italian sausage soup with stewed tomato and vegetables guaranteed to warm their bellies and their hearts.

A Furnace to Melt the Bronze

March 1422—On this gray and breezy morning at the end of March, it was business as usual for Niccolò as he took long, quick strides to reach his studio, murmuring to himself, "I will request Paolo to come early if he can, perhaps around 8 in the morning." Then he paused for a minute when a tiny bird hopped in front of him and then he whispered, "Hi little bird," and continued on his way as he continued, "If Paolo is not available in the morning, then I will start work earlier and he can join when it's possible, though, he has done a fine job preparing the tools ready for the next day and tidies up the place every day before he leaves to go home so I do not have to worry. I have already done the Prophet's two arms and shoulder and today I want to finish part of his layers of clothes and feet."

He suddenly realized that he was almost at the piazza when he saw Luigi from the bakery waving his hands like he wanted to talk to him. The baker was his late father's friend so Niccolò called him "uncle" which Luigi liked very much. So Niccolò slowed down and headed towards the bakery.

"Niccolò, how are you, my dear boy?" said the baker who considered Niccolò to be still quite young. "I made special breads for you with green olives and wild berries. Please take it."

"Thank you, Uncle Luigi, that is very kind of you. How are you, Uncle?"

"I am doing fine. I am happy my business is flourishing." The baker put his right hand on Niccolò's left shoulder. "Son, I am so proud of you, Firenze is proud of you. So tell me about your new commissions from the church?"

"Uncle Luigi," his voice cracked then he took a deep breath. "The church gave me the commission of the prophet Habakkuk and Uncle…" He paused for a few seconds. "I also got a commission of The Feast of King Herod and St. John's execution from Siena which will be a bronze casting." Niccolò's voice trembled and his heartbeat raced. "Uncle Luigi, it will be my first bronze casting."

"My dear Niccolò, you will do just fine," the baker said. "You will excel. If only your dear father could see you now. God bless him and you."

"Thank you, Uncle Luigi, that is very nice of you."

Luigi handed over a bag full of different bread loaves. "See you again soon. Stop by anytime if you need anything."

"Thank you, Uncle Luigi. Have a wonderful day."

Niccolò strode briskly to his studio where Paolo greeted him with a smile.

"Maestro, I prepared all the tools in order so we can start when you are ready."

"I want to finish part of the layers of his clothes and start on his feet. We cannot finish the entire body but we will do as much as we can as long as there is still daylight. With the candles flickering, sometimes it is difficult to see as there are shadows. My friend, Antonio will start constructing the furnace soon. There will be noise and dust. Antonio told me that he will cover the workplace like a tent and ask his people to work under that, whenever possible. I might start planning and do the sketching for the scene from The Feast of Herod before the furnace is complete. Then we will be organized fully before we do the casting. Let us start working on the Prophet. We will work about two and a half hours. Before our lunch we will work on the layers of his clothes and start the feet. Then I want to make plans for The Feast of Herod and start sketching."

"Maestro, I am ready to start whenever you are ready."

They started working on the Prophet's layers of clothing until Niccolò stopped at the part where the fold of his outfit—the toga—touched the feet. "Paolo, I am going to start sculpting the feet right now."

"Maestro, I am ready with whatever you want to do."

Niccolò knitted his eyebrows and fixed his eyes on the fold of the Prophet's outfit that almost touched the feet. There was a shadowy area where the fold of the cloth was rising that Niccolò chiseled out carefully before he chiseled the feet out from the sketch on the slab. Then the clock tower announced one o'clock in the afternoon.

"Paolo, we will stop right now for lunch break," Niccolò said. "That is all we are going to work on for the Prophet today. After lunch break, I am going to tell you, and at the same time make a note for myself, about how we are going to proceed with our next project."

Niccolò told Paolo that he brought lunch for both of them. Mother Orissa, he said, made some beef stew with vegetables from Amadeo's garden in Castellina. His mother had also baked fresh bread so they have a small loaf for each of them.

"Maestro, that is very nice and sweet of her."

They chatted while enjoying the delicious hot beef stew and bread after Paolo warmed up the stew on the charcoal heater.

"The original plan of the Siena Cathedral was to make six reliefs to be completed by two local artists but the plan did not go very well," Niccolò said. "The local artists were not making any progress, so the plan was abandoned and ultimately, I got the commission. My plan will be to bring together the events in a single scene."

"Maestro, why do you want to do that?"

"Because it will help depict the story of St. John's martyrdom without explicitly showing the beheading. The scene will depict the executioner presenting the head of St. John on a platter after the daughter, Salome, asked Herod Antipas for his head on a platter. The expression of King Herod and his companions then will be changed to horror. This is another added point. I also want to include Salome's dance."

Niccolò paused and took a deep breath. "I plan to bring these elements together using continuous narrative art which includes multiple scenes of narrative within a single frame."

"Maestro, now I understand exactly why you are doing it this way."

"There is more to it." He fixed his eyes to a distance and softly said, "I am also bringing Maestro Filippo's linear perspective which I mentioned to you a while ago but do not worry. I am going to explain it again. Linear perspective is a system which creates an illusion of depth on a flat surface. All parallel lines in a painting and drawing using the system converge in a single vanishing point in the composition on the horizontal lines. The objects in the composition are rendered increasingly smaller as they were close to the vanishing point."

"I remember now that you explained this to me before," Paolo said.

"After our lunch break, we will start sketching the scene."

"Let me know how I will put the sketching paper—on the stand or on the wall or lay it on the work bench flat?"

Niccolo's brows knitted. "Hmm, that is a very good question. Let us start laying it on the work bench flat and later, I will find out where it will fit better as the work proceeds. I am starting the scene of Salome dancing in the palace, King Herod sitting on the throne facing forwards, the executioner standing on the right and a musician and Herodias on the left. Salome is to wear a sumptuous bejeweled costume, in a tiptoed position holding a lotus in her right hand and extending her left arm in a rigid gesture. She would appear frozen or, at most, moving in a dead march. Then another scene will show King Herod with his high military official sitting around a dinner table where the executioner delivers the head of St. John on a platter. Here, the expression of King Herod will be changed to shock and horror along with the military officials. One of them, with an expression of horror, has extended his fingers and both hands flexed at the elbow leaning backwards on his seat. The next one would turn his face away from the scene, while another one would cover his eyes with his palms as others remain in shock and horror."

"Maestro, you are a genius. I know what you are telling me will be depicted in the frame and, as you say, it will be alive as the people see them, they will speak to them from the past."

"Thank you for your good words, Paolo."

His assistant looked out the window. "It will rain soon. Shall we go home?"

Paolo and Niccolò closed the studio and bid each other good bye then hurried to reach their homes.

As the days passed, soon it was almost the end of March and the mornings were still cold and foggy yet the hazy sun rays bathed the city through a layer of fog.

As one passed through the avenues of trees, there was a feeling of awakening in the air. The green blades of grass started to peep through the wet ground proudly holding the dews while daffodils and tulips buds were still sleepy yet moving their heads gently with the breeze. Niccolò walked his usual brisk pace to his studio, lost in his thoughts about the furnace and bronze casting.

Clouds of thought kept passing in his mind. He was happy about the construction of the furnace in the studio. He had already finished sketching the scene depicting the feast of Herod and now he was eager to talk about his clay modeling and bronze casting with Paolo.

As he strode rapidly, he could see his breath form like a small patch of mist slowly but surely dissipating in the mist around him. When he reached the studio, as usual, Paolo welcomed him with a huge smile.

"The tools are ready for sculpting the Prophet," he said.

The maestro nodded. "We will definitely work for at least two hours on the Prophet. Then I will explain the process of bronze casting to you."

Niccolò and Paolo started working on the Prophet's layers of clothes, the toga, as the church bell rang, signifying it was 9 o'clock in the morning. Niccolò kept chiseling away the stone as his jaw clenched, eyes glued to the stone slab to make the folds of the toga more prominent. Under Niccolò's direction, Paolo continued brushing away and at times cleared the rough edges with a rasp.

There was a knock at the entrance and Niccolò looked up to see his friend Antonio standing at the doorway. Niccolò and Paolo stopped what they were doing to greet Antonio as he entered the room.

"I plan to finish work on the furnace room and everything else I need to do in a week then I will give a trial to see whether it works smoothly or not," Antonio said.

"Thank you, Antonio, you are finishing it early. That is so nice of you."

"Just want to let you know after I finish the work, we should spend some time together and go somewhere for lunch. What do you say, Niccolò?"

"Yes, that's a good idea, Antonio."

"Paolo, you are invited too."

"Thank you, Antonio."

Niccolò and Paolo diligently worked for two and a half hours on the layers of the Prophet's clothes.

"Let's take a break and we will start again after fifteen minutes. It is 11:45. We will start at noon and try to work till one o'clock if we can. Paolo, what you say? Is it all right with you?"

"It is fine with me."

They took a break to relax, sitting on two cushioned chairs doing nothing which was something that was needed after all their hard work. But all too soon, the church bell started chiming at noon and Niccolò and Paolo continued working on the Prophet, this time, Niccolò wanted to work on the Prophet's hand, the one hanging by his side.

"We can almost finish with the finer touch so that it will be done," Niccolò said.

"No problem. We can finish it."

As scheduled, once Niccolò and Paolo finished their work on the

Prophet's hand, they were ready for a lunch break. Paolo offered to warm up some minestrone soup and spaghetti and meatballs in tomato basil sauce.

Niccolò's mouth watered. "Oh, sounds delicious."

After their sumptuous and satisfying lunch, Niccolò explained the detail of bronze casting.

"I plan to follow the Direct Lost Wax Technique and will explain it in detail to you. You see, a sculptor molds the desired sculpture out of clay. This is called core. He covers the core with a thin layer of wax and makes all the details on the wax."

"Maestro, let me write all of this down." Paolo grabbed something to write his notes on. "All right, Maestro, go ahead."

"Then he attaches the wax rod—sprues—perpendicular to a wax surface covering the core. Then some channels are made side by side the wax rods from which the gas will escape during the casting process." Niccolò paused to eye his assistant. "Paolo, are you still with me?"

"Yes, Maestro," Paolo nodded as he feverishly scribbled down his notes.

"Now bronze pins, called chaplets, have to be inserted into the wax and the core. You will soon understand why. The pins will remain sticking out. Understood, so far?"

"Yes, Maestro."

"Now comes the interesting part, Paolo. Another layer of clay is placed over the entire wax covering, this means over the whole structure. Then the whole structure is baked and the wax melts. Now you see Paolo, the bronze pins and chaplets are necessary to hold the two clay shells into the mold where the wax was. That explains the lost wax technique. The gasses and air escape through sprues and the vent so as not to create the bubbles."

"Maestro, I see how the technique is devised step by step. I really applaud the person or persons who created it."

"Paolo, people acquired this technique through trial and error for thousands of years. It started some time in BC. Now, is the step for casting the metal bronze which is alloy of copper and tin heated very high to the melting point and the molten metal is poured. The mold should also be hot when the molten metal is poured so it would not crack. The outer clay core is most often scraped out to avoid interior corrosion when it is cooled. The bronze is rough and needs to be finished, a step that is called chasing which has to be done very carefully since it is a painstaking process and also time consuming."

Niccolò paused to rub his eyes then turned to his assistant. "We will keep working on the Prophet till noon and then start the clay molding of the scene of Herod's Feast in the afternoon. This will be our every day schedule until we finish both commissions."

"That is nice to know," Paolo said. "Let us finish today."

"That sounds good. Tomorrow let us go for lunch at the Osteria. The weather is getting better and it will do us some good to get some fresh air before starting the clay modeling.

After they parted ways, Niccolò headed towards home. The weather was getting a little warmer and besides the shrills of seagulls, he heard some birds chirping on a few pine trees as the western sky brushed with a reddish orange glow. Niccolò walked leisurely towards home with pleasant thoughts of a delicious home-cooked meal and a cozy bed waiting for him at the end of this fruitful day.

Salome and The Feast of Herod

Niccolò got up early the next morning happy to remember he explained to Paolo the lost wax technique process of bronze casting the previous afternoon before he returned home.

On this foggy morning while Niccolò was getting ready, he heard his mother's voice. Niccolò came quickly, closed the door to his mother's room and asked, "Is anything the matter?"

"Why you are leaving so early for work?"

"Mother, I am working on two commissions at the same time. If I start early, I can come home early so that I can spend time with you and Tia."

"That is very nice of you," his mother said, "but Tia will stay another month or so. She plans to leave the first week of May."

"I see," Niccolò said. "Mother, I want to discuss with you and Tia about hiring a helper and companion who will stay with you all day so that you will not be alone after Tia leaves for Castellina. Please give this some thought."

"That is very considerate of you Niccolò but that will be an extra burden of expenses on you, my dear."

"No, not really. I will be happy to bear that burden. I will feel very happy and relaxed that you are not alone all day."

His mother nodded. "Come back as soon as you can. I will prepare gnocchi, vegetable soup, roasted potato and will also make your favorite almond rice."

"Mother, that sounds so delicious. I will do my best to come home early."

Niccolò covered himself with his black, wooly hooded cape over his long, white outfit, and started to brave through the thick fog. The landscape of the city looked like a black outline on a foggy background.

He started walking nearly at the speed of running, feeling good that he could talk to his mother about hiring a helper before he left the house. "I must ask Paolo about whether his cousin is still interested in working as Mamma's companion, and if so, when could she start?"

When he heard the shrills of seagulls, he realized that he was close to that bridge where the wall bends at Ponte Vecchio. All of a sudden, his heart started racing, feeling like the blood was gushing rapidly all over his body and he felt warm around his face and neck. He came close to the bend and just stood there for a few minutes.

"Yes, just right here, she used to wait for me." He saw there at the same spot a seagull with closed eyes standing on one leg and resting.

Then he took a deep breath and scurried faster and when he reached his studio, he was almost panting for breath. Paolo came out running.

"Maestro! Are you all right?"

He took a few staggered breaths before he could talk. "I need some water."

"Coming right up." Paolo rushed inside the studio and offered him a goblet full of orange blossom water.

Niccolò sat down on a cushioned chair inside the studio and slowly drank the water from the goblet. After a few minutes, he returned to his normal state.

"We will start working on the Prophet in a few minutes."

"Maestro, everything is ready. Take a few more minutes to rest."

The church bells started to chime signaling that it was just 8 o'clock in the morning which was good, thought Niccolò, who said, "Paolo, I did not ask you to come this early. What made you arrive so early?"

"Maestro, you were keeping a journal regarding at what time you would like to do certain tasks," Paolo said. "I saw that and realized, unless you come early, you cannot do all the tasks you have written in your journal."

"Paolo, you have a very keen observation and you are very bright. I am glad that you are working for me."

"Thank you, Maestro, for your good words."

"We shall start working on the Prophet. From today, we will concentrate on the Prophet's toga until we are done with that. Let us begin with a part of the toga on his right shoulder. There is a knot we will first carve today and then proceed from there. The knot, which rests on his right shoulder, is not complicated. It is just a piece of the round shaped stone to be chiseled out. Then there is the fold of his toga which goes just below his neck and runs across the other side almost to the left, yet not quite, as there will be another layer of his clothing draping over it. Let us finish that much."

Niccolò chiseled out the knot and asked Paolo to smooth it then worked on the fold of toga which ran across. He did so then paused and asked for a round and pointed chisel. He wanted to sculpt the part of the clothing which would drape over it and wanted to make the grooves on that layer which would look like pleats. His jaw clenched as he worked and fixed his eyes on that area and kept chiseling out the stone until it looked like a draping layer of cloth running from his left shoulder.

The church bell chimed twelve times just as Niccolò said to Paolo, "I am going to start another fold of cloth a few inches below the one I did that will run across to the other side about the same length with a deep upwards curvature and join the cloth from the left shoulder which is draping over it."

Niccolò commenced his plan and asked Paolo to brush the marble chips he was chiseling. They both worked diligently for more than an hour and finished that fold. Niccolò took a deep breath and with relief, announced, "We are done. That is all we are doing for the Prophet today."

Niccolò took a swig of water and wiped the sweat off his brow. "Paolo, let us go for lunch to the Osteria. The walk and getting out of the studio for some time will refresh us, then we can concentrate on the clay molding for The Feast of Herod."

Niccolò and Paolo ambled towards the Osteria as the cold breeze blew through tall birch trees still bare but there were touches of green over some branches. Patches of green grass were along the sides of the moist paved road with areas where some of the daffodils and tulips with their closed buds swayed gently with the breeze.

They reached the restaurant Osteria, the brick-layered building with an arched entrance and arched wooden doors with iron bolts. Entering the restaurant, they saw a big oval-shaped furnace with log fire, yellowish blue-flames almost touching the brick-layered roof of the furnace. A large iron container half-filled with some kind of simmering soup hung from an iron hook over the fireplace as the smell of simmering soup filled the air.

It was warm and cozy inside as Niccolò and Paolo took their seats on polished wooden stools around a rectangular, polished wooden table covered with a red tablecloth.

An attendant came wearing a brown breech, a yellow long-sleeved round neck sweater, and a red apron tied to his back. "Today we are featuring sausage and vegetable soup, fresh sourdough bread, roasted sweet potato and carrots, mulled wine, beer and orange blossom water.

Niccolò ordered a bowl of soup for him and for Paolo, bread, roasted sweet potato and carrots, and mulled wine. "Is that all right, Paolo? Or would you like something else to drink?"

"Maestro, that is perfect."

"Oh, before I forget, I would like to ask you about your cousin, the one you told me could work for my mother to keep her company. Do you think she will be ready to work as a companion for my mother this coming May? It is almost the end of March."

"Maestro, thank you for letting me know. I will talk to her and let you know soon as I hear from my cousin." Paolo took a sip of water. "Maestro, tell me your plan for the scenes of The Feast of Herod."

"Well, today we will begin the clay modeling. I will start with Salome's dance. To give you a rough idea: the whole thing will be 60 cm x 60 cm using perspective. I already mentioned to you when I was sketching that there will be a banquet scene for Herod's invited high officials and military men of Galilee. I do not want to show the execution explicitly. Instead, I will show the executioner presenting the head of St. John to King Herod on a platter. When King Herod's expression will change to shock and horror, the military officials' expression will change too."

Carlo brought their food which Paolo commented, "Smells delicious."

Niccolò and Paolo enjoyed the hot sausage soup with freshly-baked sourdough bread.

"Maestro, the mulled wine goes very well with it."

"I am very glad that you are enjoying it." Niccolò looked far into the distance before facing back to their table. "The weather is still foggy and the sky is gray. It seems Mother Nature will soon be melting in rain."

"We can work at least three hours after our lunch," Paolo said.

After finishing lunch, Niccolò and Paolo hurried towards their studio as the wind blew stronger. The pointed pine trees moved strongly to kiss each other as the strong breeze whistled through the birch and oak.

"Maestro, it is starting to rain."

"Yes, it is. We are almost there."

They reached their studio just as it started raining heavily.

Paolo looked around the room. "Where are you going to start your work?"

"I will start in the furnace room as it will be convenient. The furnace is almost ready but Antonio will try to run it in two days to see if it works all right or not. The bucket of moist clay is already waiting for me at the corner and the platform with a wooden plank is ready to mold on the statue."

"I will light the charcoal heater to make the room a little warmer," Paolo said. "You can start and I will help you out soon."

"I am starting with Salome."

Paolo joined Niccolò who was in the process of molding the sculpture.

"Paolo, here is Salome standing on her tiptoes," Niccolò said. "I will detail later the face, the neck and body with her dress with enough width and length. She is a dancer so she is slim. I think this is good enough. What do you think, Paolo?"

"You are so good with your hands, it seems that the figure was already there and you are scooping it out," Paolo said.

"Thank you," Niccolò said. "She is on her tiptoes—there she is. I will carve the details of her feet later.

The church bell started chiming 4 o'clock in the afternoon as a stormy wind blew outside whistling through the trees.

"Maestro, let us go home. A big storm threatens to come and it will rain soon."

"Let us wrap the clay mold with wet cloth otherwise, it will dry up."

"I will help you," Paolo offered. "So you can clean your muddy hands."

They promptly closed the studio and set off quickly, braving the stormy weather to reach home.

* * *

Niccolò arrived at the studio early the next morning thinking Paolo was not yet there but surprisingly, he found Paolo arranging the tools in front of prophet Habakkuk.

Thank

Echoes of the Past

"Thank you for arranging the tools. Today, we will finish the folds of his clothes up to his waist."

"Okay," Paolo said. "Oh, before I forget, my cousin Emilia told me she could start working for your mother beginning the first week of May. She would like to meet your mother before that and talk to her directly."

"Of course, we can arrange that anytime in April," Niccolò said.

Niccolò started carving the folds of clothing around the Prophet's waist. "See, it has to look like it is a little puffed so I am making a few of them round so when it is done, it will look like puffed folds of clothing. The Prophet's right hand is bare and no clothing is covering that hand so we can see the neck and upper portion of his bare chest below his waist, a fold of clothing with a curvature looking upwards will be hanging below his knees.

"There will be two more long folds, one after the other with a curvature upwards, the last one will touch his feet. These folds are coming from the clothing which drapes from his left shoulder."

Niccolò and Paolo together got first the fold of clothing below the knee. Then Niccolò scooped out stone in a few places to create flat bottom recesses with variable depth so it would look like real creases of clothing more so with light and shadow.

Then the clock struck one o'clock in the afternoon. Niccolò stood up to stretch. "I think that is enough for now. We are left with two last long folds of the clothing, one after another. The last longest one will almost touch the feet of the Prophet."

Niccolò told Paolo that his mother packed some lunch for them—leftovers from last night's dinner which Paolo offered to warm up. When Paolo opened the package, he gasped in delight. "What a feast! There are gnocchi in sauce, vegetable soup, roasted potato and dessert—your favorite almond rice. Everything looks delicious."

They enjoyed the lunch of leftovers, with Paolo complimenting Mother Orissa's cooking, saying she was a very sweet and compassionate lady. After lunch, they continued with the clay molding of Herod's feast.

"Paolo, I am going to detail Salome's jewelry and her clothes. The clay is still moist so it will be easy to do everything today."

Niccolò sculpted the jewelry on Salome and designed and sculpted her seductive dress that looked like a see-through material of cloth while sculpting her face. He gave her eyes an expression of staring with lust, looking at a particular direction, pouting her lower lip, head slightly tilted to the right. The upper part of her body was covered with a thin veil through which the contours of her bosom were seen. The body was slightly curved at the waist and she was standing on her tiptoes, holding a lotus in her right hand while her left hand was extended straight out from her shoulder.

After he finished sculpting, Niccolò looked at his sketching paper and his journal to make sure he had done everything that he intended to do. Then he asked Paolo to inspect the sculpture and comment on her.

"Maestro, she looks like a Femme Fatale.'"

"Thank you for your comment, Paolo, that was exactly the effect that I was going for. I want her exactly to look like that."

"Now that you are almost done with Salome, which scene will you mold next?" Paolo asked.

Niccolò scratched his head as he considered that. "I will give you an idea of how I will proceed with The Feast of Herod and then give you an update on the Prophet." He stretched his tired arms and took a breath before continuing.

"For The Feast of Herod, I will start with King Herod and the executioner presenting St. John's head on a platter—"

"Maestro, are you going to mold the executioner with St. John's head on a platter first?" The concept of this next scene seemed to excite Paolo.

"No, I will mold King Herod and the other officials first. I will place them in their respective seats. Then later, I will detail them with expressions and body positions, such as hands covering their face and other details. Then I can create a space just below the level of King Herod and his officials for the executioner presenting the head of St. John on a platter. Then there will be other levels in the frames for the rest of the invited officials. This is the stage of molding, then waxing, then baking twice and then the metal casting. When the metal is cooled, then we have to detail it, like engraving over the casting material, cleaning and polishing. There are so many steps and it is time consuming. But we will still be ahead of schedule."

"That is good," Paolo said.

"I might be called to Padua for some other commission and Cosimo is planning to give me more commissions for the new palace which I heard construction will soon start. In the meantime, for us, mornings will be devoted to the Prophet. We will finish his clothing, the toga, in another day or two, then next, his face at least, we will devote around five to seven days to detail his expression and observe him as if speaking, lamenting and asking, 'God, why did you not do anything to save the people?' This will take some time. I do not know exactly how long he will stay with us but I suspect for some time until the church people will come to take him to his place in the bell tower."

"Wow, Maestro, we surely have our work cut out for us."

"Yes, that is quite an extensive account of the work we are involved in now and a preview of what we will be delving into for the future," said Niccolò.

The Prophet is Alive!

28ᵗʰ of March—This spring morning started bright with golden rays of the sun peeping through the grayish orange clouds, flooding the city of Firenze.

People wrapped in their woolen capes walked on the paved path near the piazza. The Baptistery stood at the corner with all its beauty and grandeur against the fluffy clouds. Vendors were pushing their business carts as busy boats carrying passengers were passing along the river.

Some of the tall trees painted their branches with soft green leaves as a number of birds chirping on the branches and a flock of birds enjoyed their flight across the sky.

Niccolò was lost in thought as he quickened his pace towards the studio thinking about his commissions to be completed in time and wondering about Cosimo's message.

"He wants to talk to me but did not mention a time but said he is currently busy. As soon as he finishes dealing with those matters at hand, he will send a message."

He felt good that Emilia, Paolo's cousin, had already met his mother. The two women formed an instant bond upon their first meeting and Tia also liked Emilia so this set Niccolò's mind at ease. In fact, Tia had asked Emilia to immediately start keeping Orissa company as Tia would be leaving for Castellina in a few weeks.

"Today I want to finish sculpting whatever's left of the Prophet," Niccolò continued murmuring to himself. "I sculpted out the Prophet's face and neck, the hollowed eyes, the parted lips. I have to check whether there's anything else left to sculpt then detail it with an expression so that I will be done within two weeks. The Feast of Herod is waiting for casting. So today I have to check everything and after baking a second time, will start melting the bronze in the afternoon and casting the metal to the scenes one scene at a time. The second time baking will be some time in the morning as the mold should remain hot while I am casting the metal otherwise it will crack."

Niccolò was completely immersed in his thoughts until he suddenly realized that he reached the studio when he heard, "Good morning, Maestro, the tools are all ready for sculpting."

"We will start working on the Prophet," Niccolò said promptly. "Let us see whether we missed anything." Niccolò started to examine the sculpture from the head of the Prophet to his face, neck and body, the folds of his toga, and his feet. He took a deep breath and said, "Nothing is missing, but his eyes should be more hollowed and sadder, the parting of the lips should be more prominent. I want him to look like he is in pain and distress, create an image of him in anguish. I will try to make the sockets of his eyes deeper, his head more tilted, his lower jaw dragged down a little and show linear creases on his forehead and on his face, deepening the creases on both sides of his nose." He paused for a few seconds. "Paolo, do you know why I am keen to create a melancholic look for the Prophet?"

Suddenly, Niccolò's expression changed as he drew closer to the unfinished sculpture, he began speaking to him: "I say Zuccone, speak to me right now. You were not afraid to question God about the injustice he allowed on the people of Judea. So now, speak to me! Your eyes are sad and void, your lips are parted as if you want to speak yet I cannot hear you speak. Speak! I sculpted you with metamorphic marble that is translucent like our skin and your body is sinuous which will encourage the eyes of the people to move around you with their anguish and complaint to God, reminding them of their own spiritual and personal struggle with their own relationship with God. Come alive and speak to me now!"

Niccolò kept screaming at the Prophet. "Speak to me, you fool, speak to me!"

An alarmed Paolo shook Niccolò as he called, "Maestro! Maestro, remember we must focus on our work, please. We have to put the mold of Herod's feast for baking for the second time in the oven. You told me that it has to be warm to hot when we start casting the metal, otherwise it will crack. Are you with me, Maestro?"

With an expression of incredulity on his face, Niccolò stared at the Prophet. Gradually he snapped back to the present and took a deep breath. "We shall now go back to work on the Prophet."

Paolo scratched his head. "Maestro, do you think we are going to be done with the Prophet soon?"

"No, it takes time to smooth the rough edges and polish it the way I want."

So Niccolò continued working on the Prophet, trying to smooth out the rough edges. Thirty minutes passed, when Paolo reminded Niccolò to take the mold out. Niccolò could not believe that thirty minutes could pass by so quickly.

"Are you sure it's been thirty minutes?"

"Yes, Maestro."

The church bell chimed twelve times. "Paolo, when would you like to take a lunch break?"

"You decide what's best for your schedule."

"I want to continue working another half an hour."

Paolo sighed. "That is no problem."

As soon as Paolo finished talking, the sounds of horses galloping could be heard in the background. The sound became louder and louder as the horses drew closer.

"I think the messengers are coming to our studio."

Paolo was right, a horse carriage arrived and stopped in front of the studio. Two men dressed in navy blue breeches, beige shirts and doublet with brown vests and black hose, covered with a short black mantel and brimless scarlet caps got down from the carriage and bowed in front of Niccolò. They opened a scroll and read:

"Cosimo de' Medici is inviting Maestro Niccolò to meet him at the palace. The time and the day will be scheduled accordingly to suit Maestro Niccolò's wishes."

Niccolò consulted his schedule and asked Paolo, "Do you think that between 9 and 10 in the morning will be good, when you can work on polishing the Prophet and in the afternoon, we can continue casting the relief of The Feast of Herod?"

"Maestro, that is good so that we can do the casting after lunch."

Niccolò turned to the men. "Yes, I accept the invitation from the Honorable Cosimo and I shall see him on Wednesday, the 30th of March at 9 in the morning which is two days from now." He said this with startling revelation.

"Thank you, Maestro," one of Cosimo's men said. "Please state where you would like us to pick you up? From your home or your studio? And we can give you a ride back when you return."

"Please pick me up from my home and a ride back to my studio," Niccolò requested.

"We will be very pleased to do that, Maestro."

The two palace messengers bowed then left the studio.

"Paolo, I think this will be the commission for Cosimo's new palace. I must tell him I am currently working on these two commissions right now." Niccolò raked his fingers through his hair as though a bit overwhelmed at the moment. "We will be almost done with the Prophet in another few months although the church will not be ready for the Prophet until 1423."

"Maestro, that is all right. We can keep him here covered and protected."

"Yes, Paolo. That is correct." He sighed. "Let us have our lunch break and in the afternoon, we can decide what we will do tomorrow and assign some areas for you on the Prophet's sculpture to work on Wednesday morning."

Niccolò and Paolo began work on the bronze casting, this time the scene of the executioner presenting St. John's head on a platter to King Herod. Niccolò carefully poured the liquid bronze on the mold including the high officials and said to let it cool.

"I hope the liquid bronze covered the whole scene," he said.

"Maestro, to me, it looks like it is all done but you can confirm it."

"Hmm, you are right, Paolo, it does look good. Tomorrow morning, we will be working together but Wednesday morning, I am to meet with Cosimo. You can start polishing the part of the toga that layers from his left shoulder."

"Yes, will do, Maestro."

"Tomorrow morning, the 29th of March, we will start with the Prophet, finishing whatever is left and then we will start to detail."

Paolo peered through the window. "Let us go home soon as the daylight is fading and it will be difficult to see what we are working on."

Niccolò agreed and they soon closed the studio and began walking toward their homes.

* * *

The horse carriage from the palace arrived at Niccolò's cottage to take him to the Medici Palace to meet Cosimo as previously scheduled. As the horses trotted then galloped faster, inside the carriage, Niccolò's heartbeat quickened with anxiety and nervousness.

On this Wednesday, the 30th of March 1422, the sky was gray and Firenze was still under the last grip of winter. The cold wind was whistling through the tall trees as small patches of frost were seen on the red-tiled roof of the houses. There were patches of frost on the ground. On the way there, memories of going to the palace to work on Beatrice's sculpture seized Niccolò who tried his best to shove these images away by focusing on his current projects.

"I finished casting all the scenes yesterday which is good as it will be cooled and we can look at it thoroughly tomorrow afternoon to check whether the casting is complete or not," Niccolò murmured to himself. "Paolo is working on polishing the Prophet's toga right now." Niccolò was lost in thought, still anxious about what kind of commission Cosimo will give him. The carriage was almost at the gate of the palace when Niccolò spotted two palace guards with their blue outfits and scarlet caps who promptly opened the gate and greeted him, *"Buongiorno"* as he got down from the carriage.

"Maestro, we are here to accompany you to the Honorable Cosimo," one of the guards said.

Niccolò was happy to follow them, remembering his first visit as they passed through the garden and then climbed up a few steps to the tapestry room where Cosimo de' Medici conducted meetings with his guests.

Niccolò arrived at the entrance of the familiar room, having been here before. Beautiful tapestries hung on the walls featuring scenes of beautiful ladies playing lyre, children playing. The others featured beautiful landscapes with green grass and flowers with a flock of deer frolicking.

When Niccolò entered the room, he saw Cosimo in his long scarlet outfit with a matching cap sitting on a red-cushioned chair with golden handles. His face was triangular with a pointed nose and sharp, black sparkling eyes. Cosimo greeted Niccolò with a handshake and a smile and asked him to take a seat on a red-cushioned chair.

"Buongiorno Vostro onore," Niccolò addressed Cosimo.

Cosimo asked his attendant to offer some pastries and water to the guest.

"I am fine," Niccolò said. "I do not eat anything until lunch."

"Benvenuto amico mio," Cosimo said.

Niccolò slightly bowed. *"Millie Grazie."*

"My friend, our new palace will start construction soon. We are proceeding with the plan of Maestro Michelozzo. Maestro Brunelleschi's plan was grand and unique but we thought it would be too grand so my brother and I chose the little modest design. So I plan to commission you to create a sculpture which you will sculpt with as much creative freedom as you desire—from the materials you choose to the way you want to sculpt. I would like the sculpture to be a unique one as it will stand in the palace courtyard as a showpiece. There will be more sculptures for the gardens but this piece for the courtyard is the most important."

"Signore, I am at present working on two commissions at the same time. At the end of this year, I will be done with the Prophet and the church will take the sculpture and place it in the bell tower sometime in the next year. Then there will be more space in my studio. With your permission, I would like to choose the material but I will agree with you about sculpting whichever particular hero or saint you would like me to sculpt."

Cosimo considered this for a moment. "Hmm, I like your idea of a hero. Do you have any suggestions?"

Niccolò clasped his hands eagerly. "Well, it is just a flash of thought that came to me. What about the young David who killed Goliath?"

Cosimo looked far into the distance and then his eyes lit up. "It is an excellent idea. But you have already sculpted David in marble, correct?"

"Sir, that is very different as it is in Gothic style that is in the past," Niccolò explained. "I am not in that time. I am reborn. There is not much expression in that sculpture. It is a copy of a marble sculpture in Gothic style.

Now, I sculpt figures who speak and move and share feelings with whoever comes near them."

Cosimo nodded. "My dear Niccolò, I am deeply moved you have explained this to me. As I said, I give you all the freedom you need to sculpt a figure to your specifications."

"Signore, it will be in bronze—that much I can tell you at present."

"My dear man, feel free to sculpt wherever your hands take you with the vision of your eyes and mind together. I have seen firsthand the genius of that when you sculpted Beatrice's likeness."

As much as he tried to ward Beatrice from his mind, there she was again, in his thoughts as images of her posing for him invaded his mind. He pushed those images away and focused on the task at hand.

"Thank you, *Vostra Eccellenza*, I will start planning at the end of this year and begin thinking and sketching within two years as it will take a few years to finish."

"Take all the time you want, my friend," Cosimo said. "Do not hesitate to contact me if you need anything. I will surely make time to attend to whatever you request."

"And now, sir, with your permission, I shall bid you farewell as my assistant is waiting for me in the studio. Thank you for entrusting me with this project." Niccolò slightly bowed and the two men parted ways.

When Niccolò walked to the palace gate accompanied by the guards to find the carriage waiting for him, he continued to mentally shove aside memories of his time taking this same walk at the end of his days working on Beatrice's sculpture. *That was in the past. It is now the present,* he urged his mind.

"Please take me to my studio," he told the driver.

"Yes, Maestro," the carriage driver said.

Niccolò was very excited and pleased that Cosimo addressed him as a friend and gave him the freedom to sculpt the figure in the style he most desired. The road and the landscape moved backwards fast as his mind spun forward even faster.

He was very eager to tell Paolo everything about the meeting with Cosimo. The carriage reached the studio just as the church bells chimed eleven times. Paolo met Niccolò at the door to greet him.

After Niccolò waved to the driver as the carriage took off, he turned toward the entrance happy to be back in the studio.

Paolo brought him a goblet of orange blossom water and the cushioned chair with walnut handles to Niccolò who sat down and took a deep breath.

"I feel good and relaxed." He motioned Paolo to sit down. "I will tell you all about the meeting I had with Cosimo."

Paolo sat down and leaned forward eagerly.

"I am most honored that Cosimo addressed me as his friend, then he talked about the construction of his new palace which will begin soon. He said he is giving me a commission to sculpt a figure which will be placed on the new palace courtyard and emphasized that it has to be unique and different than any other sculptor has done so far but he has given me the freedom to choose the subject of the figure, the materials, the technique and the procedure, and freedom to take the time I need to sculpt it." Niccolò leaned forward eagerly towards his assistant. "Paolo, I chose to sculpt David and I want to do it in bronze."

Paolo clapped his hands. "That is excellent, but why David and what will it stand for?"

"Paolo, that is a very good question. This version of David will stand depicting a nude boy who has slain the mighty Goliath with an expression of innocence and victory yet at the same time, will show his humility and grace to God."

"You depicted everything with your chosen few words," Paolo said.

"You can tell me in detail how you want to proceed with this new project during lunch break. I prepared the tools you need to work on the Prophet. I also polished part of the Prophet's toga which layered from his left shoulder."

"Paolo, it is now 11:30 and we can work for one hour and a half before we have our lunch break. Let me see what still needs to be done on the Prophet and you can continue polishing what is left of the toga."

Niccolò and Paolo continued working on the Prophet with Paolo diligently smoothing out the rough edges of the toga which layered from the Prophet's left shoulder. Niccolò concentrated on the face of the Prophet, fine tuning his expression.

Hours passed until the church bell announced it was 2 o'clock in the afternoon. Paolo saw how Niccolò was deeply immersed working on the face of the Prophet, he did not care to disturb him so Paolo continued working, thinking to himself, *My hands are tired and I am hungry. I need a lunch break.*

Meanwhile, Niccolò was so absorbed in making the Prophet's eyes sunken deep in the sockets until the expression of a tired and sad look on the Prophet's face suddenly became obvious especially with the effect of light and shadow. Niccolò stood back and marveled at his own work, crying out loud, "Paolo! Paolo! Look, he is lamenting, he is alive. The Prophet is alive!"

Paolo rushed to face the front of the sculpture. "Maestro, I see that! How amazing, you are a genius." Then Paolo's expression changed as he rubbed his sore hands. "Maestro, we need a break."

Seeing his tired assistant, Niccolò descended from the clouds back down to earth. "Sorry Paolo, I forgot about our lunch break. Let us have an extended lunch break. My hands feel tired too."

"I will warm up the vegetable soup with corn, potatoes, tomatoes, leek and herbs. There is Tagliatelle in tomato sauce and some boiled eggs."

Niccolò noticed Paolo's weary tone and felt guilty for making his assistant tired and hungry. "That all sounds delicious. I am sorry for a late lunch break. I just became so absorbed with perfecting the expression on the Prophet's face, his eyes. We shall discuss the new commission and after lunch we will just go over the scenes of Herod's feast to find out whether the casting is complete or not.

Instead of rushing, Niccolò and Paolo enjoyed a leisurely lunch not wishing to be in a hurry today.

Since Niccolò finished casting one scene of Herod's feast yesterday, today he and Paolo checked the scene of The Feast of Herod if anything was missing.

"Paolo, the figure of David will stand on itself without any support—the first ever sculpture and also the first male nude with other added features and expressions."

"Maestro, how big or tall will it stand?"

"Not so big—about five feet or so. We will finish polishing the Prophet within the coming few months, say about June or July. Then we shall continue examining the sculpture to see whether anything is missing and inspect all the parts, especially the toga, to see if the layers of the toga are properly done or not and check whether they are all polished properly."

The church bell chimed three times. "Maestro, you wanted to look at Herod's feast. So how about we start that to see if anything is missing?"

"That is a very good idea. Let us check the casting."

Niccolò inspected, scene after scene, to see if anything was missing then he and Paolo did a thorough check and found the casting was perfect.

"It looks fine," Niccolò said. "Tomorrow afternoon, we will start the process of engraving, which is time-consuming and tedious, and then polishing."

"That sounds good," Paolo said. "Shall we close now and go home?"

"Not quite yet," Niccolò said. "Before I forget, I want to mention that we will continue to work on these two projects for a number of months. The Prophet will be gone sometime next year, The Feast of Herod will stay with us because we need more time to complete it. And we will hold on to it until the church tells us they are ready since it will be placed in the cathedral in Siena. In the meantime, I will start to plan and sketch David. I am thinking of starting work on the sculpture of David soon as we might finish sculpting David early before Cosimo is ready to bring it to his new palace." Niccolò scratched his head as he processed his thoughts. "What I mean to say is that the construction of the new palace and its courtyard might not yet be finished in time to place the sculpture in the place where Cosimo wants it to be. But that is good as it will leave us plenty of time to examine and assess the sculpture thoroughly if we complete it ahead of schedule. That way we can take our time determining whether anything needs to be added or any particular area needs some more detailed work. Oh yes, one more last thing which is most important is that David will appear alive and express his feelings of joy for the victory of defeating Goliath who was slain and David will show humility to God for his grace—his emotions will glow like light on his face and on his tender body. That is my vision."

"That is a very powerful vision," said Paolo, looking a bit unsettled. "Maestro, I think Mother Nature is threatening us with a possible meltdown through rain."

They both peered through the open door and saw the cool and moist breeze blowing through the tall trees as flashes of lightning appeared to pierce the sky.

The weather prompted their decision to close their studio. Filled with the anticipation of finishing current projects and starting a new sculpture ahead, Niccolò and Paolo walked towards their respective paths, feeling light on their feet despite the hovering dark clouds and the rain that showered on them lightly as they headed to their homes.

Niccolo's Vision of the Bronze David

Spring in Florence—Despite it being springtime, this morning seemed to be hazy as the sun was lazy to rise. The tall trees were dressed in their fresh green leaves as they were simmering in joy in diffused sunlight. The air was filled with the chirping songs of the birds. Along both sides of a paved path, the tulips, daffodils and the blue bells proudly displayed their colors as a blast of sweet fragrances from the flowers with spring breeze filled the air. Some passersby were still dazed, walking slowly while others quickened their pace, stopped often to catch their breaths, as others with their knitted brows and reluctant expressions contemplated the outcome of the day.

A tall figure—by now, familiar to the city as the favorite son of Florence—wearing a long, white outfit and long black mantel, picked up his pace, lost in his thoughts, kept murmuring to himself, "I am glad the church took the Prophet who I hope is somewhere in a niche in the bell tower. Paolo had asked me why I screamed at the prophet so hard? I love him. I respect him very much. He questioned God about the injustice he allowed to the people. But what a fool he was as he spent night and day crying to get some answer. He was in extreme agony and despair but, did he get the answer, I am wondering? I am guessing—probably not and that hurts me a lot. After I finished sculpting, he was alive, standing in front of me but I could not hear him. It seemed his lips were moving but no sound came out and that frustrated me. Anyway, we took care of him almost every day for a year, dusting him, and before we left our studio, we covered him with fine pieces of cloth so that dust in the air would not settle on him. The Feast of Herod is still in the studio. I hope the church of Siena makes an arrangement soon to place it inside the church. We worked hard and still we are taking care to keep the relief nice and shiny. Our studio is busy—there is always some work going on in the studio on marble and other stones. Paolo is getting some work independently so I am happy about that."

As he continued walking, he looked up at the sky and around him to see if anyone was listening to his self-musings. Anyone in the present or the past or even the future who might hear his thoughts that might transcend time and become echoes of the past well into the future. And still his mind kept racing. "Mamma is doing all right at present. Emilia has been taking good care of her. Tia will arrive back home soon to spend some time with us and if Mamma agrees, she will spend some time with Tia in Castellina and she will invite Emilia to accompany her, if Emilia accepts the invitation."

Then his racing thoughts slowed down as his mood shifted and his breath staggered. "I do not want to think about the time when Mamma will be no more. She is getting older." He stopped for few minutes, took a few deep breaths and continued self-contemplating to take his mind off disturbing thoughts. "I am going to concentrate on David's sculpture, sketching and planning to sculpt David. I want to depict him as a hero and I will make him so unique a sculpture that the people of Firenze have never seen."

Niccolò could smell the aroma of freshly-baked bread. *I have not seen Uncle Luigi for a while, I hope he is all right*, he thought. Suddenly he heard someone calling his name. It was uncle Luigi who Niccolò was happy to see.

"Niccolò, I do not come too often at the shop these days," the baker said. "This is my son, Ludovico, who will be here every day. I want you both to know each other."

Ludovico came out and shook hands with Niccolò. "I will make sure that I catch you some time when you are on your way to the studio and you are welcome to stop by any time."

"Thank you, Ludovico."

"My dear Niccolò, have you finished sculpting the Prophet and Herod's feast," asked the baker.

"Yes, Uncle Luigi, the Prophet is done and the church people have arranged to install it in the bell tower. Herod's feast is finished and waiting to go to Siena church."

"That is wonderful, I am so proud of you, Firenze is proud of you."

"Uncle Luigi, I got a commission from Cosimo to sculpt David and will be casting him in bronze. He wants to put this sculpture in the courtyard of his new palace."

"Niccolò, you will do an excellent job. I am sure it will be one of the most unique sculptures Firenze has ever seen. I am so proud of you. God bless you, my son."

Luigi handed over a bag full of different kinds of bread.

"Thank you, Uncle Luigi, and Ludovico, please let me know if you need anything. Uncle, you stay healthy and Ludovico, it is very nice to meet you and we will keep in touch."

Niccolò set off briskly to reach the studio where Paolo met him at the door and greeted him with a smile.

"Maestro, I did not set up the tools as I do not know what you plan on doing today."

"I will start planning and, at the same time, working on the sculpture of David."

"Has the palace construction already started?" Paolo asked.

"I do not know but I will start working according to my schedule. If the palace is not ready, then that is their responsibility," Niccolò affirmed.

"Let me know what tools you need to start your work then," Paolo offered.

Niccolò considered this. "My journal, sketching paper, and pencils."

"How tall will the sculpture be?"

"Not more than five feet." The lines of Niccolò's forehead creased. "I think it will be the first unsupported standing work of bronze during this period of our time. Here's what I envision: David will stand poised with an enigmatic smile, his one foot on Goliath's severed head after defeating the giant. The youth is nude apart from his laurel topped hat and his boots as he bears the sword of Goliath."

"Maestro, what will his body be like?"

"Hmm, that is a very good question. David will be physically delicate and remarkably effeminate. The statue's physique will be contrasted with a large sword in his hand that will show how David has overcome Goliath not by physical prowess but through God."

"Maestro, why do you want him to be nude?"

"The boy's nakedness implies the idea of the presence of God, contrasting the youth with a heavily armored giant."

"What does the sculpture stand for?" Paolo's eyes danced with anticipation.

"David stands for victory."

"So how do you want me to hold the sketching paper?"

"Before we discuss that, Paolo, let me write down a few other important points in my journal which I will explain to you later. Another thing I want to tell you before I forget is that Cosimo promised to send me some money in advance soon. So I will give you some money in advance—today—that way I will feel better about all the hard work you have done to help me. I hope you are happy with the amount I am giving you for your work helping me with the Prophet."

Paolo nodded, deeply moved. "Maestro, I am more than happy with the amount. You are very kind and generous.

"The church of Siena did not pay me yet—"

"Maestro, do not worry. It is fine."

Niccolò nodded. "Anytime you need money, please let me know as I always carry a certain amount in my bag."

"Maestro, I appreciate that you are very considerate. I am very honored with the privilege of working with you."

Niccolò nodded, satisfied that he was able to compensate his assistant in the best way he could. And now, on to the business at hand. "There are many other sculptures in the niches but this one is meant to be seen from all sides. Paolo, I want him in a *Contrapposto*—a term that refers to the naturalistic way in which a human figure is shown with weight distributed to one hip and how the rest of the body shifts in relation to that."

"Maestro, what is the reason, or should I ask, what impression will it give to people when they will look at it?"

"Paolo, I really like your question." Niccolò propped his right elbow onto his left forearm, his fingers propping his chin in a philosopher's pose. "So here is how I see it: the figure is posed such that the weight rests on one leg, called an engaged leg freeing the other leg which is bent at the knee. The body is expressed in a more relaxed disposition, creating an illusion of past and future movement that gives the impression of real movement. Ancient Greek sculptors used this technique a long time ago. So David will be modeled in clay and cast in bronze."

"Are you going to start sketching?" Paolo asked.

"Yes, I will start to sketch and will explain some other aspects of David along the way as we proceed."

"All right, Maestro I am ready."

"Please bring that board and paste the sketching paper on it—the smooth one which is standing in the corner," Niccolò directed Paolo. "I will start from the head and sketch the outline of his whole body down to his leg and keep some area for Goliath's severed head and also some more place and space below."

Niccolò concentrated on sketching David by starting to make an outline of David's full figure first and asked Paolo to smooth out the small creases on the right side of the sketching paper. Then he wanted to sketch the right hand with the sword.

"Why do you want to do the right hand with the sword first?"

"You see, it should not be too far or too close to David's body and if I sketch the hand with the sword first, then I will have the idea of the space which is left and start to sketch his body accordingly in proper proportion." Niccolò's eyes remained focused. "You will understand better when I start the sketching process.

Niccolò concentrated sketching the hand holding the sword and outlined that side of the body and went down to the leg which was very close to the tapering end of the sword then sketched the outline of the severed head of Goliath.

Sensing the morning going by quickly, he stopped there and asked, "Paolo, what is the time?"

"It is past 11:30."

"I would like to sketch another hour or so."

"Maestro, that is fine with me."

"Paolo, could you please darken the sketched lines where it is lighter? And be careful…"

"I will be very careful."

"And I will detail Goliath's head later. I will outline the foot which is on Goliath's severed head and then sketch the other leg. After that, I will concentrate on sketching the outline of his body, face and head and his laurel hat then detail it. This is only the front. Then I have to sketch, on another sheet, the back of David. People will go around to view him. He is not going to be in a niche."

Niccolò continued to sketch David's leg and body and paused at the neck. "What is the time?"

"It is past 1:30 in the afternoon."

Niccolò stood up and wiped the sweat from his forehead. "I have to stop. The face and the head will take more than four hours and I have to sketch it when there will be plenty of light."

"Maestro, I think it will be better if you could start again tomorrow morning then you can work until afternoon sketching those parts."

"Yes, Paolo. Let us have lunch break and I will see what can be done in the afternoon. We might not be able to do much in the afternoon when the sunlight still fades away soon during this time of year."

"True. It is the end of April until the middle of May when the light fades away soon."

Niccolò and Paolo decided that they would enjoy their lunch break and head home early.

* * *

Niccolò, wearing his long white overhaul, picked up his pace to reach the studio. As usual, to get ready to face the day, he gave himself a pep talk: "The air smells fresh, the trees are covered with bright green leaves. There is the smell of flowers in the air and birds are busy chirping on the branches of the trees. I cannot believe the days passed so quickly. It is already the 25th of May and I am not yet finished with sketching the face of David. Ah yes, I changed my mind so that I am not only sketching the outline of the face. I will do each detail of his enigmatic smile with his head a little lowered showing his humility to God and his eyes peaceful and kind yet sparkling with joy of his victory and satisfied that the job of defeating Goliath is done. The month of May will soon end and Mother will be returning from Castellina in the first week of June. Then Tia will come and stay with us for a week or so." He paused to survey the activity in the city streets.

"I might have to work with my friend, Michelozzo, for the funerary monument of the Antipope John XXIII. So David's sculpture will be halted for some time until I finish working with Michelozzo. It will be all right as the new palace has yet to start its construction. We will be ahead of schedule with David's sculpting before the palace requests for it. I will ask Paolo to start the other commissions from Cosimo for his garden and I can supervise but I will let him do everything. Paolo has trained and worked for me for many years—I taught him everything I know. He is ready and I will give him the whole amount of money for that portion of the work. He deserves it."

Niccolò continued walking and musing to himself. "I think I am going to concentrate on sketching David with all its detail and sketch the back of David on a separate sheet."

Finally, Niccolò reached his studio where, as usual, Paolo greeted him with a smile and told him he had already prepared his tools for the day.

"Paolo, I will detail David's hat with the laurel first."

Paolo nodded, eager to hear more.

"After I finish his hat, I will detail his legs and the severed head of Goliath under his feet. Paolo, I have to talk to you about the commissions which Cosimo wants for his new palace garden. After all that you have learned from me, I think you can handle these garden commissions yourself and, if you need any help, or if you want to discuss any of your new ideas, I will definitely help you with that. Otherwise, think of this as your own project and concentrate on it. Oh, and I will give you the whole amount for that part of the work you will do for that commission whenever Cosimo pays me but I will pay you an advance when you start. I might have to work away from my studio with my friend Michelozzo on a funerary monument of Antipope John XXIII. During that time work on David will be on hold but you can continue to work on other projects. What do you think, Paolo?"

Niccolò's assistant stood there awestruck though his eyes brightened. "Maestro, what more can I say but, thank you! That is too kind of you to think that I am ready to take on a project of my own—with your guidance, of course! And how nice of you to offer to pay me generously. Yes, I do need to earn a living but I am not so greedy about money. I am just so grateful for the opportunity to work with you for I have learned so much under your guidance."

Niccolò regarded his assistant for a long moment. Aside from his mother and sister and now, his nephew, no one else was as close and as loyal to him as Paolo had been all these years. "I appreciate that, Paolo. Do not hesitate to tell me when and what you might need. You have been a tremendous help to me all these years with all these different commissions. And personally, you are very dear to me and I respect and I...love you for that."

Paolo's eyes lit up, he seemed as though he was about to give Niccolò a hug but stayed put. "Thank you, Maestro, for your good words and compassion. I will definitely let you know when I need your help."

Niccolo maintained his business tone. "Cosimo wants a half-open lotus in marble for his garden to be sculpted where water will be coming out from a section, yet to open and drip through the petals already opened and then water will flow to a stream and on the stream, there will be more sculpted lotuses, maybe two more or so to give an impression of floating white lotuses.

"Maestro, I can start that when you are away from the studio."

"You can definitely do that while I am working away from the studio and I will finish my sketching of David before I go."

Niccolò started working on David's hat and face while Paolo held the paper stretched. Then Niccolò finished sketching the hat with all the details he wanted. Before long, some time had passed that Paolo alerted him, "It is now one o'clock in the afternoon."

"Then we will have our lunch break now." Niccolò stood up to stretch to his full height and massaged his hands and arms. "In the afternoon, I will finish the laurel in his hat."

Niccolò suggested going to the Osteria for lunch. "Let us walk and have some fresh air and enjoy the spring season.

They reached the Osteria and took their seats around a table where the attendant Mario approached dressed with a brown breech, yellow shirt and red vest, a red apron tied around his back. "Today's menu is vegetable stew, boiled eggs, and sourdough bread. Drinks are beer, mulled wine and orange blossom water."

Niccolò ordered two bowls of vegetable stew, sourdough bread, and two beers. He and Paolo were pleased to be in the Osteria seated in front of the fireplace and being served by an attendant. This was a treat after long hours at work. The sight of steaming bowls of fresh vegetable stew made them hungrier and happier. The warm, freshly-baked sourdoughs were served on a basket lined with bright red cloth.

"I am so glad that you suggested coming here," Paolo said. "It is very relaxing."

"Very pleased you are enjoying it." Niccolò's expression turned serious as he fixed his gaze on Paolo. "I want to ask you a personal question, if I may—do you have plans to settle down and have a family of your own? If you do, then, do you not think it is about time?"

Paolo regarded Niccolò thoughtfully. "Maestro, at present, I do not have any such plans. I feel happy, the way I am now."

"My nephew, Amadeo, is 28-years-old. He and his friend, Stefano, are planning to get settled in the summer. Interestingly enough, both the young ladies they intend to marry are in their early twenties and they are very close friends."

Paolo nodded. "Maestro, congratulations, that is great news."

"I am glad they are planning on getting married on the 7th of August in Siena. Mother will go back to Siena sometime in mid-July and I will go there two to three days before the wedding and stay there a few days. After the wedding, both couples will go somewhere. I do not know yet the place."

"Maestro, that will be nice."

Niccolò leaned forward. "Paolo, I want to finish sketching both front and back. I will see whether my friend wants to start working right now or if he wants to start in the year of 1427. If it is in 1427, then I will, at the most, be committed there until 1429 maybe longer. David will have to wait as clay modeling and casting has to be done one after the other otherwise, it will not work. We will still be ahead of schedule. We can finish it before 1433. I am thinking if they start right now, then it will take them roughly about that time to finish. Cosimo also asked me to work on some antique sculpture for repair and reconstruction." He paused to sip some water.

"Paolo, the sculpture project for Cosimo's garden, which I am giving to you, will be an agreement between the two of us. I do not want anyone to know—it will be like any other commission that you are helping me with. The reason behind that is, as soon as someone from the palace finds out that another artist besides me is doing the sculptures, then they will pay less. I do not want that. It is still work contracted to me as I will supervise the work. I know you will do a pretty good job but I will not take any money for it."

"Maestro, shouldn't you take part of the amount? You are supposed to since you will be supervising me."

Niccolò trained his eyes on his assistant. "Paolo, I am telling you nicely but firmly—whatever I decide, that is final. It is not up for debate. No more questions."

"All right, then, I will accept whatever you have decided. Thank you."

Niccolò nodded, anxious to move on. "Let us go back to the studio and see whether we can work on the laurels of David's hat."

Back at the studio, Niccolò began concentrating on sketching the laurels while Paolo took the responsibility of going over the areas Niccolò had already sketched. He was darkening the lines of the sketch which looked lighter.

Niccolò had just completed the laurels on David's hat when, just then, they heard the trotting sound of horses, the sight of which became clearer through their window. They saw two men riding on horses coming closer to their studio. One of them, dressed in a beige hose, brown breeches, red vest and black mantel, got down from the horse and knocked on the door of the studio. Niccolò welcomed him inside.

"We are messengers from Siena here to deliver a message." The man opened up the scroll and said, "The Siena Cathedral is ready to take the sculpted The Feast of Herod and St. John's execution next week, if it is ready. Reverendo Don will come and would like to pay a visit to your studio then. We are humbly letting you know today."

Niccolò nodded. "I gladly welcome Reverendo Don here at our studio and yes, it is ready and thank you very much for letting us know. I want to know exactly when—at the end of the week or the middle of the week?"

"Maestro, it will be on Wednesday afternoon around one o'clock."

"Thank you very much." The messenger bowed to Niccolò then left.

Niccolò turned to his assistant. "Paolo, starting tomorrow we will polish the piece The Feast of Herod's almost every day to keep it shiny and we will keep it covered so that dust will not settle on it." He paused to collect his thoughts. "Let's see, today is Wednesday, that is good we have a few more days to get ready before we send it off and then we will have some space in our studio."

"Yes, Maestro, that will be nice."

"Let us finish early today and go home."

"Thank you, Maestro, I am ready."

* * *

The 15th of June 1426—On an early morning of a summer day in June, the city of Firenze was bathed by the soft rays of the sun. The city was already bustling bright with people going about their business.

Paolo got an early start as he wanted to arrange and tidy up the studio so it would be nice and clean. He was happy that by now the sculpted piece of Herod's Feast had been picked up by representatives of the Siena Cathedral and Reverendo Don came and paid fully to his Maestro.

Paolo thought aloud to himself, "How kind of Maestro to pay me more than enough. The marble pieces have arrived from Cosimo's palace and I am going to start sculpting the lotuses." Paolo took a deep breath. "It is extremely nice that Maestro is giving me the project and promised to pay the whole amount without taking anything for himself."

Paolo continued arranging the studio, creating more space now that the previous projects were gone. He continued tidying up until the studio looked clean and spacious. He arranged a fresh sheet of sketching paper and glued it to another smooth board and kept all the sketching pencils ready. *This is for sketching the back of David.* He looked at the sketching of the front side of David and was amazed to see him as if he was going to come out and talk to him. Paolo felt David's eyes were sparkling with joy yet his gaze with his face slightly down, showed his humility to God. The body was perfectly sketched which gave the impression of a young boy, yet he had slain the

Goliath whose severed head lies under the feet of the boy holding the sword on his right hand with his enigmatic smile.

As he gazed at the sketch, Paolo became emotional and his voice cracked as he said out loud, "I understand Maestro developed the ideas found on Greek vases. The statue expresses confidence and victory." Paolo took a deep breath and cried out louder, "I understand! I understand Maestro is trying to introduce the classical art period back to present society! What a realization!"

Niccolò had been standing behind Paolo, silently without his knowledge. Slowly, he put his right palm softly on the back of Paolo who jumped in surprise but smiled when he turned to face Niccolò. "Paolo, I am so happy and overcome that you understand exactly what I am trying to express. It is a very happy moment for me and it is a victorious moment for both of us."

"Maestro! Maestro! I am overcome and very happy as well!"

Niccolò nodded and patted Paolo lightly on the shoulder. "Now, let us start working. I have to talk to you about a few important things. First of all, you are invited and very much welcome to Amadeo's wedding. Please accept the invitation. This is my idea so think about it and please let your family know. If you accept, we will leave early morning on the 5Th of August. We shall arrive late afternoon on the 5th in Castellina. The wedding is on 7th so we will stay there from the 5th to the 8th of August in Castellina and leave there early afternoon on the 9th and reach Firenze in the evening." Niccolò raked his hair with his fingers. "Next topic is my project with Michelozzo will start in September so my guess is that it will be done by the end of 1428 but I will keep coming to our studio twice a week or so. There will be no problem those two days supervising you on your project or working on David's sculpture."

"Maestro, I am so relieved that you are able to come to the studio twice a week. That will be very helpful. I am moved and grateful that your family invited me to Amadeo's wedding so I will go and my family will be very pleased to know that I am invited."

"Good," Niccolò said. "Let us start sketching David's back profile, if we work diligently, we can finish at a decent time today."

Niccolò started sketching the back and then proceeded to the next area and sketched his legs, then upward to follow the hip curves and to his upper body and then up to the shoulder. He stopped and turned to Paolo. "What do you think?"

"He looks very delicate."

"That is true, one cannot figure out whether he is male or female from the back. The details of the back part will be done in another day or two."

"That's nice. Maestro, are you thinking of clay modeling and casting after that?"

"There will be more than forty days before we go to Castellina."

"Do not worry, Maestro, the clay modeling will not take much time. You are so good at it. It is the detailing that takes time."

"I think I will start the clay modeling soon," Niccolò said. "Casting itself does not take time but after that, chasing, which is painstaking and time consuming. Paolo, we have plenty of time. I will come to the studio at least two days every week and we will both start chasing together. We have more than two to three years to chase and shine it."

"Maestro, that is very good. Shall we have lunch? I brought lunch for both of us. I will warm up minestrone soup, sourdough bread and egg frittata."

"Sound delicious."

After enjoying their lunch, they continued working on David until time seemed to race fast. So when the church bell struck five times, they snapped back to the present, realizing as they looked out the window, that daylight was fading.

The sun was down on the west as the last rays of sun flooded the studio with the moving dust particles inside that started to glow in different colors. Struck by the hypnotic effect, they took a deep breath and said, "Time to go home."

"Paolo, I am almost done with sketching. Just have to go over it again carefully to see if any area is missing. I will start the clay modeling soon.

They decided to end their work day exchanging a *"Buonasera"* and headed towards their homes.

* * *

June 16th 1426—At 8 o'clock in the morning, Paolo began arranging materials for the clay modeling of David for his Maestro. He had already started the project for Cosimo's garden yet he was taking a break from that today to assist Niccolò with the modeling of David. Paolo left an area clear where David's model was going to stand on a platform. The clay buckets were all lined up and he made sure the consistency of the clay was right.

Niccolò arrived just as the church bell chimed nine times.

"Good morning, Maestro. I've been getting materials ready for you. Please let me know what you need to start your work."

"I think I have everything, Paolo. You can continue working on your project. I am going to start from David's leg and Goliath. I would not detail it but just start modeling it."

"Maestro, I thought I might watch you and learn how you start."

"That is fine with me."

Niccolò asked Paolo to bring the sketchboard where he sketched the front part of David. He looked at it and started to model. Niccolò told Paolo that first he had to model looking at it, then when everything was done, he could imprint it on the clay for details.

They worked the whole day on the lower part of David's body and grew tired at the end of the day but felt good that whatever they intended to do, they did.

Soon the bright summer days passed very quickly for Niccolò and Paolo as they continued working on David. On the 20th of July, 1426, clay modeling of David was finally complete.

Next came the task of preparing the bronze casting which Niccolò had done to cast the upper part of the body including the hat. The second time baking was already done and the model was still warm. So Niccolò eagerly finished as much casting as he could.

"Paolo, we will continue casting as much as we can then tomorrow, we can check again to see if we missed any area of the sculpture."

"Maestro, we could probably finish the casting today."

"You may be right, Paolo."

Niccolò concentrated on the casting which was a painstaking and repetitive process. Since the casting was done at the end of the day, time had flown and pretty soon, the sun went down below the horizon as the glow of the day still lingered over the city of Firenze.

Niccolò and Paolo promised to arrive at the studio early in the morning. When it was time to go home, Niccolò quickened his steps, happy and exhausted at the same time.

A cloud of thoughts passed through Niccolò's mind. "Mamma is not home as she went back to Castellina for the preparation of Amadeo's wedding but she left some prepared dishes so all I have to do is warm them up." The early evening air was filled with the chorus of birds chirping in their nests as Niccolò settled in comfortably alone.

En Route to Castellina

5th of August 1426—On this glorious warm morning, Niccolò and Paolo set out at 8 o'clock on their journey to Castellina to attend Amadeo's wedding. Piero, the carriage driver, picked them up at Niccolò's cottage in Firenze and from there, they looked forward to enjoying picturesque views of the countryside during the ride.

On this bright day, the sun shone against the blue sky as people scurried on the paved path along the river Arno bathed in sunlight, rippling away with a boat load of people onwards as the shrieks of seagulls filled the air. The horse carriage trotted along the paved path as the city's big and small buildings slowly moved backwards and the tall trees along the paved path started moving backwards, picking up the pace, faster and faster until before them lay the vast landscape of an open field, with a backdrop of hills and valleys. The horses were moving now at full speed, their manes flowing backwards as the carriage coasted past an open green meadow as far as one could see. At a distance, the hills with a bluish haze stood against the hazy blue sky. The fresh breeze of the meadow filled the air inside the carriage. Refreshed by the cool breeze, the carriage riders came back to the present.

"Paolo, have you been to Castellina before?"

"No, Maestro, I have never been there. I have never been on a long carriage ride like this and I am enjoying it and the landscape too."

"It will be much prettier as we proceed onwards." Niccolò's expression changed somewhat back to his serious self. "Paolo, we have to do some work putting the decorated arches on the site through which the two brides will walk beneath them."

"No problem Maestro, those are not difficult and also decorations with flowers and greens takes time but not challenging."

"It seems you have done this before."

"Yes, Maestro I helped decorate on the occasion of my cousin's wedding."

Niccolò called the attention of Piero, the carriage driver. "Please let me know where and when you could stop and have a break."

"I will let you know. Now we are about to take a winding path up the hills where we will come across many vineyards, olive groves and some fruit orchards."

"Thank you."

The carriage started ascending the green hills dotted with red-roofed cottages on the slopes. Silvery green olive and fruits orchards blossomed as they passed with frequent vineyards in between. Some time passed when the carriage arrived near a small village on a hilltop piazza where Piero slowed the carriage down.

"Maestro, we will stop here as we are less than five miles from Greve in Chianti. We will change our horses and you can stretch and have some lunch. I can recommend a place where you can have lunch, if you want."

"Please do, Piero."

Piero took his carriage to a red roof cottage with an iron gate that overlooked a valley down below. The lines of the pointed pines separated the cottages on the hilltop piazza. This particular cottage had a front and backyard. The green backyard went down to a slope with apple and peach trees.

The front yard had patches of yellow, red and pink rose bushes with patches of yellow and white daisies in between them. Nicely trimmed green bushes continued on both sides of the paved brick path leading to the entrance of the cottage. Piero knocked at the entrance door opened by a middle-aged lady who wore a bright, long floral dress up to her ankles and brown buckled shoes. She had a freckled triangular face, pointed nose, brown eyes and light brown hair tucked into a bun at the back of her head. With a smile, she greeted Niccolò, Paolo and Piero who introduced his two passengers to the woman who introduced herself as Isabella. She welcomed them to a dining room where three tables were set covered with red tablecloths, four cushioned chairs for each table and each had a flower vase with yellow roses. Isabella said she and her husband, Tomasso, owned this business of entertaining and hosting people who traveled this way towards Siena. Tomasso also worked at his fruit orchard during the day.

The room had two big windows with white lacy curtains drawn on one side looking down to the green slope of the hill with the apple and peach trees. Opposite the window, there was a solid white wash wall where a moderate-size oil painting of the landscape of the Chianti hills hung from an iron hook.

There was a fireplace as soon as you entered the room on the right which was not lit but there was a planter in front of it with some blooming violets gently moving with the summer breeze. Isabella presented the menu: tomato basil soup, spaghetti with meatballs, and garlic bread. The meal included fruit and cinnamon apples, fresh peaches, and cheese and a choice of red or white wine and orange blossom water.

"*Grazie tante,*" Niccolò and Paolo said to Isabella.

They ordered soup, garlic bread, spaghetti with meatballs, fresh peach, white wine, and a jug of orange blossom water.

Niccolò was pleased when Paolo asked about the wedding.

"Amadeo's bride's name is Andrea Borgia. I think her ancestors came from Spain. I am not sure, but I heard they are a very accomplished family. I wish them all the happiness in their life together."

"Maestro, that is the only thing we can do for them—to wish them a happy life together."

Isabella brought a tall, narrow jug filled with white wine and two goblets. Then she presented steaming bowls of soup and bread and wished them, "*Buon appetito.*"

Paolo and Niccolò spooned the last of their soup when Isabella served spaghetti and meatballs in thick tomato basil sauce. "*Buon Prazo,*" said Isabella wishing them both a good lunch.

They dove into their spaghetti just as a young boy around 8 to 10-years-old with navy blue breeches, a white long-sleeved shirt and navy vest put a jug of orange blossom water on the table. He had sparkling black eyes, black hair, a round face and a dimple on his cheek when he smiled.

"Maestro, thank you again to you and your family for inviting me to the wedding."

"Our friends Marcello and Angela Casini are doing all of the wedding arrangements for their son, Stefano and for my nephew, Amadeo. I want to contribute for the decorations but Marcello said we can make a contribution for flowers. I am so glad you have some flower decorating and arch-making experience."

"Maestro, it is no problem. It depends on how large the area is. I will check when I am there. Perhaps, I can finish it within a few hours."

"Paolo, let me know how much to pay you for your hard work."

Paolo shook his head. "Do not worry. This is my gift to both couples."

"You are a very thoughtful and generous person, Paolo."

"I appreciate your good words."

Isabella informed them that their carriage driver was at the door. Niccolò paid Isabella for the lunch and after saying, "*Grazie,*" they left to meet Piero who welcomed them back to the carriage.

"I suggest, when we head back to Firenze, we should make a stop at Greve but on our way to Castellina, we can make a leisurely pace along

Greve. I want to reach our destination before 6 o'clock in the evening." Niccolò agreed and the horses were changed so the carriage moved as fast as it could through the lush green hills and valleys as far as the eyes could see.

Since it was his first long carriage trip, Paolo was mesmerized by the beauty of the landscape. "I cannot believe the landscapes are so verdant."

Piero slowed the carriage down as soon as they arrived in Greve where Paolo could see the old piazza, and from a distance the medieval castle and the river running close to the city surrounded by vineyards. He was very pleased to get a taste of this old city and he was assured by Piero that on their way back they would stop for enough time to explore the city where the driver promised to take them to a special place for lunch.

The carriage continued its pace, winding through the hills and valleys for a few hours until the sun positioned itself in the western sky as though it would soon say goodbye. The hills and valleys were brushed with the soft orange hue of the sun. At a distance through the olive groves, Niccolò could see three hills standing one after the other.

"Paolo, see those hills? That is our destination. One of the homes belongs to my nephew, Amadeo."

"Maestro, it looks so picturesque."

The carriage moved at full speed as best it could as the sun slowly set below the horizon. By the time the last glow of the sun colored the sky orange, they reached Amadeo's residence where the gate and the entrance of the house was decorated with festive wreaths.

Niccolò saw a smiling Amadeo open the door and rush to the carriage with Tia at his heels and mother Orissa waving from her position at the entrance. All three of them were very happy to see Niccolò and pleased to meet Paolo.

"Maestro, I will pick both of you up at 8 o'clock in the morning on the

9th of August. Please pay me when we return to Firenze."

After Niccolò thanked the driver, he and Paolo followed Amadeo and Tia towards the entrance where upon entering the living room they were greeted with walls decorated with festive flower wreaths.

Amadeo was very pleased to accompany Niccolò and Paolo upstairs to their rooms. Paolo was pleased he got the middle room among the three bedrooms upstairs. Mother Orissa asked them to freshen up as she would serve dinner in about an hour.

Soon the five of them took their seats around the dining table covered with Tia's handmade white crocheted tablecloth. A crystal vase stood in the middle of the table with red roses along with gold-bordered white dinner plates and silverware with amber-colored napkins set for five.

One wall was decorated with a flower wreath hanging from an iron hook on the wall. Large and small candles around the dining room flickered joyfully to grace their dinner. Mother Orissa first served soup, a Ribollita, made with bread and vegetables—celery, chard, carrots, potatoes, onions, beans and tomatoes. Then there was Caprese Chicken—sauteed chicken, with sundried tomato, cheese and a dash of balsamic vinegar. The next course was parmesan meatballs with vegetables.

"Save some of your appetite for dessert," Mother Orissa said.

Amadeo poured white wine for all of them and proudly announced that it was from his winery. Conversation centered on the ceremony but mother Orissa expressed that after dinner they should sit down and discuss this further with dessert and wine.

"What is for dessert?"

"Well, I was going to keep it a secret," Mother Orissa said.

"What is it?" Amadeo asked.

"It is your favorite dessert."

Amadeo's eyes widened. "I cannot wait anymore. What is it?"

Mother Orissa smiled. "It is Zabaglione!" This egg custard dessert, made with egg yolks, cinnamon and a cup of wine was one of her specialties.

"Oh Nonna!" Amadeo rushed over to Mother Orissa to give her a big hug.

Everyone commented on the delicious dinner and soon, the Zabaglione was served with fresh strawberries in each of the five bowls on a side table.

They all took their dessert bowls and wine goblets and settled down on cushioned couches in the living room decorated with floral wreaths on the walls and around the fireplace. In front of the fireplace sat a moderate-sized, gold-colored metallic vase with red roses.

"Amadeo and Stefano and their brides are to be married in a church on the outskirts of Castellina where Stefano was christened," Mother Orissa said. "From there, a flower-decorated carriage will take them from the church and bring them back home where the reception will be held in an open space in a valley just below Marcello and Angela's house. The food will be displayed on a paved courtyard. I will provide the menu details later. There will be a wooden stage where musicians will play and a wooden floor for the wedded couples and others who want to dance.

"It will be at the farther end and then an arrangement of dining tables for guests will be close to the paved courtyard. The floral arches will be placed from the gate of the Casini house to the right paved path to the paved courtyards."

"Mamma," Niccolò said, "Paolo has offered to make the flower-decorated arches as his gift for the couples."

"That is so nice of him," his mother said. "There will more than a hundred and ten arches. The material is already delivered and fresh flowers will arrive tomorrow. Paolo, it will be too much work for you."

"Please do not worry, Signora. It will be my pleasure. I will love making

489

those arches for Amadeo and Stefano and their brides."

"God bless you, my dear."

Amadeo gave Paolo a hug. "Thank you, Uncle Paolo.

Paolo was very pleased to be addressed as uncle.

"Thank you very much, brother Paolo," Tia said.

Being addressed as though he was a part of the family made Paolo emotional that his voice almost choked and he took a deep breath. "I am so grateful to be invited here to be a part of this memorable family occasion. So, about the wedding, will the guests follow the wedded couples through the arches?"

"Yes, then there will be the procession of men carrying the Cassoni," mother Orissa referred to the decorated wooden chests full of everyday use articles for the brides like clothes, jewelry, cosmetics from both the brides' houses.

She further explained that the floats with sculptures made with sugar, cheese, and fruits will also pass. People singing, dancing with a group of musicians will also move through the arches. There will be a juggler and at the end, there will be fireworks but the main fireworks display will be later after the guests finish dinner. The musicians will perform music after everyone settles down.

"Mamma has compiled some epithalamia," Tia said describing the wedding poems about the celebration for both couples. "Mamma, do you want some of the poems to be read aloud to them?"

"Well, you can if you want to."

"All right," Tia said. "I will read one of them." She looked at her son. "Sorry Amadeo, if it is too embarrassing."

"Actually, I am overcome and amazed to see Nonna's enthusiasm for poetry."

Tia began reading the poem:

"On this beautiful day in summer

Stefano has married Luccia

Luccia married Stefano

On this beautiful day in summer

Amadeo has married Andrea

Andrea married Amadeo

They are married and they are now together

Like nut cake and honey, honey and nut cake

Like soup and ladle and ladle and soup together

Let us pray and wish you a lifetime of happiness,

Your wedding day will come and go

May your love forever grow."

Niccolò clapped his hands. "Mamma, it is beautiful. Who is going to sing and when?"

"All of us will sing after they get married and leave the church, we will shower them with rice," Tia explained. "There will also be showers of confetti which will be small packages of almonds soaked in cognac wrapped in paper. Mother will lead us and we all will join to start the chorus."

"You and Marcello along with Paolo will be in one carriage with Stefano and Amadeo and Angela, Tia and myself will be in another one," Mother Orissa told Niccolò. The marriage ceremony will be Monday morning at 11:30. It is a good day—it stands for wealth. "Niccolò, Stefano's bride's last name is Visconte, they are related to the original Visconte family of Milan. Bride Luccia's father, Giovanni and mother, Sabrina settled in a cozy corner at a foothill between the boundary of Castellina and Siena. Andrea's parents live a few miles away from them. Both brides' families are close-knit and very friendly to each other. Both the brides' families are arranging a getaway for the couples for two weeks. They will likely leave the early afternoon on the 8th of August and the couples will probably stay in Cortona."

"That is a very nice idea to get away from all the stress of the wedding ceremony and its preparations," Niccolò said.

"Marcello and Angela made special arrangements for both couples in Stefano's studio, two wedding chambers and all other necessities for the 7th and 8th of August," his mother said.

"I am amazed to see both Angela and Marcello's efforts to make the wedding ceremony a unique experience for both couples," Niccolò said. "Mamma, I heard Cortona is a charming town in the Chiana valley in the province of Arezo in south Tuscany. It is a scenic hilltop town."

"I am so glad that Uncle Marcello, and Andrea's and Luccia's parents arranged our stay in Cortona," Amadeo said. "I am very much interested in the history of the town and so is Stefano. When we were in school, we used to plan on visiting Cortona. We read that it is an old town ruled by the Gibeline family in the 11th and 12th century. Gibeline, who was in the imperial side, was established as the center of the Diocese by Pope XXII in 1325. Before it was dominated by the Etruscan People, these people came from central Italy. They established their culture; their way was much like the Romans."

"I am so glad you and Stefano are so much interested in Cortona," Niccolò said.

"Niccolò, what have you decided to wear? It has to go somewhat with Amadeo's outfit, right?" Mother Orissa looked at her grandson. "Amadeo, please let your uncle know what you are wearing."

"All right, this is what I decided," Amadeo said. "Since Andrea's outfit is a jewel-toned blue velvet long flowing dress with gold buttons all the way down to the ankles, I decided to wear a maroon doublet and underneath, brown loose-fitting breeches held by a jeweled belt, a linen silver tunic, leather-soled, silver-colored hose tied directly to the breeches to its belt or a snug-fitting doublet's jeweled metal belt. Over the top, a crimson velvet robe and a jeweled belt which will go as low as my hips on the side, a metal dragger will be hanging and there will be a pouch also in front of the belt to hold some currency. On my head, there will be a rich color Moire hat with white rim. I chose the maroon with a pearl string around." Amadeo turned to Niccolò. "Uncle, what do you plan to wear?"

"I have my brown breeches, yellow long-sleeved silk shirt with ruffles and brown vest with gold designs, silver-colored hose with brown boots," Niccolò replied.

"Uncle Paolo, what about you?"

"Oh, I will wear red breeches, a beige long-sleeved shirt with ruffles both around the cuffs and in front, a red vest with gold design, beige hose and brown boots," Paolo said.

"Good, that takes care of everybody," Tia said.

"Nonna and Mamma have their own plans," Amadeo said. "They want to surprise us."

"I asked Tia if she can make a flowing outfit in yellow brocade then I can wear that with a red turban-like cap with a gold and diamond brooch—the one my father gave my mother as a gift. I can wear it in the evening party," Niccolò said.

"Is she really going to make it? That would be wonderful," Amadeo said.

"Let us go to bed," Mother Orissa said. "We will get up tomorrow and start making arrangements for the ceremony and figure out what each of us will do."

"Brother Niccolò," Tia said. "I will take some measurements for your outfit right now. It will not take long. Then I will make your outfit after breakfast so it will be done in a matter of two hours or so. Then we will all eat tomorrow at the Casini's home but I will make breakfast here. A very good night to everyone and sweet dreams."

A Wedding in Castellina

Sunday the 6th of August 1426—The morning sun flooded to light the hills and valleys of Castellina, the beautiful town Niccolò and Paolo arrived at last night to attend Amadeo's wedding. Niccolò gazed at the undulating green hills, captivated by their beauty as he stood there by the window. He found he could not move and for a while, it seemed time had stopped and he was one with nature.

"Good morning, Maestro." Paolo's voice snapped him out of his reverie as he saw his assistant standing just outside the door of his guest room.

"Good morning, Paolo. Sorry, I am a little late."

"Not a problem. The rest of your family is waiting for you to join them."

Paolo and Niccolò went downstairs and proceeded towards the dining room where Amadeo, Mother Orissa and sister Tia were waiting and sitting around the dining table. Good morning greetings were promptly exchanged with Niccolò and Paolo's arrival.

"Mamma baked some fresh cookies and I made some caudle," Tia said. "Do you know how I made it? With bread crumbs, sugar, honey and saffron mixed together then boiled, then I added egg yolks, and at the end, sprinkled a little salt, ginger and sugar."

Paolo licked his lips. "Sounds delicious."

Tia turned to Paolo. "Please take your seat and enjoy. You have to work hard making those flower decorated arches."

Niccolò surveyed the spread. "Usually, I do not take breakfast in the morning but I will have some cookies and also the hot drink."

"Lunch and dinner will be at the Casini house," Tia reminded. "I told them to make lunch simple like a salad and some bread. Dinner will be served at their house between 5 and 5:30 this evening. We all have to go to bed early to get some rest for the big day coming up on August 7th."

"Uncle Paolo, I will take you to where the materials for the arches are stacked and the flowers already arrived or will be arriving soon."

Niccolò raised his hand. "Paolo, I can help you if you teach me how to do it."

"No Maestro, it be will easier and faster if I do it myself. After I am done someone has to transport those and put them one by one where they are supposed to be."

"Uncle Marcello has arranged people to help transport. I will coordinate that—do not worry."

"I must say hello to Angela, Marcello and Stefano," Niccolò said. "I want to go around and check out the whole set up of the wedding reception."

"Of course, we will all go," Tia said. "Stefano will pick us up to go to the Casini's. The materials and flowers are all in a covered hall outside Stefano's portion of the studio. We can see the whole set up of the wedding reception from there. Two wedding chambers are being set up and furnished for both couples to spent the night there."

"I will stay at home here at Tia's," Mother Orissa said. "I have few things to do."

"I will request Stefano to give me a ride back home after I see the setup of the wedding reception," Tia said. "I have to make Niccolò's long brocade outfit. Mamma, shall I gather your portion of lunch from there?"

"It is not necessary," her mother replied.

Just then, they all heard a horse carriage sound and Stefano appeared. "Hello, everyone! I am here to give you all a ride. My mother packed a lunch for Nonna in case she wanted rest instead of going to our home."

"Oh, how sweet and thoughtful of Angela to do that. God bless her," Mother Orissa said. "Please tell her I will join them for our early dinner."

They all got inside the carriage and Stefano drove them to the Casini house which was already busy with people working inside and outside for the preparation of the event. In the courtyard, people were thoroughly cleaning the floor. Part of the yard was already clean so they were putting some tables on those areas where food will be displayed. The courtyard was bordered with a designed iron railing showing creepers and flowers all around. People were cleaning and decorating them with green leafy wreaths.

Paolo was escorted to the covered hallway where the materials for the flowering arches were stacked. Niccolò and Tia went to the other side of Stefano's studio where the two wedding chambers were. Inside the chamber, curtains were lacy white backed up with thick, maroon raw silk. The bed was all covered with satin, white bedsheets with pillows covered in white pillowcases. Two mahogany tables were placed on each side of the bed with decorated lamps. The floor was covered with a saggy red carpet. The headboard and walls were decorated with floral wreaths. The other wedding chamber was decorated the same as the first one and the entrance of the second one was just opposite to each other.

Niccolò and Tia went to the paved courtyard where people were still working. They stood there watching, at the far end of the compound, workers busy decorating the wooden-floored covered stage. There were a bunch of different people working on the open compound arranging tables and chairs for the guests. Niccolò and Tia wanted to sit down outside for some time before meeting Marcello and Angela. As Tia pointed out the area where arches will be placed, Niccolò inquired about the time.

"Let me see, there is a wall clock just inside the entrance." While she went to check the clock, Marcello came out to greet Niccolò and the two shook hands.

"Angela is arranging lunch," Marcello said. "She will come out soon to call everyone to eat. Your assistant, Paolo, is very sincere and artistic. I went to the hallway and there he was, already finished with more than fifty arches. He started making them at 10 in the morning and it is now 11:30. I am amazed. I heard that he refuses to be paid for the work. What is the reason?"

"He told me that this is his gift to both couples," Niccolò said.

"Wow," Marcello said, "it is a very expensive gift." He eyed Niccolò. "Maestro, are you comfortable sitting outside? If not, you can go inside?"

Just then Tia approached them. "Brother Niccolò, I am going to pack my lunch and go back to my home. The appointed carriage driver is here to give me a ride. Remember, I have to make your flowing outfit."

"Why don't you relax and enjoy yourself here?" Niccolò said. "When Paolo finishes the arches, you can both go back together after lunch. We will come back here again for our early dinner tonight."

"That sounds good." When Tia left, Niccolò walked to the hallway to check on Paolo and was amazed to see he was almost finished with his task.

Paolo was pleasantly surprised to see Niccolò. "Maestro, I am pretty much done. I did a few extras in case a few of them break as they are transported."

"Paolo you did an excellent job! I love how the flower decorations of the arches were made with white and pink miniature roses intertwined with green creepers."

Paolo stretched his arms up then rolled his shoulders. "Maestro, these arches, first of all, should be sprayed with water now in the evening and early morning tomorrow."

"All right, Paolo. Marcello will be here soon and I will let him know."

As soon as Niccolò finished his sentence, Marcello arrived amazed to see the arches. "Wow, they are all beautiful."

"Marcello," Niccolò said, "Paolo advises these arches should be sprayed with water now, in the evening and early tomorrow morning."

"Absolutely," Marcello said. "I am going to ask those responsible to place them one by one where they belong to water them. Let us go for lunch. Angela is waiting for us."

The three men entered the house just as the workers assigned with the placement of arches started to take a few at a time to install them on the ground.

Marcello, Niccolò and Paolo headed to the dining room where Angela was waiting for them. The table, big enough for eight people, was covered with an amber-colored tablecloth. In the middle stood a vase with red roses.

A big bowl full of pasta salad and loaves of fresh-baked bread complimented the table spread that included six gold-bordered white dining plates set with silverware and white cloth napkins.

Angela welcomed them with a smile. "I am expecting Amadeo and Stefano to join us soon.

Niccolò, Paolo and Marcello took their seats as Angela started serving the food.

"There is not much for lunch but I made some cannoli to make both grooms, Stefano and Amadeo happy."

"Here we are!" They all heard Stefano's voice and soon both young men took their seats at the dining table.

"Ooo, Mamma made cannoli," Stefano cheered.

"We were just talking about the fact that both of you like cannoli," Angela said.

"Can't wait to eat it," the young men said.

"Stefano, please describe your groom's outfit to Uncle Niccolò," Angela said.

"Oh, it's almost the same as Amadeo, just a different shade."

"Let us hear you describe it."

Stefano chewed then swallowed his food. "I am going to wear a brown doublet, maroon breeches held by a jeweled belt, a beige tunic with beige leathered soles, a burgundy robe on top, a jeweled belt, a burgundy Moire hat with a rim of pearl with a yellowish tinge."

"Wow, that sounds very impressive," Niccolò said.

"We will be very much preoccupied for tomorrow's wedding event from now until the evening so I thought I should let you all know my plan."

As they continued eating, everyone listened intently as Angela outlined the schedule for the wedding preparations. She suggested that since the evening will come and go quickly, that everyone should go to bed early as tomorrow, the people taking charge of the event will arrive around 6 in the morning to serve people food and drink. They will set up a schedule on their own and carry on the tasks required for helping the grooms dress up for the wedding. In fact, Angela continued, this specialized team is willing to provide assistance to anyone needing help to prepare. For the ladies, there will be a certain group of women specializing in helping them with wedding essentials. Additionally, a team of organizers will be on hand for general supervision of the entire event.

Angela also stated that carriages will be decorated by the grooms' side where both grooms will ride carriages that include both grooms and also the grooms' side of the family. Marcello, Niccolò and Paolo will be riding in front.

"The other carriage will include myself, Tia and mother Orissa riding next to the groom's carriage and a few more carriages will follow the first two with important invited guests," Angela clarified. "We have to leave promptly at 9:30 in the morning as the wedding will be at 11:30. So it is important to be ready in time to reach Siena just before 11:30. The ministers of the church already posted a notice for a week on the door about the wedding.

The church of Siena selected two ten-year old boys from the town to ring the wedding bells.

"Thank you, Mamma, for outlining the schedule and planning for the wedding ceremony," Stefano said.

Everyone bid goodbye and confirmed their meeting at 5:30 for dinner. Almost as soon as they parted ways, a few swift hours later, everyone gathered at the Casini family home again. Stefano and Angela rushed out the door to receive Amadeo's family. Angela greeted and helped Mother Orissa down from the carriage. The older woman handed a pot to Angela. "Almond rice," Niccolò's mother said.

When everyone heard "almond rice," they became very excited and thanked Mother Orissa. Very much like lunch, dinner that evening was a simple affair: beef stew with fresh vegetables, pasta with meat sauce and Mother Orissa's almond rice.

The conversation around the dinner table centered on Marcello's outfit.

"I want to keep it simple," Marcello said. "Brown breeches with a brown vest with gold works, a light-yellow long-sleeved silk shirt and beige leather sole hose, a dark blue velvet cape and a circular dark blue Bourrelet, Rondel, for a hat."

"That is nice," Mother Orissa commented.

Marcello asked Mother Orissa whether she planned something fancy to wear.

"Oh, I have a red brocade with an Indian-design long dress and a red, almost see-through but not quite, scarf with gold work that will fall on my shoulders and I will wear my gold accessories. The brocade is brought by an Indian merchant whom my husband had bought the outfit from."

"Oh, Nonna," Amadeo said, "You will look so pretty."

"You will look fabulous," Stefano chimed in.

"Sister Tia, what about you?" Angela asked.

"Oh, I thought I would surprise all of you but it is all right if you know now. I will wear a very light, sea green flowing dress with sequins which will look like stardust. The long sleeves will be see-through with ruffles at the end. My hair will be arranged in a bun at the nape of my neck with gold star hairpins. Then I will wear a tiara and my three-row pearl choker with a square-shaped sapphire in the middle."

"Wow, you will be a pretty mother of the groom," Angela gushed.

"Speaking of another mother of the groom, what about you, Angela?

"I plan to wear a light-yellow brocade long dress with lavish trims, round shoulders, a lace-up back, and a square front neckline. I will wear my ruby and diamond necklace and ruby drop earrings, a light-yellow lacy hood and a wreath tiara."

"That is so beautiful," said Mother Orissa.

The evening slowly set in though the light outside continued to linger. Angela and Tia, both busy mothers-of-the-groom announced it would be time to retire soon to assure a good night's sleep so all will wake up refreshed for August 7, 1426—a huge event that is sure to mark the test of time. Soon, Amadeo's family bid goodnight and hopped into the carriage and before long, the trotting and clapping sound of horses' hooves echoed through the hills as stars twinkled and a sickle moon peeped with a smile as a night bird called to welcome the evening.

* * *

The brink of dawn on the 7th of August lit up with an orange glow as the green hills flooded with the orange hue of the sun. The chirping of the birds could be heard around the groves close to the house.

The sound of a carriage and horses close to Amadeo's cottage and Stefano's house as well as an assortment of voices were heard from people helping to prepare for the wedding of Stefano and Amadeo. Most of the activities centered around Stefano's home were originally supposed to take place at the bride's house but as Marcello had a large place and knew a lot of people around town, many of whom worked for him in his winery and fruit orchard, he offered to host the event as both brides' families were newly-settled in Siena so it was somewhat inconvenient for them to arrange a reasonably big event such as a double wedding.

At Amadeo's house, Mother Orissa was the first to wake up early and freshen up. She then retreated to the prayer room at Tia's section of the house to pray before the altar to ask God to bless the marriages of Amadeo and Stefano.

Pretty soon, the sound of horses' clip-clapping was heard echoing through the hills as the carriages decorated with long wreaths made with flowers and greenery formed a procession.

Tia made the hot drink, caudle, mixing bread crumbs, honey and sugar and boiling it before adding egg yolks then sprinkling it with cinnamon, salt and sugar. Mother Orissa baked cookies and fruit tarts.

Niccolò, Paolo, and Amadeo came down from their rooms to join Mother Orissa and Tia around the table. After good morning greetings were exchanged, Tia urged everyone to take hot drinks and cookies as they have to start getting ready.

"If you need help putting on your outfits, there are men waiting to help," Tia reminded them.

"I need someone to help but do not worry, I will call soon after I finish my drink," Amadeo said.

"I am almost ready and I do not need anyone's help," Niccolò said.

"Same here," Paolo chimed in.

Mother Orissa kissed Amadeo's forehead. "God bless you, my dear.

Here is a present for you: a gold chain to wear around your neck. It was your Nonno's and now, it is yours. Your grandfather's family tradition for the groom is to wear a gold chain before the wedding."

Amadeo was confused and emotional. "But why me? Shouldn't Uncle Niccolò—"

"Your Uncle Niccolò told me a while ago when I asked him whether he would get married and settle down," Mother Orissa said hastily, "that he is married to his art. So the tradition has now been handed down to you, my dear grandson."

Mother Orissa hugged Amadeo who was overcome with emotion. "Thank you, my dear Nonna. You are so thoughtful."

Tears rolled down Tia's and Orissa's cheeks.

"I am so happy that Amadeo got father's gold chain," Niccolò said. "I think father would be very happy wherever he is right now."

Orissa wiped her tears. "Shall we get ready? We have to leave at 9:30."

Tia faced Niccolò. "Dear brother, your flowing brocade outfit is ready. Will you wear it right now or this evening?"

Niccolò clasped his hands. "Oh, how wonderful, thank you. I will wear it this evening."

After they went to their respective rooms, Niccolò and Paolo emerged ready in no time. They looked very handsome in their outfits with brown boots, vests with gold works and ruffled, long-sleeved shirts. Niccolò's tall figure with black brown wavy hair up to the nape of his neck made him especially attractive.

Paolo appeared bright and happy. "Oh, mother Orissa looks so graceful and elegant," he told Niccolò. "The wreath made with light yellow roses in the middle of her head holding the short veil up to her neck makes her look exquisite."

"And look at my dear sister with her sea green, flowing dress looking so pretty," Niccolò told Paolo. "She surely looks like she came out of the clouds with stardust on her dress and…oh my, here comes my dear nephew, Amadeo who looks so triumphant with a flowing crimson robe."

Amadeo gathered everyone in a group hug. "I appreciate everyone's efforts in making this occasion special. Just think when I return to this house, I will be a married man!"

All of them boarded the carriage to the Casini family's house where Stefano, Marcello and Angela waited at the entrance. Stefano looked victorious dressed in his burgundy robe, Moire hat lined with yellow pearls. Marcello looked unique with his blue velvet robe and dark blue Rondel hat and Angela looked gorgeous with her yellow brocade dress and her diamond and ruby necklace and ruby earrings with an accent of a beige lacy hood on the top of her head. The flower-decorated carriages waited for them at the entrance.

The first one decorated with yellow and red roses with greenery in between long wreaths ran parallel to each other from the top of the carriage coming down on both sides of the carriage all the way around except the two side doors for passengers to get in. A bunch of red roses were glued on the doors. Drivers of the carriages dressed up in their dark blue breeches, silver hose and long-sleeved shirts and on the top, a long red cape and dark blue hat. Stefano, Marcello, Niccolò, Amadeo, and Paolo got inside the carriage.

Mother Orissa, Tia and Angela went inside the second carriage decorated with white and pink roses with greenery. Both carriages were positioned so that the second one was next to the first but just a little behind. Both carriages started slowly as people around working for the event cheered and showered rose petals. Two musicians walked along the carriages playing the lute for some time then the carriage slowly accelerated its pace as the music began sounding fainter and the musician's figures became gradually smaller and smaller until they eventually disappeared. Now, through the green valleys and winding hills, the carriages continued moving in their usual pace.

Carriages for the invited guests trailed just behind the two carriages carrying the wedding party. For a while the carriage was far behind but after some time, it seemed they had caught up to stay on course behind the two leading carriages.

The driver of the lead carriage with the two grooms, along with Marcello, Niccolò and Paolo, announced that it will take another thirty to forty minutes to reach the Siena Cathedral. This announcement took Niccolò and Paolo by surprise.

"Oh, I did not know the wedding will be held at Siena Cathedral," Niccolò said.

Marcello nodded. "I am sorry I forgot to update you—the church at the outskirts of Castellina had some problem last minute and is undergoing some repairs."

That explained why Niccolò had heard Siena being mentioned in the wedding plans yet was not sure. "Ah, that is all right, more than all right as interestingly enough, my sculpture Herod's feast is installed somewhere in the Siena Cathedral." A warm feeling surged through Niccolò as he voiced this fact aloud. "It is sheer destiny that Paolo and myself will soon be going there. It is quite serendipitous."

"Maestro, indeed it is," Paolo added excitedly. "To think that we shall soon set eyes on the sculpture we had diligently worked so hard on now prominently displayed for all to see."

Stefano nodded. "It is an honor that we are going to get married there."

"That is a very remarkable coincidence, Uncle," Amadeo said. "I remember that evening *il prete* came to Uncle Marcello's house and Uncle Niccolò accepted the commission. It somehow did not seem that long ago and now, here we are."

The carriages arrived in front of the cathedral.

"This is an old church in Siena dedicated to the Assumption of Mary," Marcello said. "The cathedral was designed and completed between 1215 and 1263."

They all gazed at the cathedral, mesmerized by the beauty of the illuminating white and greenish black stripes with the addition of red marble on its façade.

The carriage driver informed them that black and white are symbolic colors of Siena linked to black and white houses of the legendary founder of Senius and Aschius, the sons of Remus. "I hope you are all familiar with the story of Remus and Rumulus," he said.

As everyone got down from the carriages, there were cheers from the crowd of local folks who were all welcome to witness the wedding. The grooms and their party waited anxiously for the bridal party to arrive as it was already fifteen minutes past 11 in the morning. Suddenly, they heard the clip-clapping sound of a horse carriage.

When the carriage stopped in front of the cathedral, everyone already gathered expecting the brides to come out of the carriage but instead, people dressed in colorful breeches and half robes appeared and said, "We want to speak to the grooms."

At once, Stefano and Amadeo rushed in front and one of the persons approached them. "Are you really and sincerely waiting for your brides?" he asked.

Stefano and Amadeo did not reply as their minds went blank with this unexpected turn of events. Amadeo's eyebrows furrowed and Stefano pressed his lips with a blank stare as the man said, "I am Ricardo, a representative from the brides' side and I have a very important message."

There was complete silence from the grooms' side and the locals gathered. The messenger took a deep breath and slowly uttered, "We are sorry, dear brothers, but the brides have changed their minds." With those words, airy, awkward, tense silence filled the air and it seemed time had stopped.

After a few minutes of silence in which everyone stood still in shock, suddenly without warning, a piercing sound shattered the once silent crowd as fireworks lit up the sky followed by the intense clip-clapping of the horses with the rolling sound of carriages. The crowd started cheering as they were convinced that person from the bridal party was making fun of the grooms.

The sound of the carriages increased in intensity, louder and louder until carriages decorated with red and yellow roses were seen approaching towards the cathedral. Soon, the carriages stopped in front of the cathedral and two brides alighted from the carriage, their faces covered with veils. As they glided with their parents towards the entrance of the church, Amadeo and Stefano gazed longingly at them with both shock and admiration as though they were an illusion, a mirage.

Andrea, Amadeo's bride wore a long, dark blue velvet trailing dress up to the ankles with golden buttons lining the bodice and skirt. It featured long sleeves and buttons down the length, a Cotehardie underneath—usually brides wore a chemise—a breast band and silver stockings. She had on pearl teardrop earrings, a three-layered pearl choker with a sapphire in the middle. Over the top of her dress was a long trail, light blue, see-through beautiful cloak with a gold border. As she took a step forward, her pearl and diamond tiara gave off blue and yellow colors with the rays of sun while her face was covered with a veil. She glided like a swan with her father towards the entrance of the church to pick up the flower bouquet which was kept by her groom.

Luccia, Stefano's bride, accompanied by her parents, moved towards the cathedral in a long trailing dress up to the ankles, a yellow brocade in the body and see-through loose, long sleeves and on the top, a white long train, see-through cloak with a gold border. She was adorned with a ruby and diamond necklace and dangling ruby and diamond earrings. Her face was covered with a thin veil and there was a gold crown on her head which looked like an engraved gold band with a star in the middle. Her father was in navy blue breeches and dark cap and a short yellow cape, while her mother wore a long, silver brocade dress with long sleeves, a pearl necklace and pearl teardrop earrings.

Both brides with their parents entered the cathedral with the bridesmaids dressed in olive green flowing dresses with two-stringed pearl necklaces and teardrop pearl earrings.

As wedding guests for both the bride's and groom's parties entered the cathedral from a different entrance, they were mesmerized with the pictorial effect of black and white marble stripes on the wall and columns which definitely struck their eyes.

The pulpit, made of Carrara marble, expressed the Gothic style still showing classical influence. The floor was mosaic. As one looked up, the whole message of the pulpit was dedicated to the doctrine of salvation and the Last Judgment. The top level featured seven scenes narrating the life of Jesus.

The guests took their seats including mothers and grandmothers of the brides' and grooms'. The brides Luccia and Andrea gracefully walked down the aisle of the cathedral towards their grooms Stefano and Amadeo, the mosaic floor just below the pulpit on the right and below the decorated altar above which the lower part of the lantern was visible.

Though the cathedral imbued silence within, joyous vibrations echoed from wall to wall and from pillar to pillar inside the cathedral. The priest appeared on the pulpit and announced the names of the couples to be wed. He explained that the two couples will be wed at the same time, one after the other and he will announce the names of the couples who will repeat the vows one after the other. After the exchange of vows, they will say "I do" when the priest asks them to do so. Then the rings will be blessed by the priest one after another and the brides and grooms will be asked to exchange wedding rings to each other then there will be a blessing by the priest and minstrels will sing liturgical songs.

After the explanation, the real ceremony began as every word from the vows the priest uttered echoed from wall to wall—the same effect occurred with the words uttered by the couples. The hall kept on echoing "I do, I do, I do, I do" for some time that the entire congregation became so energized and joyous. After the exchange of rings, the priest blessed the couples who kissed as the crowd cheered. Rose petals showered the couples as they walked down the aisle. Wedding bells in the church tower started ringing as the couple exited the wide doorway amid a river of joyous cheers that continued to flow in small and big tides inside the cathedral. Outside the cathedral, the couples were greeted with showers of rice grains and rose petals.

Confetti, in the form of small packages of almond soaked in cognac, showered over the cheering crowd and with that, mother Orissa's composed epithalamia began as the crowd harmonized the part "they are honey and nut in cake, ladle and soup and soup and ladle, their love will forever grow," with the cheering, the ceremony of breaking the glasses was done and the crowd cheered even more.

While all the revelry was going on, Niccolò and Paolo quickly broke away from the group to hastily hunt for Herod's Feast. In the huge cathedral, all seemed lost when, at first, they could not locate it until Niccolò stood frozen as Paolo peered in the direction of his Maestro's gaze. Amid all the cheers of the crowd in the cathedral, there was the familiar art piece, the result of several hours of hard work by Niccolò and Paolo, truly a labor of love. Then Niccolò and Paolo hurried back to join their group.

Both wedded couples were escorted to the carriage and the driver of the coach started heading towards Castellina.

The families of the wedded couple got into their carriages one by one and the procession of carriages headed towards Castellina leaving the cheering crowd behind.

Within time, the carriages arrived in Castellina at 3:30 in the afternoon as it took about three hours to reach their destination as they stopped for some time at a place to feed the horses and gave them water to drink.

Upon their arrival, the guests and crowd cheered the wedded couples as more showers of rose petals pelted their carriages. The people in charge of the wedding reception came running to welcome the newlyweds and all others who attended the wedding. After the couples emerged from the carriages, Niccolò and Paolo walked through the flower-decorated arches painstakingly made by Paolo. The revelers all headed towards Marcello's and Angela's house as others followed the brides and grooms through the arches. Both wedded couples were cheered on as they walked to their designated place to sit and have their lunch and refresh themselves for the late afternoon triumphant procession of Cassonis and other floats with events and entertainment including jugglers and fireworks.

Guests and parents headed to their own designated places to eat lunch and rest. By 5 o'clock, everyone, including the newlywed couples, gathered at the paved courtyard where plenty of cushioned chairs were situated for the guests. The newlyweds who sat on reserved floral decorated chairs happily gazed into each of their beloved's eyes as they intermittently observed the revelers. An imaged of Beatrice in a wedding dress invaded Niccolò's mind which he briskly cast away, anchoring himself in the present moment.

Everyone sat eagerly waiting for the procession to start. A booming sound signaled the commencement of activities with fireworks shooting up the sky as guests "oohed" and "aahhed" at the spectacular show above. Next, floats drawn by horses formed a procession with big swans made of sugar slowly passed by. They were followed by a float of a couple made out of pineapple rowing a boat of scooped out pumpkin making its way, followed by a figure made out of cheese waving a flag. The procession continued until suddenly, someone jumped out of nowhere and started playing the kettle drums, followed by the decorated Cassoni, a chest holding the dowry and the brides' everyday articles on open carriages pulled by horses carried through the arches. Musicians gracefully walked through the flower arches playing their lutes, their sweet tune filling the early evening air. People were just catching their breaths as they began to relax from all the excitement when jugglers jumped up and about, impressing the audience with their clever tricks.

Finally came a circular, spectacular fireworks display that lasted for quite some time, drawing more "ooohs" and "aahhs" from the spectators.

Then an announcement broadcasted that guests take their seats for dinner and that there would be more musical entertainment during the wedding feast as well as more fireworks displays and then the floor would be open, inviting everyone to dance.

For the wedded couples and their families, a particular area was reserved close to a makeshift stage where musicians prepared to perform and near the designated area for dancing. Lines of gaslight posts illuminated the reception area complimented by large hanging covered lamps lighting the entire section.

The wedded couples took their designated seats as family members from both the brides' and grooms' side took their assigned seats. Guests waited for the moment when the brides and grooms would drink from the "love cup"—trophy-like cups with handles brought by attendants. The two grooms took big gulps before handing the cups over to their brides who finished the beverage amid the cheers of the guests who then proceeded to drink from their goblets.

Before serving the food, the attendants brought knives made with metal spoons and mugs made of wood. Reception attendants brought food on wooden platters: first course was fruit, wafers and cheese, and then pottages and then varieties of roasted meats such as mallard, pheasant, woodcock, partridges, and stuffed chicken. Next course came the tarts, pastries and finally, candied fruit.

The brides and the grooms had their first bites of food signaling the guests to follow and soon everyone started enjoying the sumptuous feast. Between courses, the attendants cleaned and wiped down the tables before the next course was served.

The guests brought gifts to the newlyweds and female members of the grooms' family offered heirloom rings passed down from one generation to the next. These rings welcomed the brides into their new families.

The brides and grooms then gave small tokens of appreciation to guests. Wedding events continued to flow smoothly with an announcement before each event and during the feast while minstrels, bards, and musicians entertained the guests during interludes.

The feast continued until it was announced that the newlyweds would take to the dance floor followed by their parents. Dance music started with a violin and drumbeats in the background. Then Niccolò, dressed in a flowing yellow brocade outfit and a red turban-like cap on his head with a diamond and gold setting brooch pinned at the front of the turban, started to play his lute as everyone cheered. Soon the dance floor began to fill first with the wedded couples who swayed in rhythm for a while, followed by their parents and grandparents. For the next hour or so, the merrymakers swayed to the music as the newlyweds at one point appeared to float on the dance floor in wedded bliss.

The attendant and friends arrived sometime after to accompany the wedded couples to their nuptial bedroom and helped them dress for bed and retreat to their individual flower-decorated bedrooms where the beds were decorated with rose petals.

Some of the family members and friends were present. Then priests, one for each couple in their own nuptial bedroom performed a ceremony ensuring fertility and blessing upon the union.

Then one of the friends in each bedroom reminded them the carriage and their personal belongings were prepared for their getaway travel to a beautiful small town in Cortona in the Chiana valley in south Tuscany for two weeks.

The priests ended the ritual with a final invocation and blessing and then everyone left the brides and grooms in their respective nuptial rooms.

The feast and celebration with music and dance continued until the weary but merry guests gradually began leaving amid the darkness piercing the sky punctuated by the sharp shrill of night birds as the dreamy moonlight flooded the hills of Castellina.

Music slowly became fainter and fainter until it faded like a dream as two owls hooted to each other before silence fell on the Castellina hills.

Preparations for the Wedding

April 16th 1965—On an early spring afternoon, Samir and Amita were eagerly waiting for Sharmi to arrive from Durham. Knowing that Rudy was busy looking for a registrar's job at work, they did not hear from Rudy for the last two weeks. Yet they were worried because it wasn't like Rudy to not communicate as he never failed to call them every few days. Samir called several times and there was no reply at his residence and he called a few times at his work but could not reach him.

Sharmi was busy with her thesis and took an additional few more days to submit it. She was supposed to turn it in at the end of March but instead she submitted her thesis on April 14.

Sharmi came back from India around the middle of January overwhelmed with anxiety about her thesis, the stress about telling her parents about Rudy, and tired from traveling to India and back to England so Amita and Samir decided not to call too often to give Sharmi some space to study, work and decompress.

Rudy was also busy with work and studying as he intended to get through the first part of his FRCS (Fellow of Royal College of Surgeons) Exam which was supposed to be in March. He used to call often and communicate with Samir and Amita about what was going on in his life except for the last two weeks.

Samir was just thinking about calling Rudy again when the phone started ringing. When Samir picked up the phone and heard Rudy's voice, he was relieved and very happy yet upset that Rudy didn't bother to communicate for a while.

"Where were you all this time? Why didn't you call us?" Samir inquired.

"Please do not get upset," Rudy pleaded. "I'm going to tell you all about it when I see you. I have some good news to share."

"Are you coming to our place?" Samir said anxiously. "Where are you?"

"Yes, I'll be going to your house within an hour."

"Who called?" Amita's interest was piqued after the phone call.

"You'll be surprised—Rudy called to say he's coming here about an hour from now."

"Did he communicate with Sharmi recently?" Amita began, "I didn't ask—"

The phone started ringing again. "Must be Sharmi just arriving at the bus station."

She was right. Samir took the telephone from Amita. "I'm about to leave now to pick you up," he told Sharmi.

Soon after Samir left to pick up Sharmi, Rudy arrived at Samir and Amita's house. Amita and Rudy were happy to see each other.

"What's going on? You never called and we tried several times but no answer."

"I am so sorry," Rudy said, "do not get upset. I can explain. The good news is—I got a registrar post at the Regional Neurosurgical Institute at Newcastle. I was occupied with so many things and one of them is—I passed the first part of the FRCS Exam!"

"That is exciting, congratulations!" Amita said. "Have you been communicating with Sharmi?"

"Not for the last ten days or so," Rudy said in a remorseful tone, "she has been pretty occupied herself with submitting her thesis. I knew she planned to submit it on April 14 and that she's coming here to visit you so here I am. I think Sharmi will be surprised to see me because I had not told her I might be here as I wasn't sure whether I would be able to come as my on-duty schedule has been so erratic. I was on-call this weekend and later it changed so that's why I could come."

"Rudy, are you still planning to get married in Venice?"

"Yes, but I inquired about a Hindu wedding in front of an open fire pit and was told it will not be allowed in a gondola. So I am thinking and suggesting to see if we could do Hindu wedding rituals at the hotel by booking a conference room or, if it is possible, in a cozy, cemented, stretched out courtyard of the hotel close to the waterfront and then get a marriage registrar to get our marriage registration certificate on a gondola. Only six people are allowed in a gondola. Depending on the number of people attending, we can reserve a number of gondolas we need. We can tour on a gondola for some time and have the grand dinner and dance at the hotel in the evening.

"A Hindu wedding ceremony has to be during daytime but that will be okay as there is a time difference between Kolkata and Venice with Kolkata being ahead four and a half hours, for example, the auspicious time in the evening at Kolkata is 6:30 and will be 2:30 in the afternoon in Venice."

"That is wonderful," Amita said, "we can figure it out. It is pretty good, Rudy, that we will have time this weekend to discuss all the details. I'm glad Sharmi will be joining us soon." Her eyes brightened. "Oh, I hear the sound of the car."

"I have talked to some hotels in Venice also," Rudy said. "Yes, let's all get together to discuss the preparations."

"This is so exciting, Rudy," Amita said.

Sharmi and Samir greeted Rudy warmly and were very happy to see him.

"Hello, my dear friend, you made us so worried," Samir said. "What is going on?"

"Sorry I will explain," Rudy said. "Let us have some tea together. I'll make tea for all of us."

"That would be very nice," Sharmi said. "I need a cup of tea very desperately. Rudy, I am really surprised to see you here." She cast him a somewhat hurt expression.

"Sorry, my dear Sharmi, but the last two weeks I was going through a roller coaster. Events kept swirling around me beyond my control." Rudy caught his breath. "Let me make tea, then I will explain."

"I bought macadamia nut cake and spiced apple cake for our tea time snack," Amita said.

"Thank you, I wanted to have something with tea," Rudy said listlessly. "I guess I'm hungry."

Rudy made them all tea as Amita sliced and served the macadamia nut cake. Amita asked Rudy to discuss the information he gathered so far about arranging the wedding at Venice.

"This is what I found out after calling the hotels and asking about gondolas in Venice," Rudy said. "There is a hotel called St. Regis in the center of Venice on the waterfront. The La Fenice opera house, Doge's palace, and other cultural highlights are very close by. Some of the area's most notable landmarks include St. Mark's Square and the Campanile are also close. There are rooms we can book with a view of the waterfront and the piazza. The rooms are very nicely furnished and lighted and sounded pretty good to me. I also inquired about the wedding in a gondola which is not possible as we have to have an open fire pit for the Hindu rituals.

"I asked the hotel about booking a room or their extended courtyard on the waterfront to do the rituals and I thought it would be nice to do the Hindu wedding in the hotel and then do the registry marriage in the late afternoon in the gondola as only six people are allowed in one gondola. We will book the gondolas depending on how many people will attend."

"Sounds good," Samir said.

"Now we have to set a wedding date and I have to start booking. There is not much time left."

"Sharmi, you have to tell us which date is good for you," Amita said. "Your family should approve and select the auspicious date for the Hindu rituals."

"After my family approved our union, my sister and my mother had already looked into possible dates and consulted the priests," Sharmi said. "The dates they came up with are in the first week of May and if that's not possible, then June 6."

"What about your final interview for the thesis?" Amita said.

"Oh, the board already conducted my interview when I submitted my thesis," Sharmi said. "I was late in submitting my thesis so they have already approved it."

"So you are done?"

"Yes, I've already earned my doctorate." Sharmi's voice remained calm after all the stress she had been through, it was nice to make this matter-of-fact announcement.

"Wow, let us celebrate!"

"What a nice surprise!" Rudy said, giving Sharmi a hug and a kiss on the cheek. "I remember you told me that you have finished your thesis and I wanted to come and see you but you said, 'Please wait, we will celebrate later.' Now I know why."

"I wanted to surprise you," Sharmi told Rudy then turned to Amita and Samir. "I wanted to surprise all of you."

"I'm so very happy for you, Sharmi," Rudy said, "And so delighted that you and I have achieved what we both set out to accomplish. I just told Amita about it and—I got the registrar job at the Institute."

"Hurray, what a coincidence!" Samir said. "Looks like everything is coming together."

"That is so wonderful!" Sharmi exclaimed. "How fortunate that we both have accomplished our goals. Now we can move forward with focusing on our wedding."

"Yes," Rudy said. "We have to select the date. Let's order tonight's dinner from the kabob place so that we don't have to worry about cooking today and devote more time to discussing the date and wedding arrangements."

"Let us enjoy the tea and start thinking about the date of the wedding," Amita said. "Today is April 16 and the first week of May will be here too soon. What do you think, Sharmi?

"It will be less than a month's time," Sharmi said.

"What about June 6?" Samir said.

"That will be around two months or so," Amita said.

"What do you think, Sharmi?" Samir said.

"It's all right with me," Sharmi said. "I'm not making arrangements so much. Rudy and my family in India have agreed to do the arrangements."

"I can make arrangements if I know how many people will be coming from India," Rudy said. "We also have to make a list of people who are eager to come and join us in Venice from our department at work and our friends' circle from here."

"From India, two or a maximum of three will come to the wedding," Sharmi said. "I will invite six of my friends from Durham, but I don't know how many can actually attend the wedding in Venice."

"For our Indian community, you have to arrange a party in Newcastle sometime later," Samir said. "It is not possible for them to attend the wedding at Venice, so we will think about that later."

"This is the plan," Rudy said. "I am going to invite people who are close to me, have them let me know whether they can make it or not. I also plan to invite the person who helped me find a house officer's job in Bury and by the way, I want to invite my artist friend in Florence whom I first met on the ship SS Roma while I was traveling to England. I went to see him after I got the job in Bury. This Italian friend introduced me to the famous sculptors of Florence between the 15th and 16th centuries. He works at Uffizi in Florence and his special area of expertise is on Niccolò who lived between 14th to 15th century Florence. This particular artist inspired me deeply; he had a vision that is universal even to this present era and he said that 'creativity is like an endless stream; it flows to all the areas of work. When the stream flows through the creator, he is the one who can guide it and make it unique and alive with its magic touch.'"

The passion with which Rudy explained his enthusiasm and admiration for Niccolò Bardi is evident in the way Sharmi, Amita and Samir leaned in closer to listen with intense interest.

"This sculptor's philosophy resonates with my own work as a doctor so my area of work is also like an endless stream of creativity," Rudy said. "I have struggled and am still struggling to get somewhere. I have not reached there yet to make it unique but I am inspired and I will try hard to get there."

Amita, Samir and Sharmi were overcome with emotion when Rudy finished talking about the inspiration behind his motivation to do better. They all said this is the right direction and inspiration to go on towards living your life.

"Wonderful," Samir said. "We wish you all the best."

"I am sure you will reach where you want to be," Amita said.

"I pray all your dreams come true," Sharmi said.

Rudy squeezed his fiancée's hand. "They are already coming true."

Samir clasped his hands together. "Okay, back to the wedding plans: let's go step-by-step. So if the date is June 6, then Sharmi will inform her family and then they will confirm which date they are able to come and where their destination would be whether Venice or Newcastle. If it's Newcastle, they have to arrive much earlier."

"I think it is better for them to arrive in Venice a day or two earlier than coming to Newcastle," Sharmi said. "My brother and sister will be bringing with them our family priest who will conduct the wedding ceremony. His father was also a priest who did all the sacred rituals for our previous generations. This priest is a graduate from Calcutta University but continues to be a priest as a part-time profession. They will bring the ingredients and materials—everything needed for the wedding ceremony—like a special permit that will need a special letter or proof that we are going to get married on the specific date. All these ingredients are for the Hindu rituals."

"That will not be a problem to show proof that we are getting married," Rudy said. "For the registry marriage, the marriage registrar will announce it a month before and I can request a copy of it."

"Rudy tell me how you want to proceed with the arrangements of the wedding," Samir said. "I am ready to help with whatever you need."

"I will book the hotel and the space for the Hindu wedding rituals and the gondolas," Rudy said. "So we need to know how many people will be attending."

"Before making the list, talk to the people you want to invite to first see whether they are able to attend the wedding in Venice," Samir said. "I will also try to talk to friends whom you want to invite so, that is the first step."

"I will try to book rooms at St. Regis within two or three days," Rudy said. "So I need to know how many right now, like four rooms including one for you and Amita. What do you suggest for how many days?"

"How about for three to four days?" Samir said. "But you don't have to pay for us."

"Samir, what about if we say six to seven days? That way we can make a day trip to Florence and other places nearby," Rudy said. "You leave the paying to me and the rent for a space for the Hindu wedding rituals for a day."

"That sounds like a good and exciting plan," Amita said. "For the day trip, we can share. It will be nice because we can get a group rate as there will be seven people. I want to ask about the wedding attire for both of you."

"My outfit will be a red Banarashi saree with gold work all over, a matching red silk blouse and a red petticoat for wearing underneath the saree," Sharmi said. "A red see-through Banarashi red veil with gold works will drape over my head and will drape down below the shoulder. For the accessories: a long, gold necklace, a choker with gold beads, golden bangles—six for each arm, matching gold earrings, a gold tiara, a silver intricate and elaborate design, a silver anklet with tiny bells, an intricately designed white crown made with a plant material called *shola*.

"For the groom, Rudy will wear an off-white, loose-fitted, silk embroidered top with gold and pearl buttons in the front, a six-yard cotton material with gold border which runs along a fine linear beige or brown parallel weaved in lines. Altogether, three to four along the five-feet width on both sides will run along the six yards of white cotton material that has to be worn by the groom tied around the waist and wrapped around neatly below the waist. The garlands made with white tube roses and red roses for both the bride and groom will be brought by my sister and brother. On the groom's head, there will be a conical white decorated crown, a *topur*, made by *shola*, a plant material.

"Besides this, there will be what we called '*Tatta*' in Bengal. In this country, they will say dowry providing the bridegroom their essential articles to start their life like clothes, cosmetics, bedcovers, embroidered pillowcases, etc. As we will live in England, they are not providing the kitchen set, dinner or cutlery set," Sharmi said.

"That is quite a lot to bring from India," Amita said.

"Today is very special," Samir said. "We got good news of Sharmi's doctorate degree and Rudy's registrar job and him passing part one of the FRCS. Let us celebrate."

"We're not cooking and the food from the kabob place is delicious," Amita said. "But my favorite is Rudy's fish curry."

"All right," Rudy laughed, relieved all of the stressful work requirements for both him and Sharmi were now behind them. "I can cook tomorrow. Thank you for your compliments."

"Sharmi," Amita said, "it would be nice if you could call your mother and sister tomorrow about the date and wedding plans. I think they are anxiously waiting. Oh, did you call and let them know that you finished your thesis and earned your degree?"

"No, not yet," Sharmi said.

"Oh no, you have to call and let them know," Amita urged.

"Call them after breakfast tomorrow or around noon," Samir advised. "They are five and a half hours ahead of us."

"What do you all think about the hotel reservation in Venice?" Rudy asked. "Should it be from the 3rd, 4th or 5th of June?"

"I think June 3rd will be ideal and also for the newly-married suite from the 6th," Amita said.

They spent the rest of the night catching up on all that had happened in the four months since they had last been together. They were most excited about the wedding as it would be the first time they would visit Venice. Their imaginations ran wild thinking about the city and its architecture.

"I read that the Grand Canal and the big piazza are both fascinating," Samir said, "One can see the Grand Canal at a distance. Some ships are docked and others blowing their horns and sailing away to faraway lands. It all sounds so dreamy."

"I saw pictures of big mansions and unique buildings on either side of the Grand Canal," Rudy said.

"I love the pictures of the narrow canals around Venice with cozy mansions and hanging balconies accentuated with colorful flowering plants drooping down towards the water," Amita said.

"And I can imagine the curtain of dusk and diffused lights from the mansions playing hide and seek with the darkness and at the background, the lulling sounds of the oars of gondolas returning home breaking the silence of the evening," said Sharmi, utilizing her poetic talents that was lulling her to sleep. "I'm feeling sleepy imagining peaceful evenings in Venice."

"Me too," Amita said with a yawn.

"Goodnight to all."

* * *

17th of April 1965—The four friends were greeted by a clear spring morning with no fog and the sun was up in the sky as soft rays of sun flooded the red rooftops of the buildings whose windows were still foggy.

The tall trees outside with new green leaves joyfully swayed with the gentle breeze down on the patches of grass. Daffodils shook their heads with the pink and red tulips as a few birds happily chirped on the branches while others hopped joyfully from one branch to another.

Inside the households, people were just waking up with a hot, steaming cup of tea and a newspaper in their hand.

Sharmi and Amita busied themselves preparing breakfast as Samir was trying to light the fireplace while Rudy went to fetch the weekend newspaper. All of them wanted to sit and enjoy their breakfast around the fireplace.

Then Rudy helped the ladies with breakfast, volunteering to prepare the pot of tea with four cups, saucers and teaspoons along with sugar and milk on a tray to place on a side table. They all brought their breakfast items on a plate individually and sat around the fireplace.

"This all looks so good," Samir said. "Perfect combination of toast, bacon and fried eggs sunny side up and fried half tomatoes."

"Excellent, my favorite, thank you," Rudy complimented the ladies.

"Let's enjoy our breakfast leisurely and around 11 this morning, Sharmi will call her family about the wedding to tell them the decided date and place, etc.," Amita said. "We will all be here to help remind her about the list of things to mention to them."

"Yes," said Samir.

"I agree," Rudy said, "good to remind her if anything is missed."

As planned, Sharmi called her sister in Calcutta to inform them all of the travel plans and the June 6 wedding along with the Venice, Italy venue. She also told her family that Rudy would be reserving the rooms there and for them to let him know how many people will be coming including the priest.

Urmi relayed their inquiries to her mother who was happy to know that the wedding date had been decided.

"The priest and your Uncle Sunil happily agreed to go and will do the rituals," Sharmi's mother said. "They have to return before the 9th of June as your brother, Subir, got an opportunity to go to Germany for higher studies and work there at the end of May so he cannot attend."

"Rudy is arranging to reserve the hotel in Venice from the 4th of June for Urmi, Uncle, and Priest Dhiren," Sharmi said. "Rudy will buy tickets to reach Venice on the 4th and return on the 8th of June. Urmi can go back on the 10th or 11th."

"That is all right with me," Urmi said.

"That is all right with me too," said Sharmi's mother. "Please get the certificate or proof that there will be a wedding which includes Hindu rituals so that they will allow the materials for the rituals to go through customs."

"Yes Ma, I will send you that as soon as possible," Sharmi said. "I have another news to tell you. Ma, *Pronam* to you and Baba— I finished my Ph.D. Thank you for everything and most especially for your support."

"You make me so happy!" Sharmi's mother gushed with excitement, "your father will eventually come around and be happy for you, I can assure you that but you understand he is from a different generation so it is difficult for him to adjust and face the changing world."

"I am so proud of you, Sharmi, with all the past difficulties, you made it," Urmi exclaimed. "So happy for you!"

Mother, Sharmi and Urmi all became very emotional as tears rolled from their mother's eyes. "I pray for you and your journey of a new life in a foreign country."

Sharmi's conversation with her family seemed to go well and Amita, Samir, Rudy and Sharmi were all relieved from the tension that had existed previously.

"Amita and I will happily represent Rudy's side of the family and Sharmi's uncle, priest and her sister Urmi will, of course, represent Sharmi," Samir said. " There are rituals in a Hindu wedding to be done that is why I am telling you it's good to have representatives from both sides."

"Let's drive somewhere and spend time looking at nature and welcome spring," Amita suggested. "After all the pressures of life, we can relax and celebrate."

"Yes, with all the wedding preparations, we will likely not be able to get together till end of May," Sharmi said. "Then we will all be busy packing for Venice."

"That's true," Samir said.

"Let's at least go outside to breathe some fresh air to see and sense the colorful touches of spring no matter where we go," Rudy said.

Happy to be reunited again, the four friends were in the mood for rejoicing all that spring offered after the gloomy few winter months of rain and storm. But such is life like the weather, Rudy mused.

"The month of May will be a busy month," Samir said. "Tuesday, June 1st, Sharmi will be back in Newcastle at our place and Thursday, June 3rd we fly to Venice. The flight leaves at 11:30 in the morning from Newcastle Airport and our nonstop flight will arrive in Venice at 4:30 that afternoon. We have to start our journey from home at 10 that morning."

"We can pack everything on the 2nd of June so we'll be ready to leave in the morning," Amita said.

"Ah, my friends," Rudy interjected. "This weekend we should relax and enjoy since we are not going to get together till June 1st." Rudy paused to allow his friends to brace themselves for more good news. "I was informed that I will be officially getting the keys to a bigger place for married people."

"That's so nice," Amita gushed, "then we can start arranging a few things. Sharmi, you can bring some of your belongings from Durham where you are living now and store them in your new apartment."

"Yes, I think I'll do that," Sharmi said. "Amita this is so exciting!"

Then the four friends went downstairs to the garage and got in Samir and Amita's car, their hearts light as Samir started driving to enjoy their weekend.

* * *

Days had passed by so fast that Sharmi could not believe she was already packing her essentials to take an early morning bus ride from Durham to Newcastle and soon, the day she, Rudy, Amita and Samir had been counting down towards was finally upon them—Tuesday, the first day of June.

Sharmi's friend, Carolyn gave her a ride to the bus station. Before saying goodbye, she hugged Sharmi. "We will all be there, the four of us. Congratulations!"

Sharmi was happy her friends were all going to Venice to attend her wedding. "Thank you, Carolyn. Are you all planning to arrive on the 4th or 5th of June?"

"I think we will arrive on the afternoon of the 5th," Carolyn said.

They hugged each other and Sharmi settled in the bus. As it started slowly moving, Sharmi and Carolyn waved to each other before the bus left the station.

Sharmi took some more of her belongings from her Durham apartment to keep in her and Rudy's new apartment. She had been doing this for her last few trips and at present, she left a few things there as she still had to continue working in her department for a few more months.

Sharmi realized the bus was going through the hilly areas of Durham. She was enjoying the view now as she was relaxed a bit more than before.

She thought about how Rudy did a good job already furnishing the apartment, buying everything new, from the bedroom set to the living room and kitchen sets. He would still spend a huge amount of money for the wedding and then additional expenses for the days they would spend in Venice after the wedding. Sharmi got excited when Rudy told her he would plan a trip for just the two of them to Switzerland.

Sharmi returned to the present with a jolt, realizing the bus had arrived at the station in Newcastle-upon-Tyne. Since it was early afternoon, Sharmi took a taxi as Amita was planning to take off from her work from June 2nd to return to work on June 16th.

Samir and Rudy were also taking off from June 2nd with a return work date set for June 16th. Sharmi was the only one back to work on the first of July in a new position working as a teaching assistant in the department of English at Durham University on Tuesdays and Thursdays.

When Sharmi arrived at Amita and Samir's place, she took time to arrange her belongings in the room where she usually spends the night, then started cooking. She thought she would surprise them by cooking some simple Bengali dishes.

She cooked pulses seasoned with turmeric and fried spices and mixed seeds like cumin, black cumin, fenugreek, and Mustard seed with a tablespoon of cooking oil in a sauce pan and added the cooked pulses in it then added salt and a teaspoon of sugar and sprinkled with chopped cilantro. She was very happy as the pleasant smell filled the air. Then she started cooking rice and at the same time found some frozen herring inside the fridge.

She cleaned the fish and cut it into pieces and marinated them for ten minutes with some plain yogurt and then added half a teaspoon of turmeric, a dash of red chili powder, one teaspoonful of mustard powder, salt then about a tablespoon of oil.

She mixed it thoroughly and put it again in a sauce pan and started cooking it in low heat. She was very careful and checked it every five minutes. She then added a few pieces of green chili and found that the fish was cooked thoroughly. Sharmi then put the whole thing in a nice white bowl and sprinkled some chopped cilantro leaves.

She was very proud of herself as this particular dish looked very delicious to her and being a Bengali, fish was the favorite food.

What else do I need? she thought. *So far, there was rice, pulses, Dahi herring fish…Oh I can fry some aubergine.* She took a purple eggplant, cut it into pieces and sprinkled some turmeric powder and salt and started to fry them when she heard footsteps and Amita's voice.

"What are you doing?" Amita surveyed the spread of spices and ingredients.

"Cooking dinner. I am almost done."

"Wow, it smells good. Did you have lunch?"

"No, my mind has been preoccupied so I concentrated on cooking," Sharmi said.

"Now, take a rest," Amita insisted. "I will make some tea and I made banana nut bread so I will slice that for you and there are some cookies too."

"What time is it?"

"Fifteen minutes past 4 in the afternoon," Amita said.

"Let me put all these away and then I will relax," Sharmi said.

"I will take care of this and serve them at the dinner," Amita said, "you are not allowed to do any more chores."

Amita made tea and sliced banana bread then put the floral-designed tea cozy covered teapot on a tray then added strawberry-designed cups, saucers and a few serving plates for the banana bread. She also included a sugar pot and warm milk in a jug for the tea. She then placed the tray on the corner table and rested on the comfortable sofa and asked Sharmi to come and join her.

"Sharmi," Amita said, "this is the start of our vacation."

Sharmi was very happy to join her.

"Thank you, my dear friend, for cooking dinner," Amita said. "We will have time today to talk and plan how we will arrange things for the wedding and how to divide the responsibilities as to who is going to do what on that particular day."

"I can't believe that the day has come and tomorrow we will pack our bags for our trip to Venice," Sharmi said. "The wedding attire and accessories will arrive from India."

"Yes, that will be fun," Amita said. "For the wedding arrangements, we have to reach Venice and start arranging things there."

"Until my sister, uncle and the priest arrive in Venice, we cannot do anything as they are bringing all the things for the Hindu wedding," Sharmi said.

"We will arrive at our hotel around 4:30 in the afternoon on June 3rd and we'll get settled in our hotel and ask which room or extended paved patio they will provide for the ritual of the Hindu wedding," said Amita. "The floor or part of the floor has to be without a carpet then we can do the artwork on the floor with our viscus rice paste with our right hand's fingers close together so we can dip it in the bowl and take some of the semiliquid paste and start filling the circle on the ground with design. The circle will be drawn before with two to three feet in diameter with chalk attached to a string. One person will try to hold one end of the string down to the floor and the other one with the loose end where the chalk is tied go around on the floor to draw a circle. Next is to fill the circle. In the middle will be a flower with petals, after a line around it, we can draw the creeper and then paisley and some other design like wavy lines. When we start the project, it will come automatically what design to be done next so that the ritual could be done close to the circular artwork and it will dry and will look very nice. I will also draw with this mixture the Seven Steps of your married life you both will step one after another on the floor when the priest will ask you to do so and he will explain to you what each step means in the journey of your married life."

"Thank you, Amita. It is so thoughtful and sweet of you to think about all the details. I will help you with the *alpana*, the circular artwork on the floor."

"Thank you, Sharmi. I will do the Seven Steps myself drawing the outline of small feet. You aren't supposed to do that, all right?"

They heard some footsteps and guessed they belonged to Samir and Rudy. They saw the two of them coming towards the room where Sharmi and Amita sat.

Both of them seemed tired but happy at the end of their work day and pleased to see the teapot and banana bread.

"I am so glad that tomorrow I will work until lunch and then I am home and then on the morning of June 3rd we are leaving for Venice," Samir said. "Oh, what fun we will all have in Venice!"

"I feel the same," Rudy said, then eyed the afternoon treats on the table. "I am glad tea is ready and there's banana bread to go with it. Looks delicious."

"Rudy, are you working tomorrow?" Samir asked.

"No, but I have to go in the morning just to finish some patients' discharge summaries."

"Then you should spend the night here," Samir suggested.

"Please do Rudy," Amita said. "Sharmi already cooked dinner."

"Oh, that is nice," Rudy said, smiling at his fiancée. "Tomorrow, I have to stay as we are leaving early morning to the airport."

"No problem," Amita said, "Have you packed your bags yet?"

"I did, but after I finish my patients' summary, I will go and take care of the rest of it," Rudy said. "By the way, I cooked some fish curry so we can have it tomorrow for dinner. All we need is to cook some rice."

"No problem," Amita said. "We have to pack our things for our trip to Venice soon after we finish our breakfast. We can start packing after we finish our tea today and then we'll enjoy dinner. Sharmi's started packing and found that she's already packed her things for Venice. Most of her things, like the wedding outfit and accessories are coming from India, she just has to arrange her cosmetics case."

Amita called Sharmi to select her saree, one was blue with silver work all over and the other was fuchsia with gold work all over. Sharmi selected the fuchsia saree. The accessories were easy as they go with her gold long necklace, and *jhumka*, gold dangling earrings. She also packed the blue one with pearl accessories.

Amita asked Sharmi, "Did you pack your sea green saree with silverwork and your lovely pearl accessories?"

"Yes."

"The rest of it is easy: pack our western outfits for both of us," Amita said. "I am packing Samir's Indian outfit like silk *kurta*, a silk shawl, and six yards long made of cotton material called *Dhoti*. Sharmi, I am almost done."

"I am done too," Sharmi said. "I will check it tomorrow again and then close the suitcases."

The evening was pleasant and everyone praised the dinner cooked by Sharmi as quite delicious. Complementing their dinner in the background was a record playing a Tagore song. They also put a record of Shenai, a musical instrument played at weddings. *Sur* is tune or tone and the word *nai* means reed or pipe. It is a woodwind with a double reed and metal or a wooden flared bell at the other end. Its sound is thought to create and maintain a sense of auspiciousness and sanctity.

Amita and Samir teased both Sharmi and Rudy. "Your days of single existence are biding you goodbye soon. Think it over because from here, there is no return."

Everyone laughed heartily and later, the recorded music of Shenai was then packed carefully in Amita's suitcase. To top it off, conversations with Sharmi's family went very well—everyone was happy about the upcoming nuptials. A wonderful start to what promised to be a memorable destination wedding ahead.

A Wedding in Venice

3rd of June 1965—The plane started to descend when Sharmi, Rudy, Amita and Samir peered down through their windows as the plane started circling.

The sea green water of the Grand Canal with the gondolas looked like a painted landscape. The four friends were excited the wedding was actually happening in Venice! For Rudy, as he peered down from the airplane's window, a warm feeling surged within him. Italy was not only going to be the site of his wedding to Sharmi but also the first time he would set foot on the soil that produced such great artists especially the one whose life and works meant so much to Rudy—the great Niccolò Bardi.

"I can't believe we are going to land soon at the Marco Polo airport in Venice," Amita said.

Once they claimed their luggage, they hired a cab to reach the hotel St. Regis. After checking in and settling in, the four of them thought they were in their fantasy land. The waterfront furnished rooms were so magical that they were all enchanted looking around the hanging balconies with an array of colorful flowering plants drooping towards the water. The hotel's stretched-out waterfront patio garden featuring the lapping serenade of gondolas with people made them engrossed in that moment, feeling as though time had stopped.

Amita awoke from this trance and called everyone to come out at the stretched-out patio of the hotel. "We have to start doing the artwork on the floor where the wedding rituals will take place and plan for this evening."

Rudy snapped back to the present. "I will call the front desk to inquire about the place for wedding rituals and restaurants where we could dine."

He returned after fifteen minutes. "The front desk told me we have a choice: we can have the stretched-out patio with the attached covered place for sitting or a small room inside. I saw the room on the same level as the front desk. It looks too small. To me, the patio will be better. It is open and gondolas' passengers cruising along this branch of the canal might wave or cheer which might bother some people attending the wedding ceremony but I think it will be fine. What do you think?"

"To me, it will be interesting," Samir said, "people can observe an actual Hindu wedding taking place and might even be nice if these spectators spread some added cheer on to you and Sharmi," he addressed Rudy.

"Did you ask permission so that we can start doing our artwork?" Amita inquired.

"Yes, they will keep a sign for people to stay away from it," Rudy said. "At any rate, the early afternoon tomorrow which is the 4th of June to the evening of the 7th it is reserved for us. You can start your artwork today. The hotel staff will post a sign alerting people that the space is reserved for a wedding."

"What is our plan for the evening?" Samir wanted to know.

"Well, it is 6:45," Rudy said, "we have a dinner reservation at 7:15. The dining area is nice—you can see the Grand Canal at a distance. The tables we reserved are on the terrace in the evening. They told me that the lights from the buildings will reflect on the water and will look spectacular."

The four friends went to the dining area where the tables were covered with white tablecloths with shiny silverware displayed on the terrace close to the water of the branch canal. Each table had a small candle in a glass holder and a small vase with a mixed bouquet of red carnations and yellow roses.

Sharmi, Rudy, Amita and Samir took a table close to the water where it was very dreamy and peaceful. The sun went down the horizon as the curtain of dusk fell. The gondolas were all parked along the shore as the reflected lights of the large and small buildings were all broken in pieces and rippling away to an unknown destiny. In the background, the frequent crashing sound of water on the structures at the shore seemed to be lulling the silence of the evening.

The attendant came to take the order. All four ordered fresh seasonal vegetables, minestrone soup with tomato and basil.

Amita ordered Mediterranean red mullets, scallops and couscous. Sharmi ordered sea bass, vegetables and couscous. Rudy and Samir ordered medium-baked loin of lamb aromatized with three peppers. All of them complemented their dinners with a glass of red wine except Sharmi who ordered strawberry lemonade.

They took their time starting a conversation as they were lost in the moments of their surroundings. Finally, Amita spoke. "Thank you Rudy, for everything—selecting the venue, the hotel and trying to arrange all the events to be filled with moments of joy which is coming along our way and at the start of your new chapter of life."

"Thank you," Rudy said. "I am very happy to know that all my efforts have been a success. My intention is to have you all enjoy, be happy even if it is for a short time. But most especially, I am grateful to share this very special occasion with all of you."

"Thanks, my friend. We are honored to be part of this memorable event of both your lives," Samir said. He turned to Sharmi."When is your sister, uncle and the priest arriving from India?"

"At noon," Sharmi replied.

"We will all go pick them up," Rudy said. "I am renting a car from the 4th to the 11th of June and then hire a taxi from the airport. "There are seven of us so we need two cars. One will be a taxi and the other will be the rented car."

"I will stay as I want to finish the artwork," Amita said.

"I will do the same and help Amita," Sharmi said. "It will take at least two hours for them to arrive at the hotel. We will see whether the rooms are ready and take the keys and welcome them at the hotel."

"Whatever you think will be best, let me know," Rudy said. "Then Samir and I can go together to the airport if it is okay with Samir."

"Absolutely," Samir said.

The attendant brought the steaming soup with a stack of bread rolls in a basket covered with a red napkin and four small bowls filled with olive oil for dipping the bread.

The soup set the mood for dinner with sips of red wine as a complement and for Sharmi, the refreshing strawberry lemonade. Sharmi's sea bass and Amita's red mullet and scallops looked delicious. Rudy and Samir took pictures of the lamb aromatized with three peppers. They all enjoyed the preparations very much compared to their bland English dishes from the hospital cafeteria and restaurants around Newcastle-upon-Tyne.

"Rudy, have you decided the dinner menu for the wedding feast?" Samir asked.

"I have a copy of the menu which I'll read it to you," Rudy said. "By the way, I wanted Sharmi's opinion about her food choices. She said, 'I cannot make up my mind it is confusing,' so I consulted the manager and chef who helped me so here's the menu: a glass of Bellini; nonalcoholic rose cocktail; white and red wine will be served during dinner.

"Then for appetizers: canapes with feta; green apples and roasted almonds; scallops with cream of courgettes; shrimp with mango and ginger tartare; smoked ham, cucumber and lime. Dinner starts with salmon steak in thyme sauce and tuna steak with sesame brittle. There will be plates of salad in the middle of the table with shrimp and artichoke. Then a duck leg with raspberry sauce and pilaf rice; Beef filet cooked with Amarone sauce and vegetables. To conclude dinner, some dishes with typical cheeses will be placed in the middle of the table. There will also be a selection of mixed fresh fruits like papayas, kiwi, pineapples, and bananas.

"The wedding dinner ends with a lemon sorbet before eating the wedding cake, a *Millefoglie*, which translates to 'a thousand layers' with cream and berries," Rudy explained. "It will be traditionally done in front of the wedded couple and the guests as a live show."

"Wow, that's a grand menu," Amita said.

"How many guests have RSVP'd and will attend?" asked Samir.

"There are twenty-five, excluding us, which means the seven of us including the priest so that is thirty-two," Rudy said.

"How many gondolas have you booked? asked Amita.

"I have booked six," Rudy said, "for thirty people. The gondolier who will lead all the gondolas said that some guests might drop off from the list so it is okay at present, but if it happens, he will take care of it.

"Just want to let you know, they have planned how to decorate the dinner table. The dining hall is large and rectangular with light pink washed walls, a large floor to three-quarter of wall length, wooden frame glass windows with a huge landscape painting of canals and gondolas hanging on the wall, two large gold-trimmed chandeliers and some tulip-shaped light fixtures on the walls.

"The tables will be covered with white tablecloths, pink napkins, gold cutlery and gold-bordered, white dinner plates," Rudy continued. "There will be high transparent vases on the tables with pink and white roses."

"That will look so pretty," Amita said.

A waiter approached and asked what kind of desserts they preferred.

"What do you recommend?" Rudy asked the waiter.

"Signore, you must try the Napoleon," the waiter said, "it is a special, layered puff pastry. We have ice cream sundae, Cannoli... those are also very special."

When the waiter brought the Cannoli that all of them ordered, they were fascinated by the elongated, tube-like dessert crust-filled with ricotta cheese and dusted with white powdered sugar.

As the evening grew darker, the sounds of water crashing on the shore became louder and louder. Up in the sky, the stars looked down on Venice while the moon peeped through a patchy cloud touched by the moonlight as ripples of the grand canal seemed to glow like silver and magically started waltzing with anchored ships at the harbor with the blast of strong wind.

"It's about time to retire," Samir said, "have to get up early to see the sunrise."

The morning of June 4th started out spectacular with a hearty breakfast at St. Regis that featured varieties of pastries and croissants, espresso, coffee, and tea.

The morning sun had bathed the city of Venice and the day was in full swing.

Sharmi, Rudy, Amita and Samir sat around a table in the dining hall near a big window. They could see the greenish-blue water of the Grand Canal and some ships docked with a few preparing to leave. The gondolas cruised along the Grand Canal and also along other canal branches. Part of St. Mark's Square captured their vision where people walked in many different ways some striding faster, others walking leisurely while still others were completely lost in the beauty of the structures around them. They looked around, going back and forth to capture an image of certain places to keep in their memory forever.

Amita asked Rudy, "At what time will you be leaving for the airport?"

"As soon as we finish breakfast," Rudy answered. "I have to pick up the rental car and ask the front desk for a map then we will go. That is why I want to leave early. I can drive three of them in the rental car where they can sit in the back and Samir can sit in front with me."

"Will it be all right to drive around?" Amita pointed out. "The driving is completely different here compared to England."

"It will be all right," Rudy said. "Samir can guide me and look at the signs. So the two of you can stay busy doing your artwork."

"Yes," Amita said.

"Drive carefully," Sharmi said. "We will be at the patio if you need us."

Rudy and Samir bid the ladies "goodbye for now" saying they will all have lunch when they get back.

Sharmi's heart started pounding, thinking about Urmi, her sister, her uncle and the family priest coming all the way to Venice from India. She was excited while at the same time feeling uncomfortable about the efforts everyone had done to make this wedding a success.

She was also thinking about Rudy every moment and what it would be like once they were married although she rarely declared her feelings openly.

"Sharmi, let's get started on the artwork," Amita said.

"Sure."

"First thing we'll do is draw the circle," Amita said. "Three-feet diameter so from the center to one side, it has to be one and one-half feet. I measured the string at the end of it and tied the white marker. Sharmi, you hold the other end very tight pressing it on the ground. Are you secure?"

Sharmi nodded. "Yes."

"All right," Amita said. "I am going around with the marker pressing it on the ground. Steady Sharmi, hold it tight. Going around, it is marking nicely. I am almost there making the circle. Oh, finally it is done. Wow, it's a perfect circle."

"Oh, I'm glad," Sharmi said. "Now I can breathe easily."

"The liquid white color made with powdered rice water and some glue is in the plastic bowl," Amita said. "I'm starting at the center a small circle with it that will be filled up with this white color later. See, I put my right fingers close together like a cone and dip it in the white color and quickly start drawing with color-dipped fingers in the circle on the floor."

Amita kept on drawing different designs going from inner-smaller circle to outer-bigger circle. The circular spaces were filled with creeper, others with paisley in between with wavy lines with the last outer larger one with big conical petals. When she finished, the time was past one in the afternoon.

Amita got up and sighed. "I will stop now for a while and start after lunch again."

They heard the voices of Samir and Rudy and behind them was Urmi, Sharmi's sister, who came running to Sharmi and hugged her tightly. Both sisters were overwhelmed with joy and emotion. Uncle Sunil approached Sharmi and patted her on her back. With tearful eyes, he said in a soft voice, "I have not seen you for so long. Give your uncle a hug."

Sharmi gave a big hug to her uncle. Priest Dhiren said, "Hello, I have not seen you for a while. It is interesting that I have come to see you in Venice to conduct your wedding ceremony."

"Thank you Dhiren-*da*," Sharmi referred to him as "*da*," short for "*Dada*," meaning elder brother.

"Let us go for lunch," Rudy said. "Dhiren-*da* any food restrictions for you?"

Dhiren said, "I do not take meat."

Priest Dhiren and Uncle Sunil were very impressed with the hotel and the dining area at the waterfront with gondolas cruising by.

"All of us will enjoy lobster in a special sauce, sauteed vegetables and rice," Rudy announced.

Everyone clapped in delight. Urmi was very eager to converse about the wedding ceremony.

"Urmi, let us enjoy lunch then we will take you to your hotel room," Amita said. "Sharmi and you are going to stay there today on the 4th, 5th and also the 7th the night after the wedding night when couples do not stay together especially at night in Bengal. There is a superstition around that night long, long ago as it happened to a couple leading to the death of the groom. From there, it is branded as *Kaal Ratri*, Black Night."

"I am pleased to hear that as our mother also told me to abide by that," Urmi said.

They all enjoyed lunch. Rudy and Samir accompanied the priest and Uncle Sunil to their room and told them to rest for a while and they will be called when needed.

Urmi, Sharmi and Amita went to Urmi's room.

"There are a number of suitcases," Urmi said, "one suitcase is specifically for Sharmi's wedding attire, jewelry and the groom's attire." Urmi showed the jewelry and asked Sharmi to rent a vault from the hotel management to keep it there. Sharmi was pleased to see the attire which was lovely, so were the jewelry.

"Excuse me," Amita said. "I am going to the patio to finish the artwork. You two rest and catch up."

"I'm going to help you," Sharmi told Amita, "Let Urmi rest and we will come back and wake her up from her jet lag nap."

"Yes, I am feeling sleepy, especially after the delicious lunch," Urmi said.

Amita and Sharmi left Urmi in her room and headed to the patio to continue the artwork on the ground that they started earlier. They worked for a couple of hours.

"I'm happy it is done," Amita said. "Let's both look at it from different angles to see how it looks."

"I think it looks very beautiful," Sharmi said.

"But tell me if it's as good as it's done in Kolkata."

"Of course, it's as good and even more than how it's done by the standards in Kolkata," Sharmi reasoned.

"Oh, what time is it?" Amita said, suddenly frantic.

"It's 4:30," Sharmi said, "let's go wake up Urmi to tell her it's tea time."

"Also what has to be done for tomorrow—all the materials for the wedding rituals have to be unpacked and arranged in the proper order. By the way, did you see the Seven Steps? I did those close to the open fire pit, close to the waterfront that will be safe."

"Yes, I saw that," Sharmi said.

Sharmi and Amita went to Urmi's room to wake her up but she was already awake.

"I slept for some time but most of the time I was resting," Urmi admitted.

"We were talking about planning for tomorrow and arranging the things for the wedding ritual," Amita said.

"I will help you, *Didi*," Urmi referred to Sharmi with the term of endearment reserved for an older sister. "You're not supposed to do anything. Brides are treated like royalty as they are starting their new journey in life.

"First of all, we select a place for the *Malabadal*—the exchange of garlands— where the groom will stand around four young banana plants to be placed in each corner. The bride is usually carried by male relatives, four of them each holding the wooden slab, one on each corner. She will be sitting on a thick polished rectangular wooden slab covering her eyes with a triangular leaf and has to go around for seven times. Then she will be lifted at the same level as the groom and exchange garlands three times and for a few minutes, they look at each other, mostly the two pairs of eyes meet together while a veil is placed over their heads. These are very private moments of exchange of expression through their eyes. If banana plants are not available, we can put some other plants," Urmi said.

"There will be banana plants arriving this evening," said Amita.

"Both the bride and groom have to sit down on the floor," Urmi said. "When Uncle and the priest do the ceremony, giving away the bride to the groom will be at the fire pit where there will be a ceremony and the Seven Steps journey to their married life."

"I have already selected the place of the fire pit and already made the Seven Steps on the ground and the *alpana* artwork," Amita said. "We will take you now to see it and arrange to have some cushions for them to sit on the ground. The site will be decorated with pink and white roses intertwined with creepers."

"Both of them can drink liquids all day, buttermilk is usually offered," Urmi said. "Ma packed some sweets, like *Sandesh*, prepared with the protein of curdled milk *chana*, like cheese, cooked with sugar in low heat. It gets cooked and turns like a solid dough then from that, small pieces in different sizes and shapes are made. Those were offered to our image of the goddess, Durga. Now that it is holy, they can have those with their liquid drink, if they wish, no other solid foods. After the wedding, they can eat whatever they want."

Amita nodded, then said, "Let's go join the others."

"When do we unpack our suitcases?" Urmi inquired. "I want to take out the things we need for the wedding rituals and the gifts. Do you want to display these in open boxes or trays? Usually, that's the way it is done. If not, let me know. In the western world, they call it dowry but in India these are gifts from the parents, family members and close friends to help the newlywed couple have things for their new home and items for personal use like new clothes, toiletries to start their life together."

"We can specially display the beautiful sarees and handmade home décor," Amita said. "They are beautiful."

"Priest Dhiren-*da* has all the things for the wedding rituals: the iron pit where the fire will be lit, special pieces of wood for lighting the fire, sandalwood paste, a trident grass head called *Durba*, red twined thread, paddy grains—rice grain covered with its skin; they are needed for offering prayers and also when the couple will be blessed by the priest and their elders and two gorgeous garlands of white tube rose with an accent of red roses in the middle of the garland. The garlands are all kept in the hotel's refrigerator to keep them fresh. Also turmeric paste which is usually applied to both the bride and groom's bodies. Before they go for a shower, there is a short ceremony with blowing conch shells which is done separately in the groom's place and also in the bride's place between midmorning and afternoon of the wedding day. The purpose is to clean and disinfect and the result is the skin looks brighter," said Urmi.

While Sharmi appreciated her sister was a wealth of knowledge, she was becoming restless. "Let's go. I am thirsty for a cup of tea."

Amita, Sharmi and Urmi went to the stretched-out patio to see the completed *alpana* artwork designed by Amita. Urmi was amazed to see the artwork on the floor close to where the wedding rituals will be conducted.

"It's so beautiful," Urmi said. "Oh, what a great site to do the wedding rituals, I am so impressed. I will take photos and we also brought movie camera equipment."

"That's wonderful," Amita said. "Who will be in charge of it?"

"Uncle Sunil will set it up and when he will be busy with the wedding rituals, then I will take care of it," Urmi said.

"Very nice that you could take on so many responsibilities," Amita said.

They went to the hotel lounge and saw Samir, Rudy, priest Dhiren and Uncle Sunil. They join Rudy to order tea and some light snacks. They were all happy to be reunited again. Then Rudy announced that dinner will be at eight in the evening as tomorrow will be a busy day for arranging and preparing for the wedding day. Rudy said he just had to confirm the particulars regarding the gondolas, the marriage registrar, catering service and hotel management will take care of the rest. Rudy assured them that after confirming the necessary arrangements, everything should be set.

Priest Dhiren and Uncle Sunil expressed needing help with unpacking the suitcases.

"I think I can manage to unpack it myself but with the arrangement and order of the delicate materials for the wedding rituals, I could need some assistance with those," Priest Dhiren said.

"I can help you," Urmi said to the priest, "just let me know when. Dhiren-*da*, you have to see Amita's *alpana* artwork on the ground and the *sapta padi* artwork of Seven Steps."

The evening set in slowly as the seven of them gathered on the terrace dining area for another pleasant evening at the waterfront. They all ordered *Sarde Savor*, fried sardine-fillets marinated in vinegar, onion, raisin and pine nuts as an appetizer.

Samir and Rudy ordered *Fegato alla Venezia*, liver, stewed onions, caramelized onions served on a bed of polenta.

A special dish with rice, vegetables and shrimp in tomato basil sauce was prepared for the priest. Uncle Sunil ordered *Risi e bisi*, made with rice, prosciutto, peas, butter, onions and parsley.

Amita and Sharmi ordered *Bigoli Salsa*, pasta resembling spaghetti in salsa. Urmi ordered the same special dish as Dhiren: rice, vegetables, shrimp in tomato and basil sauce. They all ordered fritoli, made with flour, eggs, butter, nuts, raisins, sugar, made in the shape of balls, deep fried and dusted with sugar.

For the beverages, *Soave,* a white wine of Venice and lemonade for Sharmi were served.

Uncle Sunil and Priest Dhiren were extremely happy to be on the waterfront terrace relaxing with the gentle breeze, the lulling sound of water on the shore and the spectacular moon rise beyond the horizon made the landscape magical.

"I feel I am in a dreamland," Uncle Sunil said. "Thank you, Rudy, for selecting this romantic place for your wedding."

"You're welcome, Uncle," Rudy said.

The waiter brought their food one after another as they all enjoyed their meals with *Soave* wine and the last serving of *fritoli.*

Uncle Sunil was very excited. "It reminds me of some sort of sweet in Bengal, where they make a syrup and put these into that to be soaked."

"What is it called?" Amita asked.

"I think it is called *Rosh bara* or syrupy balls," Uncle Sunil replied.

Everyone agreed and started enjoying the *fritolis.*

Rudy reminded them it is just past 10:30 in the evening. "No rush, just letting you know so everyone is aware that it's time to say goodnight."

They gazed one more time at the outline of sleepy Venice and said "Good night" to each other.

* * *

On the 5th of June, the table occupied by Rudy's group by the big window offered a magnificent view of the waterfront's branch canal shimmering with the orange color of the sun's rays. At a distance, a ship blew her horn to announce her departure. The movement of the ship created a motion in the water that it seemed the canals woke up from their sleep and suddenly started crashing on the shore causing the seagulls to shriek and circle the area above.

Sharmi, Amita, Samir, Uncle Sunil and the priest came together. Sharmi took her seat at the window. She looked very pretty. Uncle Sunil sat close to Sharmi. The day felt a little different to Sharmi, the lovely bride lost in her thoughts, feeling as though time was running too fast as today was indeed the day before her wedding. Suddenly as she sat, her mind flashed back to her recent visit to India, thinking it was like being on a swing as she pondered the mood of her family that vacillated from sometimes high and bright to sometimes low, sad and uncertain. In the end, most of her family agreed with their union and her mother insisted on getting married within a few months as is customary in Hindu weddings especially in West Bengal when some months were not auspicious times to get married. Sharmi wore her red-bordered parrot green saree and red blouse she adorned with a red coral necklace that reached to the middle of her chest, two round, gold earrings with shiny gold balls that moved when she turned her head.

She had two red bangles on each hand, her hair secured in a bun and a few half-opened white rosebuds placed around the bun with one in particular peeping through behind her right ear. With her face looking very bright with a bindi in the middle of her forehead, she seemed to be in a pensive mood.

Then Rudy came and sat close to Samir. When he turned to the corner to gaze at Sharmi, his eyes suddenly sparkled and gleamed, his face became radiant, the corners of his lips turned up. Sharmi lifted her face and when her eyes suddenly met his, she shyly looked down, blushed and started smoothing her saree to calm her self-consciousness.

In Bengal, brides were not supposed to show their expression too much preferring to appear in a quiet, pensive mood.

When breakfast was served, the plates came with brioche, pieces of Venetian cake with nuts and raisin, and another pastry filled with chocolate complemented espresso and coffee.

"While in Venice, eat like a Venetian," Samir remarked as the breakfast was so different from England.

Uncle Sunil had already taken a big bite of cake. "It is delicious and the espresso goes very well with it. Four of us are going to fast tomorrow: myself, Priest Dhiren, Rudy and Sharmi but we can have espresso so that will be nice."

"After breakfast, we have to start arranging things for the wedding rituals," Priest Dhiren said. "We must have some place for the *Malabadal*—the exchange of garlands—an area for the firepit and also for *sampradan*—giving away the bride. But if there is not enough room available, we can arrange all this in the same place one after another."

"Please don't worry," Amita said, "we have an area which is spacious enough to accommodate all that. We have already demarcated the areas individually. We will show you after we finish our breakfast."

"That is very nice," said the priest, "then it will be easier to arrange as I packed the things for the rituals separately and already marked which one is which."

After breakfast everyone had their share of work arranging the things for the wedding. Priest Dhiren was amazed to see the *alpana*—the beautiful artwork on the floor and pleased to see the selected areas for the different rituals.

The stretched-out patio seemed to him an ideal area with a view of the waterfront. And as the hours ticked by, in the evening they all gathered for a simple dinner as, according to Priest Dhiren, the couple must eat a vegetarian diet so everyone had rice and vegetables cooked in tomato-based sauce and ice cream.

In India, the bride and groom were not supposed to see each other the day before the wedding. In a foreign country, it was different and they all had to adjust.

"Good night, everyone," Sharmi said.

Urmi told Sharmi, "I will soon join you."

Rudy waved his hand as he and his bride-to-be exchanged a warm look and smiled. The rest of them sat for some time to watch the city of Venice lay in slumber with the sound of water crashing on the shore.

* * *

Wedding Day, 6ᵗʰ of June 1965—The big day that greeted them at 8 o'clock in the morning was bright as the gondolas started cruising along the branch canal and at a distance on the Grand Canal, a big ship had just arrived and docked.

The busy scene with people coming out of the ship and boxes being loaded from the ship to motor boats and the movement of the ship and boats resulted in small waves throughout the branches of the canal which started crashing at the buildings along the shore. There was some kind of unknown excitement in the morning air with shrieks of seagulls diving into the water as the traditional recording of Shenhai started playing in the background filling the air around the stretched-out patio. Samir had requested that hotel management play the record featuring music from this flute-like instrument with a bulbous end while the wedding rituals would be going on.

Amita and Samir, along with Rudy, arrived at the stretched-out patio where they asked Rudy to stand on a rectangular area which was specially decorated with artwork on the floor. Rudy wore a beige cotton Indian top with a round neck and loose-fit sleeves and body over dark navy-blue pants. Around him stood four banana plants in planters placed in each corner of the rectangular area. Amita, dressed in her red-bordered beige saree with a red blouse, started blowing the conch shell. Samir, in his Indian gray top and dark pants, put the turmeric paste on Rudy's face and forehead which was usually done by a family member. Then all the family members would have fun putting the paste on each other and the rest of it usually got sent to the bride's place to put on her and her family members. But here, Samir put the turmeric paste on Rudy and Amita as well.

Then Rudy and Samir went away to shower and freshen up.

Meanwhile, Urmi, dressed in her maroon saree with green blouse, was accompanied by Sharmi who was asked to stand on the same spot. The bride was wearing a yellow saree with a red border and red blouse. Amita then blew the conch shell and Urmi nicely smeared Sharmi's face with turmeric then put it on Amita who in turn put some on Urmi's face. Urmi then put small bowls made of clay on the four corners of the rectangular area where Sharmi stood and asked her to break those clay bowls with her heel. Sharmi performed this old tradition indicating that she was breaking away from her bachelorette life and on to a different, new life.

And they all had fun smearing each other with turmeric paste after which they took showers and changed their clothes. It was a long Bengali wedding tradition to brighten, clean and disinfect the body and skin. The wedding ceremony would start at 2:30 in the afternoon which would be 6:30 at night in India, a very auspicious time in the twilight of the evening. The bride also had to get dressed and, after putting on makeup, her face would be decorated with sandalwood paste. It would take at least two to three hours.

Amita and Urmi helped set up the areas of the rituals: the first area for the exchange of garlands; the second area for *Sampradan,* giving away the bride; and the third area, the firepit.

Amita and Urmi both took Sharmi to Urmi's room in the hotel and began the process of dressing up Sharmi who refused to have professional makeup artists do her makeup so Amita and Urmi tried their best to apply makeup to Sharmi's already pretty face and after doing so they styled her hair in a bun honoring the old tradition to make a frilly wreath with red and gold ribbons with the red one first then the gold one.

She already put on her red silk blouse and red cotton slip, the red Benaras saree with gold work tied nicely and pinned and secured in proper places before putting on jewelry. Urmi and Amita wanted to decorate her face with sandalwood paste. First they put a round red Bindi on her forehead then made sandalwood paste which they dipped the rounded end of the hairpin in then started drawing tiny specks of sandalwood around the Bindi and continued putting tiny specks over both eyebrows and went down to both temples and ultimately curved down to both her cheeks.

The artwork of sandalwood paste would dry in time and would look very nice. Then it was time for the jewelry: putting six gold bangles on each arm, the long gold necklace up to the middle of her chest, gold dangling earrings and lastly, a gold tiara. Then the red veil had to be tied.

"Oh," Urmi said, "we forgot to put *alta*." She was referring to a red dye usually put on with a thick swab around the side of both feet and also in between the web of the toes. Both feet had to be dry. They put some old newspaper under her feet to let it dry.

"The only thing left is the garland and the crown," Amita said. "Those will be ready before she goes for the exchange of garlands. Let us see how Rudy's doing. Samir and Uncle Sunil are both helping him dress up like a fine Bengali groom."

Amita described Rudy's outfit that consists of a special off-white silk top with a round neck and loose long-sleeves. The front of the top stayed open at the upper one-third with buttons placed there and a twelve-yard special cloth with a fine gold border. First thing was to hold at the middle portion with two hands, one on each side of the upper end, after the cloth went around the back and then brought in front, the two ends tied on the waist half its length would be pleated of which two inches of the upper portion would be tucked in the waist and hanging in front and the other half-pleated tightly would go between the upper portion of the thigh and groin to be tucked at the back. On the forehead, there will be sandalwood specks over both eyebrows but would stop just before the temple. The garland and the conical crown would be the last to put on just before the ceremony of the Exchange of Garlands.

The guests had already arrived and eagerly sat on the stretched out patio as Rudy, accompanied by Samir and two other doctor friends, came out to the patio where the priest and Uncle Sunil announced the groom's arrival.

The first part of the ceremony, the Exchange of Garlands, commenced as Sharmi's friends and family cheered the arrival of the groom while Amita and

Urmi started to blow the conch shell one for each as the priest and Uncle Sunil performed the rituals to welcome the groom and asked Rudy to stand on the area of the Exchange of Garlands.

Then Sharmi, the bride arrived, carried by four men who were the husbands and partners of Sharmi's friends from Durham University. She sat on a rectangular, polished, thick plank of wood with each of the four holding a corner of the plank. Rudy's heart throbbed immediately upon setting his eyes on his lovely bride. Sharmi remained sitting on the plank almost at lotus position her eyes covered with a *paan* leaf, a betel nut leaf. Then she was taken around the groom for seven times as the guests cheered and called out the numbers as the conch shell blew loudly. Since the ceremony was out on the patio facing the waterfront, the gondolas with people cruising along the canal cheered and waved. They were fascinated to witness a part of a ritual of an Indian wedding.

After taking her around seven times, the bride was brought at the level of the groom where they exchanged the garland for three times. Next was the "*Subho Dristi*," when usually the bride and groom look at each other as a veil was placed over them, kind of a private moment with the inner feeling of love as their eyes met and locked. *Subho Dristi* meant a combination of benignant, gracious, fortunate, prosperous and happy. And though meant to be private, some guests couldn't resist taking a quick peep anyway for fun as they thought the couple appeared to be soaking in love and affection as if they set eyes on each other for first time and could not bear to look away from each other, a warm-hearted gesture that made everyone very happy.

Next came the second phase of the ceremony, the *Sampradan*, in which the bride and groom sat separately on cushions placed on the floor facing each other. At this time, a silk shawl was placed over the groom and the priest took the stretched-out right hand of the bride and placed it on the groom's right hand. Then the hand of "*sampradata*" who was giving away the bride—in this case it was Uncle Sunil who stepped in the place of the father, joined hands and said the name of a particular Bengali month—*Jaistha*—in the period of the waxing moon and the genealogical background of the bride and groom and offered the bride to the groom who answered, "I am honored."

Then the couple received each other with mantras. The bride's mantra: "I respect you with all my mind and all my heart. May there be no barrier between us. Let us remember our divine creator."

And the groom's mantra: "I respect you similarly in the presence of all."

Then on to the third part of the ceremony where the priest at this time tied the knot between the shawl of the groom and the veil of the bride.

The Lighting of the Fire, the fourth phase, was when the priest prayed to Agni, the fire that "May Agni protect the couple."

In the fifth phase, the bride prayed: "May my husband live long and prosper."

And the groom prayed for his bride and their prosperous life together.

Then the bride followed by the groom went around the fire and the groom offered some ghee with a spoon that was like butter so that the fire kept on burning.

The sixth part of the ceremony, called the *Saptapadi,* featured Seven Steps the bride and groom would take one after another close to the fire that had already been marked on the ground. As the priest kept on reciting, the bride and groom would repeat:

Our first step: for nourishment of life

Second step: for our success

Third: for loyalty to each other

Fourth: to quest the source of bliss

Fifth: To do good for all creatures

Sixth: for prosperity

Seventh: to be sacredly illuminated

At the end of the seventh step, the bride and groom faced each other as she said, "With Seven Steps you have become my friend, may my friendship make one with you, may your friendship make one with me."

In the seventh phase, the final acceptance, the bride and groom then held each other's hands and said the following: "Happily, I hold you in marriage, I am your husband/wife. Let us grow old together happily as beloved, as friend, as guide, be with me with the grace of divine assisting, let us build together an ideal home. Let our hearts be united, let us share our sustenance, let us bind together in truth and in mutual love and joy. May we live a hundred autumns to see a hundred autumns and hear a hundred autumns."

Then the groom placed the red vermillion on the bride's parted hair in front with his ring. There was no separate ceremony for exchange of rings yet; a ring was always given to the bride from the groom's side and a ring for the groom from the bride's side.

After the vermillion ritual, everyone cheered and congratulated the bride and groom.

Then came the blessing by the priest: "May you succeed in your pursuit of Dharma—duty, virtue, morality, spirituality and referring to the power which upholds the universe and society; *Artha*—prosperity and *Kama*—love, desire and pleasure personified, cosmic desire or creative impulse and called the firstborn of primeval chaos that makes the creation possible."

Then the bride and groom said, "We will."

And the priest said, "May the fruits of this sacred wedding be blessed with the grace of God. It is only through the fullness of ourselves can we seek fulfillment."

OM SHANTI…OM SHANTI…OM SHANTI…

Everyone then cheered as two conch shells simultaneously started to blow, one by Amita and one by Urmi, first together then one after another.

The gondolas on the canal stopped for a while so that the passengers could see the wedding and they cheered along with the wedding guests.

Then two gondoliers started singing their song *"Barcarolle"* in a six-eight rhythm as the sun on the west emitted soft, orange rays flooding the canal, flowing merrily, simmering in gold.

The bride and groom bathed with the soft hues of the sun's rays and the couple looked glorious, mesmerized as they held hands and together looked at the distant golden horizon, like two figures in a painted landscape in Venice, frozen in time forever just when the recording of Shenhai, the Indian flute-like instrument music performed by the renowned musician Bismillah, played in tune with the cheers of the guests and friends.

Samir approached Rudy. "Congratulations, my friend. The gondolas are here for us to take a cruise along the canal. They are all ready to welcome us on board."

After being in a dreamlike state, Rudy snapped back to the present. "Thank you. We will be there within half an hour."

Amita approached them and hugged Sharmi. "We will now have our snack. Sharmi has to eat a little something though she is fasting and also all the gondoliers should be offered some snack as that is our Indian custom."

Rudy squeezed his new wife, Sharmi's hand as they gazed into each other's eyes. Now that the ceremony was officially done, their life of celebration was just beginning.

Maya Mitra Das

A Gondola Wedding in Venice

For Rudy and Sharmi, the bind that would forever be marked in their hearts as the day they made their union official began with the magic of Venice.

The six gondolas ready to pick up riders from the St. Regis all had colorful silk cushions decorated with flowers. The head gondolier was tasked to lead all the gondolas: the first one for newlyweds had a sofa for two, like a loveseat. It was smaller than an ordinary sofa and the cushion was bright maroon silk designed with silver-colored flowers. There were red cushioned seats with back rests for another four people including the marriage registrar.

There were floral decorations with white and pink roses intertwined with greenery. The wreaths ran along the length of the gondola on both sides with a bouquet on each side of the tapering end with pink and white roses.

The one for the newlyweds was decorated as all the others but additionally had a floral wreath that wrapped all around the loveseat and two tubular golden-colored metallic bases on either side of the loveseat with red roses. The lead gondola carrying the bride and groom would cruise in front. Behind them, the two lead gondolas carrying guests would cruise along at the same speed together. Behind these, two more would be cruising the same as the other two. And the last one with the musicians, carrying a cello, violin, lute and two vocalists rounded out the procession.

The guests from Durham University, Sharmi's circle of friends, would play individually and serenade the couple together. The serenade featured instrumental as well as vocal performances given outdoors as a grand romantic gesture to woo a woman with a meaningful song.

The gondoliers were dressed in a pair of black pants, black and white striped top, a wide-brimmed straw hat and a bright red sash tied around their waists holding their single instrument—the oar in their hands.

The wedding event proceeded as seamlessly and as magically as a movie reel: After the Hindu wedding rituals were over Sharmi, the bride, changed her attire, a sea green Benares saree with silver borders and a silver floral design all over the material with a matching blouse. She adorned teardrop pearl earrings, a three-strings pearl necklace, a light blue see-through veil draped down covering the middle of her head beyond the shoulder, a flower crown with white tube roses, two or three parallel lines of stringed flowers went around from the front of her forehead tied at the back of her head with strings attached to it at both ends. The front featured an arrangement made with a stringed flower which looked like a triangle. On the apex of the triangle, a tiny red rose was placed to make it prettier.

Urmi, the bride's sister, dressed in a thick, sky-blue silk saree with a round-neck blue blouse. The saree had a silver border and silver work all over the material. Her black wavy hair was arranged in a bun and a pink rose was placed on the right side of the bun. She was further adorned with shiny silver jewelry, earrings that looked like dangling small intricate mesh bells hanging from a stem with tiny balls hanging at the end.

The silver necklace was two inches broad with an intricate design resting around her neck, two silver bracelets, one on each wrist, and a red maroon Bindi on her forehead. Amita wore her fuchsia Banares saree with gold design. She was further adorned with round, gold pearl-set earrings, her long, three-stringed pearl necklace dangled below her chest with a pendant designed with ruby and pearl.

Rudy, the groom, was dressed in a western outfit of black trousers and white shirt with ruffles and a red tie with black jacket. Samir was also in a dark, navy-blue western outfit with navy-blue trousers, a white shirt and navy-blue jacket with a striped blue tie. They were in the lead gondola.

The marriage registrar boarded the lead gondola. The gondolier asked everyone to settle down.

"First, the registrar should get ready and ask the couple to take their vows," the gondolier said. "I will ask all the other gondolas to slowly circle us so that the gondola with the bride and groom will be in the center while the ceremony is going on."

The marriage registrar conducted the marriage with vows and issued the legal certificate of marriage to the bride and groom. The other five gondolas kept on circling the central gondola with the bride and groom. The gondolier kept the gondola with the bride and groom sailing in a slow motion while the other gondolas kept circling. Everyone cheered from all gondolas as a few small bouquets of roses were tossed to the bride and groom's gondola. Urmi and Amita blew the conch shell and the sound traveled far away and dispersed all around and ended up with the crashing noise of the water on both banks.

At the lead gondolier's command, other gondolas changed their formation. Two gondolas followed the lead gondola followed by the other two behind and then the last one featuring the musicians that followed them.

Then the lead gondolier started the serenade, "*O Sole Mio*"

Che bella cosa na jurnata 'e sole,

N'aria serena doppo na tempesta!

Pe'll'aria fresca pare gia na festa...

Che bella cos ana jurnata 'e sole.

* * *

Ma n'atu sole cchiu bello, oi ne',

'o sole mio sta nfronte a te!

'o sole, 'o sole mio

Sta nfronte a te, sta nfronte a te!

* * *

What a wonderful thing, a sunny day

The serene air after thunderstorm

The fresh air, and a party is already going

What a wonderful thing

A sunny day

He stopped and two other gondoliers followed with their gondolas started singing:

But another sun, even more beauteous, oh my sweetheart,

My own sun, shines from your face!

This sun, my own sun,

Shines from your face, it shines from your face!

Two gondolas which followed these two refrained the stanza. The last gondola which was following the last pair of gondolas had two vocalists. One of them started singing accompanied by a cellist:

When night comes and Sun

Has gone down

I start feeling blue

I'd stay below your window

When night comes and the sun has gone down

The other vocalist, accompanied by violin, sang:

But another Sun

That brighter still

It's my own sun

That's your face

The sun, my own sun

It is your face

It is in your face.

The people in all six gondolas seemed to be drunk with music. A few of them started humming the tune while others held each other swaying sideways. The gondolas which were not in the group but passing by filled with tourists would join the celebration and cheer as the gondoliers passing by would catch a few familiar lines and join the singers for a few minutes as the people would hum and sway with the rhythm of cheers.

The bride and groom after some time got closer and closer together and the guests were happy to see Sharmi's face and upper body closely ensconced on Rudy's chest.

Then the vocalists took a break when the musicians playing the violin, cello and lute started Shubert's serenade from the Swan Song wedding quartet as time passed by like in a dream. Everyone came back to the present when the gondolas started to turn and announce that it was almost time to return to St. Regis where they began.

The sun went down on the west horizon which was curved almost touching the waters of the grand and branch canals that started simmering like liquid gold.

The city of Venice bathed in gold floated on green water when the seagulls shrieked to their last dip for fish in the water. The wedding group of six gondolas in their formation were serenaded by the violin and lute on their way back to St. Regis.

* * *

For the wedding reception, the dining hall of St. Regis highlighted the pink washed walls, the high ceiling hall decorated with wreaths made with pink and white roses with greenery placed on the wall at intervals. The tulip-shaped wall lights were all lit up and two large, gold trimmed chandeliers hung from the ceiling on each side on the top of the large, decorated dining table.

Tall thick candles were placed on golden stands at different corners of the room. The table was covered with a white tablecloth, gold-colored cutlery and pink napkins placed with gold-bordered white dining plates. On either side of the table, two high transparent vases were placed with pink and white roses with greenery, for the bride and groom. Two gold-framed cushioned chairs with red brocade work with handles were placed at the head end of the broad table. The guest chairs were gold with maroon silk cushions.

The guests of the bride and groom entered the dining hall when the music of "Four Seasons" by Vivaldi began playing in the background. As the bride and groom entered the hall, everyone cheered. Sharmi looked like a dressed-up doll walking gracefully close to Rudy who stood nearly six-feet-tall. They took their designated seats as the guests began slowly taking their seats designated by guests' name tags as two hotel staff members assisted the guests in finding their seats.

The dinner started with a glass of Bellini and a non-alcoholic rose cocktail as red and white wines were kept aside to be served with dinner. Appetizers were served soon after the drinks and included: canapés with feta, scallops with zucchini cream, and shrimp with mango. Red and white wines were offered when the main entrée was served.

By now, the background music had started featuring Beethoven's "Moonlight Sonata," as the guests started to cheer and the champagne was poured in individual champagne flutes.

The cheering crowd beckoned some gesture from the groom—preferably a kiss—to show emotion publicly which was almost unheard of and unseen in the Bengali culture. It was really an amazing scene to see both the bride and groom shyly looking at each other and blushing, almost unsure of what to do next to meet the demands of their cheering guests. Finally, Rudy took the plunge bravely, and with the presence of mind, drew closer to Sharmi and gave her a hug and a quick peck on the cheek which seemed to satisfy the guests who returned to concentrate on their dining.

The dinner entrées started coming one after another starting with salmon and tuna steak; shrimp and artichoke salad; duck leg in raspberry sauce with pilaf rice; beef fillet with amarone sauce and vegetables.

Then the guests noticed one of the doctor friends of Rudy from Newcastle-upon-Tyne raise his glass, wanting to toast the newlyweds. The champagne had already been poured in the flutes when the friend said:

"The time has come to toast two people as they embark on their life together. So here's to the lovely bride and here's to the groom, here's to the marriage in full bloom. Here's to a long, happy life for a brand new, grand new husband and wife!"

Everyone cheered and raised their glasses. "Cheers!"

The dinner followed with typical cheeses, a selection of mixed fresh fruits like papayas, kiwi, pineapples and bananas. The wedding dinner ended with a glass of lemon sorbet which was ideal before eating the wedding cake.

Millefoglie, the traditional Italian wedding cake, translated as "a thousand layers," with cream and berries arrived on the scene as the experts appeared pushing the wheeled cart and set the cake right in front of the bride and groom and the guests.

Then the music started for the first dance:

"Love me tender, love me
Sweet, never let me go
You have made my life complete
And I love you so…

Rudy could not wait any longer as he gracefully glided on the dance floor holding Sharmi closely to him, moving and swaying with the music carrying her to his land of fantasy.

The guests hummed the tune as they sat watching the newlyweds, the wave of the humming tune vibrated wall to wall and high up the ceiling creating ethereal waves of sounds that kept on moving for a while.

The guests were more than excited to get on the dance floor when Dean Martin's tune started playing:

Don't you know that I care for you?

Send me the pillow that you dream

So darling, I can dream on it too...

Gentle expressive sounds emitted from guests as couples glided and swayed, holding each other, closely dreaming in their own fantasy lands. More favorite and popular songs kept on playing as guests would dance and then take rests in between songs.

Then finally the wedding cake was served after Sharmi and Rudy, holding on to the knife together, jointly sliced the cake.

Then the dance floor came alive again with swinging and swaying couples and popular songs. As Rudy watched the happy faces at their wedding, he recalled recently reading about the wedding of Niccolò's nephew, Amadeo whose wedding also took place during summer time five centuries ago. *Yet another way I am connected to Niccolò*, Rudy thought.

As the hours passed, the lights dimmed further as moments became dreamier when the Beatles song "Yesterday" started playing. Urmi and Amita got up and escorted Rudy and Sharmi to their wedding suite at the St. Regis where the room was facing the waterfront. Through the glass window, the sky studded with stars was seen through a patchy white cloud as the moon peeped through and the soft light beamed through a window into the room.

The wall of the room was decorated with flowers and petals of red roses covered a snow white bed with big pillows. Two bed lights on either side were dim and Amita and Urmi said "Good Night" with a smile.

Later, the two bed lights grew dimmer as Rudy pulled Sharmi closer as they snuggled on the soft bed while the waves of the canals crashed and played their serenade in the moonlight.

Niccolo's Surprise Invitation to the Palace

30th of July, 1428—Niccolò and Paolo examined the bronze-casted David closely, the result of both their efforts chasing this sculpture since September 1426. Twice a week when Niccolò would come from Michelozzo's studio where he worked with him on a funerary monument, he would devote time to David as he and Paolo continued each stage it took to make David come alive.

Paolo was ready to continue the chasing process on David when he heard Niccolò's voice. "I want to go over the sculpted figure before we start to chase the sculpture again. Paolo, do you want to know why?"

"Yes, Maestro."

"Because David is the first free-standing nude male so far in history. He is just a young boy. I wonder, how did he become brave enough to encounter the mighty Goliath? So I want to make sure, when you look at him, it will give you the impression I am talking about."

"I understand, Maestro. But the sword on his right hand is too big. I wonder Maestro, why do you want the sword in his hand?"

"Paolo, I want you and everyone to understand that David killed Goliath, not by his own strength, but by the grace of God."

"Maestro, I understand what you are talking about. Which part of the body are you going to start chasing at present?"

"I will leave the face for later. We will start the two hands. Another thing, Paolo, I think the project with Michelozzo will finish before the end of this year. We're hoping to be done before November."

"Oh, Maestro, that will be very nice."

"Paolo, just to remind you about the chasing process—we have to work on the front of the metal surface by hammering with various tools that raise, depress, punch or push without removal of surplus metal from the objects after chasing. In other words, it is a technique used to define or refine the forms of a surface design."

"Maestro, I understand now."

Hours passed before the church bell tower struck one—time to remind them that it was lunch time.

"Let us have our break," Niccolò said.

Paolo's eyes brightened. "I brought some salad, vegetables cooked in tomato basil sauce and rice."

"Sounds delicious for a summer afternoon," Niccolò commented.

While enjoying the delicious meal, Niccolò updated Paolo on project-works-in-progress.

"Paolo, I heard the construction of the new palace has already started so it will most likely be done between 1432 to 1433."

"That is nice David will be exhibited in their courtyard!" Paolo said excitedly. "I wonder where exactly? I hope it is in a covered place."

"After we finish, I want to show my mother the finished sculpture so I plan to bring her to our studio so she can see it," Niccolò said.

"That is very good idea," Paolo said. "She will be very happy."

Niccolò grew silent, pensive. "You know, Paolo I am worried. She is becoming frail."

"I understand your worries about her." And then, because he could not think of anything else to say, Paolo simply patted Niccolò gently on the shoulder and decided to change the subject. "Maestro, someone from the Medici Palace came looking for you and I told them that you will be at your studio today. He said he will be back."

Niccolò snapped out of his gloominess. "Paolo, I hear horses clip-clapping. That could be him."

Paolo looked out the window. "You are right. I see a person getting down from the carriage now."

The messenger from the Medici Palace approached and handed a message from Lady Contessina, Cosimo's wife, to Niccolò who opened the message.

He could not say anything for few minutes after reading the note. His face was flushed and eyes focused at a distance.

"Lady Contessina has requested you to accept the invitation as little Matteo would like to meet you soon."

Paolo looked very confused so he turned to his Maestro for clarification and an explanation.

After a while, Niccolò took a deep breath. "I will accept the invitation from Lady Contessina whenever she wishes me to visit them."

"I will relay your reply to her ladyship and will inform you as to the meeting day and time. Thank you, Maestro."

When the messenger left, Paolo silently observed his Maestro.

Niccolò sat down for few minutes lost in thought, his mind traveling back as he heard voices, echoes from the past. Finally, he returned to the present. "Paolo, Lady Contessina is inviting me to the palace to meet Matteo, the six-year-old son of Beatrice. Apparently, Beatrice and Matteo will be visiting sometime in October. I have been informed that Matteo had seen the marble sculpture of his mother and liked it so much that he wants to meet the person who sculpted it."

"Maestro, that is so wonderful. Even though I have not yet met him, I really like this little boy. He is inquisitive and has a special talent to be able to admire an artistic creation."

"Yes, Paolo, the boy seems very special." Niccolò paused and sighed. "For me, the chapter with Beatrice is closed. She is accomplished where she belongs and I belong to my world—to my art. There is no common ground between these two worlds. They both rotate in their own axis and go around in their own path destined for them."

Paolo nodded sympathetically. "Maestro, I do understand your feelings."

And the two of them took a few moments to ponder the future.

* * *

Days seemed to pass very quickly to Niccolò who kept balancing working with Michelozzo and his visits twice a week to work with Paolo at the studio.

Then all of a sudden, it was the 20th of September, 1428. *Where did the time go?* Niccolò thought as he arrived early that afternoon at his studio very happy to announce that he had already completed his task with Michelozzo—at least for now as he might have to go back to help his friend put some finer touch and cleaning if need be.

Paolo, who was in the middle of putting some finer touches and cleaning, was relieved to see him. "Maestro, if you wish to rest for a few days, you can. I will take care of things here, preparing and arranging everything and we can continue again with whatever is left to be done."

"We will start again in the morning and work on David starting two days from now," Niccolò said.

Paolo nodded. "I am so pleased to see you back in the studio."

Fall already started painting the leaves orange and brown. The air was cool and the sunrays were softer as the sun was a late riser and usually went down early in the afternoon on the west.

To avail of the sunlight, Niccolò and Paolo arrived early and started their work of chasing David and then left the studio as early as 4 o'clock in the afternoon.

As usual, working diligently made time fly so swiftly that all of sudden, Niccolò and Paolo found themselves on a cool morning in the middle of October in 1428. When Paolo arrived at the studio, he was surprised to find a note from his Maestro telling him to carry on without him and continue working on David's torso and that his Maestro would join him sometime in the afternoon.

Paolo frowned. He could not think of any reason or remember any conversation with his Maestro indicating he would be late especially since Niccolò had always been a meticulous planner. So Paolo continued to work as his Maestro instructed him to do but had to stop at some point to examine the sculpture. He was amazed that quite a lot had been done except some finer details on his hat, portions of his face and Goliath's head.

When Paolo took his lunch break, he could not help but feel a bit sad. Even though he had grown accustomed to working alone on the days Niccolò had been working with his friend, on this particular day, it felt as though a dark cloud had hovered over their studio. So after lunch, Paolo busied himself with work again, diligently chasing the area of the sculpture as he was tasked to do until the church bell chimed three times. He was about to continue working just when Niccolò showed up at the door.

"Maestro, I am glad to see you!"

Niccolò's expression was serious. "Let us sit down and I will let you know what happened."

"First of all, Maestro, have you eaten anything for your lunch?"

"Yes, the palace staff fed me," Niccolò quickly said. "Paolo, I was at the Medici Palace at the invitation of Cosimo's wife, Contessina, as you know, to meet Beatrice and her young son, Matteo." He sighed. "Beatrice looked the same yet more of a mother figure and affectionate in a motherly manner. Lady Contessina was, as usual, very graceful and accommodating. They were all trying to tend to me with lots of care, affection and respect. Beatrice's boy, Matteo, was adorable with big, sparkling dark eyes. He had a dimple on his right cheek. He was dressed in maroon breeches, beige stockings, a beige shirt and a red vest. He greeted me with a smile and shook my hand like a little gentleman. I was so amazed to see him so spontaneous and charming. Matteo had asked me about sculpting so I tried to explain to him the process as much as I could. I showed him how sketching is important before a figure is to be sculpted. So I sketched his outline and asked their attendant to bring me a slab of stone then put the sketched paper on the stone and traced it, then chiseled it out from that stone. He was very attentive and his big eyes sparkled and grew wider with wonder."

Niccolò took a few seconds to catch his breath. "Beatrice is going to supervise the library in Florence which Cosimo is very interested in building so she will be visiting Florence two to three times a year. She had married a man who came from a military family and settled in Certaldo, one of the metropolitan cities of Florence which is around 48.4km from the city of Florence and the birthplace of Giovanni Boccaccio, a famous writer born in 1313, author of The Decameron and a great humanist."

He paused to collect his thoughts. "Paolo, did you know that Certaldo was inhabited by the Etruscans? The remains of their temple and inscriptions are still there, then it became a Roman colony from the 12th century and was under the control of Alberti counts from Prato and by the end of the 12th century, Alberti counts were forced to accept the rule of Florence."

"Maestro, I am so glad you gave me some background of this place Certaldo which has a historical background and I am happy to hear about your visit with Matteo who sounds like a bright and adorable boy. It is really very admirable for Lady Beatrice to take on the responsibility of the new library. And I am so relieved you have joined me for work. So what is your plan for whatever time is left for today?"

"We will continue the chasing work on David. If we only have a few hours to work on it today and maybe even finish it, we can take time to add the finer touch and at the end, polish it."

"That sounds like a good plan," Paolo said.

The next morning, Niccolò was feeling good after visiting Beatrice and her little Matteo the day before. Niccolò spent this time searching from deep inside him for an answer as to why he was imbued with this sense of calm and satisfaction that filled his heart after such a long time. Prior to reuniting with Beatrice, he had been nervous about seeing her again after all these years of wondering how she was doing in her new life. And now, seeing her fulfilled in her role as a mother and patroness of the arts had given Niccolò some much needed closure to move on.

"While she is married now with a child, she is still beautiful," he mused to himself. "I believe the intense attraction between us and the feelings shared between the younger versions of ourselves has evolved into some deeper emotion and respect, a more mature feeling of love and affection that has transcended to a level beyond this daily life and is suspended to this higher level where there is no decay and distortion." He took a deep breath and released a long exhalation. "I feel safe and nourished," he affirmed.

* * *

On his way to the studio, Niccolò contemplated about how time had flown so fast and that time waits for no one. Whether one is prepared or not, certain matters occur beyond one's control. He maintained this thought as he headed toward the studio, processing his day with his usual musings to himself.

"How can it already be the 18th of December 1428?" he voiced aloud. "Just a few more days of work and then a break for Christmas and the New Year. Paolo was not willing to take a carriage ride from his home to the studio but still agreed to a ride back home at the end of a work day with me. It is all right if it makes him happy. I am going to make a work plan for the rest of the days before the Christmas break and talk to Paolo."

The carriage arrived at the studio and Paolo came out by the entrance to welcome Niccolò who got down from the carriage. After an exchange of greetings, Niccolò beckoned to Paolo.

"Let us sit down and make a plan. We are going to take a break during Christmas as my mother wants to go to Castellina to visit my sister, Tia on the 21st of December. She wants me to arrive at Castellina on the 23rd so there is only four days left." Niccolò examined their work-in-progress. "Paolo, what do you think? Where should we concentrate next on the sculpture?"

"I think it is a good idea to continue the chasing work on David's sculpture. It looks like we can finish it in about three to four months so by the New Year. Maestro, can you believe that it will soon be 1429? Then if we can finish the chasing, we can polish it and then finally bring mother Orissa to visit David in our studio."

"Excellent idea! You have grown to be an amazing sculptor, Paolo, and I am grateful to you for remembering how much my mother wants to see David."

* * *

Time flew as fast as a bird flying south in winter and soon the dawn of a spring morning in 1429 swiftly greeted Niccolò and Paolo at their studio as they continued working on David.

The chasing process seemed to be taking longer than expected. Niccolò was very careful not to compromise any part of bronze David the way he envisioned him.

"Maestro." Paolo's voice snapped Niccolò from his thoughts. "I am glad we are still working on the chasing of David."

The creases on Niccolò's forehead deepened in wonder. "Why do you say that?"

"Well, since we are taking our time to finish chasing, then polishing David will not take very long so then, as we had planned, we can have mother Orissa visit our studio this year. The weather has been so unpredictable and harsh. The wintery weather still persists with so much rain off and on. It would be too cold for mother Orissa to visit David at our studio."

"Paolo, you are so thoughtful and you are absolutely right. You know she is not so strong anymore and seems to be getting more frail. I doubt how long she will live." Niccolò paused to breathe more deeply. "I have asked a physician to visit her regularly with his assistant apothecary. The physician is very good but he told me that, according to his assessment, she will live a maximum of two years, even that is also doubtful depending on how she will be this coming winter." Niccolò paused, shaking his head. "I do not want to think about it but that is the reality. My sister, Tia will be visiting often and that is comforting for both my mother and myself. I want to continue working in Firenze as I do not want to leave the city. I want to stay close to my mother."

"I completely understand," Paolo said solemnly. "And I am here for you if ever you need me for anything."

Niccolò acknowledged Paolo with a grateful nod and the chasing of David kept on going and going until the days gradually grew warmer and the air was filled with the chirping sound of birds and the once nude trees were now all dressed in their shiny green leaves as patches of daffodils and tulips moved gently with the breeze.

Niccolò and Paolo diligently continued concentrating very seriously on the painstaking and time-consuming chasing process that they almost lost track of the days that turned into months.

By the end of July, they finally finished the work of chasing then took a few days to clean and closely examine the sculpture to see whether anything else needed to be added.

It was a bright morning in the middle of August when Niccolò and Paolo began polishing David. They were determined to polish the sculpture before bringing mother Orissa to the studio to see the finished sculpture of the bronze David.

"After the initial polishing and cleaning, I will hire a carriage to bring mother Orissa to see the bronze sculpture. I know someone named Romero who will drive the carriage very slowly and make the seat comfortable with pillows so that my mother can lie down with her chest and the upper portion of her body propped up and then carry her from the carriage to inside the studio with a reclining padded sofa. Paolo, she has difficulty breathing when she lays down flat."

"I am so glad you have made a special arrangement for her."

"I asked Tia to accompany her to the studio so my sister is arriving two days from now."

They both kept working on bronze David and decided to clean and polish it as much as they could. The motivation to finally finish the project weighed heavily on Niccolò so that he could bring his beloved mother to the studio by the end of August since in September the weather may change. It would be the beginning of the fall season so he decided on a date for the visit—the 28th of August.

Paolo concentrated on arranging the studio so that it would look a little tidy and clean and managed to put the sculpture of David close to a window where the sunlight usually bathed that corner of the studio. A welcome banner Paolo made and painted orange and green hung at the entrance of the studio.

Niccolò was very happy to see Paolo's efforts to make the visit very special. On the 28th day of August, mother Orissa and sister Tia rode in a carriage driven by Romero and along the way, familiar faces waved as Luigi's son Ludvico came out of the bakery and handed over a bunch of freshly-baked bread and vegetable vendors came running alongside the carriage to hand over a basket of different fresh vegetables. Mother Orissa was very happy to receive these acts of kindness and warm feelings from those they encountered.

And when she arrived at the studio and saw the welcome banner at the entrance, she was absolutely overcome with joy. Paolo and Niccolò stood at the entrance of the studio as the carriage driver and his assistant carried mother Orissa in a chair and brought her inside the studio accompanied by Tia as both mother and daughter were overcome with emotion to see the sculpture of David. Niccolò's mother shed tears of joy and kept on saying, "God Bless both of you!"

"Without God's grace, this unique creation would not be possible dear brother," Tia commented. "Niccolò and Paolo, you have made us very proud. Firenze is proud of you."

The joyous moments were treasured in memories as a blast of cool air blew through the window and a flock of birds chirped on the branch of a birch tree and the boatload of people cheered with usual joy passing along the river Arno.

All too soon, Niccolò's mother and sister announced it was time to return home. Mother Orissa kissed her only beloved son on his forehead and handed over a box of homemade food for lunch. Niccolò's face lit up in satisfaction that everything he planned worked very well and the carriage slowly but surely became smaller and smaller and ultimately disappeared, leaving behind an echo of clip-clapping horses that lingered for some time before fading away. Niccolò was left standing at the entrance all this time even when the sight and sound of the carriage faded away until he finally sat down for a while in silence.

"Mother is going to fade away soon," Niccolò said solemnly, finding his voice.

Paolo's expression grew sullen. "I understand your anxiety and feelings but let us remember and keep this image of her in our hearts: that your mother was so happy and proud she had a chance to see the sculpture. And she gazed at it for a while as if she could not take her eyes away from the bronze David. All this unseen energy will live forever with the sculpture, Maestro."

"Paolo, you are very thoughtful and wise. Your words are a comfort to me, thank you."

Days and months passed as Niccolò and Paolo continued the work on David's sculpture giving it the finer touch wherever and whenever needed and refined and polished the sculpture meticulously. They estimated it would be approximately around March or April 1430 that Niccolò would inform the palace that the sculpture is finally complete.

And by spring 1430, indeed the sculpture of David was deemed officially finished and Niccolò happily informed the palace officials who sent a message back that Cosimo de' Medici was extremely pleased and would be making arrangements soon to transport the sculpture to the newly-built courtyard. Though some sections of the palace were still under construction, the courtyard where David's sculpture would be placed was complete.

And so, after some time, the day Niccolò had been dreading had finally come on the early morning of the 23rd of April 1430. At the cottage, Niccolò and sister Tia sat by the bedside of their beloved Mamma who had not been feeling well for the past few days. She was propped up due to difficulty in breathing. Last night was so rough that a physician came in the evening with his apothecary and tried different medications.

But mother Orissa's breathing issues worsened that the physician advised to prop her upper body with pillows and gave her some mixture to drink to calm her down as she was agitated, moving her hands and legs as if she wanted to get out of bed. Tia slowly gave her mother medicine drop by drop so that she would not choke.

After a while nothing more could be done—her heart was failing.

Niccolò and Tia each held their mother's hands one on each side as they spoke softly to her, helplessly asking if there was anything they could do. Mother Orissa could only respond by nodding her head as she tried several times to say something to her children but could not.

Finally, Mother Orissa became calm after Tia gave her medication, her breathing became slower, and she started to fade away. Yet, she tried hard to keep her eyes open to gaze lovingly and longingly at Niccolò and Tia for the last time as the light of her eyes grew dimmer even as she willed her weary eyes to stay open. Then her breathing became staggered, at intervals, then there was a pause before starting again, a few more, until the pauses in between breaths became wider and wider and then with one last jolt of breath before a long sigh, her whole body finally settled peacefully on this spring morning. The silence and stillness that followed lasted for a long while until a blast of cold breeze through the window and the chirping of the birds on the branches of her blossoming apple tree resumed and relaxed as the woman who had once tended her vegetable garden and fed the birds wore a blissful expression on her face so radiant that her whole being settled softly in eternal peace.

Rudy Feels Connection to Niccolo in Florence

Hotel St. Regis, Venice, 8ᵗʰ June 1965—Tables for breakfast at the balcony close to the waterfront were ready for people to take their seats for their first sustenance of the day. The morning glow of the sun brushed the small ripples of the Grand Canal that were happily dancing towards the shore. The Eastern sky imbued an orange red through a few fluffy, white clouds. The sun tried to look down below at a distance as a ship at the harbor blew its horn and the seagulls were busy diving down in the water, their shrill shrieking filling the air.

Rudy, Sharmi and Urmi took a table close to the water. Watching the ripples of the water while intermittently stealing glances at his new bride, Rudy felt so refreshed and brand new on these first mornings as a newly-married man.

"Amita and Samir are late." As soon as Urmi finished the sentence, Amita and Samir arrived and said, "Good morning."

They took their seats as the attendant approached them for their breakfast orders. Friends and family from India and England who attended the wedding left, one by one, on the 7ᵗʰ of June. Urmi stayed in Venice and Amita and Samir extended their vacation for another four days as they all wanted to visit the city of Florence. All five of them decided to take a train ride from Venice to Florence. Then after a four-day tour of Florence, Urmi would fly back to India from Florence and Amita and Samir would fly back home to Newcastle.

Rudy and Sharmi planned to take a train back to Venice and stay at the St. Regis Hotel before flying back to Newcastle on the 19ᵗʰ of June.

But since today was only June 8ᵗʰ, everyone aimed to focus on the present and all the beautiful sights they were excited to see. After breakfast, they took a cab to the train station where they boarded the train just in time. Soon the train started chugging along through the beautiful landscape with rolling hills and green valleys and within a few hours, the train reached the city of Florence. Upon their arrival, they took a taxi to their hotel at Machiavelli Palace in the historic city center of Florence. They were thrilled to have a spectacular view of the Duomo from their hotel rooms. As he stood by the window, viewing the Duomo, Rudy couldn't help but feel connected to Niccolò Bardi, his mentor who transcended time, for this was the famous sculptor's home.

On this summer afternoon in Florence, the sun shone gloriously over the red cupola of the Duomo as Rudy's group of five ventured with vigor to explore and enjoy the Duomo with their guide, Tomasso. Rudy was so eager to retrace the steps of Niccolò Bardi and imagine what life must have been like during his time.

"The Duomo is also called 'The Basilica Santa Maria del Flore,'" Tomasso said. "'Duomo' is the Italian word for 'church.' All cathedrals including the Duomo of Florence were designed with four perpendicular arms. The entire building has the shape of a cross symbolizing the crucifix: a long arm west to east called a nave and a short arm from north to south transept, the area where the nave and transept meet is called the crossing. The outside of the building is covered by a geometric pattern of marble blocks. The Duomo of Florence was meant to emphasize the size.

"The inside area of the crossing is about 140 feet," Tomasso continued. "You all have to stand and feel the extreme spaciousness of the place. The entire cathedral is incredible. The dome is called a cupola. In 1417, it was commissioned to Brunelleschi and Lorenzo Ghilberti who left the commission for other works on the Duomo. Brunelleschi got the inspiration from the Pantheon of Rome and took up the monumental task."

The five of them gathered closer and gazed up.

"Oh, I feel dizzy," Urmi said.

Amita and Sharmi commented that they felt both lost and humbled by the experience of being near the Duomo while Samir and Rudy agreed.

"It is incredible," Samir said.

"Unless you are here, one cannot feel the spaciousness of the Duomo," said Rudy in awe, thinking about how lucky Niccolò was to have lived amid such splendor.

"Thank you all for your comments," Tomasso said. "The area of the dome had to cover a 140-ft. crossing that was so long no one knew how to build it thinking the heavy dome would not be safe, that it would collapse. But with a lot of calculations, Brunelleschi decided to build with slight points rather than smooth the round top—a diagonal arch or rib across a gothic vault. The dome was made up of two ogivali—an equilateral arch whose radius is same as the width—shaped cups connected with each other without any support. Inside, Brunelleschi invented a double shell system where the smaller version with less weight of the dome held inside the outside shell."

Silently to himself, Rudy marveled at the genius of Brunelleschi who Rudy had read was one of the early mentors and influences of Niccolò.

"Allow me to go back in time to a little history," Tomasso said.

He explained it was designed by Arnoilfo De Cambio at the end of the 13th century on the foundation of church Santa Reparata and finished in the 15th century around 1436. The church was dedicated to Santa Maria Del Flore in reference to a "Lily," the symbol of the city.

"The statue of each architect can be seen outside to the right of the cathedral, both admiring their work for eternity," Tomasso continued. "The church was consecrated as soon as the dome was in place. The façade was only half finished then. The exterior is covered in a decorative mix of pink, white and green marble."

Tomasso scanned the group of tourists. "Okay, everyone, the clock you see above the entrance inside the church was designed by Paolo Vecello in 1443 in accordance with 'Ora Italica' where 24 hours of the day ends at sunset."

"Oh look, it is still alive, showing the time," Samir said.

"Now friends, I must tell you about the biggest artwork within the cathedral which is Giorgio Vasari's fresco of 'The Last Judgment,'" Tomasso said. It was designed by Vasari but painted by his student. You all should pay close attention to three pieces of the fresco, one of them Dante, before the city of Florence." He waved to the group. "Well, friends, it's time to say goodbye to you all. Have a wonderful time in Firenze."

Samir, Amita, Urmi, Sharmi and Rudy said, "Thank you and goodbye."

Checking their watches and seeing it was fifteen minutes before seven in the evening, the tired and hungry group wanted to go back to Hotel Machiavelli for dinner.

As the sun set on the west, a soft glow of the sun brushed the Duomo softly in orange and the sky was also painted with orange as a cool breeze blew through the pointed pine trees. The five friends headed to the rooftop restaurant where they were welcomed by the maître d' who showed their their seats.

They all ordered bruschetta and Chianti wine except Sharmi who ordered lemonade. Then they ordered lasagna and for the second course, a rack of lamb and artichoke for Samir and Rudy. Amita ordered veal while Sharmi and Urmi ordered a seafood combo, a plate of vegetables and a salad that came with it.

The five friends enjoyed course after course of their dinner that was complemented by the view of the city from the rooftop. Even though the sun had set, a reddish orange light still flooded the Duomo which looked magnificent as a blast of evening breeze blew through the lemon container plants around them, emitting a fresh lemony smell that wafted through the air.

Rudy was excited to share his passion for Italian art and culture with his friends, especially with his new wife, Sharmi, whose face still imbued her bridal glow. "I'm excited for you all to meet my friend, Flavio, who has a degree in renaissance art and sculpture and works at the Bargello National Museum. He is very kind enough to meet us at our hotel lobby at 10 tomorrow morning. Then, he's generously offered to be our guide to Uffizi, Bargello, and the Accademia Gallery so we are going to spend the next two days touring with him."

"That's so wonderful," Sharmi gushed, clasping her hands.

The five friends enjoyed their dinner, excited about the next two days of being treated to a very fulfilling art tour with none other than Rudy's friend as their guide.

The sunlight slowly merged in the twilight of the night as the evening illumination cast a glow on the city accompanied by a refreshing cool breeze. When the waiter came to inquire about, *dolce*, their dessert, Amita immediately asked for the tiramisu and so did Urmi while the rest wanted gelato and pannacotta to be shared from one serving.

The evening sky spread its veil with a dome of studded stars over the city of Florence whose lights sparkled at less crowded roads when the noise of the traffic started tapering off and the city was preparing for its slumber. Rudy's group of five slowly walked toward their rooms to retire for the evening.

* * *

9th of June 1965—When Rudy, Sharmi and their friends woke up on this summer morning, the sun was not warm yet the city of Firenze stirred slowly from its slumber and soon became bustling with activity. As soon as Rudy and friends finished their breakfast, they sauntered over to the lobby to meet Flavio, Rudy's friend and their tour guide.

Rudy would be forever grateful to this friend who introduced him to the art and life of Niccolò. Flavio, who stood waiting in the lobby of the Machiavelli Palace hotel, was about five-feet-seven inches tall, with black brown wavy hair parted in the middle. He possessed an aquiline nose, a triangular face and big, sparkling black eyes. Flavio wore a light blue long-sleeved shirt, navy-blue trousers, and dark navy-blue jacket. He walked up to them and, with a big smile, shook hands with Rudy and welcomed everyone with, *"Buongiorno."*

"I planned for us to visit the Accademia to see the hall of sculptures and then visit and study Michelangelo's David," Flavio said. "Then we will visit Bargello Museum and study Niccolò's works, have a lunch break and then I will take you to Uffizi which takes more than a day but I will mention a few important things and then you can take your time exploring whichever artworks you would like to see on your own. How does that sound?"

Everyone chimed. "Sounds excellent." Rudy's ears in particular perked up upon Flavio's mentioning that they will be viewing the works of Niccolò.

Rudy and his group ventured to Accademia Gallery after walking through the hall of sculptors. They all stood in front of Michelangelo's David with awe, staring spellbound at the enormous sculpture in white marble.

"The history of the statue began prior to Michelangelo's involvement," Flavio said. "A block of marble from a quarry town in the Apuan Alps in northern Tuscany had been sent to the office of the Florence Cathedral who had plans to commission a series of twelve, large Old Testament sculptors for the buttresses of the cathedral. The cathedral gave the commission to Augostino to sculpt David but Augustino only got as far as the beginning to shape the legs, feet and torso and roughing out some drapery then his association with the project ceased for reasons unknown. This was around the late 1460s.

"In 1500, an inventory of the cathedral described a figure of David a year later. The cathedral was determined to find an artist and the block stone was called a giant raised on feet so that a person experienced in this kind of work might examine it and express their opinion. Leonardo da Vinci and others in the committee were consulted but it was a 26-year-old Michelangelo who convinced the opera that he deserved the commission." Flavio paused to look at the group. "Does anyone have questions? None? All right, so I will proceed." He started pacing ever so slowly as though deep in thought.

"On August 16, 1501, Michelangelo was given the contract to undertake the challenging task that began on the 13th of September. On June 25, 1504 when the sculpture was nearing completion, a committee of 30 Florentine citizens, including many artists like Leonardo da Vinci, insisted that the sculpture should be placed in Palazzo Vecchio next to the entrance of the Civic government. So it was installed in the same place they had originally intended to put it."

"During his sculpting process, did anyone go and watch him sculpt in action?" asked Rudy who recalled reading about the many times people would watch Niccolò sculpt his famous works. One of those curious onlookers included Niccolò's beloved Beatrice, Rudy remembered reading.

"Absolutely not," Flavio replied, "Michelangelo was very strict about that—no one could go near to watch or ask him anything. The 17-foot marble statue of David symbolizes civil liberties and has been the embodiment in the republic of Florence. The eyes of David with a warning glare were fixed towards Rome where the de' Medici family lived. David looked tense, ready for battle, the veins bulging out of his lowered right with his left hand holding a sling draped over his shoulder and down to his right hand about to move, an expression heightened into *contrapposto*. The classic pose caused both hips and shoulder to rest at opposite angles, giving a slight same *contrapposto* at that part emphasized by the turn of the head to left by contrasting the positions of arms. David was depicted as an example of prepubescent male nudity with large hands as he was about to battle and was a symbol of strength and youthful beauty." He paused to catch his breath, looking at the group. "Friends, any questions?"

"I supposed David was a 14-year-old boy, though the figure looks like a strong adult man except for the genitals," Amita said. "So the expression and body contour did not depict a prepubescent male?"

"That's absolutely right," Flavio said.

The group of friends expressed curiosity about the life of Michelangelo.

"As both of you are physicians, it will interest you to know that Michelangelo was a very good anatomist." Flavio nodded at Rudy and Samir. "Michelangelo had a lifelong anatomical interest that was as much of a reflection of the culture of his times as it was that of his inimitable genius which made him a better student of anatomy than most. At that time, art students had to study anatomy and artists also performed dissections conducted by physicians. The artists also formed part of the Florentine guild of Physicians and Apothecary. The discipline of art and science had blurred the edges in high renaissance. Michelangelo wrote treatises for artists and collaborated in an anatomical test for students of medicine. Michelangelo suffered from gouty arthritis and kidney stones often and he died of fluid overload and obstructive nephropathy."

"Flavio, we are very grateful that you have given us some very important aspect of his life and health," Rudy said.

"After our lunch break, we will all meet at the entrance to the Bargello Museum where we will study the works of Niccolò Bardi," Flavio said.

I can't wait, thought Rudy as the group headed to the restaurant.

They all went to treat Flavio out for lunch as a way of thanking him for being their tour guide. There was a bit of time left so Sharmi, Urmi and Amita browsed a bit in the shops before they all arrived at the entrance of the Bargello Museum.

"You all can explore after I finish my guided tour with you," Flavio said. "I will take you to the sculptures which need some explanation as they are 'must see items.' But first is Niccolò's St. George slaying the dragon. There is the marble statue of St. George then there is St. George and the dragon below him depicted in a low relief that narrates the scene of the full story in what likely was an example of the relief *schiacciato* or a Bass Relief that Niccolò invented; when a relief is curved into a flat surface, the field is lowered, leaving the field which is not sculpted seem higher. This necessitates a lot of chiseling away and takes a long time. This technique involved extremely shallow carving throughout which would create a far more striking effect of atmospheric spaces than before. The sculptor is no longer modeling his shapes in the usual way, he paints them in chisel."

Listening to Flavio's narration, reminded Rudy about his reading of how Niccolò created the St. George statue and about Niccolò's various sculpting techniques.

"I think that is all about the bass relief," Flavio said. "We will now study the 'Bronze David' sculpted by Niccolò which is in bronze casting. He is nude except the military boots and a shepherd's hat with a laurel wreath and a young man with long curls." Flavio paused to look at the group. "I'm curious to know, what is your impression of this sculpture? I know what Rudy's answer will be but how about a comment from one of the ladies?"

"Well, compared to Michelangelo's sculpture of David, this Bronze David really does look like a boy," Amita said. "His body doesn't look muscular and I love his smile with his head slightly lowered."

"He does look more like a boy," Sharmi agreed. "But who killed a giant? The sword is so big. I wonder how he did it?"

Rudy smiled at Sharmi, pleased that his new wife was showing interest in one of his favorite artist's works. Since he had read about how Niccolò created Bronze David, Rudy was awestruck at seeing the actual sculpture. But the feeling was bittersweet as Rudy called reading how grief-stricken Niccolò was when Mother Orissa passed away shortly after bronze David was completed. The only consolation was that at least Niccolò's mother got to see her son's sculpture and his studio, Rudy thought.

"He looks so calm and looking down which is not exactly the pose we expect," Samir said.

"His figure looks so feminine from the back," Urmi said.

"You are absolutely right," Flavio said, "that was what Niccolò wanted him to look like to give people the impression that he was a boy. All of your impressions and questions are very good. Niccolò wanted to depict David as a 14-year-old boy who stood against this tyrant. Niccolò symbolized the victory of humility represented by David over the tyranny represented by Goliath. David smiles with his head slightly down as he acknowledged the victory with the grace of God."

"Most of Niccolò's works are very expressive," Rudy commented. "Little children really look like children as if you can feel their emotions and see them joyous and playful."

"That was what he wanted to depict through his sculptures," Flavio said, "he used to say 'I want to make them alive.' Rudy, I'm sure you have read about this. You can see his sculpted figure in a niche in Uffizi. He used to say while teaching others 'the creativity flows like a stream of energy inside the body of the creator.' The creator's responsibility is to guide the stream to come out and manifest. It could be in different areas of life and work in different people but it is same."

Rudy reflected on this wisdom from Niccolò that he had always found useful in his own life and career.

"The energy is real and alive," Flavio continued, "so the manifested creation surely will be alive."

Florence mesmerized everyone in the group with its culture and its people, the city itself with its grandeur.

Rudy was absolutely immersed and lost in thought as he saw Niccolò's sculpture standing in the niche at Uffizi. His friend Flavio was with him to explain everything in detail but he himself wanted to be alone with the sculptures created by Niccolò. Some unseen energy was drawing him to them. He went back alone to see the bronze David, the Madonna and Child. With penitent Mary Magdalene, Rudy stood there for what seemed like hours together with her to sense the depth of Niccolò's anxiety and suffering to make the sculptures alive. Being in the area of neuroscience and dealing with the brain and its connection, Rudy understood all of what Niccolò had felt.

The anatomy and physiology of that system and whatever we have so far to record the activities, he thought to himself, *it is very superficial.* It struck him that the brain and its connection is a state of mind; there is no anatomical structure called "mind," neither a real proof of how the mind spreads and takes over.

The sun was going down as the last rays of sun flooded the city of Firenze. Rudy felt that something inside was telling him to visit the marble figure of Niccolò at Uffizi. Before leaving Sharmi with the group for a while, he said, "I will return to the hotel after an hour or so."

It may have sounded strange to the rest of the group but Rudy knew that Sharmi understood his interest and connection to Niccolò.

"All right, we will wait for you in the lobby," Samir said.

Rudy almost ran to Uffizi just as the sun's orange glow illuminated the marble figure that Rudy gazed at for a while silently then murmured, "Give me some signs that I can follow to harness the stream of creative energy to manifest what I want. It is different than yours but it is surely creative."

The rays of sun went down the western horizon as the twilight of night slowly spread its veil. In the evening twilight, the marble figure looked very soft and real with the gentle breeze while the light and shadow playfully moved over his face gently and the dark shadows under his eyes became even darker. Rudy could see his eyes come alive as the shadows around his lips moved and he could hear in the distance what Flavio had said, echoing Niccolò: "The creativity flows like a stream of energy inside the body of the creator. It is the creator's responsibility to guide the stream…"

Rudy felt goosebumps all over his body and he murmured, "It is my imagination, it cannot be true." He looked at the figure for the last time then started striding rapidly almost at the speed of running to reach the hotel. He felt energized and refreshed as he picked up his pace faster and faster to be with Sharmi and their friends.

A gentle breeze blew through his face and body as the seagull's shrill filled the air. He felt comforted seeing Sharmi, her sister and his friends waiting for him in the lobby as a warm wave of gratitude for finally seeing Niccolò at last enveloped him.

Honeymoon in Florence

Florence, 12th June 1965—On this day, Rudy's group of five would return to being a group of four again as at 11 this morning, Urmi would be flying back to India via Air France as there was no direct flight to Calcutta from Florence. Then she would change planes in Rome and from there, go directly to her final destination.

Rudy and his friends started off early so her luggage would go directly from Florence to India which Urmi felt relieved about. It was very hard for all of them to say goodbye. She had spent all this time with them to commemorate a very special event—her sister's wedding—and going on art tours. Urmi commented that she was very fortunate to have been able to attend the wedding and grateful to her brother-in law, Rudy, for arranging all the tours.

As the sisters hugged, tears rolled down their eyes and soon everyone hugged Urmi goodbye.

"We part for the time being. See you all soon," Urmi said. "Being here for Sharmi's wedding was a happy moment I was fortunate to come and share with all of you."

Urmi waved and went through the gate as the four friends stood watching for a while until Urmi was out of sight.

"Let us all plan for the rest of the day," Rudy continued. "After we have lunch, I was thinking about taking a sunset boat ride along the river Arno. I was told it is about a 45–50-minute ride that includes drinks."

Samir, Amita and Sharmi all said it was a great idea.

"Amita and Samir, you have two more days here before you leave on the 15th of June mid-morning back to Newcastle," Rudy said. "That same day we'll be taking a train back to Venice where Sharmi and I will stay for three to four more days."

"I am thinking we should all take a day trip to Pisa and Tuscany to see the Chianti hills, visit an old town and then come back," Samir suggested.

"That is an excellent idea," Rudy said.

Amita and Sharmi agreed with Amita being especially excited about visiting the Chianti region.

"I heard the landscape is very pretty with hills and valleys all green with olive orchards and vineyards in between," Amita said.

Samir and Rudy suggested contacting a tour guide immediately to book the trip.

After a quick panini lunch, the group decided to go back to their hotel to reserve the sunset tour which would meet at Piazza Metana at 5:30 in the evening. They also booked tours for Pisa and the Chianti Hills for the 13th of June.

The four friends arrived at the meeting place to board a *barchetta*, a small boat. Amita, Samir, Sharmi and Rudy comfortably sat on their seats feeling relaxed at the end of the day. There were only about ten people on the boat navigated with a long wooden pole. Slowly the boat started gliding along the river as each passenger was offered a glass of wine, except Sharmi who opted for ginger ale.

Landmarks they passed included Ponte Vecchio, where Rudy remembered reading about the place where Niccolò encountered Beatrice some mornings as the sculptor strode to his studio—and Ponte Santa Trinita and traditional buildings that lined the river banks. As the tour guide provided information about the various points of interest, Rudy felt a strange sense of déjà vu, as though he had been here before, and he realized he had—through the sensory experience of reading Niccolò's vivid, atmospheric biography, which he realized read like a novel.

"Folks, what you're now riding in, a *barchetta*, is a small boat entirely made of wood," the tour guide said. "In fact, the original four boats still exist."

The boat continued cruising smoothly along the river, passing by famous landmarks, one after the other as people along the river banks waved on the shore.

The city blushed with orange and red hues of the setting sun. The ripples of the water blushed with red happily danced towards the shore while the seagulls' shrieks serenaded in the background. The sun appeared as the orange ball started to dip down in the rippling water of Arno where the water of the river glittering in gold waltzed together with the horizon as the *barchetta* cruised by.

All the guests on board appeared nearly lost in their own dreamland as the *barchetta* rocked sideways with gentle movements as the evening slowly drew its curtain. When the boat anchored at the piazza where they started the relaxed guests were ready to wind down for the evening.

The four friends all looked forward to the day trip to Pisa, San Gimignano and Siena the next day.

The visit to Pisa began in the morning as the rays of sun flooded the Piazza Miracoli's green courtyard which looked greener against the white marble structures and those that stood magnificent all around the piazza.

The visit began with a walk along the medieval wall to the ancient entrance of Porta Santa Maria from where one could admire the whole architecture of marble structures which stood out on the green meadow of Piazza de Miracoli. The Leaning Tower, Baptistery and cathedral were all sights to behold.

Carlo, the tour leader, guided Rudy's group to the Leaning Tower of Pisa. When the four friends stood in front of the tower, they were amazed to see that it was truly leaning. The tall marble structure looked so unique that Carlo provided a brief background of this leaning tower.

"Hello everyone and welcome to the one and only Leaning Tower of Pisa which is the campanile of the Pisa Cathedral," Carlo said. "It is known for its four-degree lean, the result of unsatisfactory foundation. Its height is 55.86 meters on the low side and 56.67 meters on the high side. The width of the wall of the base is 2.44 meters, its weight estimated to be 14,500 tons. The tower, which has 296 steps, began to lean during its construction in the 12th century due to soft ground which could not support the structure's weight. Then it worsened through the completion of construction in the 14th century. The bell chamber was added in 1372. There are seven bells for each note of the musical major scale."

"I wonder if the bells are heavy, then wouldn't they add more to the tilt if it is still tilting?" Samir asked.

"You are absolutely right," Carlo said. "They took out all the bells for some time. The city of Pisa did some remedial work which reduced the tilt to four degrees." He paused to gesture to the tower with his hand. "You all can climb up the steps if you like at your own pace after I finish the tour of the cathedral and the Baptistery."

Carlo asked Rudy's tour group to follow him to the Baptistery.

"Pisa Baptistery is a Roman Catholic ecclesiastical building in Pisa," Carlo relayed. "Its construction started in 1152 to replace the older Baptistery. Designed by Diatisalvia whose signature can be read inside two pillars dated 1153, the Baptistery was completed in 1363. Now, if you follow me, I will show you the pillars."

Entering the Baptistery, they were amazed to see the size and the architectural beauty of the building. Everyone marveled at seeing the signature of the designer.

"This is the largest Baptistery in Italy," Carlo continued. "It is 54.86-meters high with a diameter of 34.13-meters. The Pisa Baptistery is an example of the transition from the Romanesque style to the Gothic style."

"What is the difference between the two styles?" Sharmi asked.

"Good question," Carlo said. "The lower sections are Romanesque style with rounded arches while the upper section is in Gothic style with pointed arches. Does that answer your question?"

Even with her literature studies, Sharmi had always been fascinated with architecture. "Yes, thank you."

"The Baptistery is constructed in marble," Carlo continued. "The portal facing the façade of the cathedral is flanked by classical columns. Inner Jambs are of the Byzantine style. The Intel is divided in two tiers—the lower shows St. John, while the upper shows Christ between Madonna and St. John flanked by angels and evangelists. The bronze sculpture of St. John is at the center of the font." He beckoned the group with a hand gesture. "Come, all of you, please stand close to me so you can see it better. The Baptistery was also constructed on unstable sand so it leans 0.8 degrees towards the cathedral. The exterior of the dome is clad with lead sheets on the east and red tiles on the west giving a half gray and half red appearance from the south."

He scanned the group. "When we walk to the cathedral, you will see what I mean. Now, I'll give you fifteen minutes to walk on your own before I take you to the cathedral. I'll meet you at the entrance. Enjoy."

After fifteen minutes, the group gathered near Carlo who asked them to follow him to the cathedral where he began narrating a brief history of this structure. "You all know that this is a Roman Catholic cathedral dedicated to the Assumption of Mary."

"When was the cathedral built?" Rudy asked.

"The construction began in 1063 and was completed in 1092," Carlo replied. "Additional enlargements and a new façade were built in the 12th century and the roof was replaced after damage from fire in 1596. The cathedral was made with loot money from Sicily after defeating the Muslims. The exterior is mostly made of white and gray marble. The dome of the cathedral is elliptical. The original wooden doors were destroyed. The bronze doors were made in the 17th century by a Florentine artist.

"Let us look now at the interior of the cathedral which is subdivided at the front into a central nave flanked by two side aisles on either side and with a transept and apse in three naves covered with black and white monolithic marble columns having Corinthian capitals."

"The ceiling looks interesting," Amita said, gazing up.

"It is a coffered ceiling with gold leaf," Carlo said.

"The lamp at the center of the nave is very fascinating," Sharmi remarked.

"It is indeed," Carlo agreed. "It's called Galileo's lamp because the legend says that the great scientist formulated his theory of isochronism of pendulum while watching from the roof of the nave. He noticed during mass that it was taking the same amount of time to sway back and forth."

Carlo clasped his hands. "Okay folks, here with Galileo's Lamp, I end my tour with you. Let me know if you have any questions and I'll be happy to answer them."

After thanking Carlo and bidding him a goodbye, Rudy and his friends took a car to St. Gimignano, Siena and the Chianti Hills.

As the town of Pisa moved backwards slowly through green meadows and winding roads, the car started careening along the hills dotted with small, picturesque red-roofed cottages that seemed as though they were hanging on the slopes of the mountain. Amita and Sharmi became immersed in the beauty of the landscape as Rudy and Samir marveled at the view which they remarked looked very much like a moving painting.

All four friends agreed that a day tour was not enough to see all the sights in the cites and the countryside and promised to return for a longer stay sometime in the near future.

It took them about one hour and a half to reach St. Gimignano where Matteo, their tour guide stood waiting at Piazza Duomo in the heart of the square in front of Collegiate Church. The four friends approached Matteo who held a banner with Rudy's name.

Lorenzo, the rental car driver asked Matteo, "When would be a good time for me to pick them up to go back?"

Matteo checked his watch. "Let's see, it's now 1:30. Come back around 5 p.m."

"That is all right," Lorenzo said. "It will take me a little over 45 minutes to Firenze so you will be there just before 6 tonight."

Matteo started narrating the tour while walking with Rudy and friends. "San Gimignano is a small town in the province of Siena, Tuscany in the north central part of Italy known as the town of towers and with its hilltop setting and circulating wall that form an unforgettable skyline. Within the walls are the well-preserved buildings and churches including both in the Romanesque and in the Gothic style."

Amita raised her hand. "I am still confused, could you please explain the differences between Romanesque and Gothic?"

Matteo nodded. "For the Romanesque style, there's no definite beginning date as the proposed date ranges from the 6th to the 12th century. In England, it's referred to as Norman Architecture known by its massive quality and thick walls with round arches, sturdy pillars, barrel vaults, towers and decorative arches.

"On the other hand, Gothic style, from the 12th to the 16th century, typically features masonry buildings characterized by cavernous spaces with the expanse of walls broken by overlaid tracery. The rib vault, flying buttresses, and pointed arches were used as a solution to the problem of building very tall structures while preserving as much natural light as possible as stained-glass window panels rendered startling sun dappled interior effects. One of the earliest buildings combining these elements was the Abbey of Saint Denis, Paris from 1135 to 1144." He nodded to the group. "Please take your time looking inside the buildings. I will tell you which one of the buildings and take you all close to the church."

Matteo looked back at them. "Oh, and if you are wanting to try typical Tuscan food, I can point you towards some restaurants."

They all visited the church and a few buildings before sitting down for lunch. Among the restaurants Matteo suggested included Ceppo Toscano.

After the four friends scanned the menu, Sharmi and Amita ordered Ribollita, a soup with cabbage and beans and Pasta Pappardelle with Ragu sauce.

Rudy and Samir ordered salad and beef steak prepared specially with dry-aged beef from a Chianina cattle featuring thick cuts at least three fingers wide, slightly charred outside but soft and succulent inside.

Matteo bid them farewell after helping them choose a restaurant and decipher the menu then asked them to stand just outside the restaurant in the piazza where the cars usually stay to pick up passengers. After they all thanked Matteo, they dove in to enjoy the local Tuscan specialties as they sat in the dining area that looked antique and made of stone.

While enjoying their food, Samir said, "We should take it easy tomorrow, the 14th of June. Just pack our things and enjoy the day sitting around and talking for our last day in Florence."

"I would love to do the same," Rudy agreed. "We'll also be leaving at the same time to catch our train back to Venice where I just want to relax at the hotel St. Regis which is very nice." He paused to squeeze Sharmi's hand. "And it would be nice to enjoy the rest of our honeymoon strolling around and watching the gondolas pass along the canal. When we go back to Newcastle, I have to start preparing for the final and part two of the FRCS (Fellow of Royal College of Surgeon) exam in addition to working in my new position as a registrar."

"So what about your plans when you return, Sharmi?"

"Well, I have plenty to do. I don't have to take any more exams but I will be busy with my post doc research and with my teaching assistant's job. "I am working for two days at present so I might ask my professor if I could work on Tuesdays and Wednesdays. I want to stay there from Monday evening, work and teach Tuesdays and Wednesdays and come back to Newcastle by late afternoon on Wednesday."

"Where will you stay? Do you have your own place?"

"I can arrange to stay with my friends there first and then see later on whether I can have a small place to rent."

Everyone agreed that would be a good idea.

Amita stretched. "Oh, we have had a wonderful break from our routine and life back home."

After checking the time, Rudy said, "It's almost 5 p.m. We should go out and stand by where the car will be waiting for us."

They were right on time as Lorenzo, the driver was waiting outside and soon they were headed back to Florence. They were all tired yet very happy and satisfied with their day trip. As a couple of them took a nap, the car winded through the hills and valleys while the sun was cruising towards the western sky. The hills and valleys flooded with the sun's orange spill, moving backwards as time passed by until they came to a wide-open space and Lorenzo said, "We will reach Firenze in about fifteen minutes."

Then Sharmi, Rudy, Amita and Samir suddenly awoke from the pleasant memory of the day thanking Lorenzo for the pleasant ride through the countryside.

That evening back at the hotel, with Sharmi sleeping next to him, Rudy sat up in bed as a reading lamp cast soft light over his shoulder and on to the pages of Niccolo's biography.

Niccolò's Detour to Padua

Niccolò's world was shattered. He was utterly devastated after the passing away of his beloved mother, Orissa, in the spring of 1430 for he had known her his entire life—all of his forty-four years. His only consolation during his time of grief was that his mother had seen the bronze David sculpture. For years prior, he had wanted his mother to see David which was then completed, but since the palace had not taken the sculpture as construction was still going on, his mother had the good fortune to visit Niccolò's studio ensuring that she finally, happily got to see where he worked and that made him happy.

Memories of that time filled Niccolò's mind as he recalled how gleeful and proud she was of the accomplishments of her only beloved son. Two weeks after her visit, she fell ill with high fever, was plagued with a cough, difficulty breathing, and within a week, she had left this world.

His whole world that had rotated around his mother for whom everything he did—from the mundane household task to sculpting the most challenging work of art—had been in her honor. The emptiness he felt was almost unbearable. He had lost his father when he was young and even back then, it felt like he was standing on shaky, unstable ground as he lost all his support and never had a chance to show his father what *he* wanted to be and what his father wanted him to be. Then there was his mother, who had always been there for him and for his sister—solid as a mountain protecting them from all possible storms of life.

He remembered, after days of hard work, he would return home weary in body and mind but the weariness would melt away with a hot delicious meal complemented by the comforts of home as his mind would be refreshed by his mother's encouraging words and affectionate smile.

His sister Tia's presence at their small, cozy cottage after their mother's passing somewhat filled the painful hole inside his heart for Niccolò could not do any sculpting for some time. It was as though his heart had stopped beating when his mother passed.

The pain lodged in his heart would torturously flash back time after time to when he would work long hours yet Mother Orissa would wait patiently for her son and never complained when Niccolò told her that he would be home late.

Niccolò kept being bombarded with thoughts and details about the days and events that would have helped his mother cope a little easier. He spent a lot of time thinking "What if I did this?" and "I should have done this," and "Why did or didn't I do that?" Niccolò thought more deeply about the feelings and concerns of his mother and the small gestures of concern and care from Niccolò always made Mother Orissa very proud and happy and he wished he had done more of that.

Time was the best healer, he heard, yet to him, "time was like a big aggressive monster swallowing slowly everything in its path and satisfying its appetite."

At times, Niccolò would take long hikes from his studio when he could not concentrate. Paolo wanted to accompany him but Niccolò would refuse, telling him he wanted to be left alone. One afternoon when he was very restless and was striding rapidly, a concerned Paolo followed him. When Niccolò turned around and saw Paolo, he became upset and screamed, "Why you are following me? Stop following me!"

"Maestro, you told your mother that as long as you live and your two hands work, you would keep on sculpting—this is your world. Your mother was happy and understood you and she said, 'I will be happy, if you are happy and I pray to the Almighty for you to succeed and persevere because life and art will not always be easy.'"

They stared at one another amid the bustle of the city around them.

"Maestro, do you think your mother would be pleased if you stop doing everything you love now?"

Niccolò stopped then, his eyes went distant and he took a few deep breaths.

Slowly, he came back to the present. "Paolo, let us go back to the studio."

From that conversation, some time had passed and gradually Niccolò resumed his routine and soon became busy when he was commissioned for the Duomo, the main cathedral in Florence, as part of a larger program that sought to embellish the appearance of the Duomo's interior façade prior to beginning his work on Cantoria in 1433.

The Cantoria commission piece was meant to provide a stage for members of the church choir. Cantoria, meaning chancel, was the area in church near the altar which provided a standing room for the choir and clergy.

Niccolò carried out the work where the Latin cross-shaped section of the cathedral in Florence intersected with the Cantoria sculpture, a rectangular structure with balconies or galleries that appeared in relief making allusive representations to singers.

This time period was Niccolò's Poetic Classical period when he worked for the Medici family between 1433 to 1443 in Florence. The Florentine people coined the name for him for his creative expressions on sculptures.

Niccolò had to juggle between the two works: the Cantoria and the Annunciation of Mary in Santa Croce in Florence.

"I am going to sculpt the Annunciation very differently," Niccolò told Paolo one day. "It will not include doves or any other details. It will be dynamic and expressive."

"Maestro, I cannot wait. It is amazing to see your unique and amazing ideas come to life."

Paolo had always been a sincere, loyal friend of Niccolò who never failed to take good care of him even during the hardest of times as Niccolò's moods would swing from grief to anger and back again in a vicious cycle. Niccolò would also emphasize that he did not like to be nurtured by someone else. Paolo thought to himself that probably it was because Niccolò had only one person who nurtured him and that person was gone.

Yet, despite all that, the bond between the two of them grew more stronger so that they now could not live without each other's care and company. All those years of creative collaboration had evolved into a deep appreciation and friendship.

Niccolò had spent significant time in Rome in the past studying the great artists of the ancient period, carefully assimilating many of their stylistic formal elements. Paolo pointed out, "Maestro, I can see the use of putti, or winged children who appear to be singing and dancing through a narrow space. Are you returning to classical form?"

"Yes, Paolo, I am glad you noticed it." He considered the evolution of his techniques over the years. "Paolo, when you view as a whole, there is an ornamental richness with its many motifs representing children, flowers and plants. Many columns came together with cantilevers and the inlays of gold, green and red accompaniment of the figures in mid-movement on the shafts of the column you see I am trying to make the effect to be of magnificent dynamism."

"Maestro, I definitely see that. You are not just a genius but an insightful one."

In 1435, near the altar of the Cavalcanti chapel in Santa Croce in Florence was the Annunciation of Mary influenced by classical media in gilded "Pietra Serena," a gray sandstone. Niccolò focused on the dramatic interaction of the two participations rather than usual: Mary caught in motion had just arisen from a chair, a book open in her hand, right foot off the ground. What Niccolò believed and truly felt in his heart that he concentrated on, recovering the beautiful style of ancient cultures. Mary positioned her leg and foot while her hips and shoulders were turned on opposite sides when a drapery of clothes covered her leg. Mary's expression seemed to be startled by the appearance of the angel. This was very atypical of the usual annunciation. Niccolò already planned to sculpt this differently. After it was finished, Paolo could not believe that it was so expressive. He kept gazing at it.

"Paolo, why you are so amazed?"

"Maestro, you told me what your intentions were as I was assisting you, yet I cannot believe that it turned out so lively and it seems it is happening before me."

"Thank you, Paolo. There are more commissions coming so be prepared."

From about 1437 to 1443, Niccolò was working on the decoration of the old sacristy of San Lorenzo built by Brunelleschi from 1418 to 1428. The decoration was carried out with bronze and polychrome stuccos comprising the whole arched relief above the bronze doors of the altar walls showing St. Thomas, St. Damian, St. Stephen, and St. Lawrence. The two bronze doors were divided into ten compartments each with apostles and martyrs.

In 1443, Niccolò told Paolo that he was about to start work on two more ambitious pairs of doors of the sacristy. He was lured to Padua by a commission for a bronze equestrian statue of a famous Venetian condottiere, Erasmo da Narni, popularly called "Gattamelata," meaning honey cat, the nickname for the fallen military leader. Niccolò was not sure at first, but the Paduan senate unanimously wanted an equestrian statue as the city wanted to honor Erasmo after his death.

The statue was highly controversial at that time as it was an equestrian monument glorifying a man who was not a ruler. Niccolò wanted to depict Gattamelata as a composed, alert, watchful leader—the depiction of forces of character and reference to the power of real people would flow with the Renaissance theme of individualism and humanism. The horse would possess the alert, self-contained and courageous air of the ruler. So Niccolò agreed to take the commission at Padua.

Paolo became sad and wanted to follow him to Padua but Niccolò wanted him to take the responsibility of the studio in his absence.

As a result, Niccolò had immersed himself in his work in Florence for many years. It was really a dilemma for him to move to northern Italy. On his way to Padua, memories of Florence—his cozy parental home—seemed to be spinning in his mind along with images of the familiar place and faces of the people around him. The roads, even the familiar trees he could see passing backwards as they stood there silently becoming fainter and fainter.

Then he took a deep breath and pulled himself together, reminding himself that this was a great piece of artwork he was going to create in Padua—the Gattamelata. Niccolò found it humorous that the funny-sounding name, meaning "honey cat" was the nickname of the mercenary who fought for Venice. Niccolò envisioned that the statue would be on an elliptical base and Erasmo would be dressed in military gear wearing an armor with a sword at his side. His body would be in natural proportion to his horse which would indicate achieving a high level of naturalism. Erasmo would be shown as someone who conveys intelligence, courage and confidence, a triumphant figure who rides on a horse with its hoof on an orb—a symbol of power in the tradition of an equestrian statue reminiscent of depicting a famous emperor. Yet this statue would be the glorification of someone of lesser rank who seemed to be more in line with humanist practices of honoring individual achievement.

Niccolò settled in with a group of sculptors who helped him as Paolo would occasionally visit him but could not help him in this particular commission. Niccolò proved himself such a master in proportion and excellence of so great a casting that he could truly bear comparison with any ancient craftsman in movement, design, art, proportion, and diligence—it astonished all who saw it.

The city of Padua wanted to honor Erasmo after his death and they did so by placing the equestrian statue of him in front of the main church in the city.

Years rolled by and Niccolò received praise for his work. The city and the people of Padua wanted him to stay and offered him amenities, a life of comfort and money. The people took care of him when he was not well, a team of doctors treated him vigilantly but the result was the opposite—he was determined to leave saying, "if I remain any longer in Padua, I would forget everything that I ever knew." Being so greatly praised there by all, he would be glad to return to his city where he would gain nothing but censure, since such censure would urge him to study and enable him to attain greater glory.

Niccolò finally came back to Florence after almost ten years. While he was away, he was exhausted and not feeling as strong. He had not been well for a period of time and was treated round the clock by a team of doctors.

But despite that, he was glad to be back in his own beloved city of Florence. It seemed he could breathe easier and regain his strength being in his own studio with his assistant, Paolo and close friends, and back in his own little cottage.

Niccolò and Paolo were glad to be back working in their studio together. By now, it was 1453, a glorious morning in spring when the sun was partly covered with grayish white clouds and the city bathed in the soft rays of sun while the river Arno merrily streamed along with noisy people in boats as a gentle cool breeze blew the pointed pine and the birch trees. The air was filled with chirping birds on the branches of the trees and the frequent shrieks of seagulls dipping and diving in the water. *It feels familiar, it feels like old times, it feels like home…indeed, it is home,* thought Niccolò.

"Maestro, do you hear what I hear?"

"What is it you hear?"

"The sound of a carriage heading to our studio."

As always, Paolo was right. When a carriage stopped in front of the studio. Two people got down, one was a bishop in a long flowing dress and a cross hanging from his neck down to the waist, and the other was his attendant in a brown brief up to the knees with black stockings, a brown vest and yellow shirt.

The men walked through the entrance of the studio and immediately asked for Niccolò to which Paolo quickly informed his Maestro of their presence. When Niccolò reached the entrance, the bishop recognized him at once.

"Welcome back to Firenze, my dear—"

"Welcome Your Eminence, please come in." Niccolò invited the men to sit down on two chairs usually reserved for their lunch breaks.

"My dear Niccolò, I am here to inform you that the cathedral wants to commission you to sculpt the penitent Mary Magdalene."

Niccolò sat in pensive thought as his breathing staggered. "Pardon me, Your Eminence, as you are well aware, I just returned from a long stay in Padua and I am not so strong. I had been seriously ill."

The bishop nodded. "I am sincerely sorry to hear that and I hope that you have fully recovered. So that is why we encourage you to take your time as your expertise is of great value to us. This is a very important commission and we cannot think of anyone else more suitable to create this sculpture." The bishop paused, eyeing Niccolò intently. "You choose your own material, your own technique. If you agree, we will provide you with everything necessary to meet your every need. Niccolò, you must have faith that, by the grace of God, you will get your strength back. We will pray for you. Please consider—"

"Your Eminence, I will choose wood," Niccolò promptly and confidently replied as though he had been thinking about this type of sculpture all along. And indeed, he had been considering using wood. He was just waiting for the perfect opportunity to execute his unique plan. *This must be part of God's plan for me*, he thought.

Despite his efforts at staying dignified, the bishop gushed, "Bless you, my dear Niccolò!"

After the carriage left, Paolo eyes moistened. "Maestro, I truly believe this will be your greatest work."

Niccolò's brows furrowed. "Why do you say so?"

Paolo closed his eyes and placed hand over hand on his heart. "I feel it will be."

Niccolò softly chuckled and affectionately patted Paolo's shoulder. "Let us walk over to the Osteria for old times' sake."

As Niccolò and Paolo walked leisurely, a gentle breeze caressed Niccolò as he and Paolo were serenaded by the chirping of birds and the lapping of boats that brought him back to present time Florence.

He felt refreshed knowing he had something new to look forward to. "Paolo, I am so happy we got this commission. And you're right. I will create something so remarkable that the whole world will know about and many centuries from now, people will talk about, Paolo. Mark my words."

Back to Newcastle After the Wedding

June 25th 1965—After their wedding and honeymoon in Italy, settling into their new routine became an adjustment for the newlyweds Sharmi and Rudy. One afternoon in late June, Rudy came home from his work to find Sharmi in the kitchen of their apartment preparing dinner. As a newly-married couple, they were happy, still in a daze reminiscing about their grand wedding ceremony in Venice followed by a few vacation days with their friends in Florence where Rudy connected even more with Niccolò then finishing up their honeymoon back in Venice before flying back home.

Rudy joined Sharmi in the kitchen to prepare cups of tea for them. Then he went to the living room with their tea, eager to sit down, relax and chat. With a pleasant smile, Sharmi joined Rudy.

"How was your day?"

"It went very smoothly," Rudy replied. "Not so much work which is fine for me so I can prepare for my final FRCS. Work here is not so busy. You know, Sharmi, it is all right for the time being to work there. I will get more time to go to the library and study and, to tell you the truth, there is not much neurosurgery going on there—actually none."

Sharmi appeared very anxious. "So what are you going to do?"

"I'll continue working there until I finish my final exam, then I will find some other job, maybe move to some other place."

Sharmi looked a little concerned but wanted to be supportive. "We can probably do that."

"I want to appear prepared and confident for the examination which is usually around middle of December," Rudy said.

"Oh, it's almost the end of June," Sharmi said, "so there's only around five and a half months left."

"That is all right," Rudy said. "I'll try to concentrate with all my energy."

"What are the possibilities?" Sharmi wanted to know.

"The possibilities of getting a registrar position in Newcastle seems to be grim," Rudy said. "I will look around and maybe try at Birmingham to check if they have a position there." He paused to sip his tea, his brows furrowing at the prospect of once again relocating to another place. But he tried to look on the bright side. Sharmi was now by his side. He would never again walk alone in the field of uncertainty.

"Let's change the topic," he suggested. "I'm not on call this weekend so let's dedicate one day visiting our friends and enjoy spending time with them."

"Amita and Samir called and asked whether it is possible to spend a day with them," Sharmi said. "I told them I would ask you first."

"That would be great," Rudy said, "we haven't seen them in almost two weeks."

"I think it's only been just ten days since we haven't seen them," his wife said.

"So, Sharmi, what do you think?" Rudy said. "Wouldn't it be nice if we leave our house after breakfast and head to their place, spend Saturday night there and come back home on Sunday after breakfast with them?"

"I think it's an excellent idea but won't you miss your study time?"

"I'll study about three hours tonight so I can enjoy Saturday."

Sharmi smiled. "I'll call Amita right now and tell her we are coming."

Sharmi dialed her friend's number. "Amita, how are you both doing?"

"We're fine," Amita replied on the other line. "Are you both settled in your apartment?"

"Yes almost," Sharmi said, "listen, Amita, Rudy is eager to visit you and so am I. We wish to come over soon."

"Wonderful. You can come right now."

"Oh, that's nice of you," Sharmi said. "but I think we'll start from our home Saturday after breakfast then stay with you Saturday and come back Sunday. Would that be okay with you?"

"Sharmi, you can have breakfast with us that morning. Start soon after you both get out of bed and get ready right away. We're not that far."

"All right, we'll do that," Sharmi said. "Can't wait to see you both. Bye for now."

Once Sharmi put the receiver down, she went to Rudy. "Amita's happy we'll be coming over and wants us to be there earlier to join them for breakfast. So she was insisting we go to their place tonight but I suggested we start out tomorrow morning."

"That's wonderful," Rudy said, "we'll do that so after dinner I will study for at least two hours."

"Good to hear," Sharmi said. "So I'll leave you to your studies then. I have to read a few things myself to help the research students in our department."

As the summer evening set in, the glow of the sun flooded their cozy apartment as they sat around their kitchen table to enjoy the home-cooked dinner of chicken curry and rice.

Rudy was determined to study for at least two hours. He looked at the clock. "The evening is still young. It's eight o'clock."

"No excuses and no procrastinating," Sharmi teased her husband, "Study now, please because the sooner we do our studying and reading, the closer we are to enjoying some time off." She yawned. "Although, I don't know how much I can do tonight. I am feeling rather sleepy already."

Rudy smiled at his wife's adorable quirk. "So what do you plan to do?"

"Well, since I don't work on Monday, I can just catch up on work that day while you are at work," she replied.

After a few hours, Sharmi went to bed while Rudy concentrated on studying for his examination.

* * *

June 26, 1965—On a bright early morning, Sharmi got up to start getting ready for their overnight stay, packing essentials in her bag and also Rudy's.

I'm glad I asked him to put his things in one place so that it will be easy for me to pack quickly putting all his stuff inside the duffle bag, she thought to herself. *Oh, he is still in bed. I have to wake him up so he could get ready.*

Sharmi was about to wake him up when she heard his voice.

"Sorry, I woke up late. I'll be ready soon."

Then Sharmi and Rudy were all set to go when the phone started ringing. Sharmi picked up the phone.

"Breakfast is ready," said Samir on the other end, "I hope you're on your way."

Rudy took the receiver. "It's now half past eight. We'll be there within thirty minutes."

Rudy and Sharmi reached their friends' place around 9 that morning and the four of them squealed with joy upon seeing each other again, excited to catch up.

Amita invited everyone to sit around the table where they started filling their plates from the spread of breakfast items: poached eggs, bacon strips, fried tomato, toast, and tea.

"This is a wonderful spread of breakfast food," Sharmi said. "Thank you."

"Did you manage to arrange things around the apartment?" Amita asked Sharmi.

"I did as much as possible so that I can find things handy and easy to reach."

"Rudy, how's it going at your work place?" Samir asked.

"Work is fine and the people are nice to me," Rudy began, "but there's not much work to be done. In a way, that's ideal for me so that I can prepare for my final FRCS exam,"

Samir looked puzzled. "What do you mean by not much work?"

Rudy sighed. "I mean there are no neurosurgery opportunities going on there. Mostly it's patients with head injuries who are admitted to that center. It's all right for me now, this is a registrar position, a good earning job, more than the house officers and not so much work which means I have time to study for my final FRCS exam. I'm not complaining but it would be good for me to work in situations that challenge me."

He cast his wife a smile of gratitude. "Life is a little more comfortable now that Sharmi took over the cooking and other household chores which I try to help her with but she insists that I relax after work and dedicate time to studying so for the time being, it is pleasant."

"At least you are concentrating on your final exam so that's good," Amita said.

"Yes, and if I get through the final exam in December, then I can look for other places of employment," Rudy said.

"Which places will you be looking for positions?" Samir asked.

"I told Sharmi I'd like to find a registrar job in neurosurgery at Newcastle," Rudy said. "It will be tough so I might try in Birmingham."

"That sounds like a good idea," Samir said. "But it might be tough for Sharmi to commute to Durham as it will take more travel time."

Sharmi sighed. "I'll figure it out. I only work for two days a week so may be on those days I will probably get home late."

"Well, it's fine to see you both have good plans," Amita said. "I'm telling you now that in a marriage, it's going take a lot of work, compromise and sacrifice. But don't worry. Your devotion, support and respect for each other's dreams will prevail."

"After the registrar position, you need to be a senior registrar for some time, am I right?" Samir asked Rudy.

"You're absolutely right," Rudy replied, "without that training, one cannot get a consultant's job." He paused to breathe deeply. "Consultant's job or not, I want to be a well-trained neurosurgeon. If possible, I want to go around different institutions in the world where renowned neurosurgeons are practicing neurosurgery. I wish to watch the experts and learn from them. But right now, I have to concentrate and get through my final FRCS."

Samir patted his friend's arm. "You're going to get through it and pass the exam with flying colors."

Rudy nodded gratefully. "Okay, now let's enjoy our day."

"After we left Venice, did you travel anywhere else in Italy?" Amita asked.

"No," Sharmi replied, "but one day we visited an art gallery where the old masters' paintings were, then cruised along the Grand Canal in Venice and watched the sun rise from our hotel room and the beautiful sunsets from the patio of our hotel."

Samir nodded. "That was a great way to relax over there."

Amita sighed. "Oh, we do miss exploring in Venice and Florence and nearby towns." She clasped her hands eagerly. "Do you want to go for a ride today?"

"Well, maybe we can go for a walk or just ride around the area or go to a park and walk around there," Sharmi suggested. "But I think it will be best to just stay here to chat and relax."

It was one thing to actually be on vacation somewhere but now that the friends were all back to their working and studying routines, they all agreed to stay at Amita and Samir's to catch up, relax and chat.

Sharmi and Amita went to the kitchen to check what was in the refrigerator to plan for a light lunch and a typical Bengali dinner.

"I have some pieces of Chad fish," Amita said.

"Oh that will be nice," Sharmi said, "I usually make a preparation with mustard, turmeric, just a small piece of green chili and salt, mix them all together then pour about one teaspoon of mustard oil to mix with the other ingredients then add pieces of Chad then transfer these in a bowl with a cover and steam it."

"That's nice and doesn't seem to be very messy compared to frying the pieces before cooking."

"Frying Chad is really difficult and messy," Sharmi agreed. "It's oily and the air will be filled with a fishy smell. If you want, I can cook it and you will see how easy and not too messy it is."

"I have already prepared Dal, made some mixed vegetable curry and fried pieces of aubergine and steamed rice," Amita said.

"That will be enough for dinner," Sharmi said.

"So what do we do for lunch?"

As soon as Amita finished her sentence, Samir entered the kitchen. "I'm going to make lunch for us."

Sharmi clapped her hands. "That would be wonderful."

"I'm going to make gumbo," Samir said proudly.

Amita and Sharmi cast puzzled expressions at Samir.

"Gumbo?" Amita said. "I've never heard of it."

Despite the unfamiliar dish, Sharmi was curious. "What is it?"

"It's a kind of stew where you include so many vegetables, pieces of meat, seafood like fish and shrimp," he replied.

"How did you find out about this dish?" Amita wanted to know.

"Well, through some visiting nurses from America who were talking about it," Samir explained. "I liked the idea and asked them for the recipe. It's not bland, it is spicy so I thought it would be quite tasty for our palate."

So Samir started preparing the gumbo, first getting a big saucepan. He then chopped vegetables like okra, bell pepper, squash, onions, and celery.

He showed Amita and Sharmi the ingredients he took from the refrigerator and the freezer. "I bought Andouille sausage, medium-sized prawns which I'll use to make the broth with prawn shells and put the prawns later when the vegetables are already cooked.

Amita came forward to help Samir who said, "Now, I need two bay leaves, one teaspoonful of paprika, the same amount of salt, garlic powder and onions."

"There's no garlic powder," Amita said. "I have fresh garlic."

"Even better," Samir said, "Now we can put diced onions and garlic and oh, we have to make roux…"

"How do you make that?" Amita said.

He paused trying to decipher recipe notes he scribbled. "You take some flour and just keep on cooking in oil and when it turns brown, then that is the roux."

"So one has to be careful and try to regulate the heat while cooking," Amita said.

"It takes half an hour to forty minutes to cook the whole thing," Samir said.

"Samir, you start cooking and I will help you make the roux," Amita said.

Samir made the broth with the shells of shrimps in a medium-size sauce pan. He was pleased to be cooking something gourmet that no one in his immediate circle had ever made before.

When the broth was ready, all the vegetables were added to the sauce pan with two fried bay leaves, a teaspoonful of paprika, one teaspoonful of salt with chopped garlic and onions. Then all the ingredients started to cook in the sauce pan.

The roux that Amita made was also added into the sauce pan.

Sharmi, in the meantime, had prepared the Chad fish for dinner.

Amita started cooking her mixed vegetable curry, chopping chard and pieces of potato. Within an hour, preparation for dinner was done by Sharmi and Amita.

Samir's gumbo had been simmering for the last forty-five minutes. "It will continue to cook with frequent stirring, about another hour or so.

After checking the time was 11:30, Samir continued to check the gumbo, reminding himself that he still needed to add chopped parsley.

As Sharmi and Amita went to relax in the living room, Rudy took the opportunity for two and a half hours to concentrate on studying. Even though he felt a bit awkward studying when he should be visiting with his friends, Amita and Samir assured him it was okay if he spent a few hours studying between late morning and early afternoon so he could join them. When he was told that lunch would be ready by 1:30, Rudy took advantage of the time before lunch to concentrate on preparing for the final FRCS examination.

Soon, Samir was happy to announce the gumbo was ready. The whole house was filled with the aroma of gumbo. Samir called everyone to take their seats around the dining table and Rudy arrived first.

"I'm ready to have my delicious lunch," Rudy said. "Oh, the aroma makes me hungrier. Can't wait."

Sharmi and Amita sat around the dining table and Samir, who was all dressed up with an apron and chef's cap, started serving each person.

"What about you Samir?" Sharmi said. "Come and join us."

"Yes, I will join you soon as I serve the gumbo," Samir said, "it doesn't take that long."

The four of them complimented "Chef Samir" on making a delicious gumbo.

Amita and Sharmi said they had already prepared dinner in advance.

"So there's plenty of time for us to talk and enjoy ourselves," Amita said. "What about you, Rudy?"

"Well, I think I'm done with studying for today," Rudy replied. "Now, I just want to enjoy the rest of the time relaxing and spending time with you all. We cannot afford to visit anytime soon till December. Until my final FRCS exam is over. But maybe, Amita and Samir, you could come and stay at our place when I leave for Edinburgh for my examination."

"Absolutely, no problem at all," Samir said, "it will be our pleasure, right, Amita?"

His wife nodded. "Yes, that would be good for us to keep Sharmi company while you are away."

Rudy nodded. "So for today, let's enjoy spending time with each other."

The summer evening drew its curtain. There was still light as birds were still chirping and the gentle summer breeze blew through the tall trees and the ravens cawed in the background.

Rudy and Sharmi planned to leave on Sunday afternoon so there was no rush—just relaxing and being present in the moment as the background music of Ravi Sankar's sitar accompanied by a Tabla recital with a solo in between continued playing, moving the musical debut to eternity, soothed their senses like a promise of tranquility.

Celebrating and Planning

Samir, Amita and Sharmi sat around the kitchen table at Sharmi and Rudy's apartment in Newcastle. The afternoon sun slanted towards the west as the soft rays struggled through the window at intervals. The blast of wind blew through the tall trees as brown and yellow leaves fell off with a twist and a turn amid the cyclone wind only to crawl under the trees to rest as a misty haze hovered.

Perhaps the weather had something to do with the three friends who had been anxious about Rudy and his whereabouts.

"I think there are several trains that run between Edinburgh to Newcastle directly," Amita surmised.

"I know that but…" Samir remarked somewhat cantankerously. "But I was expecting a call at least. I recall the last time Rudy left us wondering how he was doing. Doesn't he realize we're his friends? We're like family, so we worry."

Sharmi's eyes were downcast, her shoulders slumped. "I worry that may be the exam did not go well."

Samir took a deep breath as if willing himself to purge unpleasant thoughts. "Let's not think negative. I'm going to make us all some tea. We all need a cup of tea very badly."

Sharmi started to get up from her seat but Samir held up his hand.

"I know where things are," he said, "you need not worry."

It was 4:30 in the afternoon when Amita picked up the phone to call the Newcastle Railway station. She talked to someone for a few minutes then turned to Sharmi and Samir.

"I think—I hope—we will hear from him in a few minutes or maybe see him within half an hour," she said.

Samir's eyebrows furrowed. "How can you be so sure?"

"I'm not sure," Amita said. "It's just that I've been told the train from Edinburgh just arrived."

No one dared to comment whether Rudy would be on that train or not. As soon as she stopped talking, the telephone rang.

Amita picked up the receiver and gave it to Sharmi.

Sharmi stood a bit frozen as if she dreaded what might be said on the other end. "Hello." Her voice was feeble, unsure.

Rudy's voice on the other end sounded very excited. "I will be there in about a half an hour. I bought some snacks from an Indian grocery shop in Edinburgh. Just make some tea."

Sharmi tried to decipher the tone of her husband's voice. "All right, Amita and Samir are here." She wanted to tell him they were anxious about him but she kept silent.

"Wonderful," Rudy said. "I'll be there as soon as I can."

Sharmi, Amita and Samir were relieved and guessed that it must be good news.

Samir also thought of expressing his worry now dissipated by the fact that Rudy was on his way there. "Oh, let him come but may be we should plan for a celebration?"

Certain it was likely close to dinner time, Amita glanced at the wall clock. "It is 5."

Sharmi nodded as if sensing Amita's concern. "Don't worry, I have already cooked a few things for dinner. Rudy bought some snacks from Edinburgh so we can enjoy those with our tea."

The three of them were excited and anxious so much that any little sound made them jump and think, *Oh! This must be Rudy...*

The doorbell rang and all three of them exclaimed, "Ah, what a relief!"

"After all that anxiety, the doorbell seems to be the sweetest sound I've ever heard," Samir said.

Sharmi rushed to open the door to find an excited Rudy sweep Sharmi off her feet, briefly picking up her petite figure, scooping her up in a warm hug.

Samir and Amita approached Rudy who he each hugged.

"All right, everyone—I finally got through my final FRCS exam!" Rudy announced with glee.

Immediately, his wife and two friends leapt up in jubilation as they all joyfully cheered.

Samir patted his friend on the back. "Well done, Rudy. "Now, how about some tea and those snacks you brought which we keep hearing about." Samir winked.

Rudy smiled. "Yes, I got some Bengali sweets."

Samir's eyes widened. "Oh, like what?"

"Well, there's *Rasamalai*, you know, it's cheese balls made from curdled milk, cooked in syrup then boiled for a few minutes in condensed milk, remember these?"

They sat around the kitchen table to indulge in this calming ritual of a cup of tea complemented with the snacks Rudy bought for them.

Outside, the weather had changed as the wind began blowing and howling strong as lightning flashed.

"Samir and Amita, you should spend the night here, not only for one night but you might as well stay for the weekend."

"What about splitting it?" Amita said cryptically which caused brows to furrow.

"What you mean?" Rudy said.

"I mean, how about we spend the night here then tomorrow is a Saturday so all of us will go to our place and have a party to celebrate your successful completion of the exam?" Amita suggested. "You can both stay there then return when you have to go back to work. You're both not working on Monday, correct?"

Rudy turned to Sharmi who nodded. "Yes," he said to Amita, "that will be all right. Maybe we can come back Sunday evening. But what about you two? Won't you both of be working?"

"No," Amita replied, "this coming Monday we're off."

"Then it's settled," Rudy said, "Looking forward to a nice celebratory weekend."

"I've already cooked dinner so we can all relax," Sharmi chimed in.

Samir patted his fellow doctor friend. "Rudy, I'd like to hear about your final exam experience."

Rudy scratched his head, recalling the anxiety he felt before the exam. "I was terrified but I psyched myself up into believing that I am calm and well prepared."

Rudy took a deep breath then let out a long exhale. "There were three examiners sitting around the table who kept on asking questions. One will finish, while the other one will start. All I remember is that I did not stop and kept right on going. When they finally stopped, I was very exhausted but happy that I could answer all their questions."

"Rudy, when you found out that you passed the exam, what was the first thing that came to your mind?"

He took another deep breath. "Well, at first, I didn't believe that it was really true. I was in daze. Another local doctor—Albert was his name—also got through the exam and he came and shook my hand and said 'Let's celebrate.' I was so tired. I wanted to call Sharmi but I couldn't. I was so drained."

Rudy explained that Albert, his new friend, said, "Wake up, this is a special day," and then he took me to a pub called The Sheep Held Inn, Edinburgh's oldest pub having opened its door in 1360 welcoming reams of historic guests like Mary, Queen of Scots, and recently, Queen Elizabeth II and many poets and writers.

"The pub was located downtown in the picturesque city of Edinburgh. The look of the place from the outside was very unique and impressive to me. The outside wall had been painted in a silvery, gray color with black window frames. The doors were painted black with black-painted wooden panels running across the building horizontally and vertically. The history of the place goes like this: sheeps reared in Holyrood Park in Duddlingston were slaughtered here and the meat was sent to the market. Duddlingston village is halfway between the royal residence of Cragmiller Castle and Holyrood Palace.

"King James, like his mother, the Queen of Scots, was said to have stopped many times and even played skittle in the courtyard behind the pub. So it was very interesting to be there. We ordered drinks like Scottish Ale, which is lighter and malty and of low alcohol content. Albert was the one who ordered everything. I was so tired and hungry that I didn't have the energy to look at the menu. Albert ordered a burger and I said 'the same' and it was fortunate the burgers were delicious served with green salad. It was really a treat. After we finished our lunch, he gave me a ride and, on the way, I stopped at an Indian grocery store and bought these snacks for you so that is all about my time in Edinburgh."

"That is wonderful," Amita said. "I'm glad you had a nice experience."

"Rudy, aren't you feeling light, as if some heavy load was lifted from you?" asked Samir.

Rudy raked his fingers through his hair. "Definitely. Now I have to start hunting for a neurosurgery job. That's the next step."

"Don't worry," Samir assured him, "there will be an opening for a Birmingham neurosurgery job soon."

Rudy's eyes widened. "Really? How do you know?"

Samir smiled as though he was keeping a secret. "I just know."

Amita rubbed her palms together. "All right. No more job-related talk. There will be plenty of time this weekend to talk about that later. For now, let's get ready for dinner. Sharmi worked so hard to cook us a delicious meal."

Amita paused to eye her friend whose head was slightly bowed. "Sharmi, you've been so quiet. What's on your mind?"

Sharmi looked down at her fingers on her lap. "I was very anxious and nervous at the same time since Rudy left for Edinburgh so I am so glad that you both came." She cast Amita and Samir a grateful look. "I was praying so hard. I don't think I had ever prayed so intensely like that before. Mainly for Rudy's sake, just concentrating on only positive thoughts. But it was hard. When you concentrate on trying to think positive, the negative thoughts appear like dark clouds and keep on gathering. So anyway, good thing I focused my thoughts on cooking a delicious dinner to keep me distracted while I was anxiously waiting for your arrival." She smiled wanly. "And now that you're here and that the exam went well, I think I'll sleep like a baby tonight."

Rudy gently patted his wife's hand, concern flooding his eyes. "I am so sorry it was hard on you. I understand how you feel. And I truly appreciate your prayers." Then he slowly got up and stretched after the long train ride. "Now, if you'll excuse me, I'd like to take a warm shower and change into some comfortable clothes."

"Feel free to slip into your pajamas," Samir suggested. "Ladies, do you mind?"

Amita and Sharmi shook their heads. "Not at all."

"Why don't we all change into our comfortable clothes?" Amita advised.

"I'm so glad you gave us permission to change," Samir said with a little laugh.

Sharmi and Amita started arranging the dining table.

"What dishes did you cook?" Amita asked Sharmi.

"Oh, I cooked Dal with green peas, fried aubergine that I sliced in pieces, then dusted them with turmeric powder and salt then added a dash of chili powder and fried them individually until they were dark brown. I also cooked cabbage with pieces of potato and added a tomato."

"How do you cook that?" Amita asked.

"You put two tablespoons of cooking oil in a sauce pan then put a few cumin seeds on the hot oil, add two bay leaves, add potato pieces then fry for a few minutes then add a quarter teaspoon of turmeric, a dash of chili powder, add some crushed ginger root and one teaspoonful of cumin powder. Cook the whole thing for a few minutes then add the chopped cabbage and chopped tomato. Cover the sauce pan and reduce the heat. The whole thing will cook for some time then you add some salt. I add salt later as the volume of cabbage becomes small in quantity when cooked for some time, the water content in the sauce pan will dry slowly. Then add a teaspoonful of sugar and just before you take it out from the stovetop, add a pinch of ground clove, cardamom and cinnamon—then it's done."

"Sharmi, that sounds so elaborate," Amita said, laughing.

Sharmi shrugged. "Once you try cooking it, it becomes easy over time. Oh, and I also made lamb curry for a change and plain rice."

"Wow, Sharmi you cooked up a feast for us!"

They heard Samir's voice. "What's the menu for tonight's celebration dinner. Smells good."

Amita beamed. "Sharmi's serving her special for the day."

"Are you all ready for dinner? You'll find out soon what's on the menu," Sharmi said.

They all sat around the dining table very excited that Sharmi cooked lamb curry which was their favorite, all fully aware of how long it took to prepare. Everyone was pleased to start dinner with rice, dal and fried aubergine and they found the cabbage curry was unique with rice and last, and best of all, the lamb curry with plain white rice was considered a real delicacy for them.

After finishing each course, they praised Sharmi for her excellent culinary skills to which Sharmi replied jokingly, "I should be a chef."

After dinner, Sharmi served them all bowls of special homemade yogurt that tasted a little on the sweet side—thick and creamy. The entire feast left everyone satisfied, impressed and full. All the while everyone enjoyed a glass of wine with their dinner except Sharmi who had ginger ale.

Everyone gathered in the living room after dinner with their wine glasses to plan for the next day.

"I'm going arrange a party Saturday evening for Rudy," Amita said. "We will order food—so no cooking."

"That's nice," Sharmi said. "Where do you want to have breakfast?"

"We'll get up early tomorrow to have breakfast at a coffee corner close to us. We will have a very simple breakfast and for lunch I have a pot of leftover stew we can warm up and eat with bread rolls."

"That sounds nice," Samir said.

"Amita, you plan everything so perfectly, like our Paris trip," Rudy said.

"What's your plan for the evening party?" Samir asked Amita. "Can you give us a clue?"

"Yes," Amita replied. "I will order Biryani and plain rice, vegetable kofta, tandoor chicken, mango chutney. Dessert will be some kind of crepe with filling, something very special. When you try it, you will get an idea of what it is exactly."

Outside, the weather changed and as the wind blew, it whistled through the trees so loud that, at times, you could hear the blast on the windows. Through the closed window pane, one could see the drizzle against the street light. The wet roads flooded with amber streetlights with mist and fog which looked very different and mysterious as if there was a dark tunnel leading to an unknown place.

The roads were empty except for an occasional car that would pass by. A young couple braved the wet footpath, treading close to each other as they tried to balance while holding their umbrella.

Inside Rudy and Sharmi's apartment, the flickering flames of the fireplace broke the monotony of the static living room as the shadows of the décor started dancing on the wall.

The four huddled closer together to plan their future. Rudy had his plan all mapped out: to finish neurosurgery training in Birmingham where he hoped to get a job soon and then come back to Newcastle to finish his registrar and senior registrar training in Newcastle and later, planned to visit neurosurgical centers around the world.

Samir was all set to be a consultant soon. He planned to continue working at the same place that offered he and Amita stability they needed to leisurely trot around the globe whenever chance they get.

Amita had been gradually ascending to a higher position expressing she would someday become the head of the department.

Sharmi's plans included continuing her research on the subject of religion and literature.

Soon, the combination of their hearty meal and their intense future planning discussion made them all tired and sleepy. The weather was a perfect antidote to lull them to sleep as the harsh wind continued to blow with occasional flashes of lightning with the incessant drizzle and whistle of the wind. Then the couples retreated to their respective rooms to snuggle comfortably in their warm beds.

Training and Globetrotting

With a stroke of luck, hard work, and determination, Rudy acquired work in Birmingham where he placed all his energy and enthusiasm into his new position.

The only drawback of the move to Birmingham was the hardship it created for Sharmi who now had to travel to her workplace in Durham which was farther and took more commute time. While working two days a week, she kept her spirits up and continued adjusting to the flow of their new lives.

The new location and position energized Rudy to work even more than his share, a work ethic his consultants took notice of. And it paid off as Professor Brodie Hughes, one of the consultants, was very impressed by Rudy's drive and work ethic.

Though it was more work than play, Sharmi and Rudy kept on moving forward to reach their future goals: Rudy's dream to be trained in neurosurgery in the UK then travel to different parts of the globe to work with people who had their name and fame in neurosurgery and learn from their expertise.

Sharmi supported Rudy trying to fulfill his dream by determining to help him as much as she could. But she had dreams too—hers was to continue her research on the subject of literature and religion at Durham University.

The days and weeks seemed to pass with getting up in the morning, going to work for a busy schedule all day at the hospital, on calls at nights, on call on every third weekend of the month. There were busy clinical rounds of patients with the consultants then catching up with reading journals, clerical tasks like writing notes on the patient's condition, patient care and follow up after the patients had surgery and then again when patients get better. They he had to complete their discharge summary and talk to them at the time of their discharge and advise them about the routine of the follow up.

Then there were outpatient clinics where already discharged patients would come for follow-up appointments. The new patients would show up with their ailments to be examined by the physicians. There was only one-half day in a week off and the weekends—not all but an average of one weekend a month when Rudy was working which would start Friday after 4 in the afternoon until late morning Monday.

Life rolled on faster as time passed by sooner. And on the days after work on his day off, Rudy would find himself revisiting and re-reading Niccolò's biography which had still inspired him now as it had then—that one can achieve great things through passion for one's chosen position in life. For Niccolò, it was sculpting, for Rudy, it was neurosurgery. What got Rudy through seemingly endless hours and days of work was the enthusiasm for one's chosen career instilled in him through his reading of Niccolò's life as though the great sculptor had always been there as his mentor transcending time.

There were Friday evenings to catch up with one's social life meeting friends or paying attention to one's spouse. It was almost near the end of his registrar's job in Birmingham that Rudy's consultant, Professor Hughes helped him to get a Senior Registrar's job in Newcastle. The day Rudy was selected seemed to him that he had stepped closer to his future dream. Working at Newcastle would help shorten Sharmi's travel time so she could relax a little more. The move back to Newcastle meant that Rudy would be back to his familiar place of work resulting in forging an even deeper bond with their longtime friends especially Samir and Amita. Returning to Newcastle was like going home and indeed, for Rudy and Sharmi, it was home.

While Sharmi and Rudy were very excited about moving back to Newcastle, securing the Senior Registrar job had proved to be an even greater challenge for Rudy as he and Sharmi discovered that there were 25 centers around England who offered Senior Registrar jobs, one position for each center, occasionally two at some places, which meant that a selection board would give first preference to British medical graduates who were trying equally as hard to land a Senior Registrar job and they were also well trained and well qualified. Being a foreign medical graduate, Rudy would obviously fall behind them but credit went to Professor Brodie's efforts that landed Rudy his position, an opportunity which Rudy and Sharmi were grateful for.

So happily, they were Newcastle-bound and before accepting the new job, Rudy and Sharmi stayed with Amita and Samir for a few days before moving into their own place in Newcastle. The reunion among the four friends was fun and magical; they were so happy spending time listening to music, talking for hours, watching their favorite Indian movies at night and cooking and eating home-cooked meals together.

When Rudy started his new job in Newcastle, he found the workplace demanded a demonstration of his ability to get along with three different consultants with three different personalities.

Professor Brodie Hughes was very interested with Parkinson's disease and surgery of other movement disorders. So when he had to deal with patients with subarachnoid hemorrhage—this condition occurred usually from bulging blood vessels that burst into the brain—Professor Brodie would refer the younger patients to Mr. Jack Small and older patients to Mr. Eric Turner. If a patient was admitted under him, the patient had to wait for three weeks before he or she would be investigated for fear of a poor outcome.

If a patient was admitted under Jack Small, he would investigate immediately if an aneurysm, a bulge of the wall of a blood vessel, was found. He would take the patient to the operating room and ask the cardiac surgeon to expose the heart by opening the chest and stand by Mr. Small, who after exploring the area of the brain close to aneurysm, would ask the cardiac surgeon to stop the heart for a few minutes. During this time, Mr. Small would clip the aneurysm to prevent bleeding.

The surgery was very dramatic and the patient would go home intact whereas in Mr. Turner's case, a patient while waiting, would die or become disabled from further bleeding.

Rudy was amazed to see the difference and decided to become an aneurysm neurosurgeon. Fortunately, his senior registrar's job in Newcastle gave him the opportunity to do many aneurysm surgeries. The senior neurosurgeon was very confident and comfortable with Rudy's performance so he gave Rudy the freedom to do most of the surgeries, which was indeed an honor for Rudy to have the opportunity and experience to become very confident performing an aneurysm surgery.

As time passed, Rudy realized that he had to learn and refine the technique from the great aneurysm surgeons of the world, a dream he had always had. At this point, he definitely wanted to visit all the centers around the globe.

So he decided to do just that footing the cost and expenses himself using his hard-earned money. And as usual, his beloved wife, Sharmi had encouraged him to follow his passion even considering all her hardships carrying on alone.

Rudy took a leave of absence from work to visit Norway, Sweden, Finland, Germany, Switzerland, Japan, and Canada. In the United States, Rudy visited Massachusetts General Hospital in Boston and the Mayo Clinic witnessing how each of these famous surgeons tackled the challenges and rewards of aneurysm surgery. Some surgeons impressed him and others not so much, but all the while, Rudy formulated several ideas about aneurysm surgery while taking copious notes. He realized a CT scan would give the living pathology of the brain without even seeing the brain. So the condition of the brain had to be respected before embarking on a clipping of aneurysm. At the same time, if there was no reason to delay, the sooner one clips the aneurysm, the better one could stop the recurrent bleeding. In addition, Rudy thought that with the bleeding, the anatomy becomes distorted and the area harboring the aneurysm would look like a jungle.

Rudy used to think the aneurysm, a bulge of the blood vessel, was like a cobra with fangs within the jungle. One had to know the anatomy of the jungle and, with that knowledge, if one did not disturb the apex of the aneurysm where the bleeding was taking place and expose the neck to obliterate with the clip, then the result would be better.

Rudy always reminded him and his colleagues who worked with him that one had to know the *value* of the circle of Willis and the vasospasm—a sudden narrowing of the vessel—and the *role* of the circle of Willis, the area where several blood vessels join at the bottom of the brain and mainly supply blood to both the front and back hemisphere of the brain.

"Looking at it with our naked eye properly and concentrating on the unique technique with our hands, we would usually get unbelievably good results," Rudy said.

While working as a Senior Registrar, Rudy got his master's degree from Newcastle University, writing a thesis on the Circle of Willis. He decided to get a second FRCS from London—having acquired the first one from Edinburgh. After he obtained the second one, Rudy realized that he had a good period of neurosurgical training.

Meanwhile, Sharmi had been anxious to return to India. At this point in their lives, they had been blessed with two beautiful children—a boy and a girl. In 1971, the whole family went to India looking for a job and spending a holiday for the first time in ten years.

Then came an invitation to attend a meeting in Bombay on the west coast of India. This prompted a flashback as Rudy remembered the time he started his journey to the UK from this same port years ago to board the ship SS Roma. Now, he was back, this time heading to a place called Benares where Sharmi's sister lived and then to Kolkata. It so happened that on their way to Kolkata, Rudy and his family found out that a war had started between India and Pakistan, a fact that plagued their vacation in darkness as they reached Kolkata.

Rudy tried different institutions looking for a job and everyone in those institutions advised him that he would be better off in England.

So Rudy became disillusioned, realizing that India, his home country, did not want him and there was so little scope in England. In the middle of this gloomy period, Rudy got a call from Professor Bill Sweet from Massachusetts General Hospital asking if Rudy was interested in working there.

Rudy accepted the invitation to work there as a Senior Resident and at the end of the year he returned to England.

Rudy left the U.S. for several reasons: he realized that all his qualifications earned in England were of no value to the U.S. Also, he had to start from the very beginning again. Then being accustomed with all kinds of free treatment for all, no matter if they were rich or poor, a privilege that appealed to him more, he was in total shock when he found out how many people without insurance were treated in U.S.

Ultimately, Rudy realized that he still held the Senior Registrar job in Newcastle even while he left to the U.S. on sabbatical and was very happy to return back home again to Newcastle by the end of December 1974.

Finally settled back in Newcastle, Rudy thought how his time spent around the world and working in Birmingham was similar to the time Niccolò spent ten years working on the Gattamelata in Padua before he finally returned to Florence. Rudy relished that for both he and Niccolò, life had come full circle as they both found their way back home.

Niccolò Sculpts Penitent Mary Magdalene

A misty spring morning in Florence, 1453 —A spacious room of the cathedral workshop was arranged for Niccolò to sculpt Mary Magdalene. A tall figure with a flowing white overhaul and a white, broad headband around his head entered the room followed by his assistant, standing five feet nine or ten inches tall, dressed in brown breeches and a yellow long-sleeved shirt, holding in one hand a heavy bag and in the other hand, his white overhaul.

The soft sunrays brushed the big trunk of the poplar tree which was solid not being scooped out to make it hollow—Niccolò wanted it that way. Many times, he had closed his eyes and envisioned how Mary Magdalene would look like.

The assistant scanned the room with his bright sparkling eyes. "Maestro, let me arrange the room properly then it will be easy for you to work."

"Paolo, please leave the heavy big work bench with the poplar tree trunk there near the window so there will be plenty of light and kindly arrange the sculpting tools. I do not want to scoop out the trunk and make it hollow."

"Maestro, are you sure?"

"Yes, I am absolutely positive," Niccolò asserted. "I do not want to be restricted by any rules and regulations of wood carving as other sculptors have done and continue to do."

Paolo blinked his eyes in confusion. "Maestro, have you had any training in wood sculpting?"

"No, but I understand that wood cracking is a problem with wood sculpting, Paolo, you will soon find out why. The position of the figure in the trunk will be done in such an ingenious way that the chance of wood cracking will be minimum." He examined the wood. "The difficulty of sculpting with wood is that the long hair on the sculpture would not fall smoothly. It will be more in matted ropes, sticking to her face and wasted body."

Paolo nodded. "That is absolutely true, Maestro, I am so amazed that you grasped everything so fast and you know so much. All these years I have been so lucky to work and assist you."

Niccolò took a deep breath eager to begin. "Let us start with an introduction of our new subject so that we can better understand her. Mary Magdalene of Magdala was a leading figure among the followers of Jesus. According to the gospel, she stayed with him at the moment of his crucifixion and was the first to witness his resurrection."

Niccolò closely examined the huge poplar tree trunk with the sun casting its mighty rays on it. He gestured Paolo to come and examine the poplar closely. "Mary Magdalene will stand over six-feet tall made of wood and stucco. She will depart from the smooth marble and bronze sculpture. This is how I envision her to be: she will be staggering and unique in the sense that she will be expressing the inner thoughts and feelings through her emaciated body by fasting and abstinence to such an extent that every part of her body reflects a perfect and complete understanding of human anatomy."

"Wow, Maestro, that is definitely a different vision than what is traditionally done and in wood no less. When are you going to start sketching?"

"Yes, Paolo, but the problem is the tree trunk is not so smooth as marble. It will not be easy to put the sketched paper and outline the figure on the trunk of the wood. Yet it will help quite a lot so please fix the sketching paper on the board."

"Right away, Maestro."

"And I will let you know which particular tools I need for wood carving after I finish my sketching."

Paolo scratched his head. "Please give me a list so I can search whether we have these in our studio and if some are missing, I can go acquire these tools."

"Hmm, I see your point. Well, the most important ones are a chip carving knife, a drill press, and, what else?" He paused, scratching his head as he kept thinking. "Oh yes, a band saw, mallet, hardwood and rubber, carving knife, gouges, bent and spoon gouge. V gouges are the workhorses of wood carving. A skewed chisel cutting edge is angled back from the leading edge at a forty-five-degree angle, and a carpenter's chisel." He caught his breath. "That is all I can think of—oh, I forgot about the chainsaw."

"Maestro, I will start looking for them while you sketch."

"In the meantime, I will do the outline and lower part of the body—the face and upper part of the body I will finish tomorrow," Niccolò said.

"Please proceed with whatever way you think would be best," Paolo said.

Niccolò nodded. "I will start carving the body after I finish sketching."

He then proceeded to concentrate on sketching while Paolo went out looking for the tools, first granting permission from cathedral authorities to search for wood carving tools in their storage.

The morning flew by fast and soon, it was afternoon when Paolo returned to Niccolò's work station.

Paolo was slightly out of breath from his exhaustive search. "Maestro, I gathered almost everything except the chainsaw."

Niccolò was still working on his sketching. "Do not worry. I already have one and whatever we request, the cathedral will provide. We do not need that immediately."

"I could not carry all of them so I have to go back and bring the rest."

"That is all right, Paolo. Let us have a lunch break first."

"I brought some food but I have to warm it up," Paolo said.

"There is a kitchen where we can go to warm up the food," Niccolò said.

"And there is a small table that I can set up for us," Paolo said. "There is one chair in addition, there are several stools here."

"We need plates and spoons," Niccolò said.

"I got everything and kept them in one of the closets," Paolo said. "And I brought orange blossom water in a clay jug and two wooden glasses for water and got spoons, bowls and plates for us which I plan to keep here while we work in this workshop."

Niccolò nodded in acknowledgement. "Good. Now, I will explain to you how I want to present Mary Magdalene to the viewer. The moment the viewer sees her, Mary appears to be caught up in a personal moment between Christ and herself. She does not invite viewers directly by her look but the openness of the sculpture will draw them closely to her space. The viewer will be drawn into the moment of quiet internal conversation and contemplate her story and perhaps their own spiritual life."

Niccolò concentrated on the sketching of Mary Magdalene with Paolo right by his side observing. As scheduled, Niccolò finished sketching within a few days. Now the challenge was tracing the whole sketch on the poplar trunk. The uneven surface of the trunk had to be evened out with a tool first, where you could hold the tool, which had a sharp metallic edge attached to it, and with a sweeping motion, the rough surface would ultimately be smoothed out taking the rough surface of wood out of it.

Paolo held the sketching paper while standing on a bench. The sculpture would stand six feet tall; extra wood had to be removed from the trunk. Paolo helped Niccolò remove the extra wood by sawing it from the poplar trunk.

Eventually, much time had passed—very fast it seemed—and they soon found themselves nearly at the end of August 1453. Niccolò had his vision of how to depict Mary Magdalene after being ill in Padua and realized the physical and emotional toll the illness had on his body. At present, he could almost feel the emaciated physique of Mary Magdalene whom he wanted to sculpt in a different way. And so Niccolò deliberately chose wood instead of a smoother material such as marble or any other stone to sculpt something uniquely staggering and psychologically telling.

Eventually as days and months passed, Mary Magdalene's sculpture started shaping up in the cathedral workshop. Day in and day out, Niccolò showed up to the cathedral workshop where Paolo waited for his Maestro while arranging tools in the morning then helped and followed his directions and specifications as the seasons changed from summer to fall to winter. Occasionally, when the days were short, they would go home early. But time in the workshop was time well spent.

All too soon, the 20th of December 1453 fell upon them and the wooden sculpture of Mary Magdalene continued to take shape—standing tall with her wasted body, looking like she found some strength to continue her penitence. There was slight *contrapposto* of one leg—bent at the knee—and with the other leg placed forward, it seemed like she was trying to move forward in a state of dynamism.

Niccolò beckoned Paolo to bring the two arms he sculpted separately.

"Paolo, I want to screw the arms now and we will see how she looks. Her hands will be placed in a gesture of prayer but still will not touch."

"Here is one arm," Paolo said, handing it over to Niccolò, "when you finish working with that, I will give you the other one."

"All right," Niccolò said. "Today we will do just the arms and examine her carefully to study her expression."

Niccolò took time to put the arms and hands on both sides together by screwing them at the joints below the shoulders. "See how her hands are placed in a gesture of praying but still do not touch?" Niccolò told Paolo after placing both arms. "She wants to keep on praying. As a believer, she has hope in salvation despite her physical weakness, she is gaining strength to continue her penitence."

"I understand what you are trying to say—"

"But do you really?" Niccolò's expression changed. His eyes looked far into the distance and his tone of voice rose as he started talking forcefully, his face flushed.

"Paolo, you must know, sculpting Mary Magdalene will offer a powerful insight and reality of the mental state. She is the symbol of powerful human expression and dynamism. She is not shown surrounded by angels and ascending to heaven. She is alive! She is alive, Paolo!" Niccolò's voice rose higher and higher. "She is alive and suffers as any one of us would in her circumstances."

Paolo was quiet, appearing to absorb all his Maestro said. "I understand now how you want her to be presented."

"Mary's face is the most psychologically telling part of the sculpture," Niccolò continued, enthusiastically. "Her lips are parted as if she is being caught in the middle of a sentence. Her hands are not joined together and she gazes outward with intensity. Her hollowed cheeks, missing teeth, matted hair, sunken eyes are evident from the toll taken from both her sinful and her reformed life as an ascetic."

Paolo nodded. "What are some aspects you want to concentrate on the sculpture right now?"

"We have to sculpt separately the bundles of hair then stucco it on the sculpture. Then with different gouges, we must work on her face to make everything vivid, most likely scoop out more wood. The bundles of hair will cover her body. There is much to do there around the level of her waist. I want to put a bundle of hair going around like a belt. At the end, we have to paint her in gold color." He stopped to catch his breath.

"By the way, when we sculpt the bundles of hair, I think we have to paint those bundles in gold, before we glue them on the sculpture and again paint another layer of color after we glue them. We shall see. For now, let us start with the bundle of matted hair."

"All right, Maestro."

While Niccolò concentrated on making the matted bundles of hair, he told Paolo he will continue work on the matted hair until the 23rd of December so both of them can take a break.

"Tia, Amadeo and his wife will be arriving on the afternoon of the 23rd," Niccolò informed his assistant. "This year, Tia wants to celebrate Christmas and New Year at our house and she is bringing a helper. As always, your cousin is there to help our household. As you know, she has been helping us for long time since mother Orissa was living, we are very fortunate. So Paolo, I am also inviting you to join us if you can."

"That is really nice of you, thank you. I will try during the Christmas holiday to visit you and your family. It has been a long while since I saw Amadeo."

"Amadeo and Andrea's two boys are studying in Padua, so are Stefano's children. They are all at Marcello and Angela's house spending Christmas there so Tia, Amadeo and Andrea will go back on either Tuesday the 3rd or Wednesday the 4th of January. So we can start working on Thursday, the 5th of January. What do you think?"

"That is fine with me."

Niccolò and Paolo continued working diligently to sculpt the bundles of matted hair.

Then on the 23rd of December, 1453, when the soft rays of the noon sun passed through the misty glass window and illuminated Mary Magdalene's disheveled appearance and tortured expression, Niccolò suddenly cried out loud:

"Paolo! Paolo! Come look! She is reliving a moment of thankfulness and grace from Christ and glimpsing hope."

Paolo reached his arms up to stretch. "Maestro, you are right, her expression looks so real. I can see her emotion."

Niccolò noticed Paolo's weary countenance. "Let us take a break and go have lunch at the Osteria today. I will close the studio so we can go home after lunch."

"Maestro, please have a wonderful time with sister Tia, Amadeo and Andrea. I will definitely try to meet you all during our Christmas break."

Niccolò and Paolo headed towards the Osteria as the wintery breeze blew through the tall cypresses along the roadside while bare birch and maple trees stood there shaking their frosted branches. The sun hid beyond the gray clouds that were threatening to melt down in rain.

Upon reaching the Osteria, they took seats close to the open fire oven where a big iron container with steaming beef stew was suspended by an iron hook from the brick-layered ceiling of the open fire oven. The delicious aroma filled the air.

Niccolò and Paolo enjoyed lunch with freshly-baked bread and a big bowl of beef stew with hot anise drink.

* * *

On a cold morning the fifth day of January, 1454, while Niccolò was getting ready to go to his studio after his sister, Tia and family left yesterday afternoon, he reflected on the past few days of celebration. During Christmas Eve, Tia and Andrea decorated their cottage where the smell of pine added with the smell of cooked food accompanied with waves of cheerful chatter punctuated by their crushing laughter filled the air.

On Christmas day, everyone sat around the fireplace with hot beverages and food, talking about the present and past filled with golden memories of their parents, especially Mother Orissa who they missed yet whose presence they still felt. Armed with a platter full of home-baked varieties of pastries, Paolo took time from his own busy family festivities to visit Niccolò and his family.

Suddenly, the clip-clapping sound of a horse-drawn carriage that stopped in front of his cottage snapped Niccolò back to the present. After a few minutes, he heard a gentle knock at his door and he wondered, *who was it and what could be so urgent that they had to show up at his doorstep?*

When Niccolò opened the door, the carriage driver bowed. "The Honorable Cosimo de' Medici has asked me to tell you that starting today, my duty is to pick you up every day from your home and give you a ride to your studio and, at the end of the day, pick you up from your studio and give you a ride back to your home or anywhere you would like a ride to, I shall always be at your service."

Niccolò looked at him blankly. "I am fine and I can walk. I do so every day."

"Maestro, please understand, Signore de' Medici has specifically assigned me this service for you. He urges you to please, do not refuse."

"Well, I understand you are doing your job. But I must speak to Signore de' Medici to inquire as to why he is doing this extra favor for me."

"Maestro, it is very simple. He wants you to not waste your energy and tire yourself out walking in rain or during the hot summer to reach your studio. He believes your energy must be spent on sculpting and creating art."

Soon after, the carriage's clip-clapping sound reached the cathedral workshop prompting Paolo to come out. He was amazed to see his Maestro getting down from a most elegant carriage.

Before the carriage pulled away, the driver, Ruperto, told Niccolò that he will be coming back to pick him up just before 4 o'clock and he will wait until he finishes his work. If he needs to come sooner than that, then he should let him know.

As Niccolò bid the driver, "See you later," Paolo was very anxious to know what was going on.

Niccolò explained that it was Cosimo's desire that Niccolò be transported to and from his place of work by carriage on a daily basis. He also said the carriage driver would be available for any of Niccolò's other travel needs.

Paolo was very pleased. "Maestro, it is about time they recognized you in the manner that you deserve by attending to your needs."

* * *

Mid-morning, spring of 1454—On a particularly sunny day, the cool breeze blew through the tall birch tree's long branches. Some remained covered with small green leaves while some were not quite fully open, trying to unfold, still dazed in a wintery dream. But birds who welcomed spring were hopping and singing their songs while the river Arno kept streaming happily with boats loaded with people.

Niccolò and Paolo kept busy working on the bundles of matted hair of the sculpture.

Paolo rubbed his hands and squinted his eyes. "Maestro, it seems as though there's no end to this."

Niccolò sighed. "Paolo, please understand the whole body of the sculpture will be covered with matted hair—she is six-feet-tall. Do not worry, I think we are going to finish her hair by the end of spring. Just a few more bundles and then we start painting her in gold by summer when the paint will dry out soon."

"I understand." But Paolo's tone sounded deflated.

Niccolò paused from his task. "Listen, after Mary Magdalene, I do not have any other project to work on. People know I am not as strong as before. Signore de' Medici had already offered me a villa on a hill just on the outskirts of Florence with all sorts of amenities and a staff to look after me. But I am not going to take that. I intend on staying in the city in my own humble cottage."

"Maestro, as long as you have your studio, I will continue working with you so you can teach me how to get better and better—"

Just as Paolo uttered that last word, a priest from the cathedral appeared at the entrance of the workshop asking Paolo about Niccolò who welcomed him inside their work space.

"Don Reverendo, welcome to my work place." Niccolò invited the priest to sit down on a cushioned chair.

"I am here to discuss some important matter with you," the priest said, somewhat cryptically.

Niccolò nearly held his breath in suspense. "Yes, Don Reverendo?"

"My dear Niccolò, we have a few more workshops inside the cathedral where young artists are being trained to sculpt and I wonder if you could take charge of the teaching? Currently, there are two young sculptors who are trying hard to teach but what we need is someone with your expertise and experience to supervise all of them."

"Don Reverendo, while I am most honored by your offer to teach, you do know at present I am very much occupied with Mary Magdalene's sculpture, and you are aware that commission came straight from the cathedral."

"Yes, yes, I am very well aware of that matter, yet I implore you to consider this offer as everyone from the cathedral is asking—no, *begging* you to accept this role. To make matters more convenient for you, we shall wait until such time when you will be ready to join the team in charge of honing the skills of these young sculptors. In fact, the Honorable Cosimo de' Medici would very much appreciate your contribution of time as he is involved with the program. Niccolò, please do us the honor of accepting our request."

Niccolò looked at Paolo whose eyes sparkled in favor of this opportunity. The great sculptor sat down quietly for a few minutes as Paolo and the priest waited. Finally, Niccolò looked up, and said, "All right, I will accept."

The Domopera clapped his hands. "Bless you, dear Niccolò, you have made us all very happy!"

Niccolò and Paolo bowed to the priest who made his way toward the door, his long, black cassock rustling with the movements of his stride until it became fainter and fainter as he proceeded through the corridor.

Paolo clasped his hands eagerly. "Maestro, you got this very important job so you do not have to think about whether or not anyone will give you another commission."

Niccolò nodded his mind at ease. "You are right, now I do not have to think about my daily expenses for my basic needs of survival. And you will be here in my studio and I will see to it that you get more commissions through my circle of friends who are associated with people who have money to spend for the enrichment of art."

It was an early afternoon when the sun was still up in the sky, that the sound of a carriage clip-clapping on the cobblestones alerted Niccolò and Paolo to board the carriage towards their home. The blast of a cool breeze refreshed them as Niccolò felt somewhat relieved and Paolo was content that his Maestro obtained an important teaching job ensuring financial security for the rest of his life with no worries about daily expenses.

Niccolò and Paolo decided to finish the bundles of matted hair in the near future, targeting a completion date for this portion of the project by the end of May. They continued working diligently to get the bundles of hair done then began the next stage in the process—painting the individual bundles in gold.

Summer went by swiftly for Niccolò and Paolo who were relieved that the painting was done for the entire bundle of matted hair. Now, it was time to attach the piece onto her body. In the process of doing that Niccolò said, "Golden hair is a reminder of her former beauty and sensuality while on the other hand, matted bundles of hair are a symbol of her neglect of worldly things during her life as a hermit."

"Maestro, I fully understand what this particular sculpture represents."

"After getting all the bundles attached to the body, we have to go back again to work on her face. We want to work on her disheveled appearance and the tortured expression on her face."

"Maestro, I will ask you about a few more details when we work on that part of the sculpture."

It took more than the estimated time to attached the bundles on the body of Mary Magdalene but it turned out to be well worth the effort.

Niccolò stood back to assess the sculpture. "I am glad this time consuming, tedious process is finally complete and we have to paint one more time with gold color. But before that, I will go back and work on the face of Mary Magdalene."

"Maestro, that sounds good and when you finish everything to your satisfaction, we can finally paint the whole sculpture."

Soon the autumn season was upon them as the leaves of trees started to change colors and a breeze brought the message of a cool winter ahead.

Niccolò begin focusing on fine-tuning Mary Magdalene's face, giving it an emaciated appearance with visible, protruding cheekbones and making the eyes more sunken by taking out the wood by gouges.

"Maestro, why would you want to do that?"

"I want to make Mary extremely thin representing the physical effects of fasting and to such an extent that every part of her body reflects a perfect and complete understanding of human anatomy. She left her past behind and her present is a story of repentance and redemption—both are wrapped up together in one image and now, her entire life is out in the open for viewers to see."

Again, more months flew past until they reached the spring of 1455 when one afternoon, the breeze was still cool and fresh as the scent of daffodils and tulips wafted through the cathedral workshop. The birds were hopping on the branches of the trees dressed with dewy, fresh green leaves while indoors, Niccolò and Paolo busied themselves painting Mary Magdalene in gold. They were almost at the end of their task as all that was left to be done included putting the last coat of color and then thoroughly examining every inch of the sculpture to determine if there was any crevice they missed.

The days passed by painting then meticulously checking the parts of the sculpture, giving special attention to the little spaces in between the matted bundles of hair on the body and the face where the matted hair stuck on her protruding cheek bones. Later on, as the weather changed, the summer heat helped the sculpture dry out faster.

One afternoon in the fall of 1455 as the sun's soft rays touched the disheveled, haggard-looking, penitent Mary Magdalene, Niccolò excitedly beckoned his assistant.

"Paolo, come quick! She is alive! I can hear her talking! Can you hear her?"

"Maestro, no, I cannot hear her but, to me, she is a reminder of her former beauty and sensuality and her neglect of worldly things during her life as a hermit is evident in the touch of the grace of Christ that seems to be suspended between her beautiful fingers."

The rustling noise of the Domoperas' long cassocks were heard at the door. Paolo and Niccolò saw the three of them entering awestruck by the sculpture's paroxysmal expression of faith and penitence and moving vision of her body's downfall which enriched and extended the emotional changes of this work of art.

"My dear reverends, this penitent Mary Magdalene offers a powerful reality that we are invited to view. This sculpture urges us to see Mary as a human being, dynamic and expressive—not a saint surrounded by angels ascending to heaven for she is alive!" Niccolò's voice rose higher and higher, echoing beyond the work room and down the long corridors of the cathedral. "She is alive and suffers as any of us would in her circumstances. You see how her eyes look onward as if she were waiting for something, her hands placed in a reverent gesture yet still do not touch, symbolizing she has hope and finds the strength to continue. One leg is slight *contropposto*, while the other leg moves forward. There is a dynamism." At this point, Niccolò's voice became emotional yet triumphant for in piecing together Mary Magdalene in this state was akin to symbolizing his own journey of overcoming adversity through the challenges of work, life, regret, and great loss only to emerge more resilient. And as he described Mary Magdalene to the priests, it was almost as though he was describing himself.

"My dear reverend gentlemen, Mary Magdalene is not only a symbol of remorse, Mary Magdalene is a symbol of courage and survival."

Rudy's Encounter with other Neurosurgeons

On a gray and windy morning, Rudy, who had been a senior registrar, was on track towards the next step—becoming a consultant. Mostly through to the late 1970s, the chance of getting a position of consultant for an Indian doctor was very difficult. But again, Rudy's hard work and determination helped him secure the position of senior registrar fellowship. Though neurosurgery requires a longer period of time, Rudy's wait was worthwhile as there was the possibility that a senior neurosurgeon would likely retire in the near future.

In the department of neurosurgery, there were three neurosurgeons, one who was very influential and renowned and had his own way of dealing with the surgery of aneurysm of the brain, a bulging in the wall of the artery due to weakness. Which usually ruptures and bleeds inside the brain, the cause mostly due to atherosclerosis.

To start it, a professor explained to Rudy that his way of dealing with the condition was, instead of going to the small branch where the bulging was, he wanted to clip the main artery from where the small artery branched. It worked in a few cases but mostly due to vasospasm, patients suffered from less blood supply to other areas of the brain resulting in weakness and loss of sensation of limbs and mental disabilities.

Rudy tried to explain to other neurosurgeons, "Professor, I did clinical research on the importance of the Circle of Willis in aneurysm. The circle of Willis at the inferior side of the brain where the internal carotid artery—the main artery that supplies blood to the brain branches into smaller arteries that supply oxygenated blood to over 80 percent of the brain. Professor, I ended up in Newcastle University and submitted my thesis."

Rudy suddenly remembered his visit to Florence where he had envisioned and heard the tour guide explaining the famous sculptor Niccolò's work in 15th century Firenze. Niccolò had been the one who started sculpting *contrapposto* that is when the sculpted figure would stand on itself without support at the back. He was the first one who invented the method when he was asked by his assistant and other rising sculptors "What is ahead for future generation of artists and the artistic world?"

Niccolò took a deep breath and exhaled, started slowly, "Creativity flows like an endless river flowing through all the areas of work and profession. When the stream flows through the creator, he is the one who can guide and make it unique and alive."

The clock tower started chiming and Rudy came back to the present with renewed confidence, strong enough to explain his case.

"This is what I see with the bleeding, the anatomy gets distorted and the area harboring the aneurysm is like a cobra with its fangs within the jungle," Rudy stated. "We have to know the jungle with that knowledge. If we do not disturb the apex from where the bleeding takes place, we just expose the neck to obliterate with the clip."

"That is just your imagination," the professor countered, "I do not agree and the department will not help you either."

Rudy was very disappointed and it seemed that the walls were closing in on him, yet something came from inside him, telling him not to quit. So with his strong determination, he tried to find ways around it. At last Rudy somehow managed to get permission to carry on with the surgery the way he wanted but there was the big question: What if he fails and the patient's condition gets worse?

On a gray morning that turned out to be stormy and misty, Rudy left home in the wee hours while Sharmi was still in bed. He did not want her to know that he was anxious and nervous for this important surgery that would test and prove his abilities.

The patient was already prepped and his younger assistant ready, welcoming Rudy with a smile. "Sir, we are ready."

Rudy scrubbed up quickly as the patient was under anesthesia. Then the scalp was prepped and marked. With the scalpel, skin and muscles were lifted off the bone and folded. Next, small bur holes were made in the skull with a drill. The bur hole allowed entrance for a speared saw like a jig saw, called a craniotome. Rudy outlined a bone window and cut open the flap to expose the covering layer of the brain. The bone flap was set aside which would be replaced at the end.

The covering layer called dura was opened to expose the brain. Retractors which were stainless steel blades with handles were used gently to open a corridor between the brain and skull. Rudy located the artery and followed the aneurysm. Then very gently, Rudy handled which one he could rupture. The neck of the aneurysm was prepared for clipping. Rudy took the titanium clip with a tweezer and clipped the neck all done—no bleeding and with great relief Rudy took a deep breath. The clock at the operation theater made some clicking sound which caused everyone to look and realize that it was just 9:30 since they started at 8 in the morning. It took another half an hour to close the wound.

The anesthetist gave a thumbs up to indicate the patient was doing all right.

Rudy was overwhelmed with joy and so were all the staff assisting him. Afterwards, Rudy announced that he wanted to do more surgeries like this and see the consistency of the results and all the staff members agreed to help him.

He nearly ran through the blizzard to his home which was warm and cozy. Once inside, he stretched his arms to hug Sharmi who came running to greet her husband. They embraced themselves tightly without exchanging words. The flickering flames of the fireplace lit up Sharmi's face while the shadows started dancing on the wall.

Time seemed to stop when Rudy pulled Sharmi even closer to him as he kissed her.

From then on, Rudy managed to operate on a number of aneurysm patients from different areas of England and also from other countries such as France, Italy, Egypt and Greece. After the procedure, they all went home feeling better without further bleeding and disability. The news of his success spread like wildfire far and wide. Soon after, Rudy received an invitation to an international neurosurgical conference in Bermuda. Rudy was happy yet anxious as he told his wife, "The conference is in Bermuda. I hope my project would not get lost like ships that vanished in the Bermuda Triangle."

To further support him, Sharmi accompanied Rudy to Bermuda where he presented his paper showing his results and where neurosurgeons from different parts of the world attending the conference cheered Rudy on for his wonderful presentation.

To the shock of everyone present, one of the British neurosurgeons shouted from the audience: "Black magic! Black magic!" And booed.

The rest of the audience disapproved this kind of behavior.

Then Professor Harkinson stood up. "The views of Dr. Sen are only his personal expression and not the view of the hospital. In fact, the professor's paper showed that some of his patients did not make it at the end and others became disabled."

One audience member picked up the microphone and countered his comments very harshly. Most of the attendees cheered Rudy at the end, even awarding him with a thunderous applause aimed to put this interloper in his place.

At the end of the conference Rudy rushed over to Sharmi who sat in a corner of the conference hall.

Sharmi smiled. "Your ship is well on its way to a faraway land."

Then they walked out of the conference room holding their hands firmly.

A blast of moist, cool breeze blew through their hair and face reminding them of their birthplace, Chittagong, a land they left far, far away and in the midst of the breeze. They could hear the famous quote from Xuanzang, the Chinese traveler who commented that Chittagong is a sleeping beauty arising from mist and water—an Emerald by the sea.

Rudy's Unique Procedure Gains Momentum Globally

Rudy's unique technique of treating aneurysm became well known that it was featured in articles in various publications and in addition, Rudy was invited to various conferences and centers to give lectures and to operate on aneurysm. The young neurosurgeons from those countries wished to be trained by Rudy.

As a result, young neurosurgeons from India, Pakistan, Greece, Spain, Italy, Sweden, Syria, Iraq, Iran, Egypt, Brazil, Argentina, Guatemala, Australia, and the U.S. came to Newcastle hospital to work, to get training, or just observe Rudy working and operating on patients for a few days.

Rudy was happy to train around 100 Indian neurosurgeons and he even had a most celebrated patient—the President of India, Mr. Venkataram's wife who had a brain hemorrhage. Prime minister Rajiv Gandhi was advised to contact Rudy who went to New Delhi and pleaded with the patient to get the angiogram done in All India Medical Institute (AIMS). She refused and insisted on going to Newcastle for everything. That event helped accelerate Rudy's reputation towards international recognition.

The next interesting event that happened at the time was the Japanese Society wanted to arrange an international conference inviting all the top aneurysm surgeons from different countries. To Rudy's amazement, they invited Rudy be the representative from the U.K. While each representative was carrying the flag of their respective country, for Rudy, it was hilarious to be holding a Indian passport while he was carrying the British flag.

Rudy grew accustomed to treating patients from different countries so patients were coming as private patients and would pay heavily to the hospital that way the authority allowed Rudy to take such patients.

It seemed the success of light shone on Rudy very brightly and that his dreams were coming true with each accomplishment and each achievement.

In Newcastle, Rudy became the favored neurosurgeon for neurologists and they made sure that Rudy stayed in Newcastle and by the late seventies the neurosurgical world became Rudy's oyster.

From near and far, he continued getting invitations from all over the world to give lectures on his unique procedure or to perform aneurysm operations. He even provided surgical advice by telephone to Borneo and advised a doctor from New Zealand about removing a clot from the brain.

Rudy continued working harder and harder, he could not even stop traveling all over the world. To him, it seemed as if he was floating and being swept up in a stream of energy with no escape. It was a very unique and often surreal feeling.

But just then—amid riding the wave of success— out of nowhere, tragedy struck as the news arrived that Rudy's bright young son, who was on his way to becoming a physician from a prestigious medical college in London, had a tragic accident. The news shattered Rudy and Sharmi who rushed there to visit their son. Then it was hope against hope to feel and believe that their beloved son would not leave them, yet the dark curtain of death fell on the bright, young man. That even the strong bond of his parents' love could not hold him enough to stay in this world.

And that world fell apart for Rudy and Sharmi as life changed completely around them. Thinking that somehow it was his fault, guilt consumed Rudy—that what had happened was a result of his neglecting family duties as he was completely engulfed with his world-is-your-oyster realm of neurosurgery.

Then all that he spent his life dreaming of—becoming a successful neurosurgeon—became to him, at least at that moment—the bane of his existence. So much that Rudy wanted to quit neurosurgery, in fact, he wanted to quit *everything*. In his darkest moments of grief, Rudy turned to the pages of Niccolò's biography again, and there he found solace, especially in the part of Niccolò's life where he had lost his beloved mother. And so, before going to bed, Rudy allowed himself to share his own grief with that of Niccolò's, a moment of comfort transcending time.

Sharmi's pain and guilt grew equally as deep and intense as a mother's grief could be as she mourned the loss of a child that she herself had brought into this world. *What else could I have done?* Played torturously like a broken record in her mind.

What else is there in the future? What else is there right now?

Mornings and evenings seemed to be the same—all dark—no light—no solace.

With seemingly no way out, no hope. Not ever.

Dear friends, like Amita and Samir, reminded Rudy and Sharmi of their beautiful daughter whose life had just started to blossom and that she was still here in this world to bring her parents light and love. All was not lost, their friends would say.

For Rudy and Sharmi's daughter was a beautiful combination of her parents—one of the brightest students studying in the medical field. At around the same time, Rudy's friend, a doctor from Hyderabad, almost forced him to complete the book Rudy was writing on the subject of Subarachnoid Hemorrhage.

Eventually, Sharmi's pain and suffering lessened a bit by the passage of time when her attention started to focus on her daughter. Sharmi also had a dream one night that she saw her son flying away with angels just above their home in Newcastle.

* * *

Before the family tragedy, Rudy had been visiting all the neurological centers in India and it struck him painfully that from the east part of India in Bengal Kolkata, patients had to go to south India for any treatment or care for any neurosurgical problems.

After researching the matter, it turned out that the infrastructure for neurosurgery was not there and also the neurosurgeons were not there to treat the patients with empathy. Rudy could not bear the miserable state of affairs in Kolkata, the city which made him a doctor. So he wanted to do something about it but when tragedy struck, after a period in which he doubted whether he could go on with neurosurgery, eventually within time, he felt that good work would be his salvation.

Then suddenly, like a grace from heaven, it came to him—the dream of creating a National Neuroscience center and Neurological and Neurosurgery center in Kolkata. And with this newfound mission that combined his passion with his determination to help those in need, this started to form like a cumulus cloud soon to be precipitated.

The need to share this idea prompted Rudy to discuss the project with Sharmi and his daughter, Anjali. For the first time in a long time, Rudy's idea gave his family a reason to hope, to happily sit down and talk about a very important mission—a live-saving mission.

"It is going to be a huge project," Rudy said, "the money that we have saved so far will not be at all sufficient."

"You know, I don't need anything, money or property from you," Anjali said, "so you can put whatever you meant to save for me into your project. I am established enough in my career and can handle my future finances."

By then, Anjali was a professor of anatomy at Bristol.

Rudy and Sharmi patted their daughter's hand.

"It's very sweet and nice of you to let us know your feelings," Sharmi said.

"It is still a small amount compared to what we are embarking on," Rudy said.

"So what do you plan to do?" Anjali asked.

"I will approach the owners of large, successful businesses to request for donations and I will travel all over the globe to ask people who are well established for donations," Rudy said. "Also doctors from India living abroad and as well others I know very well."

"You must have land to build it," Sharmi said. "Do you have an idea where?"

"I have an idea of where I want it to be built but I don't know whether I will get a piece of land there," Rudy said. "And even if I do know where, I'm not sure whether it will be affordable. I'm thinking perhaps in a center of the city. Maybe I'll go around and meet people and ask them to donate a piece of land. It wouldn't hurt to ask at least."

"So it appears this is a huge project that needs investing in tremendous effort to get it accomplished," Anjali said.

"You are absolutely right," Rudy said. "I have to travel back and forth to India, not only to India, but also around the world to ask my friends for help. It is my ultimate challenge but also my greatest contribution to the field of neuroscience and neurosurgery. To bring neuroscience in the highest order—this I take as my ultimate mission.

"I am not looking for recognition like 'Neurosurgeon of the Millennium,' a brain operating theater, nor a Medal of Honor by the World Federation of Neurological Societies or an Honorary title of Doctorate degree by the Newcastle University."

"Ah, but you missed mentioning a few. One of them is an OBE by Her Majesty the Queen," Anjali said in a teasing tone. "You don't look for these yourself but people have recognized your work and rewarded you as a token of their appreciation. They gave you these awards to be treasured and carry those as an example to others so that they get energized to work for the good of humanity."

"I know I cannot compete in communicating with the younger generation," Rudy chuckled softly. "You win, Anjali."

The idea and the dream of the neuroscience institute started to crystalize in Rudy's imagination. He was restless and could not sleep soundly at night.

So one foggy morning when the sun rays struggled to peep through the tall pine trees in his backyard, he paced fast with his smoking pipe on his lips, fixing his gaze at a distance then murmured, "I can start around two to three days from now. I have to start somewhere, sometime. No more time to doubt about the uncertainty of the future."

He seemed suddenly energized as if he finally got the answer he was searching for and hurried inside the house to call Sharmi. "I'm going to Kolkata in few days. I know someone who lives close to the place where I would like to build the institute."

"Where is this place in Kolkata?" Sharmi had been washing dishes and was twisting a dish towel with her hands.

"You know the graveyard in the lower circular road where the poet Michael Madhusudan's grave is? Somewhere around that area."

"Well, it might be very difficult to find a place there," Sharmi said. "It is a centrally located place."

"I know," he said, his eyes sparkling like that of a child's—full of wonderment. "But I feel I will somehow find a place there to construct the institute."

Sharmi tossed the dish towel aside and she and Rudy held hands. "This is your dream, Rudy, and I support you on your journey towards whatever brings you happiness and peace."

Rudy squeezed his wife's hands. "Thank you, my dear, Sharmi. For being my wife, the mother of our children and my pillar of strength all these years."

So Rudy started his journey to Kolkata just two days after his discussion with Sharmi. When he reached Kolkata, he started to search for a piece of land. He researched the area and with help from his friends, he was able to find a list of names of the residents around that area. He started going door to door to acquaint himself with the locale and the residents who lived there. He visited and discussed matters with the city officials. Initially, he was offered a piece of land which, it turned out, was not so good and had several problems attached to it.

He thought of what could be the ideal piece of land but unfortunately that was under the control of some higher authorities of Kolkata.

Rudy could not give up the idea of acquiring land to fulfill his dream of bringing help to neurosurgery patients to the part of the world he will forever fondly refer to as his hometown as it would be the ideal place.

So, he persevered, making many visits to the offices of the authorities of the Kolkata City council and managed to make them uncomfortable for not being able to provide him with an answer.

After getting through all the bureaucracy of business dealings, in the end, Rudy acquired the piece of land he wanted, making note that Rudy's approach of pushing the city authorities to their limit proved to be fruitful.

Rudy was so happy that he was able to obtain everything, with legally valid documents, that once elusive piece of land to build the Neuroscience Institute of Kolkata. A wave of relief swept through his mind and heart after realizing he cleared his first hurdle as a piece of land was so important in manifesting his dream of where a Neuroscience Institute would stand.

Rudy visited the gravesite of Michael Madhusudan Dutt and read the inscription on the tomb which was a poem the poet wrote and translated in English himself just before his departure to England:

"Forget me not, Oh Mother

Should I fail to return

To thy hollowed bosom

Make not the lotus of thy memory

Void of its nectar honey."

Rudy remembered reading that Michael Madhusudan was a poet, writer and playwright born on the 25th of January 1824 and died on the 29th of June 1873 at the age of 49. He created blank verses in Bengali poems and received an education in the English language and additional tutorship in English at home. His father intended for western education to open doors for a government position for his son. Michael Madhusudan developed an aversion to Indian culture and a deep yearning to become accepted into European Culture.

Rudy's dream was to give something unique to the city of Kolkata who made him a physician. He murmured to himself, "I am nowhere near the great poet. I just want to be inspired by the inscription so that a miniscule of my effort could be of some help to this city."

It was a very emotional moment for Rudy—he succeeded in accomplishing his first step. Now he had to go around the globe to collect money from people who could afford to donate. He was determined yet anxious and nervous as well. He called Sharmi who was happy to hear the good news about acquiring land and encouraged him further.

"You're very lucky to get that piece of land," she said. "I didn't even dream that you would get that particular piece of land but look how far you have come now."

Feeling encouraged that he cleared his first hurdle, Rudy started to plan how to raise the money. He kept imagining how people were going to treat him when he requested for funds. He then resolved to rise above of all sorts of people he might encounter—especially from those reluctant to invest money. So first he started with a group of his doctor friends including Samir, who, thankfully, thought that it was a good project to invest in.

During the course of Rudy's tireless journey he realized, to his dismay, the people who were initially excited about the project in the beginning didn't maintain their enthusiasm in the long run. Unable to stay focused, they were not confident about the outcome and they considered that not only was this a risky venture but one in which would be a group endeavor that required much of their time and money that might wreak havoc on their own careers so, to them, it didn't seem like a good investment after all.

So Rudy was on his own. He took a quantum leap and started trotting around the globe for funds.

Around Kolkata, rich businessmen could afford yet, they asked: why should they? Rudy realized some people wanted their name to be remembered even after they pass away from this world. Since time seemed to swallow everything in its path, people were desperate not to be forgotten before time ran out. So having their names imprinted on a wall, clinic or a section of the hospital would ensure their legacy. Rudy was right. People would donate funds for the sake of having their names recognized throughout time.

Soon he started gathering donations, traveling all around the globe as much as he could including the U.S., Canada and many other countries. At Newcastle-on-Tyne, the doctors and nurses encouraged and helped him as best they could.

It was a joyous moment when on one auspicious day, an Indian priest came to perform the sacred rituals on the land to start the process of construction.

When the arrangements of construction started, the place became busy with people carrying construction materials and the air was filled with their excited conversations. As the trucks filled with building materials lined up around the block, an unusual hub of activity on that spot aroused the curiosity of onlookers eager to find out what was going on and what would be built in that piece of land. Soon more people would gather around the area interested in the construction, talking amongst themselves as they stopped to look at the site.

On busy afternoons, Rudy would visit the site when his anxiety would plague him and for comfort, he would assure himself that: *This construction will go as smoothly as possible.*

As the days passed, Rudy would visit the construction site as frequently as he could.

One late morning in the spring of 2006, a local Indian priest came to administer the rituals of prayer to "Bhumi," the earth where the multi-story Neuroscience Institute and Hospital would stand and the prayer to Mother Earth would sustain, hold and protect the structure.

Interestingly enough, there was a christening ceremony of the institute by the bishop of a church. As the construction started, it was a huge process, one that made Rudy happy yet still anxious as he repeated an affirmation to calm himself: *The construction should go smoothly so that enough money will flow like a stream.*

As Rudy continued visiting the construction site, he would be there to witness the project's milestone such as when the building was being raised floor by floor. Rudy would look at it, often fantasizing and envisioning the finished building in his imagination. And so it happened that one fine morning as Rudy stood in the middle of the high-rise building—holding Niccolò's biography in his hand—surrounded by unfinished concrete walls and juts of pointed iron rods and half-done pillars, he suddenly became jittery and doubtful and started questioning himself. *Would it ever be done? What would happen if I ran out of money? What will happen to my dream to build the best possible Neuroscience Institute in Kolkata, the city who made me a physician?*

And then suddenly, in a moment of calm, the realization hit him: Niccolò had experienced moments of doubt and uncertainty even amid his past accomplishments, even on the wings of success. It was natural to want things to run smoothly. Rudy took a deep, cleansing breath and focused on his blessings: his family and his dream to heal the world and his beloved India through the wonders of neuroscience one patient at a time was coming true.

In the background, the busy city of Kolkata kept on dancing with the chorus of so many people's busy footsteps as their voices sang while walking along the road amid the sound effects of different transport vehicles with the backdrop of the seasonal veil of summer's sultry heat followed by torrential rain and water-logged roads. From a cool wintery blast to spring with its chorus of different birdsongs and their chatter on the branches of big Banyan trees—the city kept on going eternally.

Niccolò's Vision and the Future Sculptors of Italia

15ᵗʰ century Florence—As summer quietly gave way to fall, the season kept knocking on the door of the octagonal Baptistery which stood against the blue sky where white clouds were grazing lazily.

Inside the famous Baptistery, a studio lay abuzz as the sun rays reflected on different sized marble slabs strewn all over the floor. The young rising sculptors were chiseling out their figures from their marble slabs as some young artists were murmuring to themselves. Some were frustrated, sighing often, while others stood whispering to the unknown figures, beckoning them to emerge from the slab. They were channeling their master who, while sculpting, would do the same.

Niccolò had been requested by the personnel of the Baptistery to supervise the rising sculptors working at the studio inside the Baptistery in Florence.

He was now in his mid-seventies wearing his usual long, white flowing dress and a turban-like head cap through which his gray hairs were peeping. His forehead showed deep horizontal lines as he watched very closely the young trainees while at the same time, looking at the sculptures of his own creation inside the Baptistery.

A younger sculptor came and asked him, "Maestro, will you ever stop?"

Taking a philosopher's pose, his right elbow propped on his left forearm, index finger on his chin, Niccolò replied, "Yes and no, at the same time. It is relative. Even when my hands are at rest, my mind keeps on working and beautifying the figure."

"So, are you thinking in a different perspective now?"

Niccolò placed his hands on his hips. "Are you asking me whether I have changed my perspective of my artistic endeavor? Well, it depends how one looks at it."

Niccolò continued making his rounds in the studio, observing and chatting with the students. He stopped for few minutes when he saw a student was having difficulty chiseling the part of a sculpture's trunk. He approached that student and showed him how to hold the chisel properly so that it would not slip from the particular area. He stood there until he was satisfied that the young sculptor mastered the technique. When he saw that the young artist started to confidently chisel again, he went back to where he was before and continued his conversation with the previous student.

"You see, my dear, Carlo," Niccolò said. "The difference is, my hands and mind used to work continuously together. There was no space or time to enjoy my creativity myself. I was confident of my own opinion of beauty. Now, I stop and think and my eyes scan and perceive the light of the beauty which gives off from the objects of my creation. From there, I transcend to a different perspective—beyond the light of my eyes."

Marco, who was quietly working in a corner, came forward. "Maestro, what is ahead for the future generations of artists and the artistic world?"

Niccolò took a deep breath and exhaled. "Creativity flows like an endless stream—flowing through all areas of work and profession." He paused, flashing back to his days in Padua when he was sick and lying in bed, thinking his end was near as physicians there took great care of him until slowly, but surely, he recovered and became stronger.

Regaining his composure, he stood tall despite the stiff joints and back pain that had plagued him of late. "When the stream of creativity flows through the creator, the creator is the one who can guide the process and make it unique and, with the artist's magic touch, everything comes alive. The creative stream is a transmission of feelings of the artist's experience. It enables us to find ourselves and lose ourselves at the same time. Art devours the whole person with the fire of the soul.

"When I cry out loud after finishing a figure: 'He is alive! He is alive!', what I really mean to say is that art is not to represent the outward appearance of things, but their inward significance."

Niccolò stopped, his eyes cast far into the distance beyond the window that offered a magnificent view of the rest of Florence.

"Maestro! You have bestowed upon us your wisdom about artists and the artistic world," exclaimed one of his students excitedly. "Though it is hard at present to understand it all, it will remain in our hearts forever."

On this fall afternoon as the sun went down in the horizon and the soft sun's rays brushed the window panes of the Baptistery, there was a blast of strong cool breeze blowing outside, through the tall trees. The leaves began painting in fall colors, twisting and turning until they fell on the ground one by one and started to rustle together.

Suddenly, the trotting sounds of a horse carriage drew nearer and clearer towards the Baptistery with frequent interruptions of the shrieks of seagulls.

"Maestro!" Carlo called, "your assistant, Paolo, has arrived with the carriage to give you a ride home."

The tall, frail figure stood up, brushing from his clothes the debris which formed a rainbow of dust clouds with the reflected rays of the setting sun. The young men, who had been his students for quite a while, carefully observed Niccolò moving slowly towards the open door, their attention still focused on their Maestro's figure as it became smaller and smaller until it gradually disappeared.

The sound of the carriage moving faster with the whistling sound of a strong wind dominated the afternoon for some time. Then distant echoes of the carriage dissipated when the cold blast of wind continued whirling over the Baptistery. As the sun dipped then set, its golden orange color painted the Baptistery in gold, painted the river Arno in a rippling gold stream as the shrieks of seagulls continued questioning the unknown as its ethereal spirit traveled far, far away, eventually disappearing in the evening silence.

Epilogue

After reading the last chapter of Niccolò's biography which he had practically read many times throughout the years and brought with him on his travels, Rudy walked through the construction site mindfully, breathing heavily just as a car stopped in front of the unfinished building. The passenger inside the car was a renowned film actor and producer who asked his friend, the driver, "What is going on here?" he said as he watched the construction and the tall man who was walking inside the unfinished building.

His friend explained, "They are building the Institute of Neuroscience of Kolkata and the man responsible for the project is a renowned neurosurgeon. I heard that his dream to build an Institute of Neuroscience and Neurosurgery in Kolkata is becoming fulfilled."

"Excellent! Excellent!" the actor said, "call the team from the studio. We are going to film it and make a movie!"

The actor got out of his car and approached Rudy who was very happy, honored and surprised at the same time. The actor requested Rudy's permission to film at the construction site, stating that he himself would be playing the role of Rudy in the film.

Rudy was overcome with emotion and granted the actor permission to film a movie based on his life and his neurosurgeon's dream and all that came with it.

Rudy's dream crystallized every day, bit by bit, resulting in a twelve-story high-rise building with the capacity of treating around two hundred patients in the fields of Neurology, Neurosurgery, Neuro rehabilitation, Neuropsychiatric, Neuropathology, Neuroanesthesia, Neuroradiology and Interventional radiology, and Neuroendocrinology.

It would later come to be ranked as one of the number one medical facilities around the world specializing in neuroscience and neurology.

Finally, all Rudy's hard work came into fruition in the form of a grand opening ceremony of the new hospital, a truly memorable occasion when none other than the honorable President of India presided over the ceremony. With his wife, Sharmi, and his daughter, Anjali, by his side, and his dear friends Amita and Samir in the audience, Rudy was a mixture of happy and emotional as his eyes went far off into the distance as a voice started ringing inside of him. Rudy listened carefully and smiled. It was the voice of Niccolò saying, "Creativity is like a flowing stream. It flows inside the creator. It is the creator's responsibility to guide the stream to…"

Thunderous applause caused Rudy to snap back to the present as he witnessed everyone cheering as the President of India commemorated the ceremony at the entrance of the building by cutting the ceremonial silk ribbon.

Rudy silently repeated the words in his mind: *This is just my offering at the feet of the big city of Kolkata who gave me the chance to be in this noble profession.*

In the background, the big bustling city of Kolkata kept on gyrating with the chorus of people walking by as a concert of percussive sounds from the horns of cars, buses, and trams accompanied by the slow, pleasant chimes of wedding bells from a nearby church filled the air with magical moments captivating, bewitching and enthralling the city of Kolkata as the celebration continued, dazzling her in an eternal dance.

The End

Author's Note

The idea of this book project began in 2018 while I was trying to relax and enjoy the view of the landscape outside my home in Northern California. It was a fine spring day when the trees were all dressed up with young, green leaves rippling with joy.

On the ground, a bunch of daffodils swayed with a gentle breeze as two blue jays continued a long conversation on a branch of a blossoming magnolia tree. I just happened to remember a discussion on medicine and art in which Trousseau in 1869 said, "The worst man of science is never an artist and the worst artist is he who is never a man of science."

In early times, medicine took its prominent place at the side of poetry and painting and today, people have attempted to make a science of it, placing it beside mathematics, astronomy, and physics. So what he means to say regarding the progress of science is that there is a rapid decline in the so-called "human elements of a health care provider" which dilutes the age-old doctor-patient relationship. At that moment or realization, the telephone started ringing and it turned out to be a call from a dear friend from England, a renowned neurosurgeon, who lived by this motto: to help people with neurological disorders while also reaching out to those in need, providing the best medical care to those who could not afford it.

My idea at that moment crystalized during my telephone conversation that "artistry flows in all areas of profession" which resulted in the creation of my first novel.

I was very excited to depict a great man at the other end of the time spectrum—an artist from 15th century Italy who was passionate and completely one with his art, fusing his story with that of the life and work of my neurosurgeon friend in his present time. So the artistry evolved in a completely different form—an amalgamation of real lives fused into fiction through two characters whose fully-realized lives depicted those of their real-life counterparts in a narrative which flowed and mingled happily with the past.

Armed with that inspiration I started and completed my first novel with fond remembrance of my aunt, Bina to whom this book is dedicated, for she had been like a second mother to me. She used to say about the journey, "You have to have a goal—keep on moving towards it with all your concentration."

So, I kept on moving, always forward on my journey.

When I was young, my mother had been busy with her career volunteering to help less fortunate people and was a rising politician and assembly member (senator). So, I would cling to my Aunt Bina. While my aunt was studying at the University of Calcutta, I used to wait for her in the common room, keeping myself busy scribbling with colored pencils, creating imaginary landscapes and figures, eagerly waiting when her class would be done. That is how I remember where I came from, where I now stand and who I am—as a result of my aunt's love, care and guidance every step of my life.

Maya Mitra Das
March 24, 2023

Acknowledgments

First of all, I have to thank my young friend and creative writing teacher, Janice De Jesus, MFA, for her help and encouragement with every step from the start of writing my first novel.

The subject matter was somewhat complicated as I decided to write a historical fiction account based on two characters who lived apart in different times and space. One was a renowned artist who made his mark in the world which will continue forever, and the other whose artistry in medical breakthroughs will endure with each human life he saved long into the future.

The skillful knowledge and wisdom of Janice De Jesus made my journey smooth and pleasant. She is the real "Guru" of my creative writing life as she was the one who taught me what creative writing is all about.

I really appreciate the expertise of Dr. Robin Sen Gupta OBE, Doctorate of Medicine Honoris Causa (New Castle University) FRCS (Eng), FRCS (Edin) for making me understand his area of work and dedication in the field of Neurosurgery to serve humanity. The knowledge of Dr. Sen, who is an Emeritus Professor of Neurosurgery and a consultant, founder and chairman of N, NC and the Institute of Neuroscience, Kolkata, India, proved to be valuable in providing the much-needed background for my novel.

Many thanks to my other Guru, Katherine Kunhiraman, my Bharatnatyam dance teacher, who introduced me to the term "historical fiction" as she herself was in the process of writing volumes on the 18th dynasty pharaoh, Tutankhamun.

My gratitude goes to my Saturday Creative Writing class for their comments and encouragement.

My thanks to my family who were constantly supporting me and tolerating my ups and downs.

Last but not least, I thank my publisher, especially Paul Willington, senior book coordinator at Ink Start Media LLC for his hard work in helping me gather my words in a presentable package to share with readers.

About the Author

Poet and writer Maya Mitra Das was born in India and came to the U.S. in 1973. She studied internal medicine and pediatric medicine in India, England, and the United States, earning her M.D. and PhD.

Dr. Das received her training at Downstate Medical Center and State University Hospital in Brooklyn, New York.

She completed two fellowships, one for the department of hematology at UCLA Medical Center and the second at the University of California, San Francisco for radiation oncology.

Dr. Das served on the medical staff at UCSF Children's Hospital in Oakland, California working with Sickle Cell Anemia in children.

Among her many hobbies includes performing Indian classical dance, Bharatnatyam, playing classical music for piano.

Her historical fiction has appeared in her full-length collection of short stories *Silhouettes of Time*; in anthologies, *Tremors: Short Fiction by California Writers* and *Insight, Hindsight and Flights of Fancy*.

Her poetry has appeared in her book *Rhythms Primeval*, the anthology, *Tuesday Poetry* and two narrative poems anthologized in *What's in a Name?*

She has also authored a number of scientific papers.

Echoes of the Past is her first novel.

Maya Mitra Das, author Silhouettes of Time, fictional short stories Rhythms Primeval, poetry www.mayamitradasauthor.com

www.silhouettesoftime.com, www.mayamitra.com

maya.mitra@gmail.com

Other books by Maya Mitra Das

Silhouettes of Time, 2016, a collection of short stories

Rhythms Primeval, 2017, a collection of poetry

Anthologies

Tuesday's Poetry, 2013, Acalanes Adult Education and Barnes and Noble Poetry Workshop Member's anthology

What's in a Name?, 2014, a collection by the OLLI Concord, CA Writing Group

Tremors, 2014, short fiction by California Writers

Insight, Hindsight and Flights of Fancy, 2018, a collection of short stories by Shadow of the Mountain Writers Guild